WAITING FOR SUMMER

BOOK TWO

ANNA-MARIA ATHANASIOU

For the three men in my life: Marios, George and Michael. I was recently told that I was the luckiest woman in the world because I have three men that love me. I am the luckiest woman in the world, because I love them; totally, completely and unconditionally.

CONTENTS

SUMMER

Place me on Sunium's marbled steep,
Where nothing, save the waves and I,
May hear our mutual murmurs sweep;
There, swanlike, let me sing and die:

'The Isles of Greece'
by Lord Byron (1788-1824)

1

HEAVEN

It was the last week of May. Summer was nearly officially here and Sylvie felt her whole being uplifted. Was it really because summer was finally arriving, or was it because she was about to spend four days and four nights with the sexiest young man she'd ever had the good fortune to fall upon? *A bit of one and a lot of the other*, she mused.

Last night, Nick had sounded a little strained when she'd called. Sylvie had been in her room packing the last of her things. *What to pack?* She put in what she'd need for her business meeting, but then what? She rifled through her wardrobe. Sundresses? Shorts? She pulled them out and threw them on her bed. Cocktail dresses, skirts, vests, bikini, swimsuit… crap, she didn't know. She could never pack light. She envied anyone who could throw together a few key outfits and look fabulous. Sylvie looked down at the ever-increasing pile of clothes and frowned to herself. To hell with it – she decided to pack all of it. Then she opened her underwear drawer. She had it split into two, basics and sexy. Most of her basic underwear was looking well worn and she'd hardly ever worn the sexy stuff – hell some still had the tags on. She ripped off the tags and packed them, discarding the basics section altogether. She looked over at the twelve pairs of shoes she'd bagged. Maybe for four days it was too many. She packed her nude stilettos, two wedges, a pair of gold peep toes and some jewelled flip-flops. Then she reluctantly put the rest away, but not before throwing in her black and white peep toes and a pair of cream Converse. She'd discreetly washed and packed Nick's shirt and placed it in her suitcase when her phone beeped a message.

'Can u talk? x'

Sylvie called him immediately.

"Hi." His voice was soft.

"Hi, I was packing." Why did she feel so nervous? She closed her eyes and tried to dispel her constant worrying thoughts. *He'd realised this was stupid. He couldn't go through with it. She wasn't right for him. She was too old for him.* The list was endless.

"Me too. I want to see you. I need to see you."

"Oh Nick, I…"

"I know Markus is still there. I just wanted to hear your voice. This is so incredibly hard."

"I know. For me, too." Sylvie allowed herself to relax. So he did still want to go with her. She felt the wave of relief flow over her.

"Dad came round." He paused to wait for a response, but Sylvie fell silent. "He just came to say bye. It made me feel pretty shitty." Her heart sank and her initial worries came flooding back again like a torrent.

"I see… do you want to cancel?" Sylvie whispered. Crap, she couldn't cope with this roller-coaster of emotions. Up so high, then way down low.

"No! Of course not. I just wanted to tell you, so you know that I do understand how you feel, because I feel it too. Today, in the shop, you told me that you didn't want to hurt him. Neither do I. I know you have a history with him and that you really don't want to make it any harder than it needs to be. But I really can't bear this, this not being able to be with you. Four months I sat back, Sylvie. Four months, I waited to see if anything was going to happen between you two. I know we've only been together for a few days, but I feel it's been much more. I got to know you over those months too. Shit… I'm not really making sense."

Sylvie could hear him opening up a packet of gum and it made her smile. His words made her spirit soar, from the depths of despair back up to the height of elation.

"Nick, in less than twelve hours we'll be together. We can talk it through then." He sighed at the end of the phone. "How much gum have you gone through?" she asked, trying to lighten the mood.

"Don't ask. I could have smoked an entire carton tonight!" Sylvie giggled at his exasperated tone. "Sylvie, you're killing me. You know that, don't you?" Sylvie laughed, allowing herself to relax again, his words erasing all her previous doubts.

"What are you wearing?" His voice changed from exasperated to sultry.

"What?" Had she heard right?

"What are you wearing? I want to picture you."

Sylvie clenched her eyes shut and grinned to herself. She looked down at her navy sweat pants and vest. Smirking to herself, she replied. "A smile," she whispered. Well he couldn't see, so what did it matter?

"Oh fuck," Nick groaned. "Now you really are killing me. How the hell am I going to sleep now?"

"Sweet dreams, Nick. I'll see you at the airport." Sylvie sat on her bed, hugging her knees, feeling thoroughly pleased with herself as she spoke. That was the exact reaction she'd hoped for.

"You're lucky Markus is home, so help me... ah!"

"Goodnight, Nick."

"Goodnight, baby."

<hr />

She Pulled into the Larnaca Airport car park and scanned around for Nick's Jeep. They'd arranged to drive up separately, just as a precaution. Sylvie was being paranoid, she knew, but she really didn't want anything to go wrong. The sun was beating down, causing the air around the airport to make heat waves rise up from the tarmac. Thankfully, she had worn a cool halterneck dress. *It must be in the thirties*, she thought.

Failing to spot his Jeep, she turned to open up the boot of her car to retrieve her suitcase. She'd call Nick once she was inside. As the boot lid rose, she felt a warm kiss on her shoulder and an arm curl its way around her waist. Sylvie jumped before giggling.

"Heaven," he breathed into her ear. Sylvie leaned back into him and Nick trailed kisses up her neck. "You smell delicious. Let me get that." Sylvie moaned and turned to face him.

"Hi." Her eyes drank him in. His hair dishevelled and his eyes hidden behind his Ray Bans. He leaned her up against her car and kissed her fully, taking her face in his hands. Sylvie wrapped her arms around him, allowing herself to be swept away by him. Then he reluctantly pulled himself back from her and stroked her face. Sylvie furrowed her brow, showing how displeased she was.

"Come on, let's go check in. If I carrying on kissing you, we'll never leave. Jeez, I've missed you!" He grinned as he reached into the car and effortlessly pulled out her suitcase, all the while keeping his arm around her. "Today couldn't come fast enough." He pulled her close and kissed the top of her head. He reached down and swung his large holdall over his shoulder. Sylvie shook her head as she locked the car. She remembered how Chris would moan about the amount of clothes she packed. Nick leisurely pulled her suitcase as they made their way to the departure lounge.

"Ready?" He looked down at her. Sylvie nodded wistfully. He kissed her forehead and squeezed her waist.

Within fifteen minutes they had checked in and were sat in the business class lounge in a booth. Luckily, there were not many people, so they both felt as if they could relax at last. Nick sat next to Sylvie and had his body turned to face her. He was breathtaking in a light blue shirt and faded jeans. His hair untidily framed his face, which glowed, and at last Sylvie could see his piercing blue eyes.

"I thought this moment might never come, sitting with you here. It has been the worst two days of my life." He reached over and stroked her face. "I haven't been able to relax or concentrate on anything."

"Me too," Sylvie murmured.

"My dad was quizzing me last night. I think he suspects I'm seeing someone, or maybe Mum told him."

"Maggie?"

"She grilled me on the day we watched the DVD. She suspected I was seeing someone. So I told her that I was. She was worried."

"I know, she told me too." Nick cocked his head and edged closer to Sylvie.

"I bet that made you feel uneasy," he smirked. "What did you say?"

"Nothing. I just sat and listened."

"And?"

Sylvie felt herself flush. This was too heavy a discussion to have in an airport lounge. "She's worried… worried that you'll get hurt." Sylvie cast her eyes down to her lap where her hands rested and she started to rub her finger. Nick lifted her chin and fixed her with his eyes.

"Hey, don't do that. We knew this was tricky." He leaned over and slipped his arm around her shoulder so that she could rest her head on his shoulder, then took the hand she was rubbing and frowned before kissing it. "We need to talk about so much and I know you're finding this overwhelming, but please don't let all this baggage spoil our time together. We've got four days, Sylvie. Four whole days to sort all this out. Four days of just you and me. Four days of heaven." He lifted her chin and kissed her gently. Then he kissed her on the forehead.

"Heaven," she whispered, and in that moment Sylvie knew she only wanted to be held and kissed by this man. This remarkable young man, who despite personal cost, wanted to be with her. Something she was struggling to comprehend, but at the same time was totally intoxicated by. She was drawn to him so forcefully that it frightened her. From the moment he had pulled himself out of the pool at Maggie's, she'd known she was done for. Now, four months later, she was in his arms. Their flight was called and they both reluctantly rose from their seats.

"Come on, baby." He held out his hand and Sylvie took it as they walked in the direction of the gate.

The ride in the taxi to the Grande Britannia Hotel was an experience as ever. Sylvie couldn't quite get used to the erratic driving at breakneck speed that seemed to be the norm in Athens. Leaving the quiet island of Cyprus and being thrust into the fast pace of the capital was always a shock to the system. It had been almost a year since she'd been here, and even though she was excited that she was here with Nick and that she'd be representing her company for the first time, she was full of mixed emotions.

She associated Athens with Chris and that fated last journey, and that made this trip bittersweet. She gazed out of the window and looked at the vaguely familiar roads and tried hard to shake off her apprehension.

"Are you okay?" Nick squeezed her hand as he watched her. Sylvie turned and nodded weakly, scared to speak in case her voice gave her away. He pulled her closer and wrapped his arm around her shoulder. He couldn't work out what she was thinking, but he knew it wasn't anything to do with him and their situation. From her expression, he knew it was something he couldn't ask her about. Her eyes were so melancholy that his heart broke. He sighed, resigned to the fact that this was a subject he couldn't press.

The Grande Britannia was a stately hotel in the heart of Athens. Chris and Sylvie had always stayed there. It was very opulent and with its heavy brocade and gold, reminded them more of a hotel that you would find in Paris.

Sylvie loved it here: the views from the rooms faced the Acropolis hill and at night the Parthenon was lit up. The church of St. George could also be seen on Lycabettos Hill, another favourite of Sylvie's, where she had drunk fresh lemonade with her family as a child, and then as an adult had cocktails with her husband. As they approached the entrance, Sylvie began to feel uneasy. Maybe she should have booked a different hotel.

Nick took her hand after paying the taxi, as the doorman took care of their cases and led her through the luxurious lobby to the reception desk. A pretty receptionist Sylvie vaguely recognised smiled at them as they approached. Sylvie saw her face change to shock, then quickly recover back to her professional stance, as she hurriedly picked up the phone and quickly spoke to someone, before greeting them.

"Good afternoon Mrs Sapphiris, so nice to see you again." Her tone was genuine but wary, as her eyes darted to Nick, who was more than a little surprised at her greeting.

"Good afternoon. Thank you. It's nice to be back. I booked a suite under Sapphire Developers. I…"

Before she could finish, she felt a presence next to her, as the receptionist's eyes rested on a man who was now by her side. Sylvie turned to see who it was and was instantly faced with Mr Zavos, the manager. He was a middle-aged man in his early fifties, short and slim with grey hair and impeccably dressed in his black suit. His eyes were dark but friendly and his smile was genuine.

"Mrs Sapphiris. How lovely to see you again." He had his hand outstretched and Sylvie immediately smiled and shook it.

"Mr Zavos, it's lovely to see you." His eyes moved to Nick and he outstretched his hand. "I'm sorry, this is…" Sylvie hesitated. What was she going to introduce him as? She decided that Mr Zavos really didn't need to know the nature of their relationship. "Nick Steed. Nick, this is Mr Zavos, the hotel manager."

Nick smiled and shook his hand. "Pleased to meet you. Your hotel is very impressive."

"Thank you. Is it your first time here?"

"Yes, I've only ever stopped over in Athens, before flying on, so I'm looking forward to Sylvie showing me around." Nick slipped his arm around her waist, making it obvious as to what kind of relationship they had. So much for keeping Mr Zavos in the dark!

"I noticed that you booked a suite, Mrs Sapphiris."

"Yes."

"I took the liberty of upgrading you up to the Presidential Suite.

Unfortunately, the Royal Suite was already booked. Otherwise I would have preferred to have given you that. I hope that's alright?" He directed the question to Sylvie, and his eyes seemed to be trying to convey something that Nick couldn't quite grasp. "It's the least we could do in the light of… well, you are a very valued customer of ours."

Nick felt Sylvie stiffen slightly and he could see her start to rub her finger. He squeezed her to him in an attempt to reassure her, though what about, he wasn't sure.

"That's very kind of you, but it really wasn't necessary."

Mr Zavos shook his head slightly, indicating it was nothing. "Dr Dracos has left you a message. Kiki made sure it's in your room." He motioned to the receptionist. "If there is anything you need, please don't hesitate to contact me directly. I'll let you settle in. Mr Steed, it was a pleasure to meet you."

He held out his hand again and Nick shook it. "Thank you. Likewise."

And then Mr Zavos turned and shook Sylvie's hand but this time, he also clasped it with his left hand, enveloping her hand between both of his, and his face showed an emotion Nick couldn't quite fathom. Almost as a protective gesture, fatherly, and his face was tinged with sorrow. No, more that he wanted to show he was genuinely caring. Nick found the gesture almost too familiar. Then he nodded curtly and left them.

Sylvie quickly signed the register, leaving their passports. Nick then guided her to the elevators and they rode up to the fifth floor in silence. Nick pulled her close and kissed her head, breathing in deeply. He really wished he knew what was going on. He couldn't work out what Sylvie was feeling and he just wanted to make her forget. Sylvie turned to him and smiled, and he bent down and kissed her gently. She closed her eyes, and he could feel her whole body relax as she wrapped her arm around his neck. The elevator stopped, and they reluctantly pulled away from each other.

"Okay?" Nick asked tentatively, searching her face for some clue as to what was bothering her. Sylvie smiled weakly and nodded. Nick took her hand, and she followed him as he headed towards their room. He walked with urgency and once outside the room, he expertly slipped in the card key and opened up the door.

The room was, of course, magnificent. It comprised an entrance which led through to a twelve-seated dining room. There was a sitting room with amazing views of the Parthenon, an enormous bedroom and a sumptuous bathroom with a huge bath and wet room. It was all classically inspired with chandeliers and columns, all in muted tones of taupe, cream and gold. There were fresh flowers in every room and champagne on ice, along with a well-stocked bar. Their luggage was already in the room. As they entered, they were greeted by a man in full livery.

"Good afternoon, Mrs Sapphiris, Mr Steed. My name is Andreas. I am your butler. Welcome to The Grande Britannia. Would you like me to unpack your things?"

Sylvie stood wide-eyed, as she tried to take everything in. She turned to Nick who was smiling and shaking his head in disbelief, and then shrugged. "Thank you Andreas. That would be lovely."

"Very well." And with that, he curtly nodded to them both and vanished into the bedroom.

"I could get used to this. Maybe we'll never leave," Nick smirked and raised his eyebrows, fixing Sylvie with his eyes. Sylvie giggled and Nick instantly felt relieved as he saw Sylvie relax.

"Let me get my laptop set up." She went over to the desk and placed her briefcase on it, then reached in and pulled out the laptop, discarding the case.

"I'll fix us a drink. What do you fancy?" He came up behind her and nuzzled her neck. His touch sent sparks through her whole body. "Champagne? I think it's your favourite. Laurent Perrier Rosé."

How did he know? Sylvie turned to him, puzzled.

"It's what you were drinking at Celle."

Sylvie looked stunned. *He remembered.*

Nick's eyes rested on her briefcase and his brow furrowed slightly at the monogram C.S. He looked back quickly, hoping she hadn't noticed.

"Sounds great," she said.

"We should sit out on the balcony, take in that view." His eyes flitted to the bedroom, indicating that they weren't alone, so they'd have to wait. Sylvie giggled again and nodded, then kissed him softly on the lips. Within seconds, Nick had her pressed up against him, holding her hard and kissing her harder. She didn't know if it was the fact that they hadn't touched each other in two days or the tension she was feeling being here or whatever, but she wanted this so desperately. She needed him with every inch of her being. She wound her hands into his hair, holding his head tight so that their kiss deepened and she could feel his heat. His hands moved down to her behind and pressed her onto him.

Sylvie moaned and his hand slid under her dress and ran up her leg, causing her to gasp.

"Oh, Sylvie, I've missed you," he murmured in her ear. "I can hardly wait."

He pulled away and took a deep breath. He closed his eyes in an attempt to calm himself and then said, as he reopened them, "Champagne, then, on the balcony." It was as if he was reconfirming it to himself in an attempt to pull himself together.

He walked over to the bar and started to peel off the foil. Sylvie steadied herself on the desk, trying to calm down her thumping heart and after a moment, she set up her laptop. She shook her head. She hoped Andreas was a fast unpacker! It took a couple of minutes for her laptop to warm up. She moved over to the coffee table, where she saw an envelope with her name on propped up on a magnificent bouquet of white roses. She opened it up, and inside was a card.

Welcome to Athens.
I look forward to finally meeting you.
Dimitris Dracos FRCS (Plas)

She then joined Nick out on the balcony. He stood up and handed her a glass. She dropped the card on the table and Nick glanced at it. He raised his eyebrows.

"He's the buyer of our building. He's a plastic surgeon. The building will be his new clinic."

"Impressive. You've never met him, then?" Sylvie shook her head. She didn't want to get into the fact that only Chris had dealt with him.

"Only spoke on the phone. I need to be at his office on Monday. Our lawyers will be there too. It shouldn't take more than an hour. Apart from that, the rest of the time is ours." She looked at him shyly.

"Cheers, or should I say *ya mas*?"

Sylvie raised her glass and was taken aback. "*Ya mas*. So you know a bit of Greek, then?" she asked, as they took their first sip and then sat back down.

"You could say that," Nick said cryptically. He looked out over the view and struggled to find the right words. "That's why we're here, isn't it? To find out more about each other." He glanced over to her, trying to judge her mood. "Maybe I should start. Do you want to ask me something or shall I just ramble on?"

Sylvie looked at him and screwed up her nose. This was going to be hard. "So you've never been to Athens?"

"No, just the airport. I often get connecting flights from here to the South of France, Italy, the Caribbean. I take it you've been a lot, judging by Mr Zavos's greeting."

Sylvie took a sip from her glass in order to delay her response. "Uh-huh, as a child we came a lot. It's how I learned my Greek. Then with the business, we came out maybe twice a year. Well, I came out twice a year." Sylvie omitted the fact that Chris was here every month.

"Your husband, Chris, came out more often, then?" Sylvie nodded but avoided his eyes. "That explains it, then."

"Explains what?"

"Mr Zavos. This suite." He raised his hand in the air and gestured. Sylvie smiled weakly. "Maybe this wasn't the right place for us to get to know each other," Nick mused.

Sylvie shot her eyes up to his face and she could see he was pained and unsure. "Oh no, I'm sorry." She reached over to his hand. That was the last thing she wanted to do.

"Sylvie, I don't know what the hell's going on." He ran his fingers through his hair. "You're not giving anything away. There's something wrong, and it's nothing to do with my father. This is something else, something to do with here. I sensed it the moment we got in the taxi. You tensed up, you tried desperately to cover it up, but I could tell. Right now, I feel like I'm intruding. That exchange between the manager and you–"

There was a muffled cough and Andreas stood in the threshold of the balcony. "Excuse me, Mr Steed, Mrs Sapphiris. Your things are unpacked. If you need me for anything, please press number one on your phone. If that's all, I'll bid you a pleasant afternoon." Nick rose from his chair to face him.

"Thank you Andreas. We will." Andreas curtly nodded and hastily left the suite.

Nick walked round to where Sylvie was sitting and crouched down to her level, lifting her chin up so that their eyes met. "You're going to have to talk to me, Sylvie." His voice was soft as he brushed back her hair. "If you want this to work, you're going to have to be honest with me and tell me what's upsetting you and bothering you. I can take it. I know you have a past. I'd rather know than imagine that it's something else."

Sylvie watched his expression soften as he spoke and she felt herself melt. He truly cared; she could see it in his eyes as he searched for answers in her face. She'd been so used to keeping everything inside, hiding her thoughts in order to protect the people she loved, it was hard for her to open up. Where to start?

There was so much to explain. She wanted this to work with Nick, she knew that for sure and if it meant she had to let her guard down, make herself vulnerable, then so be it. After all, this was what these four days were about. She nodded. Nick kissed her forehead and stood up. Taking her hand, he pulled her up and grabbed their glasses in his other.

"Enough talking for now. Grab the bottle, if I don't get you into bed soon, I'll take you here and now on the balcony." His voice was oh so low and white hot. Sylvie's whole body ignited. She grasped hold of the bottle as she was practically dragged through their suite to the vast bedroom.

2

REVELATIONS

"Oh, Sylvie!" Nick cried out as he collapsed gasping against her, his forehead resting on hers, and she tightened her hold on him. She could feel the sweat on his naked, toned back. He opened his eyes and looked deep into hers. "I can never get enough of you. I mean it." He kissed her forcefully and she moaned into his mouth. "You make me feel alive."

"Oh Nick, I never thought… I still don't." Sylvie shook her head. Why couldn't she just say it, say how she felt? That he was the most incredible man she'd ever been with. That her connection to him scared her. She was full of doubts and fears, doubts that someone else had implanted in her and now she was desperately trying to shake off. What did he see in her, really? She still couldn't get her head around that.

"I know, baby, I know." He stroked her face and brushed back her hair. He slowly pulled himself out of her, and she turned to face him as he propped his head up on his bent arm.

"You're very hot." Sylvie ran her finger down his chest, gathering small beads of sweat.

"Am I?" Nick arched his eyebrow, smirking at the double entendre.

"Yes very." She mockingly pushed him, but he grabbed her hand and yanked her close, then mirrored her action by running his finger down between her breasts.

"So are you." He spoke softly and Sylvie felt herself shudder at his touch. She looked away shyly. "You really have no idea how hot you really are, do you?" Sylvie felt herself flush. "Sylvie, you are so unbelievably sexy. The fact you don't realise it only makes you more so. You are so confident in other ways, but why can't you see that you're beautiful and sexy and all kinds of wow!" She shook her head in disbelief. Nick pulled her close and then rolled back on top of her, propping himself on his elbows. "What is it, Sylvie? Tell me. I can't see you full of sorrow. Does this place make you sad?" He gently stroked her hair and his eyes were soft with concern. Sylvie took a deep breath. She didn't want to spoil the mood, but she knew she would have to tell him.

"Tell me, *please*," he pleaded, his eyes burning into hers, searching for all the answers. Sylvie closed her eyes, agonising over how to say the words, then in a split-second, she decided to just spit it out.

"Chris died in this hotel."

Nick's hand stopped and Sylvie watched as he swallowed. After a moment, he continued to stroke her hair and shift a little. Sylvie tried to read his expression. He was obviously shocked, though he tried hard to hide it. Wait until he hears the rest!

"I'm so sorry. That explains the manager and why you were so tense."

"I need a drink," Sylvie muttered. *I need Dutch courage, a lot of Dutch courage*, she thought. Nick was up in a flash and within seconds, he handed her their glasses, quickly filling them. Then he put the bottle on the bedside table. Sylvie sat up and gulped down the contents of her glass. Nick immediately refilled it and took his. He sat cross-legged and naked next to her, warily observing her. "He wasn't alone." *Shit, she'd actually said that and out loud too!*

Nick stopped mid-gulp, frozen for a couple of seconds. *Holy fucking shit!* No wonder she was so on edge. He scooted over to her and Sylvie started to shake. She pulled herself up and wrapped the sheet around her as she took another gulp of her champagne.

"It's okay, Sylvie. You don't have to say any more. I don't want to upset you, really." Sylvie raised her hand, motioning him to stop.

"No. I need to tell you. It's not fair you not knowing. I don't want to hurt you or make you feel that this is anything to do with you and me. You need to know this." She closed her eyes, trying hard to calm herself. "Chris was having an affair. He brought her here and while he was arguing with her, he suffered a fatal heart attack and died." Nick's mouth dropped open and his beautiful blue eyes were wide with disbelief. "And you thought we only had your father to talk about." Sylvie watched Nick's shock and tried to lighten the mood after the bombshell. He sighed and nodded his head. "Ask me anything. I've said it now." She drained her glass again and Nick refilled it and then his.

"So you found out after he… died?"

Sylvie shook her head.

"I found out a week or so before." Sylvie paused, trying hard not to relive the whole ordeal. The confrontation in Celle's car park, and Chris's forlorn expression in her rear view mirror. "I saw some messages on his mobile and realised. I was hoping it was just a fling, but it had been going on for at least six months and then I realised that he was bringing her here. I confronted him the day he was leaving." She took a sip of her champagne.

"I told him that I wouldn't put up with it and that by the time he was back, I'd have all his things packed and that he'd need to move out." She took a deep breath and closed her eyes. All the while, Nick's eyes never moved from her face. "It was one of the hardest decisions I ever made, Nick. He begged me to forgive him and he promised it was over, that he would end it. But I was hurt and I wouldn't – well, I couldn't – forgive him. He was trying to break it off with her. They were arguing and he…" She took a sip from her glass and for the first time since she started talking, she looked at him. "The manager was the one who sorted out all the arrangements. He was very discreet and understanding." Sylvie looked down at her glass, while she allowed Nick to process the information.

"So no one else knows what happened?" His voice slightly higher as he absorbed this bombshell. Sylvie shook her head.

"Well only me, the woman, Mr Zavos and Zach. He had to deal with all the logistics. I wasn't in any fit state."

"Not even… I mean, the rest of the family?" Nick was dumbfounded. *How had they kept that quiet?*

"I didn't want the boys to know. I didn't want them to see their father in a bad light. It would have only hurt them and anyone else if I'd told them. It was bad enough that I knew – and Zach. The woman thankfully didn't want to tarnish his name either, or maybe it was hers, but she did me the favour and kept quiet too. Zach took it bad. Very bad. He thought he was to blame."

"Why?"

"She worked for us. She was Chris's secretary. I hired her." Sylvie snorted. "Zach thought that if he'd known, he'd have stopped it and then maybe Chris wouldn't have died. He felt he should have realised, especially after the last time." Sylvie's eyes focused on Nick as she spoke. The champagne had made her relax so she had opened the floodgates and let everything come out.

"Last time?" Nick's eyes widened, and Sylvie nodded as he gulped his champagne and refilled both glasses again.

"Maybe I should stop. It's probably a bit too much to take in."

"No, no. It is, but I want to know, please."

"When Chris and I had Markus, things got a little strained between us. The business was growing and he was working hard. I had two small children that took up all my time and well… you know how it is… well actually, you don't." She snorted. "The children took priority and Chris got neglected. It was hard for me to do everything. Chris was very high maintenance. He needed me to be around. He loved his children, but he found it hard that they were always put first. He wasn't used to it. He'd always been number one, even as a child. He was an only child, you see. He needed my constant attention, and I was really not in the position to give it – well, not to the extent he wanted. Instead of being understanding, he pulled away. So the inevitable happened: he found someone who was happy to give him what I couldn't. Unfortunately, she became more of a problem as their affair continued. She wanted more and it became obvious to her that he was basically using her. Things got a little ugly, resulting in her… suicide. Zach was around to help clean up Chris's mess."

"Jesus Christ, Sylvie." He ran his hand down his face and rubbed his stubble.

"No one knew about that affair either. Just me and Zach. That's why he really felt guilty about Dina."

"Dina?"

"The secretary. Zach was with them every day and he never realised. He felt he should have."

"So the manager, Mr Zavos, knew about Dina?" Sylvie nodded. "And arranged for… the body? I see. And Dina, she doesn't still work for you?" His previous feelings towards the over-familiar Mr Zavos seemed petty in retrospect. He was obviously a gentleman and his solicitous attention to Sylvie was more than justified.

"No, she resigned. I haven't seen her since she left, except the night of Celle's opening."

"She was there!" Nick asked in disbelief. Sylvie clenched her teeth as she nodded. "Is that why you were so upset?" Sylvie nodded again.

Nick sat still for a while, going over everything in his head. It was all making sense now. Why Sylvie clammed up whenever Chris was mentioned. He remembered their lunch with Markus and Thea Miria. They had spoken so fondly of him and Sylvie had been silent. He'd mistaken her reaction for sorrow and mourning, when it was actually a lot more than that. Disappointment, anger, betrayal – God only knew. She'd had a lot to deal with over the last eight months. Her husband's affair, his death and then having to hold the family together by pretending that their marriage was this idyllic love story.

"Too much?" Sylvie asked as she looked at him through her lashes, warily. "Got a lot more than you bargained for? I'm sorry, I should have been a little gentler. I'll understand if it's a bit overwhelming."

"What do you mean?" Nick looked puzzled.

"Well, I've a lot of baggage and I'd understand if you'd find that a lot to handle." She wanted to give him the option to back out. She didn't want him to feel obligated to her.

"Why are you saying that? Sylvie, I don't give a flying fuck about your ex. To be honest, it's made things a lot clearer. I thought you were still mourning him, that I couldn't compete with this… this… enigma. Every time he was brought up, you would crawl into yourself and I thought you'd never get over him. That I didn't stand a chance of getting close to you. That night, after the opening, you said you had a secret that you could never tell. Is this what it was?"

Sylvie nodded again. She'd forgotten about that – or rather, Nick had made her forget.

He took a deep breath and ran his hands through his hair. "Sylvie, I know I didn't know Chris, and by all accounts he was a good man. But he fucked up." He took another deep breath and took her glass and put it next to his on the bedside table. He reached over and took both her hands and pulled her up so that they were facing each other, only inches apart, kneeling. He stroked back her hair and clasped her face. "If you were my wife, there wouldn't be a woman who could ever come between us. Not even Aphrodite herself would make me want to betray you. I love you, Sylvie. I think I loved you from that first time I took you home, on that awkward car journey. I remember how you kissed me goodbye, and how I could hardly contain myself. I did everything I could to keep away, but then did everything just to get a glimpse of you, be close to you. I want to be with you – always. Can't you feel that? Don't I show you that?"

Sylvie's eyes filled with tears as he spoke his tender words, words that she so wanted to hear.

"I just don't get it, Nick. How can you? I gave him everything and he betrayed me. I know he wasn't fully to blame the first time. But this last time… When your heart is broken and you see the man you love fall for someone else, push you aside, let someone else into what you felt was untouchable, not once but twice, and both times with women who are younger than you, you begin to question yourself. It makes you feel unworthy, that you don't deserve him. I'm scared that it'll happen again, that I'll fall in deep and then…"

"And that's what you feel, that you're not worthy? You think that because of how he treated you that I can't really love you, or that I'll wake up and decide this isn't for me. Is this what this is all about?" Nick whispered in disbelief.

Sylvie closed her eyes tightly as tears trickled down her face. Nick gently stroked them away. "Please don't cry, Sylvie. I won't do that. I told you I don't do casual. I've only ever had two girlfriends in my life and both left me! It should be me who's full of doubt. But I love you, Sylvie. You mean everything to me." He pulled her face to his and kissed her, their mouths locked as he gently eased her back down on the bed and pulled away the sheet. He trailed kisses down her neck down between her breasts, then up to her lips.

"I love you. I don't know how else I can show you – that until you came into my life, I was just living, and now you are here, I'm alive. I want to be with you and no one else, ever." Sylvie grasped his hair and brought him back to her mouth and he groaned. She held him close as she gently moved him so that she could position herself over him. His eyes were filled with wonder as she straddled him. He gently took hold of her hips and raised her so that she could lower herself onto him. As she did, she arched her back and let her head roll backwards, feeling every inch of him.

"Ah." He cried and then pulled himself up, so that their faces were an inch apart. "Oh baby." He held her close, never taking his eyes off her, and they were lost, lost in each other.

"I love you too, Nick," Sylvie whispered as they moved in perfect unison. Nick's eyes slowly closed as he revelled in her words, the words he'd longed to hear. He drank in her need for him. "I'm just so scared."

She knew she was letting her guard down, that she was allowing herself to be vulnerable. But just one look at this beautiful, strong and utterly wonderful man made her forget everything. Her doubts, her fears, everything – all she wanted was him. Nick grasped at her face, then down to her hips as they both continued to move perfectly together, gradually faster and faster. He stroked her back and kissed her lips, her cheeks, her eyes and before he could answer, he opened his eyes as Sylvie arched her back and cried out. Seeing her let herself go was all he needed, and he was undone as he clung to her, finding his own his sweet release.

They lay wrapped in each other's arms, Nick gently stroking her arm as she nuzzled his chest, half her body draped on his. The sun was setting and the room glowed orange.

"I could stay here forever." Nick kissed her head as he spoke. "You hungry?"

"Mmm."

"Is that a yes, then?" he smirked.

"I don't want to move." She gripped onto him tighter.

"We could get room service."

"Yes. I really can't be bothered to get dressed."

"Naked dining it is, then." He let his hand slip down to her behind and he squeezed it. Sylvie let out a giggle. He pulled her chin up and kissed her. "How are you feeling?" His eyes searched hers.

"Exposed. I've never told anyone, other than Zach. I've spent the best part of this last year trying to hide the truth to protect everyone."

"You've sacrificed a lot. Your feelings, I mean. No wonder you suffer from stomach cramps." He started stroking her arm. "I'm glad you told me. It explains a lot. Come on, let's order some food, then sit on the balcony and look at this fantastic view."

"I know. It's really something." Sylvie turned to look out of the window.

Nick pulled her back to him, his eyes fixing intently on hers. "I meant *this* view."

Sylvie's heart soared. How was she ever going to get used to this?

3

KICKING THE HABIT

Andreas set up the table in the dining room as Sylvie spoke to Dimitris Dracos on the phone. Nick was lounging on one of the sumptuous settees, dressed in a hotel bathrobe and pretending to read some literature left in the hotel. His eyes kept flitting to Sylvie as she paced around the room. He was listening intently to her conversation.

"Yes they are lovely, thank you. Yes, Mr Zavos is looking after me. Ten o'clock Monday morning suits me fine. I'll call Spiros and make sure that's alright with him." Sylvie glanced across at Nick, feeling him watching her. She grinned shyly. "I'm enjoying my time here, relaxing, taking in the sights, you know... Well, maybe we can discuss that on Monday... No I haven't seen it, only pictures... Thank you, our company always endeavours to reach our clients' expectations." Sylvie flushed at something he must have said. "Well that's very kind of you... Yes, so until Monday... Thank you, I will. Goodbye, Dimitri." She pressed her phone and shook her head.

"Everything okay?" Nick tried hard to sound casual, though her reaction to the phone call made him feel a little tense.

"Yes, fine. We sign over on Monday morning."

"Your first official duty as MD?"

Sylvie grinned and nodded, feeling a little daunted. "I better call Zach quickly." She picked up her phone and dialled. "Hi Zach... I'm fine. Yes I spoke to Dimitri. Monday morning we'll do the signing." Nick got up from the settee and walked to where she was pacing. He gently came up behind her and put his arms around her waist. She smiled as she squeezed his arm with her free hand. He pulled her hair away from her neck and started kissing it. "Yes, can you get in touch with Spiros and tell him to be there by ten?" Sylvie rolled her head back as she spoke, trying hard to concentrate. "Oh just staying in tonight, getting room service. Yes, I will try and enjoy myself, Zach." She emphasised the last sentence, as if she was reassuring him. Sylvie was jolted to her senses when she heard a discreet cough. They both turned round to find Andreas standing in the doorway of the dining room.

"Excuse me. Dinner is ready. Would you like me to serve?"

Sylvie raised her hand up, signalling to give her a moment. "Zach, room service just arrived. I'll call you tomorrow. Okay, sweetie… I know… me too. Bye." She turned off her phone.

"Thank you, Andreas. We can serve ourselves," Nick answered, once he was sure Zach was off the line.

"Very good, Mr Steed." And with that, Andreas disappeared.

Sylvie giggled nervously. "That was close."

Nick shook his head. "I feel like I'm having an affair. God, I can't wait 'til everyone knows. This sneaking around is very tiresome. Come, let's eat. Wine?" They moved over to the dining room and Nick pulled out Sylvie's chair.

"Red? Okay." Sylvie nodded. He poured the wine into her glass and then pulled her bathrobe to reveal her shoulder and planted a tender kiss there. He took his seat and poured wine into his own glass. Sylvie lifted her glass.

"Ya mas."

"Ya mas," Nick replied, and he watched her as she took a sip.

"It's delicious. Châteauneuf du Pape. My favourite." Sylvie replaced her glass and picked up a wholemeal roll, pulling it apart. She reached over with her knife and, carefully slicing up some butter, slowly spread it over both pieces, then gently placed them on Nick's side plate.

Nick smiled wryly. *How was such a simple action so sexy?* He took hold of her hand and kissed the inside of her wrist. "I love that you do that."

"Do what?"

Nick motioned to the buttered bread roll.

Oh! She looked surprised. She hadn't really thought about it. It was an instinctive, unconscious act. She realised she had always done it for Chris, because she always liked to look after him. She wrinkled her nose.

"So, what do you know about this Dimitri?" Nick asked, as he cut into his stifado and popped it into his mouth.

Sylvie furrowed her brow. "Are you really interested?"

"Of course. It's a big thing for you what you're doing. I want to know everything about you, your business, your family. That's one of the reasons we're here, isn't it?"

"Okay, then. He's a very talented plastic surgeon who had a practice in London. He was married to an English woman. That's why he lived there. She died five years ago in a car crash, so he decided to come back to his homeland and set up a surgery here. He has a son who's also a plastic surgeon, and a daughter. They both work with him. He's very rich and has tapped into the ever-increasing business of cosmetic surgery."

"Oh, I see. So he panders to middle-aged women who want to look young." As he finished his sentence, he instantly regretted it. He closed his eyes momentarily and then returned his gaze to Sylvie. She had a tight smile on her face. "Shit, I'm sorry. I didn't mean…"

"That's okay. I know what you're trying to say." She dropped her eyes down to her duck, and cut into it. "He actually finances a lot of medical reconstructive surgery from the money he makes doing the cosmetic work. You know, for people who have been burned, or been in accidents, that kind of thing. The rest, though, is middle-aged women who want to look young." She smirked up at him.

"And you've never met?"

Sylvie shook her head as she chewed.

"He seemed very… chatty on the phone."

"Well we've spoken a lot over the past month, regarding the signing over."

Nick pursed his lips together and nodded. "I'm sorry about my comment. I didn't mean to generalise. It's just… it's something I don't really get. You know, the plastic surgery thing."

"That's because you're young and look… well you look like a Greek god, Nick. You're perfect, so why would you ever want to change or improve anything? Not everyone feels so comfortable in their own skin."

"Mmm." Nick was clearly embarrassed by her honest comment. "I think that's a little over-generous." He squinted his eyes and shifted in his seat.

Sylvie shook her head. *Surely he could see how good-looking he was?*

"How do you feel about it? Would you go that route?" He stopped suddenly, his fork suspended in the air, the rich tomato sauce dripping back down to the plate, and looked up at her. "Have you?"

Sylvie burst out laughing. "I'm not sure if I should be flattered or offended. No. I. Haven't. Would I? That's harder to answer. I always thought 'Not a chance in hell', but as you start to feel old, it does cross your mind. A nip here or a tuck there." She shrugged. "I'm too chicken anyway."

Nick reached over and grazed her cheek with the back of his hand. "Don't ever. You are perfect." And his blue eyes burned as he spoke and Sylvie realised that he actually meant it. *Wow!*

"Zach – he's your partner, right?" Sylvie nodded again as she tasted another morsel of her duck in sweet walnut sauce. "You're close to him?"

She quickly chewed and swallowed. "Very. He's like a big brother to me. Chris and Zach were school friends, so I've known him ever since I came over from England. Over twenty years now. He has my back and I couldn't have got through the last eight months without him. He's the kindest, sweetest man I've ever known. He doesn't have a bad bone in his body." She paused thoughtfully. "I love him." Sylvie felt goose bumps cover her body as she spoke and her eyes welled up from the depth of emotion she felt for her confidant and partner. "I've never told him that. Maybe I should."

Nick leaned over and tenderly wiped a tear from her cheek with his thumb then put it in his mouth, savouring it. Sylvie grinned shyly. She swallowed hard as her heart started to race again. "He's married to my best friend, Lilianna."

"I remember seeing them at the wedding. The petite blonde? She's the one that realised you were seeing someone, right?"

"She knows me better than anyone. How I've kept *this*" – Sylvie waved her hand between the two of them – "from her, I don't know. I'll have to tell her though. She worries about me, a lot. They are both like family to me." Sylvie pushed her plate away and took a gulp of her wine. "I think it's my turn now." Nick raised his eyebrows and conceded with a nod. "Tell me about your business."

"It's not very complicated. I earned money while I was at school, then afterwards as a water-ski instructor and lifeguard. I took over the shop I have now with a small loan and then started sourcing yachts – boats for wealthy clients who wanted them for prestige rather than anything else. My business grew quickly, mainly because of the influx of wealthy Russians and then from word of mouth. Christian manages the shop for me. We're old school pals."

"So you always wanted to live on a yacht. You never wanted your own property? Like a house, I mean?"

"I do own a property." Sylvie looked puzzled. "The shop is mine, I bought the whole building. The first floor houses my office and a two-bedroomed flat and the top floor is a three-bedroomed penthouse. Christian lives in the small flat and I rent out the top floor to an offshore company."

"Oh." Sylvie didn't know what to say. He seemed to surprise her all the time.

"I just never needed that much space. The yacht works for me and if I need anywhere else to crash, I have my mum's or Christian's sofa." He smirked.

"What about Brigitte?" she asked. Nick's eyes clouded over and he took a gulp of wine. "It's okay, you don't need to tell me." Sylvie looked away at the view of the now-floodlit Parthenon through the open French doors.

"Not much more to tell. I was very much in love with her. I was prepared to take her children and marry her. They were adorable and that's what hurt too. I got very close to them and when she left me, I lost them too."

Sylvie could see the hurt in his face. *Children, he obviously wants children*, she thought to herself. Well that wasn't going to happen, not with her. Sylvie looked over again to the Parthenon, trying hard to think of a suitable response.

Nick took the bottle of wine and refilled their glasses. "I met her through her ex-husband. He was a friend of my father's. He'd been the architect for some of his buildings out in Dubai a few years back, and then Dad had designed their house out in Cyprus. Dad introduced me to him when he needed to sell his yacht, when he and Brigitte divorced."

"Julian worked out in Dubai?" interrupted Sylvie.

"Yes. After Mum and Dad divorced, he went back and forth from Dubai. He did quite a lot of work out there. He did think about moving there permanently but he couldn't bear to be away from us." Nick snorted. "He did do very well over there though," he added wistfully.

"I never knew," Sylvie muttered, stunned at this new information. It explained his extraordinary wealth.

"One good thing came of it." Sylvie quickly turned to face him. "Elenora met Pavlos because of my breakup."

"Really? I didn't know that."

"Uh-huh. When I went MIA, I went to the South of France for a couple of months. I left Christian in charge of the shop and checked in with him. I literally fucked everything in sight and was wasted every night. I thought I'd be able to block out the pain. Pathetic, really, and it didn't work. I was pretty disgusted with myself after six weeks. It's not really me – I just wanted to act out and I couldn't face coming back to my family. I got my shit together and actually made some very good contacts over there. All the rich and famous hung out there, so I got to meet a lot of them." He paused only to pick up her hand. He played with her fingers as he spoke. "I sourced yachts for a lot of them who were clueless, and made a serious amount of money within a few weeks. Pavlos and I had been in the army together and he was back after finishing his studies in England. He came over to the house to find me – you know, to catch up. Of course I wasn't there, but Elenora was and he ended up talking to her all afternoon. They went out on a couple of dates and within a few weeks, it became obvious they were serious."

"That's so romantic. What made you go back?"

"Christian told me my sister had a serious boyfriend, which freaked me out. I've always been over-protective of my sisters. So I decided to bite the bullet and return. Thank God it was Pavlos. He's a great guy. He really looked out for me when I was in the army."

"He is, and they're really sweet together." Sylvie remembered how they kept touching each other the night of the DVD, and how it made her feel that she couldn't be that way with Nick. The image of Julian forced itself into her head and she clenched her teeth. They were going to have to get round to that topic soon and she really didn't have the stomach for it – literally!

He saw her expression change as she spoke. "What is it? What are you thinking?" Sylvie shook her head, embarrassed. He pulled her onto his lap and she draped herself around his neck. "Hey, come on, tell me. Whatever it is. At this stage, I think there's very little that can shock me."

Sylvie grinned; that was true. "Well, I remembered how tactile Elenora and Pavlos were last Wednesday, and I remember feeling almost jealous that they could be that way and we couldn't." She sighed hard. "And of course there's the obvious."

"Obvious?" She looked up into his beautiful young face and felt her heart leap.

"Yes, the obvious. You being younger than me. You wanting children. Our families. The list is quite long."

He pulled her closer and kissed her lips gently, his eyes wide open and burning. "Do you love me?" His voice was quiet and hoarse. Sylvie closed her eyes and nodded. He breathed deeply and the tension in his body released. "Then all of that can be sorted out. Sylvie, I don't want to be anywhere else. You are the most important thing to me. You are my heaven."

They sat there for what seemed like an age, neither one of them wanting to move. Nick continued to stroke her arm as they sat, and Sylvie rested her head against his chest, breathing in his intoxicating scent. She realised that this was the longest time they'd ever spent together.

Nick broke through the silence first. "What would you like to do tomorrow?"

"Whatever you want, I really don't mind."

"Ideally I'd just like to spend it in bed with you, but it seems a waste not to actually see Athens after you dragged me out here."

Sylvie giggled. "Okay, we'll do Athens, then."

"Okay. Right now, though, I want to do you." He nuzzled her neck as he spoke.

"Oh really? How about a bath?" Nick's eyes widened as he remembered the last bath they'd taken.

"Now you're talking." His voice gruff and full of mischief. "I hope the tub's big."

"Oh, it's big, Nick." Sylvie raised her eyebrow and slowly stood up, unwrapping herself from his arms. Then she slowly started to undo her robe. Nick's eyes were transfixed, totally captivated by her as she allowed the robe to drop to the floor. She stood there naked in the dim lighting and the reflected glow of the Parthenon. She took his hand and at a leisurely pace, led him to the bathroom.

Sylvie didn't know whether it was the combination of the wine and champagne, or the fact that she'd confessed her innermost secrets that made her feel so unashamed and so connected to him. All she knew was she wanted this man's hands, mouth, body on her. She fleetingly thought back to the 'fucked everything in sight' as she tried hard to look graceful, while he willingly followed her. *Well, at least he'd sown his wild oats, then.* That thought didn't sit well with her. Who was she kidding? *All those taut and tight thong-clad hotties in the South of France and their 'Voulez-vous coucher avec moi?'* Well he was here with her now. By his own admission, he'd said he could have had any young girl, and she knew that was true. By some miracle, though, he was here, devouring her up with his molten gaze.

She turned on the taps and allowed the water to slowly fill up the large tub as she poured in the bath oil. Nick was beside her as she turned to him, his eyes wide with wonder. Sylvie pulled at his robe tie and loosened it. He gasped as the robe fell open, and Sylvie pushed it over his sculpted shoulders, letting it drop down onto the bathroom floor. Nick stood stock-still, watching her every move, totally in awe of her. She kissed his chest and smoothed her hand over his toned stomach, gliding across to the muscle over his hip bone. *God, he was perfect.* She loved that muscle, it led straight to… He let out a deep moan as he reached for her head. Interrupting her train of thought.

"Oh no… no touching yet," she whispered, as she gently took his hands and placed them at his sides.

"Oh, Sylvie, what are you doing to me? I just want to –"

"Patience," she mock-scolded him, her voice barely audible over the water filling up the bath. She smoothly kissed his chest and moved slowly down his body again as he tensed his fists and feet, knowing exactly where she was heading. Sylvie lowered herself and knelt in front of him, glancing up at him through her lashes.

"Christ, Sylvie, you're gonna kill me." On hearing his needy tone, Sylvie took him in her mouth and started to suck. "Argh, Jesus, sweet Jesus."

She held on to his hips to steady him as she sucked, moving her mouth up and down his extensive length. He moaned through clenched teeth as she moved faster, taking him deeper. Nick exhaled deeply as he let his head fall back, relishing every second. His fingers tensing, itching to touch her.

When she felt that he couldn't take any more, she stopped and rose up, kissing him passionately, this time allowing him to hold her. He pulled her up to him, grasping at her thighs and head. Then, in one swift movement, he was on the floor, dragging her down on top of him. Sylvie lowered herself onto him, her breathing becoming increasingly faster and shallow.

"Oh baby, that's it. Aah." As Sylvie moved up and down, he matched her every move. He held her waist and lifted her, her eyes flickering shut, revelling in his touch, his total desire for her. She had never felt like this… this want. It was almost unbearable.

"Take my hands." His voice husky. Sylvie clasped on to each of them and leaned forward, moving slowly at first. Then, seeing his clenched jaw and his eyes burning into her, she started to move faster, Nick matching her every move.

"Oh that's right. Faster, Sylvie. That's it…" His words setting off the fuse. Sylvie looked down at this incredible man as she let herself go, crying out his name as she reached her climax and seeing her undone by him. Nick too found his release, thrusting into her, crying out through clenched teeth. Sylvie collapsed onto his chest, gasping, as Nick wrapped his arms around her.

Slowly, Sylvie pulled herself up, her breathing still shallow and quick, and glanced up at the tub.

"God, you're beautiful." Sylvie flushed shyly, his comment taking her by surprise as he breathed heavily.

"Let me turn the water off," she mumbled, as he reluctantly let her go and watched her reach over and turn off the taps. She held out her hand to him.

"Come. Bath." He lifted himself off the floor and took her hand. He kissed it tenderly and stepped into the bath.

He smiled seductively at her, then cocked his head to the side. "Lay on me, this time?"

"Let me get our drinks first." Sylvie skipped out to the dining room and picked up their glasses and the wine and headed back to the bathroom. Nick was lying back in the water, his eyes closed.

"I see you've got a feel for it."

"Yeah, who'd have thought? Come on, this tub is far too big for one." Sylvie put down their glasses and the bottle and stepped in, nestling between his legs, lying back against him. "You smell wonderful." She took his hands and put her fingers in between his and grasped them tightly.

"I really don't want to leave this place. You realise this is the longest we've ever spent together?"

"I know. You're not sick of me are you?"

"No, silly." She splashed him.

"You must be good for me. I haven't had one stick of gum today. You've made me kick my chewing gum addiction! The only problem is I've substituted that addiction with another. You!" He kissed her neck, then rubbed his nose over it.

"Oh, I approve of that one." Sylvie squirmed.

"You realise that I'll need you with me then, every day, twenty-four-seven. I don't know what I might do if I can't get my fix." Sylvie turned around to face him as she smiled at him.

"Sounds serious."

"Deadly," he whispered. He pulled her face up to his and kissed her softly at first, then harder, urgently. "Sylvie, you own me." His expression intense, raw, his comment flooring Sylvie with his honesty.

"I'm not going anywhere," Sylvie mumbled into his mouth.

"Good."

4

INSECURE

Sylvie's eyes fluttered open as the sunlight streamed in through the windows. It took her a couple of seconds to register where she was. Nick was resting on her chest, his arm around her, and his knee resting on her leg. She slowly bent her head down to take in his smell and then she gazed down the full length of his body, drinking in every contour. *Ho-ly shit!*

Her fingers itched to stroke his back but she knew it would wake him. Sylvie turned to see if she could see the time on her watch, which was just out of reach on the bedside table, but it was no use. Judging by the noise on the street and the sunlight, it must have been around seven. The French doors had been left open and the voile curtains flapped in the breeze. Sylvie smiled to herself; she'd slept without her eye mask for the first time in years and she'd slept past six. Nick was definitely having an unusual effect on her! Normally, Sylvie would have been desperate to get out of bed – she never lingered once she'd woken. Today, though, she wanted to stay. *Mmm.* Stay and be wrapped in this glorious man. She couldn't stop grinning to herself.

Yesterday had been a night of real revelations. It had felt good to finally tell Nick the truth about Chris. She never thought she'd have been able to. It was a part of her life she really didn't want to relive or discuss again, but Nick had made it almost easy. His honesty and concern were so refreshing, it had totally disarmed her. She'd never experienced that with Chris. She was always too concerned about how he might react or if his feelings would be hurt. Her feelings were always secondary to his. Nick didn't make her feel that way. In fact, he made her feel the complete opposite, like her feelings were the most important.

Sylvie gently stroked Nick's back as he tightened his hold on her. It was no use, she'd resisted for as long as she could. Her hand was literally drawn to him like a magnet. He let out a stifled moan and stretched his shoulders. His hand caressed her arm as he slowly lifted his head to look up at her, resting his chin on her chest, his stubble prickling her.

"Good morning, beautiful."

Oh my! Even with bed hair and slightly swollen sleep-filled eyes, he was breathtaking. Sylvie's heart lurched. She smiled tightly, thinking that she must look like a crumpled brown paper bag. Why the hell hadn't she got up and sorted herself out? "Morning," she whispered.

Furrowing his brow, he reached up to her face and ran his finger over her mouth. "What's wrong?"

What's wrong! Nothing. Apart from I just woke up next to God's gift to women and I must look like a bag of spanners! Sylvie shook her head.

Nick pulled himself up closer to her. "Hey. Did I do something?"

Oh no! He'd done absolutely nothing, except to reaffirm her anxieties, just by being! "You've done nothing. It's not you, really. It's me." Her voice soft and reassuring. "Let me go to the bathroom." Her few moments of bliss seemed like a distant memory, faced with her oh-so-present insecurities. She slid out from under him and padded over to the bathroom as he turned to watch her, his face intense and pensive.

Once inside, Sylvie quickly went to inspect her face. Shit! Dark circles, blotchy and sallow. She turned on the tap and reached over to her toothbrush and started to vigorously brush her teeth. Who was she kidding? He wasn't going to stick around now. Their first morning waking up together, it was like Beauty and the Beast! She quickly peed, then splashed cold water on her face and patted it dry, then slipped into one of the robes they'd left there last night. She caught sight of their wine glasses and the bottle on the side of the bath. She closed her eyes, summoning up the picture in her head of the two of them. Her eyes dropped to the floor where they had been. Last night was –

Nick knocked on the door, interrupting her thoughts. "Sylvie, are you alright?" he demanded, his voice strained.

"I'm fine." Her voice was almost as strained as his.

"I'm coming in." And before she could protest, he flung open the door and stood there in all his glory staring at her, as she swung round in shock. His head slightly cocked to one side, assessing her mood. "What is it?"

Sylvie closed her eyes and buried her face in her hands. He was up to her in a millisecond, wrapping his arms around her.

"Hey, don't. Please, Sylvie, what is it? I'm thinking the worst here. Tell me, please." He stroked her hair and dropped kisses on the top of her head. "I can't see you this way, please just tell me." He held on to her for what seemed like an age, totally baffled and bewildered as to what had made her so upset. His heart was pounding as he tried to keep himself calm. Then, thankfully, Sylvie spoke.

"Oh Nick, I just don't get it." She looked up at him, her eyes full of tears. She swung round so her back was facing him as she looked at him in the reflection of the mirror. His eyes rested on hers. "Look!"

He softly gazed at her, puzzled as to what he was supposed to be looking at.

"Can't you see how this looks? I used to laugh at men who dated young girls old enough to be their daughters, and now look at *me*." She closed her eyes momentarily and shook her head as if she couldn't believe it. "And look at you," she finally whispered, sighing deeply.

Nick's face softened as he visibly relaxed and pulled her to him. "Is this what this about? I thought we'd covered this. I thought…"

Sylvie turned round again to face him, stepping back slightly. "I thought that when you'd see me, really see me, that you'd realise that maybe, this, you and me –"

He reached over to her and pulled her close again, almost in a vice-like grip. "You thought that I'd have a change of heart? Do you think I'm so fickle? That I'd tell you that I love you and then because your hair isn't combed or that you haven't put your make up on, or God knows what else, that my feelings would change?" His eyes were searching hers for some indication or confirmation that this was in fact what she was feeling. He loosened his grip and held her face gently, his expression anxious. "Sylvie, my sweet, sweet angel, why on earth would you think that? I love you. Have you so little faith in me?"

Sylvie saw hurt in his eyes and her heart twisted, knowing that through her insecurities she had caused him pain. Nick swallowed and the muscle in his cheek flinched. He pulled her head to his lips and murmured into her hair.

"I'm not him, Sylvie."

Sylvie's clenched her eyes shut as it dawned on her that Nick had worked out where her insecurities lay.

"I would never hurt you. He was the insecure one, not you." Nick softly kissed her and smoothed back her hair, allowing a smile to curl at the edge of his mouth. "You are the sexiest, cleverest, sweetest, kindest, most unselfish woman I have ever met. He was a fool to have never cherished that. I am the luckiest man alive, being here with you." The tears that Sylvie had been forcing back tumbled freely down her cheeks. She flung her arms around his neck and kissed him hard. Nick moaned as he freed the robe tie, allowing him to feel her soft skin as he let his hands wander freely over her smooth back and behind.

Sylvie pulled back a little and Nick wiped her eyes and cheeks with his thumbs, then licked them, grinning back at her.

"I just find it hard, Nick. I'm not used to this, I –"

He put his finger on her lips, effectively stopping her. "I don't want any more doubts. I've told you I don't play games. If I didn't want to be here I wouldn't be. Come on, let's get ready. I don't want to hear any more about it. Well not for now, anyway. We had an incredible evening last night. Sylvie, baby, I'm ecstatic I'm here with you. I've been longing for this. I waited four months." He grasped her face again and kissed her. "Shall I order breakfast? I'm starving!"

She nodded weakly, not wanting to ruin his good mood. She'd have to try and deal with her insecurities later.

"And then you show me Athens." He was grinning, and it was infectious. Sylvie started to smile. "That's better. That's one of the things I notice about you. You always smile."

Sylvie took a deep breath and momentarily closed her eyes. "Okay, what shall we have?" She really couldn't face anything; her stomach was in knots.

"I'll go and get the menu." He bounded out of the bathroom, allowing Sylvie to take in the perfect view of his firm behind. *He was beyond yummy*. She slowly followed him out, retying her robe. He'd slipped on his boxers and was leafing through the menu. He gazed up at her as she stood by the window. "They have everything, I'm going to have pancakes with bacon and eggs – oooh, and croissants. You?"

"Just some porridge and some stewed apricots and prunes." Nick wrinkled his nose in disapproval. Sylvie shook her head. If she ate half of what he ate, they'd need a winch to get her out of the hotel room! He leaned over to the phone and dialled Andreas.

Sylvie slipped back to the bathroom and started to run the shower. She allowed herself to calm down after her outburst, the warm water washing away her doubts. God, she was being so emotional these days.

He was still here, for goodness sake. She'd have to try and get a grip. If she was a blubbering mess all the time, he'd probably not want to be with her. After all, he'd only ever seen her confident and calm. She started to feel nauseous. Saliva started to fill her mouth as she desperately took deep breaths to calm her over-sensitive stomach. Porridge would help.

After washing herself and her hair she wrapped her hair up in a towel and then pulled another one around her body. Wiping the steam off the mirror and opening the door so she could re-examine her face, she saw that she looked a little more flushed and her skin had plumped up. She put her vitamin drops in her palm, then patted them onto her face, then rubbed in her face cream and eye cream. Then she applied a little concealer and blush, bending over the vanity unit so as to get closer to the mirror. As she was brushing on her mascara, Nick strolled into the bathroom.

"Has anyone ever told you that you have the sexiest eyes?" He gazed at her in the mirror. Sylvie smiled shyly, not knowing what to say. "It was the first thing I noticed about you." *Oh!*

He came up behind her and pushed up against her so she could feel him on her behind. He stifled a grin as she looked wide-eyed at him in the mirror. He had a wicked glint in his eye. "Now this, this I like." He had his hands on her hips and he pulled her closer to him, and leant down to kiss her bare shoulder. He slowly stroked her bare back and shoulders as Sylvie closed her eyes. *Holy shit, they were never going to leave this hotel room.*

"Oh God. Sylvie, you look… I can never have my fill of you."

Sylvie moaned as he slowly reached down to the bottom of the towel and he slid his hand up the back of her thigh. "I want you so bad. Like this." He looked at her in the mirror asking her permission. Sylvie stared at him in the reflection, her eyes transfixed on his, then slowly closing them, she revelled in his caress, as his hand stroked her now-burning skin. He slid down his boxers and gently lifted and folded back her towel, leaving it still wrapped around her middle, his eyes momentarily leaving her gaze to marvel at her behind as he continued to stroke it. The whole scene was so seductive, so erotic, it was as if she was watching someone else – it was almost voyeuristic.

As he slowly slid into her she gasped and he closed his eyes. His expression was of pure ecstasy. Sylvie gripped the sink with one hand and then, realising she was still holding her mascara brush, she released it into the sink and held on to the vanity marble as he slowly moved.

His eyes reopened, burning into hers. Her towel was still in place, making it feel illicit, forbidden even.

"Oh Sylvie." He was picking up the pace, holding on tightly to her hips as Sylvie watched him, and then her eyes rested on her own face. She could hardly recognise herself, flushed, her eyes bright and her mouth almost pouting. Sylvie pushed back to meet him with every thrust, totally mesmerised by the scene as it unravelled before her. It was so sensual and carnal, his desire for her and hers for him.

Nick cried, "Oh baby, this is gonna be quick." She watched him as his eyes bore into hers, his face determined. His hand moved up to her breast, squeezing and kneading, and Sylvie cried out as she could feel herself being pushed higher.

"You are –" but before he could complete his sentence, Nick tensed, his eyes clenched shut and seeing him become undone, undone by her, she too reached her climax. He fell onto her back gasping, wrapping his arms around her. "Incredible," he said, finishing his uncompleted sentence.

After a moment, when his breath started to slow down, he started planting soft kisses down her back as Sylvie tried to catch her breath, while she rested her forehead against the cool vanity. *Wow, where did that come from?*

"I've wanted to kiss your back from the night of the pre-wedding dinner." He looked at her in the mirror and Sylvie lifted her eyes, locking onto his in the mirror. "You wore that backless dress and I had to sit and look at it all night. Then when we danced, my hand was a centimetre away from it. I needed all my self-control not to reach up and stroke you from here" – his fingers caressed the nape of her neck and agonisingly slowly, he stroked down her back, loosening the towel so he could reach the dimples at the base of her back – "to here," where he planted a kiss. Sylvie's whole body trembled. "It was pure torture." He straightened himself and pulled out of her and then dragged his boxers back on.

Sylvie turned to look at him as she readjusted her towel. Then she kissed him hard on the lips, taking him by surprise. "You say the most romantic things sometimes. I never know what to say."

"I'm telling you how I feel, Sylvie. I want you to know, I need you to know. So you can stop doubting me. Doubting this." He pulled her to his chest as she wrapped her arms around him. There was a knock at the door. "That'll be breakfast."

"I thought we'd just had breakfast," Sylvie giggled.

"Mmm and it was soooo tasty."

Sylvie gasped, recoiling in embarrassment.

"Here, put this robe on. I'll get them to set it up in the dining room, is that okay?" Nick handed her one of the robes hanging on the door.

"Perfect." *Like you*, she thought.

"Like you." He winked at her as he left the bathroom. *Whoa! Did he just…? Spooky!*

Sylvie quickly towel-dried her hair and combed it back. She'd dry it after breakfast. Nick was already out leaning over the balcony, watching the activity below. Andreas was setting up the table. He smiled at her as she stepped through the threshold.

"*Kali mera*, Andreas." Sylvie greeted him in his native language.

"*Kali mera*, Mrs Sapphiris. I hope you slept well."

"I did, thank you."

"Well everything's ready. Will you be needing anything today?" Andreas looked over to Nick and then back at Sylvie. Nick shrugged and looked at Sylvie. "Laundry, reservations, taxis," Andreas suggested.

"Oh… um, we're not sure yet."

Andreas smiled and nodded. "Don't hesitate to call me. Enjoy your breakfast. Good morning." And with that he retreated.

Nick came over and pulled out a chair for Sylvie. Once she'd sat down, he took the chair next to her. "I have to say that I am enjoying someone else doing all the work. It's very novel for me. I suppose you're used to it."

Sylvie's face dropped in shock. "What do you mean?"

"Well, you have staff, don't you?"

"Yes, but Marcy doesn't do everything for me." Sylvie reached over to the teapot and popped in the tea bags.

"Oh."

"She's part of our family. She's been with us for twenty years. She helps me out with the house, and Teresa, her daughter, is like a sister to my boys. To be honest, I really don't need her, now the boys are grown. But like I said, she's like family."

"She's been with you for twenty years?" he said, his expression surprised. "I didn't realise."

"Yes, she came over to help when the boys were young and Chris and I were setting up the business. Chris was never a 'hands on' father. He liked the fun bits. Nappies, vomit and sleepless nights were not his thing. Marcy's like an aunt to Alex and Marcus."

Sylvie poured the milk into the tea cups and then their tea. Nick was slicing through his pancakes, which were dripping in syrup, as Sylvie lifted her cup to take a sip. The smell of the milk wafted to her nose and she felt her mouth fill with saliva again. She quickly put down her cup and clasped her hand over her mouth.

"What is it? You've gone…" His face was full of concern and his voice sounded shocked. Sylvie swiftly got up and ran to the bathroom, just making it in time to retch over the sink. Nick was by her side. He rubbed her back as she retched again. Once she'd stopped, she straightened up.

"I just need my antacids, I'll be alright." Nick rummaged in her wash bag and fished them out as Sylvie brushed her teeth again.

"Are you sure you're alright?" He pulled her close to him and took her face in his hands. "You look better now. Christ, you turned green at the table."

Sylvie laughed. "I've always had a sensitive stomach. I don't know – the milk just smelt funny. I suppose because it's different to back home. I'll just have my tea black."

They returned to the table and Nick poured Sylvie a fresh cup of black tea and then he picked up his own, ignoring the handle, and gingerly sniffed it. It smelled fine to him and he took a huge gulp. Sylvie looked at her porridge and pushed it away, deciding on the stewed fruit and croissant instead. She felt a lot better but she didn't want to risk it. Nick devoured his six pancakes, eggs and bacon.

"You eat like my boys. I don't know where you put it."

Nick grinned. "I'm going to jump in the shower and then we can go take in the sights. That's if you're up to it?"

Sylvie popped two antacids. "I'm fine, really. I'll get dressed, then." Nick stood up and then bent down to kiss her softly on the lips. Sylvie closed her eyes as her heart began to swoon. They were actually going to go out in public today. Together. Sylvie allowed herself to get excited.

She quickly gulped down her tea, then found her navy silk Bermuda shorts and an ivory vest that had been carefully hung in the walk-in closet. *Andreas sure knew how to unpack*, she thought to herself. She then pulled out her red wedges and a small red bag that Lilianna had bought her. Slipping on her silk nude bra and thong, she walked over to where the dressing table was and flicked on the hair dryer. She bent down, allowing her hair to fall so that she could roughly dry it under the force of the dryer, slowly massaging her scalp. She didn't hear Nick come out of the shower. He had a towel wrapped around his waist and was towel-drying his hair when he stopped dead in his tracks and gasped at the sight of Sylvie bent over double.

He swallowed hard and dropped the towel he was holding and lazily walked towards her, drinking her in. Once behind her he grazed his knuckles down her right bottom cheek and she instantly shrieked and flung herself upright. Nick laughed loudly and Sylvie marvelled at how stunning he looked.

"That's a very interesting way of drying your hair." He pulled her close. "God, you drive me insane, do you know that?" He kissed her hard, holding her head steady with his hands. "Get dressed – otherwise we'll never leave this hotel room." He mumbled into her mouth. "Mmm… minty. I like minty." He was referring to the residue left from her antacids.

"You're so bad!" Sylvie mock-scolded him, enjoying every second of his obvious approval. She was so glad she'd opted for sexy lingerie.

"Oh yes, I know I am. I'm very, very bad." His eyes filled with wicked mischief. He kissed her again, squeezing her tightly. "Quickly put something on before I peel you out of these." He ran his index finger round the lace top of her thong. Then he pulled away, his erection evident through his towel. Sylvie retreated hastily and slipped into her laid-out clothes as Nick shook his head and sauntered to the walk-in closet.

Was it always going to be this way? Sylvie thought, as she brushed her hair back, then applied some lipstick. Were they always going to be so… so… hot for one another? She couldn't remember if she'd been that way with Chris. This felt naughtier somehow. Really naughty! Well that's probably because it was. She really was tasting the forbidden fruit. She remembered with Chris she'd been shy and inexperienced which had made her feel a little nervous. With Nick, though, she didn't. It was carnal sometimes, like in the bathroom this morning. But it was also intense and passionate, like yesterday, after all her revelations. What affected her the most was that she could let herself be swept away by him, yet also take control without feeling vulnerable or embarrassed. He made her feel that way. He made her feel sexy and confident. He made her feel loved.

5

BACI

Nick emerged from the closet in a light blue polo, a pair of sand-coloured Bermuda shorts and sneakers. He reached over to put on his watch and then quickly rubbed in some hair product. The whole process had taken not even five minutes, and he looked good enough to eat. Sylvie shook her head. It really wasn't fair how little time men needed to get ready. Or maybe it was just Nick. The smell of his after-shave wafted through the suite. *Mmm.*

"So where're we going?" asked Nick, as Sylvie put the last of her things in her bag.

She slung it over her shoulder as she replied, "I thought we could go to the museum first, then down to *Plaka* for lunch."

"*Plaka?*"

"It's an area of Athens I love: small restaurants, cafes and shops, and its right under the Parthenon," Sylvie explained.

"Sounds great. I'll call Andreas to get us a taxi." As the elevator arrived down to the lobby, Nick grasped Sylvie's hand. She looked up at him, taking in his beautiful eyes. They matched the colour of his shirt perfectly.

"Are you ready?" Sylvie cocked her head, not understanding what he was trying to say. "This is our first time out together. In public." She nodded shyly as he leaned over and kissed her forehead.

They walked into the lobby, which was buzzing with guests. There was a large party of tourists who seemed to be checking out. Mr Zavos was talking to the concierge, when he spotted them walking towards the entrance. He stopped what he was doing and strolled over to them.

"*Kali mera,* Mrs Sapphiris, Mr Steed. Your taxi is waiting. I hope everything's to your satisfaction." He shook both their hands and smiled warmly at them.

"*Kali mera,* Mr Zavos. Yes everything is perfect, thank you," Nick answered, as he slipped his arm around Sylvie.

"Yes, thank you so much. The suite is fabulous." Sylvie smiled.

"Enjoy your day. I believe you're going to the museum today. It really is quite special." His comment was directed at Nick. Sylvie presumed Andreas was keeping Mr Zavos informed of all their plans.

"Thank you, we will." They all shook hands, and with a curt nod, Mr Zavos returned to the concierge.

"I like him," Nick commented as they walked out of the entrance.

"Me too."

"I like him because he looked after you. He's a good man."

"Yes, he is."

The taxi wound its way through the heavy Saturday morning traffic at breakneck speed. The taxi driver periodically shouted abuse at fellow drivers. Nick glanced at Sylvie nervously as they travelled in petrified silence.

Once they'd screeched to a halt, Sylvie smirked, "Yeah, I know. Takes a bit of getting used to." Nick nodded his agreement. They both leapt out of the taxi after Nick paid, and headed for the museum entrance.

The museum itself was an impressive neoclassical building with columns and marble stairs leading to the main doors. Nick kept hold of Sylvie's hand as he guided her to the ticket office, momentarily releasing her hand as he reached into his pocket for his wallet to pay for the tickets. The museum was already quite busy with tourists. They started to walk leisurely round the different artefacts. Sylvie pointed out the array of pottery that was dated between 1000 to 2000BC. There were the gold-handled weapons and beautiful gold masks. They came across some statues dating back as far as 4000BC. He watched and listened intently to her obvious enthusiasm, his eyes wide with pride. She obviously loved being here and she talked with such passion.

"Can you believe that some of these statues are *four thousand* years old?" Nick raised his eyebrows, sharing her disbelief. "These statues here are relatively new, around 100BC." Sylvie turned to Nick as she spoke. They were in front of a large marble statue of Aphrodite, Eros and Pan. "New. Well, new in comparison to the others," she huffed. "That makes them over two thousand years old. Remarkable condition, considering their age." She gazed at the statue. "She's so beautiful and serene," she mused almost to herself, then looked back at Nick as he continued to smile at her.

He squeezed her hand, her words mirroring his exact thoughts on her.

"What?"

"Nothing. I'm just enjoying my very personal guided tour. You are right, though. This statue is really quite beautiful."

"It is, especially considering how long ago it was made and how primitive their tools would have been back then." She glanced back at it wistfully. Nick pulled her gently to him so her back was up against him and he nuzzled her ear.

"She's still not as beautiful as you though," he whispered. Sylvie giggled.

"That's because about she's two thousand years older than me. At least I'm not the oldest woman in the museum!"

Nick laughed. *Finally! She was joking about her age.*

"Second oldest… oh no look." He motioned to an elderly lady in her seventies with a fiercely coiffured blue rinse, and a heavily powdered face. "I think that maybe she's slightly older than you, so that would make you the third oldest."

Sylvie swung round, her expression in mock-horror, wide-eyed and her mouth open.

Nick grasped her in a vice-like grip, effectively holding her arms as she tried to wriggle free, laughing at her lovingly. "Don't you glare at me with those beautiful eyes!" He chastised: "You started it." He sniggered. Then he quickly planted a hard kiss on her lips, making a smacking noise. He felt her body instantly relax. "You're the best-looking woman in this museum, Sylvie. In fact, you're always the best-looking woman in any room." He released his hold and tenderly stroked back the hair from her face. Holding her chin, he kissed her softly this time. "I mean it."

She squirmed and flushed at his comment. *Oh, he said the sweetest things!*

"Come on, show me the rest."

Sylvie took his hand and they carried on the tour, marvelling firstly at a bronze statue of Poseidon. "This should really interest you. Poseidon, god of the sea." Sylvie pulled him in front of the magnificent statue.

"Wow, it really is something. He looks very austere. Commander of all he surveys."

"Definitely," mused Sylvie.

Then they moved on to a bronze statue of a stunning naked man found in a shipwreck. Sylvie gazed up at it, taking in every contour.

"Hey, stop staring. Are you trying to make me jealous?" Nick teased.

Sylvie shook her head and smirked. "Well, he is very…" She pretended to search for the correct adjective, sucking on her teeth. Nick pulled her sharply away from the statue.

"Never mind what he is. Come and show me the gold art and masks. I'll show you later what he is."

"Don't tell me *you're* jealous of a bronze statue!" She laughed in total disbelief, as he continued to increase the distance between her and the statue.

"I'm jealous of how you're ogling at it."

Sylvie snorted. After they had admired the last of the artefacts, they made their way out back onto the street. The sun was high and strong. Sylvie slipped on her sunglasses as the glare bouncing off the white buildings was fierce. Nick rummaged in his pocket and slid on his Wayfarers too.

"So to *Plaka*, right?"

"Yes."

"Is it far?"

"A couple of kilometres."

"So we could walk?"

Sylvie nodded.

"Is that okay? I really don't feel like getting thrown about in a taxi again."

"Sure. We can pass by *Syndagma*?"

"*Syndagma?*"

"The parliament building, where they have the soldiers changing guard."

"Sounds very touristy, so I definitely need to see that."

They lazily walked down the busy streets. The noise was quite overwhelming: cars beeping, screeching of brakes, men shouting. Nick gripped her hand tightly as they weaved in and out of pedestrians.

"A little different to our sleepy island?" Sylvie commented, clearly loving the atmosphere.

"You could say that! It's crazy."

"I know, but I really love it. I love the buzz. It reminds me of when we used to come when I was a child. Good memories."

"You were amazing in the museum. You really love the history…"

"I do. I'm fascinated by old things. They give us an insight into our past, our roots. They achieved amazing things, beautiful things. Even then, people wanted their homes to look beautiful. You saw the pottery, the paintings. It wasn't just practicality – even their weapons were exquisite."

"So they had interior designers even then?" Nick joked, slipping his arm around her waist.

"Yes, I suppose you could say that," laughed Sylvie, putting her arm around his waist and hooking her thumb in his waistband. "I find it inspirational."

"So you've been to it a lot, then?"

"Every time I've come to Athens since it was made – well, almost. I mostly came on my own. I brought Alex and Markus a few times. They really loved it. Well, they'd done a lot of the history at school, so it brought it alive for them. Chris didn't really share my enthusiasm."

"Well, I loved it. I loved that you love it and that you took the time to show it to me. My very own personal guide." He stopped in the middle of the street, halting the agitated pedestrians behind them, and bent down to kiss her tenderly on the lips. The pedestrians started to catcall and whoop, to Sylvie's horror, probably because she understood their lewd comments. Nick sniggered against her cheek. "I take it that's 'Get a room' in Greek."

"Hmm, something like that. Slightly more colourful though," laughed Sylvie.

They eventually reached the outside of the parliament building, where there were a large number of tourists taking photos of the soldiers dressed in the national costume. The pigeons swarmed around them as a few tourists had thrown down crumbs. Nick fished out his iPhone.

"Come on. If I'm a tourist, I need a photo too."

Sylvie went to take the phone, but Nick shook his head.

"No, no, of both of us." He turned around and walked to a man who was taking photos of his children. "I'm really sorry. Would you, please?" He motioned with his phone to Sylvie.

"*Si*," the man answered, in a thick Italian accent. Nick quickly ran over to Sylvie and dragged her to where the man was and handed him his phone.

"Just touch here." He explained and the Italian tourist nodded and beamed up at them. Nick took Sylvie by the waist and pulled her close. "Now smile for the camera, baby," he whispered in her ear and Sylvie smiled, not because he'd asked her but more because she just couldn't stop herself. The Italian man put up his thumb, indicating it was a good photo, and Nick bent and kissed Sylvie. Without being prompted, the Italian man secretly took another shot of them, smiling to himself, then handed over the phone.

"Thank you." Nick beamed as he took back his phone and scrolled to see the result. When he came across the second photo, he looked up at the man who winked at him.

"*Baci.*" His voice sang as he spoke and then he made kissing noises, explaining the word.

"Oh, *baci,*" Nick repeated, as realisation hit.

"*Si, baci.*" He beamed again, then motioned he had to go. "*Ciao,*" and with that, he went back to his family.

"How nice was he?"

"He was sweet," agreed Sylvie. "Come on, I'm thirsty and starving, Plaka's just up this street here." Nick slipped his phone in his pocket, but not before sneaking a second look at their photo. Sylvie closed her eyes and took a deep breath as he squeezed her again and kissed her. "*Baci,*" she muttered against his lips.

"Mmm. Let's go eat."

It took ten minutes to reach *Plaka*, which nestled in the shadow of the Parthenon. The streets were narrow and rammed full of people, tourists and locals alike. The noise level was just a little lower than out near the main roads, only because of the lack of cars. Sylvie guided Nick through the people, ignoring the incessant calls from different restaurateurs to come and sample their cuisine, the smell of garlic, fried fish and rich sauces heavy in the hot midday air.

Eventually, they arrived at a small square, and Sylvie headed for a simple-looking restaurant called *Byzantino Taverna*. The tables were covered in blue tablecloths and the chairs were traditional wooden and woven seats. A short, grey-haired man wearing a white shirt and black trousers greeted them with a face-splitting smile.

"*Po, po, kalo sorises* Sylvie!" He hugged her warmly, as he was genuinely shocked and equally pleased to see her. He then turned to look at Nick.

"It's so good to see you again, Lefteris. This is my friend Nick. Nick, Lefteris is the owner."

"I'm very pleased to meet you." His accent was thick as he struggled with the words.

"Me too." Nick shook his outstretched hand.

Lefteris eagerly pointed to a table and motioned them to take a seat.

"Come. Sit." He called to one of the waiters to get some water and a small carafe of ouzo and some dips. "So, how are you? So, sorry about Christophoros. I was sock, real sock." He emphasised the 'h' and the 'sh' sound was replaced with just 's' as he spoke his broken English. He did the sign of the cross three times over his head, chest and shoulders and looked skywards, shaking his head. Sylvie smiled tightly. "*O Zacharias* tell me, last time he here." He mixed the two languages as he spoke. The waiter arrived and placed everything down on the table, nodding his recognition. Sylvie smiled tightly at him.

"*Efharisto*, Lefteris."

"Sorry, eh, I make you sad. *Ela*. Sit. Nick, please. Let me pour you ouzo eh, then go and see what you eat." He dropped a little water in two glasses, then poured the ouzo in. The clear liquid instantly turned milky, then he dropped a couple of ice cubes in. The strong smell of aniseed wafted up to where they were still standing. Lefteris pulled out a chair for Sylvie and she sat down, turning her face to Nick, who'd stepped back to allow them to talk. She patted the chair to the left, adjacent to her, and he willingly sat down, removing his sunglasses and leaving them on the table. "Okay, I leave. *Kali orexi*." With his blessing, Lefteris quickly retreated back to the kitchen. Sylvie rubbed her finger nervously.

Nick immediately took her hand and kissed it, looking at her intently through his lashes. He could see she was feeling uncomfortable, as her eyes were fixed on her glass – or so he thought, as she hadn't taken her sunglasses off.

"Hey, baby," he whispered, then stroked her hair back off her face, removing her glasses and placing them next to his. She turned to look at him. "It's okay. At least he knew." Sylvie furrowed her brow, not understanding. "I mean you didn't need to explain."

"Oh, yes, I suppose so. I'm sorry. Maybe we should have gone to a place I didn't know. I didn't think." She shook her head, then repeated her apology. "I'm sorry."

"Why are you apologising?" He scraped his chair closer to her.

"We were having such a lovely time and… well, now…" She couldn't get the words out. She'd ruined the mood.

"Hey, stop that. I'm having the time of my life. I'm glad we came here. It obviously means a lot to you. It makes me happy that you'd want me to be part of this." His hand motioned in the air. "I love seeing you with people that genuinely like you. It makes me feel proud and lucky, really lucky."

"Thanks." She lifted her hand and stroked his stubbly chin, and he leaned into it, then turned slightly to kiss it.

He leaned over and picked up their drinks and handed her one. She took it and they clinked them together. "*Ya mas*," they said in unison, and then Sylvie took a large sip, while Nick tentatively put the glass to his lips and took a smaller one. As he swallowed, he closed one eye.

"Don't you like ouzo?" giggled Sylvie, looking at his face.

"Never tried it," admitted Nick, almost ashamed.

"Oh God! What do you think?" her surprise evident.

"It's an acquired taste. It's strong, really strong. Like potent liquorice."

"Very potent. I'll get you something else."

"No, no. I want the full Greek experience. It's just I don't really do spirits, but it's not unpleasant." He took another sip. "Maybe I should eat something though."

Sylvie giggled and nodded. She took some bread and dipped it in a grey creamy-looking substance, then offered it to him. Nick willingly opened his mouth and she put the bread and dip in. "Mmm, what is it?"

"Aubergine dip. More?"

He nodded and she dipped it in, collecting a larger dollop. When again offering it to him, he bit down on the bread, then took her hand as he chewed, fixing her with his blue eyes. He pulled her hand closer and licked her thumb where some dip had dropped.

"Delicious."

Sylvie's stomach filled with butterflies as she smiled at him. "You are bad."

"Oh yeah, baby." He wickedly raised his eyebrow and smiled a very sexy smile, then released her hand. She sighed, trying to keep her butterflies in check. She placed a plate in front of him, then systematically served each and every dip onto his plate. She spooned some salad and carefully placed that on his plate too, his eyes never leaving her face.

"What?" She flushed under his constant gaze.

"Nothing." He smiled and his eyes sparkled. "So what do you recommend here?"

"It's all good. We can go in the kitchen and look in a minute." Nick looked puzzled. "You choose from the kitchen. So you can see what it is. Come on, I'll show you."

Sylvie stood up from the table and reached out her hand. Nick took it and gracefully pushed his chair back and followed her to the kitchen at the rear, peering into the huge pots and oven trays. The smell was amazing, and the temperature in the kitchen was at least ten degrees higher.

"Look, there's baked aubergines in tomato, *gouvetsi* – that's rice pasta with beef," Sylvie explained, "roast chicken and potatoes, spinach pie, meatballs in the oven, lamb fricassee, beef in a lemon sauce, beans in tomato, and over there are any number of fish that they can fry up."

"You're right. Everything looks delicious. Um, what are you going to have?" Nick watched as an elderly lady spooned the pasta dish onto a plate for another customer. She gave him a toothy smile.

"I always have the aubergines, they are so nice here."

"I can't decide. I think the lamb, but I want to try the beef too."

"Have them both and we'll get some chips. They make them fresh and they sprinkle oregano on them."

Sylvie spoke to the elderly lady in Greek, placing their order, and then they went back and sat at their table. Nick took another sip of his ouzo. *It wasn't so bad actually*. He was getting used to it.

"So, shall we continue where we left off?" Sylvie stopped mid-mouthful and turned to look at him. "I mean getting to know one another."

"Sure. What would you like to know?" Sylvie's stomach constricted. She wasn't really sure if she wanted to confess all in such a public place.

"You haven't told me much about Alex. I know I've met him, but what's he like? Is he anything like Markus?" Sylvie's whole body relaxed. Now this topic she had no problem with.

"No, well they both have a similar wicked – and sometimes an inappropriate – sense of humour, but Alex is very laid-back and sensible. No extreme sports for him. He's calm and gentle but strong. Very strong actually. He was a great help to me when… well. He helped Markus too. He was close to his dad simply because he was easy, and Chris could entertain him when he was younger. He misses him, a lot. They bonded over alpha male stuff. You know: action films, football, basketball, they played pool and some violent video games too." Sylvie took a good drink of her ouzo. "I need to call him; see when he's getting back. He's supposed to be finishing his exams on Tuesday, so he should be back by the weekend, hopefully before."

The waiter arrived with their main courses. Lefteris came over to check that everything was alright. Nick could see that he genuinely cared for Sylvie and he kept using terms of endearment as he spoke to her. Nick managed to eat everything that was brought and also tried Sylvie's aubergines. "Boy, I'm stuffed!"

"Where do you put it all, really? Well I think you need a walk to digest and then we can go up to see the Parthenon. The sun won't be so strong, then."

Nick asked for the bill and paid, after arguing with Sylvie.

"Don't even think about it, Sylvie. You're giving me my personal guided tour. The least I can do is take you to lunch." Lefteris was over like a shot, seeing them rise from the table. He hugged and kissed Sylvie and he shook Nick's hand, telling them he hoped to see them both very soon. He stood at the entrance of the restaurant and tearfully waved them off.

Nick slipped his arm around Sylvie's waist and she put her arm around him, hooking her thumb in his waistband again as they lazily walked through the narrow streets. They were both a little giddy from the potent ouzo. Sylvie stopped into a small grocery shop selling local produce and bought a couple of jars of *vissino*, sour cherries in syrup, and a jar of *mastica*, a sweet made from tree sap, for herself and Lilianna. As they turned into a small street with tourist shops, Nick's phone rang. Clearly surprised, he released Sylvie as he fished it out of his pocket. He looked at the number and raised his eyebrows.

"I'm sorry. I really need to take this." Sylvie nodded, showing him she didn't mind and that he should answer. "Hello, Serge, how are you? … Good. Yes, I'm on holiday. Yes…" Nick's eyes focused on Sylvie. "… with my girlfriend."

Sylvie smiled shyly. *There was that word again.* She really found it bizarre being called a girlfriend, but hearing it from Nick's lips made her heart swell.

"No, that's okay. What can I do for you?" Nick held on to her hand as he spoke, idly playing with her fingers. As Nick listened intently, Sylvie mouthed to him that she was going to look at the rather smart-looking jewellers specialising in Byzantine-style jewellery. He nodded and reluctantly let go of her hand.

Sylvie pushed open the shop door and was immediately hit with the smell of burning incense and cool air, thanks to the air conditioning. It was beautifully set out and it reminded her of the museum. There were pictures on the wall of original antique jewellery, and glass cabinets housed a large collection of copies and original designs.

The owner was a slim man in his early thirties. He had long dark curly hair in a ponytail. He was pale and wore round John Lennon glasses. He looked like someone who should have been around in the late sixties.

"Good afternoon. Would you like any help?" His English was good, though his accent was strong.

"I just came in to look, if that's okay."

"Of course. Everything is handmade," he explained.

"Your work is very beautiful. Did you make them?" He nodded modestly. Sylvie looked at all the glass cases, one by one. There were some very simple designs in matt gold that looked very similar to the ones she'd seen in books. Along with those, there were some exquisite ornate designs that were like works of art encrusted with bold stones and fine details of leaves and grapes. As Sylvie scanned the cabinets, her eye caught sight of a beautiful ring that had a large cobalt blue oval stone set in a gold ring of tiny gold balls. It was simple, yet stunning.

"Can I see this?"

The owner opened the drawer and placed the tray on the counter for her to look at. He pulled it out of its case and held it out to her.

"Please, try."

Sylvie slipped it on her ring finger, the one she always rubbed. Maybe it was time to put something new there to rub, rather than just skin. It looked fabulous and it fitted perfectly. She held her hand up to admire it.

"It's very beautiful."

He nodded modestly. She looked over to the tray and noticed some earrings in the same design but with a drop and much smaller. Seeing her look, the owner pulled them from the cushion and handed them to her to examine closer. He then brought a table mirror for her to see what they looked like as she held them up against her ear.

"I love the colour. It's so rich." The owner smiled kindly. She looked again at the ring and thought, *what the hell!* "I'll take them both." The owner raised his eyebrows and curtly nodded. Sylvie was sure she'd just bought them purely because he was the most un-pushy salesman she'd ever come across in Greece. They were beautiful though – and blue, she loved blue.

He reached over to retrieve a white leather box, which he flipped open and set the earrings in. He then reached for another box and gestured for Sylvie to give the ring to put it in. "I think I'll keep it on."

He smiled gently and put the earrings and the empty ring box in a white carton bag with 'Byzantinos' in gold writing on the side. Sylvie handed him her credit card. He looked down at the name.

"You are Greek, Madame?"

"Yes, from Cyprus. I'm here on holiday."

"Well, then you get discount, twenty percent. Always to our Cypriot cousins, overseas."

"Oh, thank you. *Efharisto.*" Sylvie beamed.

He rang up the amount and Sylvie pushed in her pin number. He handed her back her card and the receipt. "*Efharisto* and *ya sas.*" Sylvie picked up her bag and stepped back out into the harsh heat of the afternoon. Nick was just finishing his call.

"Okay, Serge, a week on Friday. I'll email you everything you need. I will. Bye." He switched off his phone, replaced it in his pocket and walked over to where Sylvie was standing in the shade of the building.

"Been shopping, I see." Sylvie lifted her hand and wriggled her ring finger, showing him what she'd bought. He took hold of her hand and admired it. "That's ve-ry nice, very Greek, very beautiful. Like you." He kissed her palm.

"And some earrings to match," she grinned, sounding pleased with herself.

"Really? I didn't think you liked jewellery."

"Are you mad? All women like jewellery. The bigger the better." She was shocked that he would even think that.

"You never seem to wear any. Just your cross and your watch. I just thought that you weren't that bothered for it." Sylvie took a deep breath and smiled. He was right; she didn't wear any jewellery, and her hand touched the small gold and diamond square cross that hung round her neck.

"Most of my jewellery was bought by Chris. I have a whole box-full at home. My parents bought me this cross when I was twenty-one as my original christening cross got stolen."

"Oh, I see."

"Lilianna bought me my diamond-drop earrings for my fortieth birthday and I wear those. But the rest – well, I don't really want to wear them anymore."

"I'm glad you bought these then. From here, with me." He stroked her face and pushed back her hair, then kissed her. He seemed to be preoccupied for a moment.

"Is everything alright? I mean the phone call?"

"Yes. It was that Russian client of mine, Serge. He has a couple of friends who want yachts, so I said I'd find him what he's after. It'll mean a real trip to the South of France this time." He laughed as he remembered Sylvie stressing about his decoy trip. "You should come too. This time I could give you a personal guided tour. I know Cannes very well."

"Yes I seem to remember you telling me quite colourfully too." Her thoughts shot back to *'fucked everything in sight'*.

"Come on, let's go see the Parthenon, and then I really want a very private and personal tour of this." He ran his middle finger from her lips down her throat and then he stopped just between her breasts. Sylvie's whole body trembled as she put her hand over his and a very wicked smile crept over Nick's face.

6

PERSONAL TOUR GUIDE

Nick emptied his pockets onto the desk and plugged in his iPhone to charge. Their suite had been cleaned and there was a fresh bowl of fruit and some luxurious-looking chocolates on the coffee table. Sylvie put the jars she'd bought into her suitcase, which was stowed away in the closet. Her eye caught sight of her silk aqua top. It was hanging with the rest of her clothes.

"You brought back my top?" she called to Nick.

"Oh yes, I forgot to tell you. Andreas must have hung it up."

"I brought back your shirt. He's hung that up too," she smirked.

"Can I borrow your laptop? I need to send out a couple of emails. Get the ball rolling."

"Sure, I'll put it on. I'll call Alex while you work. Where do you fancy eating tonight?" She had turned on her computer and was waiting for it to warm up. Nick came up behind her and snaked his arms around her waist, then softly kissed her neck. Sylvie moaned.

"Up to you. You're the boss," he whispered.

"Mmm."

"You smell delicious." He swept her hair to one side so that he could get to her throat.

"I really need a bath. I'm hot and –"

"Yes you are. Very." He smiled against her neck as Sylvie rolled her head back.

"That's not what I meant," she murmured. "Okay. If I'm the boss…" Sylvie turned around to face him. His eyes were sparkling. She took his face in her hands and kissed him softly. "…you are going to do

53

your work." She kissed him again slightly harder this time. "I will call Alex." She kissed him again, and this time Nick pulled her tight. "I'll get Andreas to book us a table on the roof terrace here for nine o'clock." Nick kissed her hard, leaving her breathless. She pulled back and he feigned his disappointment. "That will leave us approximately three hours before dinner for us to… relax, have a bath, or do anything else you can think of." She spoke softly and seductively, then stepped back and Nick groaned.

"Sylvie, you are a tease and you don't play fair." Sylvie ran her finger down from his neck slowly over his chest and taut stomach to the waistband of his shorts, hooking her finger inside and then jerking him towards her. Nick gasped and his eyes ignited.

"If we continue, we'll never get anything done. Now, go on. Send your emails. I'll run a bath and once I've spoken to Alex, I'll come and get you." She kissed him hard and he moaned into her neck. Then she released him, and this time he was breathless. "Deal?"

Nick pursed his lips. "Deal, but I'm telling you now, I won't be long."

Sylvie moved away from the desk and pulled out the chair for him. He sulkily sat down. Then she bent down and whispered in his ear. "Oh I hope not."

Nick moaned and threw his head down on the desk as Sylvie giggled and ran off in the direction of the bedroom. He straightened himself, then slipped off his sneakers and socks, then started to type.

Sylvie got Andreas to book their table, then she called Alex. He was stressing over his last exam on Tuesday. He'd managed to book a flight for the Wednesday so thankfully, he'd be home for when Markus would be discharged. She quickly took out her white strapless fitted dress with a skinny black belt and checked if it needed ironing. It looked perfect. Maybe Andreas had ironed it. Come to think of it, all her clothes looked immaculate. How lovely! She pulled out her black and white peep toe stilettoes and a matching clutch. Then she laid out her never-been-worn ivory strapless bra and matching lacy thong.

Nick was typing away at her laptop looking engrossed, as she slipped into the bathroom and turned on the taps. She heard him momentarily stop, then restart again at what seemed a faster pace. Sylvie smiled to herself. She wriggled out of her shorts and camisole and slipped off her shoes. She checked herself in the mirror: not bad for a forty-four year-old. She leisurely sauntered into the sitting area where Nick was still bashing away. He briefly looked up at her through his lashes, and a smile curled over his lips. He continued to type as she came up behind him, his eyes still fixed on the keyboard.

Sylvie leaned over him and ran her hands slowly down his firm chest and he took a deep breath, but still did not acknowledge her. She smiled to herself. *So he was playing hard to get. Mmm, well we'll see about that!* She reached down further and he sat back slightly, making it easier for her. Slowly she took hold of the hem of his shirt and pulled it up as he lifted his hands from the keyboard, allowing her to remove it. She dropped it on the floor. Nick closed his eyes for a moment and licked his lips, then continued to type, stifling a smile. Sylvie then knelt down by his side and ran her hands up his taut thighs, skimming over his ever-growing erection, then to his waistband. She ran her fingers around the top of his shorts, slowly caressing him, and then expertly unbuttoned them. Nick swallowed hard and clenched his teeth, all the while typing. Sylvie then, achingly slowly, pulled the now-straining zip down. Before she was even halfway down, she heard him take a deep breath again.

"Fuck it!" He grabbed her by the shoulders and lifted her on to his lap, his hands in her hair and his lips pressed hard against hers. Sylvie moaned and grabbed his neck as she deepened the kiss. "Oh baby, you are one hell of a sexy –" He groaned as she silenced him with her mouth. In one swift, fluid manoeuvre, he lifted her up as he stood. Sylvie gasped and he glanced at the laptop. "Hit the send button!" he growled. Sylvie reached down and tapped the keyboard. "Enough work – time for bed!"

Sylvie clung to him and giggled. She kissed his neck. "Bath," she whispered, as he strolled purposely towards the bedroom.

"Bed," he insisted.

"Bath," she breathed into his ear, gently nipping his earlobe.

He stopped and looked into her eyes. "Bath it is." He bent down and kissed her. "How can I refuse? One look into those oh-so-sexy eyes." Then, changing direction, he headed for the bathroom.

Once they were in, he gently placed her down and then stripped off his shorts and boxers, tossing them aside. Sylvie had turned off the taps and tested the water. When she turned around, he was inches away from her, his eyes now blazing. "I think you're a little overdressed. Let me help you out of those."

Nick reached behind, dropping a kiss on her shoulder, and unhooked her bra. Then he pulled down the straps, removing it. He then knelt down and slipped down her panties, keeping his eyes on hers. She stepped out of them and Nick straightened himself. He took her face in his hands and pulled her to his lips and she melted into him. His arm ran down her back to her waist as he jerked her close to him.

"I love it when you're bossy," he murmured into her neck. "It's a real turn-on."

"Really?" With her index finger, she stroked down the length of his nose and to his lips as she spoke.

"Uh-huh." He kissed her finger and then kissed her fully on the mouth. "Can't you tell?" He smiled wickedly as he pushed his hips up against her so she could feel his erection. She smiled and let her hand slip downwards to that muscle just above his hip and she stroked it and then moved down. He groaned and grasped her behind and again, he lifted her, and then placed her down on the floor.

"Jesus Christ, Sylvie, what are you doing to me?" He was over her as she lay on the cold, hard marble floor. "God, I love you."

He brushed back her hair and she wrapped her legs tightly around him. He slowly eased into her and she arched her back to meet him, his eyes wide and bright as he revelled in her total surrender to him. Sylvie ran her hands down his chest, grasping, as he eased back out again. He kissed her tenderly, moving down to her breasts, suckling them softly. She cried out. "Ah!"

He moved steadily in and out as she gripped onto his arms, her eyes closed as she felt him pushing deeper with every thrust. Sylvie ran her fingers into his hair, then pulled him up to her so she could see his face.

"I want to see you. I love looking at you." Her words fuelling him, he groaned.

Nick took her hands and pulled back. He kneeled back on his heels, not breaking their connection. He let go of her hands and held on to her hips and Sylvie lay back, resting her behind on his thighs and her shoulders on the cool floor. He started to move faster as Sylvie watched him, watching the pure passion and desire in his beautiful young face. His eyes fixed on hers. She could feel herself quicken, his beautiful face full of wonder as his eyes burned into her.

"Oh Nick, I love you," she gasped.

"Oh baby," Nick cried out. Hearing those words were enough to push him over the edge, and seeing him undone, Sylvie pulled herself up and grasped his neck as she too fell apart, clinging tightly to his neck.

He stroked her hair as she held on to him and she sat there relaxed and content, not wanting to let go. He kissed her head and she nuzzled up closer to him, her legs wrapped around him and his legs now outstretched sitting on the cool black marble floor. "You smell wonderful." He took in a deep breath.

"We should get in, but I don't want to move."

Nick squeezed her closer and Sylvie sighed. It was only their second day together, and she felt so at ease, as if this was the only place she belonged. They hadn't even talked about Julian, or about speaking to Alex and Markus, but she knew they'd have to, sooner rather than later. The thought depressed her. She was so incredibly happy. She hadn't felt like this for what seemed like a very long time. It was all because of Nick. He made her feel this way; he made her feel loved. That's why she felt so at peace, here with him. She lifted her head off his shoulder to look at him. His eyes were dreamy and his cheeks a little flushed. Broaching those subjects, facing reality, was something she wasn't looking forward to.

"Let's get in. The water will get cold." She kissed him softly and peeled herself off him.

Sylvie stepped into the bath, pleased that the water was still warm enough. Nick waited for her to sit down, then he also stepped in and nestled between her legs. Sylvie wrapped her arms around him and rested her legs on his.

"That feels wonderful." He spoke softly and rested his head back against her shoulder. "How's Alex?" He played with her fingers as he spoke. "When's he back?"

"He's fine. His last exam is on Tuesday. He managed to get a flight out on Wednesday, just in time for Markus's discharge."

"Oh." He carried on playing with her fingers. She knew where his line of questioning was going. "So, will you tell them? About me? I mean – us?"

Sylvie sighed: *why was this so complicated?* When it was just him and her it was so simple. "Yes, I will. It won't be easy." Her voice was quiet, and Nick sensed her apprehension.

"You don't have to do it alone. I can be there with you. We'll tell them together." Sylvie thought about how she envisaged her conversation going and shuddered. She really didn't want Nick witnessing their reaction. She knew it wouldn't be good.

"No, I really need to tell them alone. They're going to be beyond shocked and they'll say stuff I really don't want you to hear." Nick turned around to face her. The water sloshed over the sides.

"What do you mean? What stuff?" He brushed her hair back off her face as she smiled weakly.

"Well, put yourself in their shoes. Your mother shacks up with a man young enough to be her son. He's also a colleague's son. Your father hasn't been dead for a year yet. It's quite a lot to take in, however open-minded they are." She forced a smile and Nick pulled himself up to kiss her. "Remember, they've only ever seen me with their father, and to all intents and purposes, they thought we were the perfect couple."

"If they know you want this? That it makes you happy?" He paused a minute, then added cautiously: "You are happy? I mean about this?"

Sylvie closed her eyes and nodded her head slightly. "Nick, I am more than happy. What this is – what we have – scares me. We've spent so little time together, yet I feel that we have known each other… well, for a long time."

He knelt up in the bath and pulled her to him so that they were in the same position as they had been earlier on the bathroom floor. "I feel it too, Sylvie. You have made me so happy, the thought of not being with you" – Nick paused and swallowed and shook his head as if he couldn't even say the words – "we'll work it out, baby." He kissed her forehead and she nuzzled into his shoulder. She knew eventually Alex and Markus would get used to the idea. They were not her biggest concern. Her biggest fear was Julian.

Sylvie opened her eyes, feeling a little disorientated. After a moment, she realised she was lying on the bed. She reached over to the bedside table for her watch to look at the time. Eight? She'd slept for an hour. What was it these days that she managed to be able to nap? She'd never napped. It was probably the ouzo and walking around – oh, and the sex. Definitely the sex! She smirked to herself. After Sylvie's seduction of Nick in the bathroom, they had then moved to the bedroom. She had to admit, it had been a lot more comfortable than the cold hard marble. Nick had made love to her again, but this time he had been gentle and tender. It reminded her of the first night after the opening of Celle. Then he had taken everything a lot slower, taking in every inch of her. She hugged her pillow trying to control her giddiness. She could hear Nick in the bathroom and was tempted to steal a glimpse of him.

Sylvie sat up and ran her fingers through her tangled hair. *Crap, it must look like a haystack!* She felt a little woozy as she pulled on the robe. Once she felt steady enough, she tiptoed to the bathroom. Nick was standing by the sink, totally naked, shaving. Luckily for her, she was out of his field of vision so she could admire him as he painstakingly dragged the razor over his lathered face. As he finished the last stroke, he tapped the razor hard against the sink, then bent down to wash off any excess lather and to rinse out the razor. Why was watching a man shave so sexy? Sylvie slid out of view. She almost felt guilty for her flagrant intrusion of this private moment. Her heart thumped as she made her way to the bar. She was parched and needed some water.

After drinking almost half a litre of water, Sylvie went back to the bathroom. Nick was in the shower, rinsing the shampoo out of his hair.

"Hey, sleepyhead, you're up."

"Yeah, I really don't know what came over me. I never nap."

"You coming in?" Sylvie's eyes appraised him fully as his eyes were closed. He tilted his head back, trying to rinse out the suds.

"If I come in, we'll never leave. I'll just wait until you've finished."

He opened his eyes and smirked. "I think you might be right. I'll make a deal with you. If you don't come in now and just sit there and watch, that means I can sit and watch you."

Sylvie flushed. *Shit, had he seen her watching him before?*

He eyed her seductively. "Well?"

"Okay." She tried to speak steadily. He quickly rinsed the suds from his delectable body, then he opened the huge glass door of the shower, leaving the water running, and stepped out, grabbing a towel for his waist and then another for his hair. He stepped out of the way and waved his hand slowly towards the shower, signalling her to enter. All the while, his eyes blazed.

"All yours, baby."

Sylvie instantly felt extremely conscious that she was going to have to shower in full view of his burning gaze. The thought was daunting, yet so extremely erotic. It was like she'd be putting on some sort of peep show. *What the hell, she could do this!*

Slightly unsteadily, Sylvie stepped towards the shower, allowing her eyes to meet his. Keeping his gaze, she undid the robe and let it slide down her shoulders and then drop to the floor. Gracefully, she stepped into the shower, then turned to close the glass door. Nick was mesmerised. He lowered himself onto the small padded stool, then leaned back against the vanity unit, propping himself up on his elbows.

Sylvie stepped back under the cascade of water and tilted her head, smoothing the water over her hair. She then poured shampoo in her hand and slowly rubbed her hands together. Reaching up, she gradually worked the lather through her hair. Tilting her head back, she rinsed the suds out, and in doing so, allowed her back to arch.

Nick shifted in his seat, transfixed by the floor show, wondering whether he'd be able to control himself. *She hadn't even started on her body! Fuck, this was beyond sexy. He should have just pulled her in with him.* Sylvie ran conditioner through her hair tips, then picked up the body wash and poured it into her hands. She lathered it up, then purposefully rubbed the length of each arm, across her décolletage and down between her breasts. Then, lifting each arm in turn, she rubbed under them and round each breast, achingly slowly. Nick re-shifted in his seat and took a deep, controlled breath. Sylvie turned to face the shower and allowed her hands to slide down her smooth stomach and further down between her legs, her leg slightly bent so as to obscure Nick's full view. Nick sucked on his teeth, realising he was fighting a losing battle. It was almost unbearable. Sylvie smiled slightly to herself.

Nick's reaction spurred Sylvie to find the whole scenario so erotic and sensual. She revelled in his desire for her. In her last attempt to break him, because now she wanted him – having watched him shave in secret, then shower in all his glory, she needed him more than ever – she turned her back to him and bent ever so slowly down to wash the whole length of her right leg. Before she could move to her left leg, Nick gasped and within a second he had ripped off his towel and swung open the glass door.

"We're gonna be late for dinner," he growled, as he lifted her up and she wrapped her legs around him. Nick held her tight as he violently kissed her, pressing her up hard up against the wall.

"Oh I hope so," Sylvie moaned at him.

───

Mr Zavos was standing talking to the bar staff as Nick and Sylvie entered the terrace bar holding hands. He smiled warmly at them and came straight over to speak to them.

"Good evening, Mrs Sapphiris, Mr Steed. May I offer you an aperitif?" He stretched out his hand.

"Good evening." They spoke in unison as they shook hands in turn.

"A glass of champagne maybe?" He motioned to the bar.

"That's very kind. We're a little late for our reservation…" Nick apologised, but Mr Zavos waved his hand as if it really didn't matter.

"You're on holiday. Relax, you are in Greece now. Hardly anyone comes on time. Come sit." Sylvie slid onto the bar stool, even though her dress was a little restrictive. She'd pinned her hair up leaving just the back loose so as to show off her new earrings. Nick stood by her side, wearing a white shirt with a fine pale blue strip and a pair of dark blue trousers. His hair was perfectly dishevelled and had taken him all of thirty seconds to style. The absence of designer stubble made him look younger. Well, actually he looked his age tonight. He was beyond breath-taking.

Sylvie looked round the restaurant at all the couples. Most of them looked well matched, apart from a very dark middle-aged man sitting with a platinum blonde twenty-year-old. Sylvie sighed inwardly. She suddenly felt very conspicuous. It felt like everyone was looking over at them. This is how it was going to be. People would be staring and judging her. She turned her attention back to Mr Zavos as he handed them both a glass, and they all clinked glasses.

"Mr Steed, how did you enjoy your first day in Athens?"

"Please, Mr Zavos, call me Nick. It was fascinating."

Mr Zavos nodded. "Then you must call me George. The museum? That is where you went today?" He directed his question to Sylvie.

"Yes, and please call me Sylvie." Mr Zavos smiled and nodded.

"George," he repeated.

"Sylvie gave me a very thorough private guided tour. Some of the statues are remarkable. I particularly liked the one of Poseidon." Nick took a sip of his champagne.

"Yes it is. His temple at *Sounion* is impressive too. Did you manage to get to the Parthenon today?" His interest was genuine as always, and for the first time since Sylvie had known him, he seemed to relax.

"We went to *Syndagma* and *Plaka* and then up to the Parthenon," Sylvie explained.

"That was really something. Very eerie and powerful as the wind whistles through the columns. It really is incredible."

George smiled at Nick's enthusiasm. "I'm glad you enjoyed your first day, but I feel that even though our ancient monuments are of great interest, it may have more to do with your personal tour guide." He motioned to Sylvie, smiling broadly. Nick slipped his arm around Sylvie's waist and kissed her forehead tenderly.

"I think you're right, George." Sylvie felt herself flush.

"What are your plans for tomorrow?"

Nick looked at Sylvie, shrugging.

"How far is Sounion from here? It's been a while since I went." Sylvie was mulling an idea over.

"By bus, about an hour. By taxi or car, thirty minutes. We do have a tour from here but I believe it goes on Wednesday."

Sylvie pursed her lips, trying to work out how they could get there. "I'd love to show Nick. He sails, so I think it would something of great interest. The temple of Poseidon, god of the sea." She gazed up at Nick as she finished her sentence.

Nick looked at her lovingly before turning to George. "I don't really fancy going in a taxi. A car might be better. We could hire one. I have to say, I don't relish driving a car here though."

"It's a straight road once you're on the beach road. On Sunday, the traffic shouldn't be too bad." George put down his glass. "I can bring you up a leaflet on car hire while you have your dinner and then you can decide."

Nick squeezed Sylvie as he looked back at her. "What do you think?"

"Sounds good. There are great fish tavernas there too and a beach, so it would be a lovely day out."

"I'll let you go into dinner and I'll be up with all the information shortly." Mr Zavos nodded his goodbyes and left them to go into the beautiful terrace dining area, which was overlooked by a magnificently lit Parthenon.

They sat at right angles on a secluded table lit with small tea lights and the reflective light of the Parthenon. Sylvie chose a light dinner, as her stomach was feeling a little delicate. Salad, then some sea bream and steamed vegetables. Nick chose enough food for at least another couple of people. Sylvie picked up a bread roll and absent-mindedly tore it in half, then carefully buttered it and placed it on Nick's side plate. As he watched her, a smile crept over his lips. When she released the bread, he picked up her hand and kissed the inside of her wrist. The wine waiter brought their wine and after Nick tasted it, the waiter poured it quickly and left them.

"Isn't it a beautiful setting? Sitting, eating and looking at one of the wonders of the ancient world? I really don't want to leave here." Her voice was quiet and tinged with sadness. After all her apprehension and worries, she really couldn't have wished for a better time and it was only their first day.

Nick lifted her chin up. "Hey, baby, don't be sad. Do you know how many more times like this we are going to have? I meant what I said; I want you to come with me to the South of France. I want to leave a week on Friday. By then, we'll have told everyone and they'll just have to get used to it."

The waiter arrived with Nick's lobster ravioli and Sylvie's crab salad. Sylvie picked at her food as she watched Nick start to devour his ridiculously huge starter.

"I want to be the one to tell your father. I think it's only right." Nick stopped dead, his fork suspended. He paused, then placed it back down again. The muscle in his cheek clenched.

"Why?" He looked at her, his eyes darkening. He did not look happy. Maybe she should have spoken to him about this somewhere more private.

"I just think he should hear it from me. If he has to say anything, I'd rather he said it straight to me."

Nick sat back in his chair and ran his hand through his hair, then took a huge gulp of wine.

"If he's going to go off the rails, Sylvie, I want him to do it to me, not you. This isn't your own personal problem, Sylvie, it affects us both. Having said that" – he paused, taking a deep breath in an attempt to calm himself – "I would rather I spoke to him myself, alone. I don't want to have to subject you to… well, whatever it is he's going to say."

Sylvie looked down at her plate and played with a piece of lettuce with her fork.

"You never told me what went on between you two. I understand it's something you don't want to discuss or tell me. I'm not happy about it, but I get it. You've known my dad for a long time and there's a history, but this – well, this concerns me, and if he wants to point fingers or accuse anyone of anything I'd rather it be me. You've had more than your fair share of shit to deal with over the last few months. You really don't need this too." His voice softened as he spoke.

He reached over and took another gulp of wine. Sylvie continued to play with her salad. Nick closed his eyes and sighed. He didn't want to argue with her, but he knew how his father would react. He'd seen how much his dad had fallen for her. Julian was going to take it badly, and Nick also knew that Sylvie hadn't realised to what extent his father would be prepared to go in order to be with her. Nick had seen his father with a number of girlfriends over the years. The way he'd reacted to Sylvie was like nothing he'd ever witnessed before.

Nick took her hand and pulled himself closer to her. "Sylvie, baby, I know what this is. You're trying to take the brunt of everything so that I don't get hurt. That's why you won't let me be with you when you tell Alex and Marcus. You're trying to protect me." Sylvie closed her eyes, trying hard not to cry. She knew that things were going to get really messy and she didn't want to be the reason Nick fell out with his family. If she was the one to tell Julian, maybe she could talk him round. Maybe he could understand that he really belonged with Maggie and that she was never going to be anything other than a friend. Then he might accept her relationship with Nick.

"Well maybe you can protect me from your family, but I refuse to let you take the fall for mine. I will tell them, once you've told Alex and Markus. Please Sylvie, look at me." Sylvie turned to face him, her face full of angst as she looked into his beautiful worried eyes. "Hey, come on. We'll work it out." He pulled himself closer and tenderly kissed her hand.

"I don't want to be the reason you fall out with your family, Nick."

"Sylvie, they're going to have to get over it. Come on. Please, baby, let's not ruin a perfect day." His voice was soft as he pleaded; Sylvie could do nothing but relent.

"Okay, we'll talk about this later." Nick's face lit up again. "But it's still not decided," she warned. Nick's eyes narrowed, but he decided not to press her. He leaned over and kissed her softly, then turned back to his ravioli.

The rest of the meal was more relaxed. They talked about Nick's childhood and growing up with Elenora and Vicki. He spoke for the first time about his first girlfriend, who'd been Cypriot, and whose family had eventually split them up because he wasn't. It had been hard for him, but he had gone into the army and had realised that maybe he was too young to be in such a serious relationship. His time in the army had been fun. He'd revelled in the physical challenges and after all, he'd only done six months. The time had literally flown.

As they were finishing off their desserts, George approached their table with a large folder. "I hope you've had a pleasant meal."

"Everything's been lovely. Really, George. Is that the car hire leaflet?" Nick extended his hand as George nodded and placed it in his waiting hand.

"If you call either Andreas or myself tonight, I can make sure you have the car by nine in the morning. There are also some instructions as how to get to Sounion and a map."

"Oh thank you, George. We'll check it out when we get back to our room." Sylvie smiled up at him. He really was a sweet man.

"Well, goodnight, then, and I'll no doubt see you in the morning." He nodded curtly and left after they'd wished him goodnight. Sylvie stifled a yawn as the waiter came over and Nick signed the bill.

"Tired, baby?" He brushed back her hair from her face, then touched her new earring.

"A little."

"I never told you how beautiful you look tonight." Sylvie leaned into his hand as he spoke. "In all the rush to get ready, I never told you." Sylvie smiled shyly, then flushed, thinking of their rather frantic and passionate episode in the shower. "Come on. I really want to peel you out of that dress and check out that rather fetching underwear I barely had a chance to appreciate." He grasped her hand and gently pulled her up. He reached into his pocket, dropping a fifty euro note on the table. Then, putting his arm around her, he guided her back to the elevators.

The gesture was of a man much older, a man who was confident and strong. Sylvie realised that Nick had always behaved in this manner. It hadn't been brought to her attention until now, but Nick had subtly taken control whenever they had been anywhere. He had allowed her to instigate but then smoothly been the one to control it. Sylvie looked up at him as the elevator stopped at their floor.

"What is it, baby?" He leaned down and kissed her.

"Nothing. I just… I love you, Nick."

He closed his eyes and drew a deep breath, then opened his eyes to look at her. His eyes euphoric. "And I love you." He pulled her close and rubbed his nose on hers, then whispered: "Heaven."

7

SOUNION

Sylvie stretched her arms as she tried desperately to wake up. She could hear Nick talking on the phone in the sitting room. She propped herself on her elbows and turned to see what time it was. Eight-thirty! What the hell! She'd never slept until then before. Oh, except once. She grinned at the memory of 'the morning after', the morning after Celle's opening, and she hugged herself. That seemed like an age ago. Throwing back the covers, she reached for her robe and shrugged it on. Nick was still talking.

"Yes, I gave it to Andreas… Yes, I'll sign it when I come down… Thank you… Oh good, I wouldn't know where to fill it up… No, but I'm hoping she will be, but organise the other. Good. Yes, and thank you again, George. See you in about an hour. Oh definitely, I wouldn't miss that if I were you." He laughed and then said his byes and replaced the receiver.

Sylvie had brushed her teeth and emerged from the bathroom, still feeling sleepy.

"Well good morning, beautiful." Nick beamed at her as he strode purposely towards her and kissed her, squeezing her tightly. He smelled yummy as she held him close. "I ordered you a light breakfast, nothing with milk. How's your stomach this morning? Better?"

She felt a little nauseous but she didn't want to ruin his obvious good mood, so she nodded and his face lit up.

"Good. Tea?" He took her by the waist and guided her to the dining room, where Andreas must have set up breakfast. *Holy shit, how much food?* Seeing her expression, he laughed, "It's not all for you. I haven't eaten yet. I waited for you and I'm starving."

Sylvie yawned and sat down. "I can't believe how tired I am. I'm probably catching up on all the sleep I've never had," she smirked. Sylvie poured Nick's tea and then her own. He picked up the cup, ignoring the handle, and took a gulp. He always did that, she noted.

"Well, we'll have a lazy day today on the beach at Sounion. George organised everything, so whenever you're ready, we can go."

"Wow, you have been busy this morning." Sylvie's heart soared as she looked at Nick and he continued to beam at her. He really was in a good mood. He was so excited and he'd arranged everything. That was something she wasn't used to. His mood was infectious. Sylvie reached over and took a slice of toast as Nick helped himself to scrambled eggs, bacon, sausages and mushrooms. She slowly buttered the toast as her stomach turned over at the sight of the eggs. She hated eggs. Turning her gaze away from them, she placed the buttered toast on Nick's side plate. He watched her intently as his smile widened, and then took her hand and kissed the inside of her wrist. She then repeated the process for herself.

"We should get Andreas to book a table at Lycabettos tonight. It's so beautiful up there. You can see all of Athens."

"I'll call him after breakfast. You can get ready and I'll check my emails." And as simple as that, he had taken control again. Sylvie's butterflies jumped up and down in glee – she could *really* get used to this.

Nick logged off the computer as Sylvie came out of the bedroom. She'd put on a white bikini and slipped on her aqua halter top and a pair of white cropped trousers. She slipped on her jewelled flip-flops. Her hair was loose and she was holding a small backpack.

"I've put in towels and sunscreen. Do you need me to get anything else?"

"Maybe you should take some sneakers if we're going to go walking round the temple. I'll give you my flip flops for the beach."

"Sure. I'll put some on and pack my flip flops too."

Thank goodness she'd packed them. Sensible Nick – she really was getting to know him better. Nick picked up his sunglasses and slipped them into their case. He looked dreamy in a white T-shirt and faded denim shorts. He was already wearing his Converse. He waited for her patiently as Sylvie put the last of her things in the pockets of the backpack, and then they headed to the elevator.

Once inside Nick, took the backpack and swung it over his shoulder. He took hold of her hand and raised it to his lips and kissed it. "You look beautiful, Sylvie."

Sylvie flushed and reached up to his face, stroking his newly grown stubble.

"You're not too bad yourself." The elevator doors opened and they came out into a busy lobby. Nick walked over to the concierge's desk where a young man was busy organising some papers.

"*Kali mera*," Nick spoke to the concierge, his voice clear and confident. "Mr Steed; I believe I need to sign some paperwork."

"*Kali mera*. Yes, Mr Steed, it's all here. If you could sign here." The concierge indicated where, handing him a pen, and Nick quickly signed. "Your licence, Mr Steed, and here are the keys." He handed over Nick's licence and a key with a BMW sign on it. *A bit over the top for a day trip, any old car would have done*, thought Sylvie. Nick seemed excited as he picked up the backpack and turned to her. She was surprised George wasn't about to greet them as she scanned the lobby. Oh well, they'd see him later, no doubt.

"Ready?" Sylvie nodded and took his hand. "Let's go, then." He kissed her quickly on the lips and walked towards the entrance, almost nervously.

As they emerged out onto the pavement, they were greeted by George. He was beaming.

"*Kali mera,* Sylvie, Nick." Sylvie was a little taken aback. Why was he outside? Maybe he was taking them to the car. He looked slightly flushed, agitated even. How sweet of him, she thought as she shook his hand.

"*Kali mera,* George." Nick was squeezing her hand, his expression a little anxious. Sylvie's eyes rested on George's left hand; he was holding a silver helmet with 'BMW' on the side. Her eyes then moved to the pavement behind him, where a beast of a motorbike was parked with a matching helmet on the seat. *Holy fucking shit!* Nick had hired a motorbike – and not any old bike, a huge monster of a bike. Sylvie felt the blood drain from her face. She was petrified of bikes. She swung round to look at Nick. His eyes were wide and he was biting his lip nervously. He looked so young and maybe not so sensible after all!

"You hired a bike?" Sylvie whispered. He nodded slowly, trying to gauge her reaction. "A bike?" she repeated, as if she needed to be reassured that this wasn't a terrible nightmare. "You know I'm shit scared of them right?" He nodded again and tried hard to stifle a smile. She turned to look at George, who was smiling nervously. Maybe he wasn't so sweet either. He was obviously in on it. She closed her eyes and shook her head.

"I won't go fast, I promise," Nick reassured her, as he came up behind her tentatively. He knew this could go either way. He also had a car on standby if she really didn't want to, but he'd wait before he'd divulge that information. "Remember on the jet ski, I didn't go fast. It'll be fun. I promise, Sylvie." She turned to look at him. His eyes were sparkling and his face was so expectant she didn't want to disappoint him. "Don't you trust me?"

Crap! She was going to have to suck it up and ride on the back of a fucking deathtrap. *Thank God she had good insurance!* "Give me the backpack. I need my antacids."

Nick's face broke into a wide face-splitting grin as he picked her up and swung her round. "You'll love it, you'll see."

"Don't push your luck, Nick," she muttered through clenched teeth. *God, he looked so freaking young and carefree as he laughed loudly.* Once he'd set her down, George handed Sylvie the helmet and she grudgingly took it. "I take it you are part of the conspiracy?" George nodded shamefacedly. Sylvie rested the helmet on the bike's seat, then expertly took her hair, twisted it up into a bun, then slipped on the helmet. She lifted up the tinted visor. "Come on, then, let's get this over with. But I'm telling you, if you go fast, I'll hitchhike back!"

Nick all but ran to the bike and slipped on his helmet. He lifted the lid of the top case and stuffed the backpack in, then effortlessly swung his long lean leg over the seat and put the key in the ignition. He looked sexy as hell. *Maybe this wouldn't be so bad after all.* "Please tell me you've ridden one before." Her stomach cramped as she spoke.

Nick lifted his visor and grinned. "Oh yes. I had one in the South of France."

Oh!

"Come on." Sylvie took a deep breath to try and control her now-burning stomach, then carefully rested her hand on Nick's shoulder and stepped onto the footrest, slowly straddling the seat. Nick fired up the beast and the roar was almost deafening.

He turned to look at her over his shoulder, his eyes filled with excitement. "Ready, baby? I'll take it slow, I promise."

"As ready as I'll ever be." Sylvie flipped down her visor and wrapped her arms around him tightly. He took her left hand and kissed it, then flipped down his visor. He turned to George and waved, then kicked the footrest back and pulled on the throttle. The bike smoothly moved forward and Sylvie tightened her grip. Her heart was thumping so hard she could hardly breathe. Nick pulled out into the thankfully light traffic and headed down to the beach road.

Sylvie closed her eyes and tried hard to control her erratic breathing. *I hate motorbikes, I hate motorbikes! I HATE MOTORBIKES!* She screamed in her head as she gritted her teeth.

Once Nick had expertly weaved through the Sunday morning traffic, they found themselves on the main road leading out of the capital, south towards the beach and onward, past Glifada and on to Sounion. Sylvie held on tight as Nick steadily drove, keeping his speed in check. Sylvie had to admit it was thrilling, and there was the advantage of having Nick pressed against her chest. *If only Markus could see her now*, she sniggered to herself. She thought back to the endless arguments she and Chris had had about their son getting a motorbike. She almost felt guilty. As they cruised along the highway, Sylvie started to feel a little more relaxed and Nick felt her slowly ease her vice-like grip on him. He grinned to himself. He knew she'd eventually enjoy it.

Before long, they curved around one of the last bends on the Attiki peninsula and there, perched on the edge of a cliff, the temple of Poseidon came into view. It really was quite spectacular. It was hard to imagine a more perfect setting for an ancient temple, in particular one dedicated to the god of the sea.

Nick took the turning off to the right and followed the winding road up to the temple. He kicked the stand out and rested the bike, then cut the engine. Sylvie reluctantly released Nick, then slowly dismounted the bike. She unfastened her helmet and pulled it off, shaking her hair loose. Her jaw ached from the constant clenching of her teeth.

"That's better." She raked her fingers through her hair as she shook her head. Nick slung his long leg over the seat and took off his helmet, then ran his fingers through his hair. Of course, he looked picture perfect. He put down his helmet and scooped Sylvie in his arms.

"See, it wasn't so bad." He kissed her roughly and she squirmed.

"No, it wasn't, but I bet I have terrible helmet hair," she giggled.

"You look sexy as hell, especially when you took your helmet off."

Sylvie couldn't stop grinning and she felt slightly giddy. *It must be the adrenaline.*

"This place is incredible. I'm so glad you suggested it. Come on, let's go up and see it."

Sylvie retrieved the backpack and rummaged for their sunglasses. The sun was high and beating down on them. Nick slipped them on and grasped her hand as he led her up to the temple. They went over to the edge and looked down. It overlooked the clear blue sea below, and the view was breath-taking. They could see boats out over the bay and the beach, which was thankfully quiet. There were only a few tourists up by the temple. Nick pulled out his phone.

"I need a picture of this." He looked around and spotted an elderly man with his wife. He strode over to them and asked if the man would take their picture. He nodded and Nick ran over to Sylvie and dragged her up to where he thought they should stand. Nick stood behind Sylvie and wrapped his arms around her. Sylvie reached back with her hand and stroked his stubbly cheek. Nick kissed her palm, and she let her arm drop back down to his.

"Smile, baby," he whispered in her ear. As if she needed any prompting. The elderly man seemed to take a long time, but eventually he put up his thumb as if to say he was happy with the outcome. Nick ran back to him and thanked him, and the man said something that surprised Nick, and beamed at him.

Nick walked back to Sylvie with a huge smile on his face. As he reached Sylvie, he thrust out his phone to show her.

"Look." She willingly came by his side to see as he shielded the glare of the sun. There was a beautiful picture of them holding each other with the temple behind them. "Now look," he continued, and pressed the video option. To Sylvie's surprise and delight, there was a video of Nick gently wrapping his arms around her, and then she watched herself tenderly reach up and stroke his cheek, then Nick kissed it, while whispering in her ear.

"He videoed it!" Nick's voice was full of surprise and disbelief. "He has the same phone and he thought we looked so in love that he wanted to record it. Isn't that amazing?" He was clearly over the moon. Sylvie stared at their exchange and could hardly recognise the woman in the video. Maybe this wasn't so ridiculous after all, and for the first time since their relationship had started, Sylvie felt that she did deserve to be with this utterly remarkable man.

They walked leisurely round the temple, which had been roped off. Sylvie reminisced about being able to walk through it as a child, but now, due to heavy tourist traffic, the temple had been sectioned off. She told Nick about Lord Byron's poem that he was supposed to have etched at the bottom of one of the columns. Nick listened intently and was captivated by her enthusiasm. She made everything sound so interesting, that he was in awe of her. He took several pictures of the view and the temple, and when he'd finished, Sylvie grabbed his hand and led him back to the edge of the cliff, then picked up a smooth white stone from the ground, checking the weight of it in her hand.

"We used to try and hit the sea from up here when we were kids, but I was pretty crap at throwing and could never throw it hard or far enough. Here." She reached and picked up another stone and handed it to Nick. "It's okay. There are only cliffs below, so you won't hit anyone." Nick looked warily as he took the stone.

"Okay, here goes." He pulled his arm back and hurled the stone with force, then they both looked down to see where it had landed. They were both rewarded with a faint splash in the clear blue water below, and Sylvie squealed.

"I've never seen that happen, ever!" She threw her arms around Nick's neck as he squeezed her tightly, giddy with her enthusiasm.

"Anything for you, baby." He kissed her lips and she felt herself palpitate. "Aren't you going to try?" Sylvie shook her head and slipped her stone in her pocket. "Let's go down to that beach over there. George told me there's a good taverna, so we can have lunch later." He took her hand and they made their way back to the bike.

Nick took them down to the beach and organised two sunbeds and an umbrella. While Sylvie spread out their towels, Nick ordered some drinks and brought them over. Sylvie had stripped down to her bikini and was fishing out the sunscreen.

"Here, let me." He placed their drinks down and took the sunscreen from her. "Lie down and I'll do your back." Sylvie lay down and Nick sat on the edge of the sunbed and slowly smoothed the cream over her shoulders, down her back after loosening her back strap, then down each leg. Sylvie tried hard not to moan out loud as she felt his strong hands caress her now-ignited skin. She knew he was taking his sweet time on purpose, and it felt wonderful. She couldn't think of anything, other than that she wanted this man's hands on her all the time.

"There. Now you won't burn." He leaned down and whispered in her ear, then planted a kiss on her shoulder. "You have the sexiest back. Especially this part here." He stroked the dip in her back where the dimples were. "Very sexy." Sylvie trembled as his fingers caressed her back. *Holy shit, he'd totally turned her on, here on the beach!*

He sat on his sun bed, smirking to himself, knowing full well what he was doing. Sylvie turned to face him.

"Now *you're* not playing fair."

"I don't know what you mean." He feigned innocence and then gave her a wicked grin. "Here, I got you a mineral water. It helps an upset stomach."

Sylvie took a long drink. She hadn't realised how thirsty she was. "Let's swim, I think I need to cool down."

Nick laughed loudly. "Me too. That was excruciating for me too, you know," – his voice low and loaded. "Come on, I'll fasten you up." He expertly re-tied her strap and they made their way to the shore.

The water was gloriously clear and cool as they slowly stepped in. Nick held her hand as they progressed deeper, then held her close to him, face to face, her legs wrapped round his waist, once they were deep enough.

"I'm so glad you brought me here. It's really special. I've always loved the sea – and to be here at the temple of Poseidon, with you. What can I say? You sure know how to show a guy a good time." He held her closely and brushed back the hair from her face.

His expression changed as if he was trying to find the right words then, as if he was compelled to ask, he blurted out, "did you ever think it would be like this?" His eyes were cobalt blue with desire, looking deep into hers.

"You mean you and me?" He nodded his response as his eyes kept penetrating into hers, glad she had understood. "Honestly? I hoped it would be. I just – well, I really couldn't even imagine… I –" Why oh why couldn't she just say it? Say what she really felt. That the second she'd seen him pulling himself out of Maggie's pool, she knew she was done for. That after twenty-two years of marriage and all the shit she'd been through, she looked at this beautiful, incredible man and saw some glimpse of what could be. She could visualise something so true and sweet, honest and pure. She'd been drawn to him over and over, and by some miracle, he had too.

"I watched you, that day you came to my father's office when you brought the painting."

Sylvie raised her eyebrows, surprised. "You were there?" Sylvie couldn't remember seeing him there. She was positive she would have remembered.

"I was looking over the balcony as you arrived. You got out of your car in that tight red dress, all curves and high heels as you got out the painting. I remembered trying to see your face, but your hair was every-where." He chuckled. "Then you turned and the wind blew your hair back." He brushed her hair back again as he spoke softly. "And I saw your beautiful face and you were smiling." He kissed her forehead and closed his eyes as if he was trying to recapture that moment. "I was watching when you came in to speak to Dad. I was peeping through the blinds. All I could think of was that I wanted to know everything about you. And your eyes – wow, those eyes." Sylvie was transfixed as he spoke, her heart racing as he lovingly relived the memory.

"When I asked Dad about you and he'd told me you were married, I felt so cheated. Like someone was playing a horrible trick on me. Showing you to me, only to dash my hopes away so quickly. Then I saw you once briefly at the marina, one night in January. You looked drawn and sad but you were still beautiful." Sylvie continued to listen. Her eyes wide with continuing surprise and her heart still thumping, the blood racing through her veins, transfixed as he recounted every detail.

"Then I remember my mum telling me you were coming up to discuss her bedroom, so I decided that I would be there, just so that I could meet you, to see if the image of you I had was anything like reality." He momentarily closed his eyes and took a deep breath.

"I can see you now, standing next to me, wearing that yellow dress. You took my breath away." Nick took her face and kissed her ever so softly. "I remember I was in my trunks and I rushed to get changed so that I didn't waste a second being with you. I couldn't believe my luck when Mum suggested I take you home. God, that journey home was torture." He shook his head slightly and huffed. "I wanted to say so much, but I was dumbfounded. You looked so out of sorts and you kept playing with your rings, almost like a reminder that you were married. I didn't know about Chris, then." He shrugged as he thought back.

"And then you kissed me goodbye and I got to touch you. Your scent lingered on my cheek. How I didn't grab you, then and there, I'll never know." He gently stroked her cheek and his eyes were full of love. "And here we are, four months from then, and I can touch and kiss and make love to you. Someone up there knew what they were doing all along." His eyes looked skyward and then rested back on Sylvie's enthralled face. "They were showing me what heaven is like – it's you."

Wow! "I never knew… I mean, how could I… I was a ball of nerves and I thought… well, you're so young, and well… you're you and why would you?"

His eyes softened as he watched her try to express herself and he ran the backs of his fingers down her cheek.

"I saw my father that night and I quizzed him on you in an attempt to get more information about you. It was then I realised my father had feelings for you. It was then I realised just how much I wanted you too." Nick's expression changed, his eyes sorrowful and pained as he thought back to that night.

This time, Sylvie put her hands to his face and pulled him to her lips. He held her close as he kissed her back and for a moment they were lost in each other as they forgot where they were. Sylvie could only think that after all her worry and continuing doubts, listening to him re-enact those moments, she saw what she too had felt all along mirrored in his words and his incredible eyes. Something had drawn them together – it had been inevitable. Looking back over the chain of events that had led them to this day, this time finally together, she felt maybe, for the first time, that what they had was untouchable. No one would be able to penetrate this or break this. Not Alex or Markus, not Maggie, not Julian.

Nick pulled back and held her face. "I love you, Sylvie. I want to take care of you. I want to cherish and love you always and completely."

"I love you too, Nick."

8

LYCABETTOS

Nick and Sylvie sat at a small wooden table covered in a light blue tablecloth. The taverna was set on the beach. Its decor was all blue and white, with Greek music playing in the background. Sylvie listened to the distinct sound of the bouzouki as Nick poured Sylvie her ouzo, remembering how Lefteris had done it the day before in Plaka. She watched him, clearly impressed. "You remembered."

"Oh, I'm taking mental notes on everything," he joked. He then poured his beer. He thought he'd better stay clear of ouzo today as he was driving. He lifted up his drink and they clinked their glasses.

"*Ya mas.*" They said in unison. Sylvie mixed the salad and then served some on to Nick's plate. They'd ordered deep fried fresh calamari, charcoaled grilled octopus, prawns in tomatoes and Feta cheese, fried red mullet and chips. The smell was wonderful. Sylvie picked up a prawn and peeled off the shell. She repeated the gesture until all the prawns were peeled and sat in their sauce, then she picked up a prawn and held it out for Nick. He moved his head towards the heavily sauced prawn and Sylvie placed it in his open mouth. His lips closed over her fingers, licking and sucking the sauce off, effectively cleaning them.

"Delicious," he whispered suggestively. "I'd love another," he said, arching an eyebrow. Sylvie smiled shyly and handed him another, using her left hand this time. He took the prawn, then gently sucked her sauced fingers again, his eyes boring into her. *Holy shit!* She reluctantly pulled her fingers out of his mouth and he grinned.

"I think they're clean enough now." Her blood raced round her veins. He smirked at her, enjoying her squirm. She looked straight into his now-hooded eyes and then put her recently licked middle finger between her lips, sucking it gently. His eyes widened as he watched her. "You missed a bit," she whispered.

"Now *you're* not playing fair."

"Payback," she giggled.

"Shame this beach isn't deserted. Otherwise I'd take you in the sea." He pulled her face with one hand and holding her chin, he squeezed, making her lips pucker. He kissed her hard, crushing her lips, leaving her breathless. "Sea sex." He smiled wickedly. "Come with me to France. I won't last five days without seeing you. I'll give you your own private tour. You'll love it there," he pleaded, his face expectant.

"Once we get back, I'll check what my schedule is like. What will you be doing there?" Sylvie could think of nothing better than five days in the South of France with Nick.

"Serge's found me a few clients that want similar yachts to what I sourced for him. I've managed to find some. They look great on paper but I need to see them, check them out." He started tucking into his food.

"So it's 'Keeping up with the Abramoviches'?" Sylvie sniggered.

"Yeah, you could say that. Most of them just want to be able to say they've got a yacht. Each to their own." He shrugged. "I get to see some great yachts though, well out of my league, and make some good money to boot."

"Why don't they buy them new?"

"Well firstly, they cost a small fortune, and secondly, there are so many on the market in pristine condition, it makes sense to look at the second-hand market first. Most people risk it and buy off paper. But it's really important to check out a yacht personally. If there's any problem with it, it'll cost more to repair it than what I charge for my commission."

"You've done very well for yourself in a short time, Nick."

"I suppose so. I started early and my expenses are pretty limited." He shrugged, offering an explanation.

They leisurely finished off their lunch, Nick eating enough for four, then headed back to the beach. Sylvie stifled a yawn as they reached their sunbeds.

"Tired?"

"Must be the ouzo."

"Lie down and have a nap. I'll listen to some music and take in the view."

"Won't you be bored?"

"I want you nice and rested by the time we get back. I want to closely inspect your newly acquired tan."

Sylvie laughed. "I see, so you have an ulterior motive? Well you'd better reapply some more sunscreen on me then."

Nick's eyes sparkled as she spoke and she handed him the sunscreen. "Oh fuck! Now you *really* aren't playing fair."

"Just rub, Nick. Slowly." She reached up on her tiptoes and kissed him and he groaned into her cheek.

Sylvie felt featherlight kisses across her shoulders as she fluttered her eyes open. She turned slightly and squinted, trying to focus. She was met by the gaze of Nick, his eyes bright as headlights in the afternoon sun. He tied up her back strap, running his fingers gently down her spine.

"Sleep well?"

Crap, what time was it? "How long did I sleep?"

"It's five o'clock."

"Shit. For an hour and a half?" The disbelief in her voice was evident as Nick nodded.

"I thought we could have a last swim before we head off back. If you're up for it."

Sylvie sat up and stretched. *Oooh, that felt good.* She nodded and took his hand. She stood up and felt herself sway.

"Whoa, head rush." She grasped Nick's arm as he seized her waist.

"Are you okay, baby?"

Sylvie restored her balance and nodded. "Just got up too quickly. Come on, the water will wake me up." He tentatively loosened his grip and led her to the water. The sea had warmed up a little and Sylvie dipped herself under, allowing the water to wake up her senses and cool her head. It felt fabulous. Nick dived in and swam to where she was.

"Better?"

"Much."

"Good." And in one swift manoeuvre, he picked her up by the waist and lifted her high out of the water. She squealed as she grasped for his shoulders and wriggled her legs. He then threw her over his shoulder. She emerged from the water laughing.

"Now you're definitely awake," Nick laughed back at her as she playfully splashed him. He strode through the sea to where she was and kissed her quickly on the lips. "Here. Come and stand on my shoulders and dive in." Sylvie shook her head, totally unnerved.

"No way! I'm too heavy. No, I can't."

"Don't be silly – come on. I used to do it all the time with Vicki and Elenora." He turned around, his back facing her, then reached back and took each of her hands. Then he sank down into the water, allowing Sylvie to step onto his shoulders, steadying herself by gripping his hands tighter. He slowly rose up from the sea, his muscles tight and tense, like Poseidon himself. Sylvie could feel his shoulder muscles tighten under her feet. "Ready?" he called up.

"Ready." He gently let go of her hands as she expertly pushed off his shoulders and dived into the sea in front of him. She popped back up and span round to where Nick beamed at her. "That was brilliant!" she squealed.

"Again?" he asked, laughing loudly, clearly ecstatic.

"Again!" she repeated, like a small child full of excitement.

Sylvie packed their belongings into the backpack and pulled out her top and trousers. Her bikini was still very wet, so she went into the restrooms of the restaurant. Once inside, she whipped off her bikini, quickly dried herself, and slipped into her trousers and top. She didn't want to put dry clothes on top of a wet bikini, and it made her feel a little reckless. Riding a bike and going commando in one day? She could hardly recognise herself. She giggled as she held on to her bikini and walked to where Nick was waiting patiently by the bike. He eyed the bikini and cocked his head. She ignored his look purposefully and squashed the bikini into the backpack, then put it in the top case. Nick came up behind her and slowly rubbed her bottom, searching for underwear; when the realisation hit, he gasped.

"You expect me to stick to a snail's pace until we get back?" His voice was low. "You are killing me. You're going to make me get a speeding fine." His hands moved up to her front and he gently squeezed her breasts. Sylvie arched back and moaned. God, she wanted him now, over the bike if necessary.

"Holy mother of… come on, let's go. I swear I'll strip you naked and take you over this seat." He ripped his hands away and pulled on his helmet, then he flung his leg over the seat. Sylvie wrapped her hair up again and pushed on her helmet, then straddled the bike. Nick turned back to look at her, and through clenched teeth, he said, "For the first time in my life, I'm jealous of an inanimate object."

Sylvie looked puzzled and Nick glanced down at the seat. *Oh! Hmm, yes, it was quite a turn-on having something so powerful between your legs.* Nick flipped down her visor, then his own, and kicked the stand away, then turned on the engine. It roared loudly. Sylvie gripped him tightly round his waist, and he pulled on the throttle. Nick smoothly drove back onto the main road and headed back to Athens. Sylvie gripped tightly as he increased speed. *Oh hell, he was going faster. Well, serves her right, she shouldn't have teased him*, she thought to herself. Her heart pumped loudly. She didn't know if it was the adrenaline from the bike ride, the ouzo, the fact she was commando or that Nick had just made her internally combust, but she didn't care that he was going faster, she just wanted to get back so they could finish what Nick had almost started as fast as possible.

They pulled up outside the Grande Britannia, and Nick kicked out the stand. Sylvie eased herself off the seat and pulled off her helmet, allowing her hair to flow freely. Nick quickly flung his leg over and lifted the top case lid, pulling out the backpack and throwing it over his shoulder. He speedily pulled off his helmet and threw the keys at the valet. He thrust his hand in his pocket and stuffed a twenty euro note in the bemused valet's hand.

"Please park it. We are in the Presidential Suite."

"Of course, sir," the valet mumbled, and taking Sylvie by the hand, Nick almost dragged her through the doors and through the unusually quiet lobby, towards the lift. Thankfully, there was a lift waiting, and Nick guided Sylvie in and pressed their floor. Sylvie was panting as the lift started its ascent. Nick turned down and looked at her, his eyes blazing.

"You make me crazy, you know that?" He stroked her face then made himself pull back. "I hope you're not tired, because I plan to wear you out." Sylvie's eyes widened as she shook her head. "Good."

The elevator doors opened and they practically ran to their suite. Nick slipped in their key and the door opened. In a split-second, the door was closed, their helmets and backpack fell in a heap on the floor, and Nick was pinning Sylvie up against the door, his mouth on her, hungrily kissing her.

"Do you know how much you turn me on?" Sylvie shook her head. "All the fucking time. Jesus, I won't make it to the bedroom. I want you here. Now." He panted as he pulled her top off over her head and then dragged his T-shirt off.

"No problem." Sylvie reached down and hastily unbuttoned his shorts and yanked down the zip. Nick was kicking off his sneakers as she roughly pulled down his shorts and swimming trucks in one swift manoeuvre and he stepped out of them, leaving them with the helmets and backpack in a crumpled heap. He pulled her to him, running his hands all over her, feeling her, squeezing her as she groaned.

"Trousers," she muttered and tried to unbutton them, but he was pressed hard against her. He pulled back slightly and he made quick work of the button and zip. He eased them down her legs and lifted her out of them; she wrapped her legs around his waist as he held her tight. His eyes flitted around the entrance, at a loss as to where to go. Sylvie turned and motioned to the chaise. He was over in seconds and he lay her down on it. She pulled him down to her; the heat radiating off him was intoxicating, and all she wanted was him in her.

He slowly sank into her and she cried out in pure pleasure. "Oh thank God!" She was so tightly wound up from the constant anticipation of this exact moment. Her urgency almost primal.

"Jesus! Oh Sylvie, this is going to be quick." He pulled out and then pushed in hard.

"Faster, Nick. Please, I want this fast and hard, please," she pleaded, writhing with need.

"You got it baby!" He speeded up and Sylvie tightened her hold on him as she met him thrust for thrust, her hands gripping his upper arms, as he continued his punishing pace. Then, through clenched teeth Nick cried, "Oh fuck!" as he climaxed and Sylvie arched up one more time, crying out her release as she shuddered. *Finally!* she thought, as Nick collapsed on top of her, sweat beading on his tight back. All that unreleased tension had gone and she felt calm and soothed.

"Boy, did I need that," she whispered as she kissed his hair.

He looked up, still panting, fixing her with his amazing eyes. "Happy to oblige, Madame," he smirked. "Will Madame be needing anything else?" He put on a fake accent, mimicking Andreas.

"Mmm, I'd like the same again please, but slower this time and maybe somewhere more comfortable?" Sylvie carried on their game.

Nick slowly eased out of her and stood up, his eyes reignited with desire. "Your wish is my command." He held out his hand and she placed hers in his. He pulled her to her feet. "If Madame would like to walk this way, I'll see what I can do."

Sylvie started to walk to the bedroom, giggling, and then sped up as Nick quickly walked up behind her, until she almost ran and jumped onto the bed, laughing. Nick pinned her down, her arms held down by his, on either side of her face, and his whole body on top of her. He rubbed his nose along hers as her laughing stopped, replaced by deep breathing.

"Slow, you said?" Sylvie's eyes closed as she nodded.

"Anything for you baby. You're the boss."

Sylvie looked at herself in the mirror as she rubbed her moisturizer into her sun-kissed face. At least she didn't look so sallow now. Nick was lounging on the settee, flicking through the TV channels. She padded out to where he was sitting. He sat with the bathrobe loosely wrapped round him, his long tanned legs resting on the coffee table. His hair was still wet from his shower and he had brought a bottle of water and glasses from the bar. He patted the seat next to him, gesturing she join him. Sylvie roughly rubbed her hair dry as she slumped down beside him.

"Andreas said our table's booked for nine-thirty and he organised a taxi to take us and bring us back. He's found a less erratic driver for us. I told him that you'd had more than your fair share of excitement for one day." Sylvie elbowed him in the rib.

"Ow!" He feigned injury.

"Big softy. I think I did extremely well."

"Yeah I'm soft. Soft on you." He wrapped his arms around her and squeezed.

"What are you watching?"

"I was just flicking through. Here, have a look." He passed her the remote control.

She eyed him, a little shocked. That was definitely a first for her, a man handing over the remote control. *Surely not!* He leaned over and picked up the bowl of chocolates, offering her one. She shook her head. Her stomach felt delicate again and though she loved chocolate, they looked too rich. He shrugged and popped one in his mouth, then nodded, indicating they were delicious. Sylvie chuckled as she switched the channels.

"Oh wow, I haven't seen this film in such a long time." Sylvie had landed on a Golden Era film channel, showing the old black and white silent movie *The Gold Rush,* with Charlie Chaplin. "It's such a good film. Have you seen it?" Nick shook his head. It was at the part where Charlie Chaplin was snowed in a log cabin with a huge hunter and they were both hungry and had started cooking the old boot. Nick watched Sylvie giggle at the film as the scene unfolded.

"He was a genius. Look at how you can understand everything he's thinking just from his expression." Charlie Chaplin took the laces and twisted them round his fork like spaghetti, then he sucked on each of the boot nails.

She laughed, loving every moment, totally absorbed by it and Nick watched with her, pulling her close, her high spirit contagious. Before long, he was laughing unguardedly as the film continued. Never would he have felt that he could have enjoyed watching a silent movie so much. It was all because of Sylvie. She became so absorbed and so enthralled by it, he was drawn in too. She made everything seem more fascinating by her almost childlike enthusiasm.

"Oh, that was so good to see again."

Nick wiped a tear that had fallen from her cheek with his thumb. "Yes, I've never seen that before. It was actually really funny." They were interrupted by Sylvie's phone ringing. She reached over to see who was calling. Her eyes widened momentarily as she smiled at her phone.

"Hi, sweetie." It was Lilianna. Sylvie mouthed to Nick and nodded. He leisurely stroked her arm as she continued.

"How are you enjoying yourself?" Lilianna asked.

"I'm great, I went round the museum –"

"Again? God, you must have been ten times. Aren't you bored of it?" Lilianna interrupted.

"Yes, again. You know how much I love it, Lily. I also went to Plaka and bought a ring and some earrings, and today I went to the beach."

"Good for you. You're off to see the doctor tomorrow, aren't you?"

"Doctor?"

"Dracos. You know, work – the reason you're there." Lilianna joked. "Anyone would think you were in love." Sylvie laughed nervously. "Sylvie?"

"Yes?"

"Are you alone?"

Busted! Crap – how had she worked that out? "What do you mean?"

"Cut the bull, Sylvie, it's me. Are you there with you-know-who? Mr X?" Sylvie fell silent; she didn't want to lie. "You are? Oh my fucking

Lord. Who the hell are you and what have you done with my sweet naïve friend Sylvie?" she laughed down the phone.

"Lily!" Sylvie scolded as she squirmed, her face flushing.

"Okay, okay. I take it all is well. I expect full details when you're back."

"Okay, Lily. How's Zach? He hasn't called."

"Yeah, he's been busy with some office building. He'll probably call you in the morning. You sound really happy, sweetie."

Sylvie turned to look at Nick, his eyes meeting hers as he smiled at her. "I am."

"Call me when you're back so we can have a coffee and a chat. Love you, sweetie."

"Love you too."

Sylvie put down her phone and snuggled up to Nick.

"Is she okay?" Nick asked as he stroked her arm.

"Just checking up on me. Seeing I'm okay. What time is it?"

"Nearly eight; we should get ready. Maybe have a drink at the bar before we go."

Sylvie looked at the table; the chocolate bowl was empty. "Did you eat them all?" She couldn't hide her disbelief. Nick nodded sheepishly. "Where do you put it all?" She shook her head and he shrugged, almost embarrassed.

Within the hour, they were in the bar. Sylvie sipped on her Chivas, dressed in a floor-length purple silk dress draped at the front and skimming her curves, and Nick had his customary beer, looking positively edible in black trousers and a white linen shirt with a thin grey stripe. George had joined them, only to see how their day had gone. Sylvie asked him to book a taxi for the morning, as she needed to be at Dimitris Dracos's office by ten.

Takis, their taxi driver, proved to be a patient and safe driver to their joint relief, and dropped them in front of the Funicular railway, which took them up to the restaurant at the top of the Lycabettos Mount.

Of all the places in Athens, this held the best memories for Sylvie. Throughout her childhood, they had visited Mount Lycabettos every time they had come to Athens. The view was magnificent. You could see the whole of Athens, and at night it looked like a blanket of stars twinkling beneath you. The walk up to the top was steep and tiring, but the view that you were rewarded with was more than worth it. In the summer months, most people took the Funicular railway – and of course when they were going to dine at the restaurant perched right at the top of the hill.

Nick and Sylvie sat at their table, looking out over the view, as the waiter poured their champagne.

"You were right. The view is something else."

"I know, and it's so quiet up here compared to the street level too. So peaceful." Nick took her hand and kissed it.

"Thank you." Sylvie looked at him puzzled. "For my private personal tour. I really had fun today. And you... you on the back of a motorbike. Who'd have thought it?" He laughed softly. "You looked... wow, *really* sexy," he teased, knowing she would squirm.

Sylvie shook her head. "Don't get any ideas. I won't be getting on the back of one of those in a hurry. And don't think I didn't realise that you were going a lot faster on the way back."

"Now *that* was all your fault. You can't blame me for that. Not wearing underwear *and* the rest, I was ready to burst."

"Well, I think we managed to relieve any tension once we got back."

"Mmm, yes. That we definitely did." Nick leaned over and kissed her lips softly. "I look forward to more tension relief." His eyes darkened, making Sylvie swoon. "So what's good here?"

"Everything. That doesn't mean we need to order it all though." Sylvie teased. "I'm going for the stuffed aubergines and the veal."

"I think the shrimps and then porterhouse steak. What about wine? Châteauneuf?"

"Definitely." Sylvie fiddled with her fork and then reached over to the bread basket. A smile curled over his lips as Sylvie began her dining ritual of splitting and buttering a roll and placing it on his plate. He took her hand and kissed the inside of her wrist.

"Are you nervous about tomorrow?"

Sylvie wrinkled her nose. "A bit. Not that much involved, but it's the first time I'm doing something official – you know, for the company."

"Can I come with you?" Nick asked tentatively.

"I presumed you were." Sylvie cocked her head to one side.

"Oh, I thought you might feel awkward. This Dr Dracos knew Chris, right?"

"Oh, I see what you mean." Sylvie furrowed her brow. That was going to be awkward.

"Look, I'll come with you to the building and I'll leave you there.

Once everything's done, I'll pick you up and we can do something. You said it'd take an hour, tops, right?"

"Yes, maybe you're right. His office is in Glifada. We passed it today. We can have lunch there and wander round. It's really nice there."

"Sounds like a plan." He reached over and pushed her hair back. He could tell she was feeling a little uneasy. She was rubbing her finger again and Nick noticed she hadn't put on her new ring. "You caught the sun today – your cheeks are flushed. You look absolutely beautiful. Don't worry about tomorrow." He tried to reassure her as he squeezed her hand. "Why didn't you wear your ring?"

"I couldn't find it and we were in a bit of a rush. I'll ask Andreas if he's seen it." Nick nodded. He raised his glass. Sylvie picked up hers and they clinked them.

"*Ya mas*," they said in unison.

9

NICK TO THE RESCUE

Sylvie rubbed her hair to rinse out the shampoo, then reached for her conditioner, smoothing it over the ends of her hair. Thankfully, she'd woken up a little earlier today, leaving Nick asleep sprawled out and gloriously naked. Her stomach was in knots. She felt a little daunted by her task today and she really didn't know why. It wasn't such a big deal, but she didn't relish the idea of meeting someone who had known Chris well and no doubt had met Dina. She'd already retched over the sink while brushing her teeth, and whenever she let her mind drift back to that unwelcome thought, she could feel the saliva pool into her mouth. She tilted her head back and let the warm water flow down over her hair as she rinsed out the conditioner.

"What a beautiful sight first thing in the morning." Nick was leaning against the sink, dressed only in his boxers, all bed hair and stubble and tight stomach, watching Sylvie. She hadn't noticed him come in.

I couldn't agree more, she thought to herself.

"Need any help?" His eyes sparkled with mischief.

"I'm feeling rather tense this morning," she replied coyly, playing along. "Can you suggest anything for… umm… stress relief?"

Nick's eyes widened and he stepped forward. "Oh, I think I can help you with that." Within a second, he had stripped off his boxers and opened the shower. Sylvie grabbed his face and pulled him to her lips. His stubble scraping her chin and jaw as he kissed her hard. His hands in her hair and then down her back, grabbing her behind and jerking her to him. She felt his erection against her stomach and smiled as she ran her fingers down his firm chest, down further to that muscle just above his hip. Sylvie trailed kisses down his neck, following where her hands had been, and Nick moaned in anticipation, knowing exactly where she was heading, his hands grasping her hair. Sylvie knelt down in front of him and took him in her mouth, holding onto his hips. Nick closed his eyes and tilted his head back as he clutched onto the handrail, his breathing erratic and hard.

"Oh Sylvie," he breathed as she steadily moved her mouth up and down the whole length of him. She looked up at him through her lashes as he dropped his head to look at her. His eyes burning cobalt blue and his breathing short and fast, as he looked down in awe at her.

"Oh God," he groaned, trying hard to keep control. He reached down and pulled her to him and kissed her hard and deep, his hands running down her whole body, making her tremble.

"I want to be in you, now," he breathed in her ear. "Wrap your legs around me, baby." Sylvie held onto his neck, and he hoisted her up as she wrapped her legs tightly around him. Nick pushed her up against the smooth, cool, tiled wall as he sank into her and she cried out. He pushed in deeper and Sylvie squeezed her eyes shut from pure pleasure. It felt so carnal, his unrestrained desire for her.

"Oh Nick, don't stop." Nick slowly withdrew.

"Oh I won't." He pushed again and she cried out again as he continued his punishing assault. Sylvie gripped on to him, kissing him, biting his jaw and grasping at his hair. Nick groaned and thrust deep into her as she cried out his name, climaxing violently around him.

Then through clenched teeth, Nick cried out, "Thank fuck for that!" as he too found his release. He collapsed on the floor gasping, taking Sylvie with him. They sat wrapped in each other's arms, the water from the shower flowing over them. Sylvie stroked his back as he planted small kisses over her shoulders and up her neck, as their breathing started to calm.

Today was their last day together and Sylvie couldn't shake off that feeling of dread. They had been safe in their little cocoon and everything had been so perfect. Once out in the real world, she knew it wouldn't be like this. There was a multitude of issues they had to face and she found it hard to see how these were ever going to get resolved. She clung on to Nick fighting her natural instincts to cry.

Nick lifted her face up by the chin and pushed back her wet hair as he kissed her forehead.

"Better?" His voice soft. Sylvie nodded, closing her eyes. He shifted a little, the shower floor obviously hard and uncomfortable. Slowly, Sylvie unwrapped herself from his arms and gradually stood up. "Where are you going?" he pouted, as she slowly stepped out of the shower.

"I should get myself ready." Nick gracefully rose up from the floor, unsettled by her pensive expression.

"Hey, what's wrong? You worried about today?" He'd pulled her up close again.

"No. Well... yes, a bit. It's just... well, I realised today's our last day and I'm not really looking forward to going back. I'm not looking forward to not having you..." Why couldn't she just say what she felt? That she wanted him with her twenty-four seven. That she was scared this wasn't going to last out there, out in the real world. Her heart twisted and her stomach clenched and she struggled to stop the tears that were pricking her eyes.

"I know, I know. Look we have the whole day and tomorrow until lunch. We can do whatever you want. We can lounge about by the pool." He ran his nose down hers as he tried desperately to reassure her. "Or stay in bed all day." His expression mischievous, trying to lighten the mood. Sylvie's eyes shot up to his and she smiled.

"Hmm, I might be very tense after my meeting."

"I hope so." His hold on her tightened. "Come on, you get ready and I'll order breakfast." Sylvie nodded against his chest and sighed as she reluctantly let him go.

Nick emerged from the closet in his faded jeans and white polo shirt. He was rubbing hair wax in his hair, which took all of thirty seconds. Perfect. His face had a sun-kissed glow, making his blue eyes pop. Looking like a Giorgio Armani model, he strolled over to the dining room where Andreas was setting up breakfast. Sylvie could hear them talking as she popped in her diamond earrings, then picked up her wide black belt and clinched it round her waist. *Crap, she'd put on weight.* She'd had to fasten it at the next hole up. Well what did she expect? All she'd done these past few days was sleep, stuff her face and sex. *The three 'S's!* she chuckled to herself. She checked herself in the mirror. She'd put on her camel pencil skirt and a sleeveless white blouse and her black and white peep toes. Sylvie softly pinned up her hair. *Hmm, definitely more business-like.* She spritzed some perfume and headed to the dining room.

Nick wolf whistled as Sylvie walked into the room and she felt herself flush.

"Wow, you look lovely. All business and hot – really hot. I wouldn't mind being bossed around by you." He stood up and kissed her, then stood back to appraise her some more, then to Sylvie's horror he walked slowly round her, his eyes admiring her every angle. "I love this." He gently touched her hair. Sylvie closed her eyes, sweating under his scrutiny. "And I really, *really* love this," He gently rubbed her behind with his palm.

"Have you quite finished?" she scolded, trying hard to sound stern but failing miserably.

"Oh baby, I haven't even started." She shook her head and sat down but not before Nick had dashed to pull out her seat.

"Please sit down and pack it in. It's a skirt, for the love of God," said Sylvie, clearly embarrassed.

"I think I need to pay a visit to your office if this is how you dress." He dropped a kiss on her neck. "You smell like heaven." Nick sat down and winked at her.

"Tea?" She tried hard to sound brusque. Sylvie proceeded to pour their tea and Nick started piling his plate with what seemed to be even more food than yesterday. Sylvie picked up a slice of toast and buttered it carefully and placed it on Nick's plate. He took her hand and kissed the inside of her wrist and Sylvie sighed. She was going to miss this. Nick picked up his cup, ignoring the handle, and gulped.

"I asked Andreas about your ring. He said he'd check everywhere once we've left. He assured me he'd find it. He was quite upset."

"It's insured. I bought it on my card. If it doesn't turn up, I'll ask the jeweller to make me another. The monetary value doesn't bother me. It's the fact I got it here, with you, that's upset me." She screwed up her nose as she spoke.

"We'll find it, don't worry. Aren't you hungry?" He looked at the stewed fruit on her plate and a slice of toast. She shook her head. Her stomach was still unsettled.

"I'll feel better after this morning's finished. I have a real craving for *Galaktobouriko*. After I've done the signing we should go to a patisserie and get some. They make the best here in Athens."

"Whatever you want, baby. You're the boss."

"That I am. Well, today I am anyway." She giggled and took a sip of tea.

Takes the taxi driver pulled up outside Dr Dimitris Dracos's clinic at nine-fifty-five. Sylvie's stomach was burning as she gripped onto her briefcase – well, Chris's old briefcase. Nick had his arm around her. He could feel the tension as they stopped. Nick leaned over and paid Takis, then opened the door and ran round to Sylvie's side and helped her out. The building was one of the older buildings in the area, built in the late seventies. It looked in need of repair and remodelling, Sylvie thought, as she walked into the entrance and Nick pressed for the elevator. No wonder Dr Dracos had built his own clinic, mused Sylvie.

Sylvie had spoken to Zach this morning and he'd assured her the lawyers would be there with the all the relevant paperwork. They entered the lift and Nick took hold of her hand.

"I'll just see you in and then I'll leave you to it. Unless you want me to stay." He was hoping she'd ask him to stay. He hated leaving her in this state.

"No, really, I'll be fine. I'll call you once we're done."

"Sure?"

She nodded and put her best fake smile on, hoping he'd fall for it. He smiled back at her, totally unconvinced.

The doors opened and Sylvie entered an ultra-modern reception area, in complete contrast to the rest of the building. It was all white and black with green accents. The desk was glass and there were flat screens along one wall showing results of different cosmetic procedures. There were two opaque glass doors with plaques on, but Sylvie couldn't read them. The receptionist was a young attractive blonde, her hair in a tight pleat, dressed top to toe in white. She beamed at them as they entered, her teeth immaculate. Sylvie was sure it was because she'd seen Nick. She looked expectantly at him as she greeted them.

"*Kali mera.*" Her eyes sparkled.

"*Kali mera*, I'm here to see Dimitri, I'm Sylvie Sapphiris." The receptionist dragged her blatant gaze from Nick and frowned slightly at Sylvie.

"Oh yes, of course. One moment, please."

Nick turned to Sylvie and kissed her softly. "Good luck baby. I'll be close by. Okay?" He hugged her tightly and went back into the elevator, winking at her as he doors closed. The blonde receptionist's eyes widened in surprise as she witnessed their exchange. Sylvie cringed inwardly. That's all she needed, someone else reaffirming her ever-present insecurities!

Within what seemed a couple of seconds, one of the glass doors flung open and a dark slim man strode into the reception area. He was immaculately dressed in a black suit, crisp white shirt and grey tie. He had a full head of thick grey hair smoothed back, which he wore a little long for his age but yet seemed to be able to pull it off. He had a deep tan, dark intense eyes and laughter lines etched over his handsome face. He was in his early fifties and of average height. He oozed authority and charm and was utterly disarming.

"Sylvie, at last we meet. Welcome." He was in front of her with his hand outstretched, which Sylvie took and shook. He pulled her close and kissed her on both cheeks, throwing her totally off-guard with his familiarity.

"Dimitri, thank you. I hope you're well."

"Yes, thank you. Please come through to my office. I've set everything up there. Coffee?" He guided her through the glass door he'd come from. "How's your stay been?"

"I'm having a lovely time, thank you."

"You're leaving tomorrow, Zach tells me?"

"That's right."

"How is my friend Zach? Keeping busy? He told me you're very active in the business now."

"Yes, I'm still learning though. He's very well. I couldn't have done it without Zach. He's been a good friend to me. He sends his regards."

They were in his office now, which was also white and sleek. He had a large glass desk and by the back wall another large conference table also in glass with white leather and chrome chairs. There were papers set out with pens and water glasses. By the large window there were some black leather couches and a glass coffee table with coffee already set up.

"Please Sylvie, sit down. The lawyers will be here shortly. Black or white?" he gracefully motioned to the couches and Sylvie sat down, feeling a little uncomfortable under his constant penetrating gaze.

"Black, please." He sat down next to her and poured her a coffee, placing it in front of her.

"So, before we get down to business, I was hoping to arrange for us to go out for dinner, as I mentioned on the phone. You're in my home town; the least I could do is take you out. Seeing as you're leaving tomorrow, that only leaves tonight." He had turned to face her now and Sylvie flushed.

"That's really very kind of you, but it's not necessary." He smiled widely and sat forward, his voice softer, bordering on seductive.

"But I'd really like to."

Sylvie swallowed. She hadn't expected this and was more than a little surprised.

"Well you see, Dimitri, I didn't come alone." Sylvie could feel herself sweat even though his office was air-conditioned at what felt like a very cool twenty degrees. He raised his eyebrows in surprise, then quickly added.

"That's not a problem. You can bring your friend. I'll be bringing Adonis, my son, and Katerina, my daughter. They'll be here shortly, so you'll meet them."

The phone rang on his desk and he got up to answer it.

"That'll be the lawyers. Yes, Toula? Good. Send them through and get Adonis and Katerina to come too." He looked over to Sylvie as she sipped her coffee, then frowned at something Toula was saying. "Well, call her and tell her to hurry up."

How was she going to get out of this now? She didn't want to offend him; after all, he was about to hand over an enormous amount of money to her company. How was she going to explain it to Nick? How was she going to explain Nick to Dimitris? *Oh fuck!* The furnace in her stomach had just had a re-stoking!

Within a few minutes the lawyers representing Sapphire Developers and Dr Dimitris Dracos were sat around the conference table, after introductions were done. They all looked extremely young but professional. Spiros smiled at Sylvie as he arranged all the papers in order. Was it just her or did everyone look young these days? Her thoughts made her furrow her brow. She was abruptly dragged away from her musings by another young attractive man entering the office.

"This is Adonis my son, Sylvie. Sylvie, Adonis." The young man shook her hand firmly. Like his father, he oozed charm and was handsome but that was where the similarity ended. Adonis was tall and fair-skinned with hazel eyes. He had thick light-brown hair that he wore long and slightly layered. He must have been in his late twenties and was dressed in a camel suit with an open-necked white shirt. Perfect name for a perfect looking man: he was stunning.

"So very pleased to meet you, Sylvie. My father has spoken a lot about you over these past few months."

"Pleased to meet you, Adonis. That's very kind." Well he was definitely a good advert for his father's business. He was pretty much flawless.

"I believe you'll be joining us tonight."

"Well I'm not sure yet. I need to check. You see, I came with a friend," Sylvie explained rather feebly.

"I see." He smiled widely.

Oh! Another similarity with Dr Dracos senior.

"Katerina will be in shortly."

"Is she also a surgeon?"

"No, she's an anaesthetist." Sylvie nodded, feeling decidedly uncomfortable under his steady gaze. He seemed to be evaluating her, rather than blatantly appraising her like his father.

"Looks like everything's ready. Sylvie, would you like to come over so we can start the signing?" Dimitris fished out some glasses and slipped them on, then handed Sylvie a pen.

"We'll need two witnesses." Spiros looked expectantly at Dimitris.

"Well there's Adonis and Katerina."

"I'm sorry, but they can't be related to either buyer or seller."

"Oh, well Toula my receptionist could do it. That's okay, isn't it?" Dimitris looked a little frustrated. "Everyone else is out this morning. I could go downstairs and ask one of the accountants in the offices below I suppose."

Before he could make a decision, Sylvie blurted out: "My friend could do it."

Dimitris smiled widely. "Why of course, what an excellent idea."

Sylvie pulled out her phone and dialled Nick.

"Hi, have you finished? That was quick." His voice full of surprise.

"No, but we need you to be one of the witnesses on the sale and transfer. Can you come back?"

"Of course baby, I'll be there in five minutes." He couldn't disguise his eagerness.

True to his word, Nick entered the offices of Dr Dracos within five minutes. Toula willingly showed him through, all smiles, as Nick quickly scanned the room, evaluating what was going on, then walked over to Sylvie, slipping his arm around her and kissing the top of her head. Sylvie noticed he was carrying a large cardboard bag with 'Lancel' on the side. He set it down on the floor. "Everything okay, baby?"

Sylvie nodded, feeling herself heat up. Well there would be no doubt now in the good Doctor's mind as to what kind of friend Nick was. "Yes, um, let me introduce you. Dimitri this is Nick. Nick, Dimitri."

Nick extended his hand without letting go of Sylvie and shook hands with an obviously surprised and wide-eyed Dimitris. "Very pleased to meet you, Dimitri." Nick eyed Dimitris warily, though his tone was friendly.

"Welcome. I believe you may have saved the day. I hope we didn't drag you away from anything." Sylvie heard a slight trace of sarcasm in Dimitris's voice, but Nick didn't seem to notice.

"Not at all. Nothing's too much trouble for *my* Sylvie." Nick emphasised *my* as he spoke.

"And this is Adonis, Dimitri's son. Adonis, Nick." Sylvie felt Nick's arm hold her tighter as he reached over to shake hands.

"Pleased to meet you."

"Thank you for coming so quickly." Adonis smiled widely and Nick nodded and Nick instantly loosened his grip on Sylvie.

"It's really no trouble. Glad to help."

Sylvie watched over the whole scene and felt the excess testosterone fly around the room, bouncing off every polished, sleek, shiny surface in the cool office. Maybe dinner out with the good doctors would be a bad idea.

The papers were put out in sequence and in turn, Sylvie, Dimitris, Nick and Toula signed and initialled four copies each. Then the lawyers added their ID numbers and details. They were then stamped and counter-stamped by both sets of lawyers and the bank details were exchanged for the transfer to take place by two o'clock that afternoon.

Sylvie sighed as she placed all her documentation into her briefcase. Well, that was done. It hadn't been so bad after all, and Nick had been here too, and for some reason his presence had had a calming effect on her. It was like she felt safe when he was close by.

Nick had sat down on the couch, giving her some space. She looked over to him, his ankle crossed over his leg and his arm resting on the back of the couch. He looked so young and utterly irresistible. Spiros came over to her to confirm the time for the transfer, and to become more acquainted with her. As they talked, she spotted Adonis walking over to where Nick was sitting. She couldn't hear what they were talking about, but Nick seemed to be relaxed as they spoke, and at one point he laughed as some comment Adonis made. Adonis smiled warmly at Nick as he spoke to him, then shook his hand and returned to the conference table. Sylvie noticed that Dimitris's eyes flitted over periodically to them as they spoke. Sylvie took a deep breath, picked up her briefcase and walked over to where Nick was sitting.

"How do you feel?" He leaned forward and gently stroked her face as she sat down next to him. Sylvie felt herself flush as she could feel at least three sets of eyes focusing on them.

"Glad it's done."

"Let's hope there'll be many more." He always seemed to know exactly what to say. They were interrupted by Dimitris. He'd sauntered over to join them, standing seemingly casually. His focus was on Nick. Adonis watched from the conference table, smiling to himself as if he were in on a private joke.

"Nick, I invited Sylvie out this evening for dinner with my family. Naturally, she couldn't answer without checking with you first. I'd really like to thank her and her company for finishing our building before schedule. It would mean a great deal to us if you would both join us." He flashed his wide smile at Nick whose eyes flicked over to Sylvie. She shifted in her seat. He knew if he declined he'd look petty and rude which would embarrass Sylvie. She already looked uncomfortable and he couldn't bear to see her like that. He took Sylvie's hand and kissed the back of it, then turning to Dimitris, he stood up, effectively towering over him.

"That's very generous of you Dimitri. We'd love to join you. What time and where?" He felt Sylvie tighten her grip on his hand.

"I'll reserve us a table at Island. It's a restaurant nightclub on the outskirts of Athens. Let's say nine-thirty. Dinner and dancing, a perfect way to celebrate our newly acquired clinic. All thanks to Sapphire Developers." His eyes fixed on Sylvie as he spoke, then he turned to Nick and smiled his wide brilliant smile.

"Island and nine-thirty it is," Nick confirmed. Sylvie rose from the settee and went to shake Dimitris's hand. He extended it and then, as he did when he greeted her, he pulled her close and kissed both her cheeks. Nick kept his eyes on Dimitris, his muscle clenching in his jaw.

"Until tonight, Sylvie. Nick." He thrust out his hand and Nick shook it.

Nick bent down and collected the bag he had brought in. Sylvie quickly said her goodbyes to the lawyers and Adonis and took Nick by the hand, and they made their way to the elevator. They were met by a tall blonde young woman with hazel eyes and fair skin. She looked flustered as she flounced into the reception. She eyed Nick appreciatively and skirted over Sylvie.

"Katerina," called Dimitris, "you're late. We managed without you, my darling. Here, let me quickly introduce you to Sylvie. Sylvie, this is my daughter Katerina, and this is Nick, Sylvie's *good* friend." He made a point of emphasising the *good*. It didn't go unnoticed by Nick. He smiled wryly.

"Pleased to meet you both." She limply shook Sylvie's hand and then focused on Nick, gripping his hand tighter.

"They were just leaving, but we'll see them tonight. We'll be going to Island."

Katerina's eyes lit up. "Wonderful. I'll see you both tonight."

Once in the elevator, Sylvie's whole body relaxed. Nick watched her intensely. He wasn't happy about this evening's arrangements, but he knew that if he'd declined Dimitris it would have reflected badly on Sylvie. He pushed her hair back off her face and kissed her forehead.

"Well, boss, where do you want to go now?"

"I really want to sit in a café, to be honest, to have some tea and I really want some *Galaktobouriko*."

"Café it is, then. I saw a nice place just across from here."

The doors opened and they stepped out into the lobby and then onto the street. The sun was high and beat down fiercely on the pavement, reflecting off every light surface. It was almost painful. They both slipped on their sunglasses and Nick guided Sylvie to a large and rather busy café across the street, which thankfully was shaded. He chose a table and pulled out the chair for Sylvie. The waiter was over instantly.

"*Kali mera*." He handed them a couple of menus and looked at Nick expectantly. Nick proceeded to order a large bottle of still water, two English teas and two *Galaktobourikos* in word-perfect Greek.

Nick beamed at Sylvie, her jaw dropping as she looked at him, clearly shocked and impressed at his flawless pronunciation.

"I didn't know you spoke Greek. That was really good."

"I learned it at school, then Petra taught me more."

"Petra?"

"My girlfriend." Sylvie nodded. "In the army, everyone spoke Greek and I need to be able to speak it for business too," he smirked shyly.

"Why have I never heard you before?"

"Well everyone presumes I don't speak it and to be honest, I feel a little self-conscious in front of people I know."

"Well, I'm impressed." She gazed at him, clearly bowled over by his honesty. "Do you know what *Galaktobouriko* is?"

"Of course. It's a creamy semolina custard baked in crispy filo pastry and drenched in syrup." He grinned at her as she let her mouth drop open again.

She felt her mouth water as he perfectly described the delicious pastry. He made it sound so seductive, Sylvie's whole body tingled. *Fuck! Who'd have thought a description of a Greek pastry could turn you on!*

"You still don't know me very well. Remember, I've lived all my life in Cyprus." Sylvie nodded blankly. It was true, she really didn't know very much about him, but she was pleased to say she loved being shocked by him.

"I've been shopping." Nick pulled up the bag he'd been carrying and handed it to Sylvie. His eyes lighting up, he couldn't disguise his excitement as she looked puzzled at the bag.

"For me?" He nodded, his eyes bright and wide. She opened up the bag and pulled out a large cream box, again with 'Lancel' embossed on the top. She slowly pulled off the lid to reveal some tissue paper. Her eyes flitted up to Nick, his gaze transfixed on her; he looked nervous. Sylvie then ripped back the tissue to reveal a sumptuous dark-blue grained leather briefcase with a simple gold fastening. Her eyes shot up to his face and she was met with an almost shy smile. She ran her fingers over the leather, feeling the texture.

"It's absolutely gorgeous. Thank you." Her voice was barely audible, clearly moved by this gesture.

"Gorgeous gift for a gorgeous girl. You like it, then?"

"I love it and it's blue. I love blue." Sylvie nodded as tears pooled in her eyes. She didn't know why she was crying, whether it was the tension of her meeting or the realisation this was their final day or that this remarkable, thoughtful man had bought her such an exquisite gift. Nick got up instantly and knelt down by her side.

"Hey baby, don't cry." He held her as she let her tears trickle. "I didn't mean to upset you." He stroked her back softly.

"You didn't. It's just I'm a little emotional. I love it, truly." He pulled back to look at her face and gently wiped her tears away with his thumb, then licked it. Sylvie broke into a smile and the relief ran over Nick's face. He scraped the chair closer to her and sat down.

"While I was waiting for you to finish, I passed by this leather bag shop and thought you maybe needed a new one. I remembered you only had your laptop case and that." He motioned to Chris's old briefcase. "I thought you deserved your own. Now you're the boss." His smile was a little apprehensive, hoping he hadn't overstepped the mark.

Sylvie looked down at her new briefcase, smoothing over the stitching with her fingers. "Thank you, Nick. It's perfect."

"Like you," he added.

The waiter came over and placed their drinks and sweets on the table. Sylvie put the lid back on the box and put it back in the bag. She reached over and poured their tea and passed Nick his cup. He picked it up, ignoring the handle, as he always did, and gulped. Sylvie cut into her sweet, crispy filo breaking up over soft semolina cream and lifted it up for Nick to try. He opened his mouth and Sylvie popped the syrup-covered piece in. He chewed it, slowly savouring it.

"That's absolutely delicious."

"I know." Sylvie giggled guiltily. "It's my favourite. Can you think of anything else so yummy?"

"Oh yes, I can think of something, but it doesn't come on a plate," he replied, provocatively raising his eyebrows, making Sylvie almost spontaneously combust again.

BABY GEORGE

As Takis pulled up outside the Grande Britannia, the valet opened up the taxi door and Sylvie stepped out, glad to be heading back to their suite. This morning had been mentally exhausting and she just wanted a bath and to relax. Tonight was going to be an awkward evening and she was more than daunted by it. Dimitris had been overly friendly and she was sure Nick was not particularly looking forward to tonight either. They'd both avoided the subject throughout the afternoon while walking round Glifada. Sylvie didn't want to dwell on her unwelcome feelings regarding Dracos. Well it was just one night, albeit their last night. She could always feign a headache and they could leave early.

Nick climbed out of the cab, carrying Sylvie's new briefcase. He took her hand and they entered a busy lobby. To their surprise they spotted George by the reception desk, holding a beautiful baby boy. He was adorable, dark-haired, all curls and dimples.

"*Kali spera,* Sylvie, Nick." He greeted them both as they approached him. "Let me introduce you to my grandson, George. My daughter was in town so she came in to see me."

"Oh he's gorgeous. How old is he?" Sylvie gushed, putting out her finger to stroke his face. Baby George grabbed it and tried to put it in his mouth. "He's teething?"

George senior nodded. "He's seven months."

Sylvie turned to Nick and was immediately winded by the expression on his face. He had dropped the bag holding her new briefcase and his face had lit up, his eyes shining brightly. Nick leant forward and let

Baby George put his little fat dimply hand on his face. The baby then proceeded to gurgle as he moved his hand to Nick's mouth, where Nick pretended to bite his little fingers and made silly faces. He squealed with delight and giggled. Nick lifted his hands, showing that he intended to pick him up.

"May I?" he asked George senior, who was somewhat taken aback.

"Of course." Nick lifted Baby George gently out of his grandfather's arms and lifted him high in the air. Baby George squealed with delight as Nick gently swung him up and down. Then brought him down to his face and blew a raspberry on his chubby tummy. Baby George giggled and softly slapped Nick's face as he repeatedly threw him up and down, then blew a raspberry on his tummy. Each time, Baby George rewarded him with a peal of laughter as Nick made hugely exaggerated facial expressions.

Holy crap, he really wants children! Sylvie watched mesmerised, her heart swelling, and then as realisation hit, within a split-second her heart twisted tight in the knowledge this was something she wouldn't be able to give him. She remembered the quipping comment he'd made on the *Silver Lining* about them having kids. She had thought he was joking, but from what she had witnessed today, she realised he wasn't.

Nick turned to Sylvie, his smile almost face-splitting. "Isn't he amazing?" Sylvie smiled back at him and nodded. He turned to George and reluctantly gave Baby George back but not before he planted a soft kiss on his head, breathing in the baby smell. "He's really something, George."

"I know. He's my first grandchild, so he's special." George beamed at them.

"Very special." Nick agreed and Sylvie's heart clenched tighter.

Their suite had been cleaned and there were more chocolates on the coffee table. Sylvie placed her briefcase on the desk. They'd travelled up to their room in silence and she couldn't shake off that dreaded feeling that reality was creeping up on them. Their cocoon was slowly being chipped apart. Baby George had been the catalyst. Children. What kind of future could she really have with him? In five years' time, he'd realise that he wanted children and she'd be nearly fifty. She rubbed her eyes with her forefinger and thumb, and sighed. What was she thinking?

She could hear Nick in the bathroom. He was filling the bath. He came out of the bathroom holding Sylvie's ring.

"Andreas must have found it." He looked so young when he smiled.

She forced a smile. "Oh, thank goodness." Relieved, she tried to look pleased but she couldn't shake off her previous thoughts. "I'm sorry about tonight. I know it was supposed to be just you and me."

"It's okay. Business is business. If we blew them off it would have looked bad." He was up to her now, pushing back her hair off her face. "Are you alright? You look… preoccupied."

"I'm fine. I need to call Zach and then I need a bath." He leant down and kissed her softly, unconvinced. He decided not to push her. Today had been a big step and he was sure tonight would be, at the very least, strange and uncomfortable. He wasn't sure what to make of Dimitris. He was polite enough, but he seemed a little too forceful and his reaction to Sylvie didn't sit well with Nick. He'd obviously had an ulterior motive when he'd asked her out.

"I'll sort the bath and you make your call." He leaned down again, this time kissing her harder, and Sylvie melted as he pulled her closer. As he pulled away, he whispered, "Don't undress yourself. I want to watch you." Sylvie's eyes widened and her previous thoughts faded away. His voice was so sultry and wicked, her skin heated up instantly. He walked backwards a couple of steps, appraising her, his eyes blazing, as they travelled over her, making every hair stand on end. He swiftly turned and strolled back to the bathroom. How was she going to talk to Zach now? Thank God he wouldn't be able to see her all flushed and flustered.

She pulled out her phone and quickly dialled Zach's number. It rang twice and then his familiar voice answered. She could picture him swinging back on his chair, all relaxed and chilled.

"Hi Sylvie, darling. I hear all went well." She could hear the smile in his voice.

"Hi Zach. Yes, it did. How are you?"

"Oh you know. Same shit, different day." He laughed. "I spoke to the lawyers; the money was transferred about two hours ago, so we can celebrate when you get back. How are you enjoying yourself? I hope you're relaxing."

"I am. In fact, I'm just about to get in the bath." She felt herself flush. "I spent the day in Glifada, so I'm tired."

"Good for you, darling. Lily told me she'd spoken to you. She said you were having a great time. We've missed you."

"I've missed you too." And as Sylvie said it, she knew it was true. Even though her time here with Nick had been unbelievable, she'd missed Zach, today especially. He'd always been with her in every business transaction and it had felt strange him not being there today.

"Okay, I'll let you go. I'll see you on Wednesday. Take care."

"You too, Zach. Bye."

Sylvie put down her phone and picked up her briefcase, running her fingers over the monograms fitted on the buckle. Nick stood in the doorway leaning against the frame. He'd been watching her intently, wondering what was going through her mind. Something was bothering her and he knew it was something to do with him.

"Sylvie?" His voice was soft and apprehensive. She turned round, almost embarrassed that she'd been caught. "What's wrong?" She shook her head, indicating she didn't want to say. "Sylvie, please tell me. My mind is working overtime." He walked over to her as he spoke, his eyes wary and tense. "You need to tell me what's going on. I know something's worrying you, you've been so quiet all day." She closed her eyes and swallowed.

"Did I do something? Is it about this morning? Is it the briefcase?" Sylvie opened her eyes and stared into his oh-so-beautiful face. She felt her heart lurch. "Sylvie, please, you can tell me. I want you to. I need you to be honest with me. Whatever it is, we need to talk about it." He bent down and kissed her softly on the lips, his eyes wide open. He pulled back and held her face between his hands and his eyes bore into her, imploring her to talk.

After what seemed like an eternity, she spoke. "What kind of future do we have, Nick? I'm not right for you."

"What do you mean, Sylvie? Why are you saying that?" he whispered. His hands dropped from her face and he stepped back as if he'd been slapped.

"I saw how you were with George, Baby George. Your whole face lit up." He clenched his teeth and the muscle started twitching in his jaw.

"Is this what this is about? Me and children?" His voice filled with hurt, his hands running through his hair.

"Nick, you can't avoid this issue. You're so young, you don't think this is important to you now, but it will be. I'm forty-four!" Sylvie slightly raised her voice to emphasise the point. "I can't give you that. We've known each other just over a week. Say we get through all the other shit that's flying around our very new relationship and we get to, say, a year from now, maybe two years from now. You're going to want to know that there's a possibility of a family. I'll be forty-six. Forty-six!" She repeated it, hoping that it would sink in. He stood stock-still in front of her, still clenching his jaw, eyes wide.

"I'm trying desperately not to think about it, Nick, but avoiding the subject won't make it go away. I'm just too old for you. I have to face it and so do you." Sylvie rubbed her face with her hands, giving him a moment to process what she had said.

"I told you before. I don't care about your age. Why don't you believe me?" His voice was quiet and raspy.

"Because now, you don't care. Today, on the twenty-sixth of May 2014, it doesn't matter, but in a year or two or five, it will, and you will be faced with the option of staying with me out of guilt or deciding to move on. Either way, I get fucked over!" Her voice cracking as she spoke the last six words, because this was the crux of it all. Sylvie couldn't face being thrown aside yet again. All her insecurities reared their ugly heads. Her eyes pricked with tears as she tried desperately to hold on to her emotions. Nick stepped forward, his face softening as he reached for her, but she pulled back, indicating she didn't want him to touch her.

"I'm at a stage in my life that I can't experiment with my feelings. I never thought I'd find anyone, let alone so soon. But I can't just go with it and see if it'll work. I play for keeps, Nick, and if I feel or can see that in the long term the chances are slim of us lasting, I'd rather I face it now. My heart can't take any more rejection, Nick. I'm just not that strong." Nick rubbed his forehead and took a deep breath. He looked so devastatingly handsome as he tried hard to find the right words to say.

"Are you under the impression that it's only you who has doubts? Sylvie, baby, from the very start, I have had to contend with my father, who's besotted with you and to all intents and purposes is perfect for you: age-wise, professionally, where he is in his life. I have then been faced with Dr Dracos, another admirer who has made it more than clear of his intentions today towards you. Another perfect suitor for you. He's rich, handsome, done the children thing, and you're both in the same stage of your life. Why wouldn't you want to be with him, or my father? Or any other *middle-aged* man for that matter. I'm sure there's a line of suitable suitors just waiting to make their move. How do you think that makes me feel?" He ran his fingers through his hair again. "Well, I'll tell you, it makes me feel inadequate. I've got to do a lot of catch-up to get to that stage." Sylvie's eyes widened and a tear she'd tried to hold back trickled down her cheek.

"I can't lie to you and say that I don't want a family, because I do. I play for keeps too, Sylvie, and I can't envisage a day that you are not by my side and in my life. I waited four months Sylvie – four months to see if my father and you would ever get together.

"You keep saying that we've only been together for a week, but we've known each other longer. I fell in love with you over those four months. I watched you build yourself up. You are so incredibly strong, Sylvie. Look at how you've coped with every challenge that's come your way. Today was hard for you, I know. That's why I bought you the briefcase. So you could let go of another piece of your past." He tentatively stepped forward. Sylvie blinked quickly as more tears fell. "Yes, I want children, but I want you more. There are alternatives and I'm prepared to do whatever it takes, Sylvie, but I want you with me always. Please don't keep looking at the negatives. I don't. I only focus on the positives."

He wiped her tears with his thumbs, then held her face, smiling down at her.

"I love you, Sylvie, totally and completely." He kissed her tenderly and she felt her whole being dissolve into him. She wrapped her arms around him and kissed him back, harder and deeper. "I love you. Please believe me. I don't care about anything else."

"I love you too Nick, but I –"

"No buts." He interrupted her, putting his forefinger on her lips. He ran his hand down to her behind and a wicked smile crept over his face. Sylvie knew their time for talking was over. She felt her body heat up under his gaze. "Only this butt." He grinned. "I thought I was going to explode, watching you wiggling about in this skirt today. Your ass is incredible. All official and business-like. Very sexy. Dracos never took his fucking eyes off you. I nearly punched him when he kissed you goodbye." He pushed himself close to her, pressing her up against the desk.

Sylvie smiled shyly. "He's not my type," she joked.

"What is your type, then?" He kissed her neck as he spoke.

"Oh, I think you know."

"You better believe it," he growled as he pushed against her again so she could feel his erection, then kissed her passionately. "Let's go to bed," he murmured in her mouth. He rested his forehead on hers, his eyes burning into hers. Then in a split-second, something slipped into his mind.

"Wait here a moment." He let her go and walked to the bar. He splashed some Chivas in two glasses and dropped a couple of ice cubes in, then made his way back to Sylvie. She had her head cocked to one side, puzzled.

"Drink it." He spoke softly as he handed her the glass and he raised his own. Sylvie took a sip, her eyes never leaving his. "You're tense and you always seem to loosen up after a drink."

Oh. Sylvie took a bigger sip and Nick's lips curled into a seductive smile. He took a small sip and put his unfinished drink on the desk. Sylvie looked at it fleetingly, then fixing him with her eyes, she drained her glass and put it next to his. Nick's eyes narrowed slightly.

"Bed," she mouthed, because that's what she really wanted and what she needed. It had been a weird day, tense and emotional. All she wanted was to feel this sexy man's hands and body all over her.

"You're the boss." His eyes penetrated into her. "Walk this way. I really want to see you wiggle in that skirt one more time." He licked his lips and stepped back, signalling with his hand for Sylvie to pass. She smiled wryly and looked up at him through her lashes as she walked catwalk-style to the bedroom, removing her clips from her hair as she walked, her hair falling down.

"That's right baby, work it, work it." He was just a foot behind her, itching to touch her but restraining himself, loving that she was teasing him, his eyes covering every inch of her. As Sylvie entered the bedroom, she turned and struck a pose, laughing as she put her hand on her hip.

"Was that what you wanted?" She raised her eyebrow and he grinned at her, his eyes still blazing.

"Oh baby, you know exactly what I want." He stepped up close to her, then ran his fingers round her belt and jerked her up to him. "I think we can get rid of this." He made quick work of the belt buckle, then let it fall to the floor. He grasped her head, his fingers in her hair as his mouth captured hers and he kissed her hard, then trailed kisses down her neck as she rolled her head back. He slowly unbuttoned her blouse, pulling it out from her skirt, then letting it fall over her shoulders to the floor. Sylvie seized the bottom of his T-shirt and pulled it over his head, revealing his perfect torso. Nick stepped back to appraise her again.

"Turn around." Sylvie looked puzzled but turned all the same. "Unzip your skirt and slip it off." Sylvie was glad she'd had the Chivas. He knew exactly what he was doing. Fuelled by her Dutch courage, she leisurely unzipped her skirt and then pushed it down to the floor, bending all the way over. She heard his gasp as her hands almost touched the floor, her legs perfectly straight and in six-inch stilettos. She slowly stood upright and she could feel him up behind her, the heat radiating off him. Nick swiftly unzipped his jeans and stepped out of them, his sneakers and his socks. He pulled her backwards by the hips so she was flush up against him.

"You really are so beautiful." He kissed her shoulders and neck as he unhooked her bra, allowing his hands to cup her breasts, letting it drop away from her. Sylvie moaned.

"How can you say you're not right for me?" he whispered in her ear. "Doesn't this feel right, baby?" his words so soft, so seductive.

"Oh, Nick."

"I know, baby." He let his hands slide down her sides and then he pulled her panties down to the floor, kissing her spine, then her behind as he went.

"Your ass is so sweet. You taste and smell of heaven." Sylvie turned around, wanting to touch him, feel him. He was still kneeling down and he looked up at her through his thick lashes, his eyes white hot. Sylvie seized his head and pulled him up to her, claiming his mouth and holding him tight. He made her feel so desirable, it was totally intoxicating. Slowly, he guided her backwards against the bed where she slowly fell down against the soft mattress. He stood looking down at her as he reached down and swiftly removed his boxers, then kneeling down again, she lifted each of her legs while he slid off her stilettos and kissed the inside of her ankles.

"Nick, please." Her whole body trembled.

"Tell me this doesn't feel right."

"Nick, please!"

"Please what, baby?" She felt his smile against her ankles as he kissed them a second time, then pulled her down, so her bottom was on the edge of the bed. Sylvie writhed with desire, grasping at the bedspread.

"Tell me you don't want this."

"Oh Nick, you know I do."

"Tell me." His voice was almost menacing – hot and sexy as hell. Nick rested her legs on his shoulders, hovering millimetres away from her. "Tell me what you want," his eyes burning.

"I want you, Nick. I want you in me, now."

He closed his eyes as he heard the words, taking in a sharp breath. "Oh yes, baby," and slowly he pushed himself deep into her as she cried out in pure pleasure.

"Yes," she said as he slowly eased back out and revelled in her total surrender. "Nick, please." And he sunk back deeper and she cried out once more. "Faster, Nick." He held on to her hips and pulled back out. "Faster," she pleaded. He bent down so that he pushed her legs down and he rested his hands on either side of her, his face only inches away from hers.

He cocked his head to one side as if asking her if she was okay. "You want faster?"

"Yes, yes, Nick, please," her voice a hoarse whisper, and he sank in deeper as she cried out and he began to move, really move. She gripped his arms, feeling every muscle tense as he continued his delicious assault, his eyes boring in to her, as he started to tighten. He moved faster and faster, bearing down on her hard, her hands moving up to his head, pulling him closer to her, claiming his mouth as he pushed down onto her.

"Sylvie, oh baby," his breathing erratic as he climbed higher, until she felt herself being swept away. Seeing him start to unravel, she cried out her release as he too bucked deep into her and climaxed loudly in her. "Oh fuck!" He let her legs down, then collapsed onto her, rolling to the side, gasping for air as he took her with him.

"You are going to kill me!" He flopped an arm over his eyes, breathing hard. "Fuck, you're bendy!"

Sylvie giggled between breaths. "*Bendy?*"

"Yes, very bendy." He squeezed her and kissed her forehead brushing back her hair.

"I've been called many things, but I can honestly say that's the first time I've been called bendy." He rolled her back and pinned her down, resting his whole weight on her.

"I like bendy," he said, his smile wicked and his eyes wide. Then his face softened and he ran his nose down hers as his breathing started to calm. "Sylvie, I meant what I said. I don't care about anything. Only you. I love you, with my heart and with my soul."

"Nick… I love you too, and that's why I worry, why I'm scared."

"Please, Sylvie, don't overthink everything. I know what I'm getting myself into." He kissed her softly. "Come on, let's get in the bath." He stood up and held out his hand to pull her up.

Sylvie nestled between his legs as they both sunk back into the warm water.

"How was Zach?"

"Relaxed. Laid back as always. The money got transferred, so everything's been done."

Nick held her fingers and played with them as he periodically kissed her head. He'd heard their conversation and he was embarrassed to admit that he felt a little jealous. Zach obviously meant a great deal to her.

"I wasn't kidding about Dracos. He's hot for you." His voice was low and Sylvie could hear uneasiness as he spoke.

"I told you he's not my type. I know tonight's going to be a little weird. I'm not entirely sure why he wanted to take us out."

"Oh I think I know why! He wasn't expecting me and he couldn't very well back down once I arrived."

Sylvie turned round to face him. Kissing his chest, she looked at him. "Thank you for today. I'm glad you were there."

"Me too." He pushed back her wet hair. "Tired?" Sylvie shook her head. "Good, because I really want to make love to you."

"Me too." She smiled shyly. "But not here. The bedroom."

"Whatever you say, baby. You're the boss."

THE LONG AND THE SHORT

"Wow!" Nick stood open-mouthed in the threshold of the walk-in closet. He was rubbing some hair product into his hair, but had stopped in his tracks. "You look… wow!"

Sylvie flushed as she attached the back of her new blue earring which perfectly matched her outfit. She stood nervously, wondering whether maybe she should have worn something a little more conservative. After a huge amount of deliberation, Sylvie had put on her cobalt blue jumpsuit. It was almost indecently backless, secured only by a small button at the base of her neck. It fitted snugly over her behind, showing every curve. She'd paired it with her gold peep toes. Her hair fell loosely down her bare back, and she had pinned up the sides. Nick continued to stare, his eyes sparkling.

"It's not too much?" Sylvie looked down at herself, feeling extremely self-conscious. She was sure it was her earlier Chivas letting her inhibitions slide.

"Yes, it's seriously too much. I think my heart just stopped. You look sensational." He came over to her and ran his hand over her behind, then moved upwards to her bare back. His touch sent shivers all over her body. His fingers reached the nape of her neck. "If this button pops…" His eyebrows raised a fraction. "I'll need to keep you close, in case you have a wardrobe malfunction." Sylvie chuckled. His eyes alight with desire, their colour echoing her outfit. It was weird how his eyes changed, depending on his surroundings. Nick grasped her chin and kissed her.

"I'm going to have to keep you even closer, especially with Dracos around." He let her go and reached for his shirt, the shirt he'd worn to Elenora's wedding. He slipped it on over his black trousers and buttoned it up. He looked absolutely breath-taking.

"I love this shirt," she muttered as she ran her fingers over the fabric and he took a deep breath, relishing her touch. He bent down to fasten the laces of his black shoes and reached over to the dressing table.

"Here, don't forget this." Picking up her ring, he reached for her left hand, his eyes never leaving hers as he slipped it on her ring finger. Sylvie's heart skipped and her eyes widened as he looked at her, kneeling down still from tying his laces. A smile twitching at his lips. Sylvie swallowed her mouth drying. *Holy shit, what was that all about?*

"There, now. Ready?" Once he'd put the ring on, he got up from his kneeling position. Sylvie nodded, still reeling over his gesture. Was he just messing with her? She looked at her hand and started to play with her ring, then reached for her bag. Nick leaned against the dressing table as she moved around the suite. He watched her intently, gauging her reaction and mood.

She reached for her phone and quickly checked it. She looked up at Nick as he continued to watch her. He smiled lovingly at her. Sylvie smiled and slightly shook her head. No, it was just coincidence, She was doing her usual – reading far too much into it.

Clearing her head of her ridiculous thoughts and overactive imagination, she looked back at her phone. There were three messages, one from Markus telling her he'd be out on Wednesday night. One from Lilianna telling her that Melita had received an English prize at her prize-giving. She quickly texted back her congratulations. The third was from Julian. Her eyes flitted to Nick who was still watching her.

"Everything okay?" His eyes narrowed as he saw her flush.

"I've got a message from your dad."

He shifted against the dressing table and his face dropped. "What's he say?" He couldn't stop himself and he was trying hard not to go over and look at the message himself. Sylvie shrugged and pressed the open option. She quickly read it, then closed it.

> Hi darling, I hear all went well!
> Congrats on your first signing as MD
> We need to celebrate! Miss you xx

"He just congratulated me on the signing. Zach must have told him." She smiled tightly, hoping he didn't come over to check it. She was sure he'd not appreciate the last line. Nick nodded stiffly and his jaw was twitching from the clenching of his teeth. Sylvie put her phone in her bag and looked up at him. His eyes looked darker.

"Shall we go?"

Nick took a deep breath and allowed his face to relax.

"If it gets too strange tonight, we can leave early. I'll feign a headache."

Nick pulled her close and kissed her hair, closing his eyes while inhaling. The last thing he wanted was to make her feel more uncomfortable.

"Don't worry baby, it'll be fine." He hoped his tone was convincing.

Nick held Sylvie's hand as they stepped into Island. The club was set overlooking the sea. It was all white with gossamer curtains, candles and lanterns. It looked like a Mediterranean paradise. The clientele were an eclectic mix of people, from cool trendy types to the older and more sophisticated. The hostess smiled sweetly at Nick as she led them to their table where Dimitris, Adonis and Katerina were already waiting. Dimitris's eyes nearly popped out of their sockets as his gaze fell on Sylvie. He stood up, instantly followed by Adonis, smiling their patented wide smiles. Katerina sat looking at them, wide-eyed with what could only be described as apoplectic shock.

"Good evening, Sylvie, Nick." Recovering his composure, Dimitris took Sylvie's hand and shook it, then pulled her close and kissed both her cheeks. Nick still had hold of her hand and he tightened it as she leaned forward. Once Sylvie had been released, Nick reluctantly let go of her to shake Dimitris's outstretched hand. Adonis came over and shook both their hands and then Nick and Sylvie shook hands with a now more composed Katerina.

"This place is so lovely, Dimitri." Sylvie sat down next to him as Nick pulled out her chair, then he sat next to her, Katerina on his right, Adonis opposite.

"Yes we love it here. The owners are good friends of ours and the setting is wonderful, don't you think? What would you like to drink, Nick?"

"What are you drinking?"

"We're having some champagne."

"Champagne sounds good. We are here to celebrate after all." Dimitris nodded, his smile not as wide as before. Sylvie nodded in agreement. He motioned to the hovering waiter and they were immediately served. Katerina, now fully recovered, sat forward.

"So how have you enjoyed your stay here, Sylvie?" Her eyes flitted to Nick, then back to Sylvie.

"It's Nick's first time here in Athens, so I took him to the museum. We went to the Parthenon, Plaka, and yesterday we went to Sounion," Sylvie explained, as they all listened intently.

"Sounion was amazing. I loved it there," added Nick. Katerina raised her eyebrows as if surprised. "I love to sail, so anything to do with the sea fascinates me. The temple was really something."

"You sail, Nick?" Dimitris inquired, not hiding his surprise.

"Yes."

"You own your own boat?"

Nick allowed a smile to curl his mouth. "Yes. Do you, Dimitri?"

"Yes." Sylvie watched as their conversation unfolded; neither man was giving too much away. It felt like a game of battleships.

"What do you have?" Nick asked.

"A Sunseeker Predator."

Nick raised his eyebrows as he nodded showing his approval. "They're very nice. 60?" Dimitris shook his head. Sylvie continued to watch, understanding nothing of what they were saying. *Crap, was it turning into a game of 'is yours bigger than mine'?* Testosterone flying everywhere again.

"54." Dracos answered.

Nick nodded. "How long have you had it?"

"A couple of years. You?"

"A Sunseeker Manhattan," Nick replied, trying hard not to gloat.

"Really?" Dimitris sounded surprised. "60?"

Nick shook his head. "70." Nick smiled, trying hard not to sound smug as he had clearly won this round.

"That's a fabulous vessel." Dimitris was clearly impressed as he sat back in his chair.

"It is."

Sylvie couldn't stand the suspense as the whole table was focused on the two men. "Nick's business is yachts," she blurted out as a form of explanation. "He sources boats and yachts. He's an independent broker." She couldn't hide her pride as she gazed at him. Nick turned to her and smiled lifting her hand to his lips and kissing it.

"That's very interesting. Good to know. I might need you when I want to upgrade."

"I'd be more than happy to help you, Dimitri; any friend of Sylvie's is a friend of mine."

The waiter handed them their menus and Nick reluctantly let go of Sylvie's hand. The atmosphere seemed to change at the table. Nick seemed to relax a little, and Dimitris seemed to eye Nick with what Sylvie thought looked like a renewed respect. *Hmm, see. He isn't just a pretty face*, thought Sylvie. She'd been so caught up in what people thought of her being with a young man, she hadn't focused on how people viewed Nick.

"So you've never been to Athens before?" Adonis spoke softly as he eyed Nick, a smile fixed on his lips.

"First time. I've only stopped over on the way to the South of France, sometimes Spain, for work." Adonis nodded. "It's an amazing city, the little I've managed to see these past few days." He looked lovingly at Sylvie as she flushed.

"Well *ya mas*, and we hope to see you both here more often." Dimitris lifted his glass and everyone followed, clinking their glasses.

As they all perused their menus, a number of fellow guests came over to their table to talk to Dimitris, Adonis and Katerina. They were obviously well known and Sylvie couldn't help but scrutinise every guest to see if she could spot any of Dr Dracos's handiwork. The women found it hard to focus on anything other than Nick, and to her surprise, not so much on Adonis. *Strange?*

"So what do you recommend?" Nick directed his question to Adonis. Sylvie noticed he seemed to let his father take the lead and she was secretly pleased that Nick was making a concerted effort to include him in their conversation. Adonis came across as a very kind and caring man and lacked his father's assertive nature.

"I always enjoy their steaks. They do a number of sauces to accompany them. The pepper one is my favourite."

"Hmm, sounds good. Baby, what will you have?"

All three sets of Dracos eyes shot up and across at Sylvie, the endearment taking them by surprise. Was it so incredible that this man was with her? All her insecurities came flooding back and she smiled tightly. "Not sure." Her voice almost a whisper.

"How's your stomach?" His voice full of concern and his eyes soft as the Dracoses witnessed his tenderness again. "Sylvie has a very delicate stomach." He looked up at them by way of explanation, and they all nodded and continued to look at their menus.

"So, so. Maybe I'll have the salmon," Sylvie muttered as she felt the burning flare up again and she could feel that familiar nausea begin to build up. She took a sip of water and took a deep breath.

"Good choice. It'll be light." Sylvie marvelled at how again Nick had gradually taken control of the situation without being overbearing. He seemed to have a real knack for it. Most men she'd encountered tended to let their ego take control, Nick wasn't like that. He seemed to sit back and assess a situation, then react accordingly.

The waiter came and took their orders and Dimitris ordered both white and red wine. The music was getting livelier as the club section was slowly filling up. They had predominately been playing mellow lounge music and Greek until then. The waiter placed the bread and some small canapés on the table along with olives and some flavoured butter. Sylvie reached over to the bread and Nick smiled to himself, knowing what was coming. He watched her tear the roll apart and spread what looked like an olive butter carefully on the roll. She leaned over and placed it on Nick's side plate, and of course, Nick took her hand and kissed the inside of her wrist.

Dimitris's eyes narrowed as he looked on and then he smiled. "So, how did you two meet?" His natural inquisitive mind had got the better of him.

"I did some interior design for Nick's mother a few months ago. We met at her house." Sylvie flushed, hoping that he wouldn't delve too much further. Dimitris raised his eyebrows as if he found this information interesting. Nick looked at Sylvie and then turned to Dimitris.

"That's the short version anyway."

Sylvie tensed. *What! Oh no please don't!*

"So there's a long version?" Dimitris's interest was piqued. Sylvie felt herself start to panic and sweat.

"I like to think our story started a couple of years ago." He paused, took Sylvie's hand and squeezed it in an attempt to reassure her, as she looked nervous and puzzled within a split-second of each other.

"Really?" Dimitris sat forward, his eyes wide.

"Uh-huh, all thanks to my friend Pavlos. He was a friend of mine in the army and he came to see me after he'd finished his degree."

"You did your national service?" Dimitri interrupted, surprised. Nick nodded, then took a sip of his wine. Adonis and Katerina had now also leant forward, listening intently.

"I was away, on business, but as luck would have it, my younger sister Elenora was there and Pavlos ended up spending the afternoon with her. After a few dates they started to get serious, so serious that a year or so later, Pavlos proposed to her." Everyone's eyes were fixed on Nick as he paused. "So, in preparation for my sister's impending wedding, my mother decided to redecorate and my father recommended Sylvie to do it." His eyes rested on Sylvie's flushed face. He leaned over and kissed her softly on the lips. "She walked out on to my mother's terrace, I took one look at those beautiful brown eyes and I was done for."

Dimitris sat back in his chair, resigned to the fact he hadn't a chance in hell. Katerina sighed wistfully and sipped her champagne and Adonis smiled as if he was in on a private joke again.

"Well that most certainly is a longer version, and if I may say, a far more... romantic one too. Are you a romantic, Nick?"

Nick turned to Dimitris, a wry smile on his face. "Would you blame me if I was?" answered Nick, raising one eyebrow.

"Very good answer." Dimitris laughed loudly. "Well I wish you all the best. Both of you." Nick thanked him, then rested his arm along the back of Sylvie's chair and stroked her bare shoulder. Sylvie leant into it and turned to look at him.

"I like your version much better," she whispered, as the burning sensation in her stomach had been replaced by fluttering butterflies joyfully leaping about.

The evening progressed as they all seemed to relax in each other's company. Once the initial chest-beating had passed, Dimitris and Nick managed to ease in and out of various topics of conversation, ranging from their yachts to the impending World Cup. *Football! What was it with men and football?* thought Sylvie. *Well, at least they had another common interest.* Sylvie questioned Adonis and Katerina on where they had studied and the new clinic.

"We're opening it the first weekend of September," Adonis explained. "I'm looking forward to it. Our present clinic is a little limiting and obviously less discreet. We'll be able to control security better for our more famous clientele."

"You should come over for it, Sylvie." Dimitris paused, then corrected himself. "Both of you. Then you'll get to see your company's work finished."

"That sounds like a lovely idea. We'll have to see. Nick is leaving for the South of France a week on Friday for a few days and I'm hoping to go with him, so I'm not sure I'll be able to take so much time off."

"South of France?" Dimitris was obviously impressed.

"I'm sourcing a couple of yachts for a client."

"What kind?"

"Big – a little out of my league. Leopard 46."

Dimitris's eyes widened and he whistled out of his teeth. "How much do they go for?"

"Depending on the year, around fourteen million."

Sylvie spluttered her water. *Fourteen million!* Nick patted her on the back and checked if she was alright. Her face flushed from both the shock and this revelation. Jeez, he was going to make a mint, and the Russian wanted a couple.

"Must be very wealthy clients," commented Dimitris.

"Russian." Nick shrugged as if that was explanation enough and for Dimitris, it was.

The music in the nightclub section was getting louder and began filtering through to the restaurant. Sylvie had now begun to relax and was talking freely with both Adonis and Katerina. Nick continued to stroke her bare shoulder as he spoke to Dimitris about his business. His touch was making her giddy. Sylvie excused herself to go to the restroom and Katerina decided to join her. Thankfully, it was quiet.

As Sylvie washed her hands, not able to stop herself, Katerina blurted out, "Is Nick a lot younger than you?"

Sylvie stopped breathing for a split-second and then, trying hard not to look embarrassed, she replied, "Yes, he is. There's sixteen years between us." Katerina's eyes widened and Sylvie smiled tightly.

"Oh, I didn't think it was that much. I thought maybe five or six." Sylvie shook her head. Katerina, seeing her expression, realised that maybe she'd been a little tactless.

"Well you both look perfect for each other. Anyone can see he adores you." Sylvie looked a little surprised at her more-than-bold statement. What was it with the Dracoses and their probing questions? "You've seen the women in here, each one better looking than the next. Every one of them that has passed our table has openly gawked at Nick, yet he hasn't taken his eyes off you all night."

Sylvie wrinkled her nose and shrugged, embarrassed by the observation but feeling secretly thrilled. "He really is something else." She giggled and Katerina laughed, nodding in agreement.

The table had been cleared by the time they came to sit back down, and the DJ was playing more recent popular music. Sylvie found herself tapping her fingers along to the music.

Nick's eyes focused on them and then, excusing himself from Dimitris, he stood up and leaned to take her hand. "Dance with me?" Sylvie's mouth opened to say something, but with one look at Nick, she knew he wasn't asking. His lips slightly apart, a smile twitching around his lips and his eyes, *holy shit he looked so fucking sexy*. He raised his eyebrow, waiting for her to stand. It took her a few seconds to get her legs to respond. He excused them from the table and Sylvie followed him as he guided her to the dance floor. Her heart was thumping. The last time she'd danced with him was at the pre-wedding dinner and she had been nervous then. This was different. This was nightclub dancing and even though Sylvie loved to dance, she wasn't ready for this. The music changed to one of her favourites as they approached the dance floor. It had started to fill up and Sylvie was relieved that they'd be surrounded by fellow clubbers.

Nick turned to look at her, pulling her close so that his mouth was by her ear. "The last time I danced with you was torture. I couldn't touch you the way I wanted to." A wicked glint in his eye. He wrapped his arm around her, caressing her bare back. *Wow, was he really going to do this here?* Sylvie felt her skin heat up. "Ready, baby?" She nodded apprehensively and took a deep breath as the voice of Adam Levine sang out about Jagger and his moves.

Nick pulled her close and started to move to the rhythm, his hand holding hers and the other on her bare back, sending shivers up her spine. He let her hand drop, only to rest his on her hip as he guided her, their contact never broken and his hips perfectly synchronised to the music and to Sylvie. *Holy shit, this was so sexy, he was so sexy and he could dance*. She fleetingly remembered Elenora's comment about him stepping on her toes. Obviously it was the wrong kind of dancing! He pulled her close and sung in her ear something about being broken and scarred and that he held the key, then he kissed her ear lobe, giving her goosebumps. The lyrics now suddenly and uncannily had a much deeper meaning. She put her arms around his neck and gently caressed his head, her fingers in his soft hair. His hands tightened their grip on her waist, at the base of her bare back, as he looked deep into her eyes, cobalt blue and blazing. Sylvie gazed back, obliterating everything and everyone until all she could see was him. All she could feel was the music and him moving in perfect time with her to the rhythm. And for those few minutes, it was just the two of them, in their own cocoon, where no one could touch them.

The music changed and they were brought abruptly to the here and now. Nick took her face between his hands and kissed her, deliberately leaving her breathless. "That's how I wanted to dance with you."

Her knees quivered. *How could he do that?* With one sentence he'd made her whole body expire.

He put his arm around her as he guided her back to their table. He leaned down to whisper in her ear. "You want to go?"

"Yes," she breathed, because all she wanted was to be alone with him.

"I really need to get you back to the hotel," he growled.

Please! Hurry!

Dimitris was talking to a couple but as they approached, they bid their goodbyes and left as Sylvie and Nick reached the table.

"It's getting late. I think we need to get off." Nick looked at Sylvie as he spoke, ensuring he spoke for the both of them. Sylvie nodded.

"It's been a busy day for us. Thank you very much for tonight – it's been lovely. It was a pleasure to meet you all."

Adonis and Katerina went over to where they were standing. They both said their goodbyes to Sylvie and then both of them lingered a fraction too much on Nick. Sylvie smiled to herself, thinking back to her conversation with Katerina in the toilets. Nick didn't seem to notice as he pulled away from them, then turning his attention to Dimitris, he shook his hand.

"It was great to meet you. I hope one day we can reciprocate. You must come and visit us in Cyprus. I'll take you out on my yacht."

"Thank you, Nick, I'd really love that." And Sylvie could see that they both meant what they said. Dimitris then shook Sylvie's hand and pulled her close to kiss her on both cheeks. Sylvie noticed Nick stood back and didn't flinch.

"I'm so pleased I got to finally meet you, Sylvie. You are everything I expected and more. Nick's a very lucky man."

"Thank you Dimitri, thank you so much for everything." Nick reached for her hand and they headed out of the club, waving their goodbyes.

12

HOME ALONE AGAIN

Sylvie removed her earrings and popped them into their box. Then she held out her hand to admire her ring. Thank God Andreas had found it. She still thought it was strange that it had gone missing. She carefully pulled it off and then placed it in its box. Sighing to herself, she slipped off her shoes. This was their last night and she wasn't ready to go back. That very thought made her feel guilty. Nick leant up against the frame of the bathroom door.

"What are you thinking about?" Sylvie shook her head, indicating that she didn't want to say. He walked over to her and stood behind her. He put his hands on her shoulders as he looked at her in the mirror. "It wasn't so bad tonight, after all?"

Sylvie nodded in agreement. "Adonis and Katerina were really sweet, and you seemed to get on alright with Dimitri."

"He's still got the hots for you." Nick was slipping off his shoes.

Sylvie snorted, thinking back to all the women who'd been ogling Nick all night. "What?"

"You'll be telling me next that Adonis likes me too." Sylvie shook her head.

"Oh, I don't think so." Sylvie raised her eyebrows, almost affronted. He kissed her shoulder, then looked up at her. "I think I'm more his type," Nick explained.

Oh! "Really? How can you tell?"

"Experience. I've got highly tuned gaydar." He shrugged. "Plus, he didn't eye you up at all. You look so beautiful." He dropped another kiss on her shoulder. "Come to bed." Sylvie closed her eyes as he spoke. He took her hand and kissed it, then gently pulled her towards the bedroom. He'd opened the windows and a breeze wafted through the room, making the voile curtains flutter. The room had a muted glow, lit only by the Parthenon's floodlights.

Nick sat on the bed and pulled off his socks. Sylvie stood in front of him, her eyes never leaving his. He reached over to her and pulled her hips to his mouth and he kissed her. She could feel the heat of his mouth through the fabric. She grasped his hair as he rose up from the bed and ran his hands up her back, his lips skating up her neck as she moaned.

"I want to feel every inch of you," – his soft voice laced with need and desire. He unbuttoned the solitary fastening at the nape of her neck and the fabric fell away from her body, gliding smoothly down, until the whole jumpsuit was in a heap at her feet. Sylvie stood only in a silk thong.

"I really like that outfit," Nick smiled against her neck as he trailed kisses downwards.

Sylvie giggled. She let her hands slip down to his collar, then slowly unbuttoned his shirt, allowing her hands to brush against his chest and then down to his stomach. Nick held her face as he kissed her tenderly. Sylvie ran her hands smoothly over his torso to his shoulders, letting the shirt fall down his arms. Nick released her, only to let his shirt drop and then he grasped her again, kissing her with more urgency. His hand held the nape of her neck as the other skimmed down her back to her behind, where he pulled her up against him and she groaned into his mouth. In a swift movement, he picked her up and placed her on the bed. Nick knelt between her legs as he hooked his thumbs into her thong and slowly pulled it down her wriggling legs.

Nick quickly unfastened his trousers, letting them fall to the floor. Sylvie's eyes fixed on his eyes, wide and full of yearning. He was beyond exquisite and she licked her lips in anticipation. Nick pulled down his boxers and tossed them aside, then crawled back up the bed between her legs, running his hands up them as she flopped back on the bed and arched upwards.

"Nick, please, ah!" He kissed and nipped up past her hip, then slowly turned her onto her front. He continued his gentle teasing up her back, then back down to the dimples at its base.

"You smell so good." Gently he bit her hip, then again down her behind.

"Ah!"

"You taste of heaven, my heaven." He continued as she writhed beneath him.

"Nick, please."

"I know, baby." He stroked her behind and she could feel his erection against her leg. He gently pulled her hips up so that she was kneeling. "I want to take you like this. Your ass is so beautiful."

"Nick, ah!"

Then slowly and steadily he pushed himself into her and he gasped, trying to control his urge to move. "Oh yes." He held himself still and threw back his head. Then slowly withdrawing, he pushed back in deeper and Sylvie cried out.

"Ah!"

"Is that good baby?" His voice raspy.

"Oh Nick, harder."

"Yes." And as he pushed in harder, Sylvie pushed back against him, gripping the sheets. "Ah! Sylvie, no, I want this slow." Sylvie glanced up and saw their shadow cast on the wall it was mesmerising. Nick withdrew again and, deliciously slowly, filled her and Sylvie cried out again as she watched their shadows move, it was so erotic.

He tightened his grip on her hips and started to move slowly and steadily, relishing her as he caressed her behind, his breathing shallow. "Nick, I want to see your face." She gasped as he moved rhythmically. He stopped and pulled out of her. Sylvie turned around and his eyes bore into her, molten. She pushed him to the bed and he fell willingly, then lying down beside him, she pulled him to her, wrapping one leg around his waist and guiding him into her so they were on their sides. He took hold of her face and kissed it roughly, then more tenderly. Sylvie lifted the leg trapped underneath and rested it against his shoulder. Nick's eyes widened as he positioned himself between her and then thrust hard.

"Fuck, that feels deep," he cried out in awe. He held her close as he began to move, Sylvie matching his every movement, pushing against him as she looked deep into his eyes, her mouth open as she moaned. "Oh baby, you're incredible!" He pushed harder, slowly at first, feeling every fibre of her, his breathing shallow and hard. Sylvie grabbed onto his face, bringing him to her lips as she kissed him hard. He groaned, holding her close. Her hands slid to his shoulders as he pulled back. He began to move faster as she started to tighten around him. Nick closed his eyes as he tried hard to control himself as they moved.

"Open your eyes, Nick, I need to see you." Sylvie gasped as she gripped his head. Nick opened his eyes and they felt like lasers boring into her very soul. It was all she needed as she cried out his name, finding her release as he continued to move, and then with one last thrust, he too climaxed, loudly crying out her name.

His head rolled back and he continually kissed her leg which was still stretched up against his shoulder, his breathing hard. "That was… I think I've died and gone to heaven." He shook his head slightly as if he couldn't believe it. "Fuck, Sylvie…"

"I think you just did," sniggered Sylvie.

Nick laughed, loudly flopping back on the bed at her coarse remark, as she lowered her leg. "You are a very naughty lady." Sylvie giggled as he squeezed her tightly and kissed her forehead, then down to her cheeks, until he found her mouth and he kissed her deeply. He pulled back and stroked back her hair. "Very naughty and bendy."

"I like being naughty."

"Me too. I like you being bendy." His eyebrows raised twice in fast succession. Sylvie smiled, then nestled into him and she rhythmically stroked his chest. "Tired?"

"A bit, but I don't want to sleep. Not yet, anyway." She tightened her arms around him. "I can't believe how fast it's gone. This time tomorrow we'll be home." She sighed shakily, trying not to let her emotions get the better of her.

"Will you be back to work on Wednesday?"

"Yes."

"Even though Alex will be home?"

"I'll just pop in early and then I'll be home. His flight arrives in the afternoon."

"It's going to be hell after having you to myself. Then Markus is out, right? In the evening." Sylvie nodded. "When will you tell them?"

Sylvie propped herself up on her elbow to look at him. He seemed so young and his eyes gazed nervously at her. "I'm not sure. I suppose over the weekend." He looked pensive, and she knew he was trying to work out when he should speak to his parents. "Let's just see how it goes with them first, before you rush into telling your dad."

"Sylvie, it's going to be really hard. When am I going to see you? You're back at work, your house will be full and…" He sat up and held his head, trying to rationalise what he was feeling. He rubbed his face nervously. "Sylvie, I want us to be together, this waiting is unbearable. I'm worried that my father will do something that will make things a hundred times worse. I need to know that at least by the weekend, I can tell him."

"I'll tell them as soon as I can, I promise." Sylvie was sat up in front of him, reaching over to his face and stroking it. He leaned into it, then kissed her palm.

"Sixteen hours of heaven, then back to hell," he whispered. Sylvie took hold of his face and kissed him. He wrapped his arms around her and fell back onto the bed, taking her with him.

"God I love you, you've made me so unbelievably happy these past few days. I'm going to be miserable until I can see you."

"Me too." Sylvie traced his lips with her finger. "I'll try to get away."

"Will you?" he said, his eyes lighting up with hope.

She nodded reassuringly. "So we've got sixteen hours until we leave. What do you think we should do?" Her brown eyes were wide as she continued to trace her finger around his face. He licked his lips as he smiled, then flipped her over so that he was on top of her. She squealed as he held her face with both his hands and let all of his weight push her down.

"Oh I'm sure I can think of something," he growled, then kissed her hard and deep. *Oh, she was really going to miss this!*

Sylvie forced her eyes open as she heard a distant beeping sound. She slowly turned her head towards the bedside table to see what time it was. Nick was sprawled over her, half his body pinning her down, his leg completely trapping both of hers, his arm holding her far shoulder. *Crap, he was heavy.* It was no use. She'd have to wait until he woke up. It looked early as the sun was barely up. The beeping sound continued.

What was that? Then it dawned on her, it was her mobile indicating that the battery was low. Nick stirred as she rested her head back. He shifted a little, then slowly opened his eyes. Sylvie could feel his eyelashes flutter on her chest.

He kissed her softly and then looked up at her, his eyes sleepy.

"Hi."

"Hi. Did I wake you? Sorry." He smiled dreamily.

"I'm glad you did." He pushed up against her as he pulled himself up to her level, his erection evident. "What time is it?" Sylvie shrugged, then sliding out from under him, she stretched over to look at her watch.

"It's five-thirty," she said, looking apologetically at him over her shoulder. He slid his hand up her back and started kissing it softly. Her whole body trembled as his fingers fluttered over her, his lips retracing their path. She moaned as she turned round to meet his now-burning eyes. He rolled over so that he was on top of her, stroking her back and her hair while he slowly kissed her down her neck, as she arched up to him.

"So we're up with the roosters then?" he muttered as he trailed his kisses down her throat, then back up to her mouth, kissing her softly.

"Uh-huh… Oh Nick," Sylvie groaned as she grasped at his hair. Nick ran his nose up hers as he hovered. Sylvie was aching for him as she writhed under him. A smile curled at the edge of his beautiful mouth as he revelled in her need for him, and then slowly he entered her, Sylvie surrendering herself totally and completely, closing her eyes and pulling her head back. Nick gazed at her as he pushed deeper.

"Fuck-a-doodle-do." He grinned.

Would she never tire of him?

They sat silently in their seats and watched the air steward go through the safety measures, Nick holding Sylvie's hand and playing with her fingers. They'd said their goodbyes to George, promising him that they'd both be back soon. Sylvie hugged him tightly and thanked him, with George feeling a little embarrassed by her sudden outburst, but clearly moved. He'd never mentioned anything about Chris but she knew from his manner and behaviour that he genuinely felt for her. She was grateful he'd been so discreet, both nine months ago and now.

The plane started its ascent and Nick raised her hand to his lips. Sylvie turned from the window to look at him. This was going to be a lot harder than she thought. She wanted to fast-forward to Saturday when Alex and Markus would know and then Nick would be able to tell Julian and Maggie.

They'd both focused on Julian so much that Sylvie had almost forgotten Maggie. She wasn't sure how she'd react. Sylvie tried to imagine how she would feel if Alex or Markus were with a woman who was so much older. In all honesty, she couldn't truthfully say how she'd feel. She couldn't be objective – not now, anyway. She'd be the worst kind of hypocrite if she said she wouldn't be able to accept it. Whichever way she looked at it, she was basically up shit creek without the proverbial paddle. She was the one who should've known better and she would definitely be the villain in this. That didn't bother her so much. What bothered her was how it would affect Nick.

Julian would not be able to accept it. Deep down, she knew that, and Nick would pay the price. She hoped she'd be able to convince him to let her be the one to tell Julian. At least if he took it out on her, he might go easy on Nick. As for Maggie, she might not be happy, but she'd put up with it for Nick's sake. She'd sacrifice her feelings for Nick, especially if she could see he was happy. That thought depressed Sylvie even more. She'd lose a friend, and who could blame her? Why couldn't things just be simple and straightforward?

Nick let go of her hand and stroked back her hair. "You look so beautiful. I'm going to miss this face in the morning." He leant over and kissed her, then pulled her close so she rested her head on his shoulder as he wrapped his arm around her. He smelled heavenly. Oh God, how she was going to miss this too?

The house was so quiet as Sylvie entered the kitchen. There was a note on the counter from Marcy telling her there was food prepared in the fridge and that she shouldn't do her laundry, that Marcy would take care of it in the morning. Also, the garage door was broken. It was getting fixed in the morning. Well, that explained why it was wide open and wouldn't close.

Sylvie smiled to herself, thinking back to what had Nick said about having things done for you. Perhaps he was right. She pulled her suitcase into the laundry room and opened it, pulling out everything that needed washing. Her hands sifted through her clothes and she felt an overwhelming urge to cry. Her hands trembled as she pulled out her aqua top and white cropped trousers. She buried her face in them and sobbed uncontrollably. How was this ever going to work? She knew deep down that however much she felt for Nick, that she would always do what was right for him, regardless of the cost to her. Her heart ached at the thought of losing him.

As she dropped the trousers and her top into the laundry basket, she heard a dull bang against the bottom. She reached down into the basket rummaging around. Wiping her nose on the back of her hand, she eventually fell on a smooth, large white stone. The stone from Sounion that she never threw. She rubbed her fingers over its almost shiny surface. She turned it over in her hand, then popped it back in her suitcase and headed upstairs to her bedroom to unpack the rest.

Slowly and methodically, she put her things away. She put her phone on to charge and turned it on. She went through to the bathroom and turned on the taps. A bath would help, she thought. Then she retrieved the stone, washed off any residue and laid it on a small hand towel to dry on her dressing table. Her phone beeped a number of times. She wasn't sure how many but she knew it would be Zach and Lilianna texting her, making sure she was home. She really didn't want to talk to anyone right now but she checked her phone just the same.

There were messages from both of them, as she suspected. She quickly responded to them both, telling them she'd speak with them tomorrow. There was one from Thea Miria welcoming her home and from Julian. Her stomach clenched when she saw it.

> Hope u got home safely.
> C u in the morning, can't wait to catch up
> Missed you loads x

Sylvie put down her phone, forgetting to reconnect it to the charger, and looked at the stone, smiling a sad smile. Her eyes moved to where she had her nail varnishes sat in a box on the dressing table. She opened it and pulled out her favourite, a blood red colour called 'Heart Stopper'. *Very apt*, she thought, as she shook it, then opened it.

Very carefully, she outlined the shape of a heart in the middle of the stone and then filled it in. The varnish sunk in a little, so Sylvie went back to the bathroom to turn off the taps, then returned to put a second coat on. Remembering she had some craft pens in her study, she ran downstairs and rummaged through her drawers. Finding the gold, she ran back upstairs and outlined the heart with a small flourish at the base and then delicately wrote *heaven*. Once dry, she painted over the whole stone in a clear top coat and left it to dry under her UV lamp. Happy with the simplicity of her handiwork, she stripped off and made her way to the bathroom.

Sylvie sank into the water and immediately felt a sense of loss. Over the last four days, she hadn't had a bath alone. In such a short time it had become a glorious habit, one that she never wanted to kick. She had an overpowering need to see Nick. It had only been a couple of hours since they said their goodbyes at the airport, but sitting here now all alone, the bath felt too big without him and her heart broke. She sat up and put her face in her hands and let herself cry, unable to stop. Her shoulders shook as she let out all the tension, the fear, the doubt and the guilt and she started to sob uncontrollably again.

"Sylvie?"

Sylvie's tear-stained face shot up. "What the fuck…"

There he was, standing in the doorway, heart-stoppingly beautiful, his brow creased with worry, his eyes wide and bright. He strode over within a second and hauled her out of the bath, water sloshing over the sides as he scooped her up and sat down on the toilet seat, holding her to him as she draped her arm around his neck. His clothes were drenched as Sylvie clung to him, sobbing. "Sylvie, what is it? Baby, tell me." He reached for a towel and wrapped her in it as she tried to control her sobs. He stroked her hair and kissed her head, then pulled up her chin. "Please tell me." He pleaded his eyes fearful and anxious.

"How… did… you…?" she sobbed.

"I remembered your security code and the garage door was up. You left the kitchen door unlocked." Sylvie heaved with the aftershocks of her crying. "I tried to call you but your phone was off and I don't have your house number and I was worried. I wanted to hear your voice. I just had to speak to you. I didn't know what else to do, so I drove up here. I knew you'd be alone." He bent and kissed her lips his eyes almost fearful as he searched her face. "Sylvie, what's wrong?"

"I just felt so alone." He squeezed her, clenching his eyes shut. "I got… in… the… bath. It just… hit me," she sobbed.

Relief swept over him as he held her, rocking her softly until her sobs subsided and she relaxed into him.

After a while, when she was all cried, out Sylvie looked up at him. "You're wet."

"I don't care."

"I'll get up. I feel better now."

"Don't move, I'll carry you." And with ease, he rose up from the toilet seat and carried her through to the bedroom, placing her on the bed and tightening the towel round her. "Shall I get you a drink? Water? Something stronger?" She nodded. "Don't move. I'll be back in a minute." He stepped back, checked she was okay and then ran down the stairs to the kitchen.

He quickly pulled out a bottle of water and a couple of glasses, then went to where he remembered the bar was and pulled out a bottle of Chivas. He collected some ice in another glass and then bolted up the stairs two at a time.

Sylvie had sat back on her bed, still draped in the towel. Nick placed everything on the bedside table, then first, poured her some water and passed it to her. She took a gulp, then proceeded to drink the whole glass. *Crying really makes you thirsty.*

He sat watching her, his shirt stuck to him and see-through from the water.

"You should take those off and let them dry." He looked down at himself and smirked. He stood up and unbuttoned his shirt. "There's a hanger in my closet." She motioned to a door. Nick opened it and came out with his shirt hung on a hanger he had found. Carefully, he hung it on the door handle. He took off his Converse and socks, and then pulled off his jeans that were also wet. He draped them on the chair by the dressing table. His eye caught the stone and he furrowed his brow, then looked at Sylvie.

"It's for you."

"For me?"

Sylvie nodded shyly. He went to pick it up but before he touched it, he looked at Sylvie, asking her permission.

"Pick it up, it should be dry."

He reached down and lifted it carefully, then gently stroked where the heart was and then over the letters. "You made this today?"

"Yes, it's the –"

"Stone you didn't throw." He finished her sentence as he walked over to her. "It's so perfect, and you made it for me?" He repeated, as if it was hard to believe, totally moved. "I love it. Thank you." His voice was almost stunned. "I'll take you back there, Sylvie, very soon." He reached over to the glasses and poured her a whisky. "Here, take a sip and get in the covers."

He pulled back the duvet so she could slip inside and then she took a gulp of her drink.

"Aren't you to going to join me?" He bent down and kissed her tenderly, cupping her face, tasting the whisky on her lips, and he smiled against her mouth.

"You know, I never was a big fan of whisky, but lately, it's had a certain appeal to me." He sucked on her lip and she put her arms around him. He kissed her hard and then pulled back, only to get under the covers with her. She nuzzled into his chest and she felt at peace, her previous thoughts shelved for the moment.

"Why were you crying?" Nick stroked her back as he spoke.

"It was just overwhelming, coming home. It was quiet, I felt so alone and I was missing you. I realised that this was it, our cocoon was cracked and we'd have to face reality. I just don't want to. I'm tired of having to face reality, really tired. That's all I've done for so long. Our four days of heaven were the best I've had in a very long time. When I found the stone, it just seemed like a dream, and a very long time ago. It just got to me." She gazed up at him and put her hand up to his cheek. "I can't believe you came."

"Sylvie, this is where I want to be, always. I love you."

Sylvie reached up to kiss him and he pulled her so she was over him. "What time does Marcy arrive?"

"Seven-thirty."

"Good that gives us roughly ten hours. Now what are we going to do for ten hours?" He pretended to muse and mull over the idea as Sylvie giggled at him. He grasped her face in both his hands and kissed her hard. "I love my stone. It's the most meaningful gift I've ever had." His eyes were shining with pure love.

13

BACK TO REALITY

Sylvie opened her eyes, trying to process where she was. The familiar surroundings of her bedroom came into focus as she blinked. What time was it? The room was bathed in light but it wasn't from the window. It was very disorienting. She sat up, propping herself on her elbows, and searched for Nick. Gradually, her senses came to, and she realised the light was from her bathroom. She could hear water running from within. Nick walked through the doorway and stopped, his eyes wide and bright like two beautiful headlights. *Wow!*

"Sorry, did I wake you?" He stepped closer to her.

"What time is it?" Pulling herself up, she could see he was fully dressed.

"Five-thirty. I was trying to tidy up in here before I left. It's too early – you should go back to sleep."

"I'm up now." She stretched her arms up. "Shall I make you some breakfast?"

"At five-thirty?" he looked at her doubtfully.

"Uh-huh. Aren't you hungry? You didn't eat last night."

"If I remember, I was otherwise engaged." He smiled suggestively as he perched on the end of the bed. "I'll grab something on the way home."

"No, I'll get up and make you something. French toast? Do you like French toast?" Nick's eyebrows arched.

"I'll love anything you make."

"Okay, give me a second." Sylvie swung herself out of bed and padded to the bathroom naked. After brushing her teeth and slipping on a vest and panties, she emerged to find Nick standing by the window. He'd opened the curtains and window and was looking down at the garden as dawn was breaking. The distinctive, pungent smell of the Cestrum Nocturnum wafted up and filled the room.

"Your house is lovely and the garden's huge. I've never seen the back before."

"Well hopefully, you'll be allowed around in the daylight soon," she joked. His expression changed and Sylvie saw a glimpse of hope in his eyes. "Come on, let's have some breakfast." His face lit up even more and he ambled towards her, his eyes sparkling. He reached down to her and pulled her close to him, kissing her softly.

"I'm so glad I got to wake up with you this morning."

Sylvie sighed and brushed his stubbly cheek with the back of her hand. "Me too." She took his hand and led him downstairs.

Sylvie lifted out the last slice of toast and placed it on the kitchen paper for it to drain. "What do you want on them?" Nick shrugged. "Syrup, jam, sugar, honey or some Nutella?"

"Syrup will be fine." She put the serving plate down and retrieved the syrup, along with the cutlery and a plate. She set everything up on the counter and Nick perched himself on one of the bar stools. Sylvie brought over the teapot, cups and saucers and poured their tea. Nick watched her moving around the kitchen, serving him. His heart swelled as she placed a plate in front of him and she absent-mindedly planted a kiss on his cheek as she leaned over to him. Sylvie put four slices on his plate and handed him the syrup. Nick took it and put his arm around her waist, slowly sliding his hand over her behind, then squeezing it affectionately. Sylvie wrinkled her nose at him. This is what he wanted: them together, doing normal day-to-day things. Him watching her cook and sitting together while they ate.

"I could really get used to this." She took his face between her hands and kissed him hard on the lips.

"Eat up before they get cold." She perched up on the stool next to him as he poured the syrup over the toast and then sliced through them.

"Aren't you having any?" He forked a piece and placed it in his mouth. He chewed, then opened his eyes wide and nodded, indicating it tasted good. Sylvie shook her head and smiled. *I better keep off anything fried*, she thought as, she remembered she'd had to move a notch on her black belt.

The sun was up and its rays filtered into the sitting room and kitchen. As Nick ate his way through all four slices, he looked out into the garden and beyond where he could see the marina and the coastline. He scanned the room again. He'd only ever been here at night and had never really taken it in before. It felt so warm and comfortable. The whole room was airy, bright and fresh, the furnishings blending together without being contrived. It was really beautiful and serene, and it was a true reflection of Sylvie. Nick turned to look at Sylvie, who was staring into her cup.

"I'd better be going." He looked so handsome. His eyes softly blinked at her and she could tell he wanted to say something. "It's six-thirty. Call me when you're on the way to the office."

"Are you going to the shop today?" She rose up from the stool.

"I'm not sure. I'll text you. What time are you going to the airport?"

"Around four."

"Alone?" Sylvie nodded. "Good, so we can talk then." He got up from the stool and bent down to kiss her but before their lips touched, he sighed, "Whatever happens in the next few days, remember that you are the single most important thing to me. No one has, or will ever, mean what you mean to me. I love you, Sylvie. Don't lose sight of that." His honesty was disarming. Their lips locked and Nick's hands ran into her hair. She wrapped her arms around his neck as she stretched up on her tiptoes. Sylvie kissed him back hard. It felt like this was goodbye, like he wasn't sure when he would see her again. He moved his hand down to her waist and pulled her close to him and she moaned against his mouth.

"God, I'm going to miss this, miss holding you." He pulled away, leaving her breathless, then he kissed her forehead and stepped away, as if he needed some distance. "Bye baby."

"Bye," she whispered and he closed his eyes momentarily, clenching his jaw, then swiftly headed for the door that led to the garage. Sylvie slumped on the stool and closed her eyes. Athens seemed like an age away. She heard his Jeep pull out and set off down the hill and her heart tightened. The next few days were going to be horrible.

By seven-thirty, Marcy was in the kitchen, busying herself with the tidying up. Sylvie had uncharacteristically left the kitchen in a mess. She'd just wanted to get out of the kitchen once Nick had left. She showered and dressed and came down to find Marcy sorting out the laundry. The kitchen was spotless.

"Morning, Mam. Welcome back. How was your trip?" She was all smiles and probably glad the house would be filling up again and that she'd have more to do.

"Morning, Marcy. It was lovely. I could have stayed longer," she mused.

"I see you made breakfast." Marcy motioned to the washed up plate and cups.

"Yes, I was up early." Sylvie flushed. "What happened to the garage door?" She changed the subject before Marcy could comment more.

"Petros thinks it's just a fuse. It just opened and won't shut again. The electrician's coming this morning."

"Good. Well I better get off to the office." Sylvie reached for her new briefcase that she'd transferred all her things into.

"New briefcase?" Sylvie nodded and wrinkled her nose. "It's beautiful. About time you got your own." Marcy winked at her and continued with the laundry.

Once Sylvie was out of her gates, she plugged in her hands free and dialled Nick. As always, it just rang once.

"Hi baby." His voice was sleepy.

"Hi, were you asleep?"

"I must have nodded off."

"I'm sorry…"

"I told you to call me. I wanted to hear your voice. Are you on the way to work?"

"Yes, I just left home."

"I came to the yacht to unpack. I'm shattered but I need to get up and make some calls. What time is it?"

"Just after eight." She could hear him stretching. The thought made her palpitate. *Nick flexing his muscles…* "Mmm, what are you wearing?"

Sylvie grinned. "A blue pencil skirt to match my new briefcase, red peep toes and a white blouse."

"You took your new briefcase?" He sounded surprised and pleased at the same time.

"Of course."

"I bet you look sexy as hell." His voice lowering. "Shit, you're going to be wiggling around in that skirt and I won't get to see you." Sylvie could hear irritation in his voice. Wanting to distract him, she decided to play their game.

"What are you wearing?"

"You really want to know?" He laughed.

"Don't tell me –"

Then in unison, they said, "A smile." Sylvie giggled and Nick laughed.

"Not fair!" she moaned at him. "Get up and go to work otherwise I'll make an unscheduled stop by the marina and never get to the office!"

"Call me later."

"I will."

"Bye, baby."

"Bye."

Sylvie pulled into the car park of Sapphire developers and jumped out. She saw Zach's car and she smiled. At least they'd be able to catch up. She felt like she'd been away for ages. The elevator doors opened up into the reception area and she could hear Zach talking on the phone as she walked towards his office. She walked through his open door and he smiled widely as he saw her looking all cheeky and relaxed.

"Yes, Yiannis, I know, but we need to get cracking with it as soon as possible…" He blew her a kiss as he continued his conversation and she mouthed to him if he wanted a coffee. He nodded. "I don't care. We need to get on to it and get the planning permission. If we don't, it'll be September before we can start…"

Sylvie went into the kitchen area, flicked on the coffee machine and turned on the kettle. Maria would be in any minute, no doubt with a pile of papers for her to sift through. She walked through to her office and opened up the blinds, letting the sun come in. *Mmm, she'd missed that view.* She squinted, trying to see if she could spot the *Silver Lining*. It was too far away and all the yachts seemed to mingle into a mass of white. Maybe she should get a telescope. She shook her head; now she sounded like a stalker.

Her desk already had piles of papers on it. She put down her briefcase and smoothed over the stitching again. Pulling out her phone, she noticed a message she hadn't seen. It was from Nick.

Check your email

Love you x

Sylvie opened up her laptop and logged into her email. She scrolled down all the emails she hadn't yet opened, until she found the one from Nick, titled:

Grecian Paradise!

She opened it quickly, her heart racing. And there in full Technicolor were the photos of them both at Syndagma, posing and then kissing; at the Parthenon, her sitting on his knee and her arms draped around him; and then by the temple at Sounion and the video the tourist took of them. Sylvie watched it and her heart soared as she saw how tenderly he looked at her. There was a close-up picture of her asleep, flushed and on the sun lounger that she'd never seen. Sylvie's face grinned and she quickly texted him.

Thank you they're perfect, like u
You made my day, again!
Love you too x

"Why are you so happy? Glad to be back?" Zach sauntered in, all laid back and grinning at her. She looked up startled, then smiled while slowly closing her laptop. She came round from her desk and hugged him.

"Yes, of course I'm glad to be back. I missed you."

Zach kissed her cheek. "I missed you too." He pulled back and appraised her. "You look… great, like the old Sylvie. Maybe you need to get away more often." Sylvie flushed. "You've got a tan too."

"It was good to get away. What have I missed?" He came over and sat on the chair opposite her desk as Sylvie slipped back around and sat down.

"We're pushing for the final planning permission for that office block we're supposed to start at the end of July, and it looks like we might get that plot of land we put an offer for, just before you left. Julian's going to talk to the agent today for me – he knows the seller."

"That's good news. I've got all the documents from Dracos." She pulled them out of her briefcase and handed them over.

"Nice briefcase." Zach's eyes widened. "A lot more you than the old one," he smirked. "What did you make of Dracos, then?" Zach had met him on a number of occasions and had got to know him quite well.

"He was very charming." Sylvie chose her words very carefully. Zach snorted.

"He *really* liked you!" Sylvie's face drained of colour. *Shit, Zach had spoken to him? Did he mention Nick? Crap!* She really hadn't thought *that* through at all. Her stomach clenched as she went through a multitude of emotions, starting with panic and ending in: *how the hell do I get out of this?*

"You spoke to him?" Sylvie tried hard to sound casual.

"Yes, he called me yesterday. Just a courtesy call. He said you were – now how did he put it – yes, he said you were an *exceptional* woman." Sylvie swallowed hard. "He said that he was looking forward to seeing you at his opening."

"Oh, is that all?" Sylvie fiddled with the clasp on her briefcase, not daring to look at Zach.

"Pretty much."

Sylvie smiled tightly, then she remembered that Nick had signed as a witness on the sale and transfer papers.

"I think he's got the hots for you." He watched her squirm, laughing loudly. "You could do worse."

"Zach! For the love of God, will you pack it in!" He was loving it. Sylvie gave him a mock frown.

"Your other fan has been moping around too." Sylvie furrowed her brow. "Julian." Sylvie sighed. "Throw the guy a bone, Sylvie."

"Zach, it isn't going to happen. He's just a friend, so please drop it." She eyed the papers and held out her hand.

"Actually, I'll take those papers and drop them to the accountants. I need to see them about something anyway." Zach shrugged and handed them back to her. Relieved, Sylvie shoved the papers quickly back into her briefcase, scowling to herself. *How careless of her*, she thought, and then reflected on how discreet Dimitris had been. Then it dawned on her that over the eighteen months Chris had been going over to Athens, he'd probably taken Dina on a number of his trips and Dimitris had no doubt met her. He had obviously never mentioned Dina to Zach, so he had extended her the same courtesy. That thought appalled her, though at the same time she felt incredibly thankful.

Sylvie's morning passed quickly and before long, she realised that it was lunchtime. Maria had briefed her on the most pressing items she needed to deal with, and she'd spoken to her workmen with regard to Elenora's room. They had started today as scheduled. She knew she was going to have to call Maggie, but whenever she picked up the phone to dial, she ended up chickening out. She felt disloyal and she just didn't know quite how to handle it. She rubbed her ring and then outstretched her hand to admire it again.

"Well, look who's back!" Sylvie jumped at the interruption to her thoughts. Standing in the doorway, looking sheepish and almost hesitant, stood Julian. Sylvie gasped as he smiled at her. *Holy crap!* It was uncanny how much Nick looked like him. Was this a glimpse into the future, what Nick would be like in middle age? She pushed the image of a fifty-year-old Nick and a sixty-six-year-old Sylvie out of her mind as she tried desperately to pull herself together.

"Hi." She spoke quietly remembering the last time they'd been in such close proximity.

"Can I come in?" he asked warily. Sylvie smiled and nodded. He walked in slowly, not quite knowing whether he should come over and kiss her as he would have normally done. This was the first time he'd seen her since that night he'd kissed her. Sylvie decided to stay put, making it obvious that she wasn't quite ready for any physical contact. He'd made his way to the front of her desk and hovered. *Nervous Julian, that's a first*, thought Sylvie. She almost felt sorry for him. He must have been dreading this. "May I?" He motioned to the chair.

"Of course."

"You look… well."

Oh boy, he was really nervous! His voice was soft and didn't have that edge to it that Sylvie found charismatic. "Thanks."

"I hear everything went smoothly," he said, his eyes piercing into hers, trying to read her mood. He rubbed his designer stubble as he spoke. Sylvie took a deep breath as she tried desperately not to notice the familiar gestures she'd got to know so well over the last four days. The similarities were astonishing. How had she never noticed them before? It was very unnerving and most disturbing.

"Yes, it did." She smiled tightly. He ran his hands through his hair and Sylvie made herself look down at her ring. This was too much.

"Sylvie, I know you're still mad at me about what happened… I was out of order. I'm sorry. I behaved like an idiot." Sylvie closed her eyes momentarily. He was making her feel guilty. Her heart pounded and she needed to stop him before he said anything else.

"Julian, just forget it. I have. Really, it's fine." She tried hard to look him in the eye but she kept blinking nervously.

"If you say so." He brushed his trousers nervously as he leaned back, crossing his leg over and resting his ankle on his knee. His blue eyes gazed at her, trying desperately to grasp what emotion she was feeling. He decided to change tactic. "How's Maggie's going? Don't they start today?"

"Err… yes. I spoke to my men up there. They hope to be done by

Monday." She glanced momentarily at him. *Crap, those freaking eyes!* Then moved some papers on her desk nervously.

"That quick?"

"Well, it's mainly paintwork and the flooring. The wardrobes and furniture are already made; they just need to be fitted." She'd managed to look him in the eye as she spoke and his face softened with relief.

"Are you going up?"

"I won't manage it today. I'm going to pick up Alex from the airport. I'll try to get up there tomorrow, though." Julian nodded.

"Looks like we'll get that plot of land after all." He was trying hard to get her to talk. He needed to know that they were okay, that he was forgiven, but she seemed distant and nervous and he felt wretched. He'd been looking forward to seeing her again. He'd missed her terribly, and seeing her today behaving cautiously and almost aloof was killing him. He had a sneaky suspicion that he'd blown it, and he just didn't know how he'd be able to get what they had back.

"Yes, Zach told me. That is good news. That'll mean we have that project starting up this autumn."

"Roughly twenty-five houses." Sylvie nodded. He sighed, then pulled himself up from the chair, resigned to the fact that she wasn't ready to forgive him yet. "It's nice to have you back. I've missed you."

"Thanks, Julian."

"Athens agrees with you. You look lovely." He glanced down at her briefcase but chose not to comment. "See you later."

"Bye, Julian." He stalked out of her office and Sylvie's whole body relaxed as she sat back in her chair and closed her eyes. *Talk about awkward!*

Zach sauntered into Sylvie's office around two. She was catching up on her emails as he flopped down on the chair opposite her. He put down a plate with a sandwich on it for her.

"Eat something." He was munching on a chocolate bar. *What was it with all the men in her life? They ate all sorts of shit, and in huge amounts, and they were all so trim. It wasn't fair.*

"I'm not that hungry," she lied.

"I don't care. Eat it. You've not moved from here since eight. Take a break."

"I've got to catch up, Zach. Alex and Markus will be home today and tomorrow is his discharge so I'll be occupied with them. I've to go up to Maggie's at some point tomorrow too. I really need to catch up."

"Get Maria to do a bit more for you until the weekend, and then things will be back to normal. The boys will be doing their own thing by then." Sylvie sat back and stretched. She knew he was right. She just wanted to occupy herself. "What did Julian have to say? He left in a rather a hurry." He eyed her and she knew he was fishing.

"He just came in to say hi. Catch me up on the land and stuff." Zach's eyes narrowed, unconvinced.

"Okay, I get it. You don't want to tell me. All I know is that he normally spends ages here when he comes to see you and today he was out in ten minutes."

"Zach… It's complicated, really complicated, but I promise I'll let you know what's going on. Just let me get through the next few days." She hated keeping him in the dark, but she needed to talk to Alex and Markus first. He pursed his lips together.

"I just worry, that's all. What time you going for Alex?"

"I'll be setting off in a bit."

"Eat your sandwich." He got up to leave. "Call me when you get home. Okay?"

Sylvie smiled at him, nodded and watched him leave her office. Sylvie looked at the sandwich, and took a bite, chewing it slowly. She felt that nauseous feeling again as she swallowed. She popped two antacids, logged off her computer and dropped the sandwich in the bin. She packed up her stuff and headed to her car.

Sylvie quickly started up the engine and popped her phone on hands-free, then dialled Nick. Her stomach was giddy with the anticipation. She waited for it to connect and it started to ring as soon as she pulled out of the car park. It rang four times, then it went to voicemail. Strange – he usually picked it up instantly. She tried again. It rang twice, then went to voicemail. Sylvie's stomach cramped. She hoped it was because he was busy.

Nick clenched his jaw, seeing the number ring a second time. He quickly sent it to voicemail, as he'd done the first time, and then switched his phone to silent.

"Why didn't you answer it? I don't mind, I'll go get us some beers." Julian dragged himself up from the sofa and headed to the galley to retrieve a couple of beers from the fridge. Nick ran his fingers through his hair nervously. He knew Sylvie would be going to the airport and then Alex would be home. If his dad didn't leave soon, he wouldn't be able to talk to her. He hadn't expected Julian to come round until later. He'd just come by on the off chance to see how his trip had gone.

"Here." Julian handed him a beer and flopped down opposite him. "So how did everything go? You look well. Caught the sun. I thought it was business you were going for." He smirked, remembering the woman's top Nick had tried to hide from him.

"It was, but I managed to get to the beach too. It went well, and I'm going again next week… to finalise things. But I'll need to go for at least a week."

Julian raised his eyebrows. "Next week?"

"Yeah, I was planning to go on Friday but I spoke to my contacts out there and they want me out there by Wednesday."

"That's good news though, right? If you need to get out there faster?"

"Uh-huh. I need to do a bit of preparation before I go. Make sure everything's… well, organised." He could barely look his dad in the eye. "What've you been up to?" He hoped his dad would have enough to ramble on about. It'd take the pressure off him.

"It's been busy. I finished off the plans for that office block and now I'm putting another big development project together with Zach and Sylvie's firm." Nick looked closely at his father as he mentioned Sylvie's name. He'd shifted in his seat and he was biting his lip. Nick was desperate to find out if he'd been to see her, but he couldn't very well ask.

"What kind of development?"

"Houses, around twenty-five, depending how we split the plot. I was up there today."

Nick's eyes widened. "At Sylvie's?" he blurted out before he could stop himself.

Julian frowned a little. "Yes, but that's not what I meant. I meant I was up at the plot checking it out, just before I came here."

"Oh." Nick looked at his beer nervously. "I spoke to Mum. They've started on Elenora's room."

"Yes. At least it's keeping your mum busy. She feels a little down since all the wedding drama is over." Julian chuckled. "I should go up and see how it's going. I have a feeling Vicki's a little put out that her room's not been done. Maybe I should get Sylvie to do the whole house. She's done such a great job on your mum's, it makes the rest of the house look dated."

Nick shifted nervously in his seat and furrowed his brow. He knew this was a ploy to keep Sylvie close to his dad. Julian was going to try any way he could to keep their relationship constantly intertwined. Nick really hoped Sylvie would speak to Alex and Markus soon.

Nick glanced at his watch and Julian smiled to himself. He realised he'd overstayed his welcome. No doubt he needed to return those calls from earlier. He got up and put down his half-full beer bottle.

"Well, I'll let you get back to work. I'll see you before you go off again, right?"

Nick got up to see him off. "Of course, Dad."

Julian hugged him, then jumped down on to the quay. He turned to look at Nick but he was already dialling on his mobile.

He must have it really bad, Julian thought to himself as he walked back to his car.

"Hi."

"Hi, baby. Sorry about earlier, my dad was here." Sylvie held her breath as he spoke. She was so relieved he'd called, but she wasn't sure what to make of Julian's visit. "I didn't say anything," he added quickly, realising how it sounded.

Sylvie exhaled. "Oh."

"Are you on your way?"

"Yes I'll be at the airport in about twenty minutes."

"God, I missed you today."

"Me too."

"Look I need to leave on Wednesday for France. I found a yacht for Serge and the owner is leaving on Saturday."

"Oh, I'm not sure if I can come. It's short notice – I mean, that's if you still want me to –"

"Of course I want you to come." He sounded hurt. "At least you could come out over the weekend and stay for a week. I should be done by the following weekend."

"Nick, I'll need to see how everything is first. The boys, work, you know."

"I really want you to come, baby. Please think about it."

"I will. I want to, Nick, really I do." Next week seemed so far away, Sylvie was finding it hard enough to get through today, never mind think about next Wednesday.

"What time will you get home?"

"Around five-thirty. Markus should be back by then. I'll call you as soon as I can." There was an awkward silence.

"This is shitty, isn't it?" His voice strained.

"Uh-huh."

"And it's going to get worse ,isn't it?"

"Don't, Nick. Please. Today's been so hard and I've got to get through Markus's discharge tomorrow and I feel… I just… argh!" This creeping around was hell.

"I'm sorry. Did Dad say anything today?"

Oh crap, how did he know? "Just work stuff." She heard him sigh.

"You'll call me later?"

"Yes."

"All this shit will pass, you know, and then it will be you and me."

"I know, I know."

"I love you, Sylvie."

"I love you too."

"Bye, baby."

"Bye."

14

CHANCE MEETING

Alex and Markus sat on the dining room table while Sylvie and Marcy put the finishing touches to dinner. The volume level in the house was familiarly loud, and the house seemed alive again, woken up from its long hibernation. Alex was listening to Markus's army stories as he dipped his pita bread in the variety of dips. Markus was on such a high now that his military service was finished. Alex filled him in on the apartment he'd secured for them for September where they'd be staying together. They prattled on non-stop about what mutual friends were up to and who was seeing who. Marcy was smiling broadly to herself as she poured the spaghetti into the serving bowl.

"Markus, your kite board got delivered over the weekend. It's in the garage," Marcy remembered. Sylvie stopped for a moment, then continued to mix the salad.

"Really? Alex, you'll freak when you see it. I got it last week from Julian's son's shop."

Alex furrowed his brow and glanced at Sylvie. She flushed slightly. "He has a shop?"

"Yeah, man, he stocks all sorts of equipment. Jet skis to fishing gear. He's got all the latest stuff. We should go."

"Sure. Not sure what I'd be interested in though." He laughed at his own expense. He left all that extreme sports stuff to Markus.

"He sells swimming trunks too." Markus laughed loudly. Alex rolled his eyes.

"It's ten o'clock tomorrow, right? Up at the camp?" Sylvie asked as she placed the spaghetti and sauce on the table, then went to collect the salad and the grated Parmesan. They immediately started to serve themselves.

"Yeah, should be over by twelve-thirty, but they're doing it at the stadium." Sylvie nodded as she brought over a plate of grilled chicken she'd made for herself. "You're not having spaghetti, Mum?"

"Trying to cut back. I think I've put on weight."

Alex snorted at her. "You look great, Mum. Lighten up."

She sat down and put some chicken and salad on her plate. Almost instantly, both Markus and Alex reached over, and each forked a piece of chicken off her plate and popped it in their mouths. Sylvie sighed and smiled to herself, then reached over and put some more on her plate. It was like they were two and four again, only eating off her plate. *Maybe that's why I've put weight on,* she mused to herself, *they haven't been around to eat half my food!* She never had a chance to eat everything on her plate when she had her boys around.

"We should have lunch out tomorrow, Mum, after we've finished."

"Sure, whatever you want. I need to pop up to Maggie's in the afternoon though."

"Cool. Good to see that you're busy, Mum." Alex smiled up at her.

"Thea Miria's coming tomorrow too." Markus remember. "She called me to ask if she could."

By eight o'clock, they'd finished up and were watching TV. Sylvie decided she should ring Lilianna as she hadn't had a chance to yet, and she knew she'd be itching to find out how Athens went. She slipped into the study and dialled her number.

"Hi sweetie, welcome back."

"Hi Lily, how are you?"

"Oh you know… same shit, different day," Lilianna laughed. "More to the point, how are you?"

"Alex and Markus are back, so the house is buzzing."

"I spoke to Markus earlier. He was full of it. Glad it's over, eh? Anyway, although I love them to bits and their every move interests me, what I really want to know is how your trip went."

"I had a great time, Lily. The best. It's not so easy coming back to reality though."

"Shit, Sylvie, you've got it bad." Her voice was laced with concern as Sylvie's tone sounded so melancholy.

"I have. We had four days of really getting to know one another and I just didn't want it to end."

"You need to tell the boys. You sound like shit."

"I know. I'm thinking I'll tell them tomorrow. I can't do with this creeping around. It's a strain and he's finding it difficult too."

"So it's really serious?"

"Uh-huh. I love him, Lily."

"Well you don't need to be the Brain of Britain to work that out. What about his family?"

"That's going to be a lot harder."

"Why?"

"I can't say Lily, but it just will."

"He loves you?"

"He says he does."

"You don't believe him?"

"It's just I can't see how."

"Christ, Sylvie, why not? I can't believe we're having this discussion again."

"It's more complicated than a normal relationship, Lily. I can't explain it to you – not yet, anyway."

"What does that mean?" Sylvie could hear her friend frustratingly trying to process what she'd just said. "Is he someone we know? Is that why it's difficult?"

"Lily, please don't push me to tell you."

"So yes, then …" She wasn't going to give up.

"Lily, *please*."

"You said he wasn't married, but his family's the problem. So they're not going to like it, or you. Who wouldn't like you? That doesn't make sense. Everyone loves you…"

"Lily, just drop it, okay? I really don't want to discuss it any more, I know you mean well, but it really is something I'm going to have to sort out alone. I don't want it to affect anyone else."

"Why would this affect anyone else? It's just you and him." Lilianna paused as if something had just clicked. She took a sharp intake of breath. "Sylvie, when this gets out, is this is going to affect a lot of people? People we know?"

After a long moment Sylvie whispered. "Yes."

"The boys?"

"Yes."

"Zach?" she asked tentatively.

"Yes."

"Julian?"

"Yes."

"So it's someone involved with work that could really cause a prob-lem." She was running through everyone she could think of but was coming up blank. "Sylvie, I just don't know who it could be. I know you're not stupid enough to carry on with someone in the office. I know it's not Julian, as he was here all weekend moping around because you were away and he was at a loose end. He drove Zach mental with the phone calls and he ended up popping round on Monday night. He couldn't even go to visit his son because he was away on business. They seem to hang out…" Sylvie held her breath, her stomach cramped and she swallowed hard. She could almost hear the penny dropping in her oh-so-perceptive friend's brain.

"Don't tell me… Sylvie. Holy fucking shit. It's Nick!" Sylvie clenched her eyes shut and tried to steady her breathing. Her heart was racing. "Sylvie? Answer me?" Tears sprang to her eyes as she heard the total disbelief in her dearest and closest friend's voice.

"Yes."

"Jesus Christ." It sounded more like a prayer than an expletive. "Now it makes sense. Fuck, the shit is really going to hit the fan. How did this happen? When? Julian's gonna freak! I didn't realise you knew him. How old is he?" She was ranting, saying every thought that sprang into her head.

"Twenty-eight." Her voice was hardly audible.

"Shit, Sylvie, of all the men. He's really young! No wonder you've been so guarded. What will Maggie say? I need a drink." Her mind was working overtime, trying to piece everything together as she carried on conveying every thought that came into her mind, filtering nothing. "How long?"

"It's been only just over a week."

"What! How can you be so… involved? That's no time at all, Sylvie. Maybe I should come over."

"No, the boys are here I don't want them to hear."

"Sylvie, forgive my blatancy, but it's only a week. Are you off your rocker?!"

"Lily, it's not like that." Now that she'd said it out loud it did seem totally ridiculous. How were they so involved in such a short space of time?

"Well explain to me how it is, then." She spoke as if she was scolding a child. Sylvie sighed, knowing her black-and-white, no-holds-barred friend was going to bring her into the here and now as abruptly as only she could.

"It started a while back, when I first met him."

"What do you mean *exactly?*"

Thank God she wasn't in front of her friend, thought Sylvie. "When I met him up at Maggie's. I got to know him over these past four months. We had a sort of chemistry. I thought it was just me, you know – reading too much into it. I saw him a couple of times away from Maggie's too."

"You mean you went out on dates?" She couldn't hide her astonishment.

"No, it was by accident. We bumped into each other at the marina a couple of times. Then I went to the opening of Celle and he was there. He brought me home and… and, well… it just happened."

"And he feels the same way? I mean, like you do?"

"That's what he says. He said that he fell for me over the four months but he stayed back because of Julian, because he knew his dad had feelings for me and he didn't want to come between us. But once he realised that I wasn't ever going to be with Julian, he… well, he told me how he felt."

"So he made the first move?"

"Yes."

"Wow. I really don't know what to say." Sylvie clutched the phone and made herself sit down. She'd been stood rigid all this time by her desk.

"I'm sorry I didn't tell you earlier, to be honest, I thought that everything was in my imagination and frankly I was embarrassed. I mean he's so… well, you know, and well, I'm older. It's ridiculous I know."

"Sylvie, yes it's a little unconventional, but if he really wants to be with you and he makes you happy, screw convention. It's going to be messy, you know that. So over the last four months, eh? He was at the wedding – he hardly spoke to you."

"He was avoiding me."

"Avoiding you?"

"Yes, because of Julian, and he was worried I'd realise how he felt."

"Did you? I mean, could you tell?"

"Honestly, I was confused. He'd be all over me one minute, then he'd be distant the next, but Lily, I loved every minute I was with him. He's like no one I've ever met. He's honest and true. He makes me feel like I'm the only person in the world. I'm so happy when I'm with him. I mean really happy. He doesn't play games with me. It's disarming. I've never come across anyone like that." It was the first time she'd expressed what she really felt and that alone made her feel like a weight had been lifted off her.

"Oh, Sylvie."

"I feel so guilty, Lily, feeling this way."

"Guilty. Why?"

"The list is endless. I feel guilty that I've found someone so soon after Chris. I feel guilty about Julian and Maggie. I mean, I'm old enough to know better. I should have stopped it before it got so… intense. The fallout will be… well, I think you can guess."

"What does he say? Nick, I mean."

Sylvie rubbed her face, then sighed. "He said that they need to accept it and he chooses me over them. But I don't want to be the one that makes him fall out with his family, because I know that's what'll happen. I mean think about it, I'm old enough to be his mother. What future does he have with me? I'm forty-four. It's a mess, Lily." Her eyes brimming with tears, she tried to hold on but she just couldn't, and in a shuddery breath she finally said, "But I love him."

"Oh Sylvie, sweetie, don't cry. I should be there with you, this is too much for you to handle. How much pressure, for goodness sake."

"No it's alright Lily. I'm sorry. It just feels so good to talk it out. I'm going to have to tell the boys tomorrow. I can't put it off anymore. It's killing Nick too."

"I know I don't know him, but he sounds pretty special. Well he must be if *you* love him. Go fix yourself a drink, sweetie. How's your stomach been?" Lilianna smirked, knowing only too well her friends affliction.

"Don't ask. Thank God for Gaviscon. Those little tablets are my friend. That and Chivas." She managed a smile.

"Do you want me to be there when you tell the boys?"

"No, I think I need to face them alone."

"Okay, whatever you think. Call me and tell me everything, okay?"

"Okay Lily and thanks for listening. Love you."

"Love you too." Sylvie held her head in her hands and pulled herself together. She checked the time. It was nine o'clock. She went through to the lounge where Alex and Markus were sprawled out laughing at some comedy show.

"I'm off to have a bath and go to bed."

"Sure, Mum, goodnight." Markus glanced up at her.

"Make sure you turn the lights out."

"Don't worry, Mum. Goodnight." Alex shook his head, put out that she felt she needed to remind them.

Sylvie walked into her bathroom and looked at the bath. A lump rose in her throat. Maybe she'd have a shower. She stripped off quickly and then decided to call Nick before it got too late. She brought up his number and pressed the call button. It rang once.

"Hi baby, I've been going out of my mind waiting."

"Hi, I'm sorry, it's been a little mad here."

"Everyone's home, then, safe and sound?"

"Yes, it's like they never left." She sat on the edge of the bed and flopped back. It was so good hearing his voice. It was calming. "What have you been up to?"

"I've been on the phone, mainly. Xavier's managed to get me a few viewings in Cannes of some yachts so I should be able to get Serge's friend what he needs."

"Xavier?"

"My contact out there."

"Oh."

"I've missed you."

"Me too." Sylvie sighed and turned onto her front. "I spoke to Lilianna."

"Oh?"

"About us."

"And?"

"She was pretty shocked."

"How do you feel?" he asked tentatively.

"Better for telling her. She's pretty straight and I needed to hear her opinion."

"And?"

"She thinks it'll be messy."

"I see."

"She'll no doubt mull everything over and quiz me again. She really was quite shocked."

"She doesn't approve?"

"Oh no, not that. It was just a lot to take in. I think she's happy for me – well, us."

"For a minute there I thought your one ally had jumped ship." Sylvie could hear the relief in his voice.

"Lily's always got my back."

"What times Markus's thing tomorrow?"

"Ten. We should finish by twelve-thirty. I need to get up to your mum's tomorrow, just to check up on the work, show my face. I should be up there around four."

"Good, I'll get up there too. At least I can see you there. God knows when we'll get to see each other over the next couple of days." Nick groaned loudly. "This is fucking hell!"

Sylvie closed her eyes and tried hard not to get emotional. Then in an attempt to lighten the mood she said, "What are you wearing?"

Nick laughed at her question. "Oh I see, we're playing that game, are we? My jeans and a white T-shirt. You?"

"A smile," Sylvie chuckled.

"Fuck, are you trying to make me come over? Because I will. I don't care who's there!" He growled and laughed at the same time.

"Nick, no! Don't you dare." He could hear the panic in her voice and he sighed.

"Please tell them. Soon."

"I will." Her stomach clenched at the thought. "I'm going to go to bed. I'm shattered. It's been a long day and tomorrow will be just as bad."

"Okay baby, sweet dreams."

"Goodnight, Nick."

Thankfully it was cool as they all left the stadium where Markus had received his discharge papers. There was a light breeze as they made their way to the car. Thea Miria had left her car up at the house, so they all came down in one.

"So any ideas where you want to go Markus?"

"I really fancy a burger. You know, a filthy-smothered-in-cheese-dripping-in-onions burger." Sylvie looked at Thea Miria and shrugged as if to apologise.

"There's that pub by the marina, the food's good there and Thea and I might manage a slightly healthier option there, though I do feel a little overdressed." She looked down at her cream fitted dress and sky-high nude stilettoes.

"You look fab, Mum. Don't stress so much!" He hugged her affectionately. "They've got pool tables too. We could play a game." Alex had wasted many a night playing pool in his teens. It was the only sport he could play, and some maybe basketball.

They pulled into the car park and both Alex and Markus went straight in to find a table. Sylvie and Thea Miria strolled down to the pub. Thankfully it wasn't very busy and the breeze was refreshing against their faces.

"You're looking lovely, Sylvie. That break did you some good." She had her arm linked into Sylvie's as they walked.

"I did have a good time." Sylvie smiled at Thea Miria as she squeezed her arm.

"You need to look after yourself, Sylvie. The boys are big enough to get on with their lives. Live a bit." Sylvie nodded as they walked into the pub and scanned to find where the boys were. Alex was standing by the pool table listening, as Markus talked excitedly to someone just obscured by a pillar.

Alex waved at them to come over. As Sylvie and Thea Miria walked further in, the person who Markus was talking to came into view. Stood in his faded jeans and a light blue tight T-shirt was Nick. He was leaning on the pool table holding a cue, looking perfectly relaxed and listening intently to Markus. His eyes wide and his hair a little dishevelled, looking picture perfect as always. Christian was beside him, looking around nervously.

Sylvie stiffened as she registered who it was, and Thea Miria unhooked her arm. Conscious of Sylvie's reaction but giving nothing away, she followed her to where they were standing. Markus spotted Sylvie and beamed at her, she found it hard not to focus only on Nick as they approached.

"Look who's here, Mum. I was just telling Nick about this morning."

"Hello Sylvie, it's lovely to see you." His eyes glittered and he smiled mischievously.

Hell's teeth! Sylvie's heart rate doubled. He stood up straight and extended his hand for her to shake, his eyes fixed on her as she reached out. He ever-so-gently pulled her close and kissed both her cheeks, squeezing her hand and stroking it with his thumb. Her whole body erupted at his touch and she felt her eyes flicker shut as she took a deep breath, taking in his scent. *Oh God she'd missed him.* "Hello, Nick." She tried hard not to sound too breathy as she spoke, gently kissing his cheeks. As he released her, Sylvie turned to Thea Miria. "You remember Thea Miria?"

Nick turned his gaze away from Sylvie. "How could I forget. Lovely to see you again." He shook her hand and she narrowed her eyes at him and smiled.

"Lovely to see you too."

"This is Christian, my manager."

"Pleasure to meet you, Christian. This is a nice surprise. We seem to bump into you quite often down here." Her eyes flitted to Sylvie, then she fixed her gaze on Nick. Christian shifted uneasily on his feet.

"Well, this is my neighbourhood. I'm always round here." He was totally unfazed by her observation.

"You remember Alex?" Sylvie tried to divert the conversation.

"Sure, we met in the car park that time. You're just back from uni, right?" Alex nodded. "Just finished your exams, then?"

"Yeah," Alex replied, showing he was relieved.

"How do you think you got on?"

"I'll be happy if I pass." He paused, then added, "It was tough this year. I missed some work, so I needed to catch up a bit." Nick's eyes softened as Alex spoke.

"Are you having lunch here?" He directed the question again to Alex, changing the subject.

"Yeah, we really wanted a burger and they are really good here."

"Yeah they are. Do you play?" Nick tilted the cue forward as he spoke.

"I played a lot in my teens," Alex smirked.

"Well we could play doubles while you wait for your lunch." Nick's eyes flitted to Sylvie and then to both Alex and Markus.

"Sure, if that's okay. I mean, we don't want to stop your game." Alex looked at Christian who was finding it hard to focus. He shrugged, indicating he was okay with it.

"Great, we'll rack them up while you order."

Sylvie started rubbing her ring nervously. She wasn't sure if this was such a good idea. She and Thea Miria retreated to a table close to the pool table and waited for the waitress to come over.

"He's a very charming young man isn't he?" Thea Miria pulled out her glasses and put them on to look at the menu. She looked over to where the four men were. Markus was clowning around as usual and Alex was shaking his head, smiling at him. Christian was collecting the balls as Nick talked to Alex, handing him a cue.

Sylvie tried hard to focus on the menu, worried she may get caught out by her aunt. "Yes, he is."

"What will you have?" Thea Miria glanced at the menu.

"Er… I think the salmon. You?"

"Seafood pasta."

"I better get the boys to order theirs." The waitress came and took their order, then Sylvie directed her to Alex, so that the boys could order theirs. They'd started their game and Christian was taking a shot. Nick was texting on his phone as Alex and Markus ordered their meals.

"It's nice to see them enjoying themselves again. Behaving normally. It'll be hard for them this summer. They seem to enjoy pool, though. Maybe you should get a table."

"Chris was always saying we should get one." Sylvie muttered. "He never seemed to get round to it though. We could put it where Markus' drums are. There's loads of space. We were supposed to turn that into a games room."

Sylvie's phone beeped and she rummaged in her bag to find it. She had a message. She quickly opened it. It was from Nick.

You look gorgeous today
And smell like heaven
Meet me by the restrooms x

Sylvie flushed and needed all her will power not to look up at him. Thea Miria raised her eyebrow seeing Sylvie's expression.

"Everything alright, dear?"

"Yes, I just need the restroom. Can you order me a sparkling water when the waiter comes?"

"Nothing stronger?"

Sylvie shook her head as Thea Miria narrowed her eyes. She slid out of her seat and walked purposefully towards the restrooms without turning in the direction of the pool table. Her skin was tingling and she could feel her heart beating faster. She pushed open the communal door and walked through the corridor to where there were two doors and a fire exit at the end. Within a few seconds, she heard the communal door swing open. Not daring to turn around, she walked slowly towards the ladies.

"Go straight through the fire exit," Nick whispered behind her. She glanced over her shoulder to find him right up behind her, his eyes drinking her in as they travelled up and down her body. She pushed open the door and he followed. Bending down, he wedged the door with a stone so it wouldn't close. Then in a split-second he pinned her up against the outside wall.

Nick took her face between his hands and locked his lips on hers, kissing her hard. She steadied herself by gripping his arms. She gasped as he wrapped his arm around her waist and pressed her to him.

"Oh God, I missed you." He pulled away, allowing her to catch her breath. "I can't function, Sylvie. You're driving me mad." He pushed back her hair. She closed her eyes and pulled him back to her; this time, she was kissing him, running her hands in his hair. "Come to mine tonight. Get away, please," he muttered against her mouth.

"I'll try. We'd better get back."

He kissed her forehead and nodded. "You go first." Nick pulled open the door and let her go through. She strode through to the communal door catwalk-style and turned round, blowing him a kiss before she pushed it open. He stood staring wide-eyed after her, quickly shaking his head, trying to come back to the here and now.

Sylvie slipped back into her seat and smiled at Thea Miria. Picking up her drink, she gulped it down, draining the glass. "I think I'll need another. I was very thirsty."

Thea Miria sniffed and then called the waitress for another drink.

Once their food arrived both Alex and Markus came to join them.

"I'm starving." Alex smothered his chips in ketchup, passing the bottle to Markus who mirrored his actions. "He's alright, that Nick." Sylvie cut into her salmon, not daring to look up. She wasn't sure if the comment was directed at her. Markus answered, sparing her.

"Yes he is. He plays well."

"Who won?" asked Thea Miria.

"They did. Only 'cos Markus screwed up an easy shot."

"It wasn't easy," whined Markus. "One sport you're good at and you never let us forget it." Markus smirked, shaking his head.

"That's because it needs skill, patience, a good eye and tactics."

"Shut up," Markus answered without malice.

Sylvie laughed as her two sons carried on bickering about the faults of each other. It was so good to see them back to normal. They'd had a lot to get through these past months. She really hoped she wasn't going make things worse.

Nick picked up his beer and drained it. He needed to head back to the shop. He strolled over to their table and they stopped their chatter.

"Just came to say bye. It was good to see you all."

"Why don't you join us?" Thea Miria beamed, her eyes flitted to Sylvie.

"Tempting as that is, I need to do some work. I'm going up to see my mum later this afternoon, so I have to finish up first."

"Maybe we'll see you down at Curium. I might test out my kite board this weekend." Markus was leaning over and forking a piece of salmon off Sylvie's plate.

Nick watched him and his eyes widened slightly. "Sure. If you go down, call me. Sylvie has my number."

Sylvie froze. *Shit, had he just said that?* She looked up at Markus and he was nodding and chewing away, oblivious. Alex reached over to dip a chip in Sylvie's salmon sauce, then stopped. He furrowed his brow, then continued to dip his chip. Only Thea Miria was smirking as she took a sip of her wine.

"Cool," Alex replied.

Nick eyes moved to Sylvie. "Will I see you later?" Sylvie's eyes widened and her cheeks flushed as she held her breath. He cocked his head and continued. "Up at my mum's?"

Sylvie took a breath and answered "Er… yes, probably."

"Good. Bye for now, then." He smiled at everyone at the table and left.

Sylvie tried hard not to let her gaze follow him out of the door.

15

CONFESSION

Sylvie flicked on the kettle to make some tea. They'd made their way home and Alex and Markus were in the garage looking at the kite board. Alex was making some wisecrack about him being a total beach bum and Markus was retaliating in the only way he knew could, calling him lazy and boring. They were laughing as they came through to the kitchen where Thea Miria was pouring the tea. She watched them closely, revelling in their good spirits.

"So? Is it as great as Markus says?" asked Thea Miria.

"Yeah, Thea." He looked over to Sylvie who was cutting up a choco-late cake and placing it on plates. "You seem to know Nick quite well, Mum." Alex's tone had changed and he seemed a little apprehensive.

"Er... yes I do." She didn't look up at him as she reached for some pastry forks.

"I think he likes you." Sylvie's eyes jerked up to Alex's. She pushed a plate towards him, feeling her face flush.

"Well of course he likes her. She's a friend of his parents." Thea Miria interjected, nervously perching herself up on a stool.

"No, I mean *likes*, likes her." His eyes were still fixed on his mother, her lack of denial confirming what he thought.

"Nick likes Mum?" Markus furrowed his brow trying to process what his brother was saying. "Why do you say that?"

"Just the way he is around her."

Markus furrowed his brow, looking confused.

"Is that so unbelievable? Your mum is a very attractive woman."

Thea Miria looked over to Sylvie who was now looking pale and anxious. Alex's eyes narrowed as he looked at his great aunt.

"Mum?" Markus was staring at her as he saw her take a sip from her tea, her hands shaking.

Sylvie took a deep breath and forced a tight smile. She hadn't wanted this conversation now, not with Thea Miria here, but now that Alex had opened up the already-bursting can of worms, it seemed that she really had no choice.

"Yes he does," she said softly. Her eyes flitted over the three faces looking at her, all of them in various stages of shock.

It was Thea Miria who recovered first. "Well, there you are, then. Of course he likes her. Nothing unusual about that." Her voice was a little tight and brusque, trying to make it sound as if it was obvious and matter of fact at the same time.

"How do you know he likes you, Mum?" Markus's eyes were wide in disbelief.

"Because he told me." Sylvie's voice was quiet and wary.

"What! He just came out and told you he liked you? I mean *fancy*, like you?" Alex's eyes were glaring at his mother.

Sylvie closed her eyes and took a deep breath. This was going to be a lot harder than she'd anticipated. "Look, darling, I was hoping we could discuss this later, but the thing is, Nick and I have been… well, getting to know each other over the last few months and –"

"Hang on a minute, you're telling us that you and Nick have been seeing each other?" Alex's voice raised and his face had taken on a hard expression. He looked a mixture of angry and horrified as he gripped the kitchen counter. Markus sat back on the stool, trying hard to comprehend what he was hearing.

"Well yes, we have."

Alex whipped his head round to Markus. "And you knew about this?" His voice incredulous as if he was appalled that his brother had been a party to it.

"No, man, I knew nothing." Markus held up his hands as if he was being held at gunpoint and shook his head, clearly wounded by the accusation.

Sylvie's stomach was burning and she felt her cramps as she looked at her sons' faces. Alex was seething and Markus was still in shock. "Look, darling, I know it's a bit of a shock. I never thought that this was going to happen, but well… I really like him and he feels the same way –"

Alex interrupted. "So let me get this straight. A twenty-something year-old man is interested in a forty-four-year-old *widow*." He huffed in disbelief, almost spitting out the last word. "Do you see how ridiculous that looks, it's embarrassing! He's after your money, Mum, and you've been totally made to look a fool. I can't believe you. I thought you had more brains."

His comment was like a slap in the face to Sylvie and hurt on so many levels. All her insecurities came flooding back. Why else would someone like Nick be with her? Even her own son could see that this was an incredible scenario. He almost looked disgusted at her and it took all her strength not to break down. Sylvie closed her eyes and put her hand to her mouth. His words cut through her like a knife and they hurt. *Keep it together*, she willed herself.

"Alexander Sapphiris! Apologise to your mother. I cannot believe you just said that. Behaving in such a manner." Thea Miria had shot up off her stool and was glaring at him. Alex stepped back, shocked, as she carried on chastising, her eyes glaring at him. Fleetingly, Sylvie had visions of what it must have been like in one of her classrooms. "How dare you speak to her that way! Your mother has had a lot to handle these past months and if she's found someone that makes her happy, who are you to judge? Can't you see how she's changed in the past few months? She's started to look happy again."

She steadied herself as she sat back on the stool, allowing her eyes to look over to Sylvie. "Your mother is an attractive, loving, generous and sweet woman. Why wouldn't Nick want to be with her? I'll tell you this, Alex, my dear, I don't think he either needs or wants her money. He's got his own very successful business from what I can see, and a yacht to boot, and it disappoints me to think you have such a low opinion of your mother."

Alex looked down at his hands as the anger etched on his face subsided, and shame replaced it.

"Alex, I'm sorry if this is a shock. Believe me, it wasn't my intention. It just happened. He's a really good man." She looked over to Markus, whose face had recovered somewhat and he smiled at his mum. "He really cares for me, and I him."

"How long has this been going on?" Markus asked in a low voice. His eyes flitted to Alex who was still looking down and clenching his jaw.

"Er, well, we've been getting to know one another gradually over the last four months… but it's only recently been" – *Oh crap! How to say this tactfully?* – "more."

Alex's eyes jerked up to his mother's as she said the last word. "You're old enough to be his mother." Alex's tone was steady and measured but his eyes were still ablaze.

"Yes, I am." Well it was a fact and there was no point denying it.

"That doesn't bother him?" He narrowed his eyes and cocked his head as if he found that hard to understand.

"Typical!" Thea Miria chipped in before Sylvie could answer. "If it was your father – God rest his soul – who was dating a twenty-something girl, you wouldn't have batted an eyelid. In fact, you'd have been bloody proud of him! Slapping his back and saying 'Way to go, Dad'. Double standards! I'm sure Nick is well aware of Sylvie's age and it's obvious it doesn't bother him. For the love of God, it's not unheard of, you know. This is the twenty-first century, last time I checked! Only last week, Markus said he'd willingly" – she paused and coughed before using the next word – "*do* Jennifer Lopez, and she's over twenty years older than him!"

Markus's eye widened and he tried to stifle a grin. Alex turned to look at him with his eyebrow raised. "Well, I would. And don't deny that you wouldn't either," Markus apologised as Alex glared at him.

Alex shook his head in disbelief, then turned back to Sylvie. "Does anyone else know?"

"No. I wanted to talk to you both before I told anyone else. I know it's a shock, but I really want you to be okay with this. I understand it's not something you were expecting. Neither was I, but now you know, please be objective. Try to see it from my point of view."

There was an awkward silence as each one of them tried to calm down, then Markus broke the silence. "It's a bit weird, Mum. You know, to get our head round." Markus picked up his fork and gently stabbed it into the cake.

"What I need to know is on what level is it weird?" Both her sons looked up at her, unsure of what she was saying. "What I mean is: is it weird that I'm seeing someone, or is it weird that it's someone younger than me, or is it weird because it's Nick?" She watched them both as they tried to process what she was asking. Thea Miria nervously rearranged the teacup and saucer and refolded her napkin. Sylvie was glad she'd been here after all and she smiled at her; she reciprocated with a wink.

"I don't know, Mum," Markus finally answered.

"Well, if it had been someone else like… I don't know, umm…"

"Like Julian," chipped in Thea Miria. Both boys looked at her, horrified.

Sylvie swallowed hard. "Yes, like Julian. Would it have bothered you?"

Alex's eyes shot back up to his mother as Markus answered, "I think that would have been weird because, well, he was Dad's friend."

Sylvie sniffed a smile. So it wasn't just her that felt that way. "Alex?"

Alex furrowed his brow. "He has the hots for you. I mean, when Dad was alive too, not just now." Sylvie shrugged as if it didn't really matter. "That's going to be awkward. I mean, Nick's his son. Does he know?" Sylvie shook her head. "Well, I'm with Markus on this. That wouldn't sit well with me if you were seeing Julian. He's nice enough and I know he's helped you a lot and that, but he was Dad's friend. That *would* be weird."

"Do you think you could get over the fact that Nick's so young or is that going to be hard too?"

Markus shrugged, not quite sure what to say, and Alex stood stony faced, giving nothing away.

"Would you have been more comfortable if it had been someone more age-appropriate? Or is it just that you don't like the idea of me having a relationship with anyone at all?" That was really the crux of this whole discussion, whether they could accept that their mother was moving on with her life.

"I want you to be happy, Mum." Markus said softly. Sylvie smiled and sighed.

Alex rubbed his face and looked up at Sylvie. "Me too. It's just not easy for me. It'll take me a while to get used to the idea. I suppose it wouldn't have mattered who it was. I know that's selfish, but I'm being honest." He allowed a small smile to pull at the edge of his mouth and Sylvie visibly relaxed. She'd known that Alex was going to have a hard time accepting Nick, but at least he'd calmed down. His eyes had lost their fire and he looked ashamed. "I'm sorry about what I said earlier."

"I know, darling. Forget about it. I didn't purposely do this to embarrass you, you know?" Alex nodded. "Nick wanted to be here when I told you." Alex's eyes widened and his eyebrows rose in shock. "But I thought it was better if it was just us."

"He must really like you, Mum." Markus forked up some cake and wolfed it down.

"I think so. So are we okay? I mean you'll try and be accepting of it?" Markus stabbed some more cake and popped it in his mouth, nodding reluctantly. Alex furrowed his brow and then nodded curtly. Thea Miria put her hand on his arm and squeezed it. He sat on the stool and pulled his cake towards him. Thea Miria looked over to Sylvie and discreetly nodded while narrowing her eyes at her, conveying that she thought they'd get over it.

She picked up her cup and took a sip, then turned back to Sylvie. "So you decided to go for the newer Steed model, then." Sylvie's jaw dropped, Markus choked on his cake and Alex whipped his head round to a nonchalant-looking Thea Miria.

"Thea!" Sylvie cried as Alex patted Markus's back.

"Oh, come on," she laughed. "You guys need to lighten up! Jesus Johnny Jingles." Markus recovered his composure and Alex shook his head, trying hard not to grin and failing miserably. Trust Thea Miria to come out with an inappropriate comment. Thea Miria winked at Sylvie and dug into her cake.

Sylvie walked Thea Miria to her car, linking her arm. "Sorry about this afternoon. I really didn't want you in the middle of this. It must be hard on you too."

Thea Miria patted her hand and smiled. "Sylvie, my dear darling girl, I think you don't know me at all. I may be in my sixties but I feel like I'm in my twenties. I was born in the wrong decade. Did you think for one minute I hadn't realised what was going on between you and that scrumptious Nick? My work has always been about reading people, observing them as I teach. The second I saw your reaction to him I knew there was something. Then when we had lunch that day, I realised that your feelings were reciprocated. I wasn't sure if anything had happened until today, when I saw how you looked at him and he you." Sylvie smiled at her squeezing her arm.

"And it doesn't bother you? I mean, so soon after Chris?"

They stopped by her car and Thea Miria turned to face her putting her hand on Sylvie's cheek. "Chris was like my own son. You know that, and I loved him dearly, but I knew what he was like. He was spoilt and inconsiderate and I know he loved you very much." She stopped and sighed, closing her eyes. "But he was also unfaithful and to this day, I can't see why." Sylvie's eyes blinked rapidly and her hair stood on end as she looked at this dear sweet woman, sadness clouding her eyes. "Like I said, I can read people very well and he couldn't hide it. Not from me."

"You knew?" whispered Sylvie in disbelief. Thea Miria nodded. "How?"

"Does it matter?" Sylvie shook her head as tears pricked her eyes. "The fact you kept it from everyone and spared them any more heartache says more to me about you than anything you could ever try to explain. You deserve a second chance at happiness, Sylvie, and I'll always be on your side. He was a fool and believe me, I told him so." Sylvie wiped her eyes with the back of her hand as her tears slowly trickled down her cheeks. "Hey, stop that," Thea Miria softly admonished her. "Come on, now, the boys seem to be getting their heads round it." Sylvie pursed her lips together and nodded. "Just enjoy yourself. Live a little – that's always been my motto. Once things settle, I'd really like to get to know him, if that's okay with you?"

Sylvie hugged her aunt tightly. "Of course it is, Thea. I'd love that."

"Good. Maybe he has a friend he could introduce me to, eh!" She joked. Sylvie smirked.

After waving off her aunt, Sylvie went back into the house and found Alex and Markus slouched on the sofas, talking about the news their mother had just broken. They hadn't heard her come back in. "Look, I know it's hard to get your head round, Alex, but it could have been worse."

"How *exactly* could it have been worse? Tell me!" He was still angry and poor Markus was going to get it. Sylvie stepped back so she couldn't be seen, and listened as her heart clenched. She really didn't want them to fight but she needed to hear what they really thought.

"She could have ended up with Julian... I know you were wary of him before. Or it could have been someone we didn't know. At least Nick's cool. He's not going to try and be all fatherly, is he?" Markus snorted. "You've met him and you liked him. Just because he's seeing Mum, that shouldn't change." Alex huffed. "Would you rather she was alone?"

"No, of course not."

Sylvie sighed. Well at least they weren't expecting her to become a recluse.

"So, then? She's been so much better these past couple of months. You've noticed, right?"

"I suppose so." Alex answered warily.

"She has been through a load of shit and you've not seen it all, being away, but I have. She deserves a break, man. Stop making it hard for her."

"I'm not... Markus, what if she falls for this guy, I mean really falls for him, and things get serious?"

"So, what's your point?"

"He might decide that in a couple of years he wants his own family. Is he going to be able to? With Mum, I mean." He paused to let it sink in. "If he leaves her… if they break up… she'll be… I don't want to see her go through that."

"Oh. I hadn't thought about that."

"No, exactly. I just don't want her to get hurt. Like you said, she's been through enough." Sylvie's heart clenched. *Oh no, even they could see that there wasn't a future.*

Sylvie walked into the kitchen and sat on a stool, trying hard to pull herself together. She rested her head in her hands and leaned on the counter. She felt exhausted, her stomach was churning and all she wanted to do was transport herself back to their cocoon again, just her and Nick and none of these complications. The need to speak to him, see him, feel him was overwhelming. It was disturbing how much she missed him. Sylvie sighed deeply, realising she'd only chipped at the iceberg with Alex and Markus.

"Mum?" Alex's voice jolted her back to the here and now.

"Yes, darling?" She tried hard to sound calm as she looked back up.

"Are you alright? I mean, after everything? I know I was a bit hard on you and I didn't want to upset you. It's just… well, I was shocked."

"I know. No, I'm fine. A little shell-shocked, but that's to be expected. I need to get up to Maggie's. They started up there and I haven't been up yet."

"When are you going to see him? Nick, I mean."

Sylvie took a deep breath and flushed. "I'm not sure. I might go down tonight after Maggie's." Alex furrowed his brow. *Shit, she felt like a teenager asking permission from her father!*

"Has he been here at all?"

Oh crap, she didn't want to lie. Sylvie nodded and cringed, waiting for some reaction.

"Marcy?" He cocked his head.

"He's never been here when she's here."

"Oh." He slid onto the stool next to her and took her hand. "Nice ring. Is it new?"

"Yes, I bought it in Plaka." He looked like he was thinking hard, as if trying to solve a puzzle. Then after a minute, he squeezed the hand he was holding.

"I'm worried you'll get hurt, Mum. That's all." She smiled at him and got up from her stool to hug him. He got up instantly and enveloped her in his arms, squeezing her tightly. They held on to each other, Sylvie's eyes welling with tears again as she stroked his head. She knew his anger and adverse reaction was because he was finding it hard to become accustomed to life without Chris. He'd taken the role of protector and head of their family seriously, and the burden was sometimes too much for him. She was going to have to tread very carefully where Nick was concerned.

"Maybe he should come here… so we get to know him." He pulled back to look at her. "I mean… well, I don't want you going off all the time."

"I'm not sure, Alex. Won't you feel weird him coming here?"

"Probably, but it's going to happen sooner or later. I'd rather get to know him." He straightened up and seemed to pull on some inner strength. "Look, Markus and I are meeting some friends around nine tonight, so see if he can come round before, so we can… that's if you want to?"

Sylvie placed her hand on his cheek and he leaned into it. He was really trying for her, trying to get past his initial reaction and reservations. He was so different from Markus. He took things so personally and kept his emotions in check, reining them in. He tried to keep his feelings to himself most of the time. But like today when it became too much, he'd snap and he found it hard to keep his self-control. Markus tended to say what he thought without any filter system at all. If he was annoyed he'd tell you, if he was hurt he'd let you know. You knew where you were with him.

"Okay, if you're sure. It would mean a lot to me for you all to get along."

"I know, Mum. I'll try." She reached up and kissed his cheek. "It's going to be hard enough without me making it worse for you."

"Oh Alex, I am really so lucky to have you two. I don't think I'd have been able to move on if it wasn't for you." He looked at her, embarrassed. He wasn't good at taking a compliment. She looked at the clock; it was quarter to four. "I need to get off." He nodded.

"Go on, Mum. We'll see you later."

Sylvie looked at herself in the mirror of her bathroom. She looked haggard. *Confessing to your kids about a younger lover will do that to you*, she thought to herself. She slicked on some fresh lipstick and pinched her cheeks. She'd have to do. She was going to be as quick as possible up there, make some excuse to leave. She really wasn't looking forward to seeing Maggie. She felt so dishonest and guilty.

Sylvie started her journey up to Maggie's. She wasn't sure whether she should tell Nick yet. She knew he'd be relieved that she'd done it. What worried her was that he might rush to tell his parents, and she really needed a breather after this afternoon. She'd text him telling him she was on her way up to Maggie's. She put her phone on hands-free and dialled up Lilianna.

"Hi, sweetie, how was Markus's discharge?"

"Oh it was alright, a lot of pomp and circumstance. I'm not a big fan of all of that, but at least it's done and dusted. I thought you should know I told them about Nick."

"Already?"

"Well, it wasn't my intention, but I was put into a bit of a corner."

"How?"

"Oh, it doesn't really matter. The fact is, they know."

"And? How did they take it?"

"Initially not so well, but once the shock subsided, they seemed a little more accepting."

"Well, thank God for that."

"How do you feel?"

"Relieved I've told them, though now I know I'm going to have to face Julian and Maggie, and to be honest, I'm more than dreading it. I'm off there now."

"To tell Maggie?" Lilianna almost squeaked.

"No! I'm going up there for work. I haven't told Nick about the boys yet. I'll tell him later on. Otherwise he's sure to go and find them today; he's desperate to get it out in the open."

"Sylvie, I know you've got a lot to deal with right now, but Zach needs to know too. He'll probably get the brunt of Julian's reaction and he needs to be prepared." *Oh, poor Zach, having to deal with all her personal problems, again!* She'd almost forgotten about how this would affect him. She cringed at the thought of how he might react.

"You're right. I'll find time tomorrow to tell him."

"Do you want me to?"

"No, Lily. I think it should come from me." Knowing Zach, he'd want to know a lot more than what Lilianna could tell him. She owed him a proper explanation. She just hoped it wouldn't be hard on him. "I'm nearly there, Lily. I'll call you later. Thanks for being there."

"Anytime, sweetie." Sylvie smiled to herself. Maybe it wouldn't be so bad after all. Alex had seemed to have calmed down. Markus had handled the news well. Even Thea Miria was happy for her.

She hadn't had much time to dwell on Thea Miria's revelation about Chris. So she'd known about Dina? Or maybe it was Penny she knew about – or both? Sylvie mulled over that thought a while. Maybe that was why Chris had broken it off with both of them? Because his aunt had confronted him too. The very thought depressed her even more. Maybe she should talk to her about it. Sylvie shook her head, trying to clear the thought. Maybe there were more. Oh crap… she really didn't want to go there. Not right now, anyway. What's done is done. Did it really matter why, anymore? She really needed to let it go. If she knew, would she feel better or worse?

Sylvie pulled up outside Maggie's and switched off the engine. She knew she'd feel worse.

16

REALISATION

Maggie opened the door and beamed at Sylvie, hugging her tightly.

"Sylvie, you look fabulous! Athens definitely agrees with you. Come in. I thought you'd forgotten about me," she joked. Her hair was loose and she was in her uniform of faded jeans, floaty top and bare feet.

Sylvie swallowed hard feeling an overwhelming desire to turn around and beat a hasty retreat. The guilt felt like a tidal wave gushing over her. "I know. I'm sorry. I had so much to catch up on. Yiannis told me that everything's going well, though. He's very professional, so I knew you were in good hands." They'd made their way to the kitchen.

"Tea?" Sylvie nodded.

"I'll pop upstairs and see how far on they are?" Sylvie needed to get some distance.

"Okay, it looks great already. The floor has made a real difference."

Sylvie went through to the hallway and made her way upstairs. She passed Nick's room and stopped at the open doorway. She stepped through the threshold and scanned the room. It was extremely tidy. It didn't look lived in at all. She felt a little guilty snooping. There were a few books on his shelves, mostly related to boats. There was an English-Greek dictionary and a couple of photo albums. Sylvie wondered if there were any pictures of his exes in them – or worse, some of the young French hotties. There were some certificates framed on the wall, all related to lifesaving and water sports. There was one framed photo of Nick with a few other young boys, all obviously lifeguards, and a second photo of him water-skiing. Both photos must have been taken when he was in his teens. He was smiling broadly in both, all teeth and super-toned. Sylvie sighed and moved towards the door she could hear Maggie talking on the phone.

"Good… yes… well, they've put the floor in and it looks so much bigger… Yes, she's here. Okay… I'll ask her… umm, I know Vicki's not happy so maybe I should… true it will keep me occupied… alright… bye, then."

Sylvie slipped down the corridor and stepped into Elenora's room. She was pleased to see that the floor had been laid and the walls had been prepared, ready to be painted and wallpapered. The light fittings had been removed and the new wiring had also been completed. *Yiannis was a real marvel*, mused Sylvie. By tomorrow, all the paint work and papering would be completed, so that the furnishings could be fitted in, along with all the new lights on Monday.

Sylvie made her way downstairs to where Maggie was pouring their tea.

"What do you think?"

"Yiannis and his team have really moved fast. It looks great. The floor is perfect. Real wood looks so much better than laminate."

Maggie nodded in agreement. "I've got a sneaky suspicion that I'll end up redoing the whole house at this rate. Every room is starting to feel dated now. I was just telling Julian. He said I should do it. So it looks like you might be working up here indefinitely." Maggie looked pleased with herself. "Let's go outside and tell me all about your trip." Maggie's eye caught sight of her left hand. "Oh Sylvie, is that a new ring?"

Sylvie nodded and held out her hand for her to see. "Yes, I bought for myself."

"It's gorgeous. And the earrings too?" Sylvie smiled at Maggie's enthusiasm. "Just let me put my kiln on. I've got to fire up some pots. Go out, I won't be long."

Sylvie stepped out onto the terrace and looked at the pool, her heart fluttering at the memory of Nick pulling himself out of it. For as long as she lived, she'd never let that wonderful image out of her head. Sitting down, she wondered whether Julian had rung up to check if she'd actually come up. Maybe she was over thinking everything again. After all, he and Maggie had a close relationship. He probably called her all the time.

"Are you okay, Sylvie? You look miles away."

"I'm fine, just tired. I had a lot of catching up to do. Markus had his discharge today and tomorrow… well, I've got loads to do." Sylvie smiled tightly, trying hard to look Maggie in the eye and failing miserably.

"Well once things slow down a bit, I'd really like you to start on the rest of the house. There's no rush, but I think Julian may be right. Maybe the house could be done by Christmas."

"Really? The whole house?"

Maggie nodded. "Vicki's really put out that her room looks so shabby, so hers would be next, and the main bathroom."

"Okay, well let's finish what we've started and then maybe later on this month we can put something together." Sylvie shifted in her seat, knowing that the chances she'd be doing any work in Maggie's house again would be highly unlikely.

"So what did you get up to?"

Sylvie swallowed hard and took a sip of her tea. How was she going to do this? She hated lying. Her whole body stiffened and she felt herself start to sweat. "Oh, I just went to the museum and took in the sights. It was very relaxing. And of course, I had to go to our clients to complete the transfer of our building. That was pretty much it." Sylvie took another sip of tea. "What are you going to fire?" She hoped her question would change the direction of conversation.

"Well, after Elenora's wedding, one of our friends showed the coffee cups I made to a friend of theirs, whose daughter's getting married in a month. They asked me to design some small vases to be given as favours, so I've just started on those." She seemed excited.

"That's great, Maggie. You're going to have to get a bigger workshop at this rate."

"I know. It's keeping me very busy."

They were interrupted by voices in the hallway. Maggie turned round and strained to see who it was. "Looks like Vicki's back. And ooh – Nick!" She jumped up and quickly made her way back into the house. "Nick, you came up!" She threw her arms around him, kissing him on the cheek.

"Hi, Mum." He hugged her back.

Sylvie stayed out on the terrace, her heart thumping and her stomach clenching. This was going to be beyond hard. She'd have to make an excuse and leave. Vicki saw her first. She bounded out of the kitchen.

"Sylvie, it's great to see you." She leaned down to hug and kiss her.

"Vicki, what a nice surprise. How are you?" Sylvie was genuinely pleased to see her. Vicki was dressed in her business suit and her blonde hair was in a tight ponytail. She slipped off her jacket and kicked off her shoes as she sat down next to Sylvie. She looked casual and business-like at the same time.

"Glad tomorrow's Friday. You look fabulous. You've got a tan. Mum said you went away."

"Yes, for business." Vicki nodded. "The room looks great. To be honest, I'm a bit jealous now. I want my room done too." She mock-pouted.

Sylvie laughed. "Well, don't worry. I think your mum's decided to do your room next."

Vicki clapped her hands. "Great, when can we start?"

"Oh, I think we need to finish one at a time, and then we'll see." Sylvie explained. Vicki's eyes flitted to just behind her, and Sylvie knew that Nick must have come out on to the terrace. She felt herself tense.

"Nick, look who's here." Sylvie felt him come up behind her. Her heart raced and she swallowed impulsively.

Nick walked round so that he stood in front of her. He had a mischievous smile and his eyes were sparkling. "Hello, Sylvie." He leaned down to kiss her cheek, taking a fraction too long as his lips gently caressed her and his hand slowly stroked down her arm.

Sylvie closed her eyes and kissed his stubbly jaw, breathing in his scent. It took all her self-control not to moan. "Hi Nick," she breathed, as he pulled away from her.

"Mum's going to do my room." Vicki looked over to Nick, oblivious about what had just happened. Nick dragged his eyes off Sylvie and looked at his sister.

"Really?" He looked back at Sylvie, his eyes blazing. Sylvie picked up her teacup and took a sip, avoiding his stare.

"Well, mine looks so dated now. I'm going to make a drink. Do you want one?"

"Sure, I'll have some tea." Vicki got up and walked back into the house. Nick sat down next to Sylvie and dragged his chair as close as he could. Looking up past into the kitchen to check where Vicki was first, Nick then reached up and stroked back Sylvie's hair. Sylvie leaned into his hand.

"You look so beautiful." He ran his fingers over her lips. "God, I've missed you."

"Me too."

"How was today?" He leaned back and clenched his jaw.

"It was okay. I'm going to go home though. I can't stay… it's just too hard." Nick's eyes narrowed.

"Don't go. When am I going to see you?" His voice soft.

"Come to mine after here."

Nick looked puzzled. "Yours? What about Alex and Markus?"

"I spoke to them." Nick's eyes lit up and he shifted closer to Sylvie. Then, hearing Vicki coming out, he pulled back, searching for answers in her face.

Vicki put down the cups and flopped down on the chair.

"Mum's putting some dinner in the oven. Are you staying, Sylvie?"

"No, in fact I better get off. It's late." Sylvie stood up to leave, and Nick immediately rose from his seat. "I'll just say bye to Maggie. It was great seeing you, Vicki." She bent down to kiss her and then headed back to the house, followed by Nick.

Maggie was closing up the oven as they entered. "Maggie, I'll get off. I just wanted to make sure everything was going to plan."

"Aww, I thought you might stay for dinner. It's been ages since we caught up."

"I know but I need to get home. Alex and Markus are back."

"Oh, say no more. I bet its great having a house full again."

"Yes. I'll be checking up on Yiannis over the next day or so." Maggie came round to hug and kiss her.

"It's alright, Mum, I'll see Sylvie out. You carry on with dinner." Nick's eyes flitted to Sylvie as he spoke.

"Okay, Nick. In fact I need to put my pots in the kiln. See you soon, Sylvie."

"Bye." Sylvie smiled and headed for the door. Nick walked slowly behind her and when they got to the front door, Nick opened it and they both walked out onto the driveway up to Sylvie's car. Nick glanced over to the front door, ensuring no one was there as Sylvie opened her car door and got into the driver's seat. Nick knelt down so that they were on the same level.

"You told them?" he whispered. His face was ashen and Sylvie could see his concern. Sylvie nodded. "And? How were they?"

She turned to face him taking his hands. "They were shocked. A little angry, we talked it out and in the end they decided that they wanted to meet you, get to know you."

He raised his eyebrows in shock. "That's it? I thought… well, I don't know what I thought to be honest. They want to meet me, today?"

"They don't want me creeping around. Look, they're not one

hundred percent happy, so we still need to be considerate. No PDAs and stuff. But they are willing to get to know you, for my sake."

"No PDAs, eh?" Nick smirked. "That's gonna be tough." He ran his hand up her leg.

"Nick, stop it. Go back inside. They'll be wondering where you are. Come down as soon as you can."

He stood up reluctantly, then after a second, leant down and grabbed her face, kissing her hard. Sylvie melted against him as she grasped his hair and returned the kiss. Nick pulled back sharply, closing his eyes and breathing deeply. "I'll be down in an hour." His voice was strained. "You're killing me."

"See you in an hour."

"Bye, baby."

Maggie stood stock-still as she watched Nick lean in to Sylvie's car. The blood drained from her face as she processed what was unfolding in front of her.

She'd just put her vases into the kiln when she turned and glanced out of the small window of her workshop that overlooked the driveway. It was tinted, so from the outside, you couldn't look in. She'd watched them walk down to Sylvie's car and then saw Sylvie get in. Maggie was about to turn away when she noticed Nick kneel down to speak to Sylvie. The gesture seemed a little strange and overly familiar, considering they had walked to the car in silence. Maggie moved over to the window to get a better look. Her heart stopped when she saw Sylvie take Nick's hands, but what was more disturbing was how Nick was looking at Sylvie. Maggie steadied herself holding on to the workbench. She thought he was over her, over his crush. He said he had a new girlfriend. Did he still have feelings for her? Her mind was racing.

Maggie watched as Nick stood up and then within an instant, he leaned into the car, kissing Sylvie passionately. *Oh no!* Maggie gasped as her hand flew to her mouth. *No, no, no, no!* How had this happened? He'd been so happy, like he'd been back in the day. She sat back, thinking back over the past couple of weeks. Then she remembered their conversation on the night of the DVD.

She's the best thing that ever happened to me.
I've known her a while.
It's important to me that you remember this conversation.
You can see how happy she makes me.
She means everything to me.

He hadn't just found a girlfriend – it was Sylvie. She *was* the girlfriend. Maggie sat with her head in her hands as she pieced everything together. Sylvie had not been up as much, she'd been distant. Initially, Maggie had thought it was because of Julian. That maybe something had happened between them. It was always in the back of her mind that she would lose him to Sylvie. It was becoming increasingly obvious that his feelings for Sylvie were more than just as a colleague and close friend, and Maggie had been having a hard time reconciling that. This bombshell, though, was something so out of the blue, so totally unexpected. She really couldn't begin to process it.

Her attention then rested on Sylvie. What on earth was she thinking? Nick was so young. She tried hard to work out how this could have happened. She knew that they'd had a kind of friendship, a connection even, over the past few months, with all the wedding preparations and the redecoration. Nick had been around a lot and they'd built up a rapport. But from friendship to… Maggie shook her head. Funnily enough, she wasn't angry with Sylvie, which surprised her. The truth was she really liked Sylvie and even though it seemed inappropriate, she could see why Nick had fallen for her and that he was happy. It was really too much for her to try and fathom out. How had it happened? For how long? Why were they being secretive? They were obviously keeping it quiet for a reason. Then like a thunderbolt, it dawned on her. They were keeping it from Julian, because they knew he'd find it impossible to accept. *Holy shit! Julian.*

Maggie's heart lurched at the thought of how this would affect him. It would be bad enough that Sylvie didn't want him as anything other than a friend, but to choose Nick over him would be a real slap to his ego. Ironic that Sylvie would want to be with a man much younger than her, when over the last twenty years, Julian had only been with very young women. *Karma?* She shook her head, annoyed at herself for being so uncharitable. He was going to be devastated, really devastated. Over the last twenty years, Maggie had watched Julian have meaningless flings with ridiculously young women. All unsuitable and all without any chance of a future with him. Then Sylvie came along, and Maggie realised he'd fallen for her. She knew that any hope of them getting back together again all hinged on how receptive Sylvie was to Julian.

Over the last few months, she had witnessed Julian's attempts to move their relationship from friends to more, and she had seen that he'd failed. Whether it was because Sylvie was genuinely not interested in him or whether she just wasn't ready to move on with that part of her life, Maggie hadn't been sure until today.

"Mum? Are you alright?" Nick popped his head round the door, Maggie spun round to face him, his voice startling her.

"Er, yes." She smiled tightly.

"I'm off. I've got a lot of work to catch up on. I'm leaving on Wednesday for ten days."

"Oh? You've only just got back."

"I know, but I've got to go again, to finalise everything."

"You haven't told me much about this trip. How did it go?" Maggie had got up and was standing by him.

"It was good." His eyes scanned the room avoiding her face. She could tell he was nervous. "Anyway, I'll pop in over the weekend." He leaned over to kiss her goodbye and then quickly walked out of her workshop towards the front door.

Maggie watched him through the window as he jumped into his Jeep. He really did look happy. He was going away again, and so soon? Then she closed her eyes as another piece of the puzzle slotted into place. He'd been away with Sylvie. Of course, it was obvious now. They'd both been away. Maggie clenched her eyes shut. She knew Nick. She knew he was falling in deep – he'd told her in so many words that day of the DVD. He'd warned her, and he was keeping her out of it because of hers and Julian's previous interference. She just hoped that he wouldn't get hurt again.

Sylvie stirred her arabiatta sauce as it bubbled away. She looked at the clock. It was ten to seven. Alex and Markus were setting the table, discussing their arrangements for the evening.

"Do you want some garlic bread?"

Alex looked at Markus and they both looked over and shook their heads. "Better not, Mum. Don't want to stink the place out!" Sylvie smirked as she put the baguettes into the oven to warm. She drained the pasta, then poured it into the now-ready sauce. As she mixed it through, she heard the doorbell go. Her heart jumped, knowing it was Nick. *Oh please, please, please let everything go smoothly*, she thought to herself.

"It's okay, Mum, I'll get it." She was about to protest but it was too late, Alex was already striding to the hallway. She could hear the door open and then mumbled talking, but she couldn't make out what was being said.

Her ears were on fire and her heart was thumping. What was taking them so long? She steadied herself on the sink as she felt her stomach constrict. Then suddenly she heard them coming through.

"… I appreciate you wanting to meet me, officially that is. I realise it must be quite a shock." Nick walked through to the kitchen with Alex, his face was pensive and Alex seemed to be nodding stiffly.

"Hi, Markus." Nick immediately turned to greet Markus as he walked towards them. Nick fleetingly looked at Sylvie, then turned his attention back to Markus.

"Hi," replied Markus, his eyes fixed on Alex.

"I was just telling Alex that I know this must be a shock to both of you and well, I appreciate you meeting me so soon. I'm really not sure that I would have been so understanding. If I were in your shoes, that is. It shows me that your mother's happiness is more important to you than any reservations you may have about me." Markus nodded awkwardly. Sylvie stood stock-still in the kitchen, glad she had somewhere to lean against, as she watched her sons try their hardest to make things easy for her.

"Can I get you a drink?" Alex asked, his ingrained manners taking over as he walked to the fridge, glancing up at Sylvie.

"Yeah, sure."

"Beer?"

"Great." Alex grabbed three beers and quickly opened up the bottles, handing one to Nick and then one to Markus. Sylvie turned to the salad and started dressing it. The three of them said a very subdued "Cheers" and then tentatively took a swig from their bottles. The silence was deafening and Sylvie had mixed the salad at least five times more than was necessary, the lettuce was starting to look bruised. Nick spoke first.

"I'm just going to say hi to your mum… if that's okay?" Sylvie stopped mid-mix and clenched her eyes shut, glad she had her back to them.

After a split-second, both Alex and Markus mumbled awkwardly. "Sure, yeah." And then they moved to the sitting room, where their video game had been put on pause. Sylvie heard them slouch heavily on the couches and resume their loud game. Nick put his beer down on the kitchen counter and strode over to where Sylvie was standing. She turned round to face him, her whole body trembling as she swallowed.

"Hi, baby," Nick whispered so only she could hear. His face was anxious but soft. He gently stroked back her hair from her face, then ran the back of his hand down her cheek.

"Hi," Sylvie breathed.

"Something smells good," Nick smirked at her, his eyes burning into hers. He had his mischievous look on his face.

"Hungry?"

"Always." And Sylvie knew that he wasn't talking about the food. "Do you need a drink?" Sylvie nodded. "I'll get it." He leaned down and dropped a swift kiss on her lips and went straight to the bar to fix her a large whisky. Sylvie watched him as she took out the baguette and quickly sliced it up and placed it into the bread basket. His eyes scanned the room again, momentarily resting on the picture of her and Chris on the beach. He picked up the heavy crystal glass and returned to the kitchen.

"Take a sip." Nick handed her the glass and he watched her as she took a large gulp. Nick smiled, reaching over to her and cupping her face with one hand. "Better?" Sylvie nodded.

"Well, dinner's ready. I'll call the boys."

"Need any help?"

"I just need to put everything on the table."

"Let me." And just like that, he moved into the kitchen and started lifting the platter with the pasta, and the serving plate with the grilled chicken.

"Dinner's ready!" Sylvie called towards the sitting room. The noise of the game ceased and within seconds, Alex and Markus were in the kitchen, taking their seats. Nick waited to see where they were going to sit before he took his place. Alex sat first, then Markus hovered, wondering whether to sit opposite Alex, effectively splitting up Nick and Sylvie. Then he moved up and sat next to Alex, leaving the two seats free for Sylvie and Nick to sit next to each other.

Nick stood until Sylvie brought the last of the food, then pushed in her chair as she sat. The gesture wasn't lost on Alex or Markus, and a slight smile curled over Markus's lips. Alex had an almost puzzled expression.

"What game are you playing?" Nick asked Alex as Sylvie started to serve the pasta.

"Cod," Alex mumbled, reaching for the Parmesan.

Cod? Wasn't that a fish? Sylvie shook her head and Markus smirked at her.

177

"Call of Duty, Mum," Markus explained.

Sylvie nodded and mouthed "ah".

"Online?"

Alex nodded pensively. "You play?" Alex asked warily.

"Wasted many days and nights on that," smirked Nick.

"What prestige are you?"

Prestige? What was that?

"Tenth. You?" asked Nick as Markus's eyes widened, clearly impressed, and Alex seemed to warm up a little. He passed the Parmesan over to Nick and Sylvie felt the tension in the room drop a few degrees.

"Alex just got to seventh," Markus sniggered.

"I have to study *too*, remember," Alex offered by way of explanation. Markus laughed.

"Like I said, I've wasted a lot of time on it." Nick shrugged as a form of apology. Sylvie watched as her boys started to dig into their pasta and she picked up a piece of baguette to butter it.

"No doubt you'll spend the summer trying to get up to tenth now," Markus smirked at Alex and Alex twisted his mouth, trying to suppress a grin.

"Remind me again what level you are? ... Er... what's that? Fifth?" Alex mocked Markus in good humour. Sylvie shook her head. They may as well have been speaking Chinese. She hadn't a clue what they were talking about, nor did she care. At least they had some common interest, even if it was a mindless war game.

Nick sprinkled the cheese and passed it to Sylvie who only had salad and grilled chicken on her plate. He looked at her and frowned. She placed the piece of buttered baguette on his side plate and he instinctively picked up her hand and kissed the inside of her wrist. Both Alex and Markus stopped mid-mouthful. Sylvie froze, but Nick gently placed her hand back down as if nothing was amiss.

"Aren't you hungry?" he asked her softly. Sylvie managed to breathe and then screwed up her nose indicating she wasn't.

Markus recovered first. "She's watching her weight." He rolled his eyes.

Nick furrowed his brow in disapproval.

"I know, we keep telling her she's fine, but she won't listen," Alex added. His tone was almost exasperated. He leaned over and forked a small piece off her plate and Nick raised his eyebrows while smiling broadly.

"She's more than fine, she's perfect," Nick replied, softly turning towards her. Sylvie flushed, clearly embarrassed at the attention. Alex looked up at Nick as he spoke and could see that he meant every word. He sat back in his seat, his eyes still on Nick as Nick stared at Sylvie and Sylvie back at Nick. Alex took a long draught from his beer bottle, then sighed to himself. This was going to take some getting used to.

17

SIMILARITIES

Sylvie's eyes fluttered open as the sun shone through a gap in the curtains. Nick was stretched out on his front, his arm across her waist. *Boy oh boy did he look good!* She shifted slightly to see the time, six-thirty. *Crap!* That meant in less than an hour, Marcy would be here and she really didn't want to wake him. Sylvie looked back down at Nick. Well, maybe she should get over that hurdle today too. She knew Marcy would be beyond shocked, just like Alex and Markus, but at least they seemed to be trying.

Sylvie reflected on how after the inevitable initial awkwardness, her boys had warmed up to Nick. Markus had tried to lighten the mood by teasing Alex throughout their dinner. Nick had sat and observed, watching their interaction. As the evening had worn on, Alex began to quiz Nick on his business and his impending trip to France. Nick gave them a very condensed version of what his business entailed and Alex listened intently. It grew increasingly obvious to Sylvie that Nick was playing down his achievements, modestly brushing over his relatively short but very successful career. At first, she thought it might be because he didn't want to share the information, but as she watched Nick enthusing about other topics, she realised that he was trying to make them feel at ease with him. He didn't want to intimidate them or make them feel lacking in any way. Sylvie thought back to their last night in Athens where Nick had done the complete opposite to Dimitris Dracos. Of course, then he'd *wanted* to intimidate him.

By the time they'd finished dinner, Alex seemed more relaxed. Markus kept the conversation rolling, giving the impression he was fine with his mother's relationship, but Sylvie knew better. His behaviour was more to do with keeping the atmosphere light. He didn't want Alex to make things difficult, so he'd resigned himself to playing the court jester until Alex visibly warmed up. Sylvie caught sight of Markus looking pensively at Nick, when he thought no one was looking. He was also finding it hard, but she knew he genuinely liked Nick, and that had somewhat softened the blow.

Sylvie let her eyes drift over Nick as he slept peacefully next to her. She really didn't want to get up. Instinctively, her fingers stroked the small of his back and he began to stir, stretching and flexing his arms. He tilted his head to the side and slowly opened his eyes, a smile creeping over his lips. *Wow.*

Kissing Sylvie's shoulder, he squeezed her closer. "Morning beautiful," he murmured against her now-sensitive skin. "Don't tell me it's morning and I'm still here in your bed." He raised his eyebrows in mock-horror. Sylvie giggled as he rolled on top of her, effectively trapping her with the weight of his body. "And on a school day too!" He bent down and kissed her hard, then pulled back to brush her hair back off her face.

"I know, who'd have thought?" Sylvie pushed her hands into his hair and pulled him to her, kissing him fully as he groaned in appreciation.

"I really could get used to this," Nick breathed as he dropped kisses down her throat. "Shouldn't I be leaving?" He gently took her hands and raised them over her head so he could kiss her unobstructed down her side. Sylvie squirmed as she felt him smile against her left hip. Nick kicked off the sheet.

"Ah!" Nick softly bit her as he slowly turned her onto her front and he continued to kiss and nip her behind with his teeth, then back round again to her right hip, turning her onto her back again. "Nick, please," Sylvie quivered under his expert touch.

"You taste and feel delicious." His eyes blazed cobalt blue as he made his way back up. "So am I leaving?" he asked again, gazing up at her through his lashes. Sylvie grabbed his head and brought him to her lips, kissing him deeply, making him moan as he held her face. Pulling back, she looked deep into his eyes.

"No, never." Nick closed his eyes, savouring her words, then slowly he sank into her as she arched up to him. *She could definitely get used to this!*

"I'm going to have to fit a lock on my door." Sylvie mused as Nick held her close, stroking her back. He looked down at her, puzzled. "The boys are used to barging into my room… It could get awkward, or at worst, very embarrassing."

"Really?" Nick shifted onto his side so he could look at her.

"We've never locked the doors." Nick tilted his head a little as if he was trying to find the right words. "What is it?"

"You have a very close relationship with Alex and Markus, don't you?"

Sylvie nodded. "Does that bother you?"

"No, not at all. But it's very unique. You don't hide anything from one another and…"

Sylvie's eyes narrowed. "What is it, Nick? Just say it."

He sighed, then stroked her face with his fingers. "Okay, just small things I noticed, like… them eating off your plate and the straight-talking about women, barging into your room…"

Sylvie smiled. "Yes, we're close. It makes you uncomfortable?"

Nick shook his head. "No, it's just… well, my family is close but you seem to have very few boundaries with yours."

"Chris and I were always honest and open with them, so that they would always be that way with us." Sylvie's smile dropped as she thought about Chris and how she'd not been totally honest about him with the boys. That was different – it would devastate them, and secondly, he wasn't here to defend himself to them.

"I'm sorry, I shouldn't have said…"

"Nick, you can ask and tell me anything. Really." She leaned up to him and kissed him softly. *Shit, it was seven-thirty*. She was going to be late and Marcy would be downstairs. "I'm going to have to get up. I've got a lot of catching up to do." Sylvie propped herself up.

"Can you play hooky this afternoon?" Nick sat up to admire her as she stood up.

"Why?"

"Well Markus mentioned that he might try out his kite board. I thought I'd go with him. Maybe Alex will come too. If you come, they might feel better about it." Sylvie smiled. He really was trying to get to know them. Last night, he'd shown genuine interest in everything Alex and Markus had talked about, and they'd even played that god-awful war game together. The breakthrough had been when they were getting ready to leave. They were about to ring for a taxi to take them to the bar they were meeting their friends at, when Nick suggested he drop them off. They hadn't wanted to take their cars as they would be drinking and Sylvie had had two large whiskies, so she couldn't take them. Sylvie had stayed behind to tidy up.

The drive down to town had been less awkward than Nick expected. Markus was talking animatedly about some friend of theirs, defusing any possible tension. Once they pulled up outside the bar, Alex turned to Nick.

"You staying over?" His eyes narrowed as he straightened his posture. Nick took a deep breath, knowing this was make-or-break time. How he responded would affect their future relationship. Markus was sat stock-still and silent in the back, not moving.

Nick turned to face Alex and after a moment, he answered. "I'm not sure. That's really your mother's call." Alex swallowed hard, his eyes locked on Nick's. "But if you'd rather I didn't, I won't."

Alex continued to look at him, then his eyes lost their tightness. His eyes fleetingly looked at Markus who still hadn't moved. "Whatever Mum wants is fine with us." He spoke quietly and his whole demeanour softened.

"Okay. Thanks." Nick gave a slight smile and Alex nodded curtly, then turned to get out of the Jeep. The tension in the car dropped and Markus let out the breath he'd been holding, and shifted towards the door to get out. Alex leaned back into the car.

"Thanks for the lift." Nick nodded and indicated it was nothing. Markus looked in at Nick as he got out onto the pavement.

"Thanks for the lift, man. See you in the morning!" He grinned widely until he caught sight of Alex glaring at him. Then his grin dropped. "What! Lighten up, man." He shook his head and Alex's face twisted as he tried to stifle a smile. Nick grinned back at them, then waved as he pulled away. Alex slapped Markus playfully on the back and Markus retaliated with a soft punch to his stomach.

Nick allowed himself to relax as he drove back to Sylvie's. He was beginning to feel decidedly more optimistic about how everyone was going to react to their relationship. After his father, Alex and Markus were the two people Nick had worried about the most. Today though, that worry had subsided. They needed more time, which was understandable. He wondered how he would have felt if his mother had a younger boyfriend. He knew the answer to that and he knew there would have been no chance in hell he'd have accepted it. The thought was very sobering.

***

"Well? Maybe around two? I doubt they'll be up before midday if they were out last night." Nick ran his hands through his hair and swung his legs off the bed. Sylvie walked into the bathroom and turned on the shower.

"I'll check and see how much work I can finish off, and then maybe. I'll see." She called out to him before she closed the bathroom door, as she felt her stomach start to cramp. Oh hell, her stomach had been relatively good the past day or so but once she'd stood up, she'd felt that familiar feeling of saliva pooling in her mouth. Sylvie went to the sink and brushed her teeth, hoping the minty toothpaste would settle her stomach. It was no use, and she retched over the sink, making her eyes water. She quickly splashed cold water on her face and headed for the shower.

Today was going to be a tough day. She had to have a meeting with Julian and Zach around ten to go over the status of the new office block they were working together on, and hopefully they would have some news on the plot of land they'd put a bid in for. Sylvie knew her anxieties were connected to that. She'd have to find time today to speak to Zach. Now the boys knew, she wanted him to know sooner rather than later. Well first things first. She needed to introduce Nick to Marcy.

Sylvie slipped on her blue earrings as Nick sat on the bed watching her. He'd thrown on his clothes from yesterday minus his boxers after he'd had a shower, and had ruffled his hair dry with his fingers. It had taken him all of fifteen minutes to get ready and he looked perfect as always. Sylvie stepped into her navy blue stilettoes, then she checked herself in the mirror. She'd put on her pinstriped navy pencil skirt and a white vest and a navy wide belt. She picked up her matching short-sleeved jacket.

"I love watching you walk in those tight skirts." Nick's eyes widened as Sylvie turned to look at him shyly. "I mean it. Sexy as hell." He stood, and in two steps he was up close to her. "How are you feeling?" He cupped her cheek as he spoke.

"About what?"

"Telling the boys. Why, is there something else?" Sylvie's scrunched up her nose. "Your stomach?" She nodded, shrugging as if to say it didn't matter. "You should go and see the doctor, baby. You can't suffer like this all the time." He bent down and kissed her softly, his eyes full of concern.

"I will. I'll make an appointment next week, though I know he'll tell me it's stress."

"Good. How do you think Alex and Markus took it all yesterday?"

"It's still early days, but I know they're making an effort for me. Alex worries about me. It's nothing personal."

"Hey, I'm not complaining, really. If it were me, I wouldn't be so understanding. Are you ready?"

"Yes, let me introduce you to Marcy. Remember, she's like family, so she might be a little brusque."

"Brusque?"

"Just be nice." Sylvie shook her head smirking.

"Aren't I always?" He raised his eyebrows lewdly. Sylvie grabbed his chin squashing his lips into a pucker and kissed him loudly.

"Come on." She turned and headed to the door and Nick playfully swatted her behind, causing her to shriek.

Marcy was emptying the dishwasher as they entered the kitchen. She looked up absent-mindedly at Sylvie. "Morning, Mam." Then she did a double take, as her eyes caught sight of Nick behind her.

"Morning, Marcy. This is Nick. Nick, Marcy."

"Good morning, Marcy, I'm very pleased to meet you. Sylvie's told me so much about you." He smiled broadly as he extended his hand for her to shake. Marcy stood perplexed as the colour drained from her face. After a second, she extended her hand and shook it, staring wide-eyed at Nick as Sylvie and Nick gave her a moment to compose herself.

"G-good morning. Can I get you anything?" Her eyes moving from Sylvie to Nick and back again to Sylvie.

"That's okay, Marcy, I'll make us some tea. You carry on."

"The tea's in the pot, Mam." Nick coughed and slipped onto a bar stool, trying hard to contain his grin. Marcy stared at him, trying to fathom out what was so familiar about him, as Sylvie put out cups and saucers and then went to the fridge for milk.

"Hungry?" Sylvie turned to Nick, and his eyes were gleaming.

"Very."

"French toast?" Nick nodded and Marcy carried on staring. "Nick is Julian's son, Marcy." Marcy's eyes nearly popped out of her head as she realised that it was Julian that he reminded her of.

"Oh… um… I see." She furrowed her brow as she processed everything. Then in true Marcy fashion, she blurted out, "You look just like your father."

Nick let a small smile curl at his lips and he took a deep breath. "So I've been told." Sylvie had pulled out a bowl and cracked three eggs into it. She poured their tea and handed a cup to Nick. Marcy mechanically reached into the drawer and picked up a whisk to hand it to Sylvie.

"Thank you, baby," Nick said softly to Sylvie.

Marcy gasped and dropped the whisk onto the floor making it clatter. "I'm so sorry… I… oh… how clumsy." She was mortified. Nick grinned and Sylvie reached down to pick it up, glaring at Nick.

"That's okay, Marcy. Here, why don't you sit down and have some tea?" Sylvie placed the whisk on the counter and pushed her a cup and saucer next to where Nick was sitting, effectively telling her to sit down next to Nick. Marcy nodded nervously and walked round the counter and sat down, allowing her eyes to drift up to Nick. "I'm sorry, Marcy, maybe I should have warned you. About Nick, I mean." Sylvie poured her some tea and she looked up at Sylvie. "It's only been a couple of weeks, so I didn't want anyone to know." Sylvie's eyes were soft as she looked at the now-slightly-flushed Marcy.

"So you… and Nick are… um…?" Sylvie scrunched her nose and nodded. Marcy sighed, trying to think of what to say next. Then she furrowed her brow and asked, "Do the boys know?"

Sylvie smiled, knowing that Marcy's main concern was always her boys. "Yes, I told them yesterday."

Marcy sighed, deeply relieved, then she turned to Nick. "Sorry about that," she apologised.

"Nothing to apologise for, Marcy." He picked up his cup, ignoring the handle, and took a gulp. Sylvie started to beat the eggs and then she splashed some milk in the bowl and started to beat them again. Marcy got up and walked back to where Sylvie was, having regained her composure. She gently took the whisk out of Sylvie's hand and squeezed her round the shoulders.

"Let me do that, Mam. You'll get yourself dirty."

Sylvie patted her arm and gave her a knowing smile. "Thanks, Marcy." Sylvie moved out of the kitchen and sat next to Nick. "How many slices, Mr Nick?"

Startled, Nick looked up at Marcy. "Umm… please just call me Nick. I'm not sure."

"Make six, Marcy. He eats like a bloody horse," laughed Sylvie.

"Six it is, then … Nick. You two go out on the terrace, I'll bring them out to you."

Sylvie slid off the stool and walked towards the French doors leading out to the terrace, carrying her cup and saucer.

"Thanks, Marcy." Nick jumped down and followed, leaving his saucer behind him.

He'd never been out there before and he was amazed at the view and sheer size of the back garden. The terrace had a table which comfortably sat twelve. There was a fireplace and a huge built-in barbecue with gas rings and a fridge. It was a fully equipped outside kitchen. There were steps down to a huge pool which looked like it was once fenced off but had now had the fence removed. Small pathways meandered down to different levels and in the distance Nick could see a small orchard.

"It's amazing, Sylvie."

"Thanks. We've been modifying it over the years to suit our needs."

"What's that?" Nick motioned to an extended part of the house.

"That's where the boys have their drums and guitars. I wanted to make it into games room so that they could have it like a den, maybe put in a pool table, table tennis table, even. But I just haven't had time to get round to it. I never get any peace when they're home. They hog the sitting room with that god-awful PlayStation and I end up going to my room."

"I can't get over how big it is." They'd sat down at the table. "Do you use the pool a lot?"

Sylvie nodded. "I swim nearly every day. We've connected it up to a solar heater so it warms up in the cooler months." Nick nodded, impressed. "When the boys were young, we had it fenced off. I suppose we'll need to fence it off again when they have kids." Sylvie mused. Nick took her hand and kissed the palm softly and Sylvie turned to him. It felt so right, him sitting here with her. Nick brushed back her hair.

"You look so beautiful." Sylvie screwed her nose up shyly.

Marcy coughed as she stepped through the French doors holding a tray. She made her way over to the table and placed the tray laden with French toast, syrup, jam and Nutella. There was also more tea and some fruit salad.

"The fruit's for me," Sylvie explained. "Thanks, Marcy."

"Yeah, thanks, Marcy."

"It's a pleasure, Mam. Nick." She quickly turned round and left them alone.

"She's really sweet. She cares for you."

Sylvie nodded. "I know. We've been through a lot together. Like I said, I really don't need her, but she's like family. At least now the boys are home she'll be busy again. They run her ragged sometimes, but she loves it."

"She's seems okay. I mean about me being here."

Sylvie laughed. "Yes, well, give her time. She'll quiz you without any regard for boundaries. She's fiercely loyal and she'll let you know exactly how she feels about you." Nick raised his eyebrows. He decided he liked Marcy a lot. Anyone who looked after Sylvie and had her back was okay in his book. Nick dug into his toast, drenching it in syrup and Sylvie picked at her fruit salad.

Sylvie sat at her desk going over the last of her emails. The last email was from a new client asking her to design a new boutique. Since Celle's opening, Sylvie had had a number of inquiries. This one, however, interested her, as it was in one of the most prestigious hotels. It could possibly lead to redesigning a lot more within the hotel. She was interrupted by Zach popping his head through the gap in her door.

"Ready, darling?" He beamed.

Sylvie looked at the time. It was five past ten. *Shit, her meeting!* "Just finishing off." She wasn't looking forward to being in a confined space with Julian. Well, at least Zach would be there to defuse any tension. "Is Julian here?"

"Yeah, he's been here for about a quarter of an hour."

Oh! "Sorry, I'll be there in a minute." *Strange – he didn't even come to say hi.* Sylvie quickly rechecked her reply and then pressed 'Send'.

Julian was sitting at the conference table, reading what looked like a surveyor's report. He was wearing a light blue shirt, which echoed the tone in his eyes and a pair of faded jeans. He absent-mindedly ran his fingers through his hair and as Sylvie walked towards him, he looked up and removed his glasses, smiling cautiously. *Holy mother of…*

"Morning, Sylvie." Her thoughts were abruptly interrupted. He stood up immediately and dropped the report, purposefully stepping from behind the table he held out his hand for her to shake, which she took. Then, after a second he gently leaned to kiss her cheek. His ever-present designer stubble grazed her. Sylvie stiffened slightly but Julian didn't seem to notice. Zach watched the exchange over his computer screen, then he rose up to join them at the table.

"Morning, Julian." Sylvie's voice was soft.

"You look beautiful as ever." His eyes fixed on hers as he spoke. *Holy mother of…* "Here, sit down." He pulled out the chair to the left of where he was sitting. Sylvie steadied her breathing. *God it was uncanny!* Why couldn't she get used to the similarities and why had she never noticed them before?

"Er… thank you," muttered Sylvie. *Oh God, charming Julian was back!* What had happened to the sheepish one? Sheepish Julian was *so* much easier to handle. This meeting was going to be very awkward. Sylvie lowered herself in the chair and Zach came over to sit himself opposite her.

"Well, the good news is, the planning permission will be through by Monday, so Yiannis will be able to get cracking and put our team together." Zach looked thoroughly pleased with himself.

"How did you swing that so fast?" Julian had sat down leaning back on his chair.

"Yiannis knows someone there so he pulled some strings."

"Yiannis?" Sylvie didn't realise her contractor knew Zach.

"Yiannis, our quantity surveyor," answered Zach.

Sylvie forgot he was also called Yiannis. It was hard to keep up. There were so many people she still didn't have much to do with. "Hang on a minute, so we have Yiannis my contractor, Yiannis the quantity surveyor and Yiannis our foreman!" Sylvie shook her head.

Zach laughed out loud. "I know, it's ridiculous! They all have the same name."

"We're going to have to differentiate, otherwise it's going to get very confusing."

Zach shook his head and shrugged. "I think you may be right. Julian's just been going over the surveyor's report on that plot we put a bid in for."

"Oh, okay. Is everything alright with that?"

Zach beamed and looked over at Julian who was smirking. "Tell her, then." Zach said impatiently. Sylvie looked puzzled as she looked back to Julian.

"They've accepted the offer we put in. So once the papers are drawn up, we'll be going to the land registry sometime next week."

"Oh that's great news!" Sylvie was relieved, they'd gone back and forth with offers and she'd been worried they may lose it. She fleetingly realised that meant she probably wouldn't be able to get away. Her heart sunk at the idea.

"Uh-huh. Tell her the rest." Zach encouraged Julian, his enthusiasm obvious.

"It would seem that the land registry made a mistake when they initially looked at the zoning of the land. Originally, they allowed only twenty-five houses to be built, but it would seem that the way the land has been zoned, we'll be able to build another eight or ten."

"That's brilliant news!" Sylvie cried. "That means the profits will be a lot more." Zach nodded, his face alight.

"It's a big project. We're going to have to expand a bit."

Sylvie's looked over to Zach as she could see he was thrilled at the opportunity but she sensed his hesitance. This would be a huge project for him and the first of its kind. She knew he'd be feeling daunted without Chris there to help him.

"We'll do fine, Zach." She reached over and clasped his hand. "You'll just have to teach me a lot more." He squeezed her hand and grinned back.

Thankfully, the meeting seemed to go by quickly. They had a lot to go through and before they realised, it was twelve. Julian sat back in his chair, stretching his neck and shoulders. He removed his glasses and rubbed his eyes. "We've a busy few months ahead. I need to start on the plans for the houses so we can get planning passed before Christmas." Sylvie nodded, finding it hard not to stare as he picked up his coffee cup, ignoring the handle. "Did Maggie tell you about the house?" His comment brought her back out of her trance.

"Er… yes… um… I told her we'd discuss it next week once the bedroom's finished."

"Good." He smiled at her, then reached over to her left hand. The gesture startled her, but Julian didn't seem to care. "Nice ring."

Sylvie felt herself heat up. "I bought it in Athens."

"It's very… you." *Holy crap!* He let her hand go and got up from the table, gathering his papers and putting them into his briefcase. "I'll be off, then. We'll get together early next week for an update. Call me if you need me for anything else." Julian bent down and kissed Sylvie's cheek. Sylvie consciously held her breath, then let it out slowly as he straightened up.

"Bye, Sylvie, it's… nice to have you back. See you Zach."

"See you," called Zach from his desk.

Sylvie sat frozen for a moment, staring at her ring, her heart racing. "You okay, Sylvie?" Zach had come back to the table and sat beside her.

"Yes." She turned to him and forced a smile, swallowing hard and trying desperately to find an equilibrium between her thumping chest and her overactive mind.

"Things are moving quite fast. I think we'll need to get a project manager. You can't be running around for everything. And I'm not ready to take on much more."

"You might be right. I'll get HR to see if we can find someone," he replied.

"Are you alright with everything? I mean, it's our first new projects, the office block and now this residential project."

"To be honest, I'm a little bit on autopilot. Just working through everything. If I think about it too much, I think I'd be more than a little worried by it all. They are big investments and even though they'll be profitable in the long run, we're going to be stretched."

Sylvie took his hand and squeezed it. "Zach, you really are doing great. This past nine months have been… I know you miss him, especially on days like today." Zach shrugged embarrassedly. She decided to change the subject, as she could see he was feeling uneasy. Zach didn't *do* feelings very well! "I might be getting a new design job soon."

"Maggie's?"

"No, the new boutique at The Meridian." He raised his eyebrows in admiring surprise.

"So you won't do Maggie's?"

"I'm not sure…" She paused, wondering whether she should talk to him now. What the hell! It was now or never. If Nick decided to spill everything over the weekend, she wanted Zach to be prepared. "Zach, I need to tell you something," Sylvie sighed.

"Is this about Julian?"

"Sort of."

"He seemed okay today. Did anything happen?"

"Yes, but that's not what I want to tell you." Sylvie shifted, feeling decidedly nervous.

He looked so anxious. "He made a pass at you?" he asked cautiously.

"Zach, it really doesn't matter. That's not what… well, it's not important." Zach furrowed his brow and Sylvie took a deep breath. How was she going to tell him?

"Sylvie? What is it?" Sylvie closed her eyes in an attempt to calm herself. Her heart was racing. Why was this so hard to tell Zach? She looked at his worried face and realised she wanted him to be okay with this. They'd been through so much together over the past months and his opinion was so important to her, she prayed he wouldn't judge. This was so much harder than telling Alex and Markus.

"Zach, I've met someone." He cocked his head to the side and his expression changed from worried to sceptical. "It's new, but I've really fallen for him and he makes me very happy." He continued to look at her, obviously finding it hard to respond. Sylvie swallowed hard, her mouth feeling dry. "The thing is, because of who it is, I feel I need to prepare you, because… well, things may get awkward…"

"You've met someone? When?" He ignored the last part as he was still trying to comprehend what he was hearing.

"I've known him for a few months but we've only recently become… involved." Zach's eyebrows shot up and he seemed to look embarrassed.

"Sylvie, that's great really… I mean… the boys, how have they taken it?"

"They're trying to adjust to it." Sylvie looked down at her hands.

"Well… um… I hope he's worthy of you. You don't need my approval, you know that, but thank you for letting me know."

"Zach, it's a little more complicated."

"Complicated? How?" Zach pursed his lips together.

Sylvie shifted nervously. "It's Nick, Zach."

"Nick?" He looked at her bemused, obviously not piecing together the puzzle. "Nick who?"

"Nick Steed. Julian's son," Sylvie whispered.

Zach's eyes narrowed at first as he processed the information, then they widened into shock. "Julian's Nick?" His hand slowly went up to his mouth as he began to appreciate the enormity of what he had just been told. "How? When?"

"We got to know each other over the past four months while I was up at Maggie's, and then one thing led to another, and…"

"Julian doesn't know?" Sylvie shook her head. "Maggie?" She shook her head again. "I don't understand, Sylvie. I mean, when…" He rubbed his eyes with his forefinger and thumb, then rested his chin on his hand. Taking a deep breath, he softly spoke. "Julian's going to freak out."

"I know," Sylvie replied quietly.

"No, I mean it, Sylvie. I mean *totally* freak out. He's in love with you, you know that? He thinks you'll come round. This… this is going to hit him hard. It'll kill him."

"I know. That's why I wanted you to know. Nick wants to tell his parents this weekend and it's going to make work difficult. That's why I wanted you to hire a project manager, so I can lay low for a bit."

"Sylvie, fuck work, we'll muddle through that. I'm more worried about you and how Julian's going to react." He paused, trying to find the right words. "Look, it's really none of my business, but have you thought this through? I mean, he's a lot younger than you. I don't mean to be, well… you know… um…"

"You're right. He is and that's all I think about, Zach. Right now it's… it's so… Well, it's wonderful, and yet I keep thinking that we really don't have a future. But he has told me from the beginning that it doesn't bother him, the age thing. He just wants to be with me."

"Alex and Markus are alright with this?"

"They know about it and they are willing to try, for my sake."

"They're good kids, Sylvie."

"They are, and I know they're worried that I'll get hurt. So am I, to be honest. It's so complicated, and so many people are affected. I wanted to keep it from everyone until I was sure, but Nick wants it out in the open. I'm worried how this will affect him. I know he'll get the brunt of it from Julian and I don't want to be the cause of them falling out." Sylvie held her forehead. The more she thought about it, the more she knew it was going to be a lot worse than she imagined. Zach's comments had confirmed her worse fears.

She looked over at Zach and he was watching her pensively. "What is it, Zach?" He shook his head as if he didn't want to say. "Just say it, Zach. At this stage, nothing you can say will offend me."

"How did you two get together? I mean… I didn't even realise you knew him that well."

"I met him up at Maggie's. He was there every time I went up. Then, with the wedding as well, we just built up a friendship. Then on the night of Celle's opening, he was there." Sylvie shifted round to face Zach. "Dina was there that night."

"Dina? You never told me." Zach's face dropped.

"I know. Well, as you can well imagine, it shook me up. Nick was there that night and came over to say hi. I was a shaking mess and he realised something had upset me so he offered to take me home."

"And?"

Sylvie sighed and felt herself flush. "Well he told me that he had feelings for me and that he'd had them for a long time, but hadn't wanted to act on them because of Julian."

"So you felt the same way?" Sylvie nodded.

"I just thought he was out of my league, and the age thing."

Zach snorted. "Well it certainly explains why you're looking so good. He obviously has a positive effect on you. And what do you mean 'out of your league'?" He leaned over and took her hands. "Do you want a future with him?"

"Yes, but I don't see how." She sighed. "I have to be realistic, Zach. I'm worried I'll get hurt. Or, worse, I'll hurt him and the other people around us."

"Sylvie, darling there's risks in every relationship."

"I know, but at this stage in my life, I want to minimise them. I can't take more heartache."

Zach got up and wrapped his arms around her. "No one can tell you what to do, darling. This is your call, but whatever you decide, you know I'll support you." He stroked her head as she held him, her eyes welling up with tears. "Hey, don't cry, darling. I hate seeing you cry." She got off the chair and sat on the floor. Zach sat beside her, cradling her in his arms. Zach sighed and looked around, slightly shaking his head to himself. He had an overwhelming feeling of déjà vu.

"Zach I don't know what I'd have done without you." Sylvie sniffed. "You know I love you, don't you?" He smiled against her head and squeezed her tighter.

"I know, darling, and I love you."

18

CURIUM

"Hi sweetie, how you doing?" *Thank goodness she had Lilianna,* thought Sylvie.

"Not bad. You?"

"Oh you know, same shit, different day," Lilianna laughed.

Lilianna could always make her smile, thought Sylvie as she drove along the highway and headed home. "I thought you should know I told Zach about Nick."

"Oh! How was he?"

"Shocked. He thinks Julian's going to freak."

"I think so too, sweetie. Sorry." Sylvie sighed. "Where are you?"

"I'm on the way home."

"So early?"

"I promised the boys I'd go to the beach with them today. Markus is trying out a new kite board."

"Good. It'll take your mind off it."

"Maybe. I'll call you later."

"Sylvie, don't worry so much and stop feeling guilty. I know you. I haven't seen you this happy in a long time. The boys will come round. Julian's going to have to lump it. You can't choose who you fall in love with."

"I know. Thanks, Lily."

"Anytime, sweetie. Bye."

Sylvie pulled into her drive, parked up in the garage, then took her phone off the hands-free. She needed to call Nick. She just wanted to hear his voice. She pressed his number and waited for it to connect.

"Hi baby," Nick answered softly, making Sylvie's heart skip a beat.

"Hi."

"You okay?" Nick asked tentatively.

"Yes, I'm fine."

"You don't sound fine. What is it?"

Sylvie sighed. *I had a weird morning and it looks like your father's going to go nuts when he finds out!* "Nothing, really. I just came home. Are you still going to Curium?" Sylvie changed the subject.

"Yes. I just spoke to Markus. I told him I'd be there in about an hour. Are you going to come?"

"Yes, I came home to change."

"Good. So I'll see you there, then?"

"Yes."

"Sylvie?" He sounded wary. After a few seconds, he continued. "Don't do this. I know it's hard. Did you talk to Zach? Is that what's wrong?" His voice was full of concern. He knew how important Zach was to her. If Zach disapproved, it would make everything much harder.

"Yes, I told him today. He was shocked, understandably. But he just wants me to be happy." Nick allowed himself to feel a little more comfortable as he realised another hurdle had been crossed.

"So what is it, then? Sylvie, I can't bear it that you won't just tell me."

"Can we talk about this later? It's been a tough morning. Actually, it's been a tough few days. I really don't want to talk about it right now. I'm sorry, I just need a breather. It's all too much."

Nick sighed. The last thing he wanted was to add to the already rising pressure. "Sure. I'll see you down there, then?"

"Yes. Bye."

"Bye, baby."

Sylvie sat for a few minutes in the car holding her head. She kept thinking about what Zach had said and she couldn't shake off that feeling of dread. Deep down, she knew that even though everyone so far had been at best happy, and at worst, tolerant of her situation, she knew that when Julian and Maggie found out, this false sense of security she was experiencing would be shattered. The fallout would be far worse than any of them were expecting. Sylvie held on to the hope that maybe, just maybe, Julian would see past his own feelings.

"Mum? Are you okay?" Markus was standing in the garage doorway looking down at her.

"Darling. Sorry, I was miles away." Sylvie quickly forced a smile as she looked up at him. "Yes. I thought I'd join you if that's okay?"

"Cool."

"I'll just go and change." Markus beamed as she collected her brief-case. "Nick's going to meet us there." He opened the car door for her as she closed the roof of her car.

"Yes, he told me. Thanks for trying." She stepped out of the car and hugged him.

"He's alright, Mum." He hugged her back.

"Yes he is."

Markus parked up his pickup truck on the stones at Curium beach. Alex jumped out of the car and Sylvie opened her door. She scanned the beach but couldn't see Nick's Jeep. There were already a few kite boarders in the sea. Sylvie marvelled at them as they rapidly flew along the waves, then jumped up into the sky and landed expertly into the sea again.

Markus was pulling his board out of the back when he yelled out.

"Look! That's Nick, isn't it, Mum?" Both Alex and Sylvie looked to where Markus was pointing out to sea. Just past the red markers was a white speedboat. Nick was standing at the wheel as he drove it down closer to shore.

"Yes it is." Sylvie shook her head in disbelief. She didn't realise he had a speedboat too. Nick dropped the anchor, then swung out of the boat and gracefully dropped into the sea up to his thighs. He looked dreamy in just his swimming trunks. Sylvie's most favourite view, Nick wet and half-naked. He came out on to shore running his hands through his hair. Sylvie leaned up against the truck in a feeble attempt to look casual. It took all her strength not to run down and throw herself at him.

"Hey, Nick." Alex came round, effectively blocking Sylvie from Nick's view.

"Hi Alex. Markus." Nick looked over to Alex. "You're not going to have a go, then?" Alex was dressed in shorts and a T-shirt.

"No, that's definitely Markus's department. I'll sit here and watch with Mum."

Markus had come round to where they were standing. "Hi, Nick. Wind's perfect today. Did you bring your board?"

"Yeah, it's in the boat. Let me just say hi to your mum and we'll get started." Alex stiffened slightly, then nodded.

Before he could move out of the way Sylvie stepped forward past both Alex and Markus and headed towards Nick. His eyes widened slightly as she leaned down and kissed him on the side of his mouth. Nick hesitated for a second, then he put his arms around her waist squeezing her up against him. Sylvie pulled back to look at him. Markus and Alex stood for a moment transfixed, then hurriedly walked passed them to the shore, no doubt feeling awkward and embarrassed.

"Hi."

"Hi, what happened to no PDA?" whispered Nick, as he stroked her cheek with the back of his hands, his eyes searching her face as she looked into his now-sparkling eyes.

"I missed you… a lot." And she meant it from the very depths of her being. This morning had brought her into the reality of what her life was. Complicated with a capital C. She was determined to make the most of what precious time they both had together. Lilianna had been right. She should stop feeling guilty and she should stop overthinking everything.

"Me too. Are you wearing a swimsuit under those?" Sylvie nodded. "Good. Though I'm not sure I'll be able to keep my hands off you." He arched his eyebrows suggestively. "After here, I'll take you back to the *Silver Lining*."

Sylvie smiled shyly and Nick bent down and kissed her gently on the lips. Sylvie caught Alex and Markus looking wide-eyed over at them and she pulled back. *Crap!* Nick instantly dropped his hands, understanding her reason for her sudden coolness.

"I didn't know you had a speed boat too." Sylvie spoke hurriedly, clearly embarrassed.

Nick turned to the sea to where he'd anchored it. "Yes. She's my first boat. I use her for short trips. I'll take you on her later. You can drive her. Brush up on that licence you never used."

Sylvie grinned, relaxing again. She felt like a teenager being caught out by her parents. "Sounds great."

"Okay, I'll go and get my board. I think Alex and Markus have been more than patient." He grinned, then ran back to the shore and into the sea.

Sylvie and Alex sat on the pebbly beach watching as Nick and Markus flew across the sea on the waves, jumping high, then gracefully landing back down.

"They're good," commented Alex. He'd taken off his T-shirt and was leaning back on his elbows. Sylvie had discarded her shorts and T-shirt and was sitting up, leaning back on her hands in a turquoise bikini. She pulled her hair into a loose ponytail as the wind was blowing her hair around.

"Yes, I'd love to be able to do that," she mused.

"You should get Nick to teach you."

"I think I'm too old for that, Alex." As she said the words, she felt herself flush. *Not only too old for kite boarding*, she thought to herself.

Alex pressed his lips together and sat up so he was the same level as Sylvie. "He really loves you, Mum." His voice was gentle. Sylvie turned to look at him and he smiled at her. "Anyone can see that. I'm not saying it's comfortable for me to witness, because it's not. But he's really nuts about you."

"I feel the same way, Alex, and I'm sorry if that's hard for you and Markus to accept but I don't want to lie to you. Thanks for trying, though. I mean, I know it can't be easy. I'll try not to rub it in your face."

"Mum, I only want you to be happy. My reservations about Nick were that he'd hurt you, but I can see he's not that kind of person. He's putting your feelings above his. I can see that just in the last day. I mean, he didn't need to do this today, did he? He's doing it for you and that's… well, you know."

Sylvie put her arm around him and squeezed him. "I want you guys to get along. You and Markus are everything to me and I want you in this part of my life too."

Markus and Nick collected up their boards and started to fold up the kite. Nick waded into the water and pushed his board into his speedboat.

Markus strapped his into the back of his truck. "I'm starving, Mum. Shall we go down to Blue Beach and have some dinner?"

"Sure, what time is it?"

"It's nearly six. Let me ask Nick if he's up for it." Markus ran down to the shore as Nick was coming back out of the water.

"We're thinking of having dinner at Blue Beach. You coming?"

"Sure. I'll drive down there. Alex, you want to come in the boat? I'll teach you how to drive it." Alex looked over to his mum, a little embarrassed.

"Go on. I'll go with Markus in the truck."

"Okay." He got up nervously.

"Give me your sneakers and roll up your shorts so they don't get too wet." Sylvie stood up and held out her hand for his shoes as he awkwardly slipped them off and handed them to her. "Look, if I can do it, you can." She grinned and smacked him playfully on his back. Alex grinned sheepishly and Sylvie was transported back to when Alex was five years old again, grinning cheekily at her. Did mothers ever see their children as anything other than small, however old they got?

Sylvie slipped on her shorts and waved to them both as Nick helped Alex get on the boat. Nick waved back and blew her a kiss. She flushed, then turned and made her way back to the truck.

Markus was drying himself off, then he dragged on his T-shirt. "That was awesome, Mum." Markus was beaming. "He's alright, is Nick."

Sylvie laughed. "What, because he can kite board?"

"Not just that, Mum. But that helps." He chuckled. "Come on. I want to beat Alex down there. You know he'll be driving like an old lady!" They got into the truck and Markus span it round and headed down to the restaurant.

Of course, they reached it well before Nick and Alex. Sylvie and Markus sat out on the veranda looking out over the sea. The restaurant was a favourite of theirs. They'd spent most of their summers on the beach here. The waiter brought them the menus and they ordered their drinks along with salad and dips. Sylvie scanned the sea, trying to see where Nick and Alex were.

She spotted them going out deeper into the sea and she sat up, leaning forward. *Crap, where were they going?* The speedboat curved round in a semi-circle, then headed towards the shore. As it came closer, Sylvie recognised Alex at the wheel and Nick was pointing to the left of the boat. Alex nodded, then accelerated, turning the boat to the left in a tighter semi-circle, making the sea splash up in a high wave. He eased off the accelerator, then turned it a full circle. Sylvie could see he was beaming. He then slowly came back towards the shore, down the red bobbing markers, and stopped ten metres from the shore. Nick slapped him on the back and Alex awkwardly grinned at him. Once they'd dropped the anchor, they both jumped out of the boat and waded out to shore. They were talking animatedly to each other as they made their way up the stairs to the veranda of the restaurant.

"He's a natural, Sylvie." Sylvie handed Nick a towel to dry himself off. He took the towel and rapidly dried his legs and torso. *Oh hell.*

Sylvie dragged her eyes off Nick's abdominals and turned to Alex. "How was it?" She handed Alex another, his face glowing.

"It was brilliant, Mum, and you feel like you're going so fast, but it's not as fast as you think." Alex couldn't hide his enthusiasm.

"I think you gave Mum a heart attack!" Markus laughed, having witnessed her shifting in her seat all the time she was watching them.

Nick sat down next to Sylvie and she instinctively leaned towards him. Without thinking, Nick draped his arm along the back of her chair and let his fingers gently stroke her shoulder. Alex sat down opposite them and poured himself some water, trying his damnedest not to stare.

The waiter came over and they ordered some beers and then decided on the fish meze for dinner. Their dinner progressed as the three men talked incessantly about their afternoon, Sylvie enjoying the fact that they seemed to be getting along. This afternoon had most certainly broken the ice and they actually had a lot in common. Well, Nick was closer to their age than hers, so it seemed only logical that they would find a multitude of topics to talk about.

Sylvie picked at her food as they were discussing a new film that was coming out. Nick looked at her plate. "Are you okay baby?" Sylvie nodded slightly. "Your stomach?" She scrunched her nose in response. "Promise me you'll go to the doctor next week." He gently smoothed her hair off her face as he spoke.

"She's always had a dodgy stomach. Always popping antacids," Alex chipped in.

"I'm fine, really." Sylvie didn't want to spoil their dinner.

"Fine! Eighty percent of the time you're suffering." Nick sounded exasperated.

"I know, she just suffers, and the doctor gave her some pills but she doesn't take them." Markus rolled his eyes as he spoke. *Nice! Now they were ganging up on her!*

"Why won't you take them, Sylvie?" Nick looked at her, puzzled.

"It's just stress. I don't want to be taking pills for stress. They make me feel like a zombie." She muttered. It was true. Whenever she was stressed, her stomach always suffered and so her doctor prescribed a relaxant which made her feel drowsy, but she had no stomach pains or retching. So she preferred to live with the cramps.

"Oh, baby." Nick's brow knitted and he put his arm around her, pulling her to him. Alex and Markus sat back, almost giving them space for this sudden intimate moment. Nick kissed her forehead. "All this isn't helping is it? Just take something until all this gets sorted out, I hate seeing you suffer."

Sylvie nodded. "Okay," she whispered.

He reluctantly let her go and looked over to Alex and Markus, a little embarrassed, realising he'd acted instinctively, forgetting they were there. "Sorry guys," he muttered.

"No problem. S'okay," they mumbled back. They leaned forward again and continued with their dinner. Nick called the waiter over and ordered a sparkling mineral water. Once it arrived, he handed it to Sylvie.

"It'll help." He picked up her hand and kissed her knuckles. Sylvie nodded and took a sip.

Of course they managed to finish all the food, all twenty-four dishes and dessert. Sylvie sat with her third mineral water. Her stomach had settled thankfully and she'd managed to eat a little sea bream and chips.

The sun was beginning to set and the beach was emptying. Nick discreetly paid the bill and returned to the table.

"Is it okay if I take your mum home, guys?" He looked at Alex and Markus who were getting up.

"Er… sure, Nick," Markus answered, his eyes rested on Sylvie. Nick looked at Alex.

"Sure, we'll see you later, Mum."

"Are you going out tonight?" Sylvie collected her bag as she spoke.

"Yeah, we're meeting up with some friends," Alex answered.

"Okay, have fun."

"See you, Nick. Thanks for today. It was fun."

"Any time. When I get back from France I'll have more time, so we can go out more." He looked first at Alex, then Markus, and added, "If you like?"

"Cool." Markus replied.

"Sure." Alex shrugged, then smiled.

It was almost dark by the time they pulled up to the quay. Nick had let Sylvie drive the boat back, showing her how to manoeuvre it into the marina and then up to the quay. As they floated up to the dockside, Nick jumped down and quickly tied it up, then went over to help Sylvie down. He slipped his arm around her waist and pulled her close. She put her arm around him and slipped her thumb into his waistband.

They walked over to the *Silver Lining* which was beside the speedboat. Nick climbed up on board, then reached down and pulled Sylvie off the quay up next to him.

Once they were on the deck, Nick pressed her close to him and kissed her, grasping her head, then moving down to wrap his arms around her. She moaned as he enfolded her in his arms and kissed her harder as she moved her hands up his bare chest to his hair.

"I need to get you inside," Nick breathed against her neck.

"Uh-huh," Sylvie agreed. "It's so dark out here." Nick pulled out his keys and took her hand as he made his way to the door. He unlocked it and opened it as fast as possible. He let Sylvie step in first, then following her in, he flicked on the lights, closing and bolting the door behind him.

Julian had pulled up into the car park at the marina. It was eight-fifteen. He thought he'd pass and see Nick on the off-chance before he headed home. He closed his car door and sauntered down to quay eight. The lights hadn't come on and it was dark. Looking towards where the *Silver Lining* was moored, he saw Nick helping a young woman onto the deck. Julian stopped. *This must be the girl he was involved with*, thought Julian, and he smiled to himself. They were quite a distance away and he couldn't see what she was like in the dark and there were no lights on the yacht. Julian squinted hard to see if he could make out who it was, but then Nick kissed her, obstructing Julian's view. He then watched as Nick guided her into his yacht and then once inside Julian saw the lights turn on. Well, it looked like he'd need to head off home, he chuckled to himself. Whoever she was, it was obvious Nick was smitten. The intensity of that kiss alone proved it. Julian walked back to his car and headed back to his empty apartment.

Once inside, Nick pulled Sylvie up to him and stroked her face gently. "How are you feeling?"

She slipped her arms around his waist. "I'm fine, Nick. Really, please don't fuss." His mouth curled into a smile.

"Okay, let me have a shower. I'm all salty." He made an attempt to move but Sylvie tightened her hold on him. He cocked his head to one side.

"You can shower after." She fixed him with her eyes and his face changed from amused to wide-eyed elation.

"After?"

Sylvie leaned up to his ear and whispered, "Yes, after. Take me to bed."

Nick groaned. "You're the boss." In a split-second, he scooped her up in his arms and carried her through to his bedroom. Sylvie draped her arms around his neck and nuzzled his chest, softly kissing him and tasting the salty sea that had crystallized on his chest hair. He gently set her down in front of the bed. Sylvie ran her hands over his chest again and pulled him to her, holding his neck as she kissed him hard. Nick's hands reached for her bikini top and he pulled the string free, then he unclipped the back fastening and pulled the top lose, dropping it to the floor.

"Oh Sylvie," Nick gasped. He pulled at her shorts, yanking them down, taking her bikini bottoms with them. She stepped out of them, along with her flip-flops. Crouched down, he planted feather-like kisses up her stomach, rising as he trailed up to her breasts, kissing and sucking gently as she fisted her hands in his hair.

"You smell so good. Do you have any idea how much you turn me on?" he murmured, as he made his way up to her neck. Sylvie shook her head in response. "Jesus, I want you." Sylvie groaned and pushed her hands into the waistband of his swimming trucks, slowly moving them down until they dropped to the floor. Sylvie trailed kisses down his salty chest until she reached that muscle, that gloriously sexy muscle at his hip. Nick moaned as Sylvie gently bit him. "Fuck!"

"You taste salty," she breathed against his hip and he flexed himself.

"Fuck, Sylvie, you're killing me here," he pleaded, his hands in her hair. Painstakingly slowly, she kissed him across from one hip to the other and he trembled against her lips. Sylvie looked up at him through her lashes as his eyes burned down into hers. Then, slowly, she took him into her mouth as he closed his eyes, in pure unadulterated pleasure. He hissed through his teeth and she slowly but firmly moved her mouth up and down, taking him deeper every time. It was intoxicating to watch, his shoulder muscles flexed and he clenched his teeth momentarily looking down at her, then closing his eyes again.

"Oh baby!" She sucked harder as she felt him start to tense. "Stop, please. Ah! Sylvie!" and he pulled back, grabbing her from the shoulders and dragging her up to him and kissing her passionately. He kicked away his trunks and flip-flops, then lifted her onto the bed.

"You are so fucking beautiful." His eyes, white hot, eating her up as he gazed down at her, then kneeling down, he slowly started to kiss up her legs.

Sylvie groaned as she looked down at him moving up as she writhed on the bed.

"What is it?" he murmured against her hip. "I want to kiss you all over."

"Nick, please." Sylvie grasped at his hair but he gently took both her hands and held them as his tongue moved across from her hip and down. *Fuck!* Sylvie was so wired she knew she'd explode.

"Please what, baby?" he muttered against her skin, and slowly, Nick made his way down, his tongue expertly teasing the most sensitive part of her body.

"Oh Nick, ah!"

"I know baby." He carried on licking and teasing and Sylvie could feel herself surrendering. "Nick, please! I want you in me." Nick loosened her hands and moved up to her, claiming her mouth hard as he rested his elbows on either side of her face.

"God I love you, Sylvie. I could make love to you all night." And slowly he sank into her and Sylvie closed her eyes, relishing his fullness.

"AH!" She grasped onto his back as he began to move, pushing deeper as Sylvie clasped her legs up around him. "Is this what you wanted?" He looked down at her as she arched up, closing her eyes.

"Yes!" He continued to move push at first, savouring her, feeling her, as he kissed her neck, her shoulder and then back to her lips.

"Harder?" he murmured against her mouth as she gasped, breathing hard.

"Yes!" And he thrust deeper again and again. His eyes blazing as he watched her coming apart.

"Faster?" he cried through clenched teeth.

"Fuck yes!" And he thrust harder, over and over again. Faster and faster as she gripped onto his shoulders, crying out as she climaxed around him. Nick thrust once more time, groaning loudly as he too found his release, collapsing on the bed, rolling over and taking Sylvie with him, not breaking their contact.

"You're going to wear me out! Fuck!" He gasped for breath and his heart was pounding against his chest. Sylvie laughed and kissed his chest, running her tongue over the hairs on his chest.

"Salty and sexy," she mused. He shifted so he could see her.

"You're sweet and sexy." And he ran his hand down her back and squeezed her behind. "Stay with me tonight." He stroked her hair and kissed the top of her head as his breathing began to calm. "It's Friday. You don't need to get up for the office. Stay."

"I need to get up to your mum's in the morning. Check everything's okay."

"Then stay tonight and I'll take you home in the morning. Then you can go up." Sylvie tightened her hold on him. A thousand thoughts pushed their way into her mind. What would the boys think? Marcy – she'd work out where she'd been. She felt guilty that she was doing this for herself – she'd feel guilty if she didn't stay. The last thing she wanted was to upset Nick. He'd been so good to her boys today. She sighed and tried hard not to allow her constant nagging thoughts to spoil what had truly been a perfect afternoon.

Stop feeling guilty and don't overthink! What did she really want to do? Of course, she knew the answer. There was no place on earth she wanted to be, other than in Nick's arms and in his bed.

"Please, baby. Stay." Sylvie looked up at this beautiful young man who had turned her whole world upside down. Stretching up and sliding over so that she was lying fully along his whole body, she framed his face in her hands and bent down to kiss him softly. His eyes looked dreamy as he slowly closed them, then reopened them wide.

"Okay," she whispered, and his whole face lit up. *Wow!*

19

YOU INSECURE?

Sylvie woke with a start. It took her a few seconds to get her bearings as she took in her surroundings. Ah yes... the *Silver Lining*, last night. She smiled to herself. Last night had been... perfect. Nick had practically kept to his word. Well, he hadn't made love to her all night, but it had been around four in the morning by the time they'd eventually fallen asleep...

After Sylvie had made her decision to stay, Nick scooped her into the shower, making love to her slowly as the water cascaded around them. Then afterwards, he made some mushroom risotto and they ate it the living area slouched on the couch, Nick in his boxers and Sylvie in her T-shirt and bikini bottoms. Sylvie sat on his knee as they both ate out of the same bowl.

"This is so good, Nick. Where did you learn to cook? Maggie?"

"Some stuff, but mainly when I was in the South of France. Some people I knew worked in restaurants there, so I picked it up from them." He shrugged apologetically, his eyes a little wary as he spoke.

"Oh, the French hotties?" Sylvie tried hard to hide her pang of jealousy. Nick put down his fork and took hold of her chin turning her face to his.

"Hey, they didn't mean anything. They were just... a distraction. A way to forget. I can't even remember half their names."

Sylvie averted her eyes. "That many, eh?" *Of course there were many, look at him for God's sake!*

Nick lifted the bowl of risotto off her lap and placed it down on the coffee table. "It doesn't matter how many. I didn't feel anything for them, they were just… well… I know this sounds horrible and insensitive, but they were just a fuck. Nothing else."

Oh crap, did she really want to hear this? Sylvie closed her eyes, feeling an overwhelming urge to cry. *Fucked everything in sight!*

"Sylvie, what I feel for you, what we have, I've never felt before. I thought I did with Brigitte and to an extent Petra, but being with you has made me realise that what I had with them was… well it was small." He grasped her face. "Sylvie, don't think about my past. I don't. You shouldn't feel threatened by it. If I wanted that life, I would be living it. I don't. It's not who I am." He kissed her, gently stroking back her hair. "Sylvie, I love you. You own me. Heart, body and soul. Can't you feel that?" Sylvie looked deep into his cobalt eyes, overflowing with sincerity. "It should be me that feels insecure, not you." His brow furrowed as he spoke, then he shook his head as if he was trying to rid himself of an unwelcome thought.

"You? Why?" Sylvie stared wide-eyed at him.

Nick pursed his lips together, sighing. He kissed her quickly on the lips and sat back. "Never mind." He smiled stiffly and looked as if he wished he'd kept his thoughts to himself. Sylvie pulled back to look at him, tilting her head to one side. "Tell me, Nick. Why?"

"Look, I shouldn't have said anything. It's okay really, just forget it."

"Oh no, Nick. Now you've got me more than intrigued. Come on, what on earth could make you feel insecure where I'm concerned?" Sylvie's tone was incredulous, as if it was altogether impossible.

Nick closed his eyes, trying to find strength from somewhere.

"Nick, what is it?" Her tone softened, as she realised this was obviously difficult for him.

They sat in silence for a moment, then Nick spoke. "I'm competing with someone you had twenty-two years of marriage with. A history and a shed-load of memories. A business you both built up together, a home you created together and two children you brought up together. How can I ever compete with that, Sylvie? It's a whole lifetime. You are hung up on our age difference, or more the fact that I'm younger…" Sylvie slid off his knees and crossed her legs facing him. Nick turned to face her, tucking his ankle under his leg, then he pressed the top of his nose with his thumb and forefinger, closing his eyes. Nick took a deep breath and looked up at Sylvie. His eyes had clouded over and he looked anxiously at her as he spoke, unsure of whether he might be crossing a line, a very delicate and fragile line.

"You look at me and you think about my past. But that's exactly what it is: my past. It doesn't come back. Whatever's happened, it's gone. Finished. Done. But your past is with you all the time: your home, your business, your children. Yours and Chris's."

Sylvie gazed at him, her heart clenching as he opened up to her. He stopped for a minute as if evaluating whether he should continue. Sylvie reached over and stroked his stubbly chin.

He smiled weakly. "It's there all the time. And it's not like you got divorced. You didn't fall out of love with Chris – he died. You still loved him." He closed his eyes, his breathing shallow. Even worried and pensive, he was breath-taking. "That's why you feel so guilty all the time, and I get it. I understand. It's like you're being disloyal. But it doesn't make it easy for me. You look at me and you see the packaging, and that's what makes you feel insecure. I look at you and I see what's inside. That's what I love. How you think, what you feel, how you love and knowing that about you, seeing how you live your life, that's what makes me insecure. It's all part of your past. You still love Chris. He's still part of your life. The life you had with him was... it was large, huge. How am I ever going to compete? I'll never be able to catch up." He thought back to his father's words, *"How can I compete with a dead man?"* now appreciating the gravitas they carried.

Sylvie stared at him, lost for words, once again floored by his honesty. She'd never once thought of her past being so *present* in her present. It was true Chris was still everywhere in her life, but she hadn't realised how much Nick was affected by it until that moment.

Sylvie thought back over their trip to Athens. She realised now that throughout their time there, he'd tried to make it specific to them. Their trip to Sounion on a motorbike, for example. He knew she'd never been on one before and that the last time she'd been out there was when she'd been a child. He'd brought her a new briefcase, replacing Chris's old one. The time they'd spent in the museum and sightseeing: again, something she hadn't done recently with Chris, or even associated with him. And then now, his insistence that she stay here with him tonight, on his boat, in his surroundings. He'd tried subtly to make their time together have no ties to her ever-present past.

Today had been hard for him, but he'd still managed to put his unique mark on their day. Oh, and last night, dinner with Alex and Markus sitting in the lounge, in front of that photo of Chris and her. *Oh crap!* Her life with Chris was everywhere. How had she not seen it?

Nick watched her intently as she slowly put everything together. He'd told her that she still loved Chris and she knew that was true. But she also loved him. Surely he could feel that too. She'd been hurt by Chris and that had made her feel vulnerable, it had fuelled her insecurities and she still couldn't forgive him. She couldn't put that to rest, yet. Is that why she felt so guilty about Nick? Because she felt she was betraying Chris? This was all too much. Sylvie shook her head and swung round so she was sitting, her feet back on the floor and her head in her hands.

"I'm sorry, I shouldn't have said anything. You've got enough to deal with without me dumping my insecurities on you." He tentatively reached over to her and slowly stroked her back.

She turned to look at him and her heart twisted seeing him look so vulnerable, his face raw with emotion. "I need a drink," she muttered.

Nick nodded and went over to the kitchen and grabbed two glasses. He threw in some ice and then splashed some Chivas into both glasses. Sylvie watched him as he walked back to the couch and handed her a glass. She sat back and took a gulp, her eyes focused on Nick's. He sat back down, leaving his glass untouched on the table next to their half-eaten bowl of risotto. Fleetingly, Sylvie wondered why he had poured himself one. He never seemed to drink it. Maybe he poured it so she didn't feel like she was drinking alone. Dragging her thoughts back, she turned back to him.

"I never realised, Nick." Sylvie spoke softly and his gaze met hers, his eyes tense and his expression forlorn.

He knew that what he'd said would upset her, and that very thought made him feel wretched. He just hoped he hadn't pushed her too far. "Sylvie… look, I shouldn't have said anything. I need to get over it. You can't eliminate your past, or rub it out. It's part of who you are. I don't want you to do that." He was desperately trying not to make her feel worse. "In time it won't be like that – we'll have our own past." He stroked back her hair and gave her a reassuring smile.

"Is that why you bought me the briefcase?"

Nick's eyes widened slightly. "One of the reasons."

Sylvie nodded. "Is that why you wanted me to stay here, instead of at mine?"

Nick sighed and sucked on his top teeth.

Busted! "That's okay, Nick, I just wanted to know. I've been a little too wrapped up in my own insecurities to even think that you might have any." She took another large gulp, savouring the slight burning sensation in the back of her throat. Sylvie took a deep breath and thought back to Lilianna's words. *Don't feel guilty and don't overthink.*

Fuck it, she was right! "It's not just the packaging I like, Nick, by the way." She raised her eyebrow at him in a mock-scold. Nick's face visibly relaxed as the relief began to flow over him, thankful that she hadn't been upset by his confession. "I love what's on the inside too."

Nick shuffled up close to her, putting his hands on her face. "Well, I'm glad to hear it. I didn't figure you to be so shallow." He planted a wet kiss on her lips. Then licked his lips, indicating he liked how they tasted. "Second-hand Chivas is *sooo* much tastier than first-hand," he smirked. "And just so you know, your packaging is *the* most beautiful, gorgeous and downright sexy." He kissed her again harder, and Sylvie moaned against his mouth. He took her glass from her hand, placing it next to his, then gently pushed her down onto the couch, his hands running up under her T-shirt, squeezing her as they moved up to her breasts. "So fucking sexy," he breathed against her neck. Sylvie groaned, clenching her fists in his hair, temporarily forgetting everything as she allowed herself to be overwhelmed with pure unadulterated desire for this incredible man.

They had eventually ended back in the bedroom. Sylvie stretched and searched for her watch to see what time it was. Ten-thirty! Crap. How was this happening? She never slept that late. Sylvie jumped out of bed and felt herself sway. *Shit.* She abruptly sat back on the bed to regain her balance and felt her stomach start to retch. *Oh no!* Saliva pooled in her mouth and she felt that oh-so-familiar horrible feeling as she staggered to the bathroom. She just made it to the sink as she heaved up what little was in her stomach, gripping the edge of the sink.

"Jesus, Sylvie, are you okay?" Nick rushed to her side, having heard her, but she pushed him back.

"You don't need to see this!" she coughed, spitting into the sink and turning on the taps.

"Don't be ridiculous." He stood firm and rubbed her back. "Here, use my toothbrush." Sylvie nodded weakly and then splashed cold water on her face.

"I'm okay now, really. I got up too fast and the swaying of the boat…" Nick was putting toothpaste on his brush and he handed it to her. "Thanks." She slowly stood upright and caught sight of his anxious face.

"Better?"

Sylvie nodded, closing her eyes.

"You promise you'll go to the doctor?"

Sylvie smiled and nodded.

"I mean it, Sylvie. I'll take you myself. I really can't see you like this."

"Really, I'm fine now."

Nick furrowed his brow, unconvinced. "Tea? Black?"

"Yes, I'll be out in a moment." Nick pulled her close and kissed her forehead, leaving her to get herself together.

Sylvie brushed her teeth and showered quickly, then slipped on her shorts and T-shirt and stuffed her bikini into her bag. Nick was sitting at the breakfast bar dressed only in his jeans, drinking his tea, ignoring the handle. He was picture perfect as always and her sensitive stomach was now housing dancing butterflies as she took in her favourite view. The living area was spotless and there was toast and fruit salad on the counter. Fabulous view and food – what a lovely way to start the day.

"How are you feeling now? You look much better." His smile lit up his face and everything around him like a beacon.

"I am. I'm starving, actually."

"Well, I know you don't overdo it in the morning so I hope toast and fruit's okay?"

"It's perfect." She beamed. His eyes sparkled back at her as she slipped onto the stool next to him. "Like you." And she leaned over to kiss him. He pulled her to him, lifting her onto his lap as their mouths locked. He grinned widely as his hands caressed her back and behind.

"Commando again?"

"Don't get any ideas, Nick. I'm late as it is," she mock-scolded him. He twisted his mouth, showing he was disappointed. "There's always tonight." She grabbed his chin and squeezed so that his lips puckered, and kissed him hard. He squeezed her tighter.

"Tonight. I'm not sure I can wait until then."

"Patience is a virtue."

"I'm not virtuous," he said seductively as he kissed her neck. "Or patient for that matter." He smelled delicious as he rubbed his nose down her jaw line and she inhaled deeply.

"Aren't you going to let me eat?"

Nick slowly raised his head to look at her, his eyes blazing. "Okay, but only so you keep your strength up." Sylvie laughed, then reluctantly slid off his lap and sat back on her stool.

"What about you? Aren't you eating?" Sylvie buttered a slice of toast and placed it in front of him. "I had something earlier." He picked up her wrist and kissed the inside of it, never taking his eyes off her.

Sylvie flushed, revelling in his flirty behaviour. "What time did you get up?"

"About eight."

Sylvie shook her head in disbelief. "I can't believe how much I'm sleeping." She turned to him as she put her spoon into her fruit salad. "You're wearing me out."

"You better believe it baby," he growled and took a huge bite out of his lovingly buttered toast.

———

Nick pulled up outside Sylvie's front door and turned to look at her as he switched off the ignition.

"What time are you going up?" He hated saying goodbye to her. "I'm just going to change and then I'll get up there. I won't stay long. I just need to make sure everything's been finished correctly before they fit the lights and furniture."

Nick nodded. "Okay, so I'll see you later, when you're done?" He pushed her hair back off her face, then he leaned over and kissed her softly. When he pulled back, his eyes had narrowed and he swallowed hard. "I'm going to speak to them tomorrow. I can't do with this sneaking around anymore."

Sylvie nodded slightly, not knowing how to respond. "I'll call you later, once I've finished."

Nick jumped out of the car and ran round to open up the door. Sylvie stepped out and kissed him, running her fingers over his stubbly cheek.

"Bye."

"Bye, baby."

———

The sun was streaming through the trees as Sylvie drove up the familiar windy road to Maggie's house. The smell of the pine trees was strong in the fresh air. Sylvie had changed into her aqua top and cropped white trousers, as it was too warm to wear jeans. Her ponytail swung behind her as the wind blew. She swung her car into Maggie's drive and within a minute, Maggie was opening the door.

"Come to inspect?" Maggie was standing in the doorway smiling at her in a long floaty sun dress, looking like she belonged in the seventies.

"Yes. Sorry I didn't come earlier."

"That's okay. I know you're busy. You look lovely, Sylvie. You've got a tan." They hugged and kissed each other.

"Yes, I was at the beach yesterday with the boys. Nice dress – very you." Sylvie flushed and avoided her eyes as she spoke. Nick was right; they needed to come clean. She could hardly look at Maggie.

"Thanks."

"So everything's done then. Yiannis told me."

"Yes he's so fast! Go up and have a look. I'll put the kettle on."

Sylvie walked into the hallway and then went straight up the stairs. The room looked amazing, even half-finished. The hardwood floors complemented the light blue walls. The far wall, which would have the bed against it, was wallpapered in a textured light blue and thin brown stripe. The headboard was light blue and Sylvie had found cream light blue and brown bedding. All that was missing was new wardrobe fronts and the bedside tables. Sylvie had found a chrome modern chandelier and matching small lamps, which would be fitted on Monday, and a modern chaise for the base of the bed.

Sylvie found Maggie in the kitchen putting out some cups. "Yiannis is a marvel. It'll all be done by Monday."

"It's really so lovely. Vicki says she might move into it now. Here." Maggie laughed and passed Sylvie her cup. "Let's go outside, it's cooler out there; there's a breeze." As they walked out, they heard a car pull up. "Who's that, I wonder?" Maggie put down her cup and went towards the front door. Sylvie had a bad feeling Nick may have followed her up. She really couldn't face the pressure again. She sat down on the chair and waited impatiently to see who it was.

She heard the familiar voice and turned around to see Julian walking through the French doors over to where she was sitting.

"Hi, Sylvie." He beamed as he leant down to kiss her cheek. "I thought I'd come up and see how it was coming along."

"Hi." Sylvie flushed, still feeling uneasy around him. He sat down and looked at her steadily. "It should be finished by Monday."

"So soon?" He raised his eyebrows, impressed. "You've got a tan."

"Yes, I went to the beach yesterday with the boys." Sylvie reached for her tea and sipped it nervously.

Julian smiled and nodded, then furrowed his brow as his eyes travelled down to her top. "That colour really suits you."

"Thanks." Sylvie tried hard not to look at him and she started to rub her ring nervously. Julian leaned back in the chair, resting his hands behind his head and stretching, his eyes still on her. Sylvie dropped her eyes to her ring.

"Here you are." Maggie had come out of the kitchen onto the terrace and had put down a cup of coffee down for him along with some biscuits. "Aren't you going up to have a look?"

He prised his eyes away from Sylvie, as she continued to look down at her ring. "Sure, I'll go up now." He rose up from the table and strolled back into the house.

Sylvie and Maggie sat for a while talking about Maggie's new orders. Sylvie listened to Maggie as she talked away about how she was trying to find the right packaging and the problems she was faced with, but all the while, Sylvie's attention was elsewhere. She kept thinking that today would probably be the last time she'd be able to speak to Maggie as a friend. After Nick spoke to his mum, Sylvie couldn't envisage their relationship ever being the same. Julian's unexpected visit had also thrown her. It was bad enough having to deal with Maggie, but Julian too? And on top of that, he kept staring at her, which was very unnerving.

"So with any luck, the boxes should be done on time." Sylvie refocused as Maggie took a breath.

"Sylvie, it's really wonderful. Great job. For sure, the rest of the house needs doing." Julian sat back down opposite Sylvie.

"Thanks. Well, we need to see. I'm seeing someone about a boutique next week."

"Sounds good. Anyone we know?" He picked up his coffee cup by the rim and Sylvie found it hard not to stare.

"It's in the Meridian."

Julian nodded, clearly impressed, as he sipped his coffee. He put down his cup.

"Well, you see when you can fit me in, and we can do a room at a time." Maggie smiled over at Sylvie, patting her arm.

"I should go. I've got loads to catch up on. Yiannis said he checked with you that it's okay to come at eight on Monday."

"Yes, he did."

"Good. Well I'll be off." Sylvie got up, feeling a lot more uncomfortable as Julian's eyes bored into her. He looked like he was trying to work something out.

"Bye, Sylvie." Julian got up abruptly, clearly preoccupied.

"Bye." Sylvie followed Maggie through to the kitchen, then out to her car.

Julian sat back down again. He looked back into the house pensively as he watched Sylvie walk away, her ponytail swinging. There was something he couldn't put his finger on, something familiar, but not quite. He shook his head, puzzled. It was probably déjà vu. He gulped down his coffee and sighed. She still was uneasy around him. He hoped she might have thawed out a little. He'd come over today purposely, knowing that Maggie's presence would defuse the tension. She always knew what to say and how to bring someone round, but it hadn't worked today. Oh well, he'd just have to be patient.

Maggie came back to the terrace as Julian fiddled with his cup. She sighed inwardly to herself. *He has it bad and he doesn't even know the half of it.* She wondered whether she should broach the subject, or prepare him, even. She sat down and he glanced up at her. "She's done a great job, Julian. She's really good."

"Yes she is." His reply was thoughtful.

Maggie tried a different tack. "Have you spoken to Nick at all? It seems he's off to the South of France again. Wednesday, I think."

"I went by to see him last night but he was with his girlfriend." Maggie stopped suddenly, her cup in mid-air. *He'd seen Nick's girlfriend? Maybe it wasn't Sylvie after all.*

"You met her?"

Julian laughed, seeing the shock on Maggie's face and misinterpreting it. "No, no. I pulled up and he was helping her into the boat." He picked up a biscuit from the plate and took a bite.

"Oh."

Julian swallowed, then continued. "Yeah, it was dusk and I couldn't really see her. I was a fair way back. Well anyway, he took her inside, so I left. I didn't want to intrude. I just passed on the off chance."

"I see." Maggie's heart plunged as she realised that second that her hopes were dashed. He'd seen Sylvie, but hadn't even recognised her.

"So you didn't see what she was like, then?"

"Just from the back." He took another bite and chewed thoughtfully.

The phone inside the house started to ring and Maggie got up to answer it. Julian sat looking at his cup. There was something niggling at him. Something in the back of his mind he just couldn't shake. He popped the rest of the biscuit in his mouth and ran his fingers through his hair. The image of Sylvie walking away, her ponytail swinging, came abruptly into his head as he rested his hands on his head...

Then, in what seemed like a lightning bolt of realisation, it hit him like a wrecking ball. The girl on Nick's boat last night had the same ponytail. She was the same height, same figure, the same... *Sylvie!* Julian sat up straight, his hands dropping to his legs as he pieced everything together. The top, that aqua top, that was the top Nick had discreetly hid in his suitcase that night. Sylvie was wearing it today. He knew he'd seen it before! His heart was thumping. *How was this possible?* He took deep breaths to calm down. *Nick and Sylvie?*

He stood up, pacing around, trying to think logically. *It was ridiculous! She couldn't be interested in him, he was just a boy!* He rubbed his forehead as if his head was sore from the very thought. *How could she? When? Where?* No, he was just letting his thoughts get the better of him. He shook his head, trying to expel the thought and the image of Nick and Sylvie together in that clinch on the deck, but it came back loud and vivid into the forefront of his brain. He clenched his teeth and squeezed his eyes shut. Then, as if that wasn't enough, another lightning bolt jolted him as he realised that Sylvie's trip to Athens had coincided with Nick's trip to France. *No, no, no... NO!* His hand flew to his mouth and he felt the anger start to boil. He felt such a fool, humiliated.

He could hear Maggie talking on the phone. He stormed into the house and waved his hand at her as she spoke, indicating he was leaving.

Maggie excused herself for a moment and put her hand over the mouthpiece. "You going?"

Julian nodded, curtly averting his eyes.

"Are you alright? You look like you've seen a ghost."

"Fine. I'll speak to you later." And with that, he strode to the door.

2 0

CONFRONTATION

Julian gripped the wheel as he drove down towards the town. He was replaying everything back in his head over and over, trying hard to shake the image of Nick and Sylvie kissing on the deck at twilight. He didn't know what to do, where to go. He knew he'd have to find out once and for all, but he really didn't know how he was going to handle it. He looked at the time: it was one-fifteen. He contemplated ringing Zach, then thought better of it. No, he'd go round to Sylvie's. He needed answers.

The gates were open as Julian powered his car into the driveway. He saw that both Sylvie's SUV and convertible were in. He parked up and switched off the ignition. He sat a moment, trying hard to rein in his temper. He didn't want a scene but he was hurt, beyond hurt, and he needed to know. He got out of the car breathing deeply and walked apprehensively up to the door.

Sylvie was in her office looking over her schedule. She'd walked in from Maggie's and decided to see if she could fit her redecoration in, even though she was sure that from tomorrow it would be highly unlikely she'd be welcome there again. The doorbell rang, interrupting her train of thought. Strange – she wasn't expecting anyone. She heard Alex open the door and then some mumbled talk. *Must be one of his friends*, she mused, then continued scanning her screen, when she heard footsteps and Alex walked in, his face ashen. Sylvie looked up at him, then her eyes focused on Julian stood behind him, his face stony and his eyes ice cold.

"Er... Mum? Julian came to see you." He widened his eyes and he grimaced at her, knowing Julian couldn't see. Sylvie's stomach clenched and her heart froze. *Oh no, this did not look good!* She tried hard to smile.

"Thanks, darling. Come in." Julian remained silent and Alex left, closing the door quietly behind him. "Sit down. This is a surprise. Um... what can I do for you?" Sylvie tried hard to sound calm but even she could hear the waver in her voice. Julian paused a moment, then sat down on the chair. Sylvie was grateful for the desk between them. He took a deep breath. He rested his ankle on his knee and leaned back, his piercing blue eyes burning into her; his stance was misleadingly relaxed.

"That top you're wearing... where did you get it from?" Sylvie looked puzzled. This was not something she had expected to hear from Julian.

"This top?" She pulled at the silk material, confused.

"Yes." His voice was deceptively quiet.

"Er... I had it made a few years back. It's made from some Indian sari material I came across. Why?"

"So it's unique, then? One of a kind?"

"I suppose. Julian, you came here to ask me about my top?" *Where was he going with this?*

"Not exactly." He slowly smoothed his stubbly chin with his hand. "I saw the exact same top a few days ago... in Nick's suitcase before he left for France."

His eyes stayed focused on hers as the colour slowly drained from her cheeks. He put his leg down, leaning forward and clenching his hands together, then rested them on his knees. The gesture was almost threatening. Sylvie rested back on her chair trying to widen the distance between them. Sylvie swallowed hard, now knowing *exactly* where this was going. "I see."

"Do you? Well I don't. Maybe you could enlighten me." He couldn't hide the sarcasm in his voice. *Shit!* How was she going to explain this without it hurting him? Her blood was pumping through her veins and her ears were buzzing.

"Julian, I know this might be a bit of a shock, but you see, Nick and I have been seeing each other –"

Before she could finish he shot up from his seat and glared down at her. "A bit of a shock! What the fuck do you think you're playing at?" He leaned forward, his hands gripping the desk, his knuckles white from the strain. Sylvie jolted backwards from the shock. Gone was the charming gentleman and in his place was Mr Fucking Angry! She'd never heard him swear before. "You've been seeing each other?" he hissed. "My son? For how long?"

"A couple of weeks." *Fuck, he was seething!* She just hoped Alex couldn't hear. He took his hands off the desk and straightened up. "Julian, it just happened. We were going to tell –"

Again he interrupted her. "It just happened! What do you mean? It was an accident?" He snorted. "He's my son, for fuck's sake! How could you? How could you do this? After… after what I told you, after you knew how I felt about you."

Sylvie closed her eyes for a second as she witnessed the hurt in his eyes and his voice trembling. Oh, this was so much worse than she imagined.

"Did he go with you to Athens?" Sylvie mouth was dry as she swallowed hard, her eyes fixed on his. "Answer me." His voice was low as he stood still, watching her.

"Yes."

"When did this start?"

"Julian, please. I really don't want to go into details. We got to know each other and as time passed it became… more." Sylvie slowly stood up from her chair as she spoke.

"I want to know."

"Does it matter?"

"To me it does." They stood facing each other, Julian glaring at her and Sylvie wide eyed.

"I'm sorry, Julian. I didn't mean to hurt you. You know I care for you. It was never going to be more than that. You're a good friend and that's never going to change for me."

He narrowed his eyes and seemed to stiffen as she spoke. "Does anyone else know?" His voice was glacial.

"I only told the boys a couple of days ago and yesterday I told Zach. Nick wanted to tell you himself."

His eyes widened. "Does he know how I feel about you?" His tone was still cold.

"Not from me he doesn't. I never told him anything. But he knows, yes, he worked it out."

He took a deep breath and for a moment he seemed to relax. Sylvie began to feel that maybe the worst was over. She was just glad she had got the worst of it before Nick confronted him. Maybe now when they spoke, Julian would be less volatile.

Then something changed. She could see he was trying to understand something or process it. "Why did you tell them?" He cocked his head to the side as if he couldn't understand why anyone needed to know.

"What do you mean?"

"Why did you tell the boys and Zach? And why was Nick going to tell me?"

Sylvie raised her eyebrows, puzzled. "Well, because we didn't want to sneak around and because things are serious –"

"Serious!" His eyes reignited as he hissed at her. "You mean you're in some sort of relationship with him?"

"Well, yes." Sylvie answered, a little affronted.

"I thought… I thought you were just…"

What did he think? That it was just a casual affair? One look at his face and she knew the answer. He had presumed that Nick was just using her, like he himself used his endless string of young women.

"He's young enough to be your son, for the love of God, Sylvie! How could you be serious with him? What kind of *relationship* can you have? It's ridiculous. You should be ashamed of yourself!" He almost spat out the words, the last phrase stinging her like a slap in the face.

"How dare you preach to me about relationships!" She straightened herself and looked him directly in the eye. He'd gone too far. First, he thought she was some casual fuck for his son, and now he was scolding her like a wayward child! "You… you who have slept with any twenty-something with a pulse for the last God knows how long, and you're going to judge me on my relationship choices? You really don't want to go there! Have you ever heard of the phrase 'people in glass houses'?"

He was about to interrupt, but Sylvie glared at him and lifted her hand up, signalling him to be quiet. "Oh no, you've had your say. Now it's time to listen. I didn't want this. I wasn't looking for it, but it happened. What I have with Nick isn't some casual affair that will fizzle out. I don't work that way, Julian, and nor does your son. I thought you knew that. You and I were never going to happen, Julian. I know you're hurt, but would it have made any difference who I'd had a relationship with?"

"He's my son, Sylvie, and he's sixteen years younger than you!" He spoke through clenched teeth, his tone menacing, indicating it was abhorrent to him that she could even think that she could be with Nick.

Sylvie narrowed her eyes and tried another tactic. "I know our relationship isn't ideal, but I love him and he loves me and –"

He glared at her as she spoke and before she could finish, he shouted. "You love him! You've known him for five fucking seconds and you love him! Well I'll tell you one thing. This... this *relationship* you have will tear our family apart. How can I accept it? Did you ever think about how this is going to affect everyone? Me? Maggie? Have you no regard for anyone's feelings? I know what Nick's like – he's young and doesn't see the future but you... you should have known better, you should never have let it get this far."

Sylvie cringed as he spoke, reaffirming her dreaded fears and her insecurities. She could feel the tears pricking the back of her eyes and the stabbing cramps in her stomach as he continued to glare at her. He spoke the truth and his words seared into her twisting heart.

He leaned forward on her desk, looking straight at her, his eyes blazing with hurt and anger. "I may have slept with every twenty-something with a pulse, Sylvie, but I never split up a family because of it. Or hurt them." He took his hands off the desk and straightened up.

"Except your own," Sylvie whispered. The words were out before she could stop herself. The colour drained from his face.

"Don't you dare tell me anything about *my* family! All because you're fucking my son, that doesn't make you an expert on them!" he hissed.

"I think you'd better leave, Julian." Sylvie's voice cracked. *Don't cry, don't cry!* She willed herself as she glared at him.

"Yes, I think I better had."

"Forgive me if I don't see you out." She couldn't keep the sarcasm out of her voice but she just wanted him gone.

"Forgive you? Oh I will never forgive you, Sylvie." He narrowed his eyes and shook his head before stalking out of the office.

Sylvie stood waiting to hear the roar of his car engine disappearing down the hill and then she slumped into her chair and the tears freely ran down her face. Within a few seconds, she began to retch and she vomited into her wastepaper bin. Alex ran in from the sitting room having heard Julian leave.

"Jeez, Mum, what the hell! Marcy!" Marcy came running into the study within seconds.

"Oh my goodness, come, come. Go and wash your face and I'll make you some ginger tea."

"What happened, Mum? He looked pissed! What the hell did he say to you?" He was trying hard to keep the anger out of his voice.

"Give her a moment Alex, she's just thrown up!" Marcy scolded.

"I have to call Nick. He'll be going down there, I'm sure." Sylvie picked up her phone and pressed his number.

Nick stepped into the shower, allowing the water to flow over him. He'd been scrubbing down the decks and scraping the algae off the jet ski and the *Silver Lining*. He heard his phone ringing. *Crap!* He knew it would be Sylvie. He hurriedly started to rinse the shampoo out of his hair. He heard the phone stop ringing and quickly scrubbed the grime and sweat off himself and rubbed his face. He'd ring her as soon as he got out. Turning off the shower, he reached over for the towel and rubbed his hair, then grabbing a larger towel, he dried himself. He slipped on his boxers, a T-shirt and a pair of khaki Bermudas, then went to find his phone.

There was the missed call from Sylvie and he immediately pressed the call option. It rang three times and then he heard her answer. He'd been so preoccupied with his phone, he hadn't noticed that Julian had jumped on deck and was heading for the stairs.

"Nick?" Her voice sounded urgent.

"Yes, baby. Are you alright?" He turned around and was faced with the image of his father coming down the stairs. From the look on his face he realised this wasn't a social visit.

"Nick, I'm so sorry. Your dad came round and somehow he worked out about me and you and I couldn't lie to him…" Her voice was cracking as she hurriedly tried to catch him up. Within a millisecond, Nick had the full picture: his father standing stony-faced in front of him and Sylvie distraught on the phone. He fixed his stare on his father, each with their eyes burning into each other, Nick knowing that Julian would have been merciless. That thought alone made him livid, knowing Sylvie would have had to endure his father's full wrath alone.

"He was so angry, Nick, and I think he's coming down to you…" she continued.

Nick momentarily clenched his teeth and closed his eyes. All he could think about was how she'd had to face his father without him. "It's okay, baby." His voice was low, trying to soothe her. Julian flinched at the endearment. "Are you alone?"

"No, Alex is here." She sobbed.

He swallowed, trying to keep himself calm as he heard her desperately try to control herself. "Good. Don't worry. I'll call you in a bit, okay?" His voice was deceptively soft, his eyes never leaving his father's.

"Okay."

Nick placed the phone down on the counter. "What did you say to her?" he hissed, his blood boiling.

"Nothing she didn't already know."

"She's almost hysterical. WHAT DID YOU SAY?" he screamed. He couldn't control himself.

"Don't you dare, Nick! How could you? You knew how I felt about her. I told you!" They both stood facing each other a few feet apart, Nick's fists clenched by his side. "Of all the women, you had to take her – take her away from me?" Julian's voice was a mixture of hurt and anger. He rubbed his face. "You could be with anyone, Nick. You have the pick of the crop. Why her? Why Sylvie?" Nick stood silently as Julian stepped back and leaned against the wall. His voice had softened but his eyes were still blazing. "Answer me, God damn it, why?" He ran his hands into his hair.

Nick's hands unclenched and he leaned back onto the counter. "She was never yours to take." His voice was almost matter of fact, and Julian's eyes widened in disbelief.

"What do you know about what I had with her?" he replied bitterly. "I was by her side over the last nine months. I was giving her space and time to get over Chris." He moved from the wall and started to pace. "We spent days and weeks together. I brought her round. She's starting being her old self again and then you, you came in and just…" He closed his eyes and shook his head then turned to look at Nick. "I'm in love with her, Nick. I've never been in love with anyone… except your mum." His voice softened as he spoke the last sentence.

"Well you screwed up that relationship." Nick mirrored his father's bitterness. Julian gasped but reined in his anger.

"Maybe I did," he answered. "But I really thought I could have a future with Sylvie. A second chance."

"You never had a chance, Dad. I sat and watched you for four months try and move your friendship with her to something more. She was never going to see you as anything else. I fell in love with her over those months and I know she feels the same way."

Julian clenched his teeth as he heard the same words he'd heard only half an hour ago from Sylvie and he realised there was no way he could accept it. His son with Sylvie? Not a chance. "She's old enough to be your mother, Nick. Where the fuck do you think this is going to go? You think you have a future with her?" he mocked.

"Yes," Nick answered calmly.

"You really are living in cloud cuckoo land, Nick. You need to grow up! You've known her for next to no time. It's Brigitte all over again, but this time it's worse. If you continue with her… if you insist on being with her… you'll tear our family apart, Nick."

Nick closed his eyes, his mouth dry as he convulsively swallowed. "Is that what you said to Sylvie?" he spoke through gritted teeth.

"And then some!" Julian yelled. Nick's heart pounded. He knew if his father had made Sylvie feel she was going to break up their family, she would never be able to get over it. All his pent-up anger came boiling to the surface, knowing that his father may have actually managed to tap into Sylvie's worst fear. "It's not me or Sylvie that'll break up this family. It will be you." He moved forward, pointing his finger directly at his father's face. "We have had to deal with your continuing mid-life crisis for the last twenty years."

Julian went to speak but then stopped seeing Nick's burning glare.

"You walked out on Mum because you couldn't be restricted and you felt trapped. She was the best thing that ever happened to you and you fucked it up. For some inexplicable reason, Mum's still in love with you and you don't even see it. You're so wrapped up in your own selfish world. You've screwed anything and everything within a twenty-mile radius and then when a decent, beautiful, witty, intelligent, sexy woman comes into your life, you are under the impression it's your God-given right to have her, regardless of how she feels, or anyone else for that matter. It's not me who needs to grow up, Dad." He was on a roll now and he couldn't stop himself. He knew he was wounding Julian deeply as he spoke, but all he was concerned with was that if his dad had made Sylvie feel guilty, she would never be able to get past that. He couldn't lose her.

"What, you think you can make her happy?" Julian sneered.

"I know I can. And what's more, Dad, I do. You need to get over it. She's not some bimbo that's impressed with your flashy car, your swanky bachelor pad and the fact you can throw your money around."

Julian glared at him as Nick's words stung. *He made her happy?* He felt his heart break and his lungs tightened at the very thought.

"Is it the fact that she's found someone else, or is it the fact that she's with me that you cannot accept?"

They stood glaring at each other, neither one of them speaking, but their bodies were screaming and radiating anger.

"You'd better go." Nick broke first. He needed to get up to Sylvie; he knew she'd be in a state.

"This isn't over."

"It is for me, Dad. You just couldn't be happy for me could you? Everything has to be about you. Well I'm done, done with it all. Go, go now. Before I really do something I'll regret!"

For a split-second, Julian's face froze, then he turned and strode up the stairs, leaving Nick shaking as he tried hard to calm himself.

Nick needed to get himself together and fast. His main priority was Sylvie; she'd be frantic. He went back into his bedroom, closing everything as he went. Grabbing his keys and phone and dragging on socks and sneakers, he headed to the car park and jumped into his Jeep. Then he pulled out his phone and called Sylvie.

"Nick? Thank God!" she said, relieved.

"I'm on my way."

Nick rang the bell and waited for what seemed like an age for someone to open the door. As Alex pulled the door ajar, Nick quickly greeted him. "Hi Alex. Where is she?"

"Hi. She's out in the garden walking around." His face was strained.

"Did you hear what was said?"

Alex shook his head. "I just heard some shouting and then when he left, Mum was pretty shaken up." Nick closed his eyes and breathed deeply. "She still is, but she's trying to put on a brave face for me."

"I wanted to be the one to tell him. How the hell did he figure it out? We've been so careful. I'm so sorry, Alex. Really. I never wanted your mum to face that, and alone." Alex nodded stiffly. "I'll go and find her" – he stopped a second and turned to Alex – "if that's okay."

"Sure, Nick. Go through."

Nick almost ran through the sitting room and through the kitchen. He nodded briefly at Marcy, who was scrubbing a perfectly clean sink, then strode through the French doors onto the covered terrace. He scanned the garden, frantically trying to find her, then he saw her: she was crouched by a lavender bush, it looked like she was pulling at a weed.

"Sylvie." She shot up and turned to see where he was, dropping the weed she'd pulled and hurrying to him. Nick ran down the path and threw his arms around her. "Jesus, Sylvie." She clung on to him as she started to cry into his chest. All her pent-up emotions, the shock and her angst came pouring out. He stroked her head as she tried and failed to control herself.

"I'm so sorry, baby. It's over now. Hush." He kissed her head as she continued to weep. It was blisteringly hot, but Sylvie was shaking as she tried to control her shuddery breath. Nick pulled back so he could see her face. Her eyes were watery and red from the crying. He took the hem of his T-shirt and wiped her face, smiling gently at her.

"Please don't cry, baby. Come on, let's go inside."

She nodded weakly. He bent down and kissed her lips, his hands holding her head. She held on to him as she melted against his mouth. Then he held her close to him. This was where she wanted to be, wrapped in his arms. She took deep breaths, smelling his chest, which was now damp from her tears and from his sweat. *Where were they going to go from here?* She kept hearing Julian's words reaffirming everything she feared: 'tear this family apart', 'should have known better', 'never let it get this far'.

Nick pulled away and tucked her under his arm as they walked silently back to the house.

Marcy was collecting her bag as they entered the kitchen and Nick deliberately but reluctantly unhooked his arm from around Sylvie.

"Do you need me to stay, Mam?" Her face was full of concern.

"No. Thanks, though. I'm fine."

Marcy smiled at Nick and nodded and then she left, saying her goodbyes.

Alex came through from the lounge where he was playing on the PlayStation.

"You okay, Mum?"

"Yes, sweetheart. I'll be fine. Did you eat something?"

"Mum! Stop fussing. Yes, I did, now forget about that. I'm just worried about you." He looked over to Nick as he spoke.

"I really don't want to talk about anything right now," Sylvie said.

Nick clenched his jaw. He wanted to know what had gone on and he knew while Alex was around, there was no chance Sylvie would tell him. He'd have to stick it out until they were alone. "Where's Markus?"

"He went down to the beach with some friends."

"Well I'm glad he wasn't here." Nick squeezed Sylvie's hand as she rubbed her ring nervously.

Sylvie said, "I'm going to have some more tea. Nick, you want some?" Nick nodded and watched as Sylvie put on a brave face for the sake of Alex. "Biscuits? I think we've some chocolate chip cookies I made." Alex looked at Nick as he stood awkwardly by the breakfast bar.

"I'll just have some milk, Mum. You want to play, Nick?" He motioned to the lounge where the PlayStation was.

"Sure."

Sylvie smiled her best fake smile as they walked into the lounge and she fussed around in the kitchen. Once they were out of her vision, she steadied herself against the counter. She could hear them talking quietly. The kettle had finished boiling and Sylvie poured the water into the teapot. She wanted something stronger, but she knew if she drank, she'd end up tell Nick everything and she wanted to spare him whatever she could. She was trying hard to rationalise everything but right now, after seeing Nick, and holding him, all she wanted to do was forget about Julian and let the dust settle.

Nick came through from the lounge, looking at her warily. He couldn't work out what she was thinking. He walked round the breakfast bar and stood in front of her. He reached down and stroked her cheek with the back of his hand. "You okay?"

She nodded, leaning into his hand as his eyes glowed. She looked at him and her heart clenched. He was beyond perfect. She focused on his lips, wanting them on hers, and as if he'd read her mind, he lifted her chin up and tentatively kissed her. Sylvie's hands ran up his chest, up his neck and into his hair as she pulled him closer, deepening the kiss. Nick pulled her hard against him and she could feel his growing erection against her stomach. He groaned into her mouth and then pulled away breathlessly.

"Don't, Sylvie. Please." He stepped back to get some distance his eyes flitted to the lounge. "Jesus, I've never wanted you so much," he breathed. "If you do that again, I swear I'll take you on the breakfast bar and I don't give a fuck who's here."

"Sorry." Sylvie stifled a grin. "I just want you. With all the shit that's gone on today, I just need to feel you."

He closed his eyes and sucked on his top teeth. "You're killing me," he whispered.

Alex came through from the lounge. He was holding his phone, seemingly oblivious to the highly charged atmosphere in the kitchen. "Where is it? … Second drawer, okay, and your Converse and socks… Yeah, yeah, I got it! Okay. Give me fifteen minutes, I'll be there. Okay,

okay, I said I would. Chill!" He pressed off the phone, sneering at it. "That was Markus, he's down at Greg's house and he needs a change of clothes. I'll take them down for him and then we're off to play pool." He stopped a minute and then added. "You don't mind if I go?"

"No, no, sweetheart, you go. Have a good time," Sylvie answered, a tad too quickly.

"Okay, I'll just get changed and get Markus's gear. God, he's worse than a woman!" Alex shook his head, clearly exasperated.

21

EXPLANATION

They could hear Alex rummaging upstairs as Sylvie went over to the French doors and shut them, twisting the lock. Nick stood by the breakfast bar watching her intently, a wry smile creeping over her face as she floated past him, running her fingers slowly across his chest. His eyes blazed as he moaned, his gaze following her to the lounge where he heard her switch off the TV. Nick licked his lips as she slowly walked back towards him.

"If you touch me again, I won't wait until he leaves," he said softly, his voice loaded with menacing intent.

"I won't touch you, then," whispered Sylvie, sliding round the breakfast bar and to the kitchen. Then, leaning over, she blew softly into his ear. His head rolled back and he turned around, pinning her with his gaze as she leaned against the fridge. Nick edged around the breakfast bar as Sylvie's eyes widened. He looked so determined as he purposefully stepped closer. Sylvie could feel his need reflected in his eyes, her face echoing that same need. After her confrontation with Julian and his words reaffirming her doubts and fears, all she wanted was to feel that unique bond and connection she had with this incredible man.

Nick halted abruptly as Alex bounded down the stairs with a black sports bag in his hand and put his head round the door. "I'm off."

"Okay. Have a good time." Sylvie moved round so he could see her.

"Thanks, Mum. See you, Nick."

"Bye." Nick nodded and then they watched him walk to the door leading to the garage. Once it was shut, Nick began to advance on her but Sylvie put up her finger, signalling him to stop. Then she listened until she heard Alex start his car and reverse it out of the garage and onto the drive. Sylvie ran to the door and locked it, then she turned round. She found Nick a foot away from her, his eyes alight as he ran them over her body.

"Are we alone now?" His fingers twitched. Sylvie leaned against the door and nodded. "Thank fuck for that." Relieved, he plunged swiftly, grabbing her face as his mouth closed on hers. Sylvie melted into him and gripped his arms. Pulling away, he gasped, "Not here." He grabbed her hand and pulled her through the kitchen and into the hallway. They both ran up the stairs and burst into Sylvie's room.

Nick ripped off his T-shirt and kicked off his sneakers, yanking off his socks and discarding them on the floor, his eyes never leaving Sylvie. She slipped off her shoes and sat on the bed. Nick stood in front of her; bending down to kiss her, he pushed her back on the bed and he shuffled between her legs. He stopped for a second, his face pensive.

"Are you okay, baby? After today?"

"Nick, all I want right now is for you to make love to me and forget everything." She reached up to his face and stroked his stubbly cheek. He reached behind her neck and pulled the tie which held up her top. Sylvie sat up and Nick lifted it up over her head, and Sylvie sunk back on the bed as he moved down to the waistband of her trousers. He unfastened the button, then smoothly pulled down the zip. Sylvie lifted her hips off the bed so he could pull her trousers down and he dropped them on the floor by her shoes.

As he knelt between her legs she lifted herself up and grabbed his waistband. "Let me." And Nick held his hands back in surrender as he smirked at her. She popped the button, then slowly pulled down the zip making sure her fingers rubbed down the whole length of his erection. She pulled down his shorts and leaned forward kissing him through his boxers. Nick hissed through his teeth as she gently nipped him using her teeth, and before she could reach the top, he grabbed her, pushing her back to the bed as he tore off his shorts and boxers.

"You are so fucking sexy, Sylvie. Do you know that?" She shook her head coyly as he knelt down between her legs and pulled down her panties, then he reached round her back and unhooked her bra. "Well you are, very." His hand claiming her breast as he silenced her moans with his mouth. He trailed kisses down her throat and across to her breast, suckling her gently.

"Ah."

He slowly teased her other breast with his fingers and she arched up to him.

"Nick, please, ah!" He looked up at her as she writhed under his touch and he slowly made his way up to her mouth, Sylvie's hands finding their way into his soft hair. Nick pulled back to look at her as he slowly entered her. "Ah yes," she moaned, and Nick pushed in deeper, his eyes raw with desire as he gazed down at her. Sylvie lifted her legs up, curling them around him, and Nick moved, slowly filling her.

"God I love you, Sylvie."

"I love you too, Nick." She held onto his arms, gripping his muscles as he steadily moved in and out. He rolled to the side, taking her with him and she straddled him, feeling the tense muscles on his chest. Everything that had happened today temporarily forgotten, all Sylvie needed was this, this beautiful incredible man showing her how much he loved her and needed her too.

"You're so beautiful, I love watching you." She leaned back as she moved and he held her hips, relishing her, feeling her. He matched her, thrusting into her as she began to quicken. Sylvie reached down to him, pulling him up to her so they were face to face, her legs wrapped tightly around him and her arms encasing his shoulders and head, cradling him to her as Nick's arms tightened around her waist.

"Oh baby, that's it," Nick's voice straining as he tried to control his impending orgasm, his words sending Sylvie over the edge as they found their release together, collapsing against each other breathless.

Julian drove away from the marina, not exactly sure where to go. He didn't want to head home. He couldn't face an empty apartment. So he drove around trying to make sense of what he'd learned in the last couple of hours. He was finding it hard to reconcile that Nick was in a relationship with Sylvie. How had that ever happened? He knew she'd spent time up at Maggie's over the last few months. He wracked his brain, trying to remember if there had been any indications, any signs whatsoever, but he just couldn't. The truth was he was so wrapped up in her that he wouldn't have even noticed. He punched his steering wheel as he drove, then swung his car onto the road leading up to Maggie's. He needed to tell her and maybe she'd talk some sense into Nick.

Maggie was busy in her workshop when she saw Julian's car pull up. She put down her brush and wiped her hands as she watched him stride to the door. He looked agitated and Maggie felt decidedly uneasy as he knocked hard on the door. It was a couple of minutes before she opened the door.

"Hello, Julian, how are you?" She tried to smile but one look at his expression stopped her mouth from curling upward.

"I've been better," he muttered as he brushed past her, running his hand through his hair. She followed him through to the sitting room.

"What is it? You look… well you don't look right." Maggie sat down in the armchair as he slumped on the settee.

Julian rubbed his face, then leaned forward on his knees, supporting his head in his hands. "It's Nick."

"Nick?" Maggie started to panic: *what had happened to him?*

"What do you mean? Is he alright?"

"His girlfriend. I know who it is." His eyes shot up to Maggie and he watched the colour slowly drain from her face. "From the look of you, I take it you already knew."

"Suspected," she whispered.

"And you didn't think to tell me?" His voice grew slightly louder as he gritted his teeth.

"I wasn't a hundred percent sure and to be honest, I was hoping I was wrong." She shifted nervously.

"So what the fuck are we going to do about it?"

"*Do* about it?"

"Yes. Well they can't continue. I won't allow it." He sat back as if his argument was self-explanatory.

Maggie furrowed her brow. "It's not up to you, Julian, or us for that matter. They're adults. He's not a child any more. You can't ground him because he's misbehaved." *Not that he ever did ground any of their children!* Maggie thought fleetingly.

"So we're going to sit back and condone it?" His voice was getting louder as his temper rose.

"Julian, calm down please. Let me make you a coffee."

"I don't want any coffee. And I'm certainly *not* going to calm down." He gripped the settee armrest as he spoke, trying to rein in his temper. "She's sixteen years older than him! She's… she's well, she's old enough to be his mother and she should never have let it get this far. They were in Athens *together*. Did you know that?" Maggie sat silently, letting him vent. His eyes were burning and she knew he was close to exploding.

"I mean, it's ridiculous. What on earth does she see in him? He's so young. What can he offer her? They're a generation apart. He'll never have a future with her. Children – well he can forget that," he snorted. He put his head in his hands. "This is worse than Brigitte."

"Well you won't be able to buy Sylvie off like you did her," Maggie muttered.

Julian threw her a thunderous stare. "You knew she was a fucking gold-digger. We'd have paid for it tenfold if he'd married her." Maggie cringed, knowing in this aspect he was right. Brigitte's ex-husband had warned Julian about her. They'd initially sat back, hoping it would fizzle out, but Nick had fallen for her and she was looking for a new meal ticket. Julian had offered her a substantial amount of money to break it off with Nick and leave the country, which she did all too willingly, proving to them both that their interference was justified. To this day, Nick never knew.

"Have you spoken to Nick about it?" her voice was soft and wary, praying that he hadn't.

"Yes. I spoke to both of them."

"Together?" Maggie closed her eyes. *Oh, this was not good!*

"No! I went to Sylvie's first to confront her, then afterwards to Nick's."

"What did you say?" Her voice was now hardly audible.

"Basically, I told Sylvie she was breaking up our family and that the whole situation was ridiculous – that she should have known better."

"Oh, Julian! Why did you go and do that, after everything we went through with Brigitte. You can't tell people what to do. It's not your place or mine. We said we'd never do that again." She stood up and paced around.

"What, we sit back and accept it?" He looked at her incredulously.

"We don't have a choice." Her voice was stronger, as she began to see the repercussions of his hasty and obviously self-centred actions.

"You think I could sit back and accept Nick being with Sylvie?" He stood up, affronted. "Not a chance in hell!" He flung his arm around to emphasize the point.

"We'll lose him. I won't go through that again, Julian." She stared at him and he recoiled.

"He'll get over it," he said dismissively. He sat back down again.

"He won't *get over it!* He loves her!" She turned to him, her hands flexed outward as she raised her voice, exasperated.

Julian narrowed his eyes at her. "How do you know what he feels for her?"

"He told me. He didn't tell me who it was, but he told me how much she meant to him and that he wanted me to remember our conversation when I eventually got to know." She took a deep breath as Julian continued to stare at her. "He was preparing me because he knew that once… once… Well, he knew that once *you* found out, things would become difficult."

"What do you mean?"

"You want me to spell it out?" Her voice rose as she stood in front of him with her arms crossed. He sat still, not daring to answer. "He knew you'd freak out because he knew how you felt about her." Julian looked at his hands nervously. He wasn't comfortable talking to Maggie about his feelings for Sylvie. "What worries me is your motive behind you lecturing Sylvie about this and I dread to think what you said to Nick. Had it been another forty-something woman that you had no interest in, would you be so adamant that they couldn't continue?"

"So you're okay with this?"

"Stop changing the subject. This isn't about what I feel at all. I really don't think that matters, Julian. I swore I wouldn't interfere again and I still feel the same way and stand by my decision. But then again, I'm not in love with Sylvie, so maybe I can't see your point of view!" Maggie tried hard to keep the bitterness out of her voice but failed.

"Maggie?"

"What, Julian?" She stared at him, her mouth in a firm line. She wasn't going to make this easy for him. She'd done that for long enough. He actually looked embarrassed and Maggie felt herself weaken.

"It doesn't matter." He got up. "Look, I can't be like you. I won't accept it. I really don't want to talk about why." He shook his head. "I'm sorry, I just can't."

"So we aren't going to talk about the green-eyed elephant in the room, then?" Julian shot her a furious stare but Maggie stood her ground. She wasn't prepared to lose her son because her ex-husband was jealous. *No way! He'd* have to *get over it!*

They stared at each other for what seemed like an age, Julian trying to calm himself down and Maggie waiting for an answer. Maggie broke first, trying a different approach in the hope he might see sense and hopefully they'd be able to correct whatever damage he'd already done. "What if he's happy, if she makes him happy and he her? Will you still not accept it?"

Julian clenched his eyes shut. The thought of Sylvie being happy with Nick was agonising and he felt ashamed to admit it to himself or anyone else. It made him feel a failure. He'd obviously been unable to offer that to her. "I… I just don't know." His face was drawn and his eyes clouded over. "I'd better go."

"Julian, we need to talk about this. You can't just walk away because you don't want to face whatever it is that's eating you up."

Julian rubbed his face again uncomfortably. He really didn't want to get into this, and especially not with Maggie. "Maggie, it's not something I feel entirely comfortable talking to you about." He stood up again, trying hard to avoid her gaze.

"I know you better than anyone." He pressed his lips together. "Who else can you talk to?"

"Maggie please… I can't. I'm so confused and angry. There's too much shit involved…" He leaned down and picked up his keys.

Maggie watched him wrestle with himself as he turned to leave. She couldn't let him leave. She had to get him to talk to her. She knew if she didn't try to talk him round, Nick would suffer and she couldn't let that happen, not again. Maggie pulled on every fibre of strength she had. "You can't make someone love you, Julian. Sylvie doesn't love you." She spoke clearly and she tried hard to look at him in the eye. Julian slowly turned round, his face a mixture of hurt and anger. "I'm sorry if that's not what you want to hear, but you need to take it on board. She cares for you as a friend. But that's it, Julian, and you being jealous and making it hard for Nick and her will not make her fall in love with you." He carried on staring at her as he narrowed his eyes. Maggie swallowed hard and continued. "So what you're doing is trying to split them up in spite of that, for your own selfish reasons. If you can't have her, why should anyone else? Or is it just you don't want Nick to be with her? If it was some other man she had fallen in love with, would you be still so adamant to split them up?"

"I'm leaving," Julian seethed as he strode towards the door.

"That's right, Julian, why change a habit of a lifetime? Run. Leave. You're so good at that."

"Don't you dare start…" He'd turned around and strode back up to Maggie; his face was thunderous, but Maggie squared up to him. He needed to hear this and she needed to tell him.

"No I will *dare*. For over thirty years, I've sat back and let you do your thing. When it got tough, you ran. When it felt suffocating, you left. When you needed support, you were back. Everything you ever needed, I made sure you got: space, time, love, support." He stepped back, unsure of where she was going. "Now though, when things aren't going to plan, when things around you are out of your control, you want to interfere. Well you can't. Not this time. You see, before it was me you were in control of. You knew I'd do whatever you wanted because you knew I loved you and you took advantage of that. And that's fine." Julian looked down as he clenched his jaw. "I was always prepared to put your needs first; how else could I keep you close?" Her voice wavered and he looked back up at her and this time Maggie averted her eyes. She had to keep it together.

"When Sylvie came along, I knew I'd lost you. I knew there was no way I could compete with her. All the others, the many others, I knew were nothing. Distractions. You needed them to make you feel whatever it was that you felt you lacked." She sniffed, indicating she couldn't really understand and shook her head.

Julian closed his eyes. *He really didn't need to hear this, not today. Who was he kidding? He didn't want to hear it any day.*

"As time went by, though, I could see Sylvie didn't feel the same way. Oh, she cares for you a lot, but it was never going to be more. At first, I thought it was because of me. Some kind of loyalty to me." Julian's eyes widened. "But once I'd worked out about Nick and her, I knew it wasn't that. If she was concerned about my feelings, I think she would never have let that relationship develop." She sniffed again. "Julian, we can't stop this. *You* can't. However much you feel for her, you need to put it aside. For once, think about someone else."

"Maggie, I can't. I... I..." He wanted to say so much but he just couldn't. How could he tell her she was right that he was jealous of his own son? What kind of father was he? What kind of person was he? She was so selfless, she made him feel so ashamed and a failure and he wasn't ready to admit that. Not even after thirty years. He put his hand up to his forehead and rubbed it, trying to ease the pressure pushing all these unwelcome thoughts back into his head.

Maggie moved forward and reached up to his cheek. He closed his eyes, then stepped back. No, he really needed to get away. He was feeling vulnerable, hurt and confused and he really didn't want to do anything stupid. He'd done enough of that already.

"I need to go. I'm sorry." And with that, he walked quickly out of the lounge and out of the door. Julian drove away and down towards town, Maggie's words ringing in his ears. He needed to get them out somehow and he needed to distance himself from everything. There was only one way he knew how to do that. He reached for his phone and punched in the number.

Julian poured himself a large whisky and sat on his settee. It was seven-thirty. The doorbell rang and he drained his drink before answering it.

"Hi! Julian, you look like shit!" Ellie teetered in on her six-inch heels, handing him the paper bag with Chinese food in.

"Nice to see you too, Ellie," he answered sarcastically. She shook her head and her blonde hair shimmered down her back. Julian walked over to the kitchen, placing the bag down and systematically taking out each plastic box filled with food. He hadn't eaten all day but he really wasn't hungry.

"I wasn't sure what you wanted. I hope it's okay. They put every-thing on your account." She leaned over the breakfast bar and rested her head on her elbows, giving Julian a full eyeful of her ample cleavage. He looked over to her and smiled, knowing exactly what she was doing. At least he knew where he stood with Ellie. She was the most uncompli-cated woman he'd ever met. He used her and she was well aware of it. There was no hidden agenda.

"Are you hungry?" he asked.

"Not really. I can eat later."

"Would you like a drink?" She looked at his finished glass and shrugged and straightened herself. Reaching down, she took hold of the hem of her impossibly tight black mini dress and pulled it up slowly, over her perfect body and over her head. She was completely naked underneath. She tossed it over onto the settee. Julian watched her, and a smile cracked over his tense face as his eyes travelled over her, amused at her audacity.

"So, no to the drink, then?" he smirked. She turned around and teetered on her heels towards the bedroom.

"Let's not pretend that I didn't know why you called me, Julian. You need a fuck, for whatever reason. We can eat and drink later." Julian slowly walked round from the kitchen, pulling out his shirt from his trousers and followed her to his bedroom. "Lights on or off?" she called as she entered his bedroom.

"Off," he whispered.

Sylvie stepped into the bath and nestled between Nick's long tanned legs. He handed her a glass of wine as she rested against his chest. Nick wrapped his arms around her and Sylvie flexed her toes against his. Nick kissed her head and sighed. Sylvie could feel his tension. Neither one of them had spoken about their respective conversations with Julian, but Sylvie knew they were going to have to. *No time like the present*, thought Sylvie, as she took a large gulp of wine.

Before she'd swallowed, Nick muttered in a low voice: "What did my father say to you?" He tightened his hold on her and Sylvie was glad he couldn't see her face. She wasn't prepared to tell him all the details as she knew it would only upset him. She'd just keep it general. Reliving Julian's frank and hurtful conversation was not something Sylvie wanted to do in a hurry.

"Nothing I didn't already know or expect." She paused for him to comment, but he waited for her to expand her answer. "He was shocked, he thought it was… well, he thought we couldn't have a future. The age thing. He was angry, which was understandable."

"Did he shout at you?" She could hear the tension rise in his question and she knew that she had to tread carefully.

"I wouldn't say shout. He was shocked, Nick." He stroked her arm nervously, knowing full well she wasn't being completely honest with him. He'd seen what his father was like after he'd been to her and he knew Julian would have let everything rip. He had nothing to lose, after all.

"Don't defend him, Sylvie. I know he said some horrible things to you. I know what you're doing. But I won't stand for it. You can't protect me." Sylvie clenched her eyes closed. The truth was she was trying hard to forget Julian's words. She knew that they were on borrowed time and that things were going to get uglier. She just wanted their cocoon to last a little longer.

"I need to go see Mum tomorrow. I'm sure he's been up there and told her. I need to square it with her. I just hope he didn't lose it with her too." Sylvie drained her glass and set it down on the side of the bath. She slowly turned round to look at him. His face was pensive and he looked tired. For the first time since she'd met him, he looked a lot older and her heart clenched as she realised it was because of her. She should have known better. Julian was right, she should never have let it get this far.

"I'll come with you," she whispered, and immediately he shook his head.

"No way. You've had enough to deal with. I don't want you feeling guilty about my mum too." He pushed her hair back off her face and kissed her forehead. "Whatever happens, Sylvie, they're going to have to get over it. It's you and me and if it means they have nothing to do with me, with us, that's their choice." Sylvie squeezed her eyes shut. "Don't, Sylvie, please. Please," he implored as he pulled her close to him so that she rested her whole body on his and he held her tightly.

Nick held on to her as they lay in the warm water, neither of them speaking. Nick stroking her back rhythmically, Sylvie listening to his heart beat slowly, calm. The sun was setting and Sylvie shifted as the bedroom and bathroom began to darken. "Are you hungry?" She lifted her head, resting her chin on his chest. His face had softened though there was still tightness around his eyes.

"I am actually. You?"

"I could eat. Shall I cook something?" Sylvie tried hard to smile and Nick leaned down and kissed her.

"Sure. I'll help."

"Pasta?"

"I'll eat anything you cook."

Sylvie's smile grew and she gave him a quick tender kiss and gracefully stood up. Nick's hand gently caressed her back, behind and leg as she rose and stepped out of the bath.

Sylvie quickly rustled up a pasta sauce made from chicken, coloured peppers, tomato, basil and cream. Nick grated the cheese as he watched her drain the penne and mix them in with the sauce. They were both dressed in bathrobes. She poured all of it into a serving dish and then taking the cheese, mixed some of it in the dish and then sprinkled the rest on the top. Sylvie took the dish and popped it in the oven.

"Fifteen minutes and it'll be ready. Shall I show you round the house before it's totally dark? I think you've only been in my room and the kitchen." Sylvie grinned and Nick nodded.

"Sure, I'd love to."

Sylvie took him through to the sitting room where he'd played on the PlayStation with Alex and Markus.

"I forgot, you've been in here with the boys. This was supposed to be a room for me to use but since we got the PlayStation, I've been evicted!" She shook her head.

"They're good kids, Sylvie. It's quite a novelty for me, you know, having boys around. Our house was always female-orientated, what with Dad leaving when I was eight. It was always cooking, dancing, painting, even sewing! All very arty."

"Dancing?"

"Yeah, Vicki and Elenora took dancing lessons and Mum and I had to be their male partners when they practised at home." *Oh! That explained the good dancing!* "I got to learn the waltz, some jive, Latin, even a bit of Greek!"

"Really?"

Nick nodded. "All in the privacy of our lounge, mind! Wasn't very good for my image!"

Sylvie laughed. "Well our house always had the testosterone dial turned to maximum. Action films, guns, cars, loud games, football. I grew up with three older brothers too, so I never had much contact with girls. The only thing I managed was to teach my boys how to cook, and that's only because they like to eat!"

"Well I have to say, it's been a welcome change for me being around them. They're very easy."

Sylvie nodded as she took Nick through the dining room and the lounge, then into her study. Then they passed back through the house and upstairs to the other three bedrooms, each with their own en suite. Sylvie then took Nick out to the den, which was just off the kitchen where the drums and guitars were stored. It was a large room that protruded out into the garden alongside the pool.

"We wanted to make this the games room but we never got round to it. I might try and actually do it now. It'll give me something to do. We extended it a few years back."

Nick pulled her close and kissed her head. "It's really a beautiful home, Sylvie."

"Thanks. I still think it's a work in progress. Come on, let's eat. You must be famished."

They sat down in the kitchen enjoying their meal. Nick had already refilled his plate.

"I need to get out to Cannes by Wednesday. So I'll probably need to leave Tuesday." He eyed Sylvie as she played with her fork.

She knew he wanted her to go with him, but it was impossible. There was far too much to catch up on at work and Sylvie thought this might be the best time for them to maybe get some distance. Hopefully things would calm down. "I can't get away so soon, Nick. There's just too much going on at work." Nick had placed his fork down and was trying hard to read her face as she spoke. He felt uneasy about leaving her behind when things were still so volatile. "How long will you stay?"

"Two weeks maximum."

"Then maybe I could come out in the second week." She smiled weakly at him, hoping her suggestion would pacify him.

He took a mouthful of pasta and chewed slowly, his eyes not leaving hers. He nodded vaguely, not convinced that she'd ever come out. Well, he'd either try to convince her or hopefully he'd finish faster.

Sylvie took a sip of her wine, a little unsettled at his lack of resistance.

22

MORE EXPLANATIONS

Sylvie woke with a start, sitting up abruptly she glanced at her clock. It was five-thirty. Nick stirred as she lay back down onto her pillow. He turned from sleeping on his back and rested his arm over her as he shifted closer. Sylvie lay there looking up at the ceiling. That feeling of dread was ever-present as her eyes drifted over Nick's handsome face. *How was this ever going to resolve?* She knew the answer deep down: however much Nick tried to assure her, she knew they were fighting an uphill battle.

Sylvie tried hard to commit every beautiful feature on his face to her memory. He looked serene and calm, nothing like how he'd looked last night when Sylvie had tried to reason with him about his impending trip to Cannes. He tried all manner of ways to convince her to come with him. But Sylvie had maintained she'd try to come out the second week. Sylvie suggested that with everything that had transpired that maybe, if they had some distance, everyone would be able to calm down. But her real intentions were to give him space to realise that maybe she wasn't right for him. Julian's words still stung and she knew he was right, however much it hurt her. She needed to at least do the right thing by Nick. He needed someone who he could have a future with. Sylvie closed her eyes as her heart constricted and her stomach knotted.

"I don't care, Sylvie!" They were in her bedroom as Nick paced up and down as Sylvie sat on the edge of the bed.

"Nick, you're angry, I get it. But you can't excommunicate yourself from your family. Believe me, they are important –"

Before she could finish he interrupted her. He was trying hard not to lose his temper. The last thing he wanted was to fight with her. "Sylvie, please stop with this. I know you feel guilty about my dad. But he has the problem, not us. If he wants to be an ass about us, then he can go… well he can swing."

"Nick, you can't be that way. He's hurt and probably a little embarrassed. He needs time, and us rubbing it in his face won't make it easier. I'm just saying we need to be a little more respectful of his feelings, and –"

"Respectful! Was he respectful to you? Well?" He practically glared at her as he raked his hair in frustration. Sylvie looked down at her ring as she rubbed it. "Did he make it easier for you? I know he said horrible, hurtful things to you and here you are making excuses for him. Defending him! Do you have feelings for him? Is that what it is?" Sylvie's eyes shot up to his, as he continued to glare at her. She fleetingly remembered *that* kiss. She'd tried many times to erase it from her memory, but had failed miserably. Pushing away that thought, Sylvie shook her head.

"No, I care for him, Nick. He's my friend and I know that's hard for you to understand, but I want him to be happy and right now he's not. That's largely because of me." She stood up and stepped closer to him and he narrowed his eyes as he clenched his jaw. "It'll be hard on your mum, Elenora and Vicki if you and Julian aren't speaking. I know you don't want that. You can't ask them to take sides and what's more, you don't know how they are going to take it either." She reached up to his cheek and he sighed, his temper cooling. Resting his hand over hers, he reached out with his other, slipping it round her waist and pulling her to him. Sylvie rested her head on his shoulder. She nuzzled him, breathing in deeply. He smelled so delicious.

"Sylvie, I know you're pulling back because of him. You think he'll come round and you're worried about me. I can handle them, all of them."

Sylvie had decided not to push him anymore. She needed to see how

Maggie would react today. Turning, she looked back down at him; God, he looked so young. His cheeks had a flush of colour. Sylvie sighed deeply. He was beyond handsome. Her heart ached, knowing she was causing him all this anguish. She knew things were going to get worse, she just hoped Nick wouldn't get hurt. Her stomach started to twist and she felt the saliva pool in her mouth. *Crap.* She swiftly got up and ran to the bathroom, retching as she went. Thankfully she made it to the toilet in time, emptying the complete contents of her stomach.

Marcy and Petros had left for their annual holiday and thankfully, Marcy had stocked up the fridge and cupboards and insisted that Sylvie leave all the laundry until she came back. They were only away for ten days, but Sylvie enjoyed her time playing house. The boys were good at keeping things clean, so there wasn't that much to do, really. Sylvie made her tea and sat out on the terrace, taking in the view. It was six-fifteen and the sun was coming up. She felt a little chilly sat in her vest and shorts but she knew once the sun came out, she'd warm up.

"Hey, I was looking for you. You're up early." Nick had stepped through the French doors looking glorious with his sleep-swollen eyes and bed hair. Sylvie took in every feature, every dip and contour, and tried hard to hold onto it, to store it so she could recall it.

He'd wrapped a bathrobe around him. As he approached, his brow furrowed. He noticed the goose bumps on her arms and he shrugged off the robe and draped it over her shoulders, leaving him only in his boxers. Sylvie let her eyes travel down his perfect chest and down to his washboard stomach and then to that unbelievable muscle just above his waistband…

"You're cold," he muttered, trying to work out her mood.

"Thanks, aren't you?" He shook his head. "I'll get you some tea." She moved, ready to get up.

"I'll get it, you stay." Relaxing, he leaned down and kissed her forehead, then padded barefoot back inside. He came out holding a cup and placed it next to Sylvie's, then sat himself next to her.

"I'll make some breakfast in a bit. I'm not sure if the boys are home."

"They came in around three. I heard them." Sylvie raised her eyebrows.

"They won't be up for ages, then. Are you hungry?"

"Always, but I can wait. In fact I was hoping you'd still be in bed when I woke up." He looked at her through his lashes as he smiled seductively.

Sylvie stifled a smile. "Oh."

"Hmm. Oh. I could warm you up." He took her hand and started to kiss the inside of her wrist, sending tingles up her spine. *God, she was going to miss this. The way he made her feel so desired, so loved and so alive.*

He pulled her to him and she gasped. He scooped her into his arms and lifted her up effortlessly, carrying her back into the house and up the stairs. Sylvie wrapped her arms around his neck, feeling him tighten his shoulder muscles and kissed his throat, his stubble on her lips. *She was going to miss his taste, his smell, his voice, his face, his body, his touch.*

"Oh I think I'm warm enough," she whispered into his neck and his grip tightened.

"Well I intend to make you hot – very hot and very sweaty," he growled as he pushed open the bedroom door and placed her in the bed, then turned and shut the door and then wedged a chair up against it. "We need to get those locks organised." His eyes were blazing as he whipped off his boxers and clambered onto the bed between Sylvie's legs. *She was going to miss all of it.*

Sylvie sat on the bed in her underwear as she rubbed moisturiser into her arms, watching Nick towel-drying his hair. It was ten and Sylvie could hear Markus and Alex banging away in the kitchen.

"What time are you going up to your mum's?"

"I'll go from here. I want her to know as quickly as possible." Sylvie nodded wistfully. "I had planned to go around nine but I got distracted," Nick smirked. "Twice!"

Sylvie flushed. *Hmm, what a wonderful way to spend a Sunday morning.*

"How the hell am I going to survive for a week without you?" He strode closer to her and then clambered on the bed, pushing her down and framing her face with his hands, his body covering hers, kissing her soundly. "I mean it. It's going to be torture. Please come with me." His eyes imploring her to change her mind.

"I'll try and come out for the second week." His brow creased as she spoke. He wasn't convinced and he had a bad feeling she was only suggesting this so that he would go without her, but he didn't want to ruin their perfect morning. He'd keep quiet until he cleared the air with his mum and then maybe, once Sylvie saw that Maggie wasn't as upset as Julian, she may stop feeling so guilty.

"Come on, I'll make you some breakfast. What do you fancy?"

"Sylvie on toast!" He grinned, kissing her throat and Sylvie laughed.

"Well you had her *on* the bed and *in* the shower. Wasn't that enough?"

Nick's eyes burned into hers. "I can never get enough of you." His voice low and raspy. "Ever!" He kissed her again hard, then jumped back up again.

As they entered the kitchen, Alex and Markus were busy frying up French toast and grilling bacon and sausages.

"Morning! Need any help?" Sylvie asked as she was faced with two sets of slightly embarrassed eyes.

"Morning, Mum, Nick. Pretty much under control. You hungry, Nick?" Alex placed the egg-soaked bread into the frying pan, avoiding eye contact. He was still not completely comfortable with the idea of Nick staying over.

"Famished. Here, I'll give you a hand."

"Great, you can fry up some eggs." Markus handed him the box of eggs and then fished out a frying pan. "Alex likes them done on both sides. I don't." He smirked, shrugging.

"Oh, okay. Sylvie?" Nick turned to her.

Alex and Markus laughed as Sylvie flushed. "Mum doesn't eat eggs," Markus explained.

"Oh?"

"Only in things not on their own. Especially fried. She hates fried eggs. It's the smell." Alex shook his head, almost exasperated.

Sylvie watched as the three most important men in her life busied themselves. Who would have thought after only a couple of days they all seemed to be so comfortable with each other? She went over to the cutlery draw and started to set the table.

Markus looked up. "Hey Nick, do you know what they call French toast in France?" Alex shook his head, knowing where this question was going. Nick looked at Markus, bemused.

"They just call it toast!" He put on a terrible French accent and then he laughed loudly.

"Shut up Markus!" Alex smirked as Nick cringed.

Nick pulled up outside Maggie's house, not knowing what reaction he'd be faced with. He nervously walked up the path and unlocked the door. He could hear Maggie talking on the phone as he entered the sitting area; she was standing by the French doors. Focused on him, she continued to talk, smiling tightly and motioning for him to sit but he stood still, listening.

"I know… well I'm not sure. Let me find out and I'll let you know… I can't answer that right now… Yes. Let me find out, I said. Please calm down… Okay. Bye." Maggie turned off the phone and sighed.

"Hi. I take it that was Dad," said Nick. His voice was low but he couldn't hide his irritation. She pursed her lips together and nodded, her reaction indicating the conversation had not been pleasant.

"So, what did he say?" Nick tried to keep his voice calm but he knew from his mother's whole stance that their conversation had been strained.

"He's just upset," Maggie answered, purposely understating.

Nick huffed. "Upset? Well I really don't give a shit if he is. It should be me that's upset. Forbidding me to see her and God only knows what he said to Sylvie. Who the hell does he think he is? I swear if he wasn't my father –"

"Nick! Please, that's enough. You have to understand it's a shock, for everyone. We had no idea and… well…" Maggie stopped finding it hard to find the right words.

"Well what, Mum? She's older than me? That's what you were going to say, right?" Maggie stood staring at him, afraid to answer. He looked so angry and she wanted him calm so that they could at least talk everything through. "I know that's what you're worried about. That I've found someone who you feel I can never have a future with. Well I can and I will." His eyes were wide as he spoke, and Maggie could see it was difficult for him to control his emotions.

"Nick, please calm down. I don't want to argue. Yes of course that concerns me but –"

He stepped forward towards her, interrupting her. "You and Dad have no right to judge or interfere. I let you once before and it's not happening this time. How can I take advice from you both? Or how can you begin to lecture me on who I want to be with? You're not exactly the best examples, are you? Who are you to tell me who's right and who's not? Look at you both. You divorced after ten years. You're still hoping you'll get back together and Dad's a serial fucker –"

"Nick! Don't speak like that! He's your father!"

"Well maybe he should start behaving like one instead of behaving like a jealous, self-centred ass. He's thinking about himself… again! If it had been anyone else, he wouldn't have reacted this way. And I know this is hard for you to hear, Mum, but whatever he feels for Sylvie…" His voice was rising and Maggie stiffened as he spoke. Nick paused, realising he'd been more than a little heavy-handed and insensitive. "Well, it's not reciprocated," added Nick more quietly, stepping closer to Maggie as her eyes dropped to her hands. "Mum, I'm sorry, truly I am, but I think you've known how Dad felt about Sylvie for a while." Maggie stood silently, then lifted her eyes to meet his and smiled tightly, acknowledging that she was fully aware of that unfortunate fact.

"I sat back for four months, Mum, and watched to see if I thought there would ever be any chance of them getting together. I didn't blatantly decide to sabotage their relationship or break them up. There was nothing *to* break up. She only sees him as a friend."

Maggie closed her eyes for a moment and took a deep breath. Nick couldn't work out if this was because she was relieved to hear this or whether she just didn't want to hear any of it at all, but she seemed to recover and moved towards the settee to sit down. Nick followed her and sat next to her turning himself so he faced her.

"Look, Mum, the bottom line is that I love her. More than anything." His voice was quiet and his initial anger had subsided. Maggie turned to look at him, her brow furrowed.

"Nick, I don't know what to say. I want you to be happy, really I do. but I'm worried for you."

"Mum, I know you like her."

"Yes as my *friend,* I do."

"So it's just the age thing?"

"And how it's affecting your dad."

"I told you, I don't care what he thinks or feels for that matter. He'll have to get over it. My concern is Sylvie. She feels guilty and responsible for all of this and I know she doesn't want to be the one to break up our family. The truth is *I* made the move on her." Maggie sat wide-eyed, not wanting to hear the details of how her son seduced her friend. "She had no idea how I felt about her and I've been trying to convince her ever since. She means everything to me, Mum."

Maggie closed her eyes, at a total loss. Whatever she said or did it was going to hurt one of the most important men in her life. "He's taken it badly, Nick. I don't know if it's the shock or the humiliation but he's still angry."

"So you're siding with him on this?" Nick tried hard to keep his tone steady but Maggie heard the bitterness and saw it in his now pale face.

"It's not a matter of taking sides, Nick. We have to see how this will resolve without everyone getting hurt. It's very complicated, darling, please try to understand…" Nick stood up and looked down at his mother. The muscle in his cheek moved rapidly as he clenched and unclenched his jaw.

"Well at least I know where I stand."

"Nick, don't be like that. We're all reeling over this. It's a lot to take in." Maggie got up from the settee.

"Well, I'm sorry if my happiness is causing our family problems. Don't worry, I'll make sure that I won't be a burden to *any* of you anymore!" Nick stepped back and turned to leave.

"Nick, please don't go, don't leave like that," Maggie pleaded, realising how deeply this was also hurting him. Nick turned round, his face stony and his eyes exuding anger.

"Mum, it's fine. I get it. I need to get out of here before I say something I'll regret." He looked at her closely, contemplating whether he should say what was really going through his mind. Then he shook his head and headed for the door, pulling out his keys as Maggie watched on. Suddenly, she felt an eerie familiarity to his stance and behaviour. He quickly unhooked the house key and dropped it on the console table as he opened the front door and gently closed it behind him.

Nick's Jeep sped away down the hill as Maggie looked down at the key he'd left in the hallway. She picked it up and rubbed it between her paint-stained fingers as the realisation began to hit. He was cutting himself off from them, like he had done over Brigitte. She put her hand onto her forehead. She knew that it was going to be difficult but she'd hoped that they'd be able to muddle through this somehow. Maggie went straight into the sitting room and picked up the phone. There was only one thing left to do.

Lilianna and Zach sat on the terrace speechless as Sylvie recounted her confrontation with Julian. They had popped round to see her with the girls, as they hadn't seen Alex or Markus for a while.

"Holy shit, Sylvie." Lilianna took a huge gulp of her wine. Zach sat almost petrified, and for the first time since Chris's funeral, he looked tense.

"Look. I just thought you should know. I'm hoping he'll calm down. I don't want you to change anything. I mean it. Anything. I'll keep a low profile. Avoid him as much as possible. I can work from home and go in early. Please don't let what I've told you change your behaviour towards him. He's just hurt. No one knows what he said apart from you two, and I want to keep it that way."

Sylvie's eyes rested on Zach, as he seemed to come round. "I knew he'd take it bad, but to say what he said –"

"He's got a nerve, after all the young girls he's bedded." Sylvie cringed as Lilianna spoke. "Oh sweetie, it's not the same with you." Lilianna added, realising her remark was a bit too close to the bone.

"It is the same, Lily, whichever way you look at it. That's something I'm going to have to get used to."

"Just stop it, Sylvie. You know I've got a big mouth!" Lilianna leaned over and rubbed her hand, trying to reassure her.

"The truth is, I'm not sure whether I'm being selfish. I should be thinking about what's right for Nick. Is this worth him falling out with his family? When all is said and done, it's his parents." Sylvie sighed hard and reached for her wine, taking a large gulp. "God knows what Maggie will make of this. I'm going to have to face her too." Sylvie looked at her watch. It was one o'clock and she still hadn't heard from Nick. *Oh well, hopefully no news was good news.*

Realising Sylvie didn't want to be alone, Zach suggested they get some take-out and all eat together. But Sylvie convinced them to stay so she could cook. At least it would take her mind off everything. Alex, Markus, Electra and Melita were in the pool playing water volley. It felt good to have them altogether again. The last time they'd been together was at the barbecue before Chris had died. Sylvie busied herself making some rice, and then set to work on pork fillets in white wine and cream. Yes, cooking helped, she thought to herself, and before long Sylvie had rustled up some cheese-stuffed peppers and garlic mushrooms.

Lilianna watched her dearest friend moving quickly and almost mechanically around the kitchen, preparing everything in her own little world, as she cut the salad and Zach sat and umpired the water volley game. "How did the boys take it all? I didn't want to ask earlier, what with Zach there." Lilianna tried to distract her.

"Surprisingly well. I think it's because they're worried about me being alone, so they're biting the bullet. That and the fact that they seem to get on with Nick. Similar interests. Well, they are closer to his age than me." Sylvie snorted as she mixed the sauce.

"Hey, stop that. Sylvie, he doesn't care."

Sylvie shrugged and checked her watch again: it was two, and still no word. She started to worry. Sylvie checked her mobile for the hundredth time but there was still no message.

"Call him."

"He knows I'm worried. He obviously can't call me. I'll just have to sit it out." Sylvie poured herself another glass and Lilianna pushed some French bread at her.

"At least eat that, otherwise you'll be flat out and your stomach will start cramping." Sylvie picked up the bread and took a bite.

"Thank God you're here," muttered Sylvie as she looked at over at Lilianna.

"I wouldn't be anywhere else, sweetie."

Nick pulled into the car park of the marina and headed over to the *Silver Lining*. He jumped on board and strode through to the bedroom, then hauled out his suitcase. He began to pack as quickly as he could, then picked up his phone and dialled Christian, wedging it between his ear and shoulder, allowing him to continue his packing.

"Hi, Nick. How you doing?" Christian sounded chirpy and Nick almost felt bad for what he was about to dump on him.

"Hi, Christian. Sorry, but I'm afraid I need some help."

"Sure, man. Whatever." Christian sounded instantly concerned.

"I'm taking off tomorrow."

"I thought you were leaving on Wednesday."

"Tuesday actually, but anyway, change of plan. I need you to come and check the *Silver Lining* for me."

"Sure."

"I'll be away for a minimum of two weeks. So you'll be in charge of the shop too. You'll be able to contact me by phone – but Christian, only you." Nick paused, allowing him to understand where this was going.

"Nick, what's going on?" His voice was nervous and wary and he had that sinking feeling that he'd been in this position before.

"I need to get away. I'm going over to Cannes for work but I don't want anyone to know where I am. And I mean *anyone*. If you need to get in touch, either send me a text or call."

"Nick, what's going on?" Christian repeated, his voice more urgent this time.

"You don't need to get dragged into this. Just please don't let them know where I am. I'll be taking my laptop so I can work from wherever I am and you can also email me."

"Is this because of Sylvie?" Nick stopped his frantic packing and slumped onto the bed. "Nick, man, tell me."

"Yes." Nick rubbed his face. "My dad freaked out and it all… well, it's complicated. I need to get away, that's all. Sorry for leaving you in it."

"Don't worry about that. You need anything else?"

"No. Well, not at the moment anyway. I need to go up to Sylvie's and talk it through with her." As he spoke, another call came through. Nick looked at his phone as 'Vicki' flashed at him. "I've got to go. Vicki's calling."

"Okay, Nick. Take it easy."

"Sure." He hung up, then answered Vicki.

"Nick?" He knew from her tone she was anxious.

"Hi Vicki." He closed his eyes.

"What's going on, Nick? Mum says you and Dad have had a falling out and that you're seeing Sylvie. Is that right?"

"Vicki, you really don't need to be mixed up in this."

"What do you mean? Of course I'm mixed up in this. Mum's hysterical, saying you're angry with Dad. Dad's pissed at you 'cos you're seeing Sylvie. When the hell did that happen? Jeez, Nick, why the hell don't you ever talk to anyone?" Vicki sounded wounded and confused at the same time.

Nick knew he'd have to explain and he really wasn't up to it. He just needed to get up to Sylvie's; he knew she'd be worried. "What did Mum say exactly?"

"I'm asking you, Nick. Just fucking tell me!" She was beginning to lose her cool.

"Sylvie and I have been seeing each other and Dad freaked because… well, he was hoping that he'd be seeing her instead." He could almost hear Vicki's jaw drop as he spoke.

"Holy… And Mum knows… about Dad, I mean?"

"Yes. He found out yesterday about me and Sylvie and lost it with us both. He then went and told Mum. So you can imagine how that went. I wanted to break the news to her, but he beat me to it. Vicki, I'm sorry you're in the middle of it. Sylvie's worried that it'll break up the family and I'm trying to convince her that it doesn't matter."

"Break up the family?"

"Dad said he won't accept it. He used the excuse of her age but it's purely because he doesn't want me to be with her. He said some horrible things to the both of us. I'm so angry, Vicki, and well, Mum has concerns too. It's a mess. I just need some time to cool down and my main worry is Sylvie. She's going to take this badly."

"Jesus, I had no idea, Nick. You and Sylvie, eh? That's a bit of a shock. Is it serious?" She knew her question was redundant. Vicki knew her brother didn't do casual.

"Yes, Vicki. And right now, because of Dad, and Mum to an extent, our future is hanging in the balance. I can't let them do this to me again, Vicki." His voice cracked as he spoke. For the first time, he'd been able to speak frankly with someone other than Sylvie.

"Oh, Nicky. You sound terrible." She hadn't called him that since they were young and he suddenly felt that he at least had someone who he could confide in. "What are you going to do?"

"I just need some time. I need to talk to Sylvie before I decide what to do." He looked at his watch. It was two-thirty. He really needed to get up to Sylvie and talk to her face to face. "Look, Vicki, I need to go. I'll call you, okay?"

"Okay, Nick. Please don't do anything stupid."

The line went quiet for a few seconds as Nick instantly understood what Vicki had avoided saying. "Okay. Bye, Vicki."

He got up from the bed and continued to put the last of his things in his suitcase and a small holdall.

23

SUNDAY LUNCH

Sylvie started to place the food out on the table in the shade of the terrace. There was a cool breeze, making it pleasant, and Sylvie rustled the leaves of her basil plant which sat in a terracotta pot by the French doors, allowing its fresh smell to waft around. Her stomach was in knots still. Even the two glasses of wine hadn't helped. If Maggie was reluctant to accept their relationship, she knew she'd need to step back. That recurring thought kept hammering its way into the top of her mind and every time she tried to dispel it, it came racing back, stronger and more forcefully. It was up to her to make the decision and she'd wrestled with herself over and over to find the right solution. Her own pain was lattermost in her mind. Julian was right, she really should have known better. For the first time, she'd done something selfish, something that she wanted so incredibly badly, and now it had come full circle and bitten her in the ass. That thought depressed her on so many levels – that and the guilt. The guilt of hurting Nick and jeopardising his relationship with his family.

As she stepped back into the kitchen, she heard the familiar sound of Nick's Jeep pulling up outside. Her whole body slumped with relief. *At least he was here*, she thought. She quickly looked up at Lilianna, who gave her a tight smile and she all but ran through to the hallway, her heart thumping hard. All manner of thoughts raced through her head as she took a deep breath before opening the door. She prayed that it had gone better with Maggie for Nick's sake – and, she thought fleetingly, for hers too. With trembling hands she reached for the handle and opened up the door.

255

Nick was making his way up from his Jeep carrying what seemed like a holdall. He'd changed from this morning, wearing dark blue shorts and a tight, light blue T-shirt. His mouth was set in a hard line, which broke into a glorious smile as he saw her. He, of course, looked stunning and she only wished she could see his eyes, which were covered with his customary Wayfarers. As if hearing her thoughts, he removed them, revealing those amazing cobalt-blue eyes, the colour echoing whatever he was wearing. Sylvie's heart stopped for a beat, then jump-started again.

"Hi." He was up in front of her, staring down, and Sylvie could see both relief and sadness in his face.

"Hi," she breathed, equally relieved. He dropped his bag and took hold of her face, gently kissing her. Sylvie melted against him, feeling his need for her as he kissed her harder. Slowly pulling away, he smiled at her and pushed back her hair. "I was worried."

"I know. I'm sorry, baby." He turned to look at Zach's car. "You've got company?" he asked warily.

"Zach, Lily and the girls came round to see the boys. We were just about to have lunch. Are you hungry?"

"Always." He smiled. "Come on. I suppose I should officially meet them too." He tried to sound at ease as he reached down for his bag, but his voice was tense. Sylvie looked at his bag, puzzled. "I needed some stuff, if I'm staying over." He grinned. "Is that okay?"

"Of course." She looked at him, trying to assess his mood, but he was giving nothing away. As if reading her thoughts, he slipped his arm around her, guiding her back into the hallway, dropping his bag by the stairs.

"We'll talk later. Right now, I just want to forget about everything."

"Okay," Sylvie muttered, knowing deep down that it had obviously not gone well. Her heart sank.

When they reached the terrace, everyone had already sat down. There were two seats left at one end of the table. Markus was up first, ever trying to dispel any awkwardness. "Hi, Nick. Let me introduce you." Zach rose from his chair, eyeing Nick warily. "This is Zach and Lilianna."

"Hello, we met at your sister's wedding." Zach reached out to Nick's already outstretched hand, firmly shaking it, furrowing his brow. Then Nick turned to Lilianna and shook her hand.

"Nice to finally meet you, Nick," Lilianna said with a mischievous glint in her eye.

"Likewise, Lilianna," Nick responded, smiling wryly.

"Lily," she corrected. "This is Electra and Melita." Nick reached over and shook both their hands as they openly gawked at him, eyes wide and their jaws dropping, clearly shocked that this stunning man was firstly in their company and secondly was seeing Sylvie. Recovering slightly, they both looked at Alex as he stifled a grin.

"Beer, Nick?" Alex got up to go into the kitchen. "Or do you want something stronger?" Alex narrowed his eyes as he spoke to him.

"Beer's fine, thanks." Sylvie guided him to the chair opposite Zach and next to Lilianna and then she moved round to her place at the head of the table between Zach and Nick. Nick waited until Sylvie sat, then took his seat. Lilianna raised her eyebrows in the direction of Sylvie, showing her surprise and approval of his obviously ingrained manners.

"Well, everybody dig in before it gets cold." Sylvie tried to keep her voice steady, but the truth was she felt nervous. It suddenly became very clear to her that she wanted Zach to approve of Nick. Alex passed Nick his beer and he smiled down at him, giving him a reassuring wink.

"Thanks." Nick's face lost its tightness as he took his beer and he exhaled slowly.

Sylvie could tell he was nervous and that Alex's small gesture had put him somewhat at ease. She looked lovingly at Alex, who'd sat down at the opposite end of the table, and mouthed, "Thank you." He nodded slightly, then passed the salad to Electra who had to drag her eyes away from Nick in order to serve herself.

Markus started to tease the girls about their water volley skills and Alex joined in, in an attempt to lighten the atmosphere. Sylvie reached over and started to serve Nick, placing rice on his plate and then spooning the pork and sauce over it. Zach watched on, his face unreadable. Lilianna glared at Zach, trying to grab his attention, but he seemed to be oblivious, transfixed by Nick. Sylvie began to feel uncomfortable. Maybe this hadn't been such a good idea.

"So, Nick, Sylvie tells us you have a boat." Lilianna turned to him as she spoke.

"Yes, I do." Nick smiled warmly at Lilianna, then took a long draught from his beer.

Sylvie shifted in her chair as she watched Zach continue to stare at Nick. *What was his problem?* This was so unlike him – he was normally relaxed and unfazed. *Crap, crap, crap*, she thought as she reached for a bread roll and tore it in half.

"Do you take it far – what I mean is, off the island?"

God bless Lilianna, thought Sylvie. At least while she was speaking to him, Nick needed to turn to her and not be subjected to Zach's frankly unnerving behaviour. Sylvie buttered the bread roll and unconsciously placed it on Nick's side plate. Zach's eyes squinted, then shifted focus, resting on the side plate, and he seemed to be processing an unwelcome thought. For some reason, the table went quiet and everyone's attention had shifted up to their end of the table.

"I haven't had a chance yet. But I hope to over the summer. I've only had her nine months," Nick offered as an explanation. He put down his beer and his attention was momentarily distracted by the buttered roll on his plate. He smiled to himself, then turned to Sylvie. Zach was reaching for his wine glass as Lilianna glared at him, eventually grabbing his attention. Zach frowned at her and took a gulp of his wine as Nick reached over to Sylvie's hand, taking it gently and raising it to his lips, kissing the inside of her wrist.

A number of things happened at once. Zach's eyes widened as he watched this most intimate gesture and he froze, unable to place his wine glass back on the table. Then he came to his senses and he nervously coughed. Melita gasped and dropped her fork, her jaw dropping for the second time in five minutes. Electra choked on her wine and Markus patted her back, stifling his grin, and Alex closed his eyes and took a deep breath. Then, opening them, he exhaled and drained his beer. Lilianna smirked to herself and took a sip of her wine and tried hard to behave as if nothing untoward had happened.

Sylvie looked at Nick through her lashes as she smiled. She knew exactly what he was doing. It was Island and Dimitris Dracos all over again. Nick picked up his knife and fork and started to cut through the pork, his face giving nothing away.

"Are you alright, Electra?" Lilianna asked, stifling her smile as Melita scrambled down to pick up her fork and wiped it on her napkin.

"Er… yes, Mum, it just went down the wrong way." Electra blushed.

"I bet it did," Lilianna mumbled softly, supposedly to herself.

Markus tried his usual distraction tactic by making a joke about Melita's lack of co-ordination being limited not just to volley but also to cutlery, so that Alex, Melita and Electra's attention was directed to their end of the table, as they carried on with their meal.

Then out of the blue, Zach spoke softly. "You look so much like your father."

Sylvie's eyes swooped up to Nick's face as he looked up at Zach in surprise. "Yes, so I've been told." He smiled softly at Zach and Zach shook his head and huffed, indicating that he found it disorientating.

Zach picked up his fork and stabbed a mushroom. "I never noticed it before, that's all."

"He does have something of Maggie though too," Lilianna added, trying not to make Nick totally uncomfortable. Lilianna's eyes flitted to Sylvie as she took a sip of wine.

Nick shrugged awkwardly and then popped a heavily sauced piece of pork in his mouth and chewed. "This is delicious." He looked lovingly at Sylvie as he continued to chew, pointing to his food with his fork. "I love your cooking," he added softly. Forking up his next mouthful, he frowned as he heard his phone ring and he pulled it from his pocket. His eyebrows rose as he saw the caller. "Sorry, it's Elenora. I need to take this." He stopped momentarily, looking back at Sylvie. "My battery's nearly dead. Do you mind if I use the landline?"

"Of course you can."

"Thanks. Excuse me." He gracefully got up from the table but not before squeezing Sylvie's hand, and stepped inside to the kitchen.

Once she was sure he was out of earshot, Lilianna turned to Zach. "Jeez, Zach, what the hell!"

He looked up at his wife, confused. "What?"

"Are you kidding me? Why were you staring?" she hissed.

"Was I?" He looked over at Sylvie and she nodded pursing her lips together. "Sorry. It's just that… well, he looks *so* much like Julian. No, that's not right, it's more his mannerisms. And… well honestly… it's weird seeing you with someone else. Sorry." He shrugged, and Sylvie allowed herself to relax a little. At least he was being honest. Chris had been his best friend after all. She reached over and clasped his hand.

"Well remember he's probably a lot more nervous than all of us put together, so pack it in. And girls, stop freaking staring. It's embarrassing!" Lilianna added, shaking her head in exasperation. Sylvie didn't know if it was the tense atmosphere, or the fact she had been so wound up all day but she had an inexplicable urge to laugh. She clasped her mouth and started a nervous giggle. Lilianna looked on and started to grin widely as she too relented and laughed with her friend as the whole table looked on in shock, then slowly one by one, they too chuckled.

Sylvie wiped her eyes as the laughter tears trickled down her cheek.

"Oh, I feel better for that." Sylvie sighed as her laughing subsided. "I better go check on him. He's been a long time."

Lilianna rubbed her hand and gave her a reassuring smile. "It'll work itself out sweetie."

Sylvie closed her eyes momentarily and sighed. She wished she could be so optimistic.

She found Nick pacing up and down, still talking on the phone in the lounge. He was running his hand through his hair rapidly and his expression was tense.

"Like I said to Vicki, I'm not going to let history repeat itself… I know, Elenora, but if they can't at least try to accept what's happened…" He looked up and caught sight of Sylvie and smiled softly at her. She motioned that she'd leave him alone and he shook his head, waving her in and stepping closer to her. She stood awkwardly, not really knowing what she should do. Nick reached over and took her by the hand, guiding her to the settee. Sitting down, he took her with him, not letting go of her.

"I didn't want either one of them to find out this way, but unfortunately they did. I tried to express myself to them, but they can only see one side. They don't listen – or rather, they won't. I accept that. I can't make anyone like what's happened but by the same token, I don't want to listen to what they have to say either. Not anymore, anyway. They've behaved appallingly and to be honest, I'm done." Nick looked over to Sylvie as she clenched her jaw and closed her eyes, breathing deeply. She needed a drink.

Prizing her hand away from Nick's, she stood up, and his eyes followed her anxiously as she went to the bar and pulled out the Chivas bottle. She splashed a large measure into a heavy crystal glass, then went to the kitchen and fished out some ice, throwing it hurriedly into the glass. Sylvie leaned on the counter with her hands leaving the glass – now half full because of the ice – in front of her as she squeezed her eyes shut. Her stomach cramped and she was starting to sway.

This was what she didn't want. This is what she had feared all along. She could hear Nick finishing the conversation as he strode purposefully through to the kitchen. Her eyes shot open and she looked up at him, still gripping the counter.

"Sure… I'll call you. Me too." Nick hung up the phone and put it down on the coffee table, then seeing Sylvie, he frowned. Coming up behind her, he wrapped her in his arms and held her tightly, inhaling deeply. Moving her hands from the counter, she wriggled so she could place her hands on his arms, then she slowly turned to face him.

Nick stroked back her hair and kissed her forehead. "I'm sorry. I didn't really want you to hear that," he mumbled.

"It's bad, isn't it?" She rested her head against his chest, breathing in his intoxicating scent as she blinked her tears back, thankful that he couldn't see. Nick fell silent and his silence spoke a thousand words. Sylvie listened to his heart beating rapidly.

"Come on, let's go back outside. I'm starving and I've left a plateful of your delicious food out there." He spoke softly and Sylvie knew he wasn't ready to talk. Blinking her tears away, she pulled back and plastered her face with her best fake smile.

"It'll probably need warming up." She scrunched up her nose as she spoke. Nick breathed deeply as he gazed at her lovingly, his eyes ablaze. His eyes then rested on the glass behind her and he cocked his head to one side. He reached over and picked it up, handing it to her. Sylvie accepted it and took a large gulp. Then Nick bent down and kissed her, sucking gently on her lips.

"Mmm, second-hand Chivas, my favourite," he whispered seductively. Sylvie squirmed and then purposely lifted the glass to her lips. Fixing him with her eyes, she drained the glass, her eyes never leaving his. Nick's eyes widened in surprise, changing from concerned to amused. "You're very lucky there's a house full of people." His eyes glittered as he bent down to kiss her again.

"Or unlucky." She breathed against his lips. Nick groaned as his arms wrapped round her tighter and he kissed her harder. Hearing someone, Nick pulled away turning to see who it was. Zach sauntered in, stopping suddenly on the threshold of the French doors.

"Oh, er… sorry. I came in to get some more wine." He looked mortified, realising he'd interrupted. Sylvie stepped away from Nick and moved over to the wine fridge and pulled out a bottle of Chablis.

"Here you are, Zach." Sylvie handed it over to him, finding it hard to look at him in the eye. "Nick, can you get the opener? It's in that drawer." Sylvie motioned with her chin and Nick turned and hurriedly retrieved it, coming round from the breakfast bar. They all made their way back to the terrace.

Slowly, everyone started to relax, mainly thanks to the wine. They were now on their third bottle and Zach had loosened up again. The children had decided to play cards on a table further away from the rest of them. Sylvie cleared the table and brought out coffee and tea.

"I fancy a Calvados." Zach stretched as he leaned back.

"Oh yes, that sounds good. I'll go get it." Lilianna got up and headed back inside, re-emerging with a bottle and four brandy glasses. Sylvie was pouring the coffee and tea.

"Nick, are you having one?"

Nick shook his head at Zach as he watched him pour the Calvados into three of the glasses. "I really only drink beer and wine. I'm not a great fan of spirits, though I have to say my taste has recently changed." He smirked and fixed his eyes on Sylvie as she flushed. "To be honest, I don't really drink that much."

"Well don't let us lead you astray, Nick. I'm afraid we drink quite a bit. Sylvie included." Lilianna winked over at Sylvie.

Zach snorted as he placed each glass in front of Sylvie and Lilianna. "Chris was the only one who could drink anyone under the table, though Sylvie did give him a run for his money." He was almost talking to himself, then in a split-second he'd realised what he'd said and his eyes shot up to Sylvie who had frozen. There was a deathly silence as Sylvie slowly closed her eyes. Nick shifted in his chair and gently reached over and clasped her hand. Lilianna muttered an oath as she tried to compose herself, exasperated at Zach's lack of tactfulness.

"I've always been a bit of a lightweight in the drinking stakes." Nick directed his comment to Zach, breaking the silence.

Zach blinked and then turned to Nick. "Yes… um… well, I could never keep up."

"Sylvie tells me you helped Chris start up Sapphire Developers."

Lilianna and Sylvie simultaneously took a huge gulp of their Calvados as they watched on, Nick gently stroking Sylvie's hand in an attempt to reassure her. Zach shifted in his seat. Nick's comment was unexpected. He coughed nervously. "Well, that's a little generous of Sylvie. Chris set it up. I just came in to help him out. It was always his company and now it's Sylvie's."

Nick nodded, then picked up his teacup in his customary manner and took a gulp.

"Julian tells me you're doing well, thanks to the Russian market."

"Yes, they seem to be the ones with the money these days. Initially, I dealt with the European market, but I've managed to break into the Russian market now."

Sylvie gazed over at Nick. He was doing this for her, making it easy for her, regardless of how difficult and uncomfortable it made him. He'd taken control again. He knew Zach was important to her. She squeezed his hand and he momentarily looked back at her, his eyes softly returning her gaze, then he turned back to Zach, continuing their discussion. He was the single most unselfish, considerate man she'd ever come across, and fleetingly, she realised that this was a credit to his parents. Her heart soared and sank within a millisecond. Sylvie smiled at Zach as he sat back in his chair again, visibly starting to relax.

Everyone slowly began to loosen up as the two men started to talk about a number of topics ranging from their businesses to football. Sylvie's eyes kept flitting to Lilianna. She too watched on as the two men slowly started to feel more comfortable with each other and Lilianna winked at Sylvie indicating that it seemed obvious the worst was over.

It was eight o'clock by the time Zach and Lilianna got up to leave. Alex had suggested that he drive their car home and Markus would follow in his pickup truck, as both Zach and Lilianna were in no fit state to drive. They had also arranged to take Electra and Melita to the cinema in a discreet bid to give Sylvie and Nick some privacy. As Sylvie and Nick waved them off, that ever-present foreboding feeling came back. It was time to talk and Sylvie wanted to transport herself back to Athens, when things were so much simpler. Back to their cocoon.

Sylvie walked back into the house, closing the door softly behind her. Nick took her hand and pressed her palm to his lips. "Alone at last?" he murmured, trailing kisses up the inside of her arm. "Are you tired?" His eyes were fixed on hers as he gradually moved higher. Sylvie slowly shook her head as her whole body ignited. How was she ever going to let him go?

"Good, because right now, I'm desperate to make love to you." As he reached over to her shoulder, he pulled down the strap of her camisole. Sylvie moaned, allowing her hands to travel up his chest and to his head. "You smell so delicious," he whispered in her ear. Reaching down, he scooped her in his arms as Sylvie wrapped her arms around his neck, nuzzling him, and he carried her up the stairs.

As they entered the dark bedroom, Nick flicked on the lights and gently placed Sylvie on the bed. He strode over to the window, closing the curtains. Sylvie watched him as he moved seemingly at ease around the room. He turned on the bedside lamp, then turned off the main lights. Walking back around the bed, he pulled off his T-shirt and slipped off his sneakers and socks.

"We need to talk, Nick." He knelt down in front of her, reaching for the hem of her camisole and pulling it over her head. Sylvie tried hard to focus on his face rather than let her eyes drift down his taut torso.

"Later," his voice low and silky as his eyes blazed into hers. Bending back down, he slipped off her flip-flops and then gently eased her back on the bed.

"Nick… we need to talk. Work this out."

Nick knelt between her legs, his eyes emanating pure unadulterated desire. He unbuttoned the top of her shorts and pulled down the zip. He lowered himself over her and kissed her softly, stroking back her hair. "Please, Sylvie. Later." His eyes burning into hers as he spoke, his face strained. He looked so young and so breathtaking as he pleaded, Sylvie's heart twisted as she gazed back at him, her pulse through the roof. Who was she kidding, the last thing she wanted to do was talk! Sylvie took hold of his face, pulling his lips to hers and he groaned against her mouth. *Screw it!* She knew she didn't have a hope in hell.

2 4

GONE

Sylvie curled her arms around Nick's head. "That's it, baby," he moaned as he held on to her hips slowly, steadily pushing deeper into her. Raising his head up from her chest so they were face to face, her legs straddling him, he watched her writhe, arching her back. "Look at me, baby. I want to see you." Sylvie's eyes gently opened and his face was alight with love and adoration. "God, I love you." He ran his hands up her spine, causing her to shiver, all the while moving in and out as she rose and fell. He seized her face and kissed her hard and Sylvie groaned into his mouth.

"Ah."

Nick thrust harder as Sylvie clung on to him in total surrender. "Oh Nick, don't stop!" He could feel her tightening and he pulled back slightly so he could see her face, his eyes locked on hers.

"Let go for me, baby," he muttered through gritted teeth as he pushed harder and she flung her head back, his words her undoing as she climaxed, gripping on to him as she cried out. With a final thrust, Nick too found his release. "Oh Jesus, Sylvie!" wrapping her in his arms tightly, his head still cradled in her arms.

Nick eventually lifted his head again as he took deep breaths and planted kisses along her shoulder. "Come with me to Cannes," he breathed against her still-sensitive skin. "How will I last ten days without you?" He turned his gaze to her, stroking back her hair. "Please come," his eyes earnest as they penetrated into hers. Sylvie sighed, then slowly shifted, allowing Nick to move from under her. She flopped back on the bed as her breathing calmed. Nick stretched out next to her, resting his head on his elbow, turning towards her, his fingers trailing over her stomach.

After a few minutes, Sylvie softly spoke. "What happened today, Nick?" Sylvie shifted, turning to face him, reaching over to stroke his stubbly cheek. "You're going to have to talk to me. I know it's not good."

Nick momentarily closed his eyes as his nostrils flared, breathing deeply. After what seemed an age, he finally spoke. "She was shocked, I suppose. Dad had obviously gone in ranting and she was trying to be the diplomat. Making excuses for him." He turned to lie on his back so that he avoided Sylvie's face, which was now etched with concern. "I just left. I really didn't want to hear it. She's always covered for him. Whatever he does, she has some explanation ready for him. He behaves like a spoilt child. When things don't go his way he flies off the handle and she bends over backwards to make the peace again. Well, I won't budge this time."

"Oh, Nick. I'm so sorry."

"It's not you who should be apologising. It's him." He sounded angry as he turned back to face her, then his expression softened as he ran the back of his hand down her cheek. "I'm leaving tomorrow. I booked an earlier flight. My flight leaves at eleven forty-five." He leaned across and kissed her softly. "Christian's taking me to the airport in the morning. I'll need to leave by eight-thirty."

"Oh."

"You didn't answer me," he said. Sylvie looked puzzled. "About coming out to Cannes."

Sylvie swallowed, knowing she was going to upset him. "Look, Nick, I think with everything that's gone on, that maybe I shouldn't come out right now. I've got a lot to sort out here and what with the tension and –"

Nick's jaw clenched as she tried her hardest to soften the blow. He sat up abruptly and ran his hands through his hair. "You're not coming out at all?" His voice was quiet, too quiet.

Sylvie sat up and rested her hand on his shoulder. He was tense; she could feel his muscles hardening under her fingers. "Nick, please just listen. You're going for work. Once you've finished, maybe, I'll see."

He turned to look at her his face full of angst. "Sylvie, don't do this. If you can't come out now I'll understand, but at least come out at the weekend." He paused a second, then tentatively added: "Or is it that you're not going to come out at all?" He swung round, crossing his legs to face her. "Sylvie, don't feel guilty about this. They'll get over it." His voice was earnest as he implored her.

"Maybe, but at what cost, Nick? I don't want that. Maybe this trip has come at the right time. It'll give them time to calm down. I could talk to them and –"

"Oh no, Sylvie, he's said enough to you. If he ever speaks to you like that again…" His eyes blazed as he tried to rein in his temper. "No, no." He shook his head emphatically to emphasize the point.

"Nick, in a few days things will be less strained. I need to speak to Maggie. She's my friend – I owe her that. Nick, you and I, we need to get some perspective, some distance; we've been so wrapped up in ourselves –"

Nick's eyes widened as she spoke softly, then narrowing them he shuffled closer. "You think we need a break? Is that what you're saying?" He couldn't hide his horror, his voice hardly audible.

"Look, Nick, this trip is very important to you and maybe the timing is… what with everything…"

"What are you saying, Sylvie? I don't want to be apart from you. The thought of not seeing you for ten days is…" His voice trailed off as his face drained. "Don't you feel the same way? I thought you loved me?"

Of course I feel the same way! Sylvie screamed in her head. *That's why I'm doing this!* She slowly got up from the bed and reached for her robe, slipping it on, her heart pounding the blood round her shivering body. Her stomach cramped and she swallowed hard, determined to control herself.

Nick shuffled back uneasily, watching warily, her back facing him. Taking her lead, he slipped on his boxers and stood up. "Sylvie, look at me."

Sylvie knew she needed him to leave for Cannes so at least she could repair any damage their relationship had caused. Maybe if he was away from her, he'd see that their relationship was not the best for him. That thought made her heart break. She loved him so much it frightened her, because she knew if what they had could potentially ruin the relationship with his parents, she'd have to leave him. She never wanted that. How could she live through that?

Pulling on as much of her wilting inner strength as she could, she turned around to face him, her heart lurching as she stared into his incredible face, the face she had fallen so desperately in love with. Her selfish side wanted to tell everyone to take a running jump and leave them well alone. But her rational side knew that they would both pay for it later. So as she looked deep into those magnificent eyes, now full of apprehension, she spoke purposefully, hoping he'd be reasonable.

"Nick, I just think it would be better, for everyone, if we stepped back a little. Just for now. I'll try and come out, but right now I think I need to stay here and…" She watched as Nick's face changed from confused to tense, then to pained within a second. *Oh this was going to be so much harder than she'd ever imagined.* She needed to be strong, for him. She could fall to pieces afterwards but needed to get him away – away from her, so that he could get on with his life. A life he deserved.

He looked vulnerable and lost as he searched her eyes desperately. All she wanted was to wrap him in her arms again. *Why had she fallen for him? Why oh why had she not been smart and rational?* She had known it would come to this, that he'd break her heart and what was worse, that she'd break his.

He put up his hand, causing her to stop. He shook his head a fraction as he processed what he could see unravelling in front of him. He hurriedly dragged on his shorts and T-shirt with trembling hands.

"Nick, please…"

"No, no. Don't! Don't speak." He looked up as his eyes glazed over with tears. "Those beautiful eyes are doing *all* the talking. I don't want to hear you say it. I won't be able to bear it if you say it. Please, *please* don't." He quickly put on his Converse. Sylvie stood stock-still as she watched him meticulously tie up his laces. "What do I have to do? What more do I have to do?" His voice was cracking as he whispered almost to himself.

Standing back up again, he continued, his tone utterly sincere, his face totally raw. "Jeez, Sylvie. All I ever wanted was you. Is that too much to ask? Am I so unworthy?" He flung his arms in the air and then rested his hands on his head. Sylvie tried hard to swallow the lump in her throat, which had lodged itself firmly there as she stood transfixed, her feet rooted to the hardwood floor.

"Please, Nick, don't say that. We need to talk about this –"

He clenched his eyes shut, shaking his head as she spoke, then opening them suddenly as his hands dropped to his side, he interrupted her. "I'm done talking. *No one* listens to me… All the people I love won't accept what I want. They won't accept that I love you, that you are the single most important person in my life. That all I want is to be with you." He raked his hands through his hair as a tear he'd tried hard to hold dropped. Dashing it quickly away, he softly added: "Not even you."

"Nick, please…" Sylvie stepped forward. Nick's face creased as if he was torn.

Then he stepped back and put his hands up in warning. "No, don't. I'll make this easier on everyone." He stepped back again towards the door, his face desolate. He opened the door, slowly turning to look at her as if trying to commit her face to memory. "Bye, baby," he whispered, pausing a second, then he swiftly exited the bedroom, his footsteps quickening as he ran down the stairs and out of the house.

Sylvie stood shivering in the dim light of her room. Her stomach retched again and she managed to force her body to move to the bathroom just in time, as she vomited profusely over her sink. She looked up at her reflection in the mirror, her eyes red from the sheer exertion. She slid down to the floor and sobbed uncontrollably. Desolate and alone. Feeling nothing but an immense sense of loss, as the realisation began to slowly sink in and the pain lanced through her aching body. Sylvie clutched onto her knees as she rocked herself, crying unrestrained into her thighs. Her heart torn from her heaving chest. He'd gone.

After what seemed a long time, Sylvie stood up, taking shuddering breaths as her weeping subsided. Tired and weary, she dragged herself back to bed, covering herself and grasping onto her pillow. The distinctive smell of his skin still lingering on the sheets. Burying her face into her pillow, a new fresh wave of tears threatened and she cried herself to sleep.

Nick powered down the hill away from Sylvie's house, his hands gripping the wheel and his jaw clenched. He didn't know where to go. His pulse was racing as he tried to take in what was happening. Why did everyone think they knew what was best for him? He didn't want to even think about his father. He fleetingly thought about going round to see him, but he knew he'd never be able to restrain himself. No, he was glad he was leaving tomorrow. He turned down to the marina and parked up his car, still unsure of where to go. He couldn't face going to the *Silver Lining*. Rubbing his eyes, he got out of the car, dragging his holdall with him, and headed towards the shop. He'd crash with Christian.

Nick hammered on the door, oblivious that it was almost midnight.

He could hear muffled noises from within, and then the door opened. Christian stood bleary-eyed in his boxers rubbing his face. "Fuck, Nick, what the… Jesus, what's up man?"

Nick pushed passed him, dropping his bag by the small table in the entranceway. "Sorry… can I crash here tonight?" he mumbled, as he walked through to the sitting area and flopped onto the couch.

"Yeah… whatever. What's wrong?" Nick shook his head. "You want a drink or something?" Christian was eyeing him warily, knowing instinctively it was something to do with Sylvie. The last time he'd been like this was when Brigitte broke it off; then, though, he'd been angry. Looking at Nick slumped on his couch, he didn't look angry, he looked broken. Nick nodded weakly in response and Christian went to the fridge and pulled out a beer, opening it up quickly and handing it to him.

"Christian? Who was it?" Christian's girlfriend Chrissie's voice asked from the direction of the bedroom.

"It's okay, Chrissie, it's Nick," he called back, but it was too late. She'd emerged from the bedroom in a thin robe. Nick's eyes rested on the beer he was holding, almost in a trance. Christian's eyes shot to Chrissie's, glaring at her, trying to convey that Nick was not in a good place.

She stepped round so that she could see him; her hair was messy from sleep and she tightened the robe round her. "Hey Nick, you okay?" she asked softly, her eyes full of concern. Her eyes darted back to Christian and he raised his eyebrows, showing he was clueless.

After a few moments, Nick took a draught of his beer, then set it down on the coffee table and looked up at Chrissie as she stood looking at him, still bewildered. "No I'm not, Chrissie… I…" Chrissie edged closer and the sight of her concerned face tipped him over the edge, and his face contorted as he couldn't hold on to his grief any more. Leaning forward, his face in his hands, the tears sprung uncontrollably and rolled down his face.

Chrissie shot a look at Christian. He watched on, wide-eyed and perplexed. Within a second, Christian moved round to his side, not sure what he should do. Then Chrissie lowered herself onto the couch and tentatively put her hand on his back, rubbing it. "Hey, come on now." She squeezed his shoulders and he leaned into her as he tried to control his sobs. Christian strode over to the kitchen again and grabbed three glasses, a bottle of brandy and the kitchen roll. He brought them over to the coffee table and splashed very generous measures into each. Nick pulled back from Chrissie's shoulder and wiped his eyes with the back of his hand before Chrissie ripped off some kitchen roll and handed to him.

"Here, drink this." Christian shoved the brandy in front of him.

"Thanks… I'm sorry… I just didn't know where else to go." Chrissie reached over and took her glass and sipped it. Christian sat down in the armchair and gulped his drink. Giving him a few moments to compose himself, Christian watched on until he saw Nick take a welcome sip of his brandy, then he spoke. "What happened, Nick?"

Nick rested back into the couch and Chrissie turned herself to face him. "It's my parents. My dad went ape shit about me and Sylvie, and my mum's got serious concerns." His breathing was still shaky as he spoke. "Sylvie feels guilty that she's caused this and thinks we need to take a break." He gulped his brandy again and stared at the glass.

"Fucking hell, Nick!" Christian blurted out and Chrissie glared at him. "Sorry." He shrugged, embarrassed at his tactlessness.

"I wanted her to come with me tomorrow. Or at least by the weekend. But she tried to avoid it."

"I'm so sorry, Nick." Chrissie rubbed his arm as she spoke. "You care for her, then?"

Nick looked up at her, his eyes welling again. "I love her, Chrissie. She's everything to me. I might as well be a dead man walking without her." He dashed the tears that spilled over again. "I've got to go to Cannes tomorrow and I really can't face it. I wish I could blow it off… I just left because I didn't want to hear her tell me we should split up. I just didn't want to hear her say that. I knew that's where it was going." He drained his brandy and set the glass on the table. "What do I have to do? Why does this always happen to me?"

Christian rubbed his face nervously as he watched his best friend crumble before his eyes. Putting down his glass, he moved over to the couch and grabbed Nick's shoulders. "Look, Nick, right now you feel shitty about what's happened, and for the life of me. I don't get it. You both seemed… well, I've never seen you like that with anyone and… well I'll be honest, she looked totally into you. But you going to Cannes might be the best thing for you now. It's a massive deal you're putting together and by the time you're signed and finished, things may have calmed down." Nick stared blankly at him as he spoke. "If you need to stay there longer, then stay. I'll manage. Out there, at least you'll be away from it all. And if Sylvie really wants to be with you… well…"

"What if she doesn't?" Nick whispered. Christian shot a glance at Chrissie and she twisted her mouth.

"Sometimes you need to let someone go to see if they'll come back to you." Chrissie softly answered his question. "If they don't, then they were never really yours, but if they do, then … well, then you'll know."

Nick snorted. "Are you quoting sentimental crap to me to make me feel better?" His voice was laced with cynicism.

Chrissie smirked. "Yeah, that's exactly what I'm doing."

Nick looked at her as she made a face at him. "Thanks. Right now I'll listen to anything, even sentimental crap."

She chuckled at him and gave his arm a squeeze. "I'm off to bed. I need to get up for work. Unlike you two, I don't own my own company or have a laid-back boss!" She got up off the couch, then leaned down and kissed Nick's forehead. "Get some sleep, then go and make a shit ton of money in Cannes. The rest will work itself out."

"That's more like it and not an ounce of sentimentality!" Nick tried to smile, but his lips just couldn't curl.

"I'll put you a towel in the spare room. Good night." They watched her leave, then Christian splashed more brandy in their glasses.

"She's right though, Nick. Do what you need to do and give it some time."

Nick took another drink, then put down his glass. "I'm not going to give up on her, Christian."

"I know."

"As far as my parents are concerned… I just don't want to have anything to do with them. And don't tell them where I am. I'll talk to Vicki and Elenora, but that's it."

"You okay now?" Nick nodded. "So I'll see you in the morning?" Nick nodded again. "I know you don't want to leave, but Nick, it's a major deal and Serge can find you loads more clients. You can't back out now. Get some sleep, okay?"

"Sure. You're right, but it doesn't make it easier. Go on. Go to bed, I'm fine," he lied.

"Okay. Night." Christian got up and patted Nick's back, then headed to his bedroom, leaving Nick sat on the sofa.

25

IMPOSSIBLE

The next few days passed by in a blur for Sylvie. The morning after Nick had left, she'd managed to go into the office and tell Zach that she'd tried to make Nick pull back from her, hoping he'd decide on his own that it was better for them to split.

Zach sat dumbfounded behind his desk as he looked at a gaunt Sylvie. "But I thought you... well, you seemed so happy." His eyes were wide with shock. He couldn't keep up. One minute he was in shock that they were together, the next minute he was reeling because they were splitting up.

"I can't come between him and his parents, Zach," she whispered. "And he needs someone he can have a future with. I have to face facts... it's not me." Her eyes welled up again and she blinked hard to stop the tears from falling.

"Oh Sylvie, I can't see you like this. Let me talk to Julian, he might see reason..."

"No. Please don't. This doesn't concern you. I'm just keeping you informed. I'll be working from home for now, to avoid any awkwardness with him. You really don't need this."

Sylvie had sat with Alex and Markus and glossed over what had happened, trying her damnedest to sound calm and without resorting to tears. They were just as shocked as Zach. They'd worked out that things were not going well with Nick's family, but they hadn't expected Nick and Sylvie to take a break.

"He needed to go for work, and, well, we thought that we could do with some distance. To see how it goes," Sylvie explained.

Reading between the lines, both Alex and Markus knew there was more to it than their mother was letting on. They just weren't sure if it was her or Nick who'd decided. They decided not to push her as she was looking far more fragile these past few days. She'd been holed up in her office, working from home, and then she seemed to be doing an extraordinary amount of unnecessary housework, as Marcy was away.

Sylvie tried to fill her days working on the new visuals for the boutique she'd been asked to look at. She only left the house for meetings and to get groceries for the boys. Sylvie had thrown herself into a full regime of cooking and cleaning, hoping the mundane tasks would numb the constant pain. It didn't seem to work.

She obsessively checked her phone for messages, knowing deep down it was highly unlikely that Nick would contact her. He'd said he'd make it easy for everyone and Sylvie knew what that meant. He was taking himself out of the equation. No calls, no messages, nothing. Well, that's what she'd wanted: for him to want to move on. In the back of her mind, she'd hoped that he would fight back, fight for her to stay.

By Thursday, Lilianna had been drafted in to try and get Sylvie out. Markus called her when he'd found Sylvie up at three in the morning making strawberry jam. He'd been out with some friends and on his return home, the strong sweet smell hit him as he opened the front door. He found Sylvie ladling hot jam into what must have been at least twenty jars.

"Mum, what are you doing up at this time?" Even in his slightly inebriated state, he knew that no one makes jam in the middle of the night. He looked on as Sylvie tightened the lids of the jars. She looked so drawn and gaunt, it took him back to after his father had died. The whole scene was disturbing and he knew she needed help.

"We were running out of jam, so I decided to make some." Her voice was monotone and matter of fact.

"At ten past three in the morning?" Markus tilted his head as he suddenly became sober. He scraped back the stool and sat down by the breakfast bar. Sylvie took out some French bread and butter and started to spread it, placing it on a plate for Markus. Then she stopped and snorted to herself, gazing at the buttered bread for a moment.

She passed him a small dish with hot jam in. "Here, try some."

Not wanting to upset her, he spread the jam on the bread and took a bite. "It's really good, Mum."

She nodded and then continued putting the lids back on the jars. In the morning, Markus told Alex, and they decided to call in Lilianna.

She was the only one who would be able to shake Sylvie out of this downward spiral.

Maggie picked up the phone for what seemed like the hundredth time and dialled Nick's number. It went straight to voicemail. It was Wednesday and neither Julian, Vicki or Elenora had heard from him, apart from a brief text on Monday he'd sent to both his sisters saying he was fine and that he'd call them in a couple of days. Maggie sat on her sofa wrestling with herself as to whether she should call Sylvie. At least she'd know he was alright. She presumed he was staying with Sylvie, as she'd been by the *Silver Lining* and he wasn't there. She wanted to see him before he left for Cannes. She picked up the phone and dialled.

Sylvie jumped as her phone rang. She was in her bathroom scrubbing the sink down after she'd just thrown up. Seeing the number, her stomach clenched again. Well, she needed to speak to Maggie at some point. She pulled off her rubber gloves and answered. "Hello?"

"Hello, Sylvie. How are you?" Maggie asked mostly out of habit, her voice clipped.

"I'm fine. Maggie, I'm so glad you called. I wanted to explain and to apologise –"

"Sylvie, I'm only calling to see if he's okay. We haven't heard from him since Sunday and I wanted to at least try and speak to him before he left on Friday." Maggie's voice grew sterner.

"Oh… well he's not here Maggie. He left on Monday."

"I don't understand. What do you mean?"

"After he spoke to you he came here and, well, he'd booked to go on Monday. He left from here Sunday night and… well, we haven't spoken since." Sylvie tried hard to control her shaky voice.

"Why? I still don't understand. He left here telling me he wanted to be with you and –"

"I suggested we have a break, Maggie. This trip. Get some distance. I don't want to be the cause of this rift between you and him. Maggie I'm so sorry, truly I am. I didn't intend for this to happen, but it did."

"You mean you broke it off?" Maggie clearly shocked and concerned.

"Not exactly. He wanted me to go with him but I suggested he go alone so we could just all calm down. What with… well, with Julian and you. I thought if he was away, he'd maybe be less impulsive and more objective." Sylvie's voice cracked and she took deep breaths in an attempt to control herself.

"I doubt that," Maggie muttered, then added, "Sylvie, is that what you want? To break up with him?"

"I want what's best for him, Maggie. What *I* want doesn't come into the equation." Her voice was low and soft. Maggie closed her eyes as she felt an overwhelming wave of shame. It was obvious that Sylvie loved her son and she was willing to sacrifice that so that his relationship with his family wasn't destroyed. "I didn't mean for this to happen, Maggie, I didn't chase him…"

"I know you didn't. He told me it was him." They sat silent for a moment, then Maggie continued: "Do you love him, Sylvie?"

"Yes, I love him." Maggie clenched her eyes shut as she heard the words she both dreaded to hear and at the same time, was relieved to know. "But I know he can't have a future with me. Well, not the right kind of future. So I pulled back. I only wished I hadn't hurt him." Sylvie shuddered, trying to hold back her sobs.

"Oh Sylvie, I don't know what to say. A part of me wants to scream at you for getting involved with him and the other part of me is over the moon because he found someone that he's truly happy with. It's such a mess!" she added, exasperated. Sylvie screwed up her eyes as the tears kept falling down her gaunt cheeks as she slumped onto the bathroom floor. "And Julian… he's so angry. I can't get him to see reason."

"Oh Maggie, I'm so sorry. Nothing ever happened or was ever going to happen with Julian. I just never saw him that way. He's just a friend… well he was. I'm not so sure now."

"I know, Sylvie. He's behaved like an ass. He'll calm down eventually. What worries me now is Nick. I think he's gone off again and I just hope it's not like last time. I won't be able to handle that again. So you've heard nothing? Nothing at all?" Maggie asked desperately.

"No… The last thing he said, he was going to make it easy for everyone."

Maggie gasped, knowing that he was taking himself out of the picture.

Zach sat at his desk crunching through some figures when there was a tentative knock at his door. He looked at the time: it was almost six. "Come in," he called, knowing it could only be one person. The door open and a stony-faced Julian entered. "Julian. Come in. How are you doing?" Zach asked nervously.

"Fine. I brought the first drafts of the houses for you to look at." Julian's jaw was tense as he spoke.

"You've done them? That was quick."

"Well, I know we're on a tight schedule."

They were interrupted by Zach's mobile. "It's Lily. I better get this."

Julian nodded curtly and Zach motioned for him to sit down. Julian hesitated, then lowered himself into the chair opposite Zach, running his fingers nervously through his hair.

"Hi."

"Zach, Sylvie's in a bad way. I need Dr Zinon's number. She can't seem to find it. Or rather: won't. Have you got it?"

"Yes, sure. What do you mean she's in a bad way?" Julian's eyes shot up to Zach's and Zach smiled tightly, realising he should have kept his mouth shut.

"She's throwing up and not sleeping. She needs to see a doctor, Zach, to give her something to calm down." Lilianna sounded anxious and he knew she must be bad for Lilianna to insist she see a doctor.

He reached into his desk and pulled out his battered phone book. "I've found it." He quickly gave her the number and then hung up.

Julian nervously brushed his trousers as he furrowed his brow, curious to know who they were talking about, even though he was more than sure it was Sylvie. "Everything okay?" he asked.

"Umm, er… yes. She just needed a number." Zach rearranged some papers on his desk nervously. "So let's have a look at these plans, then."

"I've put them on this. You can look at them with Yiannis and we can maybe meet up Monday." He handed Zach a memory stick, then got up from the chair.

"Great. I'll call you tomorrow and arrange it."

Julian nodded and headed for the door, pausing before he left he turned back. "Is it Sylvie? That's not good, I mean?" He was itching to know.

"Yes."

"She's ill?"

"Sort of."

"Sort of? Either she is or she isn't." He sounded irritated as his forehead creased.

Zach rubbed his eyes with his thumb and forefinger. "She's just… not good. She's…"

Julian's eyes widened as he saw Zach squirming to find the right words; he stepped closer towards the desk. "She's what, Zach?"

Zach hated being put in these situations. Did he tell him? Should he tell him? Zach sighed and thought, *Screw it, he may as well know.* He'd find out sooner or later. "Sylvie tried to break it off with Nick and he left on Monday. She's taken it badly." He said it quickly, as if he just needed to get it out before he changed his mind.

Julian stood still, totally perplexed, trying to fathom out how he felt about this new information. It explained why Maggie had tried to call him numerous times today. He'd purposely avoided picking up his phone. He hadn't spoken to her after their last telephone conversation on Sunday. His first reaction was concern that Sylvie was not well. Images of how she was after Chris died flashed through his mind and his heart broke at the very thought of it. As for the fact that she'd broken it off, he had a huge mix of emotions attached to that fact. Surprise, relief, then thinking back to Nick, he felt guilt and an overwhelming sense of shame. "I didn't know. Does she need anything?"

"Lily's with her." Zach felt that was enough of an explanation.

"What kind of doctor?" Julian asked, a trace of panic in his voice. He didn't want her ill. He didn't want her to be suffering. Realisation was beginning to hit. This was the aftermath of his reaction, his over-the-top selfish reaction. She was trying to do the right thing and she was suffering because of it, because of him. He closed his eyes, trying to control his breathing.

"Her GP. Look, Julian, I've already said too much. Please don't put me in a difficult position."

"Sure. I'm sorry. I just didn't know… about Nick leaving. I'd better go. We'll speak tomorrow." He turned back towards the door and left, leaving Zach feeling utterly drained.

Lilianna took one look at the twenty jars of jam and Sylvie, and realised her dearest friend needed help. Sylvie was sipping ginger tea on the terrace as Lilianna strode directly over to her. "Hi, sweetie. You opening a side line in homemade conserves?" Lilianna asked sarcastically.

"Hi, Lily." Sylvie sat up, surprised, and tried to plaster her best fake smile on.

"Oh, Sylvie. Haven't you heard from him?" She slumped down in the chair next to Sylvie and grabbed her hand.

Sylvie pursed her lips together and shook her head.

"Did you try and call him?"

"No. He needs to have a clean break, Lily. It's the only way." The tears started to well up again. "But... I just want him to call me." She whispered because it was true. She wanted him to call her and try to convince her to change her mind. She wanted that more than anything, because she knew if he asked her to drop everything that she would. "Is that selfish?"

"No, sweetie." Lilianna sighed.

"I spoke to Maggie today."

Lilianna raised her eyebrows, clearly shocked. "I bet that was awkward."

"Awkward doesn't even cover it." She brushed away a lone tear that had escaped. "She was okay though... in the end. She didn't know he'd gone."

"Have you eaten anything? Apart from jam and bread I mean?" Sylvie shook her head. "Okay, let me fix you something and I'm calling Dr Zinon. I'll drag you there myself. Alex told me you been throwing up again. What shall I make you?"

Sylvie shrugged, too weak to fight back. She knew she didn't have a cat in hell's chance of beating Lilianna when she had that oh-so-determined face on. "Eggs on toast?" suggested Sylvie.

"You hate eggs." Lilianna answered taken aback.

"I know, but I just really want some."

"Coming up. Come on." Lilianna took her hand and pulled her out of her chair, then guided her into the house.

Nick sat in a café going over the last of his contracts. Xavier had located four yachts for him to view and he had emailed photos and all the specifications to Serge. It was now down to personal preference and negotiating the right price. Nick had been lucky and all four yachts were perfect, so it was really up to Serge's buyer. Nick knew it would take a few days before Serge's client would decide, so it gave him a chance to source a few more yachts for future clients.

He sat sipping his beer when his thoughts were interrupted by a familiar voice. "Nick?"

Nick looked up from his paperwork and immediately recognised the tall dark woman in front of him. "Hey Sandrine. What a surprise." He got up out of his seat to hug and kiss his old friend, two times on each cheek, a French custom Nick still found a little excessive.

"Xavier said you were coming." She was a stunning Amazonian chef of a small bistro she and her partner Chloe owned. She was half Moroccan and half French. Nick had got to know them well when he'd been in Cannes, MIA after the Brigitte break-up. They had lived in a small studio next to his and had become friends. Then, Chloe and Sandrine had worked in an exclusive restaurant, but had recently set up their own more casual bistro.

"How's the bistro doing?" he asked.

"It's really good. Why haven't you been down?"

"I've been busy with work, but I think Xavier said we'd come tonight." The truth was Xavier had been nagging him to go from the first night he arrived. But Nick couldn't face anyone. He'd stayed in his hotel room every night and had room service.

After his arrival on Monday, all Nick had done was to examine the yachts and negotiate with the sellers. Then he'd locked himself in his hotel room with beers and a carton of Dunhills and sat around watching old films, drinking and smoking. He'd checked in with Christian every morning and every evening, then switched off his phone. He'd had numerous voicemails from his mother. Vicki and Elenora had sent texts which he'd replied briefly to, without giving too much away. He didn't want them to worry. As long as they knew he was okay, he knew they wouldn't hassle him. Nick noted he'd had nothing from Julian – he wasn't sure what he felt about that. Mainly relieved, but he was also angered by his dad's lack of humility. What Nick found unbelievably painful was that he hadn't heard anything from Sylvie. It was now Thursday and he thought that she might at least have tried to contact him.

He'd asked Christian every time he called if anyone had asked after him. Christian had cringed every time he'd have to give him them same response. "No, Nick, no one's asked for you."

He was so desperate to hear her voice again. He'd flicked through the pictures on his phone and the video the tourist had taken of them at Sounion, just so he could see her again. It seemed an absolute age ago and they looked so happy – she looked so happy. *Why wasn't she fighting for him?* He'd picked up his phone a hundred times to call her, but he kept thinking back to that sentimental crap that Chrissie had quoted to him. *She* had to come back to *him*. She had to want to be with him more than anything – more than what his family thought or more than the guilt she felt, otherwise she'd always be feeling that doubt.

"Okay, Nick. We'll see you tonight? *Salut!*" They kissed their good-byes and Nick watched Sandrine gracefully walk away into the crowd. He packed up his stuff, paid his bill and set off towards his hotel.

It was warm and humid and Nick just wanted to get back to his air-conditioned hotel room and have a bath. He snorted to himself. A bath. He never thought he'd ever say he'd want a bath. The images of Sylvie and him in the bath at her house the very first time came to the fore-front of his mind, and he battled with himself to shove them away. He positively ached for her. He felt lost and alone. Even here, where there was nothing for him to associate with her, there were constant reminders of her. Yellow roses, red Chanel bags, red nail varnish, BMW motorbikes! He couldn't even butter a bread roll without Sylvie coming into his thoughts – not that she ever truly left them.

Entering his hotel room, he dropped his watch, key, sunglasses and satchel on the table. Kicking off his sneakers, he padded to the bath-room and started to fill the bath. He picked up his phone and willed it to ring, feeling totally frustrated and desolate as he plugged it into its charger. Then he reached for his cigarettes. He felt empty and he was dragging himself through every motion. The last thing he wanted to do was go out tonight. A bath would help.

Lilianna and Sylvie sat in the waiting room of Dr Zinon Zinonas. He'd been Sylvie's doctor from the first year she'd arrived in Cyprus. He specialised in gynaecology, but Sylvie came to him for everything from a sore throat to back pain. She wasn't keen on going to someone who she wasn't familiar with. Luckily she'd never needed any specialist treatment – she'd only ever had the usual ailments. Her delicate stomach was something they'd tackled with antacids and a mild diet and it had seemed to work until these past few weeks.

Sylvie sat looking down at her hands as she twiddled with her tissue. It was seven o'clock, and normally at this time the surgery would be closed, but Dr Zinon had made an exception for Sylvie. His receptionist was just closing up some files when she looked up. "The doctor will see you now." Her smile was fake, but Sylvie seemed oblivious.

"You want me to come too?" asked Lilianna. Sylvie shook her head and got up, heading for his office.

Dr Zinon was in his late fifties. He was balding with a slight covering of white hair around the sides cut short, and had the softest brown eyes. He smiled broadly when he saw Sylvie. "Hello, my dear. What can I do for you?"

Sylvie smiled slightly. She remembered back to their very first meeting when he'd greeted her with 'How are you?' and she'd told him that if she was well she wouldn't be here. So from then on, he'd always addressed her with 'What can I do for you?' "Hi, Zinon. Sorry it's so late." He shook his head, indicating it didn't matter, as she sat down in the chair opposite him. "It's my stomach. I just seem to be vomiting more than usual and even some smells are making me retch.

"Any diarrhoea?" Sylvie shook her head. "Cramps?"

"Sometimes."

"Is it better with the antacids?"

"Yes."

"Come over to the examining table so I can have a feel."

He came around from his desk and Sylvie got up from the chair and went over to the table where she sat up and swung her legs up to lay down. Dr Zinon carefully examined her abdomen, then carried on with all the routine checks, noting everything down but saying nothing. "I'd like you to have some blood tests done, a urine and stool sample too, just to check. I'll give you a sample box for the stool but we can do the blood and urine now and I'll have those test results back tomorrow. How are you periods? Regular? Change in flow?"

"Umm. Yes, I suppose," she answered, as they made their way back to the desk.

The doctor waited for her to sit before he resumed his seat. "Suppose? When was your last period?"

Sylvie furrowed her brow, trying to remember. She remembered she didn't have it over the wedding and it had started just afterwards – yes, that was right, she had been relieved that it didn't coincide with the wedding. "Around the twenty-ninth of April."

Dr Zinon nodded and glanced at his calendar. "Well, that's over a month now. It's the fifth today." Sylvie looked at him, puzzled.

"Any headaches?" Sylvie shook her head. Great, the onslaught of menopause. As if she needed any more reminders that she was getting older! "Why don't you pop in there and give me a urine sample." Dr Zinon pointed to the adjoining bathroom. Sylvie rose wearily and went into the bathroom, taking the plastic container with her. She felt so tired she just wished he'd give her some pills for her vomiting and cramps so she could go home. Today she wasn't in the mood for his overly thorough examination.

Sylvie emerged from the bathroom and a handed the doctor her sample stifling a yawn.

"You're feeling tired too?"

"I didn't sleep very well last night," she offered as an explanation. Dr Zinon nodded, pulling out a white strip and dipping it into Sylvie's urine sample. Removing it, he checked it; satisfied with the result, he sat forward leaning his elbows on his desk.

Then, pushing his glasses back up his nose, he smiled softly at Sylvie. "Well now, I just need to take a sample of your blood and we should be done."

"I take it that my mood swings and all the other symptoms are the beginning of the menopause?"

"On the contrary, Sylvie, it would seem that you are pregnant."

What! No! Sylvie's face drained of what little colour she had as she stared stock-still into the face of Dr Zinon. She went to say something but she was struck dumb.

The doctor regarded her as her eyes darted around the room. Then after a minute or two, she wasn't entirely sure, the doctor spoke with a good-humoured hint of sarcasm: "I take it from your reaction, this was not a planned pregnancy?"

Are you fucking kidding me! "No," Sylvie finally managed. "Pregnant?"

"Yes, I'd say three weeks. I'll need to do a scan though."

"How?" Sylvie mumbled.

"Well, the ultrasound machine is in the –"

"No, I mean how am I pregnant?" realising he'd misunderstood her question.

Dr Zinon raised his eyebrow as if to say "You really don't know how?"

Sylvie, understanding his reaction, flushed. "I don't mean *how*, I mean how, because of my age."

Dr Zinon smiled and sat back in his chair. "At forty-four it's not unheard of, Sylvie, just unusual, and if I remember correctly, you seemed to get pregnant very easily. Forgive me, but I'm asking only as your doctor. I know we are friends too, so this may be a little awkward." He swallowed before continuing, clearly a little uncomfortable. "The father? What I mean is…"

Sylvie closed her eyes, then rubbed her face as she felt the tears well up again. *How cruelly ironic!* She'd tried to split up with Nick because she knew this was the one thing she couldn't give him and now here she was, without him and pregnant with his child. A million and one different thoughts came rushing into her head all at once. The doctor stared on, realising she needed a moment to compose herself. "Would you like some water?"

"I'd rather have a brandy," she snorted, and he huffed at her, giving her a mock-stern look as reached over to the water cooler to fetch her a drink.

"Well, they'll be none of that for the next nine months." *Oh no!* She'd been drinking so much over the last few weeks. Had she done anything else, taken any medication?… No, just antacids. *Phew!* Instinctively she rested her hand protectively on her stomach. The doctor handed her the plastic cup and she took a sip.

"I've been drinking quite a bit. Is that alright? I mean… oh crap. I really did not expect this."

"Well, no more from now on. Without sounding like I'm scolding you, if you didn't want to get pregnant, what contraception were you using? I know *you* weren't on any. The father?"

Sylvie flushed, embarrassed at her stupidity. *I mean, how many talks have I had with Alex and Markus about condoms?* She'd even bought some to have in the house in case they didn't have any. Now here she was, pregnant because she assumed she was past it and because Nick obviously thought she was on some form of contraception – or also past it! "Like I said, I thought at forty-four…"

"Ah, I see. How receptive will the father be if you keep it?"

If I keep it? Sylvie's face dropped. She could never… no way. Abortion. No. That was never an option. "I will be keeping it, even if he's not in the picture."

Dr Zinon smiled and nodded. "Well, you know the drill, you've been here before. Folic acid every day, good diet, moderate exercise, no alcohol or smoking. Well, at least we know why you've been vomiting. If I remember correctly, you suffered with morning sickness with both Alex and Markus, though it seems to have started very early this time. Shall we do a scan?"

"Can I come in another day? I really can't face it."

"Okay, early next week. You know I need to keep a close eye on you. Because of your age, there are more risks. I'll need to monitor you weekly."

"I know. It's just a lot to take in."

Reaching into his desk, he pulled out a couple of leaflets and a bottle of pills. "These will give you an idea of what I mean, and this is a month's supply of folic acid." Sylvie looked down at the leaflets she had been handed. "Pregnancy and the Older Mother" screamed the first leaflet. *Talk about rubbing salt into a gaping, throbbing wound!* "Before you go, let me take some blood and I'll book you in for Monday. Nine o'clock okay for you?"

Sylvie nodded weakly, unable to grasp the wicked turn of events.

26

DONE DEAL

"Well, what did he say?" Lilianna asked impatiently as they got in the car.

"Can we get home first, Lily?" Sylvie reached in her bag for a tissue and dabbed her eyes. Why couldn't she stop crying?

"Sylvie, I'm worried here, don't drag it out. Is it serious? Why are you going back on Monday?"

"It's for my results of the blood tests, that's all." Sylvie sat quietly looking out of her window as she felt Lilianna's tension radiating from her body. She still wasn't sure whether she should tell her. Lilianna was going to freak out: well, why wouldn't she? Sylvie *herself* was freaking out.

Sylvie closed her eyes and tried hard to control the tears that relentlessly cascaded down her cheeks. What was she going to do? If she told Nick, he might think she was trapping him. If she kept it from him? She couldn't – he was the father. He had every right to know. What if he'd decided he was better off without her? He'd now feel morally obliged to stay with her. She didn't want that. What would Julian and Maggie make of her bearing their first grandchild? What would Alex and Markus think about having another sibling? How would she cope? What if she miscarried? What if… She held her head as question after question exploded in her head.

"Sylvie, please, what is it?" Lilianna pleaded as she swung her car up Sylvie's driveway.

"I'm pregnant," sobbed Sylvie, and Lilianna slammed the brakes on, gaping at Sylvie in what could only be described as apoplectic shock.

She sat looking at her in paralysed silence. Well, there was a first, Lilianna lost for words.

"But... You? ... How?" They sat for a few more seconds in silence, then Lilianna seemed to find the right gear to engage her mouth and muttered, "Jesus, Sylvie, what are you going to do?" Sylvie shook her head. "Well that explains the vomiting... and the eggs. Come on sweetie, let's get inside."

"I don't want anyone to know, Lily. I need to figure this out before I tell anyone."

"Of course. So you want to keep it."

Sylvie turned to Lilianna and nodded and Lilianna let out a sigh of relief.

"Good. I think a strong cup of tea and some ginger biscuits are in order." She leaned over and squeezed her dearest friend. "I remember you making batches of them when I was pregnant. They were the only thing that settled my stomach." Sylvie fished out another tissue and wiped her eyes dry.

"Thanks for today, Lily. I don't know how I would have coped without you."

"I'm here for you. Always."

***

At nine o'clock, Xavier banged on Nick's door. Nick stubbed out his cigarette and dragged himself up from the sun lounger where he was lying out on the balcony. He strolled over to the door and reluctantly opened it.

"Hey Nick! You ready?" Xavier stood in his faded jeans with his pink linen shirt open, showing off his black rosary, and designer loafers. He was the total embodiment of a Mediterranean player: good-looking, charming, confident and well off. He was tall and slim and impeccably groomed. Clean-shaven, his hair was shiny, brown and styled to look naturally dishevelled but Nick was sure it would have taken him at least half an hour to achieve the right effect.

Xavier and Nick had met a few years ago when Nick had escaped to Cannes trying to get over Brigitte. Xavier was then working in one of the exclusive nightclubs as the manager and Nick had frequented it. One night they'd ended up at an all-night restaurant talking, and Xavier had introduced Nick to a local businessman who was selling his yacht. With all the contacts Xavier had in Cannes, Nick had then suggested they work together in the future, splitting the commission. Nick generally found the buyers and Xavier sourced the vendors. Over the past few years, they had both done well from this arrangement.

"Yeah, just need to get my phone." In contrast, Nick looked rugged. He hadn't shaved since Saturday, so his designer stubble had become a short beard. He wore his faded jeans and Converse, a black T-shirt and his hair was untidy. Xavier frowned at him.

"You look like shit."

"Thanks, you don't look so bad yourself," Nick replied sarcastically. Xavier shook his head, smirking. "I'm really not in the mood, I told you."

"Come on. It's just a meal and then you can come home and fucking sulk again."

"Yeah, yeah. Come on, then, let's go."

Sandrine and Chloe's bistro was heaving when they arrived. The place was small but had different levels so it didn't feel claustrophobic, and the kitchen was open so that the clientele could see and hear their orders being prepared. The biggest pull of the bistro, apart from the delicious cuisine, was the pair of stunning owners. Chloe ran the kitchen and Sandrine was out in the restaurant. Everything was prepared with local produce and the menu changed accordingly. It had fast become one of the most popular restaurants amongst the young trendsetters.

Nick and Xavier entered into the noisy bistro, the air thick with exotic aromas wafting through from the hectic kitchen. Sandrine glided over to them, draped in an emerald green tight dress leaving nothing to the imagination, smiling as her eyes danced with amusement.

"You finally made it, then?" She leant over to kiss Nick first, then Xavier. "Chloe will be thrilled." She led them to a table not far from the kitchen. Nick sat down, feeling a little awkward, then glanced into the kitchen. Chloe waved at him, her blonde shock of hair covered by a red bandana, her pale cheeks flushed from the steam. The last time he'd seen them was six months ago and he'd ended up back at their apartment. Maybe this wasn't such a good idea; he hoped Sandrine and Chloe didn't expect a repeat of that evening.

"Shall I choose for you tonight?" asked Sandrine, leaning over closely, her eyes wide as she directed her question to Nick.

"Sure," Nick answered, tearing his eyes away from her and Xavier shrugged in agreement. "An aperitif?"

"I'll have a beer. Nick, what do you want?"

"I'll have a Chivas with a couple of ice cubes." Sandrine nodded and slinked off.

"She's still hot for you, Nick, and since when did you start drinking whisky?"

Nick shrugged and reached for his cigarettes, slowly taking one out and putting it to his lips. "It's packed out. They must be doing well," he commented, changing the subject. Xavier nodded in agreement. "I need to put my phone on and catch up with home. I'll go outside, I won't be able to hear a thing in here." Xavier nodded as Nick got up and sauntered back onto the busy street.

Taking his phone out, he switched it on and as he waited for it turn back on, he lit his cigarette, dragging hard on it. His stomach was in knots. He was hoping that Sylvie would have at least tried to contact him. He was finding it hard not to cave and call her. As soon as the phone connected, eight messages beeped through. He wavered for a moment before pressing the 'Open' button, then quickly scanned the messages. There were five from his mother, one from Christian keeping him up to speed on the shop and two from Serge. He ignored the first six and scrolled to Serge's. Before he could read them, a call interrupted him. It was Serge.

"Serge, how are you?"

"Good, Nick. Better now that I found you." He sounded a little irritated. "My client wants to go ahead with the sale. I sent all the relevant documentation to your email an hour ago. He wants the transfer to go through by Monday so I hope the sellers don't change their minds." Serge had always been no-nonsense and brusque. It took a bit of getting used to and most people found him rude, but Nick knew it was just his way.

"Really? Which yachts?" Nick couldn't hide his surprise.

"I've marked which ones in the email, and his final price. They are within the price range you stipulated. He went with your recommendations." Serge's voice was clipped, annoyed that Nick doubted him.

"Well, that's fantastic news. I'll be sure to get everything out to you by lunchtime tomorrow."

"Good. We'll speak tomorrow, then. And Nick, keep your phone on in case I need to get in touch," he added, a little less clipped.

"Sure, Serge," Nick smirked. "Speak to you tomorrow. Bye."

"Bye, Nick." Nick stood looking at his phone in disbelief. His client wanted both yachts. *Wow.* He really wished he could be more excited about it, but the truth was he wanted desperately to call Sylvie with the news – she was the only person he wanted to share it with. Nick stubbed out his cigarette and went back in the bistro to tell the good news to Xavier. At least he'd be thrilled.

Of course, Xavier was ecstatic with Nick's news and insisted they celebrate after their meal. Nick reluctantly agreed as they made their way to Xavier's favourite club.

They pulled up outside Le Baoli, one of the most exclusive night-clubs in Cannes. Xavier had been the manager there so he was well known. They were immediately let in, in spite of their rather casual dress. The club had both an indoor and outdoor lounge and was deco-rated in an Indonesian style. Nick's first thoughts, as he took in his familiar surroundings, were what Sylvie would make of it. They were guided to a table with light sumptuous couches sectioned off with sheer white gossamer curtains in the outdoor area. It reminded Nick of Island and he sat down with a heavy heart, pensively looking round.

It was already quite busy. Xavier was talking to various customers, moving around comfortably and clearly in his element. The waitress brought over a bottle of champagne, a bottle of Chivas, ice and water. Nick looked up at her puzzled, as she stared wide-eyed at him; she smiled and explained that Xavier had ordered them and she proceeded to open both bottles. Once she'd left, Nick poured himself a drink, dropped in ice cubes and swished them round. He brought the glass to his lips, savoured the smell, then closing his eyes, he took a sip blocking out the thumping beat of the music and the hum of voices talking above the music.

His momentary calm was abruptly interrupted by Xavier and a couple of girls who he introduced to Nick as Mati and Natalie. They couldn't have been more than twenty and Nick groaned inwardly. He just wasn't up for this kind of evening. Fake smiling at them both, he closed his eyes and drained his glass, wincing as he swallowed. Chivas was so much nicer second-hand, he thought wistfully. Xavier leaned over and told him that Sandrine and Chloe were on their way too. Nick looked at his watch and saw it was one already. He'd stay another hour and go.

Xavier poured some more drinks out and raised his glass to make a toast.

"To you Nick, thanks for pulling off the deal." Xavier beamed as they clinked glasses and Mati and Natalie giggled.

God, young women were so irritating! thought Nick. He sipped his drink, feeling decidedly more depressed and a little light-headed. The girls got up to dance, teetering precariously on their six-inch heels and swaying in their micro minis, annoying Nick even more. They looked ridiculous.

Xavier moved next to him, pouring him another drink. "What's with you? We just made a shit load of money and you look like you lost a winning lottery ticket."

"I'm just not in the mood." He shifted awkwardly in his seat; he couldn't be bothered to explain. Nick doubted Xavier would understand anyway. Pulling out his phone, he checked again for any messages, knowing it was fruitless.

"A woman?" asked Xavier, as Nick placed his phone on the table. Nick shrugged and nodded, indicating he'd hit the nail on the head. "Well call her then and stop fucking moping. I can't see you like this. I'm off to dance. *Call her.*" He emphasized the last two words.

Maybe he was right. Nick picked up his phone and motioned to Xavier he was going out to call – he'd never hear anything in the club. Xavier gave him a thumbs-up as he headed to where the girls were gyrating. Shaking his head, Nick stepped out onto a balcony away from the pounding music.

It was a warm night and Sylvie couldn't sleep. She lay back on her bed, staring at the ceiling. The constant questions rattled around in her head. She was still in shock from the news. She was pregnant. At forty-four! And for a split-second, she allowed herself to be excited about it. When she'd fallen pregnant with Alex and Markus, she'd been on cloud nine. It made her sad to think this little life inside her wasn't welcomed with the same enthusiasm. She glanced at her clock: it was ten to two.

Alex and Markus were watching some films they'd hired. Wrapping her thin robe around her, she tiptoed downstairs to the kitchen to make some camomile tea, hoping it would induce sleep. What she really needed was a large stiff drink! But camomile would have to do. Alex heard her and came in to check that she was alright.

"You still up, Mum? It's late. Can't you sleep? Are we making too much noise?" Concern was etched all over his face.

"No sweetie, I'm just restless. I thought some camomile might help. Go back to your film. I'm fine – I'll go back upstairs once I've made it." Satisfied with her answer, Alex went back to the sitting room to resume his watching. Sylvie filled the kettle and flicked it on, then retrieved a cup and placed the bag of tea in it whilst she waited for the kettle to boil. Idly, she looked down at her phone charging and unplugged it. Flicking through various apps, she went into the weather and checked out what the weather was like in Cannes. *Cooler than here*, she noted. She poured the boiling water onto the tea bag and watched it float, then she pushed it in and out with a teaspoon. She wondered what Nick would be doing. Closing her eyes, she envisaged him living it up with all the young jet set, and her heart twisted at the thought. "*Fucked everything in sight,*" – his words came back to her like a wrecking ball. Well, what did she expect? He was young, single, looked like a Greek god. Putting her hand on her stomach, she rubbed it. She was going to have to let him know, regardless of their status.

Sylvie took out the tea bag and threw it in the bin. Then taking her tea, she placed the phone back on the charger and wandered onto the terrace; it was cooler outside, and she crouched down and sat on the step to sip her tea. A buzzing noise coming from the kitchen alerted her attention. Sylvie scrambled up from the step. It was her phone on the granite worktop. Reaching across, she wondered who could be calling so late. She looked at her screen as it flashed 'Mr X'.

Sylvie's heart pounded hard against her chest as her finger hovered over the touch screen. She pressed the answer option, swallowing hard before she spoke.

"Nick?" Her voice was low and shaky.

"Sylvie?" She could hear the relief in his voice.

"Yes, Nick, it's me."

"Why haven't you called me? I waited and waited." He sounded hurt and a little disorientated and Sylvie could hear music in the background.

"Nick, are you okay, you sound funny?" God, it felt good to hear his voice; the butterflies in her stomach awakened from their days of slumber and danced around.

"No, I'm not okay… why didn't you call me?" He demanded softly.

"Nick, I…" Sylvie began to answer, then in the background, she heard a woman's voice purr in a thick French accent. Sylvie stiffened, her ears burning as she heard her speak, close enough for Sylvie to hear.

"*Chéri*, there you are. I was looking for you everywhere."

No! No, no, no… Not wanting to hear any more, Sylvie's hands trembled as she gripped onto the phone. "I can hear you're busy. Maybe when you're less preoccupied and it's a more reasonable hour we might be able to talk." She looked down at her phone and pressed the 'End call' option, but not before hearing Nick's reply.

"No, Sylvie, it's not –"

Sylvie's hands shook violently as she tried to pull herself together. *Well, he hadn't wasted any time, had he? Well, what did she expect?* She turned quickly to go back outside to cool down. As she reached the threshold of the French doors, her head began to swim and before she could steady herself, she felt herself falling. She blacked out over the small step and fell headfirst onto the cold hard stone terrace, dropping her phone as it shattered, and her teacup smashed against the floor.

Nick swiftly turned round to face Sandrine as she edged closer to him. Her dark eyes blinked seductively at him as he reined in his anger, his fuzzy head sobering up as he realised what it must have sounded like to Sylvie. He had to call her back to explain. Sandrine reached over to touch his arm and he instinctively stepped back. Her face dropped, clearly affronted by the gesture.

"I'm sorry, Sandrine… I need to get out of here. Tell Xavier I had to go… sorry." He backed away from her as he gritted his teeth, then made his way out of the club and back onto the street.

Thankfully, there was a slight breeze as Nick walked to the main street to try and find a cab, his face burning from the tension. Worst-case scenario, he'd walk back. He looked at his phone and hit the redial button, waiting for it to connect. It went straight to voicemail. Shit! She'd turned off her phone and he didn't have her home number. He clenched his fists, raising them to his forehead in a mixture of frustration and anger. He'd have to wait until the morning now. Damn Sandrine! He stood for a moment at a loss, then he started to run towards his hotel. It felt good to run as the adrenaline from his exasperation coursed through his tense body.

Within seconds, Alex and Markus were up and sprinting through the kitchen. They found Sylvie sprawled out half on the terrace floor and half in the kitchen, unconscious across the threshold.

"Holy shit, Mum! MUM!" Alex was on his knees next to her as he bent over to check her breathing. "She must have fainted." His voice was full of panic. "Mum, can you hear me?" Markus stood paralysed, looking on. "Markus, snap out of it! Get me some water. Markus!" Alex shouted, bringing Markus to the here and now.

"Sure," he replied, almost in a daze. Going over to the fridge, he got a bottle and took it to Alex.

"Get me a towel," Alex ordered. Then as he opened the bottle, Sylvie's eyes fluttered open. "Mum, can you hear me?" He stroked her hair back off her face.

"Where am I?" Sylvie asked, totally disorientated.

"Mum, you're home. You must have fainted. Don't move."

"My hand hurts... ouch." Sylvie winced.

"Markus, put the terrace lights on." Markus reached over and turned them on, still stunned and holding the towel. The whole terrace lit up and Sylvie shut her eyes from the glare. Alex leaned over her, though it was awkward as Sylvie was laid across the threshold. As soon as he looked down, his eyes focused on a pool of blood coming from where his mother's arm was. Markus had come closer and Alex looked up at him, wide-eyed with panic.

"I'll call an ambulance. Don't move her," Markus replied to his unsaid request.

"Mum, don't move. I think you've injured your arm. We're calling an ambulance, okay?" Alex stroked her head, trying hard to sound calm. He could hear Markus on the phone talking to the emergency services. Then he heard him call Zach.

"Alex, I feel cold," mumbled Sylvie.

"Okay, Mum, I'll get a blanket. Don't move." He looked frantically around, not wanting to leave her, then he heard Markus coming through. "Bring a throw from the lounge – she's cold." As he looked at Markus, he saw his brother's expression sink in renewed shock, his eyes dropping to Sylvie. "What is it?"

"She's bleeding," Markus whispered.

"I know, it's her hand," Alex replied.

"No. I mean she's bleeding between her legs," Markus mouthed, and pointed so that Alex could understand, but Sylvie couldn't see or hear. Alex's face drained of colour as he prayed for the ambulance to hurry up.

Lilianna held on to Sylvie's hand as the ambulance moved its way speedily through the deserted roads. She had arrived with Zach at the same time as the ambulance and had insisted she accompany Sylvie. The paramedic took one look at Lilianna and knew there was no room for negotiation. Her blue eyes glared at him as she pushed her way through the rear doors.

"We're nearly there, sweetie," Lilianna cooed as she stroked her dearest friend's forehead, avoiding the bruise just above her temple, which seemed to be blackening in front of her eyes. Tears were trickling out of Sylvie's eyes and running into her ears. Lilianna brushed them away with her other hand.

"Lily, I can't have an X-ray. Tell them. Call Dr Zinon. They need to know about the baby."

"Hush now, don't worry, I'll take care of it. Just relax sweetie." Lilianna was thankful that Sylvie was oblivious to the bleeding. They'd strapped her hand which had suffered a cut to the palm from the broken cup, and put on a neck brace as a precaution. Sylvie clenched her eyes shut at every bump, as the pain shot through her arm and hip. The paramedic wanted to give her something to ease the pain but she had insisted they give her nothing. Alex, Markus and Zach followed in the car up to the hospital.

Once inside the hospital, Sylvie was taken into an examining room where the on-call doctor checked her vital signs and thoroughly examined her. The rest of them stayed in the waiting room, pacing around in silence. Dr Patel was gentle and kind as Sylvie's tears continued to spring from her eyes. He spoke softly to her as the nurse measured her blood pressure.

"Mrs Sapphiris, we need to stitch your cut. Just two small stitches and an X-ray for your head and arm to see if there are any fractures. Dr Zinon is on the way." He was shining a light in her eye as he spoke.

"I'm pregnant," she whispered. Dr Patel gently lifted her left hand, which was strapped, and started to unwrap the bloody bandage. Sylvie winced as she felt a sharp pain lance through her arm and her palm throbbed.

"Yes, I know. Once we've stitched this I will need to consult with Dr Zinon. You've been bleeding and we need to do an ultrasound to make sure everything is alright."

"Bleeding? You mean the baby?" Sylvie asked, horrified. *No, no, please no!*

"There's no need to worry, Mrs Sapphiris. It's stopped now; we just need to make sure. You need to rest. Dr Zinon will be here any minute."

A fresh wave of tears rolled down her cheeks. Sylvie could hear someone approaching and the door opened. Dr Zinon strolled in; his kind eyes were tense as he smiled and greeted Dr Patel and the nurse. He then turned to Sylvie as he grabbed the chart that the nurse handed him.

"What have we here?" He shook his head, good-humouredly scolding Sylvie. "Camomile tea, eh? Maybe you should have had a brandy after all." Sylvie's face creased and let out a sob as she couldn't hold on to her emotions anymore. The relief that her own doctor was here and the panic she was experiencing about her baby was all too much. Instantly, he put down the chart and sat next to her.

"Hey, stop that. Everything will be fine."

"The baby? The bleeding?" Her eyes shot up at Dr Patel and he furrowed his brow.

"We'll check it out. It can be because of many reasons. Your cervix could have been chafed. It could even be you menstruating – it happens sometimes. I'll know as soon as I do the ultrasound. You had a nasty fall, Sylvie." His voice was soothing and he stroked her right arm as Sylvie visibly started to calm down, taking deep shuddery breaths.

"I wanted to do an X-ray to check she has no fractures to the wrist or her head," interrupted Dr Patel.

"I'd rather not. Can you get me an ultrasound in here first? Her vital signs are good." His voice was commanding. He turned to Sylvie and softly added, "They're going to stitch your hand and give you a local anaesthetic. It won't harm the baby. Lie back, and once they're done I will have a look, okay?"

Sylvie nodded weakly. Dr Zinon left the room with Dr Patel, leaving the nurse to prepare Sylvie's hand. Sylvie couldn't hear what they were saying, but by Dr Zinon's tone she could tell he wasn't happy. She closed her eyes and prayed that her baby was alright. It didn't matter if Nick was living it up in Cannes or that she was on her own. She wanted this baby so much and the threat of losing it had only confirmed that to her. Sylvie winced as the nurse carefully injected her hand.

27

PERSPECTIVE

Sylvie stared at the monitor as Dr Zinon moved the probe around inside her. Her head and hip were throbbing. The painkillers Dr Zinon had given her hadn't kicked in yet, and she was glad at least that her hand was still numb from the anaesthetic. Dr Zinon froze the picture on the monitor.

"There we are. You can see it clearly, that round ball there. Your cervix looks fine too." Dr Zinon pointed to the screen and Sylvie's eyes rested on what looked like a smudge.

"It's okay, then?" Her voice shaky and anxious.

"Yes. I'd say three weeks pregnant. We need to keep you in, though. I want total bed rest. No excitement at all, and only your boys and Lilianna to visit. No one to upset you. Your blood pressure's low, and that's probably why you passed out." His voice was a little sterner. He unfroze the picture and moved the probe again, moving closer to the monitor, furrowing his brow. Then moved it some more as if he needed to double-check. He froze the picture again.

"What is it?"

"Nothing… I'm just measuring. We'll able to see more within a week. There's no heartbeat yet." He turned to face her as her face dropped, and he smiled. "That's normal, though. Have you told the father yet?"

Sylvie sighed, relieved, then shook her head. "No one knows except Lily, and I want to keep it that way. I need to tell him before anyone else and he's away at the moment." Sylvie looked at the frozen screen, then looked back at Dr Zinon. "You think it'll be okay?"

"If you stay put and the baby shows signs of growth, there's no reason why it shouldn't be. But I mean it – no getting upset. You only get up to go to the bathroom, and you have to start eating better. I'm going to give them instructions on your diet."

"Can't I go home?" Sylvie almost whined.

Dr Zinon shook his head. "No chance. I need to keep my eye on you. I don't trust that you'll stay in bed. Just until Friday. If all is clear, you can go home." Sylvie sighed. *Thank goodness Marcy was back tomorrow.* "Now we've prepared your room, you need to sleep. How's the pain?"

"I still can't feel my hand and my head and hip still hurt."

Dr Zinon nodded. "By tomorrow, it should get better. I think your boys want to see you. I think Alex wanted to hit me when I told him he'd have to wait." He smirked as he shook his head. Sylvie smiled weakly, feeling guilty about the trouble she'd caused both her boys, and it was only going to get worse. She rested her right hand on her stomach as Dr Zinon took another close look at the frozen screen, deep in thought, and printed out the image. "Do you mind if I hang on to this until Friday? Then I'll give it to you."

Sylvie nodded at him, puzzled. *That was odd.* Well, she didn't have anyone to show it to anyway, so what did it matter?

Dr Zinon had organised a private room in the clinic and once she was settled he allowed Alex, Markus and Lilianna in. "Mum. Thank God you're okay." Markus bounded over to hug her gently. Fresh tears fell as she looked up at Alex whose face had a grey tinge to it. His eyes were red from crying. Markus pulled back and Alex edged forward, leaning down to kiss her.

"How are you feeling?" His voice was hoarse.

"My head and hip hurt, and I still can't feel my hand. It's badly sprained." She smiled weakly at them, shrugging. "I'm fine, though. The doctor wants me to stay for a few days. He's just being cautious, that's all. You must all be so tired. Go home and sleep. I'm fine, really."

Markus looked haunted as he glanced down at her hand and then gradually down her body. He swallowed hard. "I thought… for a split-second…"

"I'm fine, darling. Just weak, and my blood pressure's low. That's why I fainted." She blinked at him, trying hard to forget her phone call from Nick. She didn't want anyone to know about that.

"Come on boys, let's go. She needs to sleep, and it's nearly four in the morning." Lilianna ushered them out, but not before they gave

Sylvie a kiss. "I'll be out in a minute. Just need to get a list of stuff your mum needs."

Once they were outside the room, Lilianna came over to Sylvie, sitting next to her. "So what did he say? The baby?"

"Everything seems to be fine, but I need to stay in bed until Friday to make sure it's still growing."

Lilianna sighed with relief. "Well we both know how that feels, don't we? Time for me to pay you back. You're not to move, and I'll take care of everything. I'll bring you your clothes and laptop tomorrow. No contact with anyone who'll upset you. It's only seven days and then, when you're home, you can decide what to do. Okay, sweetie?" She gently brushed back her hair and kissed her forehead. "Now go to sleep and I'll be back in the morning. I've told Dr Zinon to put a phone in here for you to call who you want to call only."

"Thanks, Lily. How's Zach?"

"Climbing the walls! He can see you tomorrow, when you're rested." Sylvie nodded, pleased she didn't need to face anyone else. Lilianna got up from the bed and headed to the door.

"Good night, sweetie."

"Good night, Lily, and thanks."

Julian sat at his desk, sipping his third coffee of the morning. After leaving Zach's last night, he realised he needed to do some damage control. He called Maggie to find out if she'd heard from Nick.

"I sent him some messages but he didn't answer. Vicki and Elenora heard from him on Monday saying he'd arrived and that he was fine, but that's it."

He could tell from her tone she was worried, although she tried to hide it. "Has anyone been down to Christian?" Julian knew that Nick would be in contact with him.

"No. I was hoping he'd get in touch himself. Maybe I should go down and see him though."

"I'll go. Just get Vicki or Elenora to text him. Nick'll let them know he's okay."

Julian drove down to the marina. He'd decided to try and pump Christian for information. Nick was bound to be in contact with him. If Nick knew his father had been down to hassle his manager, it might make him call. He opened the door to the shop and walked through to where Christian was bagging up some swimwear and snorkels for a young couple. When he saw Julian, he stopped for a split-second and nervously put in the receipt.

Once the couple left, Julian spoke. "Hello, Christian."

"Hello, Mr Steed."

"I think you know why I'm here. We've been here before, after all." Christian shifted from one foot to the other nervously. Julian had always intimidated him.

"Mr Steed, I really don't know where he is, other than he left on Monday and he just checks in to make sure all's well here." He couldn't even look him in the eye.

"Hmm… well, when he calls, please let him know I came. I need to talk to him. It's…" his eyes narrowed as he was interrupted by his phone ringing. Zach's number flashed. "Excuse me, I need to take this." Christian shrugged and leaned back against the wall, pleased he wasn't being subjected to the Julian Steed interrogation. Julian hit the answer key.

"Zach. How are you?"

"Julian. Listen, I thought you should know Sylvie was in an accident and…"

"An accident! What kind of accident? Is she okay?" Julian's face drained of colour as Christian listened.

"She's fine now. She fainted late last night and hurt her arm and head. She's been told to have total bed rest. The doctor's keeping her in for a few days. Why I'm telling you is that she was supposed to go through the plans today with Yiannis as I'm tied up, so we'll need to reschedule our meeting."

"Forget about that, Zach. So she's in the clinic now? Dr Zinon's?"

"Yes."

"Jesus, Zach. Why is she being kept in?" Christian rearranged the counter trying hard to hear both conversations.

"He's worried about her and wants to make sure she's okay."

"Poor Sylvie. Okay, thanks for letting me know. I'll be in touch." He switched off the phone, then looked up at Christian. "I need to get off. Just tell him I want to talk to him, right?" His voice indicated it wasn't up for discussion.

"Yes, sure, Mr Steed." Christian visibly shrank.

Julian made his way to his car and checked the time. It was just after one. Getting in his car, he sat for a moment, contemplating what to do next. He needed to see Sylvie. He wanted to make sure she was alright. He started up his car and headed towards the clinic.

Christian went up to the shop front and watched as Julian drove off. Then he picked up his phone and punched in Nick's number. He knew it would be switched off, but he'd leave a message and Nick would get back to him. To his surprise, the phone rang. He waited for Nick to answer but the phone rang and then switched to voicemail. *Fuck!* thought Christian. He was screening the calls. Once the outgoing message stopped, Christian spoke.

"Nick, your dad came by… while he was here, someone called Zach called and said Sylvie was in hospital… some kind of accident. Thought you should know." He put down the phone and went back into the shop.

Nick sat at the desk in his hotel room, completing all the documentation for the transfer. He hadn't heard from Xavier yet, but it was only midday. He was sure Xavier had been out until the early hours of the morning. Nick looked down at the number calling him on his mobile. It was Christian. He pressed it to go to voicemail. He'd call him later. Right now, he needed to get everything prepared so that the transfer would go through on Monday. He needed to get back to Sylvie as soon as possible to explain things to her. He'd called her every hour on the hour from six this morning, and her phone was still off. *God, she was stubborn*, he thought to himself. He scanned and signed, then rescanned the sale and transfer and emailed it back to Serge.

Nick picked up his phone and dialled. "Serge. Everything's been sent. Once your client's signed, and the funds are deposited, the transfer of ownership will go through.

"Good. I'll call you." Serge hung up and Nick took a deep breath. He sauntered on to the balcony and lit a cigarette. Looking out onto the beach, he sighed. If his parents hadn't interfered, Sylvie would probably have come out tomorrow and he'd have really felt like celebrating. This was the biggest deal he'd ever pulled off. As it was, all he wanted was to get it over with and get back to Cyprus to explain the unfortunate incident on the phone. Why was her phone still off? His phone beeped through a message and it distracted him from his thoughts.

Nicky r u ok?

It was from Vicki. He quickly typed a reply and then went back out to the balcony.

Julian pulled up outside the clinic, his heart beating fast as he sat in the car. He was sure Sylvie would tell him to leave, but he needed to see if she was alright. He got out of the car and entered through the large double door. The receptionist looked up and smiled as he approached. Julian reciprocated and leaned over the reception desk, fixing her with his eyes.

"Mrs Sapphiris?" The receptionist blushed as she looked at her list, fumbling under his gaze.

"Yes, she's in a private room on the fourth floor. She has limited visiting though."

Julian frowned for a second, then smiled. "Oh, I won't be long, I just need to drop something off." He quickly headed for the elevator before she could object.

Once he was up to the fourth floor, Julian walked quietly through the corridor where there were doors on either side. Some were open and he could see in. The nurses were preparing the trolleys for the lunches, so he was able walk around without anyone challenging him. Eventually, he came to the final three doors. He tentatively opened the first one and peered in. It was empty. As he left, he heard the familiar voice of Lilianna and he froze outside the second door, which was slightly open. He heard Sylvie's soft laugh at something Lilianna had said and he strained to hear.

"That's better, at least your arse isn't on display now," he heard Lilianna joke.

"I hate hospital gowns. I hate hospitals full stop and I've got to stay here for another six days. I'll go mental," groaned Sylvie.

"I know, sweetie, but Dr Zinon's right. If you went home, you'd be up and down all the time, and you need total bed rest. Here he can check on you and the baby and he knows you're being well looked after."

Baby! Sylvie's having a… she's pregnant! Holy fucking… It's Nick's. It's Nick's baby. Julian leaned against the wall of the corridor as the bombshell hit him, forcing him flat against its cold surface.

Nick and Sylvie were having a baby. He closed his eyes as he absorbed the information. Nick was going to be a father, a father to Sylvie's baby. That's why she was being kept in. Was everything okay? The extent of his concern was unexpected. That was to say, his concern for the baby. *His grandchild. His first grandchild!* He was going to be a grandfather! Surely Nick didn't know. There was no way he would have gone, knowing Sylvie was pregnant. So why hadn't she told him? He took a couple of deep breaths and stood up straight, heading towards the elevators. He knew exactly why she hadn't told him. She hadn't told him because she'd broken up with him. She'd tried to do the right thing because he, Julian, had made her, and now here she was, alone and pregnant with his son's baby, his grandchild.

He stepped into the lift and pressed the button for the reception. The doors closed and he looked at his reflection in the mirror as the elevator descended the four floors. *Is this what he wanted? Sylvie alone and unhappy with his grandchild? Nick alone without Sylvie? Their family happiness denied because of him? What if she decided not to have the baby?* The elevator doors opened and he quickly made his way to his car. He needed to set things straight. He'd fucked up his own marriage and the happiness of his children. He most certainly wasn't going to be responsible for the unhappiness of his grandchild. He opened his car door and got in. He'd have to make his peace with Maggie, apologise for how he'd behaved. He'd put her through enough, it was time to man up. He smiled to himself. *Granddad. He was going to be a Granddaddy.* His grin grew bigger as the thought warmed his heart.

Julian drove up to Maggie's, not exactly sure what he was going to say to her, but he knew he had to start with an apology and not just for Sunday. She'd always stood by him and showed him nothing but her full support. He'd have to bite the bullet and take whatever she said to him.

He tentatively knocked on the door, bracing himself as he stood out on the doorstep in what must have been thirty degrees. He heard Maggie coming through to the hallway and she opened the door. She was in a navy blue bikini with a matching sarong wrapped round her. Julian's eyes widened as he allowed his eyes to travel over her appreciatively.

"Hi Julian, I was just drying off after a swim." She flushed.

"Oh, um… well I… well I just came up to see if you'd heard anything from Nick." He looked away nervously as she walked through to the terrace, and she spread back out on the sun lounger as Julian sat down.

"No, I haven't, but Vicki has had a text saying he's fine." She slipped on her sunglasses. "Do you want anything to drink?"

"Er… no. Maggie, are you okay?" He looked down at her, confused. She seemed very relaxed, considering Nick had gone MIA again, and with everything else that had gone on, he'd expected her to be flapping around and stressing.

"Fine. Did you come up for anything specific?" she asked, removing her sarong and exposing her slim toned legs. Julian stared for a moment and then turned away, embarrassed that he was checking out his ex-wife's figure.

"To be honest, I came to apologise for Sunday."

"Oh?" Maggie turned on her side and looked at him.

"Did you know Sylvie tried to break it off with Nick?"

"Yes, I talked to Sylvie."

"When?" He couldn't hide his surprise.

"Yesterday. She hasn't heard from him either."

"You seem very… well, relaxed about it."

Maggie sat up and removed her sunglasses. "Relaxed? I wouldn't say that." She stiffened as she spoke. "Julian, Nick left because Sylvie tried to do the right thing. She tried to get him to go away so that they would have some distance. That's what you wanted, isn't it?"

He opened his mouth to speak but then stopped. Maggie continued. "I tried to call him and sent countless messages, which he's ignored. Knowing Nick, he's devastated, but unless he answers me I can't help him. I know Sylvie's upset. One conversation with her was enough to confirm that. I can't do anything to help her either. She loves him and from what I can tell, Nick loves her. You made your thoughts perfectly clear to both of them, and as a result it would seem that because of you, Nick and Sylvie are splitting up. Nick will come round and Sylvie will muddle through – Lord knows she's had her fair share of drama this past year…"

Julian sat wide-eyed as he listened to Maggie talking in such a detached way. It began to disturb him. "What on earth are you saying?" he asked her, clearly shocked at her matter-of-fact summary.

"You got what you wanted, Julian." She shrugged at him, as if that was enough of an explanation.

"Not like this. You know Sylvie's in a mess don't you? Lilianna took her to the doctor because she wasn't well and now she's in the hospital. I didn't want that, I never wanted her to… I could never…" He put his head in his hands.

"Hospital? Why?" Maggie sat up, her face dropping, full of concern.

Julian looked up at her. He knew he couldn't tell her about the baby, not yet anyway. "She fainted and hurt herself. The doctor's just being cautious." Changing the subject, he asked, "How did she sound when you spoke to her?"

He looked at Maggie as her stance softened and she sighed. *Thank God!* thought Maggie; she couldn't carry on the charade. He was finally feeling remorse, finally seeing the consequences of his actions. "She sounded terrible, Julian."

He closed his eyes momentarily and clenched his jaw. All because of him. "Why were you so… cold and hard, just now?" He gazed at her puzzled.

"Because I wanted you to see what you've done, Julian. You can't make someone love you. Believe me, I know." She stopped and took a deep breath. "You forced Sylvie into breaking it off with Nick because you knew if she thought for one minute their relationship would upset you, or me, she'd break it off out of guilt, regardless of her feelings or of Nick's." She reached for her sarong and wrapped it round her. "Julian, you're going to have to make this right. Go and talk to Sylvie and apologise to her, not me. And you need to make up with Nick. How, I don't know. He was seething when he came to see me. I couldn't even make him see reason. All he focused on was that I was backing you up, which I wasn't. I was trying to make him understand."

"He'll never talk to me," he mumbled as he rubbed his face.

"Well, you'll have to make him."

"I feel so ashamed," he whispered, and Maggie reached over and took his hand.

"Make it right. I can't do this for you. If you manage to get through to Sylvie, you might have a chance with Nick."

Julian sat back and looked at Maggie as she gazed back at him. "You really freaked me out, back then. I've never seen you like that. You were so hard." His eyes narrowed.

"Well, it's nice to know that after thirty years I can still shock you."

"I'd rather you didn't," he muttered softly as she got up from the lounger.

"Do you want a drink? Coffee?" She strolled to the kitchen and his eyes followed her.

"Beer, please. You know Maggie, you should wear bikinis more often. I forgot what great legs you have. You're always covered up in sundresses and jeans."

She glanced back at him, shaking her head and smirking. "Maybe I will."

Julian fleetingly thought that she was going to make one hell of a hot Grandma.

28

VISITORS

Nick was restless. He sat out on the balcony of the Grand Hotel, smoking his way through his fifth cigarette, staring out at the beautiful view of the Mediterranean. He hadn't left the room since he came back from the nightclub in the early hours of Friday. He looked at his phone for the millionth time: still no messages from Sylvie. He pressed the voicemail option and listened to the messages, just in case he'd missed one. As the familiar voice of Maggie came on, he pressed the key to skip to the next. He skipped through the next ten messages from his mother. Jeez, she wasn't giving up. Then on the eleventh, he heard Christian speak.

"Nick, your dad came by…" He'd heard enough and turned it off. His father had eventually decided to try and find him by going to Christian. *Way to go, Dad*, he thought sarcastically. Then he put down his phone again. Still no word from her.

Well, he couldn't stay here all day. He'd be climbing the walls by Monday. It was early still and all the clubbers would be in bed, so Nick decided to go for a run, to clear his head. He dragged on his shorts and a vest, then quickly laced up his trainers. He picked up his wallet and phone, zipping them into his shorts and plugged in his earphones. Soothing music and a run would make him feel better. He glanced at the cigarette packet, then picked that up too, feeling a wave of guilt.

Nick came out onto the Boulevard de la Croisette and headed east, jogging at an even pace, glancing at the shops to his left, then at the sea to his right. There weren't many people around yet and the shops were only now opening up. He'd run for half an hour, then he'd stop by some café and take in the view, he thought wistfully.

Before long, he was passing the Palme D'Or restaurant – one of his favourites. He sighed deeply as he passed it. If circumstances had turned out the way he'd envisaged them, he would have been taking Sylvie there tonight to celebrate. He clenched his jaw and sped up his pace as he carried on down towards the marina, passing all the exclusive hotels, each of them a blur as he sped up more. There were some early risers on the beach as he powered past them.

Turning down to the right, he found himself at quay one, close to Le Baoli where he'd walked back to the hotel on Friday morning. Stopping for a moment to catch his breath, he looked round at all the yachts, taking them in. He loved it here. Sylvie would have really loved it. His heart ached at the thought. *Why hadn't she rung him? Why was her phone off?* He was in perpetual hell, darkness and silence. Monday couldn't come fast enough. Two more days; how was he going to make it through two more days? He ran his hands through his damp hair, then kicked an empty cigarette packet that was crumpled on the floor. He switched off the music on his iPhone. He just couldn't listen to any more. Everything reminded him of her. He turned back around and started his run back to the hotel.

The sun was higher now and he was beginning to feel its relentless heat on his sweat-covered skin. Slowing down, he stopped by a small shop to buy a bottle of water, not far from his hotel. As he drank from the bottle, the shop on the corner opposite caught his eye. Chugging down the remains of his water, he put the plastic bottle in the wastebasket outside the shop and reached into his pocket for his wallet.

He leafed through some business cards he had shoved in there, then he pulled out the paper he'd been searching for. He carefully opened it up. At the top of the notepaper was the Grande Britannia logo and in the middle was the letter 'N'. Why he needed to look at it, he really wasn't sure. *How could he forget that letter?* he snorted to himself. *How very apt.* He shoved it back into his wallet and crossed the busy boulevard, entering the cool air-conditioned shop. He was let in and greeted by a smart doorman. "Bonjour monsieur."

The smartly dressed assistant opposite smiled widely as Nick made his way to the counter, eyeing his sweat-soaked vest. Nick furrowed his brow for a moment, realising in his haste that maybe he was inappropriately dressed.

"Bonjour monsieur." His voice was silky smooth as he eyed Nick.

"Bonjour. I wonder if you could help me?" Nick pulled out the paper again, handing it to the assistant.

Zach was driving down to the clinic, and his head was pounding. Thankfully, the Saturday morning traffic was light. He'd hardly slept these past two nights worrying about Sylvie. Since Chris had died, he'd felt an overwhelming duty towards her. Lilianna had told him she was fine, but he needed to see her for himself. His car phone rang and he recognised Julian's number.

"Morning, Julian."

"Morning, Zach. How you doing?"

"Oh you know: same shit, different day." Zach laughed.

"Yeah, I hear you… I was ringing to see if you'd been down to see Sylvie yet."

"I'm going now."

"Oh… um… I need a favour."

Zach tensed, knowing where this conversation was going. "Oh?"

"I need to talk to Sylvie, I need –"

"Julian, she can't see anyone. Doctor's orders. They're only letting me in because I'll break the door down if they don't."

"I have to apologise, to make it right. I behaved like an ass, Zach, and I don't want her feeling guilty because of me." Zach sighed, not really knowing what to say, then Julian added. "I feel responsible, Zach. I don't want her to suffer anymore… she's suffered enough."

"Look, I'll talk to her, but it's not down to me."

"That's all I want. Thanks."

"I'm not promising anything, just so we're clear."

"I know. Please tell her I'm thinking of her and call me and to let me know how she is."

"Okay. Bye, Julian."

"Bye, and thanks again. I know I'm putting you in a difficult position."

Zach hung up as he pulled into the clinic's car park. 'Difficult position' didn't even cover it. Lily was going to freak.

Zach made his way to the elevators and pressed for the fourth floor. It was nine-thirty and he hoped he wasn't too early. He came out into the small waiting area and smiled to himself as he looked round at the familiar surroundings. It was on this very floor he'd met Lilianna over twenty years ago. Okay, it wasn't exactly the same – it had been refurbished, but it was still that very floor. He'd been visiting his mother here after she'd had her hysterectomy, and Lilianna had been a trainee nurse looking after her. He was totally smitten by her on the first day, remembering how her bright blue eyes danced around mischievously. Her blonde hair had been in a tight pleat as she quickly skipped up and down the corridors. Zach had never met such a straight-talking woman before and he was totally in awe of her. By the seventh day, Lilianna had become impatient with his lack of assertiveness and as he got up to leave after his visit, she followed him out of the door. "My shift finishes now. Do you fancy going for a coffee?"

Zach had looked at her dumbstruck and blurted out: "Sure."

"Okay, meet me in the lobby. I'll be five minutes." And then she'd flounced back into his mother's room.

"Well, did you ask him?" Zach's mother had asked. Lilianna had nodded, beaming at her. "Thank goodness. If you'd waited for him to ask…" His mother had shaken her head in exasperation at her own son.

Zach remembered they were the longest five minutes of his life.

He walked down the corridor and stood outside Sylvie's door, pausing a minute. He could hear Lilianna talking to her and the TV was on. He knocked softly.

"Come in." Her familiar voice chimed from inside. Zach popped his head through the door and was physically and mentally relieved to be faced with a decidedly fresher-faced Sylvie. The image of her the night before, covered in blood and laid out on a stretcher with a neck brace, her eyes haunted like dark pools, made Zach shiver. It would take him a while to shake that picture out of his mind. Sylvie smiled up at him as he leisurely came up to her bed and leaned down to kiss her cheek.

"Well, you're looking better." He sat on the bed close to her and took her right hand, squeezing it. Lilianna grinned. "How you feeling? How's your arm?"

"I'm fine. Just a bit achy and my arm's throbbing, but apart from that…"

Zach reached over and moved her hair away from her eyes so that he could see the bump on her head. It was a dark purple, which leached down to her brow and the edge of her left eye. "That's quite a shiner you have there," he joked, but his face was tense as he looked at it, clearly shaken by it.

"It's just a bruise. It'll go," Sylvie reassured him. Zach nodded weakly and Lilianna could see he was emotional.

"I'll go get some coffee." Her voice was low as she headed towards the door. Sensing Zach needed a moment with Sylvie, it was an excuse to leave them alone.

"Oh, Sylvie, I… Jesus, I thought, well, you looked so broken. Are you really alright? Really?" His face was ashen and anxious. Sylvie shifted closer and pulled him to her with her good arm, and he gently wrapped his arms around her. "I swear, seeing you on that stretcher… and all that blood." He pulled back to look at her, tears brimming in his eyes. "Don't do that to us again, right! Don't do that to me. I don't know what I'd do if anything happened to you." Sylvie's eyes filled up and he pulled her back in his arms as she let the tears trickle down her cheeks and onto his shirt.

"I won't, and nothing's going to happen to me," she mumbled into his shoulder. "I love you, Zach. You do know that, don't you?"

"Of course I do, and I love you."

"I know." They sat there for a while, content and at peace – Zach bewildered at the depth of feeling he had for this woman, and Sylvie thankful that through everything, he had been her constant, her confidant and her friend.

Lilianna came back with a tray and smiled as she saw them sitting facing each other, wiping their eyes. She placed the tray down and poured Sylvie's tea and Zach's coffee. Zach turned to look at Lilianna and she winked at him, knowing he'd been through hell until he'd seen Sylvie. "Better?" she asked softly, and he nodded sheepishly. "Good. Did you remember to bring the ginger biscuits?"

Zach's face dropped. "I left them in the car." Lilianna rolled her eyes. "I'll go and get them." He reluctantly released Sylvie's hand and headed for the door, but not before giving Lilianna a chaste kiss on her lips. As he reached and opened it, he turned round and said: "I'm a lucky son of a bitch, surrounded by extraordinary women." He grinned.

"Yes you bloody well are. Now go and get the biscuits!" Lilianna laughed.

They spent the best part of the morning just chatting, dunking their ginger biscuits and watching crappy TV. Dr Zinon came in to see Sylvie, pleased with her progress and glad to see her smiling. By twelve o'clock, Zach got up to leave.

"I better get off. I think Alex and Markus are coming around two." He brushed the crumbs off his trousers as he spoke. Then, looking nervously from Lilianna to Sylvie, he added, "Julian sends his best to you. He called just before I came here." Lilianna glared at him and

Sylvie narrowed her eyes. "I know he's not your most favourite person right now" – Lilianna snorted, still glaring – "but he feels like shit and wants to apologise."

"I bet he does," muttered Lilianna. Sylvie twisted her mouth, not really sure what to say.

"Anyway, at least think about it. I know you can't have visitors right now, so he won't be coming, but at least later, hear what he has to say." He leaned down and kissed her forehead. "You look tired. Get some sleep." Sylvie nodded as she stifled a yawn.

Lilianna stood up from her chair. "I'll go too. I'll be back around two with some trashy magazines, okay?"

"Sounds great. Oh, can you get me some liquorice and some pickles?"

Zach raised his eyebrows, finding her request rather bizarre, but Lilianna just nodded, unfazed.

"Sure, anything else?" Sylvie shook her head and settled down into her pillow, her eyes drooping. Why was she so tired? She'd done nothing all morning except drink tea and eat ginger biscuits. She rested her good right arm on her stomach. *Oh yes, you, you're the one tiring me out.* For the first time in six days, she felt a tiny flutter of butterflies.

Sylvie's eyes fluttered open as she looked around, disorientated by her surroundings. She could hear the faint ringing of church bells in the distance. There was a nurse jotting down some notes on a chart and as Sylvie moved, the nurse's eyes jerked up to where Sylvie was. "Good morning, Mrs Sapphiris, how are you feeling?"

"Morning. Okay, what time is it?" she croaked as she shuffled herself up to a sitting position, wincing as she leaned on her left arm, forgetting about her injury momentarily.

"Eight forty-five."

Sylvie rubbed her face. *Wow!* She'd slept twelve hours straight. She swung out of bed and the nurse was up to her immediately.

"Let me check your blood pressure first."

"Um, okay. But I really need to use the bathroom." The nurse nodded and gently helped her up. Sylvie shuffled into the bathroom and sat on the toilet. Before she could finish, she felt that horrid feeling of saliva pooling in her mouth and she retched violently, vomiting magnificently over the bathroom floor. *Joy!* thought Sylvie. Whoever said being pregnant was a beautiful experience needed to come and have a look at the amazing marbled effect of black liquorice and green gherkins regurgitated and splattered all over the floor! Sylvie shivered at the taste in her mouth. *Note to self; liquorice and gherkins tasted horrible on the reverse journey!* Sylvie got off the toilet, flushed, then proceeded to try and clean up her handiwork.

Within a minute, the nurse barged in, and saw Sylvie on all fours with toilet paper in her hand. "What on earth are you doing?" Clearly horrified to find a strictly bed rest patient cleaning the floor.

"I was just…" Sylvie tried to explain, feeling like a child being caught out.

"Leave it. I'll get a cleaner." The nurse bent down to lift her up and Sylvie staggered to her feet. "Back to bed!"

"Can I brush my teeth?" The nurse nodded, but stood and watched her, then guided her back to bed.

By eleven o'clock, Dr Zinon had passed by and had been told about the cleaning incident.

"Sylvie, that's why you're in here. Stay put, otherwise I'll cuff you to the bed," he joked. "Good to see you're eating well. Is the nausea bad?"

"Yes. I can't remember it being so bad with the boys. Maybe I blocked it out, eh? The ginger helps."

He nodded. "It's just a few more days in here," he added, knowing she was totally frustrated. "You'll still need to be careful, but at least you'll be home." He put down her chart and headed out of the door as Alex, Markus and Thea Miria walked in. He greeted them all and left them alone, but not before telling them that Sylvie would be needing to rest in an hour or so.

Thea Miria was up to her first. "Sylvie, my dear, sweet girl, what have you done to yourself? When Markus called last night, I couldn't take it in. You just don't look after yourself. You need to put some weight on." She cupped Sylvie's face between her hands. Her eyes flitted over the purple bruise around her left eye and then she looked down at her arm. "Fainted, eh?" She scrutinised her face and then sat back, allowing her eyes to drift over Sylvie's body. Alex and Markus kissed Sylvie and smirked at their great auntie's comments.

"I'm fine, Thea, really. The doctor's just being cautious, that's all. It's my blood pressure. It's low, so they're monitoring it."

"Good." Thea Miria turned to the boys who had now slouched in the two chairs. "Any danger of some coffee? Tea for your mum, and see if they've any cake."

"Sure, Thea," Alex mumbled as he got back up again, tapping Markus's leg, indicating he should come too. She effectively dismissed them as she turned her attention back to Sylvie.

"So what's going on? Alex told me that you've broken it off with Nick. Is that right?" Sylvie sighed. She really wasn't up for a Thea Miria interrogation.

"It's just for the best, Thea." Sylvie felt her eyes well and she tried hard not to succumb to their pricking. She instinctively put her right hand onto her stomach and Thea Miria's brow creased.

"I see. He doesn't know, I take it?"

"I haven't spoken to him since last Sunday. He's away in Cannes with work. I don't think he's spoken to anyone, so he wouldn't know I was in here." Sylvie looked round her room absent-mindedly.

"I didn't mean that," Thea Miria said softly. Sylvie, puzzled by her response, looked back at her aunt. Thea Miria tilted her head to one side and raised her eyebrows as if to say, *you know what I'm talking about.* "I meant about the baby."

Sylvie's eyes widened, nearly making them pop out of their sockets. *How the hell did she do that?* "How did you… I mean…" Sylvie stuttered, shocked.

"You're in the Gyni ward. You fainted, you're being monitored, your face has filled out and that teeny tiny waist of yours has opened out. You don't need to be a genius to work it out, but the fact you instinctively rest your hand on your stomach is the biggest giveaway. So I take it Nick doesn't know."

Sylvie shook her head still shocked. "No one knows, except Lily and now you. I don't want anyone to know yet, not until I've been given the all-clear and I've told Nick."

"Quite right. How do you feel?" Thea Miria's concern was evident in her face.

"Tired and nauseous."

"No, I mean about the baby."

Sylvie screwed up her nose and gave her aunt a shy smile. "I'm happy. I mean I really want this, but I'm not sure what to do about Nick."

Thea Miria nodded slowly, then, taking her right hand, she looked at her. "Take some advice from an old woman. Tell him sooner rather than later. Just think of the happiness you're feeling right now about it – it's all over your face, you're glowing, even with that purple bruise and bandaged arm. And then think that you are depriving Nick of that same happiness. He needs to know."

Sylvie stared back at her aunt. It really was that simple, and in that moment of clarity, Sylvie realised that this small smudge was their happiness and nothing else really else mattered. "How did you get so wise?" Sylvie smiled at her aunt.

"Oh, I got old and I didn't have a man around to drive me insane." She laughed loudly and as if on cue, Alex and Markus came back in, holding a tray laden with what looked like the best part of the cake section of the cafeteria.

Sylvie looked up at her boys and then rubbed her belly. *She'd rather be driven insane*, she mused.

29

HELL

Saturday had dragged by for Nick. He'd stayed in his hotel room for the rest of the day after he'd returned from his much-needed run. Xavier had dropped by in the late afternoon to see if he could coax him out for the evening but Nick had declined, deciding to eat in his room and catch up on his emails, watch films and smoke his way through numerous packs of Dunhills.

By seven o'clock on Sunday morning, though, he was stir crazy. He needed to get out of what now resembled a four-star prison cell. He got out of bed and decided he'd go for a run again. He needed to talk to Christian but he knew he'd be asleep, so he laced up his trainers and set off again, looking forward to getting out into the fresh air. Forty-eight hours left, and then he'd be able to head back home. Last Sunday, he'd envisaged spending his weekend in a completely different manner, not wishing his time away and counting the seconds until he could leave. He was in hell. *Hell!*

Nick got back to his room by eight and picked up his phone, switching it on. It was the first time he'd put it on without a flood of messages coming through. He quickly dialled Christian and waited for it to connect.

After the sixth ring, he heard a sleepy Christian answer. "Hello?"

"Christian, are you still asleep?"

"Nick! Man. No. Well yes. Give me a second. Ouch! Fuck!" Nick heard Christian stumble about and waited patiently, then once Christian had found his equilibrium: "Sorry, Nick. Did you get my message about your dad?" He sounded concerned as he spoke.

"Yeah, I'm not interested in what he has to say –"

Christian interrupted him before he could finish. "No, I mean about Sylvie." Christian's voice grew louder and urgent, taking Nick by surprise.

"Sylvie? What about her?"

"Jeez, Nick, that's why I sent you a voicemail. Didn't you listen to it?"

"No! Just tell me, what about Sylvie?" Nick's blood pumped harder as he raised his voice. He sensed from Christian's tone something wasn't right.

"He came here to ask about you and while we were talking, he got a phone call from some friend of his… I can't remember his name now…"

"Was it Zach?"

"Yeah, that's right, it was Zach. Anyway, Zach called to tell him that Sylvie had been in an accident…" Nick slumped in the chair, the colour draining from his face.

"An accident? What kind of accident? Is she alright?" His voice hoarse as he swallowed hard.

"I'm not sure, but she was taken to a clinic and then your dad left. He looked pretty shaken up. That's why I called you… Nick?"

"Yeah I'm here. When was this?" He clenched his eyes shut as he spoke, pinching his nose with his thumb and forefinger.

"Friday morning."

Jesus, it was Sunday. Sylvie's phone was still off and it dawned on Nick that that was probably why. She was in the clinic. *Fuck, how was he going to find out how she was?* "I need you to call Vicki. Ask her if she knows anything and get back to me."

"Why don't you just call her, Nick? She's worried about you."

"No, she'll try and talk me round. You know how she is, she's a fucking lawyer, for God's sake! Right now, all I want to know is how Sylvie is. The earliest flight I can get on is late on Tuesday. Please, Christian, ring her." Nick's voice wavered as he spoke and Christian knew he was beyond devastated.

"Sure, man. Keep your phone on and I'll ring you as soon as I know."

"Thanks." Nick closed his phone and stared at it for a moment. It must be bad if she was still in the clinic. He quickly dialled Serge's number. Serge answered it immediately. "Serge?"

"Nick."

"What time's the transfer going through on Monday?"

"One at the latest."

"There won't be any problems, will there?"

"Not at my end." Serge sounded annoyed.

"Good. I need to be back home on Tuesday. I'll talk to you in the morning."

"Okay, bye."

He sat back in the chair holding his head in his hands, praying it wasn't anything serious. He pulled out his cigarettes and, with a shaking hand, lit one up.

"Hi,, Vicki,"

"Yes? Who's this?"

"Christian."

"Oh. Er… hi Christian, how are you?" Vicki couldn't hide her surprise.

"I'm fine. Look, sorry to bother you, but… well, Nick wanted me to find out how Sylvie was and I didn't know who else to call." Christian put on his best coy voice in a bid to make her feel sorry for him.

"Sylvie? What do you mean? You've spoken to Nick? Where is he? When's he coming back?"

Crap, thought Christian. This was going to be a lot harder than he'd hoped. "He rang me today. He's fine. I'm not sure when he's back, he didn't tell me. Sylvie's been in an accident and naturally Nick was concerned about her. Do you know how she is?"

"An accident? No, I didn't know that. That's terrible. I could ask my mum – she should know. Hang on a minute." He heard her pacing through the house and opening a door. "Mum, has Sylvie been in an accident?" he heard her ask.

"An accident? I don't know. I know she wasn't well. Why? Who told you she was in an accident?"

Vicki paused before answering, careful not to mention Nick or Christian. "Some friend of mine." Christian smiled: ever the lawyer, giving selective information. "Don't you think you should find out?" Vicki coaxed.

"Well, yes. I'll ring Lilianna. She'll be able to tell me." Maggie reached over to her phone and dialled the number while Vicki retreated to the kitchen.

"Christian?"

"Yeah, I'm here."

"I'll call you as soon as I know."

"Great, thanks for that."

Vicki hung up and went back to the workshop where her mum was talking.

"Fainted?" Maggie sat down, clearly affected by the news. "When was this? Her arm... how did she manage that? ... I see. Julian said she wasn't good but I didn't realise it was so serious. So she's still in the clinic? ... I see... just for observation... well, of course. Thank you for telling me. Please give her my love. Goodbye, Lily."

"Well, what happened?" Vicki asked impatiently as she looked at her stunned mother. Maggie repeated what Lilianna had told her and Vicki listened, asking questions wherever she felt the information was lacking. Then, once satisfied, she went out on to the terrace to call Christian. He picked up the phone on the first ring.

Carefully and diligently, Vicki gave Christian a detailed description of the facts surrounding Sylvie's accident. Christian smirked, thinking how right Nick had been about her. Her word-for-word account left no question unanswered.

"Thanks, Vicki. Nick's really worried, I'll call him now."

"Tell him to get his ass back here, will you?"

"Sure, Vicki. Bye."

Nick sat on the balcony in a towel. He'd managed to shower while waiting for his call. He dragged hard on his cigarette, willing his phone to ring, and drank his tea. He'd played a thousand different scenarios in his head and every one of them had made him panic at the thought of anything happening to Sylvie. Abruptly his phone rang and he grabbed it, answering it after one ring. "Christian, please tell me it's good news." He almost cracked.

"She's fine, Nick."

Hearing those three words, Nick's whole body relaxed. *Thank God!* He looked skyward and mouthed "thank you". "What happened?" Now he'd somewhat calmed down, he wanted details.

"She fainted in the early hours of Friday and as she fell she landed on her left arm, spraining it badly and cutting it with either a cup or her phone that she was holding. No one seems to know which." *Early hours*

319

of Friday? That's when he called her – she was holding a phone. Nick closed his eyes, realising she'd fainted after their phone call. After she'd heard Sandrine. That's why her phone was off. *Jesus Christ, it was his fault she'd collapsed.* She must have thought that he'd moved on with some 'French hotty', as she called them. Nick rubbed his face, trying to piece everything together.

"Why's she still in, then?" *A stay in hospital for a sprained arm and a cut was a little extreme,* thought Nick.

"The doctor wants to keep her in because her blood pressure's low and he's insisting she has bed rest until Friday, just as a precaution. She's weak and he wants to monitor her."

Images of a gaunt Sylvie with tubes coming out of her flashed into Nick's mind. "Thanks, Christian. If you hear any more, anything, call me," Nick muttered.

"Okay. Vicki told me to tell you to get your ass back here."

"Well, I am. The transfer should go through on Monday and I get a flight late Tuesday. She doesn't need to know that though." Nick explained in monotone.

"That's great news, Nick! Wow."

"Yeah, I just don't feel like celebrating much, especially now." He stubbed out his cigarette that had burned down to the filter in the ashtray.

"She's fine, Nick," encouraged Christian. Nick snorted, unconvinced. "You'll see her soon enough. Come on, Nick, you've just pulled off a major deal. You should be happy. The rest will sort itself out."

"Thanks, Christian. I'm not so convinced. Call me if you hear *anything.*" He emphasised the last word.

"Sure. Bye, Nick." Christian hung up and looked at his phone. His friend had it bad. He shook his head. Chrissie came and sat by him on the sofa, putting down Christian's coffee on the table.

"How is he?" she asked as she looked at his pensive face.

"Crap! He's just pulled off a major deal and he sounded so… empty. I don't know what to do. This is so much worse than Brigitte. Then, he was angry and had some fight in him. This time he sounded like shit."

"Dead man walking," mumbled Chrissie.

"What?" Christian furrowed his brow at her.

"That's what he said on Sunday night, that he felt like a dead man walking," Chrissie explained.

"Oh. Well, I think I need to do something."

"Like what?"

"I'm going to talk to Vicki. Maybe she can talk Julian round." Chrissie sat back, unable to hide her surprise.

"What?" he said.

"It's just not like you to get so… involved."

He shrugged. "He's my best friend. He's done a lot for me."

Chrissie nodded and squeezed his arm. "Call her."

———

"Hi Vicki." Elenora was snuggled into Pavlos's chest as they sat on their sofa watching TV, their legs entwined.

"Hi. Look, I just spoke to Christian and I thought you should know that Nick's in a bad way."

Elenora got up from Pavlos's embrace and he frowned. "What do you mean?" Her previous good mood forgotten, she heard the concern in her sister's voice.

Vicki explained what had happened over the last few days in fine detail, as only Vicki could. Elenora listened in silence and Pavlos turned down the TV, realising by her expression that whatever she was listening to was obviously serious. Vicki finished with: "so I'm going round to Dad's."

"What are you going to say?"

"I'm not sure, to be honest, but I think it's down to him that it all went tits up, so he's going to have to fix it. Christian's really worried about Nick and you know he's normally so laid back about everything, so that's enough for me."

"What about Sylvie's kids? Maybe we could talk to them," suggested Elenora.

"Let me talk to Dad and I'll call you."

"Sure. Shall I get Pavlos to ring Nick?"

"He's not picking up to any of us, so I doubt he'll pick up to him either."

"Okay. Talk to Dad and we'll speak later."

"Bye."

Vicki walked through to the kitchen where Maggie was making lunch.

"I'm just off out, Mum. See you later." She turned quickly around and headed for the door. Maggie stared after her.

"What about lunch?" she cried out as she heard the front door open.

"I'll eat later," Vicki replied, closing the door behind her.

―――

Julian was getting out a couple of plates from the cupboard when he heard a knock on the door. He looked at the time. *She was early*, he thought to himself. He put down the plates and went over to the door. He ran his hand through his hair before opening it.

"Vicki?" He was surprised by her unscheduled visit.

"Hi, Dad." She barged past him, clearly on a mission. He raised his eyebrows as she walked into the sitting area. Vicki's eyes rested on the plates he'd set out on the breakfast bar.

"This is an unexpected surprise." He closed the door and followed her.

"You expecting someone?" Vicki jerked her chin towards the plates.

"Er, yes, in half an hour or so." He looked embarrassed and Vicki knew it must be a woman.

"Well, I'll get to the point, then."

"Do you want a drink? Tea, coffee?" He lifted his hand, signalling her to sit down on the sofa.

"No, Dad, I'm fine. Listen Dad, I know what's been going on between you, Nick and Sylvie." She sat down and Julian's eyes widened as he sat down opposite her. "Christian called today and said he's not good. Nick, I mean."

"Vicki, I went past the shop and told Christian I wanted to talk to him..." She put up her hand and interrupted him.

"He won't, Dad, you know what he's like. He's spoken to no one. The thing is, Dad, from what I gather..." She shifted in the chair as she tried hard to find the right words. She hadn't really thought this through and now she was here, she felt embarrassed. Julian ran his hands through his hair and let his eyes dart around the room, clearly uncomfortable. "There's no easy way to put this other than... well, your interference has caused them to split up and from what I can tell, both of them are very unhappy."

Julian rubbed his face with both hands. "I want to make it right, but Sylvie won't see or speak to me. Zach asked her and she won't. Nick won't pick up to anyone... I just don't know what to do." Vicki furrowed her brow and pursed her lips as she thought back to Elenora.

"Maybe her sons might get her to talk to you?"

"I doubt it. I behaved appallingly," Julian snorted.

"Maybe if I asked them?"

"Do you know them?"

"No, but I could go and see them, or call."

"I'm not sure."

"It's worth a try. The only other person who might be able to help is Mum."

Julian shook his head. "I don't want to involve your mum. I think she'd feel awkward… besides, I think I've put her through enough." His voice was laced with regret as he spoke.

"She still loves you, Dad." Vicki's voice was low.

"God knows why," he huffed, almost to himself.

"Dad… argh! You know, sometimes you are such an idiot!" Julian gaped at Vicki, then recovered, grinning back at her. Out of all his children, Vicki was the straight-talker.

"Well don't hold back, love, say what you feel!"

Vicki giggled. "You and Mum… It's mad… she never wanted anyone else and you just pass your time with bimbo after bimbo. You're both… well, stupid!" She glanced exasperated at the plates, then looked back at her sheepish-faced father. "I know you had feelings for Sylvie, but… well, if you care for her and for Nick, you'll get them back together again."

Julian closed his eyes and held his head in his hands. "I need to make it right with Sylvie." *I need to make it right for her and the baby.* He felt like a boulder had rested in the pit of his stomach at the thought of her suffering. Vicki was right. If he really cared for her – loved her – he'd want whatever made her happy. And that was obviously Nick. He sighed deeply, hoping it wasn't too late.

"I'll get her to see you, and then hopefully we can get Nick back here."

Julian gazed up at his daughter and smiled, then his face dropped as he heard a knock at the door. Shit, this was going to be *very* awkward.

"I think that's my cue to leave." She shot up out of her seat, wishing desperately there was another way out of the apartment. She really didn't relish the idea of bumping into his latest distraction!

Julian nervously went to the door. "I'm really sorry, Vicki." He jerked his head towards the door, then leaned to give Vicki a swift kiss. Sighing deeply, he opened the door. There, stood in all her bimboesque glory, was Ellie, dressed in a powder-blue skin-tight dress and six-inch strappy matching sandals. Her blonde hair cascaded over her shoulders and she was carrying a carrier bag of what Vicki assumed was sushi. Vicki's face drained and Julian felt himself heat up.

Ellie stood stock-still for a second, her eyes fixed wide, then she broke into a smile that didn't crack her perfectly applied make up, recovering expertly. "Hi, Vicki, how nice to see you. You look great." Her voice was breezy.

"Er... thanks, so do you," Vicki replied, her good manners taking over, bemused and utterly mortified that her old classmate was standing on her father's doorstep. They stood for a second, then Julian, remembering his manners, stepped aside.

"Come in." Ellie walked in gracefully and headed to the kitchen, glad to be as far away from them as possible.

Vicki mumbled, "Er... I'll call you later, then?"

"Yeah, sure." Julian gave a small nod.

"Bye, Dad." Vicki turned to look at Ellie who was busying herself in the kitchen. "Bye, Ellie."

Ellie turned to look at Vicki with a plastered smile still on her face. "Bye, Vicki." Then Vicki left as quickly as she could, her heart banging in her chest. *Talk about fucking awkward!* Jeez, Ellie and her dad? Vicki shuddered as she rode the elevator down to the entrance. He was old enough to be her father! She started to giggle at her thoughts. *Duh!*

Marcy and Retros arrived back on Sunday from their much needed holiday, only to be greeted with the news of Sylvie's accident. Marcy went into overdrive, cleaning and arranging the house, then she insisted she be taken to see her.

"I leave for one week and you end up in hospital!" she cried, hugging Sylvie a little too hard.

"I'm fine, Marcy, really."

Marcy shook her head, tutting. "When are you coming home?"

"Friday, if I get the all-clear." Marcy seemed somewhat pacified with this information.

"Well, don't you worry about a thing." Marcy looked round the room at the vases of flowers which were crammed on the table and window sills, then her eyes rested on Sylvie's laptop and a sketch pad. "I thought you were supposed to be resting. Is this work?" she chastised her, smoothing down the covers on her bed.

"Not really. I'm thinking of redecorating the house. So while I'm sat here, I thought I could come up with some ideas."

"Oh? Which parts?" She perched on the end of the bed, genuinely interested.

"Starting with the room we were supposed to make into a games room. I thought we could extend it. Maybe put an extension above it," Sylvie mused.

"Why? You already have a spare room." Marcy looked puzzled.

"I thought Alex and Markus might want a bit more privacy, sort of make it their wing. It's big enough. Then maybe do out my room. It depends." *And I'm going to need a nursery.* Her hand was resting on her stomach as she spoke.

"Well, we'll see. Just get better. Do you need anything?" Sylvie shook her head. Marcy bent down to kiss her goodbye.

"Thanks, Marcy. I feel better now you're back. I was worrying about the boys."

"That's my job, Mam, to look after you all."

―――――

Monday morning finally came and Nick felt a little more optimistic for the first time in seven days. He glanced at his watch. Seven-thirty. He decided he'd go for his run again this morning; clear his head. The walls in his hotel room were closing in on him again. He padded into the bathroom and splashed cold water on his face, rubbing it vigorously. His beard had grown and it made him look scruffy. *He should shave before he got back*, he mused.

―――――

"Hello?"

"Hello. Is Alex there, please?" Vicki fiddled with a pen on her desk as she spoke, trying hard not to sound nervous.

"Sorry, he's out. Can I take a message?" Marcy grabbed a pen, ready to write down.

"No, that's okay. Does he have a mobile I could catch him on?"

"Yes. May I ask who's speaking?"

"I'm Vicki, Vicki Steed, Nick's sister." Vicki cringed, hoping whoever it was didn't know too much about the rather delicate situation.

"Oh. Yes. Do you have a pen?" Vicki quickly wrote down the number and thanked Marcy.

"Hello?"

"Um… hello, is that Alex?" Vick fiddled vigorously with her pen again. *Shit, maybe this wasn't such a good idea.*

"Yes? Who's this?" Alex was just unlocking his car as he received the call.

"My name is Vicki. Vicki Steed, Nick's sister…"

Alex stopped dead on the pavement. "Oh. I see." His mind was working overtime, trying to fathom why she was calling him.

"I'm sorry to bother you… er… I hope I'm not disturbing you."

"No, not at all. How can I help you?"

"Well to be honest, I wanted to talk to you about Sylvie – I mean your mum – and Nick."

Alex took a deep breath and opened his car door, sliding into the driver's seat. "Oh, what exactly do you want to talk about?" He sounded defensive, though he was trying and failing to hide it.

Sensing he was affronted, Vicki changed tactic. "Well to be honest, I think they're both unhappy apart and I wondered whether we could do something about it." She clenched her eyes shut and counted to ten. *Shit, what if he told her to take a running jump and keep her nose out of their business?*

After what seemed like an eternity, Alex responded. "Yes. I can only speak for my mum, of course, but she's not taken it well." He paused a second, then added. "Does your dad know you're talking to me?"

"Yes. In fact, that's why I wanted to speak to you. He wants to apologise to Sylvie but she won't see him and I was hoping, well, that I could persuade you to get her to at least hear him out." She cringed.

"I'm not so sure about that…"

"Can we meet up and maybe talk about it, say for a coffee?"

"Look, I know he's your dad, and you mean well, but he was pretty tough on her and…"

"I know, Alex. Believe me, I know how he can be, but I'm doing this for Nick, not for him. Please meet up with me so I can explain. If you're still wary after we've talked, then I'll drop it." Vicki crossed her fingers, hoping he'd cave. She just needed to put her case to him and she knew he'd agree. She just hoped he'd meet her. She heard him take a deep breath, then after a few seconds, he spoke.

"Okay, we'll talk, but I can't promise anything. Firstly, my mother is pretty headstrong, and secondly, I'm not sure if I want your dad anywhere near her, especially now." Alex's forehead creased as he realised he'd maybe been a bit too harsh. "No disrespect, Vicki, but I think you can understand why."

"Sure, Alex. I understand. So are you free now? I'm just about to go out for lunch."

"Now? Er… okay. Where?"

"Costa Coffee in ten minutes?"

"Sure, um… How will I recognise you?"

"I'll be the only woman wearing a business suit in June," she laughed. "Oh, and I'm blonde." The relief she felt was unexpected.

"Cool, see you in ten, then. Bye."

"Bye."

Alex put down the tray on the low table where Vicki was sitting. She'd selected a table on the far veranda that was secluded – he presumed for their privacy. He lifted off the iced coffee she'd ordered and his iced tea, disposing of the tray on a neighbouring table. He then positioned himself opposite her. She looked up at him, smiling nervously.

"Thanks." She slipped off her thin jacket, pleased they were shaded from the hot midday sun.

"So what does your dad want to see my mum about, exactly?"

Vicki took a deep breath, a little surprised by his bluntness. Alex furrowed his brow and Vicki wasn't sure if he was angry, his eyes hidden behind his aviators. Alex leaned back in his chair, looking deceptively relaxed, but the truth was he was trying to hide his anxiety. Firstly, at how he was going to handle whatever Vicki was proposing, and secondly, because he was a little in awe of her. She wasn't what he expected at all. Alex looked at her as she fiddled with a sugar packet; her face was sweet and she had wide hazel eyes that sparkled. Her blonde hair was up in a pleat but a few tendrils had worked their way loose, softening her businesslike look. Alex couldn't keep his eyes off her mouth. It was full, and she nervously kept licking her lips; it was wonderfully distracting. Vicki disrupted his train of thought.

"Well, if I can be frank, Alex, he knows he's been out of order and he wants to make amends. Nick won't talk to anyone and Dad thinks if he makes it right with Sylvie, maybe she'll be able to get Nick back."

Alex took a drink of his tea. "And then what?"

"I'm sorry, what do you mean?" Vicki looked at Alex, puzzled.

"Will he be okay with them being together, or is this just for him to get Nick back talking to all of you again?"

"No, he wants whatever they want. Look, my dad behaved… well, he behaved like an ass." Alex snorted a laugh at her choice of words. "And he's realised that Nick and Syl… your mum wanted to be together, but because of my dad's overreaction, your mum suggested they have a break."

Alex leaned forward as he learned more of the circumstances of their split. "And he'll be okay with them being together?" She could hear the disbelief in his voice. "He was pretty fucking mad when he came round. What's changed?"

"To be honest, I don't know," Vicki answered truthfully. "He just seems to have had some kind of turnaround."

"Even if he has, I'm not sure Mum will agree. The doctor told her not to get upset. What's my guarantee he won't upset her again?"

"I could go in with him if you'd like and you could be there too."

"I'm not sure I want to hear that conversation, to be honest."

Vicki chuckled, seeing him inwardly cringe. "Tell me about it!" She laughed and Alex stared, mesmerised by how her face lit up.

Shaking his head, he smiled and rubbed his chin. "I'll ask her… that's all I can do. If she agrees, then we'll decide on the schematics."

Vicki shrugged, feeling a little more relaxed. "Please try and convince her. Tell her I'm asking about her too… oooh, and that she still needs to do my room out," she joked, hoping to diffuse any last bit of tension.

"I will," Alex said softly.

"Families, eh?"

"Yeah!"

"So you're studying to be an architect?"

"Yeah, final year."

"Apart from sorting out family dramas, what are you doing over the summer?" She leaned forward as she spoke.

Alex planted his elbows on the table, resting his chin on his hands. "Hanging out with friends and my brother mainly." Vicki took her first sip of her iced coffee and Alex's eyes focused on her lips puckering around the straw. She looked up at him through her lashes.

"No girlfriend?"

Alex eyes widened at her forwardness. "Er… no."

Vicki nodded, seemingly happy with his response.

"What are you doing over the summer?" Alex asked tentatively.

"Nothing planned… not yet, anyway."

"You're not into extreme sports like Nick, then?"

Vicki grinned and shook her head. "Oh no, I like my feet safely planted on the ground."

"I couldn't agree more," laughed Alex, and Vicki giggled back.

30

APOLOGY

Nick looked down at the computer screen indicating the transfer had been made, and smiled a small smile for the first time in eight days. Xavier was whooping and jumping around like a chimpanzee.

"Fuck, that was the easiest money I've ever made!" He almost screamed.

Nick shook his head. "I'll transfer your cut now. Usual account?" asked Nick, once Xavier had calmed down.

"Yeah. And then we celebrate!"

Nick twisted his mouth and rubbed his chin. "I've got a couple of things to organise before tomorrow, and to be honest, I thought I'd see a few more agents, keep the ball rolling." Xavier shrugged. "There. You're a hundred and sixty thousand euros richer." Nick swivelled the screen so that Xavier could see and he patted Nick on the back.

"Thanks, man. Go do what you've gotta do and get back to that woman who's turned you into such a mess."

"Thanks, Xavier."

Nick stepped past the security guard, glad he was more appropriately dressed this time, and the sales assistant beamed warmly at him as his eyes travelled over Nick.

"Bonjour, Mr Steed."

"Bonjour, Monsieur Mendoza. Is it ready?" Nick asked anxiously.

Mr Mendoza straightened his sharp tie, stretching his neck before answering. "All the adjustments have been made as you requested." He reached under the counter and lifted out the red leather box, opening it, then turning it to face Nick – but not before he admired its contents one last time.

Nick leaned forward and gazed at the open box and his face almost split in two as he grinned. "It's perfect." He reached into his wallet and handed over his credit card.

———

Zach sat in the armchair next to Sylvie as she meticulously read some contracts he'd brought in for her to sign. He flicked through the TV channels and then turned his attention to her sketchpad, picking it up to look at whatever she was working on. Sylvie fleetingly looked at him and shifted uncomfortably.

"What are these?" He leafed through two pages, turning the sketchpad horizontal and putting it at arm's length to appraise them better.

"Just some ideas I'm working on."

"It looks like a baby's nursery."

Sylvie kept her eyes down on the contracts, pretending to be distracted and feigning interest. "Huh, it's for a client."

Zach nodded, satisfied with the answer, then flicked over to the next page. "This looks like a games room."

"Yes, I'm thinking about redoing out the extension for the boys. They need some privacy." Sylvie signed the bottom of the contract and then initialled each page. "There. Done. Zach, do you think you could please organise me another phone? Mine was smashed when I dropped it and once I'm out of here, I'm going to need it."

Zach put the sketchpad back down on the bed and turned his attention back to her. "Sure, I'll do it today. I'll get Maria to transfer everything on it so it's prepped up for you."

"Thanks. I think Alex has my SIM card."

He stood up and leaned over to kiss her cheek. "You're looking a little better today."

"I'm bored," Sylvie moaned. "I hate being cooped up."

"Four more days." He took the contracts and headed for the door. "Julian asks how you are every day."

"Zach… don't start."

"Just letting you know, that's all." He winked at her, blowing her a kiss before he closed the door behind him.

Sylvie picked up her sketchpad and turned back to the nursery. Maybe she shouldn't be making plans until she got the all-clear on Friday. At least until she knew everything was okay. She looked at the calendar on her laptop. Friday the thirteenth. *You have got to be kidding me!* she thought, as she instinctively rested her hand on her stomach. *Wonderful!*

Alex lay on the bed next to Sylvie as they watched some repeat of an old comedy show they used to love. It was six-thirty and Markus had gone down to get some drinks from the canteen. Alex had avoided asking her about Julian yesterday, mainly because he'd been too nervous of her reaction and he didn't want to upset her. But he'd received a phone call from Vicki, and the truth was, he wanted to do it for her. He was a little perturbed at his feelings towards Vicki; he was sure it was wrong to fancy your mother's boyfriend's sister.

"I met Vicki yesterday," he blurted out, thinking now was as good a time as any.

"Vicki?" Sylvie had her head on his shoulder.

"Vicki Steed."

Sylvie took a second to register, then sat up, clearly surprised. "Vicki? How do you know her?"

Alex shifted up as Sylvie stared wide-eyed at him "She called me up and we met."

"Why? I don't understand." Sylvie felt her heart start to thump. *She knew this was something to do with her or Nick or…*

"She's worried about Nick. He hasn't spoken to anyone and won't answer his calls. He just sends texts to say he's fine." Sylvie closed her eyes. *No, no, no…*

"Julian's tried too and well… Vicki says they think Nick will talk to them if he knows that Julian's okay with you and Nick."

"Alex, look, what happened between me and Nick, I really don't want to get into it –"

Alex straightened up, turning to face Sylvie. "No, Mum, listen. You don't understand. Julian's realised he was wrong and wants to make amends. Vicki apparently had it out with him and he just wants you and Nick to be happy. But Nick's refusing to talk to them and so…"

Sylvie sighed, realising where this was going. Her stomach tightened. "You're asking me to see Julian so he can explain. Is that where this is going?"

Alex nodded slowly, seeing his mother's eyes harden. "Just hear him out. By all accounts, he feels shitty."

Sylvie snorted. "So he should. Talk about the pot calling the kettle black!"

"Eh?" Alex looked at her quizzically.

"Never mind." Sylvie was glad no one had heard the conversation she'd had with Julian. Maybe Alex might not have been so eager for them to make up if he had. She shook her head a little, clearing her mind. *What's done is done*, she thought. After all, she hadn't held back either. Sylvie instinctively rubbed her finger, searching for her ring, fleetingly wondered where they'd put it, then looked up at Alex again. "So Vicki actually called you up?"

Alex nodded, allowing a small smile to creep across his face. "She also told me to tell you that her room still needs doing."

"Did she really? That's sounds like her." Sylvie raised her eyebrows and she felt a small glow as she thought of Vicki, her bright eyes and cheeky smile. "She's quite a straight-talker, isn't she?"

"Yes. *And* very persuasive." Sylvie narrowed her eyes at Alex and he looked down at his hands, then nervously added. "She told me she was doing this for Nick, not for Julian."

"Do *you* think that's why she's doing it?"

Alex nodded.

Sylvie sighed, remembering how close Nick was to both his sisters; this was obviously hard on them too. "Well, call her up, then."

"Now?" Alex couldn't hide his surprise.

"Yes, now."

Alex pulled out his phone and dialled up Vicki's number. Sylvie looked on as she saw Alex flush when Vicki answered. "Hi Vicki, it's Alex… Oh do you?… yeah, not bad, you?" He laughed at something she said and then added. "Yeah, you know what they say: same shit, different day… no, not much. Maybe go play pool with my brother… Sure, what time do you finish?"

Well, well, well, another Sapphiris falling prey to a Steed! Sylvie stifled a grin, then coughed, interrupting their conversation. His eyes shot up to her face.

"Anyway, I'm here with Mum and she's willing to talk to Julian…

yes… well, you put forward a good argument." Alex laughed again at her reply.

Oh my God, he was flirting with her! Sylvie suddenly felt awkward. Alex moved the phone from his mouth to speak to her. "When do you want him to come?"

Sylvie thought for a minute. "Tomorrow morning, about nine o clock."

"Did you get that?… I will. Yeah, call me when you're done. Okay, see you in a bit. Bye." He pushed the off button and turned to his mum. Alex flushed nervously.

"So you're meeting up with Vicki, then?" she smirked at him.

"Stop it, Mum. Alright, we're just going to play pool. Markus will be there too and some other friends."

"I see. Well she's a really nice girl, Alex."

"Yeah, she is."

As Nick looked around the *Silver Lining,* he smiled to himself. Christian really was a good friend. It was immaculate and he'd stocked up his fridge and cupboards. Nick set his suitcase on the bed and started to unpack. It was one in the morning and though he'd been travelling, he didn't feel tired. His focus was on Sylvie. He had to go see her, and make sure she was alright. He felt himself almost relax at the thought of seeing her again. It was going to be a long wait until the morning; at least he was home. Just one more night.

Julian slid back into his car, carefully placing the bouquet of yellow roses and white stargazer lilies on the passenger seat. He felt nervous, and though he'd rehearsed what he was going to say to Sylvie a hundred times, he just wasn't sure how she was going to react to him. The truth was, he didn't even know how he was going to react to her either. Julian checked the time: eight forty-five. He started his car and headed up to the clinic.

Nick pulled up into the wasteland at the side of Dr Zinon's clinic. These were the advantages of having a four-by-four Jeep, he mused. He turned off his engine and sat for a minute. He rubbed his chin, feeling his beard. He should have shaved. Reaching over to the door handle, he heard the familiar sound of a car engine and he looked up through his windshield as Julian's car passed in front of him. Sitting stock-still, he watched his father park up and step out of his car. Reaching back into the car, he watched him retrieve an enormous bouquet of flowers. Nick studied his face and could see he was nervous, then his eyes rested on the flowers. He remembered they were Sylvie's favourite. Julian straightened his shirt, checked his reflection in the car window, then locked his car. He crossed the road and strolled into the clinic's reception.

Nick sat rigid in his seat, thousands of questions buzzing in his head. For Julian to be taking flowers, it must be his first visit. Well, Christian said she was being kept in with limited visiting. He sat there contemplating whether he should go in too. He didn't want Sylvie to witness him and Julian arguing. She'd had more than enough to deal with, so he'd have to sweat it out until he came out. *Hell!*

Julian tentatively knocked on the door and waited.

"Come in," Sylvie's familiar voice chimed from within. He walked in and was greeted by a bruised, slightly sallow-faced Sylvie lying on her bed with the wheeled table over her and her laptop and sketchpad on it. She couldn't help but smile slightly, even though she was unsure of what to expect.

"Hello, Sylvie." Julian edged in further.

"Hi."

"These are for you." He came up to where she was lying and Sylvie took the flowers.

"They're beautiful. My favourite. Thanks."

"May I?" Julian motioned to the armchair next to her and Sylvie nodded. Sylvie placed the flowers on the table, moving the sketchpad onto the bed, then pushing the table away to the side. Julian turned the chair to face her before he nervously sat down.

"How are you feeling?" *Oh, so we're going to do pleasantries first?* thought Sylvie. Her blood was pumping through her veins and she took deep breaths to calm herself. *He should be the nervous one, not her,* she thought to herself. Julian brushed his trousers with his hand, then looked up at her with his clear blue eyes blinking rapidly. *Oh, he* was *nervous. Good.*

"Better, just a bit achy. But my blood pressure's better." Julian's eyes narrowed as he focused on the bruise along her temple and down to her left eye, then at her left arm still bandaged. "My head's just bruised and this" – she slightly lifted her arm – "is just a sprain and a couple of stitches. I should have them out on Friday."

Julian pursed his lips together and his eyes flitted to her stomach, then up to her face. "I think you know why I'm here today. Thanks for seeing me, especially after… well, I'm not very proud of how I behaved or how I handled everything."

"It's thanks to your very persuasive daughter and my trusting son that I agreed. They assured me you just wanted to explain yourself. I hope you don't prove them wrong."

Julian smiled tightly, realising Sylvie wasn't going to make it easy for him. "Sylvie, the reason I'm here is to apologise to you and that I don't want to lose my son. These past two weeks, I've done a lot of thinking. A lot of thinking regarding my behaviour, both in the past and especially in the last couple of weeks. My family is the most important thing to me and I've messed that up… You were right about hurting them," he whispered. "I've hurt them over and over, and each time, they've forgiven me unconditionally." Sylvie shifted round as he moved forward a little. "I love them above everything. I won't lie and say that when I found out about you and Nick it didn't hurt, because it did. But it was my pride that got hurt most. Once I saw the consequences of my reaction, I knew I couldn't live with myself. Nick loves you, I can see that and what you did – sending him away – I know you did it hoping that he'd either get over you or that I'd calm down… whatever your reasons, I know it wasn't because you wanted him to go. You were just trying to protect him."

Sylvie swung her legs round to face him and they dangled off the bed. "Julian…"

He put his hand up, asking her to stop. "Let me finish," he muttered. "I still have feelings for you, that won't change. What has changed is that I want you to have whatever will make you happy. Before, I was wrapped up in my own feelings, being selfish, believing foolishly that if you were mine, if we were together, then I would make you happy. But seeing you those few days, I saw how much you'd changed. I could see how genuinely happy you were and I was living in the illusion that that was down to me. I now know it wasn't. I'm sorry for what I said to you. I was well out of order. I wish I could take it all back, but I can't. At least I can try and make things right though, right between me and you, and hopefully between you and Nick."

"I'm sorry too." Sylvie's voice croaked.

Julian fixed her with his eyes. "Don't be. Everything you said was true. I just don't know how I'll be able to make it up to Nick. You haven't heard from him either, have you?"

Sylvie took a deep breath, closing her eyes trying not to get emotional.

"Just very briefly on Friday."

Julian frowned. "What did he say? I mean, was he alright?" The concern was evident in his voice.

"It was very short; I didn't really get to say much." Julian's brow creased. "It wasn't pleasant, Julian," Sylvie added, making him understand.

"I'm sorry. He can be headstrong and stubborn… I can't think where he gets it from." Julian's mouth twitched and Sylvie's eyes shot up to meet his, which sparkled with amusement.

"Me either," chuckled Sylvie.

"So, are we good? Am I forgiven?"

"Yes, we're good." She saw his whole body physically relax as she spoke. "How's Maggie?"

"She's pissed at me, but who can blame her?" He shrugged. "As long as Nick gets back, she'll be fine." Julian leaned forward, picking up her sketchpad and flicking through the pages. "I thought you were supposed to be relaxing."

"Just a couple of jobs I'm thinking about. I'm bored." He studied the drawings, stopping at the baby's nursery. He rubbed his face with his hand as he studied it closely, his eyes meeting Sylvie's nervous gaze.

"It's only two more days." He put down the sketchpad. "It's really beautiful." His eyes rested on the nursery design.

"Thanks," Sylvie muttered, unable to look him in the eye.

"Well I'd better go. I'm going to pass by Christian, see if he can tell me anything. If you hear from Nick, please let me know."

"Of course."

He stood up, then leaned down and kissed the top of her head, lingering a fraction, then he turned to leave. "If you need anything, anything at all, it's done." His eyes creased as he spoke, and Sylvie could see something different in the way he looked at her. She couldn't quite put her finger on it, but something had altered.

"Thanks, Julian. Here, let me give you my number here. My phone's wrecked so you can only reach me on this."

"Thanks. Take care."

As soon as he left, Sylvie looked at the hospital phone next to her bed. If Julian was alright about them being together, or rather he could put up with it, then she wanted to let Nick know. She just hoped she wasn't too late. She picked up the receiver and dialled his number.

Nick sat impatiently waiting for his father to re-emerge from the clinic, when his phone rang, distracting him. He looked at the number and not recognising it, he was contemplating whether to send it to voicemail or to reject it, when he saw his father strolling out of the clinic entrance. He leaned forward to see if he could work out what kind of mood his dad was in.

He watched as Julian fished out his phone and called someone. "Zach, I just left her."

"And?"

"We're good." Julian beamed.

"Thank fuck for that."

Julian laughed at his friend's expletive. "Can you do something for me?"

"Sure."

"Do you have the plans to Sylvie's house?"

"Er…yes. Why?" Zach asked, clearly puzzled at his question.

"Can you get me a copy?"

"Sure. Why do you want them?"

"I'd rather not say, Zach, but I can assure you it's nothing to worry yourself about. It's just an idea." He laughed again, sensing Zach's concern.

"Okay, then, pass by and I'll have a copy ready for you."

Momentarily, Nick's attention was distracted as his phone stopped ringing, then he refocused on Julian. He was laughing down the phone at whoever it was and he was obviously thrilled at something. Nick's heart lurched. It was Sylvie. She'd made him feel like that. *Maybe she'd decided to give his dad a second chance, or she'd thought Nick was living it up in Cannes with numerous young women and she was moving on.*

Nick quickly started his engine and edged it onto the road. Julian finished his call and waited for the road to clear before crossing over to where his car was, when he saw Nick's Jeep heading away from the clinic. He was back! He ran over to his car, jumping in and starting it up. He'd have to hurry to catch up to him.

Looking up the main road, he saw the Jeep head in the direction of the marina. Julian waited for the traffic to clear, then followed the same route Nick had taken through the old town.

Nick picked up his phone and called Christian.

"Hey, Nick."

"Christian, get down to the *Silver Lining* and get her started up. I'm coming down and I need to get off immediately."

"Sure Nick. What's up?"

"I'll explain later. Please just do it." As he hung up, the familiar number of his father's phone came up. He pressed 'Reject' and put his foot down.

Damn it! Julian slowed down at some traffic lights. *I'll never catch him now*, thought Julian as he flung his phone down on the passenger's seat. As soon as they turned green, he sped off, praying he'd be able to catch up with Nick. Julian finally reached the car park and pulled over next to Nick's Jeep. Thank God he'd anticipated where Nick was heading. He locked up his car and headed towards quay eight. Julian frantically scanned the quay for the *Silver Lining*, unable to find it, then his eyes focused on a yacht sailing just past the buoys. *Shit! He'd taken her out already!* Julian immediately turned around and headed for the shop.

Nick sailed out and headed to the only place he knew he'd be alone. Right now, he couldn't face anyone. He picked up his phone and called Christian.

"Nick?"

"Yes, I've taken her out. I just need some time to myself. Can you manage for a few days?"

"Sure. What's happened, Nick? Didn't you see Sylvie? Is she okay?"

"No I didn't see her. My dad was there and… well. Look, I just need some space. I'm turning off my phone and I'll call you. If anything important comes up, send me a message."

"Nick, I'm not sure you should be on your own. Come back and crash at mine."

"I'll be fine, really."

"Okay, man. If you're sure. You need anything, just call, okay?"

"Okay, thanks. Bye."

As Christian put down the receiver, Julian walked in the shop. Christian sat down on the stool to steady himself. "Hello, Mr Steed, how are you?"

"Fine. I've just seen Nick leaving. Do you know when he'll be back?"

"Er… no. He just said he was going for a few days."

"Do you know where?" Julian glared at Christian as he spoke who physically recoiled under his stare.

"No."

"If he calls, tell him I need to talk to him. It's very urgent."

"Yes, of course." Julian quickly left and pulled out his phone, dialling the number he'd saved earlier.

"Sylvie? He's back and he's gone out on the *Silver Lining*."

31

UNLUCKY FOR SOME

Sylvie put down the phone and flopped back on her pillows. Thank God he was back. She hugged herself, unable to stop smiling. She hoped all had gone well for him in Cannes. Just another forty-eight hours and she'd know if their baby was okay, and then she could tell him. *Where had he gone? And why hadn't he come to see her?* Maybe he'd tried to call her, and of course her phone was off. *Did he know she was in the clinic?* Well, he hadn't been to the house because Alex or Markus would have told her. *Crap! This was so frustrating! Argh!* Sylvie got up for the umpteenth time to go to the toilet, feeling nauseous as she sat down. Maybe she could persuade Dr Zinon to let her out earlier. As she got up, she promptly threw up violently into the sink. *Double argh!*

Wednesday dragged and dragged, and only her visit from Lilianna and Zach distracted her a little. Marcy came with Petros, laden with fresh apricots from his orchard. They were so juicy and delicious. *Not so much coming back up the other way, though!* Marcy collected Sylvie's clothes and brought some fresh ones, then they all left her alone with her nagging thoughts and questions.

Dr Zinon came in on his rounds early Thursday morning. "Well, you are looking better." He looked pleased with himself as he spoke.

"Better enough to go home?"

He raised his eyebrows and shook his head. "I'm sure you can last one more day."

"I'm bored and restless."

"Good, that means you've been doing nothing, just as I ordered. Now sit tight and if all's well in the morning, you can go."

Sylvie pouted, annoyed. "When I get out…"

"Get out? You make it sound like prison!" chuckled the doctor as he jotted down her blood pressure.

"Well, it is – or rather, that's what it feels like. Anyway, when I get out, will I be able to do normal things again?"

"Normal? What exactly do you mean?"

"Well, can I go to work?"

"Yes, but don't overdo it."

"Swimming?"

Dr Zinon nodded.

"Sailing?"

He arched his eyebrow.

"Well, I mean, can I go on a boat?"

"As a passenger, you mean?"

"Yes," she replied.

"Then yes."

"What about… well, sex?"

"If your cervix has healed, then yes to that too. Anything else?" He shook his head as he chuckled.

"No, I don't think so."

"Good. So I'll see you this evening."

Nick sat in his makeshift office on the *Silver Lining,* going through the paperwork that Christian had left for him. He took out his iPhone and started to download some of the pictures he'd taken of yachts that some agents were selling. As he filed them, he looked through his music file and decided to reorganise it. He needed to keep occupied. He knew he'd have to go back soon and face whatever was waiting for him, but right now all he wanted was to be alone. He lit another cigarette and started the laborious task of reorganising his files.

Sylvie's eyes shot open. *Thank fuck it's Friday*, she thought as she scooted herself up and swung her legs off the bed. Friday the thirteenth. She sighed, hoping it wasn't a bad omen. Sitting for a moment, she waited to see if the horrible nausea was going to come, and to her delight it didn't. She pulled herself off the bed and padded to the bathroom... before she reached the bathroom door she felt her stomach convulse and she retched. Running to the sink, she just made it, empting her stomach's contents into the sink. *Where the hell did that come from?* She turned on the shower and while the water warmed up, she vigorously brushed her teeth. Once showered, she rubbed her hair and dressed in her blue Bermuda shorts, a cream camisole and she laid out her red wedges. Marcy was a marvel.

Marcy had packed her a small suitcase with everything she thought Sylvie might need. All she needed was the all-clear. Lilianna and Alex had brought down her car last night, so she could drive herself to wherever she needed to go.

Sylvie looked at her watch. Eight forty-five. Dr Zinon would be here in fifteen minutes, giving her time to blow-dry her hair and eat her breakfast, fried eggs on toast. Sylvie sniggered: *who'd have thought being pregnant would give her an appetite for eggs?*

By nine o'clock, Sylvie was packed up and ready as Dr Zinon walked in. "Morning. Nice to see you're optimistic. Let me check your urine and then we'll go for the ultrasound." He handed her a plastic cup and she dutifully went into the bathroom.

Dr Zinon dipped the white stick into the plastic cup and then carefully examined it, frowning a little. Sylvie's heart dropped. Was there something wrong?

"How's the nausea?" he asked, distracting her from her worrying thoughts.

"Horrible. I'm sure it's worse than when I had the boys. I'm starving all the time and then I just throw up anything I eat. The only thing that eases it is the ginger biscuits."

The doctor nodded thoughtfully. "Right, let's go down for the ultrasound. Ready?"

Dr Zinon carefully inserted the probe and the screen instantly showed wavy white and black swirls. Sylvie glared at the screen, willing it to show her some form of life.

"Well it seems your cervix is well healed." He winked at her and Sylvie flushed, knowing full well what he was implying. "That doesn't mean you can start swinging from the chandeliers" – he laughed as Sylvie blushed – "but sex is okay." He continued to move the probe gently around and then he froze the screen, leaning forward to look closely. His brow creased as if he was puzzled, and then he smiled wryly.

He unfroze the screen and moved the probe again, then he paused the image again. "Can you see that there? That small round black thing within that circle?"

"Yes," Sylvie answered warily, holding her breath.

"That's your baby. There's still no heartbeat yet."

Sylvie slowly exhaled as the tension drained out of her and tears pricked her eyes. "And it's okay?" she whispered. "It looks fine to me. It's grown, which is what we needed to see. Its heart should show up in a week or so." He turned to look at her as he spoke leaning back in his chair. "Relieved?"

"More than you can imagine. Thank you." He handed her a tissue as the tears spilled down her cheeks. *Thank you, thank you, thank you.*

He waited until she composed herself, then moved the probe again, pausing the image once more. "You see that there?" He pointed to the screen this time at a similar black circle.

"Uh-huh." Sylvie looked at it, puzzled.

"That there is your other baby. You're having twins."

Sylvie's eyes shot to Dr Zinon's face, which was regarding her with a wide smile. She looked dumbstruck at the screen, then back at the doctor, trying to let the information sink in. After what seemed like an age she whispered, "Twins?"

"Yes, that explains the excessive nausea and the slightly raised hCG levels. I couldn't be a hundred percent sure but on your last scan, it looked like two. They're fraternal. Look, you can see the two sacks. See here." Dr Zinon pointed with his pen. Sylvie looked blindly at the screen. "Sylvie? Are you alright? Sylvie!"

"Yes sorry, it's just… twins?"

He grabbed her hand and squeezed it. "It's a lot to take in."

"I'll say. Twins," she repeated to herself, blinking rapidly. "How? I mean… Er… I suppose there are more risks now too." Her heart froze for a second.

"Sylvie, if you're careful, rest, and look after yourself, there's really no reason why you shouldn't have a normal pregnancy. Do you want a printout?" Sylvie smiled for the first time since the good news. "How about the father? Is he back yet?"

"Yes, that's why I'm itching to go."

"Of course. Here." He handed her the printout and she looked at her two little smudges. Her heart thawed and swelled. *Twins! Wow!* "Let me take out those stitches and then you can go."

Sylvie wheeled her small case to her car and lifted it into the boot.

She slid into the driver's seat, buckled up her belt, then put her new phone on hands free. She dialled Lilianna.

"Hi sweetie. So what did he say?"

"Everything's fine. I'm just leaving now."

"Oh Sylvie, that's wonderful news. Where are you going?"

"I need to find Nick. He needs to know."

"Do you know where he is, then?"

"I've a fair idea. But I need some help."

"What can I do?" Her voice was instantly business-like.

Sylvie smiled. Lilianna was such a good friend. "I'm afraid you can't, but I know someone who can. I'll call you later. Tell Zach the news for me."

"Okay, sweetie. Good luck."

"Thanks."

Sylvie quickly called Alex and Markus, telling them she had the all-clear but needed to sort a couple of things out. Then she headed down to the marina, glad her car was an automatic. Her left palm was still tender where the stitches had been and her wrist still felt weak. She readjusted the bandage as she waited at the red traffic lights.

As she drove down to the marina, she spotted a card shop; its display caught her eye. Pulling over rather abruptly, she quickly ran into the shop and selected a card. Then once she'd paid for it, she got back into her car, quickly wrote a message on the card and popped it into her bag. Within ten minutes, she'd parked up her car, then walked over to Nick's shop. Christian was seeing to a customer as she entered, explaining the different types of flippers they stocked. He did a double take as she walked over to the cash desk and stood patiently waiting. He smiled apologetically at her and she shrugged, indicating she could wait. After a lot of deliberation, the customer chose his flippers, paid for them and left.

"Sorry about that. How are you?" Christian asked, clearly concerned, as his eyes flitted from her head to her arm.

"I'm fine. I need to speak to Nick. It's urgent."

"Well he's not here." He answered cautiously, as Sylvie's tone was almost curt.

"I know. But you know where he is, right?" Christian squirmed as she quizzed him. "Look, Christian. I know where he's gone and I need you to take me there. I can't go on my own, firstly, because I don't have access to a boat and secondly, because my hand still hurts. I could hire a boat and risk it, but my doctor told me I had to be careful and take it

345

easy and I'm sure you wouldn't like me to put myself in any danger. So I'm left with little choice. Are you going to help me or not?" She all but glared at him.

"He told me he didn't want to see or speak to anyone."

"Well, I'm not anyone, am I? Christian, please, I have to see him." He stood still, weighing up his options as Sylvie stared at him willing him to crack. "It's very important I speak to him… face to face. I love him, Christian."

Her eyes welled up as she spoke and Christian sighed. "Okay, I'll take you."

She breathed her relief and beamed at him. "Great. Now?"

"Do I have a choice?"

"Not really," she smirked. "I have my suitcase in my car."

"Suitcase?"

"Yes… I'm hoping he'll let me stay."

"Oh. Let me lock up and I'll meet you at quay eight. We'll take the speedboat."

Within ten minutes, Christian was helping Sylvie into the speedboat. He expertly pulled out of the marina and headed west. The sun was strong and Sylvie felt her stomach retch as Christian increased the speed, the boat cutting through the calm cobalt sea. Sylvie rubbed her finger, looking for her ring, but remembered she'd had it taken off her as her fingers had swollen after her fall. Thankfully they'd resumed to their normal size. She couldn't remember where she'd put it. Maybe Marcy had taken it home. She smiled, thinking that she'd lost that ring twice already in almost as many weeks.

The sea spray felt refreshing as it periodically splashed onto Sylvie's face. Christian turned to look at her. "You okay? It's not too bumpy?"

"I'm fine. How much further?"

Christian pointed to the horizon and Sylvie shielded her eyes to see. There, on the not-too-distant coastline, was the *Silver Lining* about a hundred yards from the cove. The cove he'd taken her that first time out on his yacht. Sylvie felt her stomach tighten with apprehension. "Five minutes tops and we're there." Sylvie nodded.

As they approached, Christian slowed down and cut the engine, allowing the speedboat to bob and drift up to the stern of the yacht. He leaned over and pulled the speedboat flush against it, allowing it to bang against the floats around the stern. Sylvie noted that the jet ski was also tied up to the back. Sylvie precariously stepped onto the back, then kicked off her shoes. She didn't want to break her neck, now she'd finally got here.

"I'll wait here. Make sure everything's okay before I leave."

Sylvie rummaged in her red bag and handed him her card. "Call me in ten minutes." Christian nodded and she leaned over and kissed his cheek. "Thank you."

He flushed at her warm gesture. "Good luck."

Sylvie turned around and carefully climbed up the steps leading to the deck, then entered through the open door and tentatively stepped down the four steps into the main living area. She scanned the normally immaculate sitting area, only to be faced with a coffee table littered with beer bottles and half-eaten food. There were several crunched-up cigarette packets on the table and on the floor, along with shoes, socks and a beach towel. Her eyes focused on a side table where a pile of papers was crudely stacked, and resting on the top was the stone from Sounion she had made. She smiled to herself.

Sylvie looked over at the kitchen area, which was in an equal state of disarray. There were plates in the sink and a brimming ashtray on the breakfast bar. She could hear the shower going. As she strained to hear the sound of the cascading water, it abruptly stopped. There was the faint smell of Nick's aftershave, but the smell of stale smoke was overpowering and for a split-second Sylvie wondered if she was on the wrong yacht. Then suddenly she saw him, his familiar figure leisurely coming through from where the bedrooms were. There he was, in all his picture-perfect glory, a towel wrapped round his middle; with another he rubbed his hair dry, his face looking downwards. He looked heartstoppingly handsome, and Sylvie took a few seconds to admire his perfect physique: his taut torso still glistening from the shower, his firm legs and thighs and strong lean arms flexing as he continued to rub his head. He was stunning, exactly as she remembered him – except for a beard – and wet, like the first time she'd ever set eyes on him. Her heart hammered against her chest and her ears buzzed. The butterflies in her stomach jumped for joy again. She gripped the banister in an attempt to steady herself.

He turned so his back was facing her, still oblivious to her presence. Dropping the towel he was holding on the counter, he reached for a cigarette, lighting it, then dragging hard.

"Please put that out," she whispered, taking him totally by surprise as he swung round, the shock evident in his startled, tired, dark-circled, but still magnificent eyes.

He stood taking her in as she shifted awkwardly on her bare feet. His eyes lit up and the tension that had been there seemed to vanish. He lifted his cigarette to his lips and dragged on it, and then as he exhaled a steady stream of smoke, he stubbed it out into the overflowing ashtray; his eyes never left hers. His expression hardened a little as his eyes flitted over her, then ever so quietly, he spoke. "How did you find me?"

"Does it matter?" she whispered back, and she licked her lips nervously. He shook his head and a small smile touched his lips. He slowly stepped towards her as he ran his fingers through his hair. Sylvie stood rooted to the floor, almost paralysed. Within seconds, he was standing in front of her and he gently pushed back her hair, revealing her bruised temple. His eyes narrowed and he sucked on his top teeth. Then he gently ran his fingers down her arm, sending electric shock waves through her entire body.

She shuddered as he tenderly lifted up her hand to inspect it, and he momentarily clenched his teeth while squeezing his eyes shut as if in pain. "It's just a sprain and a couple of stitches."

He opened his eyes as they blazed at her. "Oh, Sylvie, you really are a sight for sore eyes." His face contorted as he spoke and he reached up and touched her bruised temple with his fingertips.

"It's just a bruise. I'm fine," she reassured him. He lifted his left hand so that he could cup her face with both hands and looked deep into her eyes as he lowered his lips to hers, kissing her softly. Sylvie melted into him, instinctively lifting her arms to wrap around his waist, her left arm twinging as she tightened her hold and Nick kissed her deeper.

Then, releasing her, he pulled back. "God, I missed you."

"I missed you too. Nick, we've so much –"

"Shh. I just want to know one thing. Are you staying?" he held her face as he searched her eyes. She nodded, smiling shyly. He cocked his head to one side and then asked, "For good?"

"Yes, for good."

"Then everything else can wait." He leaned down again and kissed her harder and more urgently, his whole body engulfing her as she clung on to him, ignoring the sharp pain of her arm.

Nick frowned and pulled back from her as he heard her phone ring. Sylvie grinned. "It's Christian. He's brought me here on the speedboat." She fished out her phone and answered it.

"Is everything okay?"

"Yes, Christian, thanks."

"Okay, I'll put your suitcase on the back deck. I'll see you later."

"Thanks. Bye."

Nick raised his eyebrows and had a smirk on his face. Then they heard a thud on the deck and Nick looked up towards the deck, puzzled.

"It's my suitcase," Sylvie explained.

"Suitcase, eh?"

"Well if I'm staying, I need a few things."

"Who said you'd need any clothes?" He leaned down and kissed her neck. "You smell wonderful – how I've missed your smell." He trailed kisses up to her lips and he kissed her again hard, holding her tightly against him and leaving her breathless. Then, as he pulled away to hold her face, he said, "Don't do that to me again. Don't send me away."

"I won't."

He kissed her softly, then scooped down and lifted her up as she squealed from shock, wrapping her arms around his neck. "Bed."

"Bed," she agreed.

"I need to get you naked."

Sylvie giggled at his frankness. He strode purposely through the door towards the bedroom as Sylvie nuzzled into his neck. She knew they needed to talk. There was so much to sort out and explain, but seeing him again, it all became insignificant... except for... She fleetingly remembered Thea Miria's words: "*Depriving Nick of that same happiness*". She clung to him tighter, deciding to tell him tomorrow at the latest, once they'd talked.

Nick gazed at her as he carefully lay her on the unmade bed. Removing his towel, he crawled up between her legs and lay over her, propping himself on his elbows. "Are you sure you're okay?" He gently stroked her hair back, careful not to touch her bruise.

"I was given the all-clear this morning." Her voice was quiet as she reassured him. He lowered his lips to hers. Sylvie wrapped her arms around him as he rested one arm over her head and his other behind her neck, kissing her deeply with love and passion. Pulling away, he reached for the hem of her camisole, lifting it over her head, his eyes burning into hers. Then kneeling up, he unfastened her shorts and pulled down the zip without losing eye contact. Sylvie lay there, almost hypnotized by him, her breathing short as her skin heated up under his white-hot gaze.

In one fluid movement, he dragged off her shorts, taking her panties with them and discarding them onto the floor. Nick gasped seeing the black bruise on her left hip as his hands gently rested on her thighs. "Oh baby, baby." His voice was laced with concern and regret, his expression suddenly changing as he let his fingers ever so softly trace the outline.

"It's just a bruise. It'll go."

Dragging his eyes away from it, he looked back at Sylvie and she reassured him with a smile, sitting up, reaching for his face and stroking his beard. *Why was this bothering him so much?* He leaned into her hand, then covered it with his own. "I'm so sorry, Sylvie. So sorry." His voice was low and raspy, and closing his eyes, he kissed her palm.

"Nick, I'm okay, really. I'm better than okay, truly." He opened his eyes and lowered himself over, her careful not to touch her hip.

"Sylvie, you fainted after my phone call, that stupid phone call." He clenched his eyes shut again and rolled over onto his back resting his arm over his eyes. "It's my fault you hurt yourself. You heard Sandrine and I know what you thought. But it wasn't like that, honestly."

Sylvie's eyes widened as he spoke and she tried to turn on her side, but her hip throbbed and she winced, sitting up instead. "I fainted, Nick. My blood pressure was low…" She realised that this was the reason for his angst: he felt responsible.

Nick lifted his hand from his eyes and looked up at her, his face still ashen with guilt. "What you heard… Sandrine… wasn't what you think. She was, once, a while ago… before you. But there's been no one, no one else." He sat up suddenly so they were face to face, and he cupped her face as his incredible blue eyes looked deep into hers. "It's only ever been you, Sylvie." His intense sincerity floored her. One look at his troubled face was enough for Sylvie to know that what he was saying was the truth, and all her insecurities melted away. He kissed her softly and stroked back her hair.

"Nick, please don't. It wasn't your fault. I missed you so much. I kept hoping you'd call me and make me change my mind. And then when you called and… well, I heard… I thought you'd moved on." Her eyes welled up at the sickening thought of him with another woman.

"Sylvie, I love you with every fibre of my being." He took her right hand and rested it on his chest, Sylvie feeling his heart beat as she flexed her fingers on his warm damp skin. "Only for you. It beats only for you." That was all she needed, Sylvie knelt up and pushed him back down on the bed. Straddling him, she bent down and captured his mouth. Nick groaned and wrapped his arms around her as he slowly pushed himself into her, and she let out a cry.

"Ah." *God, how she'd missed this.* This intense connection they had. She was drawn to him like a magnet. She'd never stood a chance.

"Oh baby, I missed you." He pulled himself up and cradled her. Reaching behind and unhooking her bra, he gently pulled it down her arms, taking care over her injured arm and throwing it onto the floor with all her other clothes. "I need to feel you. Your skin is velvet soft. I want to kiss every inch of you." He trailed kisses from her neck down her shoulder and back, making her shiver. Sylvie moaned as she cradled his head, running her hands through his damp hair and relishing the bristles of his beard against her over-sensitised skin.

Nick slowly lowered her back on the bed, trying hard not to touch her bruise. Then slowly, he began to move. "Am I hurting you?" he whispered close to her ear as he slowly withdrew and then gently pushed back into her.

"No, please… please don't stop… I want you so much." Nick groaned as her words fuelled him on.

"I won't baby, we'll just take it slow, really slow."

Sylvie grasped on to his back with her arms, ignoring the pain in her arm and her hip. Right now she didn't care. All she wanted was him, all of him, and they moved together in perfect unison. Nick kissed her eyes, her forehead, her neck, then back to her mouth, claiming her as she let herself be engulfed in him. Sylvie arched her herself up to him, needing to close what little distance was between them, and Nick held her to him as their breathing became faster and shallower.

"Open your eyes. I want to see you." He rested his arm over her head and held her behind her neck with his other arm as she forced open her eyes. It was all that Sylvie needed to send her over the edge: seeing Nick's face radiating adoration, love, passion and desire, she cried out his name as she climaxed around him. He clung to her as he too found his release, holding her close and he buried his face into her neck, crying out her name.

3 2

THE COVE

Nick gently stroked Sylvie's back as she lay nestled under his arm amongst the dishevelled bed sheets, her leg resting over his and her arm across his chest. Nick periodically kissed her head and Sylvie sighed quietly. It felt wonderful to be back in their cocoon again.

"Are you hungry?" Nick asked. Sylvie lifted her head and rested her chin on his chest.

"A bit. You?"

"Always." He grinned. "Let me make us something. Anything in mind?"

"Er… I'd love a cheese omelette in pita bread, if you have it… Ooooh and pickled gherkins."

"Omelette? I thought you didn't like eggs. And gherkins?" He looked lovingly down at her, amused.

"I just have a bit of a craving for them." Sylvie flushed, then promptly added, "They made me eat them in hospital, so I've got accustomed to the taste."

Nick grinned. "What did the doctor tell you?" He shifted and propped himself up on his pillows so he could look at her.

Sylvie lay her head back down, worried he'd see how uneasy she was about the subject. "I just need to take it easy, rest, eat better. He suggested I stop drinking for a bit… for my stomach, and he's given me some vitamins to take." She hoped this information would pacify him and stop any more questions. She wasn't ready to tell him yet and she knew she'd cave if he pressed her.

"Well I better get cracking those eggs, then. You stay here and rest and I'll bring it to you. I don't want you doing anything."

Sylvie turned her head again to him and gazed into his beautiful face, gently reaching up with her injured hand to stroke his beard. She flinched a little and he scowled, taking her hand and kissing her palm where the stitches had been. "Stay here, I'll bring your case down too." He slid himself from under her, kissing her swiftly on the shoulder, then dragged on some boxers before striding out of the bedroom.

Sylvie lay back on the bed, wondering when she should tell him, she wanted to wait until Sunday, but Thea Miria's words kept coming back to her. She yawned and dragged a sheet over her. *God, she was tired.*

Sylvie's eyes gradually opened and it took a few seconds for her to register where she was. Looking in front of her at the light oak wardrobes, she smiled to herself: ah yes, the *Silver Lining.* Turning to the bedside table, she looked at the time; it was nearly four. Jeez, she'd slept for two hours. Yawning, she noticed her case and handbag on the chair. Lifting herself off the bed, she sauntered to her case, pulling out her wash bag, and headed into the bathroom, feeling a little unsteady on her feet. She washed her face and brushed her teeth, then brushed through her hair and tied it up into a ponytail. Coming back into the bedroom, she slipped on some navy blue panties and a camisole, then picked up her bra, panties, top and shorts, folding them and placing them in her case.

"Oh, you're awake." Nick stood in the doorway, watching her carefully. He'd shaved and he looked unbelievably young and devastatingly handsome.

Sylvie's heart lurched. "I'm sorry, I was just so tired."

He walked up to her and circled his arms around her, kissing her neck and inhaling deeply.

"Mmm, heaven. You must be starving. By the time I'd brought your case in, you were already asleep. Come on, I'll make you your omelette."

They walked out to the living area. Everything had been tidied up and was back to its previous immaculate state. "You've been busy," Sylvie smirked, and Nick snorted.

"It was a mess. I just wanted to be a slob for a bit. Not really me, though…" His voice trailed, not wanting to give too much of an explanation as to why he had lost all sense of worth. His forehead creased.

"And you've shaved. Less Grizzly Adams."

Her comment brought him out of his troubled thoughts. "Better?" he asked, cocking his head to one side.

"I love you anyway, Nick, but you do look younger."

"Is that a bad thing?" His eyes widened a little and Sylvie saw a trace of panic in his eyes.

"Not at all. It's just an observation." He sighed, relieved, and Sylvie shook her head as he moved into the newly cleaned kitchen. "You're the first person I've met that's worried that they look younger." She chuckled her disbelief.

"Well maybe it's because you've made me paranoid." He mock-chastised her as she slid onto a barstool and watched him crack the eggs into a bowl. "I've some peach ice tea if you like."

"Mmm, sounds good. I'll get it." Sylvie got off the stool and headed for the fridge. Opening it, she was surprised to find it bursting at the seams. She pulled out a bottle of ice tea and the pickled gherkin jar. She then poured herself a glass and drank it all, realising how thirsty she was. Pouring another, she remembered her manners. "Do you want some?"

Nick was pouring the eggs and cheese mix into the hot pan. "I'll have a beer."

She pulled one out of the wine fridge for him and opened it, placing it next to the cigarettes and a now-clean ashtray on the breakfast bar. She opened the pickle jar and fished one out, eating it with her fingers. *She really loved gherkins*, she thought to herself as she absent-mindedly licked her vinegary fingers. Nick flipped over the omelette and turned to look at her, mesmerised by her biting through her third gherkin.

"Well I never thought gherkins were sexy until now." He laughed as he turned off the heat, then bent down to kiss her.

"Gherkins turn you on?" Sylvie licked her fingers again as she looked at him through her lashes.

"No. You turn me on! All the time. Even smelling of vinegar." He kissed her again. "Mmm, they taste better second hand, too." Sylvie giggled. "Come on, sit down."

He pulled out the pita bread from the toaster, sliced it open, then folded the omelette and put in inside. Sylvie retook her place and watched as he placed it on a plate, adding a sliced cherry tomato on the side. He pushed it over to Sylvie with a flourish and in an over-exaggerated French accent he said, "*Omelette au fromage pour Madame.*"

"*Merci.* You're not eating?" she replied, giggling at his playfulness.

"I had something while you were sleeping."

He then reached over to the large pepper mill and sauntered over to her side.

"Would Madame like pepper?" He held the peppermill over her plate.

"Please." She opened it up her pita bread and he ground a little pepper over it.

"Anything else?" He raised his eyebrow lewdly, still in the Maître d' mode.

Sylvie pretended to think, then added: "Ketchup?"

Nick made a face as if disgusted and stepped back as if he was appalled and hurt. "Ketchup? On my gastronomic masterpiece?"

Sylvie giggled, and he reached over and handed her the bottle. Sylvie squeezed the ketchup inside the pita bread, then picked it up with her hands and took a bite. It was delicious. She closed her eyes in appreciation.

"Good?"

Sylvie nodded, chewing slowly, then swallowed. "It's scrummy." And Nick's eyes blazed as he laughed watching her take another bite.

Sylvie popped the last bit of her sandwich in her mouth as Nick finished tidying up the kitchen. He sat next to her on a stool and reached for his cigarettes, opening the packet. Sylvie's brow creased.

"Does it bother you?" He indicated to the packet as he cocked his head at her. Sylvie shook her head, because in truth it didn't. She'd always found smoking rather sexy. He smiled and then added. "But you'd rather I didn't?" She shrugged. "Then, in that case…" He crushed the packet he was still holding with one hand and deposited it in the ashtray, his eyes fixed on hers.

Sylvie smiled, remembering the wedding reception.

"I'll stop. Again. For you." His voice was low and husky as he slid off the stool and turned Sylvie towards him, grasping her face to kiss her hard. *Wow!*

───────

Sylvie propped herself up on her right side, drinking in Nick's magnificent profile, his chest still heaving as he caught his breath.

"So is this all we are going to be doing?" Sylvie smirked, as she let her fingers trail through his chest hair, now glistening with sweat.

"You're right, I shouldn't have bothered with any clothes." Nick let out a loud laugh, still breathing hard, and turned to face her.

"Well, now I've packed in smoking, you realise I need to substitute the addiction." He caressed her face with the back of his hand. "Fancy a swim?" Sylvie raised her eyebrows. "We can go out to the cove and lie on the beach."

"On the jet ski?"

Nick nodded and grinned at her obvious reluctance. "After the motorbike, the jet ski's positively tame."

Sylvie snorted. He eased himself off the couch and held out his hand to help up Sylvie. "This time I'm putting on a bikini though." She turned towards the bedroom.

"If you insist, but you realise it won't be on for long."

She turned to look at him over her shoulder as he stood openly admiring her naked body, and she shrugged.

Nick had laid out their towels on the sand and after they had cooled off in the clear blue water, they both spread out on their backs, enjoying the late afternoon sun. Sylvie relishing the tingle of the sea salt drying up on her warming skin and she rested her hand on her stomach. They needed to talk. Sylvie knew Nick was keen to avoid anything that would force him to confront his family's recent reactions and then their consequent actions.

Taking a deep breath, she decided to start the ball rolling, on neutral ground at first. Then maybe they could broach the sticky subject that was Julian Steed. "How was Cannes? What I mean is, the business. Did everything go to plan?"

Nick sat up and turned to her and she looked at him, shielding her eyes from the sun. "Yeah, it went really well. Xavier managed to find the two yachts Serge's client wanted." He grinned, his eyes sparkling, and for the first time since the transaction was confirmed he felt thrilled at pulling off such a big deal in such a short space of time. "I wish you'd been there," he added, turning to lie on his front and propping himself up on his elbows so he could look at her.

"Nick, that's wonderful. I'm so pleased for you!" She smiled widely at him, then added, "Maybe next time."

Nick frowned a little, then rested his head on her chest. "I was in hell. After I left you on Sunday, I felt like I wanted to die." Sylvie inhaled, trying to mask her gasp and steady herself. Her fingers worked their way into his damp hair. "I didn't know what to do with myself. Christian got me to go to Cannes, though. It was the last place I wanted to go."

"Oh Nick, I'm so sorry. I just wanted what was best for you." Sylvie's eyes welled as she squeezed him and he grasped her shoulder as he nuzzled against her breasts.

"Well the deal went through and Xavier was absolutely ecstatic. He insisted we go out and celebrate. All I wanted to do was talk to you, hear your voice. You were the only person I wanted to share the news with, and I couldn't. I felt so alone, Sylvie."

The tears oozed from Sylvie's eyes as she gripped onto him, wanting to comfort him. She'd done this to him because of some misguided notion that she wasn't right for him. He'd been in hell, just like her.

"Anyway, he dragged me to this club and tried to cheer me up. He even brought over a couple of young girls, thinking that's what I needed. A distraction." Sylvie stiffened slightly and he snorted at the very idea. "All it did was confirm my feelings, that I only wanted to be with you, only you. I couldn't believe you hadn't tried to call me. Not once." He shifted to look up at her, his eyes full of hurt, raw with unspoken emotion. "Why didn't you call me? Fight for me? That really hurt." He moved up, half lying on her, brushing her tears away with his thumbs.

"Nick… I'm so sorry… I thought if you had a clean break from me that you'd gain some perspective. See that we couldn't have a future. I never wanted to hurt you. I blamed myself. I should never have let it get this far. The last thing I ever wanted to do was hurt you." His brow furrowed as he listened and he gently kissed her lips, then stroked her hair back.

"Sylvie…" He shook his head and closed his eyes. "Do you think for one minute that my feelings would change, even if you did send me away?" He took a deep breath and continued. "Xavier got pissed off with me and told me I should call you. I'd had a bit to drink and it made me feel a little reckless. I'd vowed not to call you. Chrissie told me something…"

"Chrissie?"

"Yes, Christian's girlfriend. When I stayed there on Sunday night, she quoted some sentimental shit about letting someone go and if they come back to you, then you know that they truly belong to you." Sylvie smiled a small smile and Nick's expression softened. "So I was determined not to call you. I wanted you to come back to me. But the alcohol broke down my resolve and that's when I called you." Sylvie reached up to his smooth cheek and trailed her fingers down to his lips. He kissed her fingertips. "Then Sandrine came looking for me, and that's what you heard. I tried to call you back to explain, but your phone was off. I called it a hundred times and I didn't have your home number. Then Christian found out that you'd had an accident and were in hospital and I thought my whole world had fallen apart." His eyes glistened with tears as he relived the harrowing memory.

"I made Christian call Vicki to find out how you were. All I wanted to do was come back and find you, see you. Make sure that you were alright. But I couldn't leave until the transaction went through on Monday. They were the longest three days of my life. I stayed imprisoned in my hotel room, wishing the hours, the minutes away, until I could leave. Even when the transaction went through, I felt numb. I just wanted to come back to you."

Sylvie's tears continued to trickle down her face as she witnessed the pain in his beautiful face. He closed his eyes and swallowed, and Sylvie knew he was finding it hard to continue. Scared he'd stop, she stretched up and kissed his cheek and his eyes sprung open, cobalt blue and intense. "So when I got back, I didn't care that you hadn't rung me or that you hadn't fought for me – for us. I just wanted to see you to tell you that I didn't care about any of it, about anyone other than you. I pulled up outside the clinic ready to see you, ready for anything, even your rejection, and I saw my dad pull up outside the clinic. I didn't want to go in while he was there, and to be honest, I couldn't understand why he was there in the first place…" He almost sneered as his body stiffened.

"Nick, he –"

Nick put his finger on her lips, effectively stopping her.

"Let me finish." His eyes narrowed and Sylvie sighed her resignation "I waited for what seemed like forever and then he came out all happy and relieved. I presumed you'd made up and this was you moving forward. So I had to get out of there, get away from everyone. I didn't trust myself to talk to my dad and I didn't want to talk to anyone. Not even you."

"Oh Nick, Nick." Sylvie wrapped her arms around his neck and kissed him, forcing him onto his back so she could look down at him. He held the back of her head and the small of her back as she kissed him harder and he groaned against her mouth. "I'm so sorry, so sorry." And she held his face as she kissed him again, leaving him breathless.

"Fuck, Sylvie, don't ever do that to me again. Do you hear? I can't play games. I told you all that. All that matters is you and me. The rest…" He closed his eyes and shook his head. "Everyone was ringing me sending me messages. *Everyone*, and I didn't give a fuck. One word from you, that's all I wanted and I would have dropped everything to be by your side." He dragged his hands through his hair, temporarily releasing her.

"Your mum was beside herself," whispered Sylvie.

Nick sniffed and his face hardened. "You spoke to her?" Sylvie nodded. His teeth clenched and Sylvie could see he was debating on whether he should say any more, then he blurted out, unable to keep his thoughts contained: "My father?" His eyes were locked on hers.

Sylvie swallowed and breathed deeply. "Will you keep an open mind?"

His brow creased as he looked at her, obviously puzzled. "That depends," he eventually answered.

"You want to know?"

He nodded once.

"Then you need to listen without flying off the handle." He breathed deeply, then removed his hands from around her and rested them behind his head. Sylvie rested herself on her folded arms on his chest.

"Okay." His tone was still guarded.

"Okay, don't interrupt." Nick nodded again. "Well, after you'd gone, I was in pretty bad shape. Days merged into each other. Your mum called me to see how you were and I told her that we hadn't spoken since Sunday. Naturally, she was devastated that you'd gone again. She knew nothing of what had happened. No one did, except Zach and Lily."

"What else did she say?" Nick's voice was low and monotone, devoid of emotion.

"She said she wanted to scream at me, which is understandable, but at the same time, she was happy you'd found someone." Nick sniffed again, his expression softening slightly.

"By Thursday I was in a mess." Sylvie blinked rapidly, omitting the doctor's visit, and Nick's eyes narrowed as he gazed at her. "After your phone call, I passed out and I was taken to the clinic and given strict instructions to take it easy. Julian asked to see me, via Zach, but I refused to." Nick went to speak and Sylvie raised her eyebrows, halting him. "Then on Tuesday, Alex asked me whether I would speak to him."

Nick's eyes widened and he moved his arms from his head as he struggled to sit upright, anger radiating from his hardened eyes. "He went to Alex!"

Sylvie rolled onto the towel and rubbed her face in exasperation. Sitting up to face him, she kneeled and gently took his hands in hers, trying to calm him. "Please, just listen." Nick's eyes were fixed on hers, still radiating heat. "It seems Vicki had it out with him, and he admitted to her that he was out of order and all he wanted was for you and me to be happy. He knew that he had no right to lay down the law and that he'd behaved appallingly. He needed to see me to apologise, and then he hoped I'd convince you to come back."

Nick's eyes visibly cooled down as Sylvie's words penetrated.

"Vicki called Alex and convinced him to talk me round. That's when you must have seen him come to visit – on Wednesday. He was happy and relieved because I'd forgiven him and he knew I was going to call you to get you to come home."

"But you didn't call me," Nick added, hurt and puzzled.

"I did the minute he left, but you didn't pick up." Nick's brow creased as he tried to recall what happened on Wednesday. "I called from the clinic because I didn't have a phone. It broke when I fell." Then Nick remembered the call from an unknown number as he'd watched his father when he came out of the clinic. *If he'd only picked up…*

Sylvie shuffled closer to him. "All the time you were away, all I wanted was for you to call me. All I wanted was for you to try to convince me and I would have come running in a heartbeat."

Nick clenched his teeth and shook his head. "That's all I've been trying to do, Sylvie, from day one. And you. Just. Couldn't. See it. What I feel for you, what we have, it's huge. Can't you feel it?" His eyes were imploring as he pulled her to him, cradling her in his lap, kissing her head, wrapping her tightly in his arms.

"Yes I feel it. That's why I came to find you. That's why I'm here," she whispered.

The Sun was going down as Nick slowly steered the jet ski back to the

Silver Lining. Nick tided it up and helped Sylvie up on deck. "Mmm, you managed to keep that bikini on after all."

Sylvie laughed as he squeezed her bottom. "Oh, not for too much longer," she called down to him as she climbed the stairs. Nick's eyes sparkled. "Oh, don't be getting any ideas. I'm off for a shower." She laughed as he narrowed his eyes at her.

"You are a terrible tease. Okay, you get showered and I'll make some dinner." He dropped a swift kiss on her shoulder. "Baked salmon with pesto, salad and potatoes sound alright?"

"You're going to cook for me? Again?" Sylvie couldn't hide her disbelief.

"Well you are supposed to be resting, right? We can eat on the deck." She turned round to face him, draping her arms around his neck.

"You're spoiling me. I could get used to this." She stretched up on her tiptoes to kiss him.

"I hope you do."

33

SURPRISE

Sylvie towel-dried her hair as she sat on the edge of the bed. What a day it had been! She rifled in her suitcase to find her comb as she contemplated when she should tell Nick about their babies. She pulled out the card and turned it in her hand. This morning, she hadn't even known if she had one baby, let alone two. It still hadn't quite sunk in yet and she smiled to herself, screwing up her face with glee. Never in a million years did she think she'd ever be able to have children again, and to be told she was having two… incredible. She shook her head, putting down the card and slipping on a vest and cotton shorts with a stretchy waist. Everything she had was getting a little tighter. *Jeez, she was going to be humongous by the time she reached nine months.*

Sylvie could smell potatoes. Chips, if she wasn't mistaken. Her mouth watered. God, she was starving again, really starving. She groaned inwardly. *Shit, she was going to be a whale!*

Nick was placing some bread out onto the deck as Sylvie came out to join him. She gasped as she looked out at where the table was. Nick had laid it out with candles in hurricane lamps, both on the table and round the edge of the deck. The salad was already placed in the centre and at each place setting was a small plate with prawns and avocado in a Marie Rose sauce. He'd placed an ice bucket on the side with a bottle of Lipton's Peach Iced Tea and a couple of bottles of Keo beer.

Nick turned to look at her and she stood staring in bewilderment at this romantic setting he'd created under the light of a full moon.

"Oh Nick, it's so lovely." He smiled shyly as he reached for her injured hand and kissed the back of it.

"Nothing but the best for you, baby." Sylvie melted as he reached over to stroke her face. "Just give me five minutes to shower and we can start."

"Shall I do anything?"

"All under control." He jumped down the stairs and almost sprinted to the bedroom. Sylvie sat at the table, taking it all in. No one had ever done this for her before. Oh she'd been taken out to swanky restaurants and been wined and dined, but no one had ever cooked for her. She smirked to herself. *I really could get used to this.* Sylvie looked out to the shore and could see some twinkling lights from the houses up over the sheer drop surrounding the cove.

The sky was almost black and the stars seemed so much brighter. Though the candles dimly lit the deck, it was the bright full moon that flooded the deck with a bluish hue. They couldn't have wished for a more romantic setting.

The sound of music jolted Sylvie as she heard the soft instrumental arrangement of "When I Fall in Love" by Nat King Cole softly drifting up from the sitting area. Then she saw Nick stride back on deck, looking delicious in a white T-shirt and navy shorts, his hair wet and dishevelled perfectly. *Jeez, men took no time at all to get ready!* He looked nervous as he slid into the seat next to Sylvie.

"I can't believe how wonderful it is out here. It's so peaceful and beautiful," Sylvie whispered, feeling shy for some reason. Nick's faced glowed as the light from the candles flickered.

"*You* bring me peace and *you* are so beautiful." He took her chin and tenderly kissed her. Letting her go, he reached over to the ice bucket and poured her a glass of iced tea. "Hungry?"

"Famished. This looks delicious. No one's ever cooked for me… except you." The comment pleased him as his face almost split in two.

"I love this song," Sylvie mumbled as she reached over to the bread and started to butter it.

"This was playing on the radio the night I took you home from Celle. Our first night together."

As she placed the buttered bread on Nick's plate, Sylvie looked up at him, amazed that he remembered that particular detail. He picked up her injured hand and gently kissed her wrist, frowning down at the small scar the stitches had left behind. "You remembered?" Her surprise was evident in her tone.

"How could I forget?"

He kissed her scar, his eyes fixed on hers, and her butterflies did somersaults as his eyes danced. "Does it hurt?"

Sylvie shook her head, trying to calm her racing pulse. *How did he do that to her, just with a look?*

"It's just sore," she mumbled. He turned over her hand in his, so her palm faced down and gently rubbed his thumb over her fingers, his expression pensive.

"I think I might have something that might make it feel better." His eyes were locked on hers and she looked at him, puzzled. *It wasn't that bad*, she thought to herself. *He really needed to stop fussing.* She was just about to say so, when he suddenly got up.

Still holding her hand, he pushed back his chair as he moved from the table. Reaching into his back pocket, he simultaneously knelt down on one knee and pulled out a box. Not just any box, a red leather Cartier box. Sylvie gasped, her eyes like saucers and paralysed as Nick looked up at her, his hand hot in hers, his left hand holding the box as it hovered inches from her hand. He deftly flicked open the lid, revealing a platinum ring set with diamonds, with a huge central emerald-cut blue diamond. *Holy shit, was this really…*

"Sylvie, from the first night we spent together, I knew my life had changed forever. You have brought me peace, joy and unbelievable happiness. I love you with all my heart and soul. I will spend the rest of my life making sure I bring the same to you. Marry me and never leave my side."

Sylvie sat dumbstruck for the second time that day, looking down at the man she loved and adored. As her eyes welled up, she closed them, unable to comprehend how, in less than twelve hours, her life had changed so drastically. She opened them up and gazed at Nick's glowing expectant eyes. "Marry you? Why?" Her voice was tight as she stared at him, astounded.

Nick's lips curled into a smile. "Because I love you, Sylvie."

"But… how… I mean you hardly know me, I've all this baggage and…"

Nick shuffled forward, releasing her hand and placing the box on the table. He reached up and cupped her face between his hands and gazed at her, his eyes glowing. "It's very simple, Sylvie. I love you and I want us to be together forever. The rest will work itself out. I don't care about anything or anyone else. I've told you often enough." His nostrils flared as he took a deep breath and Sylvie stared transfixed on his unbelievably handsome face. "So what's it to be, baby? No or yes?"

"Yes," whispered Sylvie, still unable to process what was happening.

"Yes, what?"

"Yes, I'll marry you."

Nick half-closed his eyes as if he were drugged, leaning his head backwards, then opening them fully. They blazed with triumph. "Oh Sylvie. Baby." He stood up immediately and pulled her gently from the chair so that he could wrap his arms around her. He lifted her off the deck and kissed her neck as she squealed. "You've made me the happiest man alive." He let her slide down his body as he set her down again. He pulled the ring from the box, then, taking her left hand again, he slid the ring onto her finger, kissing her knuckles before releasing it, then cupping her face. Wiping her tears away, he kissed her hard, Sylvie dissolving against him.

Sylvie wrapped her arms around his waist and clung to his back. "I love you so much."

He lifted her up again and she gazed adoringly down at him, the moonlight lighting up his face. "And I love you."

She reached down to kiss him again and he lowered her gently. He took her left hand, holding it up to admire the ring. "It fits." Sylvie was amazed, still shell-shocked.

"N," smirked Nick as he took her face in his hands, kissing her soundly.

"N?"

"That's your ring size. Apt, don't you think?"

Sylvie's eyes widened. *Talk about uncanny! Wait a minute...* "How do you know my ring size?"

Nick laughed loudly, pure joy radiating from every pore. "Do you remember in Athens when your ring went missing?" Sylvie nodded, still not sure where he was going. "Well it wasn't lost. I asked Andreas to go get it measured." *Oh!* He kissed her again, releasing her and guiding her to her chair. Taking her seat, she tentatively stretched out her hand to look at her ring. "Do you like it?"

"Like it? It's beautiful." Her voice squeaked.

He stroked her cheek with his fingertips. "It's a blue diamond, because I know you love blue and it's rare, unique and exquisite, like you."

Her eyes welled up and tears of joy trickled down her cheek. "Oh Nick, you really say the most romantic things. I'd have loved it whatever it was," the tears rolling down her face.

"Hey, don't cry, baby." He smiled softly at her, wiping away her tears.

"You've made me so happy, Nick…" She sniffed as he dabbed her eyes with a napkin. "I love you so much… this past couple of weeks I really thought…"

He took her hand and pulled her onto his lap, cradling her as she wrapped her arms around his neck. "Hey, it's done. Finished. You and me. That's all that matters." She nuzzled into his neck, inhaling deeply, relishing his scent as he stroked her back.

After what seemed a long time, Sylvie's tummy rumbled and Nick grinned against her hair. "You're hungry."

"Very," Sylvie giggled.

"Come on, then. The salmon's probably cold by now. And the sauté potatoes."

"I don't care. I don't want to get up."

He laughed again and kissed her forehead. "I'll drag the table to the bench and we can sit there and eat."

"Perfect."

After rearranging the deck, Nick brought up the reheated salmon and potatoes, along with the pickled gherkins and ketchup. Then he sat down, allowing Sylvie to sit across his lap as they ate off the same plate, listening to a mixture of old and new slow music, from The Beatles' "Something" to Sinead O'Connor's "Nothing Compares 2U". Tony Bennett crooned "The Way You Look Tonight" as Nick periodically licked off any ketchup from Sylvie's lips after he dipped the sauté potatoes into the ketchup and fed them to her. Sylvie admired her ring, still unable to process her day. Yesterday she had been miserable, heartbroken and despondent. She smirked to herself as she thought back to the date. Unlucky for some, but not for her, not for them.

She snuggled up closer as Nick drank from his beer bottle. "Interesting mix of music."

"I made up this a few days ago."

"It's lovely. I haven't heard some of those songs in so long."

"I made it for you. For tonight."

Sylvie peered up him. "You knew I'd come find you?"

"Hoped. Like Dracos said, I'm a romantic." He bent down and kissed her softly. "Have you had enough?"

"Yes, it was delicious, even reheated," she teased.

"Dessert?"

"You made dessert?" Sylvie's jaw dropped open. *Talk about Jamie Oliver's fifteen minute meals!*

"Not exactly. I have some ginger pudding in the freezer which will take four minutes to zap, and some caramel ice cream."

You're kidding! Ginger! He shrugged cheekily, looking younger than ever. "Ginger?"

"Don't you like ginger?"

"No, no, I love it. Let me help clear, then I need to go to the bathroom."

"Okay."

Sylvie gathered up their plates as Nick picked up the salad bowl and serving dishes. She quickly dropped them on the breakfast bar and headed to the bedroom, then straight to the bathroom. As she sat on the toilet, she admired her ring. *Jeez, it was huge.* It must have cost a fortune. She shook her head at his frivolousness. He'd taken her to her word; after all, she'd told him most women loved jewellery, the bigger the better. She carefully washed her hands and dried them on the towel, mindful not to catch her ring or her scar. She stepped into the bedroom and opened her suitcase, fishing out the card and wedging it in the back of her shorts. Squeezing herself with excitement, she headed out to the kitchen where the pungent smell of ginger was wafting through the whole yacht.

Nick was scooping the caramel ice cream onto their steaming pudding. Sylvie grinned at him and her giddy mood was reflected in his face. He'd put their dessert in one big bowl with two spoons. She leaned her elbows on the breakfast bar, resting her head on her hands as she watched him.

"You were right, you know." He cocked his head to one side as she spoke. "My hand feels soooo much better now." He laughed loudly as she wriggled her finger at him, then dipped her index finger in the ice cream, taking a dollop and licking it off, her eyes fixed on his.

"If you're trying to seduce me, baby, it's working, but where you're concerned I really don't need much." He grabbed the hand she'd used to dip in the ice cream and licked her finger seductively, his eyes molten. "You missed a bit."

God, how sexy was that!

Releasing her, he mumbled, "You go up. I'll just put the ice cream away."

"Okay." Sylvie staggered up the stairs, her heart pounding, a mix of excitement and desire as Cyndi Lauper's "Time After Time" drifted around the yacht. Slipping back onto the leather bench, she propped up the envelope with the card in it against his beer bottle just before Nick stepped back on the deck.

"It smells divine."

"It does, doesn't it?" He put down the bowl. "It's still pretty hot though. As he sat back down next to her, his eye fell on the card, and he cocked his head. "What's that?"

"It's for you." Sylvie squirmed and his eyes opened, enjoying her obvious excitement.

"For me?" He picked it up and turned the envelope over. "You look very excited about this."

"That's because I am. I wanted to wait until Sunday, but I just can't."

"I can see." He laughed, her mood infectious.

"I took some advice from a dear aunt of mine. She hasn't been wrong so far." Nick grabbed her chin puckering her lips and kissed them noisily. "Open it," she mumbled, ready to burst, and Nick laughed again.

"Okay, okay."

He turned to the envelope, ripping it open, then slid out the card. Sylvie held her breath as he looked at the front of the card, his expression amused but puzzled. The front of the card had a black and white photo of the bottom of two sets of tiny baby feet. He opened up the card, still at a loss as to what the card meant, when the ultrasound printout fell out onto the table. He picked it up, still puzzled, and he turned to look at what was written inside the card.

"Happy Father's Day." Sylvie whispered the words that she had written inside the card. She exhaled and Nick shot his head round to look at her. She smiled shyly at him as he took a couple of seconds to register what she'd said.

He looked back at the ultrasound in his hand, then back at her, as Sylvie watched his eyes widen in disbelief when the moment of realisation hit him like a thunderbolt. "You're pregnant!" he cried out, as he kept his eyes transfixed on her face. Sylvie nodded slowly, unsure if he was happy, shocked, bewildered or overwhelmed. She looked at his face: *Probably all four*, she thought, as he looked back at the ultrasound. His lips curled upwards into a dazzling smile as he shook his head. "Pregnant?" He looked back at her, waiting for her to reaffirm it.

"Yes, I'm pregnant."

"But… how… I mean…" His face beamed as he looked down at her stomach. "I thought… well you said you couldn't."

"I thought I couldn't. But… Well, we never used any contraception and it just happened."

He looked back at the ultrasound. "I can't believe it." He put down the card and the printout and flung his arms around her, showering her with kisses. "Oh Sylvie, baby, my beautiful darling. We're having a baby. How do you feel? Are you okay? How far are you?" He pulled back and tentatively rested his hand on her stomach.

"About four weeks."

"The vomiting! That's why you've been vomiting! Jeez." Sylvie nodded, grinning as she watched Nick start to process everything. "Is that why you fainted?"

"Yes. When I was pregnant with the boys, I used to faint all the time." Nick's face dropped. "Only if I got up too fast," she reassured him, and he visibly relaxed.

"That's why you were kept in hospital?"

Sylvie nodded. "When I fainted, I started to bleed." Nick's face dropped again. "The doctor ordered strict bed rest until he could be sure the baby was still okay." Sylvie smiled and stroked his face. "It's okay, the baby's fine. I got the all-clear this morning."

"Jesus, Sylvie, you had to go through this all on your own." He ran his fingers through his hair.

"Lilianna helped me. She's the only one who knows. Oh, and Thea Miria… she guessed. I didn't want to tell anyone until I told you."

"Wow, I never expected this." He lifted her onto his knees and squeezed her. "I'm going to be a dad." His voice was raspy and full of emotion as he held her tightly.

"A lot to take in?" she muttered into his chest as he rocked her slightly.

"A bit," he snorted.

"But you're happy though?"

"Happy? No, I'm not happy, I'm ecstatic, I'm on cloud nine, over the moon, I cannot believe my freaking luck. Firstly you came and found me, then you agreed to marry me and now we're having a baby. I'm way beyond happy, I'm…" His voice trailed as he struggled to find the right word.

"There's more." She interrupted him and he tensed. Sylvie lifted her head up from his chest, then reached for the ultrasound. Nick shifted a little as she pointed to the first circle. "See that small circle in that black circle?"

"Ye-es." Nick looked at it and then at her.

"That's our baby. Now see *that* circle in another circle?"

"Uh-huh."

"Well, that's our other baby. We're having twins."

Nick turned to look at Sylvie who was stifling a grin. His eyes wide in stunned shock. "Twins? As in two babies?" His voice higher, clearly astounded.

"Yes that's what twins means, Nick." She mocked him as he sat still after the second thunderbolt of the night.

Nick burst out laughing as the shock began to subside. He laughed hard, throwing back his head as he held on to her tightly. Sylvie squeezed him tightly, glad she'd listened to her aunt. Seeing him so over-joyed at the news, how could she have deprived him of this even for a day?

"Oh Sylvie, I love you so much." And he kissed her hard. Sylvie grasped his hair and pushed him down on the bench as he groaned. "Oh baby, I want you so much, but not here." Sylvie sat up and Nick stood up, taking her hand. "Let's go inside." Sylvie reached up and took his hand and she picked up the ultrasound and the card, passing them to him.

Then Sylvie picked up the bowl of ginger pudding and grinned. "For after?"

Nick shook his head as he led her to his bedroom.

They entered the bedroom and Nick stopped abruptly. "Is it okay? I mean, after your fall and the bleeding?"

"Yes, it's fine. Just no swinging from the chandeliers, the doctor said." Sylvie laughed, putting the bowl of pudding down on the dressing table.

"Chandeliers, eh?" He looked at the ceiling. "Maybe I should get some fitted." He scooped her up and she squealed as he swung her round. "We're going to need a bigger yacht!"

Sylvie's eyes opened slowly. The sunlight was streaming in from the small windows where they hadn't closed the curtains. Nick's arm was draped around her, resting on her breast, her back to his front, his face against her shoulder. As she moved a little, he pulled her closer. Sylvie grinned to herself as she thought about the amazing turn of events. In less than twenty-four hours, she had got engaged to this incredible man and they were having twins. She sighed, not wanting to move, but her bladder had other plans and she really needed to get to the bathroom. As gently as she could, she reluctantly prised herself away from Nick's grasp. He turned onto his back and sighed. He looked so peaceful and so freaking young as he slept soundly. Sylvie wanted to stay and drink him in, but her need to pee was overwhelming, so she quickly headed for the bathroom, gripping onto the wall as she went. She wasn't sure if it was the pregnancy or the sea that was playing havoc with her balance, but she managed to make it to the toilet without keeling over.

As she splashed water onto her face, she looked at her reflection in the mirror and smiled. Across her right breast was a perfect indentation of Nick's fingers. She slowly traced them with her fingertips and her ring sparkled under the lights. Sylvie's heart swelled as she remembered his romantic proposal last night and the delight on his face at her reply. She rested her hand on her stomach as she thought back to his overwhelming reaction to the news of their babies, and her heart almost burst.

Sylvie reached over and started to brush her teeth, glad she hadn't thrown up yet. As she moved her toothbrush to the sides, she felt that horrible feeling of saliva pooling in her mouth and she bent into the sink as she retched up the entire contents of her stomach. *Shit!* She shuddered as she washed her face.

Once she composed herself, she decided to tidy up the kitchen before Nick got up and maybe start on some breakfast. She was starving again. Sylvie quietly and quickly slipped on a vest and panties and crept into the living area of the yacht. She scanned the kitchen and it was immaculate. She moved to the deck to check it and everything had been cleared away, apart from the hurricane lamps. *When had he done this?* She shook her head in disbelief. Sylvie made her way back to the kitchen and decided to make some tea and some French toast – *oooh yes, with maple syrup.*

Before long, Sylvie was draining off the eighth slice on some kitchen paper, contemplating whether she should make some more.

"Good morning, beautiful. You've been busy. Aren't you supposed to be taking it easy?" Nick came up behind her, wrapping his arms around her waist and kissing her neck.

"Mmm. Morning. When did you tidy up everything?"

"Last night after you dropped off." She turned to look at him and his eyes sparkled at her and he bent down to kiss her. "Sit down. I'll finish off. How are you feeling?"

"Not so bad now." She answered, surprised, because it was true.

"Good." He kissed her forehead, then let her go. "Go on, sit down. I don't want you fainting or getting tired." Sylvie screwed up her nose but did as she was told, slipping onto a stool. Nick quickly took out plates, knives and forks, cups and the maple syrup, placing them onto the breakfast bar. Sylvie watched him, enjoying the show. He really was far too handsome for one man. Sylvie focused on the waistband of his low hung boxers, where that muscle just…

"Do you want anything else? Gherkins, perhaps?" he joked, pulling Sylvie out of her trance. Sylvie looked thoughtful for a moment.

His face changed from amused to shocked and Sylvie laughed. "You have got to be kidding, right?"

"Yes. Just syrup for now. But your expression was priceless!"

"Well, I suppose I'd better get used to weird tastes and cravings," she said, and he beamed, looking thoroughly pleased with himself. "And mood swings."

"Mood swings?"

"Oh yes, horrible, inexplicable mood swings, and crying and tantrums and swollen ankles and big and fat and –"

"Okay, okay, I get the picture!" Nick held up his hands as if at gunpoint, his eyes wide with shock as Sylvie giggled.

"These next months of hell are worth every second though."

Nick's face softened immediately and he leaned across the bar to kiss her. "I want to be with you every second of it. Mood swings, swollen ankles, the whole lot included." He leaned back and put the plate with French toast down and then brought over the teapot with the brewing tea. Sylvie placed a slice on her plate and poured some syrup on it and Nick poured their tea.

"We need to set a date," he said.

"A date?" Sylvie sliced through her toast and popped it in her mouth.

"For the wedding. Would you prefer to get married sooner, or do you want to wait until after the babies are born?" *Jeez, she hadn't really thought about it.* Sylvie chewed and then swallowed. Nick was looking at her expectantly.

"I don't know. I haven't really thought about it."

Nick smiled. "Well, it depends on you."

"Me?" Sylvie squeaked, clearly surprised.

Nick grinned at her reaction. "Well if we wait a few months, you'll be showing. If we get married sooner, you won't."

"Oh. I see."

"And what kind of wedding do you want?"

Whoa! I've not been engaged for twenty-four hours and we're talking wedding types, thought Sylvie. She fleetingly thought of her wedding with Chris, which had been a huge affair, and she knew she didn't want that again. "I'm not really sure…"

Nick slid off his stool and turned her so that he could stand between her legs. He gently clasped her face between his hands. "Sorry baby. Too much, too soon?"

She screwed up her nose and nodded.

"I just…" he sighed as his hands dropped to her waist.

"What do you want?" she asked.

"Really? I want to marry you tomorrow in a church with just close friends and family. But I know that's impossible." Nick smirked.

"Oh." Nick beamed at her, then frowned as some troubling thought passed through his mind. "What is it?"

He smiled tightly and shook his head. "Nothing. Never mind, we can think about it."

He pulled away, but Sylvie grasped on to his arm. "Hey, tell me."

Nick twisted his mouth and looked uncomfortable as he took a deep breath. "I don't want to upset you, Sylvie. Leave it, we've got loads of time to make a decision."

"Nick, just tell me."

He narrowed his eyes as he thought about how he could broach the delicate subject. He took her face and kissed her softly as Sylvie looked at him wide-eyed.

"Well, don't you need to wait until… until you've been a widow for a year before you can remarry?" He pursed his lips as he spoke.

"Oh… I see. Well, yes, I think that's only…" Her voice trailed off. She started to feel like their cocoon was being cracked again. Out in the real world, there were so many things to consider, so many people's feelings. How would Alex and Markus react? Julian and Maggie? Her parents? Sylvie rubbed her engagement ring nervously and Nick took her left hand, effectively stopping her, and kissed her palm.

"I shouldn't have said anything. Sorry. I didn't mean to upset you."

"It's just all a bit too much to take in, Nick."

He nodded and held her to his bare chest, and she wrapped her arms around him, breathing in his delicious smell. "You know what everyone will think, don't you? That if we get married quickly… they'll think it's a shotgun wedding." Sylvie giggled. Nick laughed loudly and he squeezed her. "Oh Sylvie, I love you so much."

Sylvie moved so she could peer up at him and he kissed her hard. "And I love you. Let's get married once the year is up. I'll be about six months pregnant, and we'll be able to go on a honeymoon, somewhere not too far. If that's okay with you?"

"Whatever you want. You're the boss. I'll need to talk to your dad."

"My dad?" *He had to be kidding!*

"Well yes, to ask his permission. Isn't that traditional?"

"I suppose so but… well isn't it… um…" *He wasn't kidding!* Sylvie cringed at the thought of Nick speaking to her father and then finding out how young he was and that she was knocked up. *Oh crap, maybe a quickie wedding would be easier!*

"What?" He raised his eyebrows as he let her go and sat back on the stool. "Sylvie, I'm going to marry you and I'm going to do everything traditionally, by the book. This may be your second time but it's my first, my one and only wedding and I want it all, and I want it done right." His eyes narrowed slightly as he spoke with sincerity. Sylvie smiled shyly at him. He was taking control again. "So, tomorrow we need to speak to Alex and Markus" – he cocked his head to one side as Sylvie went to interrupt – "and to my parents. Then we need to see where and when." He let a smile curl over his lips.

"I thought I was the boss." Sylvie leaned her elbow on the breakfast bar and rested her head on it.

"Oh you are… you're the total boss of me, but I know this is a little uncomfortable for you so I thought I'd nudge you in the right direction."

"Nudge? That sounded more like a kick up the backside." Sylvie snorted. Nick's face dropped as she spoke. The last thing he wanted to do was railroad her. "But that's okay… you want traditional. Traditional it is." She snorted again, thinking that their relationship and situation was anything but traditional. They were surely the opposite of traditional: the anti-traditional, the unconventional, uncustomary, irregular and atypical. She shook her head, grinning at him, and he visibly relaxed. "So church wedding… big fat Greek wedding?"

"Greek, yes. Big and fat… that's up to you."

"Small and intimate. I'll be big and fat enough for everyone." She cringed.

"Perfect. And you're wearing a wedding dress. I don't care how big you are, you'll still look beautiful." Sylvie cringed some more and buried her face in her hands. She was going to be huge and in a wedding dress. *Holy fucking shit…*

3 4

HOME

Nick pulled up the driveway and turned off the engine. Sylvie finished munching on a ginger biscuit, desperately trying to settle her agitated stomach. Nick had already had to pull over twice for her to retch. He rubbed his thighs nervously.

"Ready?"

Sylvie nodded and smiled weakly.

"You're sure? If you're feeling lousy, we can tell them later." His tone was laced with apprehension and his eyes wide with concern.

"No, we'll tell them now. I'm going to feel lousy all the time so… no time like the present." She took his hand and squeezed it. Nick breathed in deeply, gave her a nod, then opened his door and got out. Sylvie was glad Marcy wouldn't be in. She really wanted to speak to Alex and Markus without anyone else around.

It was nearly twelve and the sun was beating down as Nick helped her out of the car. Sylvie could hear voices and water splashing. *They must be in the pool*, she thought. She rummaged in her bag and retrieved her keys. Nick slipped his arm around her protectively as they stepped up the stairs and unlocked the door. *God, it was nice to be home*, she thought to herself, and then she felt a twinge of guilt. This was her home and she loved it. Remembering Nick's confession about her house, her heart sank; this was doubly hard for him, stepping into another man's house. She grasped Nick's hand and squeezed it. He cocked his head, his eyes searching hers. "I love you."

He closed his eyes, relishing her words. "And I love you."

As they walked towards the kitchen, she vowed to make it *their* home. Hers and Nick's, Alex's and Markus's. They had to feel that this was all their home. Her hand instinctively rested on her stomach. It would always be the babies' home. Her thoughts flitted back to her sketches and the endless plans she'd made over the years, never finding the time to make the changes. It was time to make a change. New life and a new home.

Her heart was thumping nervously. She hoped they'd be alright about the engagement. They'd decided to keep the pregnancy to themselves until she was at least twelve weeks. Nick squeezed her hand as they walked through to the kitchen, feeling her apprehension.

"Hello? I'm back," called out Sylvie as she walked over to the open French doors. Alex and Markus were in the pool but her attention was drawn to the person laid out on one of the sun loungers under the umbrella. There, wearing a very skimpy hot pink bikini, was Vicki.

Sylvie froze in her tracks as she felt Nick stiffen. Her motherly instincts took over and she gripped Nick's arm in warning. Alex looked round from where he and Markus were standing in the pool, the volleyball falling back into the water, abandoned.

Alex regained his composure and smiled stiffly. "Hi Mum, Nick. You're back?"

There was a squeal from the sun lounger as Vicki jumped up and bounded over to Nick, flinging her arms around him. "Oh Nick, you're back!" She squeezed him tightly and Nick, thrown off-guard, released Sylvie in order to hold on to his sister. Looking up at him, then across at Sylvie, she grinned. "Thank you for bringing him back. How are you? Are you feeling better?" She stared wide-eyed at Sylvie, still grasping Nick.

"Yes, thanks, I'm fine," Sylvie answered, still reeling firstly over her open display of affection and secondly at the fact she was actually in her home.

"I missed you." Vicki squeezed Nick harder and his whole demeanour softened, clearly moved by her.

"I'm sorry."

"Is everything okay now?" Vicki leaned back as her eyes darted to Sylvie and then back to Nick. Alex and Markus had come out of the pool and were drying themselves off, coming over to where they were all stood.

Nick smirked and nodded. "Yeah, things are better than okay." Releasing him, Vicki composed herself and hugged Sylvie.

Alex extended his hand to Nick and Nick took it. "Good to have you back."

"Thanks." Nick narrowed his eyes a little but was distracted by Markus, who thrust out his hand.

"Nick."

"Markus." Sylvie moved over to them and hugged them both tightly, effectively blocking Nick from them.

"You okay, Mum?" Markus mumbled.

"Yes. Come on, let's sit down. I could do with some tea." Sylvie glanced at Nick as she guided Alex and Markus back to the house, leaving Vicki and Nick to follow. Vicki linked her arm into Nick's as she set off.

Nick pulled her back; as he looked down at her, he raised his eyebrows. "Since when are you so chummy with Alex?"

Vicki squirmed under his intense gaze. Then, squaring up to him, she replied, "Since you went MIA and I had to intervene to get you back. Why? Don't you approve?" she replied boldy.

"It's just a bit of a shock, that's all, and he's younger than you…"

Before he could stop himself, the words were out and Vicki's jaw dropped. "Well, if that isn't the pot calling the kettle black! He's only a couple of years younger, not over a decade!" Nick cringed. "And anyway, he's really mature and serious. I really like him, Nick, so don't be weird about this," she almost whined.

"Weird?"

"Yes, all protective and big brotherly." Nick sighed and furrowed his brow. He really wasn't sure how he felt about it. Vicki hadn't really had many boyfriends. Most men were a little intimidated by her. She'd concentrated on her career and boyfriends had taken a second place. He did like Alex, but now with the recent turn of events, it might prove to be awkward.

"Come on let's go in." He tried his best to sound relaxed. Vicki nodded and started towards the kitchen. "Aren't you going to put something on?"

She turned and gave him a 'what did I just say?' look, and his face dropped.

"Or maybe not," he mumbled. Vicki seemed pacified as they both went into the house.

Sylvie had made some tea and was cutting ginger into her cup.

"How are you feeling?" Nick eyed her as she poured the tea into her cup.

"Delicate. This will help."

Alex and Markus were lounging in the sitting area, having helped themselves to cold drinks, and Vicki had joined them, sitting next to Alex. Nick's eyes kept flitting back to them. Sylvie glared at him and he made a face, indicating he was less than pleased and utterly shocked. Sylvie passed him a cup of tea and put her finger to her lips, making sure he understood that he should back off. They joined the others, sitting on the adjacent sofa.

"How's your hand, Mum? Did you get the stitches out?" Markus leaned over from the armchair and picked up Sylvie's left hand, turning it to inspect the wound.

As he moved her hand, Vicki let out a gasp. "What's that?" she asked excitedly, her eyes shooting up to Nick. Sylvie flushed as all three sets of eyes rested on her ring.

"Mum?" Markus was still holding her hand and Sylvie looked over to Nick. Alex looked transfixed, unable to take his eyes off Sylvie as they all waited for an explanation.

Nick sat forward and took hold of Sylvie's right hand. "I asked your mum to marry me and by some miracle, she agreed."

Vicki's face beamed as she squealed. "Oh. My. God! That's… that's great news!" She shot up out of her seat and flung her arms around Sylvie. "Sister-in-law!" Nick grinned at her enthusiasm, then looked over to Alex who was still sitting on the sofa, his hand over his mouth. Nick's face dropped. *Crap.* Alex didn't look happy. Nick turned to Markus and he too had a stony face. *Shit.* Sylvie was going to be mortified. Nick quickly got up as Vicki peeled herself off Sylvie and plonked herself down next to her.

"I wanted to talk to you both before I asked, but the timing… well, after her accident, I didn't want to leave anything to chance. I know I should have squared it with you first but the truth is" – he paused and swallowed hard – "I love your mum, more than anything."

Alex sighed as his hand dropped from his face and he looked over to Sylvie. She smiled shyly at him and she turned to Markus, who had sat back in the chair clearly shell-shocked. "Isn't it a bit sudden? I mean, you've only known each other a few weeks," whispered Markus. Nick ran his hand through his hair nervously. He wanted them to be alright about it, because he knew Sylvie would feel guilty. Their acceptance was very important to Sylvie and he knew it.

Sylvie leaned over to Markus. "We've known each other for longer, but yes, you're right, it is sudden." Sylvie looked over to Alex, then up at Nick. Alex furrowed his brow as he watched his mother gaze up at Nick and he rubbed his face. Looking back at Nick, he stood up and strode up to him. Nick stared at Alex's troubled face, holding his breath, his shoulders tensing.

Alex put out his hand and Nick gazed at it for a second, unable to comprehend his gesture. "Congratulations... umm, don't leave her again, okay? She was a mess," he muttered.

Nick visibly relaxed, then smirked at him, as he thankfully grasped his hand and shook it firmly. Fleetingly, he wanted to correct Alex by telling him it was Sylvie who'd made him leave, but he realised at this stage it really didn't matter. He was just pleased that Alex had accepted their engagement, even if it was begrudgingly. "Thanks, and I won't."

Sylvie closed her eyes in relief, then turned to Markus. He smiled tightly. "You're happy, Mum?" he asked in a very quiet voice.

The tears welled in her eyes as she squeezed his hand. "Yes, darling, very."

His smile grew. "Good. You deserve to be." He leaned over and hugged her. "Congratulations." Releasing her, he got up and shook Nick's hand. "Look after her."

"I intend to." Nick turned to Sylvie, who was now hugging Alex. Vicki had moved from the sofa to give them some space.

Tears were streaming down Sylvie's face as she squeezed Alex. "Thank you," she whispered.

"We just want you to be happy, Mum."

Nick watched on as he said a silent prayer of thanks. He squeezed Vicki's shoulders and she leaned into him. He was grateful she was here.

Sylvie unpacked her small case while Alex, Markus and Vicki stayed downstairs to boil up some spaghetti to serve with a bolognaise sauce that Marcy had left for them. Nick lounged across the bed watching her, propped up on his elbow, his T-shirt un-tucked, revealing his tanned, toned stomach. He could see she was deep in thought as she placed her unworn clothes in the drawers and closet. "You okay?" he asked softly. Sylvie smiled and nodded. "I think they're okay about it, don't you?"

"They were shocked."

"Yes. I have to say I did panic a bit, but I think they care more about your happiness than their own feelings. They're good kids, Sylvie." Sylvie grinned. "Alex said you were a mess." His eyes narrowed as he spoke and his face tightened.

Sylvie stopped folding a T-shirt she was holding and looked up at Nick. "Yes. I was."

Nick sat up and pulled her gently on to his knee, cradling her to his chest. "Me too. You'll never feel like that again, I promise." His voice low and husky.

"Good. I thought… well, you know what I thought. It was… unbearable."

He held her tighter. "I'd *never* do that, Sylvie. Ever."

Sylvie wrapped her arms around his waist, sensing he wanted to say something more. Her biggest fear was that he'd find someone else, someone younger, better suited and betray her. Deep down, she knew that was the reason she'd wanted him to leave. Self-preservation. Suffer now so as not to suffer in the future.

"Don't you know how much you mean to me?" he murmured into her hair.

They sat for what seemed a long time, content in each other's arms. Nick realised her actions were down to her deep-seated insecurities. Insecurities planted by Chris and his betrayals. He desperately wanted to tell her that he wasn't Chris, that it was Chris who had been the insecure one. All manner of thoughts for this man, the man who'd chipped away at her self-confidence, came into his head. None of them complimentary. He'd done untold damage to Sylvie and however much Nick tried to be ambivalent about him, he realised he just couldn't. As time wore on, he began to resent him.

He scanned her bedroom, realising Chris was still very much present in her life. The thought troubled him. He'd have to suck it up though. Bottom line, he wanted to be with her regardless of the baggage. His disturbing thoughts were interrupted by the bedroom door being flung open.

Markus stood frozen in the threshold, his eyes widening in shock. "Oh shit… um… sorry," he muttered, clearly mortified and uncomfortable at the sight of his mother in an intimate embrace.

"It's okay, Markus. What is it?" Sylvie spoke softly, trying to put him at ease as she raised her head from Nick's chest.

"Lunch is ready." He eyed Nick who had stiffened slightly.

"Thanks. We'll be down in a minute."

Markus nodded and quickly shuffled out of the door, closing it behind him.

"Locks. We really need to put in a lock," snorted Nick. Sylvie peered up at him, grinning, and he softly kissed her. Pulling away, he rested his hand on her stomach. "How are you feeling?"

"Alright. A bit tired."

"You should have a lie down after lunch."

"I thought we were going to speak to your parents. Now Vicki knows, it's only right we tell them."

Nick shifted nervously. He knew she was right, but he wasn't sure how he'd react to seeing his father again. Vicki knowing had forced him into telling them sooner rather than later.

"Are you up to it?" he asked, brushing her hair back off her face.

"No time like the present. The quicker everyone knows, the quicker we can get on with our life... together."

Nick's eyes blazed as she spoke. "After lunch, then?"

Sylvie nodded as she stood up from his lap. She pulled out her sketchpad from her case and put it on the bed, then lifted out her wash bag. Nick looked down at it and idly picked it up, flicking through the pages. His face puzzled as he looked at each page. "What are these?"

Sylvie sat next to him as he turned the pad so it was landscape. "Some ideas I'm working on, for here."

He turned to look at her. "For here?"

"Well, I thought with the babies coming, Alex and Markus might appreciate a bit of privacy. So I put together some ideas to convert the extension into a den for them and maybe build above it. Put their bedrooms there, and bathrooms."

"Is that what that is?" He pointed to what looked like a games room. Sylvie nodded. He flicked over the page to a sketch of a bedroom. It looked modern yet romantic, with a huge crystal chandelier and French doors leading out to a large balcony. "And this?" He looked up expectantly at her.

"I thought I'd remodel this room. That's if you approve."

His eyes widened. "Approve?"

"Well, if you're going to be living here, you need to like it too."

Nick looked back at the sketch in wonder and then back at Sylvie. "You're remodelling it for me?" he whispered, still unsure.

"Yes, if you want me to." He clasped her face, letting the sketchbook drop. "I want you to feel like this your home," she whispered, and he kissed her hard.

"Yes, I want you to." Releasing her, he stooped to pick up the sketchbook. "I like the chandelier," he sniggered.

"I thought you might," she giggled. "I want to redecorate the whole house."

"You don't need to do that."

"Yes, I do. I'm doing this for you and I'm doing it for me too."

Nick looked back at the sketchbook and turned to the next page. "Is this a nursery?" His voice was low and soft, betraying his feelings.

Sylvie nodded. "I need to modify it, though. I did it before I knew it was twins."

"Wow, twins. I still can't believe it." He shook his head.

"Me neither."

<hr />

Sylvie picked up a piece of hot baguette and slowly buttered it.

"Wine, Mum?" Alex hovered over her with a bottle of Frascati.

"No thank you. The doctor suggested I stop drinking, for my stomach. Just some ginger ale."

"That sucks," mumbled Alex.

She placed the buttered bread on Nick's plate and he picked up her hand, kissing her wrist, then her scar. Sylvie blushed while Vicki's jaw dropped. Alex shuffled away, embarrassed by Nick's gesture. Markus grinned mischievously.

"Yeah, I know. It takes a bit of getting used to," whispered Alex so only Vicki could hear.

"So Mum, when you get married, Vicki would be our step-aunty, right?"

Sylvie narrowed her eyes at Markus; she had a bad feeling about the direction his questioning was going. Nick shifted in his seat. "I suppose."

"So Alex is dating his aunty, and if they get married, she'll be your daughter-in-law and sister-in-law, and their kids will be your grandchildren and nieces and nephews! Not your typical nuclear family, eh?"

Alex froze, the bottle of Frascati in mid-air. Nick spluttered his wine and Vicki gasped. "Markus!" Sylvie threw him a thunderous look. Then Vicki giggled. Everyone collectively relaxed as Nick shook his head and chuckled and Alex reluctantly thawed out.

"Fucking hell," Alex grimaced through clenched teeth.

"Just saying it how it is, bro."

"Well don't! Now go and get me some ginger ale," Sylvie mock-scolded him, and he grinned, loving the fact he'd have so many opportunities to embarrass them all. "Boundaries!"

Vicki looked at Nick who was stifling a smile. "When are you thinking of getting married?" Alex sat down next to her, his eyes fixed on Nick.

"We haven't decided yet, but probably mid-November." Nick took Sylvie's hand and squeezed it.

"November?" Markus placed a bottle of ginger ale on the table. "Why November?" He directed the question to Sylvie. Nick picked up the bottle and poured it into Sylvie's glass.

"Well, we thought it would be better to wait until… well. It'll be a year since Dad…" Sylvie's voice trailed.

"Oh," said Markus. Sylvie sipped her drink and Nick glanced at Vicki. The atmosphere around the table had changed from awkward and embarrassing to awkward and sombre.

Alex rubbed his face nervously. "But you'd prefer to get married sooner?" he asked softly, his eyes narrowing as he looked at Nick.

"Whatever your mum wants. I'd get married tomorrow, but I understand that's impossible and unreasonable."

Alex breathed deeply and nodded. "If you got married before the end of September, Markus and I wouldn't have to come back from England and we'd also be here to help organise it." Sylvie's eyes widened at the unexpected suggestion. "Plus it's easier for people in the summer months. Papou and Yiayia would be here too. They come out around then anyway."

"You wouldn't mind?"

Alex shook his head slightly. Sylvie looked over to Markus to gauge his reaction and he shrugged.

"Honestly? I won't lie and tell you I'm comfortable with the whole idea. Having said that, this isn't about me or Markus, or anyone else for that matter. It's what you want, what would make you happy?"

"I'm with Alex on this. It still freaks me out seeing you together," said Markus. Sylvie stiffened and screwed up her nose. "But I can see how happy you are, so I suppose we just have to suck it up."

Nick stared at them in disbelief, disarmed by their honesty. They really did 'say it how it is'. That was refreshing, albeit a little uncomfortable. It was going to take some getting used to. He shook his head and sniffed.

"Sorry," Markus added sheepishly as an afterthought.

"I think you should do it in September. It won't be so hot and you'll still be able to have the reception outside," chimed in Vicki, her hand resting on Alex's arm.

"What do you think, baby?" Nick brushed Sylvie's hair back as he spoke. Three sets of eyes widened, then darted away uncomfortably.

"Is that what you want?"

"I want whatever makes you happy." His eyes were blazing as she gazed back at him, both of them temporarily forgetting where they were.

"September, then," she whispered.

He leaned over and kissed her. "Good."

Alex coughed nervously and shifted in his seat and Vicki smiled at him, making him thaw a little. He still couldn't get used to the way Nick and his mother looked at one another. Markus eyed his brother, then turned to Vicki. "Hey, Vicki, do you know what the Greeks call Greek yogurt?"

Alex groaned and Sylvie giggled.

"Um… I think it's… er…" Vicki struggled to remember what the Greek word was but before she did, Markus interrupted her. Nick clenched his eyes shut, cringing, waiting for the inevitable punchline.

"They just call it yogurt!" He laughed loudly as Vicki gave him a murderous look, picking up her napkin and hurling it at him, hitting him square in the face. Alex laughed, throwing his head back as Markus smirked.

After lunch Alex, Markus and Vicki cleared up, allowing Sylvie to have a rest. She was exhausted. She really couldn't face any more drama. It had been eight months of drama and it just didn't seem to be easing up. She flopped on her bed and within what seemed like seconds, she was asleep.

As she woke, her highly tuned senses were flooded all at once and she could hear water running from her bathroom. She could smell ginger tea wafting from her nightstand. Feather-light kisses caressed her temple. As her eyes fluttered open, she turned and two bright cobalt eyes gazed down at her. "Hi. Sleep well?" he mumbled against her cheek as he continued to kiss her.

Sylvie stretched, relishing his touch. "Hmm."

"I'm running a bath for you."

"For us, I hope." She wrapped her arms around him, only now realising he was wearing nothing but his boxers. Her hands ran down his back. "What time is it?"

"Five." Wow, she'd slept two hours. *Crap, she needed the toilet.*

"Sorry, I need to go to the bathroom." Nick instantly pulled away, trying hard to conceal his disappointment. "Don't move, I'll be right back." She got up and hurried to the bathroom. As she sat down, she felt herself start to spin and her stomach started to convulse. *Oh no!* She slipped off the toilet and flushed just in time before vomiting her recently eaten meal. *Argh! Why the hell did they call it morning sickness? More like 'any fucking time of the day sickness'! Yuk!*

"Jesus, Sylvie. Are you okay? Shit. Stay still. Don't get up." He knelt down beside her, rubbing her back as she dry heaved over the toilet, tears springing out of her eyes. God, vomiting was exhausting. She felt her whole face contorting. Nick ripped off some toilet paper and handed it to her so she could wipe her mouth.

"Better? Here, let me lift you." In one fluid movement, he stood and scooped her up effortlessly.

"No, put me down, really I'm fine."

"Humour me. You're not fainting on me."

"I need to brush my teeth," she whined.

Nick flipped down the toilet seat and placed her on it. Then he flushed the toilet and handed over her toothbrush. He picked up the toothpaste and squirted some onto it. "There, now, you can brush them."

Sylvie shook her head in disbelief. "I'm not an invalid, just pregnant."

"I'm well aware of that, but I'm not having you keeling over again."

Sylvie brushed her teeth and then got up to rinse. Nick stayed inches away from her, a protective arm on the base of her back. She bent over the sink to spit out the water and her eyes met Nick's in the mirror, his eyes glittering with mischief as he licked his lips. He placed his hand on her behind and rubbed it.

"Now this, this looks very familiar." Sylvie pushed back against his hand and his eyebrows shot up. "Even though right now all I want to do is fuck you, especially how you are bent over, I think I'd better get you into the bath." Sylvie furrowed her brow.

"I'm fine now," she whined.

"That may be, but I don't want to risk it. Just following doctor's orders. Come on, get into the bath."

Sylvie straightened up, still holding on to the sink, just to be sure. The truth was, she was feeling a little light-headed, but she really wanted him. Well, maybe she could break him… Smiling to herself, she pulled off her T-shirt and slipped off her shorts as Nick turned off the water. He turned round and blatantly appraised her as she stood in her cream silk bra and thong. His eyes glided over her. He made her feel so desired it was heady. She'd never get over that. The butterflies in her stomach floated freely around as he stepped up to her as he sucked on his top teeth.

"You are so beautiful." His fingers trailing from the base of her throat down to her cleavage. Her breasts heaving as her breathing became shallower. Hooking his finger into her bra, he pulled her to him, his eyes white hot burning into hers. "I love you so much."

"I love you too, Nick." Slowly he sunk to his knees, holding on to her hips, pulling her to him as he kissed her stomach, then kissed across the line of her thong. Sylvie moaned as she let her hands fist into his hair.

"Jesus, I want you, so much." His nose running down from her navel to her pubic bone, breathing in deeply. "Heaven."

"Nick, please."

"Please what?" he breathed against her skin.

"I want you too," she whispered.

"I know, I know. Not here, baby." He stood up quickly and scooped her in his arms, carrying her to the bed. Placing her down, he picked up the chair and wedged it against the door. Sylvie giggled.

"Don't want to scar them for life now, do we?" he smirked. He pulled off his boxers and crawled up the bed. "You're okay?"

Sylvie pulled herself up and grasped onto his handsome face. "I'm more than okay, now kiss me." Nick groaned as he gently pushed her back down onto the bed, finding her ready mouth, his hands running down her body until he reached her behind. He squeezed it, then hitched up her leg, his erection hard against her. Trailing kisses down her throat, he loosened her bra straps and reached around her back to unhook it as she arched up against him, relishing his touch. Expertly he removed it and tossed it aside. He ran his nose down between her breasts and gently he blew on her nipple, causing it to pucker.

"Your breasts are fuller." He murmured in appreciation as his mouth closed over the nipple and he sucked softly.

"Ah!" *Boy, that was sensitive.* Nick let his hands trail down to her thong. As he continued to suckle, he pulled it down. Sylvie wriggled as Nick pulled it down further, releasing her breast and throwing her thong to the floor. He was kneeling between her legs, his hands on her hips. Gently holding her, he bent down and kissed her bruise, then trailed kisses downwards as Sylvie writhed. His skilled lips continued their journey south. Her whole body was on fire. His mouth finding her, he kissed her, then slowly let his tongue work its magic. Relentlessly sucking, licking and kissing the most sensitive part of her body. *Holy hell!*

"Nick, oh God, please!" She felt him grin and he stopped, crawling back up her burning body until his mouth was back on hers. Sylvie grasped his hair, kissing him passionately.

He pulled back, resting on his elbows and brushing back her hair from her face. "Are you ready?"

"Yes," breathed Sylvie. He smiled at the need in her voice. "Look at me. I want to see you." And slowly he sunk into her as she groaned, arching up to meet him, her eyes involuntarily closing. "Open your eyes baby," he pleaded as he pulled out slowly and she prised her eyes open. He gazed down at her, his eyes alight with love and adoration; this man she had fallen so deeply in love with, it scared her. He wielded such power over her, and she'd known it from the very first time she'd laid eyes on him. Her reaction to him was like nothing she'd ever experienced before.

He slowly entered her again and his eyes half-closed, revelling in her. She moaned, wrapping her legs around him as he sunk in deeper.

"Oh baby." He buried his head into her neck as he started to move, kissing her throat and neck. Sylvie gripped onto his back as he moved faster and his breathing became hoarse. He pulled back as he felt her start to tighten, his eyes ablaze as he thrust into her again and again. She cried out as she climaxed around him, sending him spiralling out of control as he too climaxed, calling out her name as he gripped on to her.

Sylvie played with his fingers as he tightened his arms around her. She lay between his legs, the bath water warm and soothing around them as Nick stroked her arm.

"It's very quiet downstairs," Sylvie commented as she lifted Nick's hand and kissed it.

"They were going out for a coffee, then to the cinema."

"Oh."

"I spoke to the boys after you came upstairs."

Sylvie stopped playing with his fingers.

"They were fine. In fact, I think they probably felt a little more relaxed about us."

"Really? What did you talk about?"

"I filled in a few blanks for them."

Sylvie turned herself around so that she was lying on her front up against him, the water sloshing up the side of the bath. "What blanks?"

"How we met. How we eventually got together. I didn't go into details," he added quickly, as Sylvie's face dropped.

"I should hope not!"

Nick laughed loudly, running his knuckles over her cheek.

"Need to know basis, thank you very much!" She was horrified at the thought of her children knowing all the intimate details.

"I think they felt better knowing that we'd been dancing around for four months before we actually got together. The suddenness seems to be their biggest concern. That seemed to pacify them. They're very concerned about you. They love you a lot and don't want you to get hurt."

"I know, and I them. I really couldn't have got through the last eight months without them. They mean the world to me. Dancing around, eh? I thought it was my overactive imagination." Sylvie trailed her fingers through his chest hair. "I loved the dancing around with you." She peered at him through her lashes and his eyes darkened.

"I loved the dancing around with you too." His fingers trailed down her back. "That night at the dinner, I was going to erupt. God knows how I held it together." Sylvie rested her head on his chest and he wrapped her in his arms. He felt heavenly and Sylvie sighed, content. "Vicki helped too, I think. She seems pretty into Alex." He scowled. "It looks like they'll be seeing a lot of each other this summer."

Sylvie grinned at him as he tried to look disapproving. "It's going to be an interesting summer," giggled Sylvie as she reached up and kissed him. "I love summer," she added wistfully.

Nick narrowed his eyes as he seemed to remember something. "Markus said something about that. What was it?" He strained to remember exactly how he'd put it.

"About summer?"

"Uh-huh. Something to do with you. That you really liked summer. That's why he thought it would be better if we got married in summer."

"You discussed the wedding?" Sylvie raised her eyebrows in surprise. Jeez, she'd only been asleep a couple of hours and she'd missed all this.

"Only that I said I'd want to do it sooner rather than later, and that I realised organising a wedding needed a certain timeframe. Both Alex and Markus laughed at me, saying that if you put your mind to it, you'd have it organised in a month."

Sylvie laughed. "Yeah, they know me too well."

"Vicki agreed with them, after the dinner you pulled together for Elenora."

"Well, it helped that the venue was your mum's house."

"Couldn't we do it here? You said you wanted a small, intimate wedding."

"I suppose so," Sylvie said thoughtfully, a multitude of ideas springing into her head at once.

"As long as we can get a church date, we can work round that, can't we? You won't be showing either. What do you say? Shall we try and get it organised for next month?" he added eagerly, his face full of excitement as he pleaded with her.

Wow, he really wanted this. "It'll be crazy. By crazy I mean a lot of work," she mused. "But it *would* mean we'd be married in the summer. You want to get married next month?"

"I'd do it tomorrow if it were possible. I already told you." His voice was raw with emotion.

"Then let's do it. We need to secure a church and then we can get everything else organised. Summer's always been the best time of year for me. I spend the rest of the year always waiting for summer," she muttered, still deep in thought.

"That's what Markus said!" It sounded like a eureka moment.

"What?"

"That you're always waiting for summer."

Sylvie smiled up at him as his incredible blue eyes shone brightly at her, the man she loved with all her heart and all her soul. He really was far too much handsome for one man and he loved her, truly loved her. She pulled herself up to him and kissed him hard, holding his face.

Pulling back, she looked into his sparkling eyes. All she could see was love. True love. Radiating from his stunning face. This incredibly strong, loving, generous, sweet, romantic, sexy man really loved her. Her heart went into freefall.

"Yes, I always seem to be waiting for summer…"

He tightened his arms around her, staring deep into her eyes. The woman he loved, the woman he adored. "And I've always been waiting for you."

35

EPILOGUE

People don't notice whether it's winter or summer when they're happy.

Anton Chekhov

36

ONE MONTH TO THE DAY

Sylvie looked out of her French doors onto her veranda. The sun was still hot, even though it was five thirty in the afternoon, and Sylvie was thankful of her air-conditioning today. The familiar, almost spicy smell of the *Cestrum nocturnum* had started its evening assault. It smelled glorious. Gone was her summer weekend uniform of camisoles and shorts – she'd be fully dressed today. She hugged herself with joy at the very thought. Today she was getting married!

She opened up the doors and walked out onto the newly extended large veranda, the sun warming up her cool skin. She absolutely loved summer. It was the only time of year her hands and feet weren't ice-cold. She ran her fingers over the new hot tub, then over the edging to the glass that surrounded the whole balcony. She tentatively peered over into the garden. It had been transformed and was a hive of activity. The barmen were polishing champagne glasses, while the florist was putting the finishing touches to the flowers on the numerous tables, which were scattered around the perimeter of the recently laid wooden dance floor. The distinctive smell of the white stargazer lilies wafted up to the balcony. *Wow! Her sense of smell was on overdrive!*

Each table had a tall candelabra with the lilies and yellow roses entwined round it. The caterer, her dear friend Stathis, was stressing around the large table that would house the buffet, shooting out orders to his expectant staff like rapid gunfire. There were at least twenty of them that he'd brought in, all dressed in white tops, black trousers and lemon sashes, in keeping with the elected colour scheme.

Sylvie stepped back from the edge, worried she'd be seen, and walked back into her cool room. She still couldn't believe they'd pulled it off. In a month, almost to the day, they had managed to book the same church as Elenora's wedding and arrange for their wedding to take place at her home – *their* home. She sat on her new bed and admired her newly redecorated bedroom, soon to be their room. *Yiannis was a miracle worker*, she thought to herself as she flopped back onto the bed and grinned as she gazed up at her enormous chandelier. She just hoped Nick would like it. It was one of her wedding presents to him. Her hand rested on her stomach as she thanked God that she'd only thrown up once today!

There was a quiet knock at the door and Sylvie pulled herself up. "Come in."

Alex and Markus stepped in and smiled at the sight of their mother. "Wow, Mum, you look fantastic!" Markus bounded in, sitting next to her on the bed.

"Yeah, Mum. Really," Alex added. Both were dressed in dark blue suits, dark blue shirts and matching ties.

"So do you, though I bet you're both boiling in those!"

"Thank God everywhere is air-conditioned," Markus muttered.

"Once we're back here you can take it off, sweetheart." Sylvie squeezed his shoulders as he blew air up his face making his hair fly upwards. "Better get my shoes on then. The car will be here in fifteen minutes. Where are Yiaya and Papou?"

Sylvie's parents had flown over for the wedding and though Sylvie had wanted her father to give her away again, he'd insisted the boys do it, which they were both thrilled at. Sylvie remembered the awkward conversation she'd had with him. Nick had wanted to ask his permission, but Sylvie thought she should at least explain to them a little more about how their relationship had evolved. After his initial shock, Sylvie's father gave Nick his blessing, but suggested that maybe she wasn't his to give away anymore and that really Alex and Markus were the ones who should have that honour. It also meant they were part of her and Nick's day.

"Downstairs. Yiaya's flapping around tidying up, and Papou is checking out the garden. You know how he is. Making sure everything's perfect. I think Stathis is going to explode from the pressure!"

Alex rolled his eyes and Sylvie chuckled. "I'm so glad they came."

"Yeah, me too."

Lilianna was of course her maid of honour, and Christian was Nick's best man. Melita, Electra and Teresa had wanted to be bridesmaids so desperately, even though Sylvie hadn't expected it, so they were also playing a part in the ceremony, dressed in individual styled dresses in ivory with a yellow accent.

Sylvie slipped on her ivory shoes and stood up in front of the full-length mirror in her closet. She still couldn't believe today had finally come, exactly one month to the day from when Nick proposed. Sylvie reached for her veil – well actually Elenora's veil, it was her 'something borrowed' – and started to secure it at the back of her head. There was a knock at the door and Lilianna walked in, carrying two yellow roses for the boys' buttonholes.

"Oh Sylvie, you look stunning." Her eyes were welling up as she looked at her dearest friend. "Here, let me help you." She thrust the buttonholes into Alex's hand, then stood behind Sylvie and pinned her veil on to the back of Sylvie's head, securing it where Sylvie had loosely pinned up the sides of her hair. Alex and Markus fumbled with their buttonholes, retreating into the bedroom.

"Thank you, Lily. You look lovely too." For a moment they stood holding hands, looking in the mirror. Lilianna was in an ivory shift dress and killer heels. Both of them were clearly moved and their expressions full of unspoken emotions.

"That dress. Wow, sweetie, it's perfect."

Sylvie closed her eyes and shook her head slightly, her hand over her mouth, trying hard not to allow her overwhelming sense of emotion to take over. It had been a crazy month; what with organising the wedding and the redecoration, she was still unable to grasp that today was finally here. Opening her eyes, she looked at herself in her wedding dress, a wedding dress she had found only ten days ago. Well, actually Maggie had found it.

Sylvie had been to every bridal shop in Limassol and found nothing she felt was appropriate. There were stunning dresses, which for a young bride were perfect, but for a forty-four year-old, they just seemed too much. There was also the added pressure of time. Even to have one custom-made would be hard.

Sylvie sat in her and Lilianna's favourite coffee shop, waiting for their drinks to arrive after buying her wedding shoes.

"Now shoes I can do… Wedding dresses, though, not so much." Sylvie felt exasperated. "I could have bought ten pairs, they were all fabulous. If I could just wear an ivory tux... At least I'd wear it again."

"Don't think Nick would be pleased. Not very traditional," Lilianna sniggered.

Sylvie grimaced as she recalled their endless discussions over the wedding. Nick wanted it as traditional as possible. That meant a church, bridesmaids, a wedding car, a reception with all the trimmings and of course, a wedding dress! "Traditional!" huffed Sylvie. There was that word again. "What am I going to do? I suppose I'll have to schlep up to Nicosia and see if I can find anything there. At least my shoes are fabulous, eh? Not that anyone gets to see them under a wedding dress. Argh!" She rubbed her face as Lilianna laughed at her friend, then Sylvie's phone rang. She pulled it out of her bag and smiled. It flashed 'Mr X'. Maybe she should change that now.

"Hi."

"Hi, baby, found a dress yet?"

Sylvie screwed up her face. "No, but I did find a fabulous pair of shoes."

"Well I think you need to wear something a little more than just shoes, though I wouldn't mind you *just* wearing your shoes."

His voice was low and silky, making Sylvie blush. "You're so bad."

"You better believe it," he laughed, knowing she was squirming.

Sylvie shook her head as Lilianna pulled faces at her and Sylvie recoiled back in embarrassment. "I just can't find anything that's right," Sylvie whined as she played with a spoon.

"Sylvie, baby, it's in ten days. Whatever you wear, you'll look amazing." She could tell he was concerned.

"Even a tux?"

"Not very traditional," he mock-chastised her.

Sylvie huffed again. "I know. Maybe I'll go back to the shop Elenora got her dress from. What time will you be getting home?"

"I'm just dropping Mum off at the garage. She's picking up her car, then I'll be going home."

"Okay, I'll see you in about an hour, and no peeking!"

"I won't! Nice to see you fitted a lock though," he laughed. They'd moved into the spare room until the redecoration was finished. Everyone was under strict instructions not to let Nick see their room and the door was locked every night so he couldn't sneak a peek. Marcy was on patrol during the day, ensuring the plastic sheeting covering the doorway stayed intact.

As Sylvie and Lilianna got up to go back to their car, Sylvie's phone rang. Sylvie fished it out of her bag and saw it was Maggie. "Hi, Maggie."

"Hi, I hear you're having trouble finding a wedding dress."

Sylvie smiled to herself as she heard Maggie's calm voice. She'd thought their relationship was never going to be the same again after everything that had happened, and she had been right. Their relationship had changed, but for the better. Sylvie had expected Maggie to react badly to the news of Nick and her engagement. She'd been a bag of nerves as they had approached Maggie's house. But unbeknown to them, Vicki had already told both Maggie and Julian about their engagement. Vicki knew that if Nick sprang it on either one of their parents, their first reaction would be of shock and she didn't want that. She'd seen how Alex and Markus had reacted and they were a lot more accepting of the relationship. So she'd decided to prepare both her parents, ensuring a more amiable response. The truth was, Maggie was pleased that they'd got back together. She'd never seen Nick so happy and she knew Sylvie truly loved him, and that was all that mattered.

"Yes, I just can't find the right one, they're all too weddingy... I'm not sure that's what's right... For me, I mean."

"I think I may have found something, or at least one you can modify. Have you got time? We could go there now."

"Are you kidding? I'm desperate! Yes. Tell me where and we'll set off now." Sylvie was unable to hide her relief, crossing her fingers as she looked over at Lilianna. Within ten minutes, Lilianna pulled up outside a large boutique on one of the main roads leading out of town. Maggie was parked up, waiting. They greeted each other affectionately and as they entered the shop, Maggie turned to Sylvie.

"I hope you don't mind, but I saw this dress a couple of days ago and thought that the only person I knew who could pull it off was you. So I asked the shop owner to take it out of the window. I was going to ask you first if you'd found a dress before I suggested it, but then today I heard Nick talking to you. and well –"

"The suspense is killing me, Mags. Just let her see the dress!" Lilianna said impatiently.

They walked to the back of the shop where the changing rooms were, and the shop owner opened up one of the changing room curtains to reveal an ivory, sleeveless, crystal and sequin-encrusted floor-length dress. It was stunning in its simplicity. Cut with a deep V-neck and fitted at the waist, it gently opened up to skim the hips and then went straight down to the floor. It had a split up the middle to just on the knee. Sylvie looked at it, wide-eyed.

"It's… Oh Maggie… It's absolutely perfect," gasped Sylvie.

"It's beautiful, not weddingy at all and you'll get to show off your shoes too!" Lilianna squealed, clearly thrilled for her friend.

The only part that needed modifying was the deep V-neck, so the shop owner altered it by a couple of inches, making it more bridal-appropriate. Sylvie then only needed a veil. Her 'something blue' was her engagement ring, her blue diamond, and her 'something old' was her diamond stud earrings, her fortieth birthday present from Lilianna – though Sylvie did joke that maybe she was the 'something old'!

Nick meticulously tied blue tie, then lifted off his dark blue jacket from its hanger. Maggie had already pinned on his yellow rose buttonhole. He threw his jacket over his shoulder and then looked round at his bedroom. He couldn't believe today had actually come. He'd been unable to wipe the huge grin off his face all morning. The day had dragged and all he wanted was to get to the church as soon as possible. It would be twenty-four hours without seeing or speaking to Sylvie. They had hardly been apart from the day he'd proposed. He picked up his new Omega Seamaster diving watch, his wedding present from Sylvie, and slipped it on. She'd brought it to him on the *Silver Lining* yesterday afternoon as he packed his small suitcase to take up to Maggie's. "I wanted you to have this to wear tomorrow."

Nick looked down at the beautifully wrapped box she held out to him. "Thank you." He looked lovingly at her expectant face, then bent down and kissed her, clearly surprised.

She handed it to him, beaming with excitement. "Open it," she demanded softly. He ripped off the paper and flipped open the box, revealing the steel diving watch.

Nick's eyes widened as he took a sharp intake of breath. "It's fabulous. I love it." He picked up the card that Sylvie had placed inside and read it.

Time is precious
Like you are to me
I will love you every second

> *Of every minute and forever.*
> *Yours always Sylvie x*

Nick took a deep sigh; *another hour and a quarter of hell*, he thought. Standing anxiously on the steps of the church, holding Sylvie's bouquet of stargazer lilies and yellow roses, Nick shifted from foot to foot. Christian was by his side, scanning the hill for Sylvie's car. All the guests were out on the pavement, waiting for the bride to arrive. Nick's heart thumped as he tried hard to calm down. It had been a mad few weeks and he still was reeling at the fact they'd managed to pull off the wedding in such a small amount of time. He glanced over to his parents, who were standing side by side talking softly to one another. He never thought he'd ever be able to forgive them, but amazingly their reaction to his engagement had been not what he had expected at all.

Maggie had immediately jumped up and hugged and kissed them both when they broke the news to her, the tears streaming down her face. Julian had smiled warmly, his expression almost relieved, then he had congratulated them, hugging them both. Nick still couldn't work out his turnaround, but he could see his father was genuinely happy for them. Nick had a sneaky feeling that Vicki had been an integral part of this sudden change of heart. He glanced over to her as she eagerly looked out to the hill leading up to the church.

Both his parents had played a huge part in the organisation of the wedding. Catching Nick's eye, seeing his face full of anxiety, Julian grinned at Nick, mouthing that he should relax and not worry. Nick raised his eyebrows, indicating he was trying. Then he looked at his new watch. It was five past six. She was late.

Christian leaned over. "Look. She's coming." And he motioned to the hill leading up to the church, where Sylvie's wedding car was slowly ascending. Nick felt his whole body relax as he watched the car turn sedately and park up outside the church gates.

Sylvie sat between Alex and Markus, holding their hands.

"Ready, Mum?" asked Markus as the chauffeur parked.

"I'm ready. Are you?" She turned to both of them in turn and they both nodded. Alex and Markus both got out of the car, and Markus came round to Alex's side as they helped Sylvie glide out of the car to a loud cheer, and what seemed like a hundred cameras clicking repeatedly.

"Jesus," muttered Alex as he looked up nervously, overwhelmed by the attention. Markus beamed and waved to the guests and was rewarded with another cheer.

"I thought this was my wedding day. Are you trying to steal my thunder?" Sylvie joked at Markus.

"I don't think I could do that even if I tried, Mum. You look like a movie star," he whispered back.

Sylvie looked up to the church entrance and almost stopped in her tracks. There he was, more than picture perfect, stunning in his blue suit and matching shirt and tie, his eyes wide and perfectly echoing the colour of his shirt. *How was this even possible? How was this stunning man stood waiting for her?* Her heart skipped a beat as she smiled up at him shyly and he took a deep breath, momentarily closing his eyes. When he reopened them, they glittered with pride. *Holy shit, this was actually happening!*

Alex and Markus linked arms with their mother and steadily made their way to the church entrance towards an impatient Nick. As they reached him, both Alex and Markus released her, kissing her cheek, then Nick handed her the bouquet. He gently took her face in his hands and kissed her softly, oblivious to the hundreds of eyes on them.

"You look beautiful, baby. My beautiful heaven," he whispered and Sylvie's cheeks flushed as he released her.

———

Nick tightened his hold around Sylvie's waist as he gently guided her round the dance floor for their first dance, while the band played "When I Fall In Love." Nick squeezed her closer so they were cheek to cheek.

"You smell delicious," he whispered as Sylvie blushed, glad no one could hear even though a hundred sets of eyes were focused on them. Slowly the dance floor began to fill up and as the song changed, Nick and Sylvie went back to their table. Their desserts were waiting for them and Nick sat down, then pulled Sylvie onto his knee.

"Crème caramel?"

"Your favourite."

"Yes, my favourite." He grinned. "Here." His eyes blazed as he passed Sylvie a spoon and then picked up his. The whole table watched on as they shared their dessert. Sylvie draped her arm around his shoulders.

"How's your stomach?" he whispered. Sylvie screwed up her nose, indicating it wasn't so good. "Let me get you some ginger ale."

Sylvie stood up to allow Nick to go over to the bar. It was dark, and the whole garden was lit up with fairy lights and lanterns. She watched him saunter over to the bar, happy to gaze at him without fear of being caught out. He was perfect. Picture perfect and hers!

Seeing Nick at the bar, Dimitris Dracos went over to speak to him. He'd come over especially for the wedding.

"Hey, Dimitris. What can I get you?"

"A brandy, please."

Nick asked for a brandy as the bartender prepared Sylvie's ginger ale, then turned to look at Dimitris.

"We're so pleased you came, Dimitri. I hope you're having a good time."

"I wouldn't have missed it for the world, Nick. Don't worry, Zach's looking after me. You make an extraordinary couple. You're a very lucky man." He glanced over to Sylvie as he spoke, and Nick turned to look at Sylvie, who had been dragged out of her trance and was now talking to Maggie.

"Yes I am," agreed Nick. "I didn't think I'd be in this position so soon." Dimitris furrowed his brow, unsure of what he meant. "What I mean is I never thought she'd agree to marry me."

Dimitris nodded and smiled. "Anyone could see she is crazy about you, Nick."

"Thanks. And I'm crazy about her." Dimitris laughed as Nick smirked.

"The most important thing is to make each other happy. That's what my late wife and I had, and Sylvie deserves to be happy. I don't think she's had much of that." He furrowed his brow as if recalling something. "Until now," Dimitris added thoughtfully, and Nick stared at him, feeling he was missing something in his tone. The bartender handed Dimitris his brandy and he took the glass, staring into it. He lifted it up and looked at Nick.

"*Ya mas*, I wish you all the happiness in the world together."

"*Ya mas,* Dimitri. Thank you."

Dimitris took a sip and then looked over to Sylvie. "That's your mother Sylvie's talking to?"

"Yes. Haven't you been introduced?"

"No."

"Come over and meet her." Nick picked up Sylvie's ginger ale and headed back to where Sylvie and Maggie were talking. Sylvie looked up as Nick approached with Dimitris.

"Here baby, drink this. It'll make you feel better." He leaned down and kissed her forehead as he handed her the glass. "Mum, can I introduce you to a client of Sylvie's and a friend of ours, Dimitris? Dimitri, this is my mother Maggie." Dimitris extended his hand towards Maggie and she took it, smiling.

Dimitris smiled the patented wide smile he reserved for an honoured few. "I'm very pleased to meet you." Dimitris fixed her with his dark eyes and Maggie blushed at his obvious appraisal of her. *Oh my, oh my*, thought Sylvie. This was going to be interesting!

"Pleased to meet you too. I hear you came over from Athens especially for today."

"Yes, I wouldn't have missed this." He waved his hand in the air as he spoke.

Nick took Sylvie's hand and led her back to the dance floor, effectively leaving Dimitris and his mother alone. He turned to look over his shoulder as Dimitris sat down in the chair next to Maggie.

"Did you do that on purpose?" Sylvie looked over and watched Maggie blushing at something Dracos was saying.

"He wanted to meet her." He stifled a grin, then motioned to Julian who was sat with Zach at the table adjacent to where Maggie and Dracos were engrossed in conversation. Julian was stony-faced as he looked on. "It'll do him good to see what he's missing and it may kick-start him into doing something about it."

"You did it to make your dad jealous?" Sylvie whispered, her surprise evident. Nick nodded slowly. "You think it'll work?" She glanced over to Julian. He didn't look pleased.

"Let's see."

Nick held Sylvie close as they danced to the band. Within a few minutes, Julian got up from his chair and, seemingly casually, he walked over to where Maggie and Dimitris were talking. Julian spoke to them both, smiling down at Dimitris as he listened to whatever Dimitris was saying, his hand resting on the back of Maggie's chair. Then Julian turned to Maggie and said something that took her by surprise, but after a second, she excused herself from Dimitris and took Julian's hand as he led her to the dance floor.

Sylvie looked up at Nick, who was smirking. "My evil plan worked." He laughed like a villain and Sylvie giggled into his shoulder. "Told you. Now let's hope he follows through." He bent down and kissed Sylvie on the lips softly. "Now all I need to do is get everyone to leave so that I can eventually have you all to myself."

"Mmm… that sounds like a great plan. We didn't really think it through, did we? We can't very well go upstairs with everyone still here."

"We could leave, though." His eyes widened, glowing cobalt blue as he spoke.

"You mean…?"

Nick nodded slowly, then kissed her tenderly on the edge of her mouth. His eyes fixed on hers, conveying his deepest darkest thoughts. "We could sail out and we'd be totally alone," he whispered seductively in her ear. Her whole body ignited. "What do you say, baby?" Sylvie wrapped her arms around his neck, pressing herself against him, feeling him as she nuzzled into his neck, drawing in his intoxicating scent, making her light headed.

Just as Sylvie peered up to answer, they were interrupted by Julian and Maggie. "How about a dance with your old mum?"

Nick dragged his eyes away from Sylvie, his question left hanging. "Sure, Mum." Nick reluctantly let go of Sylvie and took hold of Maggie, leaving Julian standing a few inches away from Sylvie.

"I'll bring him back to you soon," Maggie called as she winked at Sylvie.

"Fancy dancing with your father-in-law?" Julian chuckled, as Sylvie shifted uneasily from foot to foot.

Sylvie grinned at his attempt to defuse an awkward moment with humour. "I'd love to," Sylvie replied softly. Julian took hold of her hand and started to move her expertly round the dance floor.

"It's a beautiful wedding, Sylvie. You're a marvel to pull it off." He gazed down at her with what seemed like pride.

"Thanks, but we *all* did it. You included." Julian shrugged, indicating he was unconvinced.

"The last time I danced with you was at Elenora's pre-wedding dinner. And if I remember correctly, I handed you to Nick," he snorted. "I remember thinking then that I wanted us to be related…" He grinned widely as Sylvie's eyes shot up to his. "However, I didn't envisage us being related in this way." He laughed and Sylvie's expression softened as she smiled up at him, his piercing blue eyes danced with amusement as he smoothly moved around the other couples dancing.

"It's good to see you so happy, Sylvie." Julian's eyes softened as he spoke.

"Thanks, Julian. I am. Very." Sylvie felt her throat constrict as she tried not to show her emotions.

"That alone is enough for me. Nick's a fabulous kid. I'm so immensely proud of him. I'm lucky to have you both in my life."

"We're lucky too, Julian. You've been a good friend to me." Julian shrugged and cringed, indicating he wasn't so sure, and Sylvie smiled, shaking her head. "You made it right in the end, that's what counts."

"He adores you, Sylvie." He looked over to where Nick and Maggie were. "He'll never hurt you and if he does, he'll have his old man to answer to." He squeezed her to him and Sylvie felt for the first time that Julian's affection for her had changed. It felt like he was protecting her, he was genuinely concerned for her, like a brother would be. For the first time, she didn't feel uneasy with his touch or how he looked at her. "Come on, let me take you back to your seat. I don't want you getting too tired." Sylvie frowned at his comment. *That was odd.*

Dimitris Dracos had gone back to where Zach and Lilianna were sitting. Sylvie took her seat as Julian pushed in her chair. "That Dimitri was saying he may open a practice out here," Julian snorted.

"He's supposed to be very good. It might mean we get to build another clinic." Sylvie watched as Julian's face darkened and he glanced over to where Maggie was being guided by Nick back to their table. He then glanced over Dimitris who had his eyes firmly fixed on Maggie.

"He's very charming, don't you think?" Sylvie asked. Julian grunted, but before he could comment Maggie and Nick were by their side.

"Ready?" Nick held out his hand to Sylvie and she nodded.

"You're not leaving? It's only ten," Maggie whined.

"You can't leave yet, I need to give you your wedding present," added Julian.

"Present?" Nick raised his eyebrows in surprise.

"Yes but I need to show you it inside. Can we use your office, Sylvie?" *Office?*

"Er… sure." Sylvie rose from her chair, intrigued, and they all followed Julian into the house through to Sylvie's office.

Sylvie flicked on the lights and Julian moved towards her computer. He turned it on and as it warmed up, he pulled out a USB drive from his pocket and plugged it in. He nervously looked up at their expectant faces as he pulled out his glasses, slipped them on, then pressed numerous keys on the keyboard. Once he was satisfied, he turned the monitor around so Nick, Sylvie and Maggie could see.

Sylvie gasped as she gazed at the images that faded onto the screen.

There was a virtual plan of her house with the remodelled extension, including a den for Alex and Markus and two spacious bedrooms with their own bathrooms. The downstairs had been rearranged to accommodate a playroom and the office had been extended. The upstairs had also been remodelled, housing a nursery.

Sylvie's eyes shot up to Julian's as he smiled at her, then he looked over to Nick who was staring at the screen, paralyzed.

"You said you wanted to change it but never seemed to get round to it. I got your original house plans from Zach and came up with what I hope is something like you were planning." Maggie looked at the screen, finding it hard not to focus on the nursery.

"Oh Julian! It's pretty much exactly what I had in mind."

Julian breathed a sigh of relief and he looked over to Nick who was still dumbfounded. Sylvie took his hand and squeezed it, which seemed to bring him round.

After a moment, Nick looked up at his dad. "You made these plans for us? For this house?" Julian nodded warily. "Dad it's… I don't know what to say. It looks amazing. Thanks. Alex and Markus will be thrilled." Nick looked down at Sylvie as he spoke.

Julian smiled, relieved. The screen was paused on the nursery and Sylvie bent down to look closer as she recognised her original idea that she'd sketched.

"Do you like it? Did I remember it correctly?" Julian asked softly. Sylvie looked up at him, cocking her head to one side.

Nick looked at the screen, and then to his father. "You know?" Nick mouthed. Julian beamed and nodded. Sylvie's eyes widened and Maggie looked on, still unsure of what they were talking about. "How?"

"I overheard when Sylvie was in the hospital. I was absolutely thrilled. I can't believe I'm going to be a granddad." Nick grinned broadly and Sylvie's squeezed her eyes shut as her hand flew to her mouth.

"You're pregnant?" squeaked Maggie, astounded by the news. Her face was a mixture of utter shock and delight.

"Yes, Mum." Nick put his arm around Sylvie's shoulders as his face glowed, lighting up the small office. Tears welled up in Sylvie's eyes as she peered up at him. "You're going to be a grandma."

"How far are you?" Maggie focused on Sylvie, still shell-shocked at the news.

"Seven weeks," she mumbled as tears now streamed down her face.

"Oh, Sylvie! That's wonderful news." She flung her arms around her friend as her eyes welled up. "I'm so happy for you both."

"I wanted to tell you, but we were going to wait until I was twelve weeks," stuttered Sylvie, overwhelmed by their reaction.

"There's more." Nick looked at both his parents, then gently tugged Sylvie towards him and softly wiped her tears away with his thumbs, before kissing her forehead protectively and wrapping her in his arms. He looked down at her. "Hey, don't cry, baby," he whispered as his parents looked on, confused.

"What do you mean, there's more?" Julian stood up as he shot a glance at Maggie.

Nick pulled his gaze away from Sylvie and looked at his parents in turn. "We're having twins."

"Holy mother of…"

Julian slumped back on the desk chair and he looked over at Maggie as she squealed, "This feels like déjà vu."

He grinned at her. "I'm going to have to put in another nursery!"

Once Julian and Maggie had recovered from the double whammy, they made their way out to the garden, leaving Sylvie and Nick in the office. "I can't believe how well they took it," Sylvie mumbled against Nick's shoulder as he held her tightly.

"Me too. How are you feeling? I don't want you getting tired."

Sylvie smirked to herself as she remembered Julian's comment on the dance floor. She really couldn't get over the similarities. "I'm fine. While we're inside, though, I'd really like to show you what I've been working on."

Nick pulled away from her so he could look at her. "Your bedroom?"

"*Our* bedroom." She corrected. "Come on, I really want you to see it."

"Me too. It's been torture!"

She giggled as she took his hand and pulled him out of the office and across the hallway towards the stairs. As they reached the bedroom door, he could feel her apprehension and almost childlike excitement. He pulled her into his arms, clasping her face. "Thank you. I love it." His expression earnest and intense.

"But you haven't seen it yet."

"I love it anyway. I love that you did this for me, for us. I. Love. You." He bent down and kissed her hard, then swooped down and scooped her up in his arms. Sylvie squealed. "This is our threshold so I need to carry you over it." *Oh!*

Sylvie reached down to the handle and pulled it down, then she nudged the door open as Nick walked through, still gazing at her. As they entered he carefully placed her down onto the newly treated hardwood floor. Nick looked round the room, taking in the new furniture and furnishings.

The first item that caught his eye was the bed. It was new and had an enormous cream padded headboard. The room had been transformed from a romantic classic bedroom into something modern and chic. Sylvie had kept the colour palette mainly cream but had accented it with sky blue, light brown and light gold. Nick's eyes swept around the room and his eyes landed on the enormous modern crystal chandelier over the bed.

"I love the chandelier," he laughed as he raised his eyebrows in quick succession, making Sylvie grin.

"I thought you might. Come and have a look outside." She grabbed his hand as she dragged him to the French doors. Pulling back the voile curtains, Sylvie opened up the doors, revealing the huge veranda furnished with sun loungers and the hot tub, all subtly lit, and the view of the whole city reaching down to the marina.

"Wow, Sylvie, it's incredible." He walked over to the balcony's edge and looked down at the garden below. He turned around as Sylvie stood awkwardly by the hot tub. The whole veranda was lit up from the reflection of the full moon and the water in the hot tub glistened.

"You like it, then?"

He strode back to her, picking her up in his arms and swinging her around. "I love it! It's completely different. I can't believe it's the same room. And *this*." He put her down and waved his hand in the direction of the veranda. "This is just amazing. Our own private space."

"I just want you to feel at home here," Sylvie whispered, as she reached up and stroked his smooth face. "I want you to feel that this is your home."

"*Our* home. Yours, mine, Alex's, Markus's and the babies." He rested his hand on her stomach. "All of ours."

"Yes, all of ours," Sylvie sighed, and reached up to kiss him.

"Mum! Mum! MUM!" Markus's voice could be heard from the garden below as he yelled.

Sylvie smiled against Nick's mouth. "So much for private space. At least we have a lock now."

Sylvie moved to the edge of the balcony and peered over. "I'm up here!"

Markus looked around before his eyes focused on the balcony. "What are you doing up there? Is Nick with you?"

"Yes he's here."

"Well come down. They're gonna play some Greek music. He's got to dance!"

Sylvie raised her eyebrows, then nodded before turning to Nick. "You're requested downstairs. Apparently you're going to do some Greek dancing." She stifled a smile as she spoke.

Nick cringed. "Crap! I thought I'd got away with it. They've been banging on about it since the bachelor night. So much for getting away early. Come on, let's get this over with. You're married to me now, so if I totally humiliate myself it's too late!" He grimaced as he grabbed her hand and they made their way back down to the garden.

Alex and Markus stood grinning by the band, giving them their instructions as Sylvie and Nick came out onto the dance floor. "Now be gentle with him," Sylvie jokingly warned her boys. They both laughed as Nick shook his head, clearly dreading his initiation into the family.

The band started to play the introduction to "Zorba the Greek" and Alex rested his hand on Nick's left shoulder while Markus rested his on Nick's right. Nick dutifully rested his outstretched arms on both their shoulders as he waited for Alex to count them in. All the wedding guests stopped whatever they were doing, cleared the dance floor and started to clap. Sylvie stood by the edge, clasping her mouth as she genuinely felt for Nick. It was bad enough he was having to Greek-dance, but in front of a hundred sets of eyes... *Poor Nick!* Nick looked up at her and winked just as Alex counted to four and the three of them set off in perfect unison.

Sylvie watched on as Nick, Alex and Markus expertly moved around the dance floor, their feet perfectly matched to the beat and each other, each step synchronised, all three of them grinning broadly, as Sylvie stood stunned. Zach was whooping it up as he clicked away with his camera and the guests clapped louder and faster as the music began to speed up. Alex, Nick and Markus moved faster, forwards then backwards, then turning in perfect time. Julian gaped at them in shock and Vicki whistled loudly through her fingers, clearly ecstatic. They moved quickly to the left as the music got faster and faster, then over to the right. Maggie was cheering alongside Elenora and Pavlos, who was laughing in disbelief at his friend. Everyone was clapping louder and faster to the bouzouki music. The three of them moved around the edge of the dance floor, completing a full circle at an increasing speed, matching the ever-faster rhythm of the music, until the song came to an abrupt end. Then all three took a deep bow to a thunderous cheer and standing ovation.

Sylvie ran over to them and flung her arms around them as they hugged her back, forming a circle. "That was unbelievable!" she cried, the tears brimming in her eyes.

"We've been practising. Nick wanted to surprise you," Alex gasped in between deep breaths, clearly moved by his mum's reaction.

She stared at Nick as he smiled shyly, drawing air in deeply, sweat glistening on his forehead. "You were all incredible."

"Surprised, then?" he asked, as his breathing started to calm down.

"More than surprised!" Sylvie rested her hand on Nick's hot face, then grasped his chin between her thumb and fingers, puckering his lips, and kissed him hard.

"Please tell me someone got that on video!" Markus cried. "'Cos I'm not doing it again! I'm knackered!" Alex, Markus and Nick laughed loudly, slapping each other on the back, immensely pleased with Sylvie's response.

"Yes, the video man did. Don't worry!" called Zach. "The look on your face, Sylvie, it was priceless! I swear your jaw hit the floor!" Sylvie bit her bottom lip and shook her head in disbelief.

Vicki ran over to them all, hugging each of them as she handed them all napkins to wipe the sweat off their faces.

"You guys were brilliant!" Her eyes rested on Alex as she spoke and he grinned broadly. Unable to contain herself, she flung her arms around his neck again and hugged him, which he awkwardly reciprocated, trying desperately not to look at either Nick or Julian.

Nick sucked on his top teeth, stifling a grin, and moved over to their table where he was met and congratulated by everyone. Lilianna squeezed him. "You really are full of surprises, Nick. What other talents do you have hidden up those sleeves of yours?" She laughed as he smirked at her.

Once the commotion had died down, Nick pulled Sylvie back onto his lap. "So, good surprise?"

"The best." Her arms draped round his neck as she looked into his eyes.

"We've been practising for three weeks solid. I've never been so nervous in all my life!"

"I can't believe you did that for me."

"I'll do anything for you baby, anything to make you happy. Are you tired?"

Sylvie scrunched her nose indicating she was. "Yes, but not *too* tired."

Nick's eyes glittered as she spoke. "Good, then we had better get off, then."

"Yes we better had."

Nick ran his nose down hers as she spoke. His eye caught his father coming over to the table and he sighed, knowing their getaway plan would be thwarted, again. "So how long has *that* been going on?" Julian scraped a chair back for him to sit down as he motioned to the dance floor, where Alex was teaching Vicki some basic Greek dancing steps to the delight of Electra, Melita and Teresa. They were all on the dance floor, along with Elenora, Pavlos and Markus.

"About a month," Nick answered warily, unsure of how his father would take the news. Julian furrowed his brow a little.

"How old is Alex now?" He looked uncomfortably at Sylvie.

"Twenty-two this October."

Julian huffed. "He's a few years younger than her, then?"

"Yes, Dad. Some men like older women, you know." Nick twisted his mouth, trying hard and failing miserably to stifle a grin.

Julian raised his eyebrows and smirked. "So I hear. Though I never understood why." Sylvie's mouth dropped open in appalled shock as Julian laughed loudly.

Nick squeezed Sylvie tightly, grinning broadly. "Oh, Dad, you don't know what you're missing."

Julian laughed back at him as Sylvie squirmed on Nick's knee. "Touché!" His eyes rested momentarily on Sylvie as she flushed. "I'm not sure I'm ready for a third wedding yet, though." He looked over to where Vicki was stood mesmerised by Alex as he proceeded to guide her through some more dance steps. "She's got it bad." He shook his head. "So no honeymoon for you two, then?" He needed to change the subject. He could just about cope with Elenora getting married and he'd resigned himself to losing Sylvie to Nick. But Vicki too? And so unexpectedly. It was all getting a bit too much too soon.

"Well Sylvie can't fly yet. Maybe in September when Dracos has his official opening. I rather like the idea of going back to Athens and then to Cannes. I really want to show Sylvie Cannes. We'll have to wait and see – whatever the doctor says. We've plenty of time for that."

Sylvie rested her head on his shoulder, comfortable in his arms. She didn't really care where they went or even if they went. All she cared about was that she was with him.

"Mm, that Dracos says he's thinking of opening a clinic out here." Julian's tone was measured as he tried not to give too much away.

"I think he might. He really seems to like it out here," Sylvie said. Julian was about to comment when Thea Miria made her way over to their table. She looked down at Sylvie and Nick, smiling wryly.

"Well, now you're officially in the family, Nick, I thought I'd prize you away from your gorgeous bride and ask you for a dance."

Nick laughed. "Sure Thea, I'd love to." He dropped a kiss on Sylvie's head and she slipped off his knee.

"You don't mind, do you?" Thea Miria asked Sylvie as an afterthought.

"Not at all."

Nick guided Thea Miria onto the dance floor, leaving Julian and Sylvie at the table. Julian glanced over to where Maggie was now sitting with Lilianna, Zach and Dimitris and he clenched his jaw.

"You know, Julian, you can't expect her to wait around forever for you." His eyes shot up to Sylvie's. "She needs someone in her life. She only ever wanted you. If you don't man up soon, you'll lose her, for good. Dimitris is quite relentless, you know, and even if nothing happens, it'll be someone else. She doesn't have to worry about the children anymore."

"It's complicated, Sylvie."

"What's complicated? You love her, don't you? She's still in love with you. I just don't get it," Sylvie added, exasperated.

"I've done stuff that's hurt her. I'm not sure she'll forgive me," he mumbled, shifting in his seat.

"Well, you'd better find out before it's too late, Julian. Just talk to her. Are you happy being alone? If she finds someone, you know you will be."

Julian took a deep breath. The truth was, he was scared. Scared Maggie would reject him and scared she'd find everything he'd done in the past unforgivable. The relationship now was close, but for it to be more again, it would need to be honest too. He wasn't sure if Maggie could accept him again, so much had happened in their lives. "I think it'll be hard for her. We're not who we were twenty years ago, Sylvie." He ran his hands through his hair nervously.

"Thank God you're not! All those insecurities. Feeling the pressure to be the perfect partner. When you get older you just… well, you just don't give a shit anymore. You know who you are and you accept it. Yes, it will be hard, but I think she's worth it."

Julian smiled and nodded. "Is that how it worked out for you, then?" He leaned forward on the table, resting his chin on his hands, his steely blue eyes fixed on her.

"No. Not at all, actually." She looked over to Nick who was engrossed in whatever Thea Miria was saying. "It took a very persistent, confident, sweet, patient younger man to make me work it out. I'm a heap of insecurities, Julian, especially when I try to rationalise why Nick would ever want to be with me" – Julian opened his mouth to speak but Sylvie put up her hand, effectively stopping him –"but I know he loves me and to be honest, I really need to get over it. It's not easy, and it won't be for you, either. All I've done from the moment Nick and I got together was try and find every reason as to why we should never be together. From my age, to his future, to my family and his."

Julian blinked rapidly as she spoke.

"But what it boiled down to was how I felt and how Nick felt. He told me and showed me over and over again that all that didn't matter, and I didn't believe him. And when he left and I was all alone, I realised he'd been right all along." Sylvie brushed a tear that had sprung from her eye. Julian sat stock-still, focused on Sylvie as he listened to her candid reasoning. "The bottom line, Julian: could you stand to watch her be with anyone else?"

"Honestly? No. It would break my heart." He rubbed his face and leaned back in his chair. Sylvie smiled softly at him. "I think I need a drink."

Sylvie laughed. "Just speak to her. At least you'll know one way or the other."

Julian nodded, then looked up as Nick strolled back over to the table. Julian stood up. "I thought you two were leaving." He grinned at Nick.

"We seem to keep getting distracted. You must be exhausted. It's almost midnight." Nick put his arm around Sylvie's shoulders and she leaned into it.

"I am tired."

Julian smiled. "Then you should both leave. Are you staying here tonight?"

Nick looked down at Sylvie. "We were going to, but I thought we could go out on the *Silver Lining*."

"Sounds like a good idea. I have a feeling this lot won't leave for a few more hours yet. I have to say, your family knows how to throw a party, Sylvie."

Sylvie laughed. "Tell me about it, Julian!"

Nick helped Sylvie pack a small bag to take with her, after saying their goodbyes to everyone. They all waved them off as the happy couple left in a shower of rice and Nick sped down towards the marina.

Once they'd reached quay eight, Nick quickly started up the engines and guided his yacht out into the dark sea towards their cove. Sylvie sat on his lap, drinking in his scent; his body was radiating heat and she unbuttoned his shirt so she could feel him. It was a balmy night and down by the sea, the humidity was higher than up the hill where Sylvie's house was.

Nick cut the engine and dropped the anchor. It was quiet, apart from the gentle lapping of the waves against the yacht and their mingled breathing.

"Alone at last," he muttered against her hair.

"It's been a hectic day," Sylvie whispered as she held onto him tighter.

"Come on, baby, I really need to get you into bed. You're worn out."

Sylvie looked up at him, then reached up and kissed him softly at first, then she shifted so her hands reached up and buried themselves in his hair, holding him firmly. Nick groaned against her mouth as he willingly reciprocated, kissing her hard and pressing her against him.

Sylvie pulled away, breathless. "Bed," she whispered.

"You're not too tired?" His voice tight as he searched her face. His desire burning in his eyes.

"Nick, take me to bed. It's our wedding night. This is the part I've been waiting for. I can sleep tomorrow." Sylvie slipped off his lap and took his hand. He was up in a millisecond.

"Whatever you say. You're the boss."

Inside the bedroom, Sylvie gently removed her earrings and put them on the chest of drawers and then slipped off her engagement ring.

Nick dimmed the lights, then moved up behind her, bending down to kiss her neck. Sylvie rolled her head back against him, relishing his gentle touch. Nick pulled back, then reached for the zip of her dress and slowly pulled it down.

"You look like a Grecian goddess in this dress. My very own Grecian goddess," Nick breathed against her ear as he gently edged the straps off her shoulders, then let them go. The dress cascaded down into a crystal, sequined and ivory heap at her feet. "Christ, you look beautiful." He trailed kisses down her back to the base of her spine where he softly kissed her dimples. "I love these." He softly planted sucking kisses along her dimples as she squirmed, her body alight with desire.

"Nick, please," she breathed as she steadied herself against the chest of drawers. He scooped her up and placed her on the bed. Standing over her, he shrugged off his shirt and quickly unbuttoned his trousers, allowing them to drop to the floor as she drank him in. Stooping down, he removed his shoes and socks, then stepped out of them, his eyes never leaving her. Then quickly, he took off his watch, placing it on the bedside table. He kneeled down on the bed between her legs as she gazed up at the man she adored – her husband. *How was this sexy, young, unbelievably perfect specimen of a man looking at her as if he could eat her up alive? Unbelievable. Impossible. And yet…*

Nick reached down and slipped off each of her shoes, then slowly trailed his fingers up her legs as she squirmed under his steady gaze. Sylvie felt she was going to combust as his lips curled up into a smile. *Holy shit, I'm going to burst!*

"Ah." Sylvie arched upwards as Nick's lips connected with her hip and he achingly slowly trailed soft kisses up her slightly swollen stomach, up between her breasts, reaching her straining throat.

"I know, baby," he murmured against her over-sensitized skin as she writhed beneath him.

"Oh Nick. Jesus." Sylvie ran her hands up his chest and into his hair, pulling him violently to her mouth, and he groaned, heat radiating from every pore. Moving over him, Sylvie pushed him into the bed. Straddling him, clasping his hands, she pinned them on either side of his hips.

"It's my turn now." Sylvie ran her nose down his as his eyes widened burning into hers. Would she ever tire of looking at those incredible eyes? Sylvie trailed her tongue down the middle of his chest, relishing the saltiness of his sweat. Then, as she came close to the waistband of his boxers, she trailed kisses along the top until she reached that muscle, that delicious, taut, utterly yummy muscle. Sylvie nipped it gently with her teeth and Nick moaned.

"Ah! Fuck, Sylvie! You're killing me!" She looked up at him through her lashes, smirking as she continued to tantalise him. He flexed his hands. He was desperate to touch her, feel her smooth honey skin. Releasing them, Sylvie took hold of his boxers and tugged them down, letting him spring free. Nick immediately sat up, grasping her shoulders and rolling her back down on the bed while simultaneously kicking off his boxers.

"God I want to be in you so fucking much." Nick reached behind her and quickly removed her bra, discarding it. He grasped at her freed breasts and gently sucked. Sylvie cried out, arching up to him. *Fuck, that was sensitive!* His hands ran down to her silk panties, pulling them down and off swiftly, urgently. Then lying over her, Nick rested his arm above her head as he ran his other hand down her side, cupping her behind. Their breathing was erratic and shallow, their eyes locked on each other as Nick slowly sunk into her, possessing her, as Sylvie clutched on to his back in utter and total surrender.

"I'll take it slow baby, really slow." His voice was low, totally in control, seductive and heartfelt all in one breathless sentence. Sylvie gazed up into his mesmerizing eyes, having never felt so loved, so protected and so desired in all her life. Slowly, Nick started to move, his eyes never leaving hers as Sylvie wrapped her legs around him, closing what little distance was between them. Their breath mingled in between gentle kisses, and their bodies fused together as they both climbed higher and higher. Nick gently stroked back her hair as he continued to push deeper and deeper, feeling Sylvie tighten. Then with one last thrust, Sylvie exploded around him as he too cried out his release.

After a few moments, their bodies descended back down to earth. Nick shifted a fraction.

"Don't move," Sylvie whispered.

"I must be crushing you, baby." His breath was slowly calming as he rested his forehead on hers.

"I don't care."

Nick grinned. "Let me move over so I can hold you." Sylvie screwed her nose up, but reluctantly let him go. Gently, he pulled out of her, then slid behind her, engulfing her in his arms, her back to his front.

"God, I love you, Sylvie," his mouth against her hair as he squeezed her tightly. Nick's left arm over hers, his fingers stretched in-between hers.

"I love you too, Nick." Sylvie slipped her legs in between his, as she gazed at their clasped hands.

There was nothing on this earth better than being in bed with the man you adored, the man that loved you totally and unconditionally, your bodies entwined together, wearing nothing other than your wedding rings. Heaven.

3 7

HAPPY BIRTH DAY

Sylvie lay on the bed, looking down at her swollen toes. She needed a pedicure. She groaned inwardly. How was she going to give herself a pedicure when she couldn't even bend to put on her shoes? Her flat, boring, sensible, horrible shoes that she'd had to buy and now begrudgingly wore. Being pregnant sucked!

Sylvie heaved herself out of bed, for the umpteenth time, to get to the toilet, *again*. It was five-thirty in the morning and it was still so dark. Sylvie turned on the light and avoided looking at herself in the mirror. She sat on the toilet and reached over to her toothbrush and toothpaste and started to brush her teeth while she peed. Another two weeks to go. She was going mental. She was due on the twentieth of February, but Doctor Zinon had decided on an elective caesarean a week before. This meant that they would be in control. Sylvie wasn't happy with the decision. She wanted a natural childbirth like she'd had with both Alex and Markus. But Doctor Zinon was not so worried about the babies – he knew they were well and growing – it was Sylvie he was worried about. He was as tactful as possible when it came to mentioning her age, but the truth was he was concerned that natural childbirth for a 'more mature' mother, as he put it, had more risks. Both he and Nick were pretty much adamant that she should agree. So, feeling ganged up on and forced into a corner, she had agreed on the thirteenth of February. Much to Nick's relief.

It didn't help that Nick was away. He had left for Cannes two days ago to oversee the sale of a yacht. He'd tried to avoid going over, but Serge had insisted that Nick inspect the yacht before their very wealthy

416

client bought it. Seeing as Sylvie had at least two weeks before her elective caesarean, Nick had left, reluctantly. He was due back at around six that evening.

Sylvie rinsed out her mouth and splashed cold water on her face, still avoiding the mirror. She knew her face was swollen and blotchy and one look at herself would reduce her to tears. She seemed to be crying an awful lot these days. Yesterday she cried because her printer had run out of black ink. Marcy had found her sobbing in her office as she'd tried to print out an email. It was all hormones, she knew, but when Nick was around she didn't seem to feel so bad. He had the patience of a saint and nothing was too much, too bizarre or too ridiculous for him. Whatever she asked for, he instantly got it. If she yelled at him for absolutely no reason whatsoever, he apologised. Cream cheese, apricot, and walnut sandwiches at two in the morning with a side serving of sardines? No problem, it was done. No questions asked, no raised eyebrows. The previous week, Sylvie had taken a disliking to a particular T-shirt he was wearing for no apparent reason. It was gone. Vanished. Without question.

She missed him so much. They hadn't spent a day apart since their wedding day. Sylvie slipped back into bed and curled up onto his side, hugging his pillow and taking in his glorious scent. Maybe she should call him. It was six o'clock, making it five o'clock in Cannes. She knew he'd be getting up soon to catch his flight. Sitting up abruptly, she reached over to the house phone. Damn it! He was her husband, for goodness sake, and she could ring him whenever she bloody well wanted! Sylvie waited impatiently for the line to connect and felt a twinge of guilt. God, she really needed to get a grip on her emotions.

"Hello, Sylvie?" Nick's voice croaked. Sylvie instantly felt better. "Is everything okay?" She sensed panic in his voice.

"Yes, everything's fine. I just wanted to talk to you. I'm sorry. I woke you." She heard the smile and relief in his voice as he sighed.

"No, it's okay. I need to get up in an hour or so. Why are you up so early, baby?" His voice was soft. He rubbed his face and scratched his stubbly chin, trying to come round.

"I can't sleep. I keep going to the toilet and the babies are dancing about and pushing into my ribs."

"I know, baby. It won't be long now. God, I've missed you."

"Me too. The bed's cold and too big without you. I hate that you're away," Sylvie whined.

"I know, I'm sorry. I'll be back by six tonight. I land in Athens at two and my connection to Larnaca is at three-fifteen. How are you feeling?" He pulled himself up, then propped himself up against his pillows, trying to wake up, hating the fact he'd left her when she was so vulnerable.

"Tired, moody, fat, ugly and frustrated," snorted Sylvie as she rubbed her back. It really ached today.

"So no change there, then," Nick laughed.

"Are you making fun of me?" she answered, her tone clipped.

"I wouldn't dare, baby, not even from two thousand miles away," he laughed.

"I should hope not. My back is killing me today and you're not here to massage it. Maybe I'll have a bath or get in the hot tub…"

"Not a chance, Sylvie. You're not getting into either. You could slip or faint and I'm not there. You know you get light-headed. Promise me you'll wait until I'm back."

"Okay, okay. No bath or hot tub." *Jeez, he was so protective.*

"Promise?" he insisted.

"Promise," she whispered, feeling a warm glow from the inside radiating out through every nerve ending.

"Good. What are you doing today?"

She knew he was checking up on her. He'd practically banned her from the office. She'd been working from home for the last month, mainly because she'd tired herself out with the renovation in the house. The boys' rooms had been done in time for Christmas, when they came back from England for the holidays.

They had been thrilled with their own den, fully equipped with pool table and table tennis table. It had two large flat screens for their PlayStation and film watching and was complete with surround sound. The sofas from the house had been brought in for them to slouch on, along with a couple of leather La-Z-Boy recliners. It was perfect for them to have friends round and it meant they had their privacy and they didn't disturb the rest of the household. The upstairs had two large bedrooms, each with a wet room. Nick, Alex and Markus had become close over the three weeks, bonding over their boys' toys and that God-awful 'Call of Duty' game. All they bloody talked about was which prestige they were on. Prestige? *Wasn't that a pressure cooker?*

Once the new year had passed, work continued on the main house. The office had already been extended so that Nick could work from home too, and a playroom had been added. The whole floor was then redecorated and refurnished so there were no traces or reminders of the past.

The upstairs was redecorated and Alex and Markus's rooms were made into the nurseries. Though Sylvie knew that the babies would be sleeping with them to begin with, she wanted them to be ready. Everything had been finished apart from assembling of the cots, which had arrived the day Nick left. He'd promised to put them all up when he got back.

"I wanted to give myself a pedicure but I can't reach my toes," Sylvie grumbled.

"Get Lily to do it for you," yawned Nick.

"She can't. She's off to a family wedding in Nicosia and then they're going to the occupied side of the island to show Zach's mum." Sylvie sighed.

"What about Marcy?"

"She's only here until lunchtime. Teresa's back today for the weekend, so they're spending the rest of the day together." Sylvie wiggled her toes as she looked at them.

"My dad knows a beautician. She's an old client of his. Maybe you could go there. Ring him and ask him for the number. Better yet, get her to come to the house."

"Really? Oh okay, I'll ring him later. Does she do massages too?"

"I've no idea. Ask her."

Sylvie smiled to herself. He'd managed to do it again. He'd taken control and sorted everything out, even from two thousand miles away. "Did the transfer go through yet?"

"It's supposed to go through at eight-thirty this morning, so I'll check when I'm at the airport."

"Did Xavier freak out again?"

"Yes. He's rapt that he made more money," laughed Nick.

"Did you go out to celebrate?" Sylvie asked tentatively. She knew she could trust him, but the way she was feeling, she really needed to hear it from him.

"Xavier tried, but I crashed after I called you. You checking up on me?" She could hear him stretching as he spoke.

"A bit." Then after a second she asked coyly down the phone. "What are you wearing?" Nick laughed loudly.

"We haven't played this game in a while," he smirked. "You really want to know? I don't want your blood pressure going up." Sylvie chuckled. "I'm a little more overdressed since the last time we played this game."

"How so?" Sylvie asked, intrigued, knowing Nick never wore anything in bed.

"Well… apart from my huge smile, I'm also wearing my wedding ring."

Sylvie sighed, swooning inwardly. "I wish you were home," she muttered, feeling her eyes brimming. She positively ached for him.

"Me too, baby. But it's better I came here now. It would have been worse once the babies were born."

"I know. Call me from the airport and then the minute you land. I'll worry."

"I will. And stay home. When I'm back, I'll take you wherever you want. I don't want you going anywhere."

"Don't worry, the way I look and feel, I think I'm just going to laze in bed until you get back."

"Good. Watch some old movies."

"Maybe." He could hear her voice wavering.

"Twelve hours of hell," he mumbled.

"Yeah, exactly."

"Bye, baby."

"Bye, Nick."

Sylvie put down the receiver and put her face into her hands trying to stifle her tears, but it was no use. The tears cascaded down her hot face as she hugged herself.

Nick sat up in bed and checked his watch. Five-thirty. It was too early to call his dad. He leapt out of bed and made his way to the shower. He'd call after he got dressed. Nick checked his reflection in the mirror and rubbed his stubbly chin. He'd better shave before he got home. Sylvie hated his stubble at the moment. Or maybe that was just last week; *hell, he couldn't keep up!* She seemed to change her mind every minute. He grinned. *God, he missed her.* He pulled out his shaving things and started to shave.

At six, Nick was throwing in the last of his things into his suitcase. He placed the red leather Cartier box at the top of his small carry-on case. Mr Mendoza had been thrilled to see him again. Nick had headed straight for the jewellers the day he'd arrived and ordered his specific items.

"They'll be ready by Friday?" asked Nick as he handed over his credit card.

"Of course. If you like, we can deliver them to you." Mr Mendoza beamed.

"Great. I'm at the Grand Hotel. Room four-fifteen."

Nick picked up his phone and dialled his father's home number. He let it ring five times, then hung up. *Where the hell was he so early in the morning?* He clenched his teeth, thinking he was probably at some bimbo's house. The very thought infuriated him. *Well, tough shit!* He needed his dad's help. He punched in his mobile number and waited. Julian picked it up after the second ring.

"Nick? Is everything alright?"

"Yeah, fine Dad. I'm just setting off to the airport now."

"Oh good. You'll be back at six, right?" yawned Julian.

"Yeah that's right. Listen, Dad, can you do me a favour?"

"Sure, what do you need?"

"Sylvie needs a pedicure and she's stressing about it. You know how she's been. So can you get that Ellie to go to the house today and do it for her? I'm worried she'll go out and do something stupid. She's got zero patience at the moment. I caught her standing on a chair a couple of days ago changing a freaking light bulb, all because it wasn't instantly changed."

Julian laughed at his son's exasperated tone. "Yes, of course I will. Don't worry, I'll call Sylvie now and tell her it'll be sorted." Julian heard Nick sigh with relief. "It will get better once the babies are born. She'll be less… well, she'll be back to normal again. I remember your mum was the same. She kept mopping the bloody floors, saying the house was filthy all the time."

"I don't mind, it's just I'm fucking miles away and feel useless. She sounded terrible this morning and her back's aching too." He couldn't hide his frustration.

"Don't worry, Nick, I'll go and keep an eye on her."

"Thanks, Dad."

"See you tonight, then."

"Yeah. Bye, Dad."

Julian put down his phone and smirked. He looked at the time. Seven-fifteen. It was dark outside and he could hear the rain against the window.

"Problem?" Maggie stretched her arms up as she spoke.

"No. Sylvie's being hormonal and Nick's feeling it, I think."

Maggie turned onto her side and propped up her head on her bent arm. Julian slid back down into the covers, turning to face her. He pushed back her hair off her face and she smiled shyly at him.

"Good job Vicki's not here this morning. This could have been very awkward to explain."

Julian cocked his head and raised his eyebrows. "We're going to have to tell them all eventually."

"Mmm. I rather like all the sneaking around. It's so much more exciting."

Julian laughed. "Do you now? Well I have to say I agree." He bent forward and gently kissed her lips, then furrowed his brow. "I need to call Sylvie and then make some arrangements for her."

Maggie smiled. "Call her now. Then we have until about ten-thirty. That's when Vicki will be back."

He reached for his phone and dialled Sylvie's number. She picked it up after the second ring.

"Hi, Julian. How are you?"

"Fine. I hear you need a pedicure." Sylvie groaned inwardly. *How ridiculous was this? Her father-in-law and business colleague was organising her grooming!* She cringed.

"Yeah. I take it Nick's been in touch."

"The jungle drums are pretty strong in this family," Julian joked. "I'll get a friend of mine to come round." He glanced over to Maggie who was now stroking his chest.

"Great. This morning?"

"Er... no. It'll be after lunch. I've got a lot on this morning." Maggie stifled a grin as he spoke.

"Okay that's great. See you then."

Julian put down his phone and stared at Maggie as she shifted over him, taking him by surprise.

"You've got a lot *on* eh? I rather think you've taken a lot *off*." She stroked his bare chest as Julian sucked on his top teeth and he gazed up at her.

"I think you've got far too much *on*." He grasped the hem of her nightdress and lifted it off over her head. Julian shifted slightly and flicked on the bedside light switch. Then he gently moved Maggie down onto the bed and stretched out over her. She raised her eyebrows, questioning his actions. "I want to be able to see you." He answered her unspoken question as he gently kissed her neck. *Oh!*

Sylvie showered and dried her hair, then she decided to give herself a manicure, just to pass the time. Marcy had brought her breakfast in bed. She was sure Nick had given Marcy strict instructions not to let her cook or do anything while he was away. They'd bonded over their obsessive mothering of her. It was getting rather annoying now. If Sylvie wanted to do something and Nick tactfully suggested she didn't, Marcy would chip in to his defence if Sylvie started to argue.

"Nick's right, Mam. He's only worried about you." Nick would try really hard not to gloat.

Marcy set up the tray of buttered toast, cheese omelette and fruit salad on the small table. She even poured her tea! Sylvie flicked on the TV and started to watch an old romantic comedy while she ate her breakfast, wrapped in Nick's bathrobe. She put her feet up, hoping it would ease the wave of aching in her back. It just seemed so much worse today. Fed up and bored, she threw on her uniform of stretchy jogging pants and T-shirt and one of Nick's shirts, which she now couldn't button up, then went to find her shoes. She eyed the racks of killer heels longingly. Her sensible shoes sat sadly at the bottom. Sylvie shuddered at them, then picked out her jewelled flip flops and slipped them on, instantly feeling better, then made her way downstairs. Sylvie moaned inwardly as she looked outside. The rain was bouncing off the pool. She couldn't even go for a stroll round the garden. It hadn't stopped raining all morning.

By lunchtime, Sylvie was climbing the walls. Sylvie moved down to the office and checked her emails, then Marcy brought her a bowl of vegetable soup with buttered bread for lunch. It was one o'clock when she heard the familiar roar of Julian's Maserati pulling up into her drive. She heard Marcy let him in. Thank goodness for some company. *She was so bored!* thought Sylvie. Marcy had shown Julian and, if she wasn't mistaken, 'Miss Bouncy Tits' from the restaurant, into the living room.

"Hi, Sylvie." Julian beamed at her as he strode over to her and kissed her cheek, squeezing her.

"Hi, Julian. Thanks for this. I'm sure you have a lot more important things to do than pander to my needs."

"Don't mention it. Sylvie, this is Ellie. Ellie, this is Sylvie." Sylvie smiled at the blonde bombshell standing in front of her, and her heart sank. She felt like an ageing, fat whale next to the slim, pert and ridiculously young woman standing in her living room.

"Hi, Sylvie. It's so nice to finally meet you." She smiled genuinely as she took Sylvie's outstretched hand and shook it. *Finally?* That was odd.

"Thank you for coming at such short notice. I'm afraid I'm a little unreasonable these days." Sylvie apologised and Ellie giggled, her immaculate make up not even cracking. Sylvie suggested they move to the leather couches in the sitting room while Marcy made everyone something to drink.

Before long, Sylvie was soaking her feet and chatting to Ellie, feeling slightly better. Marcy left for her afternoon with Teresa, and Julian sat and watched as Ellie got to work on Sylvie's feet. Sylvie winced as she shifted slightly on the couch; her back was really aching.

Julian's brow creased as he watched her cringe. "Nick says your back's hurting you. Maybe Ellie could give you a massage." He leaned forward as he spoke.

"That's okay. I think it's the babies pushing against my back."

Before long, Ellie was gently pulling Sylvie's feet out of the UV light and wiping Sylvie's now-perfectly painted toes. She smiled up at her. "There you are. All done."

Sylvie lifted her feet up and wiggled her red painted toes and grinned feeling decidedly better. "Thank you so much, Ellie."

"That's okay. I'll leave you my card. You can call me anytime. I'll just tidy up and I'll be off."

Julian got up from his chair and picked up the bowl of water that they'd used to soak Sylvie's feet and took it to the kitchen sink.

Sylvie shifted forward to get out of her seat, when she felt a warm sensation between her legs. Ellie's face was transfixed on the floor directly below where Sylvie was sitting. A large pool of water had trickled down from in between Sylvie's legs. Her face then shot up to Sylvie. "Julian!" called Ellie.

Putting down the bowl, Julian turned to face Ellie, whose immaculate face had lost all its colour. "What is it!" He ran over from the kitchen.

"My waters broke." Sylvie replied, panic rising in her throat.

"Holy shit! We need to get you to hospital."

"I need to call Doctor Zinon. And Nick. Oh, Nick's not here." Sylvie sobbed. Ellie looked over to Julian for some kind of guidance.

"Ellie, clear up here and lock up behind you. I need to take Sylvie."

"Of course." Ellie turned back to Sylvie, smiling brightly. "Don't worry. I'll take care of everything."

Sylvie nodded weakly. "Thanks," she whispered. Julian then helped Sylvie up and she slipped on her flip-flops.

"Do you have a bag packed?"

Sylvie shook her head. "I'm not due for three more weeks… I didn't think."

"Never mind. We can get that later. I'll call Zach from the hospital and Lily can organise it." He said softly, trying to soothe her: "Are you feeling any contractions, because we need to time them?"

Sylvie shook her head. *Oh shit, the back ache! How had she not realised?* "My back pain. It was contractions!"

Julian's face dropped. "We need to get off, now!" Julian's tone was urgent. Shit, he really wasn't up to delivering his grandchildren in Sylvie's sitting room. Julian put his arm around her and guided her to the front door. Ellie ran up in front to open the door and watched Julian help Sylvie awkwardly get into his ridiculously low car. Closing the car door, he turned to Ellie.

"Good luck, Julian. Let me know how it goes."

Julian nodded curtly and rushed to the driver's side as Ellie closed the door. "Okay?" Julian asked as he started up his car.

"No. I'm scared and I think I'm getting another contraction." Sylvie cringed as the dull ache increased in the base of her back.

"Don't worry, darling. The clinic's close; we'll be there in no time." Julian turned his car round and sped in the direction of Doctor Zinon's private clinic.

Sylvie staggered in through the electric doors as Julian ran up to the desk.

"Sylvie… Steed. She's gone into labour. Doctor Zinon is her obstetrician." He was trying to sound calm, but the receptionist could see panic in his eyes. She quickly looked at her computer and nodded.

"We'll put her on the fourth floor. I'll organise a wheelchair. If you just wait a moment, Mr Steed." Sylvie bit her lip to stifle a grin, knowing the receptionist had mistaken him for the father.

"What about the doctor?" Sylvie cringed again as she felt another contraction and Julian's attention was diverted to her. He put his arm around her and let her squeeze his hand.

"I'll inform Doctor Zinon. He's on his way back from Paphos. He'll be here in forty-five minutes."

A porter brought over a wheelchair which Sylvie gratefully sat in. "They're waiting for you up on the fourth floor," the receptionist added, and handed the porter a folder with all Sylvie's details.

"Can we talk to the doctor?" asked Sylvie.

"Sylvie, let's get you upstairs and then once you're settled, we'll talk to him, right?" Julian turned to the receptionist for confirmation and she nodded. "The sister will get him to talk to you." Sylvie sighed her relief and the porter wheeled her to the elevators as Julian walked beside her, holding her hand.

"How are you doing? Any more contractions?" Sylvie shook her head. "They're about ten minutes apart?" Sylvie nodded, surprised he'd taken note.

"What time is it?" she croaked.

"Two-twenty."

"We need to call Nick. He said he'd call me when he landed and in all the rush I left my phone at home." Julian pulled out his phone and dialled Nick. It went straight to voicemail.

"His phone's not on yet. I'll try again in five minutes."

Sylvie nodded as they got into the elevator and the tears started brimming in her eyes. She couldn't have the babies without Nick. He'd been with her every step of her pregnancy. He'd been to every appointment and every scan with her. He'd read all the books on labour and been with her through every possible scenario. It wasn't fair for him not to be here now.

Julian squeezed her hand and bent down to her level. "Hey, don't cry. He'll be here soon."

Sylvie brushed away her tears, trying hard to control herself.

Nick strolled out into the terminal at Elefthérios Venizélos airport in Athens and headed towards the gate for his connecting flight to Larnaca. He fished out his phone and switched it on, knowing it would need a minute or so to connect to the local network provider. It was two-twenty. Thank goodness he only had a carry on case. He sat down at the gate and looked at his phone. Once he had a signal, he called Sylvie's mobile. It rang eight times before he hung up. His stomach constricted with a sudden sense of panic. She always answered her phone. He dialled the house phone and let that ring six times. *Shit! Where was she?* He quickly dialled his dad's phone, taking a deep breath and praying he would answer. It rang twice and Julian answered.

"Dad? I'm calling Sylvie and she's not answering —"

"She's here with me —"

"Fucking hell! I nearly had a coronary! Why hasn't she got her phone with her?" he demanded.

"Nick, her waters broke and I've —"

"WHAT!" Nick jumped up out of his seat and the neighbouring passengers jumped out of their skin as they regarded him warily. He was raking his hair rapidly as he paced around. "Jesus. Is she okay? When did they break? Can I speak to her? Fuck, fuck." A thousand questions exploded in his head as he tried hard to calm down. He racked his brain to remember all the appointments they'd been to at Doctor Zinon's surgery. All the things he needed to know.

"About half an hour ago. They're just putting her on a bed. Hang on a minute."

"Has she got contractions yet?"

"Yes, every ten minutes."

"Has she started to dilate?"

"They're just checking now. Nick don't worry, I'll make sure she's okay."

"I should be there, Dad. I should *fucking* be there. She's three weeks early, what's Doctor Zinon say?"

"He's on his way back from Paphos. He'll be here in thirty minutes."

"Dad, don't leave her. She's really panicked about the labour."

"I won't, I promise. Here. You can speak to her now."

"Nick?" Sylvie's voice croaked down the phone.

"Oh baby, baby. I'm so sorry I'm not there."

"I'm okay, Nick. Doctor Zinon's on the way and I'm only three centimetres. Please don't worry." Nick paced around the airport lounge, oblivious as his fellow passengers watched on.

"Jesus, Sylvie. I feel so useless. Three and a half hours of unbelievable hell until I'm there." She could hear the frustration and desperation in his voice.

"Nick, I don't want you speeding to get here. I'm nowhere near ready. Oh shit… oooh…"

Nick gasped. "Sylvie, what is it?"

"I'm just… having a… contraction…" Nick closed his eyes and clenched his teeth as he listened helplessly at the end of his phone for Sylvie to try and ride out the pain. He felt totally desolate as his eyes welled up. *He should be there, for fuck's sake!*

He was momentarily distracted by the announcement of his flight, which was ready to board. "Sylvie, they're calling my plane, baby. I have to go. Are you okay?" He was torn between wanting to stay on the phone with her and getting on the plane to get back to her. The last thing he wanted was to hang up. His heart clenched and twisted at the thought of saying goodbye.

"Yes, I'm fine. It's passed. Go. Get on the plane. I want you home safe. I love you, Nick."

"I love you too, baby. I'll call the second I land. Pass me on to Dad." Sylvie handed Julian the phone as her eyes welled up with tears again.

"Nick?"

"Dad, Sylvie's supposed to have a caesarean." He tried hard to sound calm as his pulse raced and his heart banged against his chest. "The doctor thought it would be safer, for her. I don't want anything to happen to her, Dad."

"Okay, I'll talk to the doctor, he should be here any minute now. Don't worry, Nick. Just get home safely, okay?"

"Okay. I'll call the second I land. And Dad – thanks."

"That's okay, Nick. I'm just glad I was there. Bye."

Nick reluctantly turned off his phone. He held his face and clenched his teeth from the frustration. He had an incredible urge to scream. Taking a deep breath, he picked up his bag and headed towards the entrance to the plane.

The staff on the fourth four of Doctor Zinon's clinic had everything set up within ten minutes. Sylvie told them she wanted an epidural, firstly because her contractions were agony and secondly, if she had to have a caesarean, she'd then be ready. Julian stood awkwardly in the corner of the room trying to call Zach again. He'd tried Maggie too, but she hadn't picked up. He tried the house and there was no answer there either. *Where the hell was everyone? Jesus!* He really wasn't cut out for this. After the third try, he scowled at his phone.

"Zach's phone's off still." He paced over to Sylvie, running his hands through his hair and smiling tightly. The quicker Lilianna got here, the better.

"They're at a wedding and then they were going to the occupied side." Julian raised his eyebrows in surprise.

Doctor Zinon, who'd arrived an hour and a half ago, looked up at them. "You can't use your phones on the north side. They're blocked."

Julian took a deep breath. *Holy crap, he'd have to stick it out!*

Doctor Zinon took a seat next to Sylvie, his face deceptively soft. "Sylvie, dear, you're about six centimetres dilated and the babies are fine." He indicated the monitor, showing their heartbeats. "Your blood pressure's not bad, but if it gets any higher, we won't be able to wait… for Nick, I mean." Doctor Zinon's eyes shot up to Julian's and Julian clenched his eyes shut momentarily. Sylvie looked up at the clock. It was nearly five o'clock and Nick would be landing any minute. "But that's not all. If you wait much longer, I may not be able to do a caesarean."

"I'm not having these babies until he's here, Zinon. If it means it's natural, then that's fine by me. If the babies are in no danger, we'll hang on."

Doctor Zinon clasped his hands together and rested them against his mouth, heaving a deep sigh. "Okay. But if I see anything that will endanger you or the babies…" Sylvie nodded a little. "Are you feeling the contractions?"

"Very slightly."

"Good, so the epidural's still being effective. We may need a top up." He got up to leave, but not before he rechecked the monitors.

Julian's phone rang. Looking down at it, he sighed with relief.

"Nick?" Sylvie asked. He shook his head and her face dropped. "Zach."

"Hi Julian. My service says I've eight missed calls from you, what's up?"

"It's Sylvie, she's gone into labour."

"Fuck. Where is she?" Zach demanded.

"She's in the delivery room at Doctor Zinon's Clinic."

"And Nick?" he asked, knowing Sylvie would be distraught if he wasn't there.

"He's due to land at Larnaca any minute."

"How's she doing?"

"Um… okay."

"I see… she's shitty."

"That about covers it."

"Okay, we're on our way. Should be there in an hour. Can I speak to her?" Zach's voice wavered.

"Sure. Sylvie, Zach wants a word." He handed over the phone.

"Hey, sweetheart, how are you holding up?" Zach's voice was soft as he tried hard not to show his anxiety.

"Oh you know. Same shit, different day," she replied, trying hard to sound cheery and failing miserably as her voice cracked at the end.

"Hey, don't get upset now. He'll be there as soon as he can, okay?"

"I know," she sniffed.

"Lily and I will be there in an hour, okay?"

"Don't speed, Zach."

"Okay. Bye."

Sylvie handed over the phone to Julian and looked at the clock. It was five past five. *Why hadn't Nick rung yet?*

Nick flew down the tunnel that connected the plane to the terminal building and rummaged in his pocket for his phone. He pulled it out and turned it on as he raced to passport control. Luckily it was quiet and he passed through quickly, then sprinted past all the other passengers waiting by the luggage carousels.

Nick looked down at his phone, waiting for it to connect to the network. As soon as he saw the bars light up, he hit the call button. It didn't even ring.

"Dad? Please tell me everything's okay?" He was running towards the parking ticket machine through the now-heavy rain as he fumbled for his ticket. Nick dashed under the shelter.

"Yes, she's fine. The doctor's pleased with her and the babies and he's monitoring everything."

Nick stopped for a second as he absorbed the information. Then he covered his eyes with his hand as the relief engulfed him and all the tension of the hour-and-a-half flight left his body. The tears sprung into his eyes and he looked skyward. *Thank you God!*

"Nick?"

"Yes, Dad, I'm here… I just…" His voice trailed off, unable to express what he felt as he tried hard to hold on to his emotions.

"Hey, Nick, it's okay, everything's fine. They're all fine."

He could hear Sylvie in the background. "Let me speak to him!"

Nick heard Julian pass the phone over. "Nick?"

"Yes, baby, I'm here. How are you doing?" He dashed his tears away and rammed the parking ticket in the machine.

"I'm okay, really. Just please get here… but don't speed. It's wet." He quickly put the money in the machine and retrieved the ticket.

"I'll be forty minutes tops, baby. God, it's so good to hear your voice. How far apart are the contractions?"

"About five minutes and I'm six centimetres."

"Good. I'll be there as soon as I can."

"Okay. Bye."

"Bye, baby." Nick sprinted across the car park, splashing through the puddles to his parked Jeep, and hurled himself and his case in.

Sylvie looked out of the window at the dark sky. In the distance, she could see lightning illuminating the whole sky as rain bounced off the window. Julian sat next to her, holding her hand. She smiled at him weakly. He really looked drawn. *I'm sure he hadn't expected this today*, she snorted to herself. She thought back over the last year and realised that Julian had rescued her on more than one occasion.

"Why don't you get a coffee? I'm fine really." She rubbed his arm gently.

"No, I'll wait until Nick's here. To be honest, I could do with a stiff drink," he grinned.

"Me too," giggled Sylvie, and Julian physically relaxed as he saw her face light up. Sylvie glanced at the clock. It was twenty to six. *Come on, Nick, hurry up!*

Doctor Zinon walked in, smiling softly. "So how are we doing? Epidural still working?" Sylvie nodded. He checked the monitors and then her blood pressure, scowling a little.

"What is it?" demanded Sylvie.

"The contractions are getting faster. Let me check how much you've dilated." Julian paled as Doctor Zinon examined Sylvie. "You've moved on fast, my dear. You're nine centimetres." He then examined her stomach. "I'd say in about ten minutes, they'll be ready to start."

"Call Nick," cried Sylvie.

Julian jumped up and punched in Nick's number. He answered instantly.

"Nick, how far are you?" As he spoke the last word, Nick burst through the doors, holding his phone to his ear, dripping wet, his hair all dishevelled, his face ashen. He looked breathtakingly handsome, his white shirt soaked, clinging to his torso. Sylvie all but screamed when she saw him.

"I'm here!" he gasped as he scanned the room, focusing on Sylvie first, then the monitors and finally over to his father.

"Thank fuck for that," muttered Julian, moving out of the way as he raked his hand through his hair. Nick shoved his phone in his pocket and strode over to Sylvie, taking her face in his hands and kissing her hard on the lips. She clung to his neck, sobbing with relief.

"You made it," Sylvie whispered.

"Just in time. Nick, the first baby's crowning." Doctor Zinon interrupted. "You're going to have to push when I tell you because you won't feel the contraction."

"Are you okay?" Nick searched her face as he pulled back from her.

"I am now," Sylvie grinned, as Nick wiped away her tears with his thumbs.

Julian retreated towards the door, giving them some privacy, when Nick turned to where he was standing. "Where are you going?"

Julian mouthed he'd better leave.

"Dad, stay. I mean, if you want to." Nick looked at Sylvie and she nodded her approval.

"Um… I'm not sure if…" He shifted uncomfortably from foot to foot.

"Sylvie, you're ten centimetres. As soon as the next contraction starts you push, okay?" Doctor Zinon's voice startled both Nick and Sylvie.

Shit, this was really happening. Sylvie blinked up at the doctor. "Okay."

Nick took her hand and kissed it.

"Sylvie, now, push now!"

Nick watched on wide-eyed as Sylvie strained herself and he gripped on to her hand.

"Okay, stop. Well done, Sylvie, now breathe. That's it, we just have to wait for the next one and… ready? Okay push… that's it, keep pushing." Two nurses had entered the delivery room and were checking the monitors and busying themselves with a number of different paraphernalia. Sylvie fleetingly wondered how they knew when to come in, then glanced up at Nick's face, his eyes fixed on the bottom part of the operating table.

Doctor Zinon glanced at Nick. "Nick, come and see. The head's out. One more push and he'll be out."

Nick looked at Sylvie and she nodded. "Go. I'm fine."

Nick moved down to where Doctor Zinon was. "Oh my God." Nick's face creased as the tears sprung into his eyes.

"Okay, Sylvie, one more push… ready? Now push."

Sylvie gripped onto the side of the bed and pushed hard. Nick's eyes widened even further as his son emerged into the world. Doctor Zinon lifted him up and handed him straight over to Nick's waiting arms, tears rolling down his face as he tipped the baby slightly so that Sylvie could see. "Oh Nick, he's beautiful."

The nurses were over him instantly, cutting the cord and wrapping him up. Nick reluctantly let his son go.

"We need to get number two out, Nick. He's impatient," joked Doctor Zinon. Nick wiped his eyes on his sleeve, then moved up to Sylvie to kiss her.

"You did brilliantly, baby. You okay?"

"Yes, I'm more than okay." She tenderly stroked his damp cheek.

Julian stood transfixed, steadying himself against the wall. *He was a granddad. Holy mother of God. A freaking granddad!*

"Dad? Okay?" Julian nodded numbly, totally overwhelmed.

"Is he alright? He didn't cry. What's his Apgar score?"

Before Sylvie could finish her sentence, she was rewarded with a small cry and she smiled. "He scored eight," called over one of the nurses as she wiped him down gently and dressed him in a tiny hospital gown and nappy.

"All their clothes are at home. We left in such a rush," Sylvie mumbled.

"I'll get them later, baby, don't worry."

Doctor Zinon checked the monitors and took a deep breath. "I think it's time. I'll tell you when to push. Ready? Okay. Now, Sylvie, push." Sylvie gripped onto Nick's hand as she strained herself to push. "That's it. Now breathe, take a break." Sylvie took deep breaths and waited for Doctor Zinon. "Ready? Push, come on, a little harder, Sylvie."

"Well done, Sylvie, that's it." Nick kissed her forehead as she pushed.

"Nick, come and see," called Doctor Zinon.

Nick moved quickly down to where Doctor Zinon was gently cradling the head. Nick's face lit up, then he looked up at Sylvie. "Push, Sylvie. Push hard." And Doctor Zinon grasped the baby and laid it in Nick's outstretched arms. The baby let out a tiny cry and Nick's eyes grew huge in wonder.

"It's a girl, Sylvie. We've had a girl."

He tilted her up again to show Sylvie, and she put her hand to her mouth as the tears sprung from her eyes. The nurses took her and quickly began to dress and clean her up. Nick was over to Sylvie in an instant, hugging her, kissing her repeatedly on her face, her lips, her head and cheeks. "You did amazing, baby."

He glanced up to where their babies were, and frowned. Sylvie turned to see what he was looking at. The nurses had placed them under heat lamps and the paediatrician was checking them. Doctor Zinon saw the concern in Nick's face. "It's alright, Nick, they're just doing all the tests. The heat lamps are just to keep them warm. Your daughter scored nine on the Apgar score."

"I want to hold them," Sylvie muttered. Nick straightened up and looked back at Doctor Zinon and then at the nurses. The nurse in charge nodded and picked up their son, bringing him over to Sylvie as she shuffled awkwardly, pulling herself into a better position.

"Here he is, Mrs Steed. Two kilos and nine hundred grams." She smiled kindly at Sylvie as she took him into her arms. "Ten fingers and ten toes. Everything where it should be," the nurse added. "Congratulations."

Sylvie looked down at him. He was perfect. "He looks like an angel," she whispered as she kissed his tiny forehead. Nick nodded. He turned to where Julian was rubbing his eyes, almost skulking by the door.

"Dad, come and meet your first grandchild."

Julian hesitated for a moment, then came over, bending down to look at his tiny grandson. "He's beautiful, Sylvie. You were… Thanks for letting me stay… It was…" He shook his head as his eyes welled up again.

"Do you want to hold him?" Sylvie asked. Julian shot a glance at Nick, who instantly nodded at him. Then he tentatively reached down and gathered the baby in his arms. He was rewarded with a wide yawn and Julian's face almost split in two. The nurse came over and handed Sylvie her daughter.

"And here's your little princess. Two kilos and four hundred grams. Ten fingers, ten toes. Perfect. And she beat her brother in her Apgar score. But don't let her rub it in, eh?" She winked as Sylvie giggled, then she looked down at her daughter. *Wow. A daughter.* She bent down and kissed her forehead.

"Well, at least I won't be so outnumbered in the house now. Two against four." She grinned up at Nick. Then she looked back down at her baby girl and frowned. "Not sure she's dressed like much of a princess, though."

They were interrupted by Julian's phone ringing.

Nick gently took the baby from him and sat next to Sylvie. "How are you feeling?"

"I'm on cloud nine, Nick. I'm so glad you made it."

"Me too. I can't believe we got one of each." He gazed down at his son and then over to his daughter.

"That was Zach. They just pulled into the car park. They're absolutely ecstatic. I'll try and call Mum too. She wasn't answering her phone earlier."

Julian came over to where they were sitting, bent down to kiss

Sylvie's, and then turned to Nick kissed the top of his head. "Congratulations. I'll go out and make some calls."

Nick looked up at Julian, his expression full of a multitude of emotions, but the most dominant one was one of utter gratitude. "Thanks, Dad. I'm so glad you were here."

Julian squeezed his shoulder. "Me too, Nick." He left grinning broadly, but not before taking one more glance at the four of them, his heart swelling with pride.

"Your shirt's a mess," giggled Sylvie.

Nick shrugged and grinned. "And you're soaked." Sylvie shook her head as she was catapulted back to that February afternoon almost a year ago.

"I'll change later."

Doctor Zinon came up to them after he'd done all his checks.

"We need to remove the epidural and put you on drip for a bit. Just a precaution. A nurse will clean you up and then we can take you to your room. Are you up for trying to feed them?" Sylvie nodded. "Good."

Within thirty minutes, Sylvie was in her room with both her babies and Nick. He'd quickly run down to his Jeep to get his case and was changing into a clean shirt. Julian had found Maggie and she was on her way down with Vicki. They'd been shopping and Maggie had left her phone in the car. Then he'd called Elenora and Pavlos. Zach and Lilianna were pacing up and down, desperate to see Sylvie. Doctor Zinon instructed that they only had five minutes with them but before they saw anyone, Nick and Sylvie wanted to call Alex and Markus. Nick set up his laptop and positioned it so that when they answered on Skype, the first thing they would see would be the babies in their plastic cribs.

"Okay. Ready?" Nick turned to Sylvie and she nodded excitedly. Nick hit the call button and waited for the screen to open up. It rang four times and then they answered. Sylvie and Nick could hear them before the picture cleared.

"It's Nick. Alex, come on!" Markus shouted.

"I'm coming."

Sylvie grinned as she watched them looking at their screen, clearly baffled. They purposefully kept out of the camera's field of vision.

"What's that?" Alex moved forward closer to the screen. "Press full screen, idiot, so we can see better. Nick, are you there?" Then suddenly, they could hear the boys gasp.

"MUM, NICK? Are those… Oh. My. God! You had the babies!" They were screaming at the screen and jumping up from their seats.

Nick turned the screen to face Sylvie as she laughed, throwing her head back. "You have a new brother and sister!"

They were truly and genuinely ecstatic, jumping about and hugging each other and punching the air. Nick stifled his laugh so as not to wake the babies, and quickly turned down the volume. After a few minutes Alex and Markus calmed down, and once they had got over the shock, they quizzed both Nick and Sylvie, wanting to know all the gory details. Nick took his laptop over to the babies so they could see them more clearly.

"We'll get a flight out as soon as we can, Mum," Alex promised.

"Good, because we've got a lot to organise." Nick turned the laptop so both he and Sylvie were in the picture. "Your mum and I want you two, Vicki and Elenora to be godparents, so we've a christening to put together." Alex and Markus stared at the screen, astounded and stunned.

"Really?" Markus squeaked.

"Yes, really!"

"Fucking hell! Are you sure? I'm not very sensible," Markus asked, genuinely shell-shocked.

"That's alright. Elenora is plenty sensible for all of you," Nick laughed loudly, then stopped himself, cringing as he remembered the babies were asleep.

"Alex?" Sylvie screwed her nose up as she spoke to him.

"Of course I'll be their godparent. I'm…" He rubbed his face, nervously wiping his eyes. "It'll be an honour. I really I don't know what to say," he said, clearly reeling.

"Good. We'll call you tomorrow and get some flights sorted. I miss you both."

"Sure, Mum."

Nick packed away his laptop, then lay on the bed next to Sylvie, cradling her in the crook of his arm.

"I think they were pleased," he smirked. Sylvie giggled and clasped onto him. "Can you feel your legs yet?"

"Yes, the feeling's coming back now. I'll be needing painkillers in a bit."

The nurse entered with some tea and toast on a tray and Nick shuffled up and dragged the wheeled table towards them. "Thank you. I have to say, I am hungry."

"We'll be bringing you some dinner in a bit." The nurse smiled sweetly, then blushed as she looked at Nick. He was pouring the tea, then obliviously buttering the toast as she scurried out of the room. Sylvie smiled to herself.

"Here, baby." He shifted off the bed and pulled the table over her. "We need to decide on some names." Nick placed himself in the seat between the cots and Sylvie, then peered over to the babies as they slept.

"Well, I like your choice for a girl's name."

Nick's face lit up. "Do you? Well, looking at her, she looks strong and feisty. She hasn't stopped wriggling."

"So Athena it is, then?"

"Definitely." Nick's eyes shone back at Sylvie as he winked at her.

"And our other little angel?" Sylvie grinned.

"He looks so peaceful and so serene."

"He does, doesn't he?" Nick gazed back down at him as he spoke.

"What about Angelo?"

Nick cocked his head to one side as he mulled over the name. "Angelo, eh? It suits him. Yes I like it. Angelo and Athena Steed. Wow." He shook his head, still trying to process the last twelve hours. *Who was he kidding, the last twelve months!* Sylvie crunched down on her toast and chewed.

"Better?" Nick moved from his chair and went over to his suitcase.

"Yes, much." Sylvie picked up her cup and sipped on her hot strong tea. *Delicious.* It was nice to get her taste back to normal. Nick picked up something from his case and hid it behind his back as he turned to face a puzzled-looking Sylvie.

"Close your eyes," he demanded softly. *Oooh,* Sylvie loved surprises. She really hoped it was some of those scrumptious macaroons they'd discovered in a small patisserie in Cannes. She really could eat a few dozen of those right now. Obediently, she closed her eyes as she heard Nick stepping closer. The butterflies fluttered in her rather tender and empty stomach.

"Okay, open your eyes." Nick's voice was soft. Sylvie opened her eyes and her gaze landed on the large square box Nick was holding open.

Beautifully displayed against the ivory satin interior was a white gold necklace. Hanging from the middle were three heart-shaped diamonds, the last of the three diamonds larger and tinted blue. On either side were matching drop earrings. They were beyond exquisite and stunning in their simplicity. Sylvie gasped as her hand flew to her mouth. *Macaroons schmoons!* she thought.

"Oh Nick, they're beautiful," she sobbed unrestrainedly. Nick immediately dropped the box on the bed and took her tear-soaked face in his hands.

"Like you, baby. Beautiful like you."

The sun filtered softly through the gap in the curtains, casting a hazy shard of sunlight on the bed. Sylvie lay perfectly still, trying hard to breathe softly as she grinned down at Athena, who was wriggling next to Angelo, still deep in sleep, his cherub lips sucking on an imaginary breast. Nick lay on his side facing them, still sleeping. His face smooth and calm; no trace of the restless night they'd all had, resulting in the babies sharing their bed, again! They were really spoiling them and Sylvie loved it! Sylvie slipped out of the bed and placed four pillows in her place to ensure 'Little Miss Wriggler' didn't fall out of their bed. Sylvie looked at the time. Five forty-five. *Crap*, she'd have to be quick. She hurriedly washed her face and brushed her teeth, then ran down the stairs.

Once in the kitchen, she set to work preparing Nick French toast with maple syrup. She placed the plate on a tray along with a pot of tea for both of them and the babies' bottles. Then she stuck a candle in the tower of toast and lit it. Carefully, so not to disturb anyone, she entered their bedroom to find Nick sat up against the padded headboard, his eyes sleep-swollen, yet wide and shining brightly like headlamps, all bed-head hair and looking good enough to eat. Sylvie's heart skipped a beat as she grinned at him.

"Happy birthday, Daddy!" she whispered as she swiftly moved over to him, placing the tray close so he could blow out his candle. He smiled so broadly it made Sylvie melt. "Make a wish."

"I've got everything I could ever wish for, baby," he said as he blew out the candle, and Sylvie bent down to kiss him swiftly on the lips.

Putting the tray down on the adjacent table, she then sat down next to him, snuggling up to him and wrapping her arms around his neck. "We've got about ten minutes before they start screaming the place down. Do you want to eat or do you want your present?"

Nick snorted, then ran his hand down her back, cupping her behind and squeezing it. Sylvie planted soft kisses on his chest and Nick moaned into her hair. "That depends. Is my present the same as last year's?" he answered seductively, reaching down to her chin and tilting up her face so he could kiss her fully on the mouth. "I want you," he murmured against her lips. Slowly, he slipped his hand under her camisole, caressing her, gently moving up to her swollen tender breasts. Sylvie moaned, reaching up and grasping his hair. "Now."

"Me too," she breathed into his neck.

Nick swiftly got up, scooping her in his arms and placing her on the large chaise longue by the window. He ran to the door and locked it, then carefully placed four pillows where he'd been lying so the babies wouldn't fall off his side of the bed. Sylvie watched with amusement as Nick bounded back to her.

"Now, where were we?" he smiled wickedly, pinning her with his piercing eyes. He stretched out over her as she squirmed under him, relishing his touch making her skin tingle. Nick pulled off her camisole, throwing it to the floor, then ran his nose along her collarbone, breathing in deeply.

"You smell delicious," he breathed.

Arching her back until she pressed up hard against his erection, she grasped his head and he moaned against her smooth skin. Ever so gently, he blew on her nipples, making them pucker. He hissed between his teeth, desperate to suck but knowing he'd have to wait. "Ah! Nick, Jesus, please."

He hooked his fingers into her panties and slid them off her legs, letting them drop to the floor then, laying back over her, he kissed her passionately, holding her head in place as he sank into her deliciously slowly. Sylvie's nerve endings were bursting, her self-restraint gone as she pushed up against him.

"You want this hard?" He pulled back as he gazed down into her eyes.

"Yes."

His lips twisted in amusement, his eyes raw as he pulled back and pushed back hard into her, watching her head fall back. "Open your eyes, baby, let me see you." He pulled back again and thrust harder and deeper and she cried out. "Faster?" he growled, his breathing growing erratic.

"Yes, Nick. Faster."

He increased the rhythm, thrusting deeper and harder as she gripped onto him, revelling in his total possession of her. His forehead glistened with sweat as he moved faster and Sylvie felt that exquisite wave radiating through her entire body as she matched his every move.

"That's it, baby, let go for me," he cried, as he thrust one more time and they both reached their climax, Sylvie clinging onto his back, her legs wrapped around him. Nick buried his face in her neck, gasping for air.

They lay there, allowing their breathing to calm, still holding onto each other.

"I think that's the best birthday present I'm likely to get today," Nick smirked. Sylvie laughed.

"Not very original of me, though. I gave you the same birthday present last year."

Nick rested his forehead on hers, then lifted his head up so he could see her face, kissing her lips softly. "Originality is overrated." He bent down and kissed the tip of her nose. "It was the best birthday present then, too." He ran his knuckles over her cheek and she leaned into it.

From their bed they could hear the babies fussing. "Well, I think that's Mummy and Daddy's time over for now."

Nick pulled out of her and stood up, holding out his hand to help her up. Sylvie reached up and took it and he pulled her gently, then stooped to pick up her strewn clothes off the floor.

"I think these are yours," he sniggered, and Sylvie quickly slipped on her panties and camisole before she went to check on the babies.

Nick pulled on some boxers, came over to the bed and sat down, leaning over as he watched Angelo blink open his eyes and Athena yawn and stretch, twisting her tiny arms. As soon as they saw their parents, they began to whimper. "Feeding time! You take Athena first and I'll take Angelo."

Gently, they gathered up the babies, cooing to them as Nick fed Angelo with the prepared bottle of breast milk, sitting up against the headboard, and Sylvie sat next to him, placing Athena on her now-tingling left breast. Her breasts felt so tender and full that Sylvie was glad of the release. After ten minutes, Sylvie unlatched Athena, handing her to Nick and took Angelo, placing him on her right breast. Nick picked up another prepared bottle and started to feed Athena. This had been their routine, switching from bottle to breast so that Nick could be a part of the feeding. It was true that Sylvie sometimes felt like a permanent milking machine, what with the feeding and expressing, but she did it for Nick.

By eight-thirty, the babies were fed, burped and changed. Sylvie and Nick took them through to one of the nurseries, putting them down for their first nap of the day. If they were lucky, they'd get two hours. Sylvie switched on the baby monitor and took the parents' unit back to their room.

Nick flopped down on the bed. "I'm knackered!"

Sylvie grinned. From the second they'd arrived home from the hospital, Nick had taken fatherhood like a duck to water. He loved every moment. From bathing to changing to night feeds, he did all of it. There was no shortage of helpers either. When Alex and Markus were home, they helped out too; Marcy was in her element, enjoying any moment she could with the twins. And of course there were Julian and Maggie, the doting grandparents. Sylvie smiled as she thought about how they'd found out about them getting back together again...

In the weeks that passed after the twins were born, it became more than evident that Julian and Maggie were rekindling their relationship. Sylvie was sure it had happened far earlier, but wisely, they had kept it from everyone. They had enough challenges to face without any added pressure from the rest of their family, so they had been shrewdly discreet until Sylvie's birthday.

Nick made arrangements for the whole family to get together at their home. He knew Sylvie had mostly shied away from having a big fuss made for her birthday. Determined to start a few family traditions of their own, Nick insisted he arrange a party for her. Sylvie grudgingly agreed. The only people missing were Alex and Markus, but Nick had wired the flat screen up to Skype from his laptop so that they could also be a part of the celebrations. Sylvie despaired at her wardrobe. It was only four weeks after the twins were born; she was still carrying baby weight and there wasn't much she could fit into. The only dress that she could get on comfortably was her wraparound red dress. It was stretchy and thankfully, the material was generous to accommodate the wraparound feature. She wore a matching camisole underneath, to make her now-larger cleavage a little more decent, and her red sling-back heels.

Everyone had gathered to sing "Happy Birthday" to Sylvie, as she flushed at the attention, then proceeded to blow out her forty-five candles on a magnificent strawberry cake made by Maggie. The twins had started to get tired so Maggie and Julian volunteered to take them up to the nursery to feed them in the quiet and put them to sleep, leaving Sylvie and Nick to enjoy the rest of the party.

"See, it wasn't so bad," Nick whispered into Sylvie's ear as she sat on his lap as they shared a piece of birthday cake.

"Mmm." Sylvie pursed her lips together, pretending she was less than pleased, her arms wrapped around his neck as he continued to eat his cake. "Did you really need to put all forty-five candles on my cake?"

Nick laughed. "That was Lily's idea."

"Sounds about right. All because she's younger than me." She squinted over to Lilianna, giving her a mock evil stare and Lilianna reciprocated by sticking out her tongue, then smirking. "I'm going to put the kettle on for some tea and coffee for everyone."

"Okay, I'll help, baby."

As Sylvie got up from his lap, Nick's hand lingered over her hips and he traced his palm over her behind. "You look beautiful in this dress. First time I ever saw you, you were wearing this dress."

Sylvie sighed, still finding it hard to comprehend how this Greek god looked at her as if she was the only woman in the world.

Once in the kitchen, they busied themselves with the tea and coffee cups. They moved around each other, perfectly synchronized and totally comfortable. Sylvie still couldn't get used to having such a 'hands-on' husband. It took some getting used to, and she absolutely loved every second of it. Sylvie reached over to the baby monitor and switched it on low. They could hear Julian and Maggie putting the babies down and then, to their astonishment, after a moment they heard what sounded like kissing noises and moaning. Nick span around wide-eyed, and focused on the monitor. Sylvie gaped at him, then turned her attention to the noises coming from the monitor. Nick's eyes shot up to Sylvie's, his expression a mixture of stunned shock and embarrassment. Sylvie giggled, putting her hand over her mouth, trying to stifle it.

"Fuck, turn it off. I really don't want to hear my parents making out! Shit! How long has that been going on?"

Sylvie shrugged and stretched over and flicked the mute button, leaving the lights still flickering, indicating there was still sound. "Aren't you pleased?"

Nick furrowed his brow, obviously trying to see how he felt about this new bombshell. "I don't know."

"I thought that's what you wanted." She moved over to where he was standing putting her arms around his neck.

"I did… do… Oh, I don't freaking know. I just don't want Mum to get hurt."

Sylvie smiled, then reached up to kiss his lips. "I think your mum knows what she's doing. Haven't you noticed the change in her?" Nick looked down at her, puzzled. "She's glowing. And she's wearing a slinky dress tonight. Very unusual for her."

"Yes... I suppose."

"Nick, let them muddle through. Maggie won't do anything she doesn't want to." Nick shrugged and nodded, still uneasy but resigned.

"Now they're asleep, I can give you your present." Sylvie pulled the tray with their breakfast onto the bed. Nick's eyes widened and he moved his eyebrows lewdly. "What, more birthday present? You are really going to wear me out."

Sylvie giggled. "You're so bad! No, I meant I bought you a present... as well as the other." Nick pouted, pretending he was disappointed, and Sylvie threw a pillow at him before she rose up from the bed. He caught it and hugged it close to his chest, covering the lower part of his face so only his amazing eyes could be seen over the top. God, he looked so young and he was a year older today. She sighed inwardly. She really needed to get over it. They'd been together a year, to the day, and had practically been inseparable. *What more did she need, for goodness sake?*

Sylvie opened up her closet door and emerged with a large rectangular white box. It was tied up with a satin bow and she was clearly excited as she ambled over to an expectant Nick.

"Happy birthday, Nick." She handed it to him and he stared at her, bemused. Taking the box, he noted it was heavy and he placed it on his lap.

"I didn't expect anything. I mean, it's been so mad these past few months and with all the christening organisation for today..." His voice trailed off.

"Open it." She was fidgeting with excitement and Nick grinned at her. He pulled the satin bow so it unravelled and slowly lifted off the lid. As soon as he saw the contents, his face lit up like a Christmas tree and his grin grew wider.

Inside was a beautiful ivory rectangular frame with two round plaster moulds. In each of the moulds were the perfect and tiny imprints of Angelo's and Athena's hands and feet. Their names under each one in gold calligraphy and today's date, the sixteenth of May, two thousand and fourteen.

"Your mum helped me do it. I thought we could make one every year."

Nick gazed at the framed moulds. "They're amazing! You're amazing. What a brilliant idea! I love it!" He carefully put down the box and dragged her into his arms, kissing her hard and loudly on the lips. Her heart nearly burst. Sylvie nestled between his legs. "How on earth did you get Athena to stay still long enough?"

Sylvie laughed. "Believe me, it wasn't easy. Come on, you should eat something. You must be starving." She pulled the tray onto her lap. "Crap. Everything's cold now."

"I don't mind, baby. I think we'll be eating most of our food cold for quite a while." He kissed the back of her head and leaned over her to pick up some cold French toast, folding it in half. He offered Sylvie a bite, which she took, then he crunched down on it. "It's still delicious, even cold," he mumbled as he chewed.

Outside, they could hear the commotion of everything being set up for the christening. They were due at the church at midday and then the christening lunch would be served in the back garden. Alex and Vicki would be godparents to Angelo, and Markus and Elenora to Athena. They had all taken full responsibility for the organisation of today, so Sylvie was enjoying not overseeing anything. In fact she'd been instructed to "butt out" by both her older sons.

Nick shoved the last slice of toast into his mouth as Sylvie pulled out her new ivory tux she'd bought for today. At least she'd be able to wear her shoes from her wedding again. It was a stylishly cut tuxedo with satin lapels and a thin satin strip down each trouser leg. Underneath, the jacket was an ivory satin waistcoat which was halter necked, extremely fitted at the waist and backless. Sylvie intended to wear the jacket for the church and then once back at home, she could take it off and feel a lot more glamorous.

Nick washed his hands in the bathroom – they were sticky from the syrup – as Sylvie tidied up the breakfast tray. He came out of the bathroom as Sylvie was bending to tuck in the bottom sheet of their bed. He ran up behind her, then squeezed her bottom, making her squeal as she flopped face down onto the bed. "I think I'd really like some more birthday present."

Sylvie twisted round to look at him. His eyes blazed as they ran over her body, making her skin tingle with anticipation. "Who am I to disappoint the birthday boy?" she replied coyly as he licked his lips.

Kneeling on the bed between her legs, he grabbed her wrists and pinned them down above her head. Sylvie gasped as a mischievous smile pulled at his mouth. "Now this time, I want this slow. Really slow," and he ran his nose down her cheek slowly towards her throat, kissing her neck as she writhed beneath him. *Oh fuck!*

Athena's arms moved wildly up and down as Sylvie carried her through to the bathroom.

"Someone's excited," Nick cooed at her as he took Athena in his arms. He tested the water for the sixth time before stepping into it, then slowly lowered himself and Athena into the warm water. Sylvie re-entered the bathroom holding Angelo in her arms. He was babbling away, then squealed when he saw Nick in the bath. Sylvie laughed, then slowly stepped into the bubbly water, sinking down gently opposite Nick and Athena. Athena slapped her hands in the water and Angelo grimaced.

"I'm sure she does it on purpose," Nick smirked. Sylvie reached over and dropped in a yellow rubber duck and frog, a sponge boat and plane. Immediately, the babies focused on the colourful items and stretched to reach them. This was another family tradition. Family bath time.

By midday, everyone gathered at the church, ready to go in. This was one day Nick was more than a little apprehensive about. The only consolation was that the twins knew their godparents well and they both liked a bath. Nothing could prepare you for a Greek Orthodox christening! Plunging the baby into the font, then pulling the baby back out of the water three times, as well as scooping water and a generous splash of olive oil over their heads, in full view of all the guests. As if that wasn't bad enough, the parents weren't supposed to help either. Sylvie squeezed Nick's hand as they walked down towards the altar.

Alex, Markus, Elenora and Vicki stood by the font after completing all the paperwork with the priest. Nick reluctantly handed over Angelo to Elenora and Sylvie passed Athena over to Vicki. All four godparents looked nervous as they turned their attention to the babies, then to the priest as he started the ceremony. Nick and Sylvie retreated to their seats next to Pavlos, Julian and Maggie.

After an hour, the longest hour of Nick's life, the twins were handed back over to their parents. Angelo was still heaving shuddery breaths from crying, but Athena was staring around at the bright lights and candles in the church, her face tear-stained but a lot calmer than her brother. Nick held tightly onto Angelo, hushing him as he rocked him slightly, kissing his damp, oily head. Angelo visibly started to calm and his eyes drowsily started to shut. "Sssh, sssh, my angel," Nick cooed, his face taut from the ordeal.

"It wasn't so bad," chuckled Markus, as Alex threw him a thunderous stare.

"Which church were you in?" he growled through gritted teeth. "I can honestly say that that was one of the most traumatic hours of my life." Alex shook his head, his face almost grey.

"God, I hope they don't remember it. They'll hate us," Elenora sniffed, clearly emotional.

"Hey. You all did brilliantly. Didn't they, Nick?"

Nick nodded blankly, still rocking a now fast asleep Angelo.

"I don't know about you guys, but I need a very stiff drink." Vicki shrugged off her jacket as they walked out of the church into the sunshine.

By two o'clock, the christening ceremony was almost forgotten and the party was in full swing. The garden had yet again been transformed, hosting beautifully decorated round tables adorned with bouquets of pink, blue, white and silver balloons. Each place setting had a set of two teacups and saucers inscribed in silver with the two letters 'A', for Angelo and Athena, all made by Maggie, for the favours.

Nick had eventually come round and was sitting still holding Angelo, who had been woken up by all the noise but seemed perfectly content, as he kept reaching over to grab things off the table. Sylvie sat beside him holding Athena, who was sucking on a muslin cloth.

"Are you okay?"

"Christ, I really don't want to go through that again," he muttered. "It sounded like he was being murdered, for fuck's sake. She was okay though," he motioned to Athena. "She just whimpered a bit."

"I think she's more like Daddy. Happy in the water. He must have taken after your dad. He really isn't so good in water."

Nick laughed for the first time in two hours. "Yeah I think you're right. We should feed them and then put them down for a bit."

"Come on, then, we'll do it inside. They'll never relax with all these people around." They both got up from the table, explaining to everyone where they were going, then headed for the living room where it was quiet.

Before long, both babies were fed and burped. As they got up to take them up to the nursery, Thea Miria came in.

"Are they ready for a sleep?" She smiled lovingly at the babies.

"Yes, we're just taking them up now," Sylvie replied.

"Can I help?"

"Sure."

"Shall I take Athena? You go out and have drink, dear, I'll help Nick." Sylvie handed Athena over to Thea Miria and wandered out into the garden.

Thea Miria followed Nick up the stairs to the nursery. Nick gently laid down Angelo who was already asleep. "He must be shattered after all that crying." Nick's face was pensive as he spoke softly, glad it was over.

"It is a bit brutal. It was probably worse because they're still so young." Thea Miria lowered Athena into her cot. Nick came over to check on Athena and Thea Miria smiled. "You really are a good father, Nick. It's a joy to watch. I suppose you're from a different generation where it's not regarded as only 'women's work'." Nick shrugged as he gazed at the twins. "No wonder Sylvie looks so happy. You're a marvel." She rubbed his arm affectionately. "You know I think of you as family, Nick, don't you?"

Nick's eyes shot up to Thea Miria's face. "And I you, Thea."

She smiled and nodded. "Chris was never any good with babies. They needed too much attention. Poor Sylvie was run ragged, until Marcy came. Even then, she had to do everything with the boys. I'm so pleased she met you, Nick. She deserves happiness. I don't think she had real happiness with Chris."

Nick creased his brow as she spoke, wondering where this conversation was going.

"I don't know how much you know about Chris."

"Sylvie's told me enough." His tone was measured as Thea Miria nodded and smiled wryly.

"Well even though he was my nephew, my only nephew, whom I loved dearly, he wasn't a very good husband. Sorry, I shouldn't be ruining your day with our dirty laundry."

Nick straightened himself, caught between desperately wanting to hear what this straight-talking woman had to say about the man he'd grown to dislike, and blocking out anything to do with him. His curiosity won. "That's okay, Thea. Believe it or not, I'd like to know."

She raised her eyebrows in surprise and there was a hint of admiration. "I'm sure you know he wasn't faithful. He was an idiot and I told him so on many occasions. After his parents died, he pretty much turned to me when he was in a jam. When he had his first affair with that Penny and she was being... difficult, I told him to man up and confess. He didn't listen." She sighed, pausing a moment. "I knew whenever he started up again, because he'd avoid coming to see me. He had a number of flings..." She paced over to the window, her face sad. "He was pretty insecure, for all his confidence and success at work. I always wondered why Sylvie was so pleased when summer came around. But now I realise it was the only time of year she had her husband to herself. This last affair, though, even had me fooled. He'd got better at hiding it."

Nick swallowed hard and he rubbed his face. The very idea that Sylvie, his beautiful, kind, loving, gentle Sylvie, had had to endure such an unhappy time made his blood boil and his heart twist. In that moment, he knew he would endeavour to make sure Sylvie never ever felt that way again. And in the same moment, he also recognised the depth of loathing he had for Chris.

"He slipped up, you see." Thea Maria turned around to face him, her eyes brimming with tears. "He was taking me home from their house and she, the woman he was seeing, called him on the car phone. There was nothing unusual in that, other than he made a point of telling her I was in the car. Basically warning her not to say anything. Of course I picked up on it instantly. He assured me he would end it. I know he loved Sylvie, but she didn't seem to be enough for him. Or maybe he just didn't love himself so much. I don't know." She sighed, deeply, visibly moved.

"You must miss him."

"I do. He wasn't all bad. He loved his boys and he was generous and kind and helped many people. Sylvie kept all of it from everyone. Especially the boys, and I will always be thankful for that. She's a strong woman, Nick. It takes a very special kind of person to put up with all that to protect the people she loves."

"I know. She *is* very special."

"I loved Chris so much... though sometimes I didn't like him." She wiped her eyes roughly and Nick quickly came over to her, grabbing a tissue and passing it to her. "Thanks. Now you... you I like. A lot." She pulled herself together and linked into his arm. "Right from the first time I clapped eyes on you. Come on, enough maudlin stuff. Let's have a drink. I could do with a stiff one."

"Me too. It's been quite a day," snorted Nick.

"Oh, I almost forgot it's your birthday today." She reached up and kissed his cheek. "Happy birthday, Nick. I wish you all the happiness in the world." She squeezed his arm as they walked towards the stairs but not before Nick took the parents' unit of the baby monitor and slipped it into his back pocket. "You know, life isn't so complicated. As you get older, you realise that as long as you love and love unconditionally, everything is just a moment." She waved her hand in the air with a flourish. "And then it passes. True love, though, that lasts a lifetime and beyond."

Thea Miria rested her head against his shoulder momentarily, then straightened up. "So your dad's off the market, I hear." Nick laughed loudly and shook his head. "Know any other rich, handsome, middle-aged men who appreciate the charms of an older woman?"

"I'll see what I can do, Thea." Nick grinned, squeezing her hand as they walked down the stairs. "Actually, I think I might know someone. He's a contact of mine."

"Really?"

"He's single and in his late fifties."

"Widowed?" Thea Miria's interest was piqued.

"Recently divorced. His wife was thirty years younger than him, and it just didn't work out."

"These young girls, eh? They just don't seem to be able to keep a man happy. Not like us more mature ones. We have the experience, you see." She winked at his as he chuckled.

"You don't need to convince me, Thea."

Thea Miria gave a throaty laugh as she re-linked her arm in his and they made their way through the house to the garden. "So when can I meet this contact of yours?"

"He's over next week. He's Russian."

"Russian? Aren't they cold and austere?"

"To begin with. But once they get to know you…" Nick shrugged.

"Mmm… well maybe this Russian needs some Mediterranean heat to thaw him out a bit. I rather like a challenge."

Nick laughed loudly as Thea Miria pursed her lips together and widened her eyes knowingly. "You are so bad!"

"Nick, you have no idea," she smirked. "Russian, eh? Well I've always been partial to ice-cold vodka." Nick laughed again, shaking his head, almost feeling sorry for Serge as they walked through the French doors into the garden.

Sylvie scanned the garden searching for Nick, then she spotted him coming out through the French doors and into the garden, his arm linked in Thea Miria's. Sylvie nodded to the band and they started to play "Happy Birthday". His head flew up to where Sylvie was standing as everyone sang to him. He shook his head in disbelief as Sylvie wheeled a birthday cake in the shape of a yacht with twenty-nine candles on it. Thea Miria released him so he could walk over to where Sylvie was.

Once everyone stopped singing, he blew out his candles.

"Happy birthday, Nick." Sylvie wrapped her arms around his neck and kissed him hard, oblivious to the hundred eyes on them. "I love you so much." She mumbled against his lips.

Nick pulled back and grasped her face between his hands and rested his forehead on hers. His eyes burning into hers. "And I love you, baby. Forever. My heaven."

The End

GLOSSARY

I realise that throughout *Waiting for Summer* there are certain traditions and facts that are specific to Cyprus. An explanation and description of these is listed below.

• In Greek Orthodox weddings, the groom waits for his bride to arrive outside the church, along with the rest of the guests. The groom gives his bride her bouquet before they go into the church.
• In Greek Orthodox christenings, the parents hand over their baby to the godparents and only once the ceremony is over can the parents hold their child. The baby is fully baptised in a font and dipped fully in the water and holy oil three times.
• Cyprus has been a divided island since the Turkish invasion in 1974. Though restrictions have been lifted for Greek Cypriots to pass over into the occupied area, Greek Cypriots cannot use their Cypriot mobile phones in the occupied air-space; their phones become automatically blocked.

The Greek words used and their translations
Thea – Auntie
Kalimera – Good morning
Ya mas – Cheers, our good health
Po, po – My, oh my
Kalo sorises – Welcome back
Efharisto – Thank you
Ela – Come

Kali orexi – Bon appetit
Ya sas – Good bye
Yiaya – Grandmother
Papou – Grandfather

Abbreviations
MIA – Missing In Action
PDA – Public Display of Affection

PLAYLIST

Moves Like Jagger – Maroon 5
When I Fall in Love – Nat King Cole
Something – The Beatles
Nothing Compares 2U – Sinead O'Connor
The Way You Look Tonight – Tony Bennett
Zorba the Greek – Mikis Theodorakis

ACKNOWLEDGMENTS

Waiting for Summer has a special part in my heart and I'm a little sad that Sylvie's story is now complete. Without the support of the three men in my life, Marios, George and Mikey, this story would never have been finished. Thank you for putting up with my obsession!

An enormous thank you to Steve McComish, Sarah Samway and James Spencer for their incredible work. You guys are truly amazing!

I will be forever grateful to my Aunty Maria who has been my constant encourager from the year dot, who listened but never judged and who has always, always been there for me! The rest of my family around the world who make me feel incredibly lucky, especially Christina, Kamini, Lee, Madga and Christina. Thank you, guys.

Big thanks to Irina my sister-in-law whose encouraging words have moved me time and time again. To my dear friends Emma and Jackie, for their enthusiasm from day one, along with their colourful comments throughout this process. They have made me feel so lucky to have them as my friends. Thank you.

A big thank you to Jaine. I'm sure I would never have thought all this possible without your unbelievable encouragement and unlimited help in the very early days.
To the two thirds of The Milkbar Trio, Sarah and Julia, thank you. You have both been incredible over the past few crazy months with your

selfless support and your unique ability to keep me sane when I was close to losing it! Thank you for supplying endless coffee to get me going and whisky to calm me down. You are both absolutely awesome!

I can never thank my parents enough. Whatever I say cannot come close to the overwhelming debt I owe them both. Every achievement I have is totally credited to them. To my brother Antony who continually pushed and challenged me, encouraged and guided me into undertaking things I wasn't comfortable doing. I know I would never have got this far without you. Thank you.

Finally, I'd like to thank each and every one of you, the readers. I have been overwhelmed by your incredible response to Waiting for Summer. You have all embraced Sylvie and her story and your comments have brought me nothing but encouragement and joy. Thank you all from the bottom of my heart for making me believe that the impossible is possible.

ABOUT THE AUTHOR

Anna-Maria Athanasiou is a wife and mother of two, who after many years of creating fantasy stories in her head decided to take the plunge and put one of them onto paper. She wanted to write a story people could relate to and consequently feel an empathy with her characters. A story that would touch the reader and ultimately make them fall in love. *Waiting for Summer Book Two* is her second novel.

Loved *Waiting for Summer*?

Connect with Anna-Maria:

Printed in Great Britain
by Amazon

55321997R00277